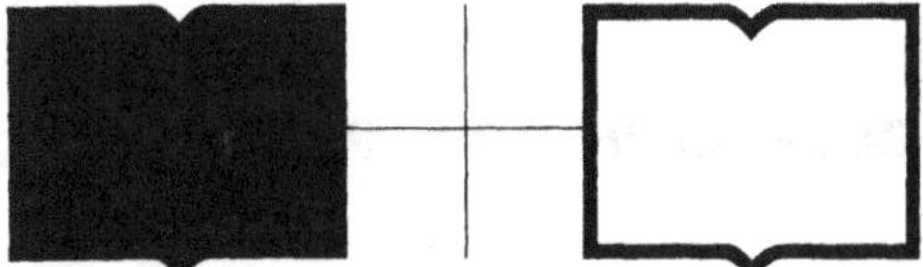

Toronto Reprint Library of Canadian Prose and Poetry

Douglas Lochhead, General Editor

This series is intended to provide for libraries a varied selection of titles of Canadian prose and poetry which have been long out-of-print. Each work is a reprint of a reliable edition, is in a contemporary library binding, and is appropriate for public circulation. The Toronto Reprint Library makes available lesser known works of popular writers and, in some cases, the only works of little known poets and prose writers. All form part of Canada's literary history; all help to provide a better knowledge of our cultural and social past.

The Toronto Reprint Library is produced in short-run editions made possible by special techniques, some of which have been developed for the series by the University of Toronto Press.

This series should not be confused with Literature of Canada: Poetry and Prose in Reprint, also under the general editorship of Douglas Lochhead.

UNIVERSITY OF TORONTO PRESS

Toronto Reprint Library of Canadian Prose and Poetry
© University of Toronto Press 1973
Toronto and Buffalo
Reprinted in paperback 2014
ISBN 978-0-8020-7504-8 (cloth)
ISBN 978-1-4426-5153-1 (paper)

No other editions.

MY LADY OF THE SNOWS

By

Margaret A. Brown

TORONTO
WILLIAM BRIGGS
1908

*" Love your country, believe in her, honor her,
work for her, live for her, die for her ; never has
any people been endowed with a nobler birthright
or blessed with prospects of a fairer future."*
                              —Lord Dufferin.

*" Canada shall be the star towards which all
men who love progress and freedom shall go."*
                              —Sir Wilfrid Laurier.

PREFACE

THIS work cannot be fully understood unless the reader is aware of the writer's motives. The book has a twofold meaning—that of a political novel, and that of the portrayal of a great love and a religious drama.

As Disraeli in his novels portrayed the political and social conditions of certain eras of his country, in a simple way this work is intended to portray the conditions existing in Canada at an era when the country was in a state of transition, with the idealistic conception of what the government of a country should be, the conception being based upon a knowledge of the inherent principles of Divine Right and upon Plato's Republic of Justice.

The scene is laid prior to the last election during Sir John A. Macdonald's administration. When there are no great questions at issue, politics are seen in their lowest form; the protective tariff had been adopted, and with the advent of machinery the old order of things was passing away; the new order had not yet brought any great issues before the people, and the election, commonly called the "Old Flag" election, was run merely on a sentiment of loyalty to the motherland.

"My Lady of the Snows" is a woman who has been born "great," and one who has based her life on principles rather than the emotions, or Plato's theory that the emotions should remain subservient to the will. In her political principles is portrayed the last lingering spirit of "Divine Right" of the "Old Regime in Canada." The "Man" in the book is the man who is thinking; the man of knowledge, of patriotism, of high ideals, he who has inherited as an heirloom England's foundational principles of greatness, her sense of duty, her code of honor and her love and fear of God; the man who realizes that the time is fast approaching when, in the evolution of history, in the very nature of things, his country must come forth and take her place in the history of nations.

In the second place: A French critic has recently said that modern books are being left unread because we live in a scientific, commercial, unbelieving world, and writers, having forgotten the poets and classics, are surfeiting the world with materialism, realism and commercial barter, and are leaving the intellectual and spiritual in man unappeased and undeveloped.

Influenced by a realization of some of the emotions, thoughts and truths which entered into the creation of Carlyle's " Hero-Worship," Goethe's " Faust," Dante's " Beatrice," and Tennyson's " Idylls of the King," the writer has endeavored to picture a great love and portray a religious drama which would appeal to thinkers and lovers of the poets and classics, and in some measure refute the materialism which is becoming so prevalent within the modern world.

The plot is based upon Tennyson's " Idylls of the King "—the unholy love of the Knight for his Lady—the poet's song of Love, free Love—the unhappy circumstances surrounding the Man's love, creating for a moment within him, despite his inherent and traditional creeds and conventions, a touch of Ibsen, that Free Will and Natural Affinity are foundations for a higher institution than the conventions of the modern world—and his mastery over such a temptation. The " Wife's " conduct is based upon Mark's treatment of his wife Isolt, whom he loves but who loves not him.

The " Visions of a New Empire," which foreshadow Imperialism, were suggested by Tennyson's description of King Arthur's Kingdom of Camelot, and were based upon the tradition that this continent, previous to the Mound Builder era and Stone Age, was inhabited by a highly civilized race, and no doubt in the evolution of history will again be inhabited by such.

Julian Hawthorne has said that any novelist truly great will subordinate events to character—that dialogue and mental history will reveal the speakers, and the speakers are the story. During the ten years the writer has been engaged upon this work, Julian Hawthorne's conception of novel writing has been instinct within her. Events we must have to make a story interesting, but events are very similar to experiences, which are monuments carved by the weapons which have wounded us most; we leave them behind and go on to character built upon knowledge; and to possess true knowledge we must have some knowledge of the origin of things which brings us into the realms of science and religion.

Carlyle tells us in his " Heroes " that "it is well said, in every sense, that a man's religion is the chief fact with regard to him. A Man's or a Nation's! By his religion I do not mean his church creeds and formulæ, but what a man does know in his Mind and Feel in his Heart, and does practically lay to heart, regarding his vital relations to the Unseen Universe and to This Universe. Tell me a man's religion and a nation's, and I will tell you what they are and what they will become. Answering to this question is giving us the soul of the history of the man and the nation. And since the spiritual at all times dominates and determines the material, the 'Man of Letters' is one of the most important personages of modern times. What his religion is, his nation's will become."

The works of the writers of the Periclean Age, an age when the world was truly great, centred round or culminated in two great thoughts—the two forces of Good and Evil, and God tames excessive lifting up of hearts. In "Faust," as in other writings of modern times, the force of Evil sometimes assumes a definite form and sometimes a mental conflict, while Good is personified in Purified Love, and Fate, Destiny and Free Will play their respective parts. Where Shakespeare moralizes on such great questions as "What is Life?" in language too austere and too pure for common humanity to approach, Tennyson appeals directly to the human heart in such words as:

> " For the drift of the Maker is dark, an Isis hid by a veil.
> Who knows the ways of the world, how God will bring them about?
> Do we move ourselves or are we moved by an Unseen Hand at a game
> That pushes us off from the board and others ever succeed?"
> " And yet we cannot be kind to each other here for an hour;
> Brave it out as we please, we men are a little breed."

The Religion in this book is outlined in the " Court of Inquiry " and practically applied in the lives of the chief characters in the book. It is based upon the vital principles of Christianity, the basis according to Carlyle being " the ultimate perfection of a principle extant throughout man's whole history on earth," and comprises a proper synthesis of faith and works; Goethe's conception that faith is a question between man and his own heart and that Greatness or Immortality must come through humility; the Socratic theory that knowledge is virtue; ignorance is the only sin; we cannot sin if we know; but love is greater than knowledge and is a gift direct from God—the Vision in the book being the same thought as Tennyson's " Holy Grail " or Plato's " Despair of Reason "—that man receives knowledge through a higher faculty than reason, that is, Divine Revelation.

Towards the close of the plot the writer found herself in a dilemma; it was easy to dispose naturally of the minor characters of the book, but the " Woman," the " Man " and the " Wife " remained—a problem. The poets purified their loves through penance and allowed them to depart in peace, but as the Woman was " My Lady of the Snows," and as She has not yet won the Immortality of Greatness, and as the writer wanted Her to develop Her in her next work to Imperialism, She could not be disposed of thus. The Man could not be disposed of because he is the man who is striving to make his country what she has been born to be. If the Woman and Man met again, and love were love, the writer was not very sure how much longer their good genius would guard them, and feared for their reputation. If she disposed of the " Wife " as Mark disposed of his wife's lover, Tristram, the writer's reputation was endangered from book critics as treating the work conventionally. As patriotism is the key-note to the book, she felt she must sacrifice her own reputation to be consistent and to save her country; but self-love is as instinct within human nature as love, and yet continued to wage war against love, when a train-master gave a wrong order and solved the problem for her.

M. A. B.

MY LADY OF THE SNOWS

CHAPTER I.

A Nation spoke to a Nation,
A Queen sent word to a Throne;
" Daughter am I in my mother's house,
But mistress in my own."

Government House was one blaze of brilliance.

The newly-appointed Governor-General and his wife had but recently arrived at their new home, and their Excellencies were to entertain for the first time the political and social world under their new regime.

The merry ting-a-ling of winter bells making gay music over a gay white world, the hollow beat of speeding horses' hoofs and the sleigh's low bass song were heard far and near in the Rideau suburbs of the Queen's City. Equipage after equipage swept in through the Lodge gateway, and up the wooded driveway—the occupants of the sleighs, through the break in the foliage, catching glimpses of the broad, gleaming, frost-bound river, the steel-like bastions which lined the opposite shore and the ice-crystalled hills beyond, while the moon swam high through the fleecy clouds of the blue dome of heaven which night had transformed into a diamond-studded canopy, and the cool, crisp northern air made the stars sparkle and scintillate and spread their rays of light like a bed of seeded pearls on the virgin snows beneath—to the main entrance of the low, grey stone Hall with its chequered shadows and lights on the whitened lawns and terraces without.

As sleigh after sleigh approaches the Hall, the massive doors open and close upon the fast-arriving guests, and the group of onlookers in curiosity await for the next to come.

At the grand entrance to Apsley House, one of the most imposing houses of the city, stood a magnificent sleigh drawn by two blacks, which were champing and chafing to get away, waiting for the occupants to convey them to Rideau Hall.

"Is father ready yet? We must not keep him waiting," said a young girl, the daughter of the owner of the house, as she emerged from an inner room to a suite of rooms adjoining the great central hall.

She was followed by her maid, who carried a long ermine-lined wrap, some flowers and a jewelled fan, and who, after depositing them on a side table, retired from the room.

"Yes, I hear him coming. Are you ready?" answered her companion, Marion Clydene, a young girl almost as beautiful as the mistress of the house, but of an altogether different type.

"Yes," replied Modena, "I have been waiting some time. You are a connoisseur in dress. Is the draping of this gown graceful? Annette is away; I miss her so much; she had such good taste, but then perhaps one grows too fastidious. What do you say, father?" she asked, as the door opened and an elderly man entered the room.

"What is it, my child?" he asked, with pride beaming in his stern but kind eyes, as he gazed on his only child.

The speaker was Mr. Wellington, the oldest member of the Cabinet, and one of the leading men of the day.

"Will I do?" she asked, not in vanity, but with the same high-born pride reflected in her eyes, as she slowly recrossed the room, the many gems in her hair and on her bosom sparkling in the semi-darkness of the subdued lights, the soft folds of her gown, with its drapings of oriental lace, falling in graceful lines about her form, and her train, with its embroideries of white lilies with their golden calyx and fern leaves, sweeping out over the soft velvet of the carpets like a peacock's gay plumage on the greensward of a lawn.

Her father's eye lighted as he felt the charm and grace of the room and its inmates. It was her own private room; everything in it was elegantly simple, homelike, artistic and inspiring. It possessed a wealth of colors, but so subdued and harmonious that they softened rather than heightened the general effect. Soft, shady rose-lights, jasmines and lilies of the valley standing on the tables and mantels, the open piano with its old airs on its ebony case, her favorite authors and magazines in the corner, all spoke of the immaculate taste of its owner.

"Look in the glass and see, my child; if you please yourself, no doubt you will do," answered her father, rather with his eyes than with his lips.

She only glanced in the mirror, but the warm blood mantled her cheeks at what she saw.

"We really do look like peacocks when we get all this war paint on," she said.

"But come, dear," continued her father, as he buttoned his great coat about him. "It is cold for the horses. Have you everything you require, Marion? What it is to possess beauty unadorned! You do not need to worry as my daughter does," he added, smiling kindly at his ward.

"Oh, I would not presume to approach Modena," replied she, looking at her friend with eyes unglazed with envy. "I feel like a waning moon beside a mid-day sun."

"The moon was made to be loved," replied Modena, as her father touched the bell for her woman-servant.

"And the sun to be worshipped; you know the moon is only the inspiration of a sentiment, the sun the source of all things."

"Then you must have inspired father with a pretty sentiment; he has paid you such a subtle compliment. I have all I want; you have all you require," said the daughter of the house as she glanced at the graceful simplicity of her companion's attire.

"One wishes one's beauty was as indisputable as yours; you have such a faculty of making one feel like a Phyllis, or an Amaryllis, or a Perdita."

"Have I? I don't see why I should, for at heart I am one myself. But I wasn't referring to beauty but to economy, but there! I had forgotten, you never read the sciences! There is such a difference between our needs and our wants. Nature is the basis of your needs; selfishness forms the motives of my frills and feathers and furbelows; you represent moral economy, I modern economy. Isn't that what Ruskin says, father?"

"Here are your wraps, my dear; we'll not stop to discuss political and domestic economy while the horses wait in the cold," replied her father, benignly.

"But why are you so anxious to-night?" he continued, as they descended, together, the broad steps which led down the great central hall.

"It is her Ladyship's first appearance, and you heard what Jack said at dinner."

"That her Excellency would expect to meet only tattooed and blanketed red men, with their beaded and ringed, red-petticoated, yellow-turbaned wives and daughters?" smilingly replied Mr. Wellington.

"Yes, and I wish to dispel the delusion and ease her apprehension at once. I hope we will be well represented to-night," his daughter rejoined, as he handed them into the sleigh.

"And you are usually so indifferent as to what other people say or think. Their frowns and smiles have never been your barometer."

" Ah, but this is different. This is not a personal matter. It is yours, all of ours, our country's reputation which is at stake. It is a duty, you know what I mean. All those things are among the necessities of life. They count very much in the game of nations."

" They certainly do," admitted Mr. Wellington, rather wearily, for he was beginning to feel sadly the need of rest and repose.

" I have been to her receptions at home in England and you may rest assured, Modena, that your advent will be quite sufficient to dissipate the hallucination at once," said Marion, as they seated themselves amidst the deep robes of the sleigh.

" Marion is thinking of Marlowe,

" ' Oh, thou art fairer than the evening air,
Clad in the beauty of a thousand stars,' "

said her father, tenderly.

Her face flushed warm, while her heart swelled with a great tenderness. It was so seldom he said such pretty things.

" Drive to Kenyon Court first, Jackson," said Mr. Wellington to the coachman.

" Do you think Mrs. Kenyon will go?" asked his daughter.

" I do not know, but I promised Keith that we should call for them."

" I do not think she will, she has gone out so little since Edna's death."

The distance to Kenyon Court was very short, and in a few minutes the sleigh drew up at the Court; but when the footman rang, a young man of splendid build and appearance, clad in a heavy sable-lined coat, appeared alone and took the vacant place in the sleigh beside the mistress of Apsley House.

" I thought perhaps if you would call I could persuade her to accompany us, but it is Edna's nameday, and I could not prevail upon her to come," said the young man, with a tinge of sadness in his voice.

" I thought so much of her to-day," replied Modena, in a low voice and in a tone which the other understood.

" Poor mother! She cannot get over it, but I think she is growing brighter. But where is Jack?" continued he, turning the conversation and addressing Mr. Wellington.

" He had an important editorial to revise; he went down to the office. He and Monteith will take a hack from the office to the Hall," replied the elder gentleman, as the horses, anxious to return to their own warm stalls, fairly flew over the ground, the balls of snow from their fleeting feet speeding in every direction and the bells floating their joyful music on the frosty air.

"I suppose everybody will be there to-night," said Keith.

"Yes, it is absolutely necessary that we should go this season," replied Mr. Wellington. "We have a heavy year's work before us; the Opposition is thoroughly aroused, and there is a great deal to be done. The politicians of to-day are very much like the knights of the fourteenth century; our responsibility, like their armor, almost smothers one; but then," he continued in a lighter vein, "if these ladies will only combine business with pleasure, they can help us a great deal in the coming contest."

"Father has grown so utilitarian of late, he must have been resurrecting Hume and Mill. For his sake one wishes the crisis was past; it augurs grey hairs and wrinkles," said his daughter.

"Hume and Mill! Their names alone are enough to send cold chills through one's veins. To regard utility as the ultimate appeal in all ethical questions is enough to cause premature old age!" exclaimed Marion Clydene from the depths of the robes.

"As De Stael thought, you'd prefer thinking that these robes were made to look beautiful and to make you look beautiful and to dream in this cold winter night, rather than to keep you warm," replied Keith Kenyon as he drew the heavy robes more closely about them, for the night was very cold. "But dream on and think so while you can. Great men and women have done so before and have been happy, why not we?" he continued, smiling at his young friend, who was curled like a dormouse in her corner of the sleigh.

"Your favorite, Merlin, changed the knight's emblazoned shield of Fame into the Gardener's Graff. Rich ripe peaches are surely preferable to and more substantial than day-dreams," said Modena.

"You are not fond of day-dreaming," said the young minister, in a low tone and with an almost personal ring in his voice, addressing her for the first time.

"One hasn't time, life is too real, everything means something, there is too much to be done; one wishes the moments were minutes, and the days weeks, and the weeks years; one has really so many real duties, that one has no time for day-dreams."

"That's what Maria Theresa said, and she lived to see forty-eight; duty without day-dreams is generally conceded to be very dull."

"Dull!" repeated Modena in exclamation, and in tones which expressed her inability to comprehend the word.

She really didn't know what it meant.

"One makes one's own atmosphere, and it's one's own fault if the atmosphere round duty is grey and vapid; and duty is generally conceded to be our weapon against the forces of forty-eight."

"How intensely practical and unromantic you are!" exclaimed Marion in disgust.

"A veritable Aristotle!" said her father, sententiously.

"Oh, Marion knows no more about Aristotle than she knows about tadpoles. She lives on Shelley and Keats," replied his daughter, knowing well her friend's dreamy, impracticable, imaginative nature.

"It's real nice to live with them, one can soar heavenward. Shelley, like Hercules, was translated from a blazing pyre to a place among the immortal gods. I like the company of the gods. Aristotle is like the peaches, he gives one indigestion," said Marion, indolently.

"We'll admit that he has given father, if not indigestion, at least grey hairs."

"But I have one consolation, I am laying the heaviest of the burdens on Keith's young shoulders."

"Young shoulders! they have seen thirty winters. I am beginning to feel quite old."

"You will soon learn, if you take life, as all men should take it, seriously and sincerely, that responsibility and position add many years to your age and many furrows on your brow," replied the elder man, gravely, and with an accent of weariness and apprehension in his voice, for he was beginning to feel the weight of many long years of strenuous labor, as the horses drew up in line with a score of other belled and robed equipages round Rideau Hall.

"Ah, here you are at last!" exclaimed Jack Mainton, as he and Carlton Monteith came out from the throng and assisted the ladies from the sleigh.

Modena, followed by the other occupants, descended. The admiring group of onlookers, who had been skating on the river, and who, through curiosity and the love of seeing the grand, as is usual in such cases, had been attracted to the entrance to the Hall, drew back and opened up a passage for her, many of them smiling as they recognized who it was, for she was as popular by reputation with the sweep and the boot-black as she was with the gay gathering now in full life behind the closed doors of Government House.

"You are last. We have been waiting. Such weather!" grumbled Jack as they ascended the steps together. "One might as well live in Greenland or at the North Pole as here."

"This is certainly Greenland, but Greenland with the roses of Mareschal, the beauty of Greece, the costumes of Worth, candelabra and gas pipes addenda. What a brilliant assemblage!" exclaimed Marion to her friend, after they had greeted and been welcomed by their Excellencies, as they stood apart for some moments before the music began.

"Who is that man talking to your father?" continued she, her eyes lighting up with interest and animation as she greeted her many friends.

The mistress of Apsley House looked over to where her father was engaged in earnest conversation with a man of noble countenance, with a brow indicative of great intelligence and with stern expression tempered with benevolent but rather sad smiles.

"Haven't you met him? Oh, I had forgotten, he has been away for a year in New Zealand taking up practical politics or something; he will come over to us soon."

"But you haven't told us who he is!"

"He is Mr. Lester Lester, the nicest man in the room, or the noblest, I should say."

"My dear cousin, I'm not surprised at your taste, but I am painfully shocked at your heresy. Lester, the leading Whig in the country, and you classing him as the best fellow! That's surely antagonistic to your principles," replied her cousin, who stood listlessly beside her chair.

"Whether it be good taste or whether it be heresy, I cannot retract anything I have said, and if you were honest you would confess you are as much of a heretic as I."

"How is that?" queried Marion.

"He thinks Mr. Lester's sister Helen is almost as perfect and beautiful as her namesake, Helen of Troy."

"You never heard me say so," replied Jack, gloomily, as he glanced across to where Helen Lester was conversing with her Ladyship.

"No, because you talk so much nonsense you have no time for common sense," replied Modena, smiling at her cousin's gloomy brow.

"Here comes Monteith; I'll tell him what you said about Lester."

The mistress of Apsley House was betrothed to Carlton Monteith, the youngest member of the Senate.

"He will but confirm what I have said," replied she, but Mr. Monteith had no time to reply before the strains of music from the orchestra were wafted to where they stood, and Keith Kenyon bent over her.

"I believe it is the arrangement we dance the first set together," he bowed and said.

Keith Kenyon was the youngest man in the Cabinet and the rising man of the day.

As he led his companion to their place in the set of honor, they were the cynosure of all eyes.

"I shall adore our new Governor and her Ladyship from this moment," said he, smilingly, to his companion.

"Why?" interrogated the dark eyes of his partner.

"For the honor of being your partner; it is almost as enviable as the ribbon our chief wears to-night."

"I am surely flattered! A compliment from the lips of a Talleyrand!"

"It is not a compliment; a compliment is a base coin tendered to one's vanity at the expense of one's intelligence. It would be impossible to offer you one."

"How nicely you infer another! I have intelligence but no vanity! and yet I am the vainest person in the room. I was admiring myself in the glass before I came, just like a peacock," she replied lightly, not wishing to admit that she saw that he meant what he said.

"The proudest perhaps, but not the vainest."

"Your compliments ascend to the height of a subtle art."

"Because they are based like all art on what is eternally true."

"Oh! Oh! But you said ' almost '; Merlin's shield of Fame still stands between you and—and—day-dreams," she replied lightly, meeting his eyes fearlessly.

"You wouldn't have it otherwise," he replied, as he took her hand as the music began.

When the set was over she was immediately claimed by Carlton Monteith, and then others followed, until an onlooker would have no difficulty in confirming Keith Kenyon's statement that the most beautiful, and even if the proudest, the most popular person in the room that evening was Modena Wellington. She danced the entire evening; she was too young to tire and too sought after to be allowed a few leisure moments with her friends, but they were all together for a few moments after refreshments, before the music began.

Jack was gazing intently at her Excellency.

"You look very serious, Jack. What are your thoughts? If you gaze much longer at her Ladyship, she will be sending her aide-de-camp to inform her servants to eject you as a wild man of the West, devoid of all manners," said his cousin, good-humoredly, to him.

"I was wondering what she thinks of us," replied Jack, gravely, as he withdrew his eyes from the face of their hostess and viewed his cousin.

"She thinks us very nice, indeed. See how pleased and interested she is in what father is telling her."

At this moment her Excellency was looking with smiling mien and raised brows at some views of the West which had been painted and left behind her by her predecessor, and which Mr. Wellington was now explaining and describing to her.

"Her good breeding makes her appear interested, but one is sure, that inwardly she is laughing at our presumption or lamenting our manners, which must savor of log cabins and the backwoods. How uncouth and undignified we must appear, and how ridiculous our aping Court Etiquette must seem to her; like a parvenu in good society or democracy in a mansion! What better opinion have they of us now than when Voltaire wrote, 'Well rid of fifteen thousand square miles of snow and ice,' or when La Pompadour said, 'The King can now sleep in peace since he has such a bugbear off his mind'?"

Jack's good-natured smile and cynicism of words irritated his cousin for a moment. She felt her face flush warm. Instinctively she felt that these were the sentiments entertained towards her country by a great many unenlightened foreigners. Had it been a personal matter she would not have cared. Her inborn consciousness of superiority made her wholly indifferent to comment or criticism; but her country! She was intensely patriotic, and it wasn't just what it might be. It was this fact which made the comments hurt.

She was about to reply, but, knowing her cousin's nature so well, she forebore, and immediately recovered her composure and good humor.

"How disappointed she will be to-night if she came expecting to meet a class of people similar to our pagan aborigines or our fur-clad Esquimaux!" was the reply she gave to her cousin.

"She sees the feathers and paint."

"They mean civilization."

"Not according to Jack's theory."

"She will have to admit we have advanced a little from the customs of Champlain and Charlevoix," said Helen Lester.

"She is wondering which clan you belong to, Modena," said Jack, laconically.

2

"She will admit you are the Queen of the clan, anyway," said Lester, as his deep-grey eyes lingered on her in meditative admiration.

"Will that add to your standing? It will please you, though; you are so conservatively fond of old traditions, age, royalty, and ancient customs and manners," said Jack, and then he smiled as he continued, "when we return home we shall look into our Almanac De Gotha, the Family Bible, and trace back to see if some of our ancestors were not Kings or Queens of the Forest Tribes. It would give such a prestige to our standing to be descended from some Esquimaux or cannibal about A.D. ——. What do you say, my cousin?"

"I say do not be profane, and I also say if that is the feeling they entertain towards us, they should come in a missionary spirit, as did Paul de Jenne or Madame de la Peltrie, and not with the insignias of Royalty."

"Missionaries generally derive more benefit than they bestow good."

"Oh! Oh! What egotism and malevolence! How ungenerous!" exclaimed someone.

"Are we not accusing them of faults and shortcomings of which we ourselves are very guilty?" asked Modena.

"That's only human nature."

"It's a human nature we should not countenance, and seriously speaking, if seriously taken, these are only *argumenta ad ignorantiam*. They give us a great deal more credit than we deserve. At heart we're only country mice sighing for our own hayricks and for some one to put a warm covering over us when the skies are stormy and cold. When we come to look at it in a right light, what's the use of pretending to be anything else or being hurt at their taking us at our real worth?" said Modena.

"How funny you look when you say that, and all the while you look like Maria Theresa, or at least like the crown of strawberry leaves," said Keith Kenyon, with a low laugh.

It was the second time to-night he had compared her to Maria Theresa.

She appeared to take no notice of it, but she knew that her blood ran warmer in her veins because of it.

"We cannot be honest and deny our primitiveness."

"Oh, please don't take life like that. If we have to live on bread and water we want to think we are really eating cake and drinking wine. One would like to see all realism buried at the bottom of the ocean. Do let us have our vanities and our ideals," pleaded

Marion Clydene, and her eyes deepened and darkened with many vague, unfulfilled desires.

"There is no vanity in the question: it is a just pride. We are just what we pretend to be," asserted the mistress of Apsley House, conscious of the integrity of her motives in life, and unconscious of any egotism or shortcoming. "Ulysses built his own house and raft, swung his scythe and guided his plow in the patriarchal simplicity of the Homeric age. We do the same. The only license put upon Homeric Kings was the time-honored customs of the community. We have violated none to-night," she continued, as she glanced round at the brilliant assemblage.

"Have we not? From the moment their Excellencies see your dress they will be sighing for the sweet delusions of youth, the time-honored customs of our country," said Keith Kenyon.

"Why?" asked she, with arched brows.

"Marion's ideals in their mind would be a tightly fitting tunic of buckskin, fringed and belled at the knees and embroidered with porcupine quills and shells, fringed leggings, beaded moccasins, eagle's plumage in long black hair, and in that necklace, instead of those pearls, bears' claws and snakes' rattles."

"And that diamond pendant on your neck would be in some dusky maiden's nose," said Jack, at which everybody laughed.

"You grow quite provincial in your thoughts and expressions; don't do so, we really cannot afford to do so," said Modena.

"You do not give them credit for much intelligence. Their education must have been sadly neglected," insisted Mrs. Sangster, who was always too much in earnest to see the humorous side of life.

"How much better are we than the aborigines?" asked Mrs. Cecil. "We're only savages painted white and some with red mountings."

"But we perfume our paint and use gloves and whitewash."

"Yes, we do," said Jack, abruptly; "when the aborigine gave his hand to, or broke bread with another, that person became sacred to him."

"What would you imply by that dark saying? That we are breaking her Excellency's bread and then discussing her? It's not a personal matter, only a political matter, and there's a moral license in politics to say all the bad things one wishes to say about another. People do not take us seriously when we say them, and there's no harm in it. I am quite sure she is telling Mr. Wellington what she thinks about us," said Mrs. Cecil.

"One regrets she does not see the best of us to-night; our climate compels us, like the humming birds and robins, to migrate to a warmer climate for five months in the year," said Modena.

"There is one thing she will regret not seeing," continued Mrs. Cecil, with an expression of mingled regret and dismay.

"What is it?"

"That which the modern world lacks, repose, harmony and dignity—our venerable, grim-visaged, long-haired sachems with their wampums and pipes of peace."

"Oh, no, she will not be disappointed, some of the Senators are here," said Jack, laconically.

"Jack, that is profane!" exclaimed his cousin, irritably.

"Well, what does she see?" persisted Mrs. Cecil, who, when she had once fastened on a subject liked to worry it well.

"You open up a wide question, and of all present the most competent person to answer the question is my lady here," said their chief, who was passing the group at the time and who now addressed the mistress of Apsley House. "She is the one who has most faith in our creeds, our country and our contemporaries."

"Before she could answer it she would have to be like the wise sage of old, 'Know oneself,' and that is too much wisdom for one so young. She does not need to know, she only needs to enjoy, and this she does, and so has found the true philosophy of life," said Mr. Lester, gallantly.

"We have been answering the question all the time with Adam Smith's eyes, seeing ourselves as others see us," replied Modena.

"If what Smith says is true, 'that society is a mirror by which we are enabled to see ourselves and judge ourselves,' then all her Ladyship can see to-night is a pack of sea-foam beauties, a crowd of cut-away cavaliers and a shoal of sentimentalists," said Jack, with his good-natured cynical brevity.

"And some satirists, too! One would infer from your looks and tone that we were a people who needed a Persius or a Juvenal, instead of being country mice," said his friend Lester.

"Were we *the* people we wouldn't do so much talking about ourselves. *The* people never discuss personalities. Her Excellency's remarks would be rich, ripe, mellow and impersonal.

"What an ungallant truism! If we don't talk about ourselves, what have we to talk about? The weather, art, war, books? Our weather is too cold to discuss, it would freeze our criticisms. We have no art; we are under age for war; and we have only other peoples' books. They talked when Hengist and Horsa were with them, and for many years afterwards. One does not need to rant or brag or boast, but one must do a little talking 'to get there,' and we're 'getting there'; there is more than talk behind our sea-foam beauties and our sweet sentimentalists," said Mrs. Cecil.

"I think Mr. Mainton was very nice to say 'sea-foam'; you know he might have said 'soap bubble' beauties; sea-foam suggests strength, beauty, purity, simplicity and the joy and light-heartedness which comes from something which in itself is typical of the Infinite; and then, too, he said 'cavaliers'; that's very nice; and he has given you credit for having in this age enough emotion to have sentiment; his words are really flattering," said her Excellency's niece, the Lady Greta.

"The Lady Greta's perception is keener than our countrywoman's," replied Jack, as he bowed deferentially to her as she passed on, but in an aside he muttered to his friend Lester, "Isn't Mrs. Cecil right? How much better are we than the aborigines? They at least had the decency to cover their nakedness, if it were only with a blanket, when they appeared at a public gathering, and that's more than can be said of us."

"It was only the half-civilized who did that; our middle classes do the same; but this monkey-gallery of ours, which we call the best, imitates the highest among our ancestors; the cannibals, you know, went to their dances and public gatherings quite full-dressed as we understand the term."

"And they knew what they were eating, too," continued Jack, again addressing the group, "good tender buffalo or bear meat served up in its own gravy and sirloin soup garnished with leeks, and weren't bothering their brains over a menu of bon-bons and bouillons, rissols and ragouts, ortolans stuffed with truffles, devilled spaghetti and oyster-cocktails—"

"What a reactionist!" interrupted his cousin. "Our ancestors may have their dishes of human broth, their bear meat and birch-bark canoes, but give me the nineteenth century, Government House and—"

"And this is ours," said Mr. Lester, as the music began.

When the evening was over and they were waiting for the sleigh to be announced, the master of Kenyon Court stood in the shadows of the hall doorway, lighting his cigar and looking at the group within, where the mistress of Apsley House stood talking with Carlton Monteith and Mr. Lester. She was a very beautiful woman, having with her beauty that supreme charm which eclipses beauty, that grace, dignity, courage and harmony which are but the heir-looms of a long line of culture, traditions and the spirit of the "noblesse oblige." Her hair was dark and waving, her skin very fair, her eyes the rich brown of the stag's throat and so deep that they shaded into violet, and were proud, meditative, inspiring, and indicative of great reserve of resource and latent power.

She wore a long, rich ermine-lined wrap, and her head was crowned by a small ermine hat, which added stateliness to her form. As they waited for the sleigh, she pushed the mantle back, and the gorgeousness of her dress and the lustre of the satin added beauty and brilliance to her distinction. But it was not so much the grace of her bearing or the beauty of her face and form that appealed to one as the sympathy and love expressed in the depth of her eyes and the sweet smile round her proud mouth.

"Her father did not read her right, when he said that no man would ever have dominion over her life, that there was no passion in her; that would depend very much on how much she loved and how much she was beloved," thought Keith Kenyon as he watched the scene within. "Her cousin Jack was right, when he said that her nature was one capable of great love. She does not care for the man she is going to marry," and he smiled at something within himself, but as quickly his face again grew grave. He was a wise man and never overrated his own powers. "She is bound to him by many ties, and she is one who would consider those ties very sacred," he reflected in after thought, and his brow drew together again in sterner lines, as he watched them take their places in the sleigh and drive away through the now fast falling snow to Apsley House.

CHAPTER II.

The Wellingtons, one of the oldest families in the country, were of United Empire Loyalist descent. Mr. Wellington's ancestor, Sir Claude Wellington, had come over from England, during the reign of one of the first of the Guelphs, as Governor of one of the New England States, and when the Pilgrim States had severed their relations with the motherland, Sir Claude, being a staunch Loyalist and firm supporter of the Crown's authority, had refused the pardon offered and rejected the inducements held out to him by the successful Revolutionists, and, leaving all he possessed, had sought a home, or rather a refuge, in a country over which the British flag yet floated. Sir Claude and his family had then disposed of their remaining property in the motherland and had bought large tracts of land from the Home Government, on which they settled, and as time passed and they became reconciled to their life, they entered political life once more, and soon became one of the leading families in the early history of the country; and as one generation succeeded another and they became identified with the birth and development of its interests, that feeling of patriotism and possession began to take deep root, as it can only generate and grow in hearts that have been bred and born in the land of their fathers. One of the wise men of old has said, " As mortars are made by the mortar-makers, so can citizens be manufactured by the law." But in oath-allegianced citizens there is not the seed or germ of patriotism. They will cling to that which suckled them as Romulus and Remus clung to their mother-wolf. This feeling may spring to life and grow in their children, but not in the alien born. One has to be born in, and intimately identified with the country, before he can become its child. His family ties must become wound in and out and around its trees and meadows, its strifes and battles, its sorrows and its joys, before it becomes endeared to one's heart. And so it was with the Wellingtons. Its struggles, its hopes, its joys, its attainments, had become theirs, doubly theirs, for the seed from the motherland had never died, but continued to blossom and bear fruit through each generation, and with the blossoms and fruit of loyalty sprang that of intense patriotism for the land of their birth; and the two flourished and grew side by side.

Until '37 they had been members of the Council, but had strenuously opposed the growing evils of the Family Compact.

The present Mr. Wellington had entered Parliament at an early age. His family had been Conservative in the true sense of the word rather than in its accepted term—that is, they believed in being governed by long-tested principles and in being governed by the best.

During their rule they had been influenced by a strong sense of duty and by a consciousness that they were the fittest to govern, and if let alone could and would govern wisely and well, their motives being altruistic and disinterested; they firmly and fully believed it was their right to govern, and that it was their duty to govern, and that they were responsible to a Higher Power and to a Higher Power alone, a sentiment no doubt, but the governing sentiment of all great men, and a sentiment that has proved the strength and stability of all great nations; but the present Mr. Wellington was wise and possessed sufficient insight to see that submission to Radical demands at the present time was the inevitable necessity, and that expediency, rather than principle, must govern, and that opposition was only prolonging events and retarding movements and changes which were in time certain to occur, because, as he sadly realized, the best had abused their privileges, and the people were almost as a unit demanding reforms in the name of right and liberty.

As far as it lay in his power to do so, he continued to oppose the extreme views of democracy, which had sprung out of the troubles of '37, but was forced by the spirit of the age to bury his old Conservative convictions, and with his co-patriots attach the Liberal to his name and accept, promote and enforce the principles and progress that the rising generation were demanding as their rights; but as year after year passed by, and as he realized that they were being deprived of their power to do good, and that each year power was slipping more and more from their order, he could not quite subdue a tinge of regret and sadness, which in later years, as the fruits of democracy and the evils so instinct within Responsible Government became more and more apparent, sometimes amounted to resentment and irony.

He had grown up side by side with men who had given their strength, their manhood, their intellect and even their life's blood to and for the young country, and who had passed away or were now passing away, and as he realized the ingratitude, the misrepresentations, the superficiality, the ephemeral and transient feelings of the present age towards those or towards the memory of those who had fought and died, at times his loyal and tender heart hardened as Scipio's had done towards the country for which he had given his all. Such feelings as these were not caused by any impatience to consummate his own plans or to bring glory to himeslf, but only came in those moments which come to every man who has the country's best interest at heart and who is governed by high standards of action, but who grows disdainful when he contemplates the frailties, the low standards, the ingratitude of human nature and the inherent corruption of modern forms of government. But as such feelings as these passed over his soul, as a wailing chord passes over the strings of a lyre, with great force of will he would rise above them into a broader and higher atmosphere, and like the brave in every line of life he would again throw himself into the fray and do what he could to fulfil the aim and object of life—that of making the world brighter and better.

He had been a strong advocate of Confederation, and had since then been intimately connected with the many movements for the welfare of the country and its people, and was at the present time second minister in the Cabinet and the Chief's personal friend and adviser.

While travelling in England he had met Marguerite Modena, who was closely related to the famous hero of Waterloo. The following year he had returned to England, and there they had been married. He brought his young bride to his home, and here in the full glow of health and eagerness of life she entered into his ambitions and plans for the civilization and aggrandizement of the infant country.

Her presence soon began to be felt; institutions sprang into life; charities were established; learning began to disseminate; elegance and refinement made their appearance in high circles, and her unconscious influence wherever she passed made life better and brighter for those around her.

But death claimed her at an early age, and when he who loved her so well laid her away beneath the sepulchre of ebony, inlaid in onyx and gold, which ever stood ready in the cloisters of the old Ursuline Chapel on the family estate at Fernwylde, he buried with her all that was brightest in his life. Life was never the same to him again; but he did not succumb to the loss. Their bonds had been too strong for even death to sever. She was ever present with him. Although an invisible and inexorable barrier divided them, it was not strong enough to keep them apart. Although he could not see her, feel her, caress her, or hear her words of love and solace, they were all there ever with him, his guide, his inspiration, his star.

Instinctive hope and philosophy had told him that this world was but an ante-chamber to be used as a preparation to a higher life where things would be better understood. She had but gone " to those blissful climes where all knowledge is gathered in the cycled times," while he was left to wander on a darkened earth " where all things round him breathed of her."

She was but waiting for him there; thus perforce had he to strive the more to make his soul mate for hers in that clearer air.

He had resolutely taken up the threads of life where they had been snapped asunder and had gone his way, giving his talents, his energies and his ambitions to his country and to the education of his only daughter.

His daughter resembled his family. The truth of the old adage, " L'enfant de l'amour resemble toujours au pere," was verified in her. The women of his house had been noble women—women who had invariably built their lives upon great principles and traditions rather than women of sentiment. His daughter possessed the qualities and attributes of the women of his house, but she had also inherited from her mother a lovable heart, an amiability, a tenderness and pliability which had softened and made more womanly her whole character.

He was immensely wealthy, possessing several mines, many houses, and various estates in different parts of the country, but the homes dearest to them were Fernwylde, the old family estate, and Apsley House, the noble and historical home of his fathers.

The first of the Wellingtons had bought Apsley House when it was but a French chateau from a member of one of the oldest families of France.

When Louis, the father of the country, had sent out the Carignans, one of the head officers, an associate of Colbert's and a pupil of the famous Lebrun, being of an aspiring and sanguine disposition, had been deeply impressed as he sailed up the great river to the Key of the Virgin Country, with the beauty, fertility and extensiveness of the world before him. Who can tell what dreams and what visions filled his mind as he stood on the heights and gazed over an unsurpassed, almost an unequalled panorama, as his predecessor Champlain, filled with the feu sacre, the Amor Patriæ, and visions of a New Empire, had stood in the door of his Chateau St. Louis on what is now called Durham Terrace and had gazed on what appeared to him an earthly paradise! He had but left a Court, one of the most brilliant that ever breathed, and united to its brilliance were both aspiration and intrigue. No doubt, as in Frontenac's mind, visions of a New France and a miniature Versailles may have entered his; at least he undertook to build himself a mansion in miniature patterned after his home in that smiling Sun-King's land.

In the midst of his pagan paintings, sculpture and architecture he died, but these were carefully preserved by his family, and years afterwards, when Quebec became the scene of so much turmoil and strife, the family removed to the Queen's City, taking with them the pagan painted ceilings, the mystic embroidered tapestries, the lancet and oriel windows, emblazoned and deeply embeyed, the valuable carvings and unique collections of art, and bought the picturesque grounds where Apsley House now stands.

The octagonal chateau was built on an eminence and the grounds laid out in lawns, rose-gardens, hothouses, and woody terraces sloping to the little lake, an expansion of a stream which ran down to feed the great river.

Surrounding the grounds were low, ivy-covered stone battlements with massive iron gates, the pillars of which were capped by bronzed lions and on the panels of which were carved the emblems and arms of the Wellingtons.

Broad driveways and walks traversed the grounds and led up

to the main entrance, which was a canopy of carved stone supported by massive pillars resting on some of the antique carved pedestals of the Carignans.

Wing after wing had been added by each succeeding generation, until it was now one massive pile of architecture with towers and turrets and soft-tinted windows standing fair and clear against the northern sky, or losing themselves in the hoar frost or rain mists so prevalent in those parts.

On passing through the massive doorway at the front one entered a large octagonal hall which reached to the dome of the house, with a ceiling of the famous paintings. Broad, heavily carved oak stairways in winding curves led to the upper stories; there were several large drawing-rooms and reception rooms with their emblazoned panels and carved mantels, and containing treasures of art from all parts of the world; state dining-rooms with polished floors and Venetian mirrors; long galleries containing, besides the family portraits of generations of Wellingtons, many paintings and pastels from convent and studio, from the classical cities of the Continent, while the library, which had done so much to make the women and men of the house ladies and gentlemen of letters and culture, was considered the best in the city.

The octagonal chateau with its colonnades of porphyry, its mystic painted windows, its mahogany carvings and old tapestries, had been left unmolested, but the present mistress of the place had taken some of the rooms for her own private apartments and had converted the others into a music room and art room combined. It was the most beautiful room in the city, with its St. Cecilias and cherubim, Orpheus with his lyre and Pan piping, peeping out from softly draped windows, while Isis, with her anemone in her hand, and Cupid with his bow, rode on high.

It was here at Apsley House, when not travelling abroad, that Mr. Wellington and his daughter spent many months in the year, but they also spent part of every summer under the maples, the oaks and beeches of their old family home of Fernwylde.

Fernwylde, a few miles from the suburbs of the city, was a remarkably beautiful and fertile estate of many acres, richly wooded, shut in, lonely and stately, away from the hum and stir of man, by a circlet of cascaded waters, heavy Siberian pine forests and the towering summits of its own hills.

In the early history of the country it had been the home of Champlain, who had chosen it for its rugged grandeur, its frowning outlines, the wild primeval aspects of its heights, in such striking contrast to the repose, the serenity and fertility of the scene which lay within its lap.

In the heart of the amphitheatre lay a little lake, lovely and limpid. On the lake shore nestled a monastery, a relic of the days when the church was the " Portals of the Poor " and " Faith was Food," now the home of a once far-famed dignitary of the church but now a solitary, a seer and a scholar, and some few Jesuit priests who devote their lives to the welfare of the poor. The monastery was long, low, moss and ivy-covered without, but rich with art and literature within, and was almost as hidden beneath the willows and larches of the lake as the oriole's nest in the trees overhanging the waters.

The monks had given to it their air of peace and repose; its cloisters were cool, calm and consoling; on the evening air its bells would chime forth their Agnus Dei, or an Ave Maria would float peacefully upward, bringing with it rest and sustenance to the villagers after their day's work was over.

It had been there longer than any of the villagers could remember. It had been there when the present mansion had been but a French chateau; each habitant loved it and felt it was part of his home, and was free to go to it when he would.

Late in the eighteenth century the French chateau had fallen to decay, and now in its place, throned on a hill in the heart of the home, an old Gothic mansion rose, homelike and stately, many-turreted and pinnacled, with its colonnades of grey stone and white marble and its stone staircases leading down the many terraces to the water's edge.

While the interior had rooms magnificent and stately, on the whole they were more comfortable and homelike. In many of the rooms were the old-fashioned fireplaces with their brass andirons and carved mantelpieces. For many months of the year fires were kept burning on the hearth, for it was its mistress's delight to run out at all seasons of the year for a few days with intimate house-parties.

When she could leave home she invariably came to Fernwylde, and the happiest moments of her life were spent in and around the old Fernery.

The old Fernery had been built by a former Wellington. It stood at some little distance from the house and was built of massive fire-proof material, and contained large vaults in which the Wellingtons, when leaving their homes, had stored their plate and valuables, but of late years there had been added picturesque porticoes, rustic arbors and alcoves, and several colonnaded rotundas, while at the western side, facing the Idlewylde, was an immense bank of ferns, from which it derived its name.

It was a spot dear to all the country round; one of those spots that tend to make a place a home, a place associated with and consecrated by old tales of love, of family joys and sorrows, loyal traditions and sacred memories.

From childhood its present mistress had dearly loved the old home, and had spared nothing to make the place beautiful and its people happy.

One felt, when approaching its precincts or when entering the portals of any of her doors, that odor and essence of beauty and refinement, that harmonious blending of good taste and magnificence, that silent sympathy and repose which only cultured people can impart to a lavish display of wealth and which alone can inspire ease and true enjoyment within those with whom one is associated.

When his wife died, Mr. Wellington had obtained the services of Mrs. Gwen, an old friend of the family's, as a companion to his daughter. The other members of the family were Jack Mainton, a nephew of Mr. Wellington's, and editor of one of the government organs, and Marion Clydene, a daughter of one of Mr. Wellington's schoolmates, who had died, leaving his only child under the care and guardianship of his lifelong friend.

Mrs. Wellington had died while her daughter was yet young, and this had caused Modena to take her place and perform the duties and receive the honors of their homes at a very early age.

Her father's position entailed much hospitality and much entertainment, and the onerous task had fallen upon her. Her early and constant association with the political world had greatly increased her intelligence and intensified her perceptions, while her responsibility and position had added age and dignity to her youth. She had reflected on and comprehended things much beyond her years, her manners and intelligence being those of a woman of mature years, whereas she was but nineteen.

She dearly loved work, and the work most congenial to her was that in which she was engaged, that of being, as in her youthful enthusiasm she believed herself to be, the Mentor and Mascot, the Lady Devonshire of her own father's cause.

She believed that great things could be accomplished socially, and was the first to introduce a new era in her country's politics.

She came from a race who possessed enough greatness within themselves to want no greatness from without. Her one desire, then, was to live well, and to live well one must to a great extent live for others. She loved the world at large, and had within her a great desire to establish conditions which would enable the people on the whole to live temperately and liberally. The cruel contrasts of civilization with which she daily came in contact were to her a constant source of thought and reflection, and engrossed her mind to such an extent that all things else seemed immaterial to her.

But, while her mind was engrossed in her father's cause of laying the foundation for these conditions and in legislating and in the administration of justice, she was also active in individual cases.

Life to her was a sacred trust; its smallest details serious and important. Like Maria Theresa, she believed that " In our position nothing is a trifle."

She was known and beloved by the working classes in many parts of the city, and there was not one on their vast estates or in the different works belonging to her father but obeyed her slightest wish. " I have not done anything but what it is my duty to do," she had once said to one of her father's employees, who had been helpless the whole winter, and who had depended altogether on her charity for the support of his wife and three little children, and who was blessing her for her kindness.

" Oh! it is not only what you give us, but it is the kindness; you do not appreciate kindness because you have been so accustomed to it that you have become insensible to it; it is different with us. It is almost as nourishing as a meal of meat and Madeira," he continued, with a deeper feeling than one would expect in so rough a miner.

But, although she was a strong advocate of justice and right to the masses, the democratic tendency of the age was abhorrent to her. " Blood tells," she was wont to think, "more than any one knows, or thinks." Generations of culture and intelligence are more capable of ruling for the general welfare of the masses than illiteracy and its companions. Our order is the product of generations of development. It is our privilege, our prerogative and our duty to rule, was her creed.

The next evening after her Excellency's reception she had gone to a Musical at Monteith House, and she had there said to Mr. Lester, who had but recently returned from studying social conditions in New Zealand, and who was expatiating the merits of the democratic basis of that country. " Equality is impossible, and were it possible it would have the tendency to vulgarity. Variety is the law of life. All republics have their slaves, from Sparta to a bee-hive. It is our prerogative to rule. It is our own fault the people rebel and grumble and do not respect us. If we would only assert and maintain our rights and privileges and make them feel we are leaders in reality and worthy of respect, as did Pitt and Colbert and Marie Antoinette, then it would lie within our power to be good and to do good; but we do not do this; we have lost our courage and our faith in ourselves as leaders, and instead of leading, we follow."

But Mr. Lester had replied, " The day has gone by for that sort of thing, as Burke says, ' Never more shall we behold that generous loyalty to rank and set, that proud submission, that dignified obedience, that subordination of the heart which kept alive even in servitude itself, the spirit of an exalted freedom.' Alas! this is the age of Equality, Right and Reason."

And Modena had looked at him, not being able to accept or to comprehend all that his truism entailed.

" If the day has gone by we should revive it again; one's feelings, as well as one's example, are contagious; and if we haven't faith and hope and ambition and a strong sense of duty, the people will not have them. It rests with us what our country will become."

And Mr. Lester had looked at her as she stood before him in all her girlish faith and fervor, and his eyes had deepened and then had saddened as he remembered.

He had had his youthful dreams and his illusions; many times he had been beaten by the rods of the world's base ingratitude. He had been in earnest, and he had cared and he had suffered. But his eyes again brightened as he remembered. The shadows of his life had begun to lengthen into afternoon, but there were many, many landmarks by the way, and his disillusions had culminated in a wider and greater hope. " Her faith and her fervor were the very essence of life," he was sure, and he bowed low and deferentially over her hand as he murmured, " Rest assured, my dear, that the unconscious influence of a good woman is greater than all social theories; you are a noble woman."

And Jack, who was a dozen years her senior, and had seen life in all forms, and who now stood beside her, pulling to pieces a withered rose and rolling the dead petals into a hard mass in the palm of his hand, was inwardly comparing it with his cousin's hopes and enthusiasms.

The rose had been full of life and beauty when it had left nature's gardens, but the heated breath of artificial life and contact with the crowded mass had withered its petals and impaired its beauty and fragrance. Unconsciously he recalled Apollo's words, "Why should I fight for the sake of those miserable mortals who, like the leaves of the tree, last but a short time and then wither and fade away. Let us refrain from fighting and let them carry on the war themselves."

But this is what Modena had no notion of doing. She did not believe the world to be a world of miserable mortals, but a world as dear as that upon which Phaeton in his Palace of the Sun had gazed with outstretched hands for the reins of the immortal chariot to light the world, and she, as he, was all ambition and sincerity. Experience and the strifes of life had not as yet lifted the rosy veils from reality or washed her eyes with the collyrium of disillusion and shown her things as they really were in their nudity.

CHAPTER III.

" How are you, Mr. Lester? Do you want a walk before dinner? I am going down to see Mrs. Byers; I heard to-day her husband was without work," said the mistress of Apsley House the next afternoon, as she met Mr. Lester coming home from the House.

She was dressed in a street costume of dark blue trimmed with sable, with hat and ruff to match, and was accompanied by her favorite St. Bernard, Nell Gwynne, and her King Arthur greyhound, Cavall.

It was a wild winter's day; heavy wracks of clouds were sweeping up from the west; great gusts of snowflakes came up the streets. while the leafless, wind-tormented trees wept, and sighed, and bowed their heads in the dull grey afternoon air.

The cold air blew in her face, tinging it with warm color, while her firm elastic step and litheness of movement told of the great vitality within.

It was fully two miles to where she was going, but she courted the long walk. She loved action. Mr. Lester had frequently accompanied her on such visits, and his face now lit up with pleasure as he raised his hat and turned to go with her.

" There are many unemployed; one fears it will be a very severe winter for some," he replied, as they resumed their way, Nell Gwynne following, carrying a basket of fruit and flowers for little Lone, who was ill.

" And what are we to do?" she asked. " I spoke to father to-day regarding Mr. Byers, and he said they had too many men now, and were only working part of the time in order to provide employment for all our own men."

"It is difficult to do anything in a case like this; one cannot offer charity. If poor, they are proud and sensitive, and the pity of the world is to them infinitely worse than its poverty. When one cannot go and say, 'Mr. Byers, we want more men and will pay fair wages,' what can one do?" asked Lester.

"When one cannot say that the government should be prepared to say it."

"Oh! Oh! that's a very serious assertion; you would advocate its engaging in public works to employ its unemployed. We are yet too young for that."

"It would be advisable as an emergency," she replied, as they passed by some large works which had been closed for several months.

"That is very fair in theory, but practice requires the money. Are we not already over-burdened with taxation?" replied Mr. Lester, as they left the thoroughfare and turned towards the lumber districts.

"We could tax the rich to furnish employment for the poor."

"How would you justify such a course?"

"Labor is the source of all wealth, and if labor fails its product should support it. Nature has her own laws, and this is one of them, or if you will permit me to use another person's words in lieu of original ones, what we want is, 'An intelligent principle of law and order in the universe embracing equally man and nature.'"

"That's Plato's definition of God. Yes, we want it, but we cannot find it. Sometimes it hides itself in funny places on cold days like these."

"That's not an expression worthy of you. That is so like our conventional religion which clips and fits the ways of Deity to suit its habits and wishes. If things are wrong, they are the result of our own actions," replied his companion, gravely.

"Then nature has nothing to do with it?"

"It is not nature that is complaining. Fernwylde wears coarse shoes, woollen stockings and homespun, and they are happy and contented. They are kings and queens on their own estates. It is not the plow-boy or the milk-maid, but the mechanic. The modern world has given us the machines. The shop has been the loadstone to the youth and the succursal of the country's sinews. It has failed for the time being. Its product should now support its source."

"Who would believe that we should ever hear you advocate Socialism! Last night you were condemning equality."

"I am not upholding it now."

3

" Then your hair-splitting is too fine for my dull eyes and mind."

" Our wealth is only a trust. We are the guardians of the goose that lays the golden egg. We must not necessarily kill the goose and distribute its bones and flesh equally among our fellow-men. It would do no good if we did. In a few years—very few—conditions would again be the same as they are now. Social grades, distinctions, barriers, all those things are a necessity. The King must guard that which he rules; he is but a hind to whom a space of land is given to plow. Duty is our weapon against envy. It is our duty to guard the goose, but it is also our duty to judiciously distribute the golden eggs equally."

" You would be a parent to the poor—guardian, rather?"

" I would have intelligence and give justice. Our aim of late has been to encourage the manufacture of machinery. We have tempted the youth from the sod. As we said a moment ago, there is now a temporary depression; we should furnish that youth with employment."

" You would encourage laziness; no, not laziness, but thriftlessness. It would only dull their invention and ambition and do for them what the machines have done—make them machines instead of artisans. The individual has his duties to perform, and his first duty is to provide for himself, and experience has taught us it is a dangerous thing to intrude on private rights or duties."

" The State has its functions to perform as well as the individual. Is not the individual's first duty to the State? Therefore the State's first duty is to the individual. Its chief object should be to provide conditions in which the people are enabled to aim at the highest and best life possible. It should provide for the happiness and welfare of the many, not the few. At least that is what Aristotle tells us, and all wise men since have upheld his philosophy. It is really the only permanent basis. It is the only basis which will endure. Ethics and politics are inseparable; we want men of intelligence at the helm, with ethics at one end and economics at the other. Our State must have been negligent in some way or we would not now hear those bitter cries. One fears and regrets that in a great many ways it is providing for the few, not the many. We have been raising our voices, but of no avail. It is so often the lost causes which are the noble ones, but since it is so, there is no use wasting one's time regretting it; all one can now do is to remedy the evil."

" The evil cannot be remedied; it is easy to philosophize, but all theories and political schemes are impracticable and unworkable, because it is an impossibility to reconcile property, poverty and population. Even your sage, with all his wisdom, in working out a theory advocated and practised infanticide. You surely would not countenance that."

"There is no need to countenance it. We give bonuses to increase the population."

"Then the theories which apply in one case will not apply in another."

"Pardon me! Don't you think they will? The principles always remain the same; it is only the outside drapings that must be clipped and embellished as the existing circumstances require. It is because men have abused their privileges and forsaken principles that we have this state of affairs. Come here, Nell Gwynne," she called to her St. Bernard, as she saw her deposit her basket on the frozen snow to defend it against the attacks of a huge mastiff that persisted in sniffing at its contents. "I am afraid we are like Plato's philosophers," she continued, smiling, "we have been sky-gazing and failed to see actions and events that are tumbling about at our feet. Poor Lone! Our philosophizing nearly cost him his hot cutlets! He may thank Nell Gwynne for them. She is like Ulysses' dog, faithful to its trust."

"Your moral would be to become like Nell Gwynne and cease sky-gazing," said Mr. Lester, smilingly.

"No, it would be a proper mixture of sky-gazing and common sense."

"You mean a mean state in life, I am afraid, that can never be," continued Mr. Lester, gravely and sadly, as they passed some thinly-clad, shivering children, who were returning home to the poorer districts after having delivered the night-men's evening lunches in the lumber districts. "It seems impossible to establish the system which your sage recommends, that of limiting or providing each man with sufficient property to live temperately and liberally. Doesn't More tell us, in his "Utopia," he saw nothing but a conspiracy of rich men procuring their own commodities under the guise and title of Commonwealth? It has ever been thus, and no doubt ever will be thus, until 'kings have become sages and sages have become kings.'"

"But surely, if men will but use the brains and muscles with which nature has endowed them, they will always have the necessaries of life, and the luxuries do not count," he continued, in an after reflection.

"They do not count if we have a society that looks at things in that light, but our society judges us by our appanages, and when one is in Rome one has to do as the Romans do or she or he is unhappy. The individual is nominally free, but he is also powerless in a world bound hand and foot in the chains of economic necessity and social demands."

"It would not make me unhappy."

"No, because you do not care for the world's opinion. You have the courage to live your own life; but yet, pardon me, if I am too personal, but your happiness is dear to me; you are not always happy. You are sad, at times almost melancholy to pessimism. You have too much of Shelley within you. You rebel against existing circumstances. You are extremely sensitive to what seems to us the cruel contrasts, the rank injustices, and the precariousness of human life. You are continually wondering why this should be. You would find the Heart behind it all—"

"Is there a Heart behind it all?" interrupted Mr. Lester.

His companion looked at him quickly.

"Pardon me, I didn't mean to say that: forget that I said it. You have found the Heart?"

"Decidedly so. And Mind, too! These contrasts are a necessity, and an evolution from the very nature of things. It has been ever thus, and I suppose ever will be. You remember the story of our own beloved Thor and his going to the land of the Jotuns with his hammer-bolt and his staunch henchman Thialfi, which, by the way, was Manual Labor, and of the great feats given him to perform —the Drinking Horn, from which he drank long and fiercely, but of no avail—the Old Woman with whom he wrestled, only to suffer defeat—and the Cat which he failed to lift—and then Skrymir's voice, the Earth, 'You are beaten, yet be not so much ashamed; these are only appearances: The Drinking Horn is the Sea, the Old Woman, Time, and the Cat is the Great World-Serpent, which, tail in mouth, girds and keeps up the whole Created World; had you torn it up, the world must have rushed to ruin.' Thor's resentment, and the Giant's mocking voice, 'Better come no more to Jotunheim;' grim humor resting on earnestness and pathos like a rainbow over the tempests of nature. And the world then was young! Ah, how little it has changed! The same World-Serpent and the same Thor cries! What you lack is philosophy. The philosophy of accepting things as they are and going on towards your Ideal. Your happiness depends upon philosophy."

"I thought happiness depended upon the heart."

"So it does, but philosophy sets the heart right."

"You are happy?"

"Yes, happy every moment of my life; happy as the birds in the tree."

"Even when you have the toothache?" Mr. Lester smiled; his companion smiled too.

"Why will you suggest such a pertinent thing?"

"Be truthful."

"Oh! no one cares to have the toothache."

"Why do you have it?"

"One wouldn't have it if one could help it; nature must answer that charge."

"There are pains in the heart for which nature too must answer. Pains which no philosophy can cure, no more than it can cure the toothache," replied Mr. Lester, gloomily, and with a personal ring in his voice. "But, there, I am talking to you in an unknown tongue. I do not believe you have ever loved. That may be a hard one on Monteith, but I believe it is true."

"What are your reasons for saying so?" she asked, not realizing any personal meaning in his words.

"Because if you ever really loved, you would have more sympathy for and less philosophy towards the sufferings of others."

"Your words would imply that great love brings great sufferings and comprehension. You think I have no sympathy, and yet I assure you I have infinite sympathy. If I could, I would take all the suffering in the world and bear it for others, but one cannot do that; all one can do is to help others bear it."

"You would do what Shelley did. You would add together every carriage and beggar seen side by side in the street and divide the result by two," replied Mr. Lester, in a lighter vein, glad that she had failed to read his personal meaning.

"No, I do not think I would. I would take the beggar up and drive him to his destination, and give him a coin or some employment, and set him down and let him climb up to the carriage."

"It takes so long to do so; and there are so many bumps and rocks in the road! You spoke in the highest terms of Mr. Byers. He hasn't yet climbed to his carriage."

"Because we have put some big hard bumps in his way—so big that he cannot climb over them."

"I do not know the man. Who is he?"

"He is one of a large family who came here from Scotland; his parents were very poor, but frugal and industrious. Mr. Byers was the eldest of ten children. His father died, and he remained with his mother and helped to feed, clothe and educate the younger members of the family, and by dint of over-work succeeded in learning a trade for himself—that of wood-carving. His wife was a young girl whom they had brought with them from home. They had loved each other from childhood, but were forced to wait many long years. At last they were married. They have now a large family of small children—eight, I think. Lone has been ill for years. The other children had the measles, followed by diphtheria, from which two died. Mrs. Byers, worn out with watching, care and anxiety, was ill for many months. Mr. Byers was forced to use the money they had saved to pay the doctor's bills and to provide nourishment for the sick. They are thrifty, honest and industrious. I have heard father say he is a splendid artisan. You have noticed those carved cornices and mantel-pieces in the north drawing-room; those are his handiwork. His work at first commanded excellent prices, but with the advent of machinery the demand for superior handwork has fallen away. Mr. Byers was forced to go to the shop and become a machine himself, but after one has spent his life in inventing and creating, it is difficult to transform oneself into a mechanical, automatic piece of blood, bone and muscle. His own soul had been reflected in his work; he took as much pride, nay, infinitely more, in an exquisitely carved toy or panel than we do in our choicest piece of statuary. The factory work was uncongenial. There were younger men more adept. He was forced to leave the factories, and now he does the best he can. Since the death of his children his spirits are broken, but he never complains. He still struggles manfully on," replied Modena, as they turned a corner where the wind blew up in great gusts from the river, causing her to pause and turn for a moment to regain her breath.

Mr. Lester sighed and did not reply, as they again resumed their way.

"In reviewing his life," continued his companion, as she took his arm to assist her against the strong gale which was now blowing, "one cannot see where he has been negligent or to blame in any way. He has not been crafty or grasping or manipulating, but has striven to do his duty honestly and simply, day by day and year by year, and has done it with great cheer and courage, and we have many men who have never done an honest day's work in their lives, living in opulence. Labor is their only capital, and that is why the government should protect it."

"You are a reactionist. You would ostracise the fruits of science," replied Mr. Lester.

"I would encourage and cultivate a taste for workmanship that requires thought, interest and pride in its execution. Doesn't Ruskin tell us it is the degradation of the operator into an animated tool, more than any other evil of the times, that is leading the masses of nations everywhere into vain, incoherent, destructive struggling for a freedom of which they cannot explain the nature to themselves. This universal cry against wealth is caused not so much by want or wounded pride, but because they have no pleasure in the work by which they make their bread. Instead of dividing labor, we have divided man. The little intelligence left within him is not enough to make a pin or nail, but exhausts itself in making a point or a head. The cry which is going up from every manufacturing town, a cry louder than the furnace blasts, is that we are manufacturing everything but man. There is more real soul, more real joy, in a man who tills his own little acre of ground, or in one who fashions his own plow-point, than in a score who are slaves to science."

"You will persist in making your world a world of husbandmen, artists and statesmen," her companion replied, as they passed a large red brick hall, which had been donated to the city by Modena's mother for a reading room and library for the laboring poor. It had been left to the trusteeship of several prominent men in the laboring classes, but these men having died or removed to another part of the country, its management had fallen into the hands of the most Radical of the workingmen, and was now used as a meeting-place for their malcontents.

As they approached the hall they noticed a banner, stretched from door to street, informing the men of an important meeting that night, to discuss their rights and grievances.

"But," continued Lester, as they stepped beneath the banner, "instead of the country generating artisans it is producing too many men such as we find in here," and he pointed to the wide-open door, through which was plainly visible the preacher's platform, backed by a crimson-lettered banner with deep black background.

"The result of the abuse of our privileges," persisted Modena, as they came in sight of Mr. Byers' cottage.

"King Arthur never abused his privileges, yet disruption crept within the Table Round."

"With the advent of women! Poor Guinevere! She was to be pitied, not condemned; her heart was stronger than her mind."

"Her love was stronger than her wisdom. What has wisdom to do with love?"

"All."

"Then you have never loved if you say wisdom has anything to do with it."

"That is twice you have told me so within the last few minutes. I assure you I have loved. I love every living thing on earth. There are attributes, appurtenances, appendages which surround many things which one detests. They offend one's taste, but beneath all these the real thing lies. It is this that one loves."

" You would put every one in the same class? You would make no selection?"

" You said all great love brings great sorrow. Is it wise to court a great love?"

" Wisdom has nothing to do with it. Fate or Destiny does it regardless of either Will or Wisdom, and when they are perverse in their selection, what is one to do?" persisted Mr. Lester.

" What one wills to do, one can do."

" You think a life-long devotion will have its reward?"

" Certainly. If you mean Mr. Byers, he will be sure to succeed in time. There he is now in his shop. Go to him, while I am within."

Mr. Lester frowned, but did as he was told, and went round the cottage to a small yard in the rear, where the owner of the place was endeavoring to put together some pieces of wood which he had carved. " She cannot understand; she does not love him," he said, as Keith Kenyon had once said, and then his brow drew together in deeper and darker lines. " Having met *him* it is quite natural she should think nothing of me," he felt, like all great and good men having a genuine humility in his measurement of himself. "There is in *his* nature what will satisfy hers; there is not in mine. I can only live well and love well, but honesty and honor are not enough to win love in return," he reflected sadly, as he reached the shop door.

Mr. Byers' little shop had been there since his cottage had been built, and for many years he had planned and dreamed of what he was to accomplish in it. There had been many pieces of exquisite workmanship gone from its doors, but the severities of the long winters and the necessities of life and its misfortunes had continually prevented his enlarging it or accomplishing in it what he had wished or dreamed.

Mr. Lester now approached him, while Modena, taking the basket from Nell Gwynne, knocked at the door and was admitted by the woman of the house.

" How are you to-day, Mrs. Byers, and how is Lone?" she asked, as she approached the invalid's chair near the fireplace.

" I am quite well, thank you," replied the little fellow, looking up from his picture book of " Cock Robin," and smiling.

He could remember no other life than the one he now led, but was fortunate in possessing a sunny disposition, and looked upon his life, with his few picture books, his little collie dog, a knife and some wood to carve as all that was desirable in life.

"Nell Gwynne has brought you and baby some fruit and some flowers and that book we spoke about the other day," she said, as she talked with him; and then, when she had taken the contents from the basket and placed some near him, she turned to Mrs. Byers.

Mrs. Byers had belonged to their sewing circle in the Mission Church in that part of the city, and Modena had learned that she was an excellent needlewoman and was anxious for work. Having six little children her time was almost all occupied with caring for them, but excellent management enabled her to devote half the day and late into the night to outside needlework. But this was difficult to obtain until her need fell under the notice of the mistress of Apsley House. On learning of the circumstances, Modena had at once secured material, paid the highest prices for the needlework, and disposed of it to public charities in the city.

It was now some half-hour before she had given final instructions as to the work and left the house, leaving its inmates happier with the prospects of comforts for Christmas.

As she emerged from the doorway she met Mr. Lester coming from the work-shop.

"When one talks to Mr. Byers, it does make one feel that our frills and furbelows, our clubs and carriages and conventionalities, and a thousand other things, are an insult to them," he said gravely, as they turned towards home.

"Did he complain?" asked Modena. "Seldom he does so."

"Oh, no, not consciously, but one can read between the lines."

"I think if you read Mr. Byers' lines aright they would justify our carriages. He does not envy them. He is a bird with a broken pinion, but because his wing is maimed he would not wish to see ours broken also. In many ways he thinks his life enviable and preferable to ours. He has a simple pity for many of our empty hearts and frivolous lives. The folly and hollowness of the life that turns night into day, and day into a pleasure-house, and which makes the gaming-table the sole field of battle, must seem to them, with their moments filled with the real things of life, a thing to be pitied, not envied. It is Mr. Byers and his kind who make one wish to distribute the golden eggs judiciously."

"But where you will see one like Mr. Byers, you will see many who are unworthy," said Mr. Lester, as they passed the hall, where many people were now beginning to gather. "No doubt if we stepped in here to-night we would hear much false logic and the expression of many unjust sentiments. It is a question which has ever worried honest men, and I suppose ever will," reflected he, and they proceeded on their way in silence for some time.

"Couldn't you help him?" his companion asked as they hurried, for it was growing very dark.

"Oh, yes, he is coming to me in the morning; but then he is only one, you know, and what is one in a hundred, a thousand, a million?" he exclaimed.

"He is one," replied Modena, "and that is everything to us now. For the ninety-and-nine you will have to theorize in the House. But here we are. Will you come in to dinner?" she asked, as they reached Apsley House, forgetting for the moment they were to dine out that evening.

"No, not in this dress; we shall see you later at Glenhurst," he said, as he raised his hat and went on into the gloom of the streets towards Maple Hurst.

CHAPTER IV.

But it seemed that the Fates had willed that the mistress of Apsley House was to be brought into the presence of the needy that day.

"Oh, father, see that woman and little child! She is completely exhausted and nearly frozen! Tell Jackson to stop a moment," said Modena a few hours afterwards, as she leaned forward from the depths of the robes, as they sped on their way to a state dinner at the residence of the Secretary of State.

"But, my daughter, we are late now, and no doubt the woman has been drinking."

"Drinking!" exclaimed his daughter, in surprise. "Oh, no, that is impossible. Do stop."

Her tone was so earnest and her distress so evident, that to please her Mr. Wellington ordered Jackson to drive up to the pavement, where the woman had sunk down, while his daughter descended from the midst of the warm robes and addressed the sufferer.

"What is the matter, my good woman? What can I do for you?"

"I am only tired," replied the woman, in muddled accents, as the cold wind swept in stinging bitterness from over the frozen river and blew the faded and torn shawl from her stooped shoulders, while the soughing sound round the eaves of the French Cathedral seemed like a mournful requiem to her accents.

"I was jist takin' hum sum clothes I had washed. I wanted the money fur pore Edy; he is so hungry." The woman's eyes were red and her voice unsteady, while the odor from her breath was suspiciously strong, and she carried in her hand beneath her torn shawl a little canteen.

"Do you live far from here? If you wait, Jackson will drive you home in a few minutes."

"Oh, no, Miss, God bless you; if you will only give a pore old body somethin' to buy a loaf of bread for pore Edy, I'll get home all right," she replied, whiningly, as the swaying lights from the post close to the Cathedral cast their lights and shadows over her ragged form.

"Where do you live?"

"Jist down there," she replied, pointing in the direction of the river. "In that row."

"Here is some silver to-night, and I shall come to-morrow and see you," she replied, without any suspicion as to the worthlessness of the cause.

She was herself of a very candid and honest nature, and people of such natures are slow to suspect others. She was stern with herself, but indulgent to others. Her heart prompted her to give, and she invariably gave impulsively. Although she had given to many charitable purposes systematically, yet she was not always satisfied with the system or its results. It seemed to her that the system had grown automatic, unintelligent, and in many places corrupt. Its formalism bound her in. She had been an ardent student of Ruskin, and his simplicity and wholesomeness had warmed her naturally warm heart and created within her, despite her inherent traditions, a desire to discard the formalism of the present day. With him, she believed that one's first duty, and generally one's life duty, is to those nearest one, and that all effectual advancement towards the true felicity of the human race must be accomplished by individual effort. She had failed to see the efficacy of aggregated organizations and had withdrawn from many. There were so many necessities which appealed directly to her. She held her wealth in trust, and she had ever considered herself a more competent and just almoner of the trust than the masses. She no more believed in the masses spending her money than in the masses ruling. "Perhaps it was only another form of egotism or prejudice or narrow-mindedness," she was wont to think, but if it were, she could not see past her own prerogatives and her own people, her own city and her own country to the beyond, and where her sympathy was awakened she gave generously.

Her cousin Jack, who was now grimly watching her, would no doubt have told her, had he spoken, that sympathy had its foundation in the imagination, and although it was a heavenly gift to possess, it was a poor guide for conduct, but he did not say so; he admired too much her earnestness; while Modena was wont to say, "I would rather be cheated by a score of rogues than suspect one honest man."

She did not now suspect the old woman.

"God bless you, kind lady, and I'll remember you in my prayers to-night," said the old woman, as she hobbled off into the darkness; dragging the child by the hand, while two ragged urchins, who had been huddled together in the shelter of the Cathedral, shuddering from the cold, piercing north wind, now humbly approached her as she turned to step into the sleigh, and begged of her to buy a paper.

Her heart melted towards the poor urchins who, despite their cold and misery, smiled in awe as they gazed upon her, as she stood like a Lady of the Snows in her white garments, ready to step into the depths of the warm robes of the sleigh.

She smiled sweetly at them as she received some more coin from her father and placed some in each little palm, and then stepped into the sleigh.

"Whatever be your fate at the dinner to-night, you may now rest assured that you have captured two little victims," said her cousin, as he drew the robes in around her.

"They were nice little boys," replied she, serenely.

Jack smiled grimly at her. "Because they admired you. You are like all other women. You are vain, even if your vanity is of a high order."

"Perhaps so, but what a gloomy world it would be without a little vanity."

"You like homage?"

"If it is merited."

"If we meet many more you will become a Philippe Egalite."

"A socialistic aristocrat! That is unworthy of you. It is a very small nature that courts— What shall I call it? vulgarity? notoriety?"

"What would you make the distinction?"

"The motive."

"Mandeville says self-love is the motive of all our actions."

"He may believe he is saying what is true, but we know his

assertion is a cynical untruth," replied Modena, with decision, as the horses stopped at the entrance to Glenhurst.

They were the last to arrive; dinner was announced a few minutes afterwards, and she went down to dinner with one of their own ministers.

"Haven't they arrived yet?" some one was asking Keith Kenyon, as the last guest was seated.

"Not yet; but they will be here in the morning."

"Which way will he go?" asked the Secretary of State, addressing the young statesman.

"I do not know."

"There will be some work for you," continued the Secretary in a low voice to Modena, who sat near him.

"What do you mean? Of whom are you speaking? I do not understand you," she replied.

"Haven't you heard of her who is coming? If you haven't you are the only one in the city in Cimmerian darkness!" replied Mr. Lester, who sat opposite her.

It was a gathering of the Tory clan, but Lester Lester, although the staunchest man in the Opposition ranks, and his sister Helen were admitted everywhere.

"Who is she? One of the Queen's daughters?" continued the mistress of Apsley House in interrogation, as the lights from the shaded candelabras shone on the tiara of diamonds that crowned her head and on her upturned face, showing there the interest, animation and anticipation in her expression.

"Not quite, but next thing to it She is Miss Lennox, the money-king's daughter from Chicago. Her father has bought up half the distilleries and mines in the country, and in future we are to be honored with their presence, their prestige and their patronage."

"Oh," said Modena, while the change in her countenance was as great as that from summer sunshine to winter in a landscape.

It was only a little monosyllable, but it contained a whole world of meaning.

Mr. Lester laughed outright at what it implied.

"You will have to rid yourself of that expression, Modena; the millions are not as supreme a purifier in your sight as if they were blood blue as indigo, but it is an exception in this case," said Mr. Lester, as he pushed aside a gilded basket of osier filled with white lilacs which stood in his way, that he might see her.

"It means a great deal to the party that gains him," said the Secretary. "They are to be at Parliament Hill to-morrow. You'll see Mrs. Sangster with them, and I'll wager that before two weeks she will have the red ribbon tied on the Lennox whip," continued he, in a low voice, wishing to arouse his guests' interest in the coming people.

Mrs. Sangster was the leading lady in the Opposition ranks. She came from an old family, was beautiful, clever, honest and intensely practical, and had accomplished much for her party. The mistress of Apsley House had realized her contemporary's sterling qualities and far-reaching influences. She was too great a lady to be moved by any feelings of rivalry or jealousy, but she was arrogant of her leadership and tenacious of her influence, and would not brook usurpation by another. If it were necessary that they—these new-comers—should join her party, why she would certainly secure them. But she wanted to be convinced of the necessity before lending herself to any movement. She would lend herself to no unwise or unworthy motives or movements.

"Why make such a fuss about one man?" she asked of the minister by her side.

"He has influence in so many close constituencies. There have been times when our majority has been very small—one, once; work is very scarce; wages very low; labor very plentiful; these conditions make the capitalists very powerful. Mr. Lennox to a certain extent will control the labor vote. It is absolutely necessary that we secure him. I trust that you will do what you can."

"He is coming to live here?"

"Yes; it enables him to attend to his interests much better."

"They will be terribly bored."

"Oh, no. You have seen those twenty big cannon all in a row on the bank overlooking the river, none of them more conspicuous than the others; but take one and place it on Durham Terrace, and it becomes a great gun. He is so much greater than anything we have here that he will become conspicuous at once. Human nature all over the world is the same. Its unfailing motto is 'Aut Cæsar, aut nullus.' He will be Cæsar; that will recompense him," the minister replied, sententiously.

"He will be Cæsar! It all depends upon what standard you use to measure greatness."

"We must use the accepted and stamped standard which our age uses."

"What is that?"

"'Gold is the pole to which the whole world turns; the whole big world hangs on gold,' sang Goethe. Isn't his song true? We now measure honor by gold, as the Carthaginians measured glory by war rings."

"You are as cynical as Goethe was when he wrote those words. You do not mean that. One cannot comprehend how you can suggest, even in irony, that gold should be mentioned with blood, tradition, instincts, accomplishments, inheritances and descent."

"It is not placed side by side with them. It supersedes them infinitely."

"Pardon me! One does not like to dispute the assertions of such a great man as a minister, but one cannot be honest with oneself and agree with you. If we look beneath the surface we shall see that gold is not the test. Greatness is measured by goodness, by development—there, I do not like that word; it is so modern and so threadbare, but so expressive—by character, by real worth and by world-ennobling efforts."

"You are describing an ideal state—not the real state. You are being misled by your own standards, as Swedenborg and Dante were deceived by their own creations," smiled the host, as their hostess gave the signal for the ladies to withdraw. "But," continued he, a little while afterwards, as they formed in groups in the drawing-room, "our argument is not to the point. I did not say great, I said conspicuous."

"One does not like your inference," said Modena; "you do not inspire one with much zeal. Have you ever met her, Lester? What is she like?" asked she, with well-bred curiosity.

"Ask Keith; he knows them." For once, however, the young statesman was not ready with a reply.

"I have seen her," said Helen Lester, coming to the rescue, "and you need not worry, Modena; her aspiration will tend towards your people."

"Why do you say that? Foregone conclusions are so suggestive of manipulations. What has been the loadstar?" asked the same minister.

"It may not have been a 'what,' it may have been a 'who,'" replied Helen, with more meaning than her light, smiling words conveyed, while the mistress of Apsley House felt that many eyes in the group were turned towards Keith Kenyon.

"What did it mean?" she asked herself. "Why had she been kept in such darkness?" Her quick instinct made her feel that there had been some reason for keeping her in darkness. "What was it?"

She felt herself prejudiced towards the newcomers, perhaps because she was the last to hear of their coming, or perhaps because she was always rather apt to shut herself up behind a prejudice of caste than to accept anything new, or perhaps because there was in the air around her something which her quick and ready knowledge of the world told her was there, but of which the world had not spoken, and which had the power to annoy her.

"Her party wanted them and she must help them," she told herself. "She must cast aside her prejudices and be just, but she could not be just without knowing, and no one seemed to wish to enlighten her." There was an awkwardness in the situation somewhere, and she felt her prejudices deepening rather than dispelling. "She would not seek a confidence which had been purposely withheld from her; it was of no importance to her whatever," and she turned the conversation to other matters, but despite herself the thought intruded itself. Things were not quite right, her serenity was disturbed, and unnoticed she withdrew into an embrasure of the window while her hostess was arranging different amusements for different guests.

She was only a little tired; she had overdone herself that day. She had spent the morning at the Children's Shelter; then the long walk to Mrs. Byers's in the strong gale which had blown all afternoon, and her exposure in evening dress on the cold pavement had been too much for her. "The events of the day had depressed her and irritated her, and she was too tired to throw them off. It was only that," so she told herself.

But she had never felt them before. From a strong sense of duty and from womanly sympathy she had gone among sorrow ever since she could remember, and she had done much to alleviate it, but her philosophy and her sanguine disposition had kept it from really touching her life. As Macaulay, the historian, had hated mathematics and the sciences, not realizing that they were an absolute necessity as a mental discipline, so had she disliked all the darker sides of life. She loved life and joy and beauty. She wanted to live in that atmosphere. She had the soul of the Greek within her. "Ugliness gave them pain like a blow." The miseries and sufferings of human existence gave her pain like a blow. The Greeks would have made even death beautiful. She would have made all things beautiful and all people happy. Even books which portrayed the darker side of human life she had cast aside. "One has no patience with such. It is their duty to feed one's soul. Why cannot they feed it with joy?" was her wonted cry. But still, as such things did exist, she had ever gone among them and had done what she could, and had then put them from her, and their existence had not made life any less pleasant for her; but to-night it was different. "Was Mr. Lester's mantle falling upon her? A few hours ago she had said to Mr. Lester that they had comforted one, and that the House must look after the ninety-and-nine; and now the Lennoxes were coming, and their attention would be centred upon them, and these other things would have to wait," she thought, with a little scorn.

She looked round on the smiling faces in the room and then her gaze wandered out into the night. The shutters were unclosed and the night was fair and bitterly cold; the dim outlines of the Laurentides, with their dusky pine shadows in the moonlight, and the frozen shafts of the Cascades, were dimly visible in the distance, while the low, hoarse song from passing sleighs was audible on the bitter cold air.

"And there are people out in that," she thought. She was disturbed in her meditations by the voice of Mr. Lester, who had approached unnoticed.

"Why that thoughtful mien? This is no place for care," he said, as he drew aside the heavy draperies which concealed her from the others.

She turned and looked at him and moved a little to one side that he might be seated, and then answered him.

"If one would close those shutters and draw to those draperies one would not think while gazing on this scene within that woe and want prevailed without," and her eyes wandered once more to where the smoke shadows were circling on the moonlit snow. "I was thinking of that woman we passed on the way."

"Your father told me about her. No doubt she had been drinking. Don't you think it probable?" replied Lester.

"Oh, I think not; not here. One sees plenty of that while travelling abroad, but not here."

"You are losing your philosophy. You have always had the good sense to accept things as they are and make the best of them. Do so still. It is really the only way in life."

"But if someone does not think and work, the evil will never be remedied."

"I should think you would be more interested in securing Lennox at the present time than in the old woman."

"It is 'Lennox,' as you call him, that makes one think of the old woman."

"My eyes are too dull to see the analogy."

"Nature only endowed us with a certain amount of ability, time and energy. We are responsible for their expenditure. For the coming months they will be expended on the Lennoxes. They might better be spent on the old woman. A loss of power, or power misspent, is always a melancholy sight."

"Why don't you tell your people that?"

4

"Our people know it or one is much mistaken in the depths of their intellect."

"Then they should leave Lennox alone and think of the old woman," smiled Mr. Lester.

His companion smiled too.

"If we did that we would have to step out, and you would step in."

"You might do so. Surely you have been experts in manipulating power and ruling long enough to please even you," added Mr. Lester, in a light vein of tender sarcasm.

"The length of the rule matters not. It's what we accomplish that counts."

"You are not growing dissatisfied. You have always looked upon your party and its prerogative as being almost divine. Are you changing?"

"Changing! What blasphemy! Certainly I think the future and prosperity of our country depend upon us. What one regrets is that it does not lie in our power to do good. We spend our time over shadows and allow substances to drift. You know the old story of how the doctors allowed their patient to die while they disputed over the Greek root from which the name of the disease was derived. We'll quarrel over Lennox and let the old woman die. These things really exist; we shut our eyes to them, or if we move, we move like snails."

"Events never move rapidly in your ranks unless reform forces them to move, and, my dear Modena, you are a veritable Hypatia! You would be the very first one to cry out against the destruction of old creeds and principles. An iconoclast in your eyes is worse than a Radical or Rebel."

"Our principles are right, and I have heard my father say, and it must be so when he says it, that he wishes there were more beautiful and gifted Hypatias in the world—that had there been, things would not be as they now are," she replied with a return to her usual mood.

"If there were, they would suffer the same fate. A modern Hypatia would be martyred by an Anarchist or a Churchman, as your Grecian was stoned to death by the fanaticism of the Christian monks. The pagans inscribed on the tomb of Isis, 'I am all that is, all that was, and all that ever will be.' and yet when Socrates tried to introduce the true Isis he was forced to drink the fatal hemlock. Truth at all times is derided, denied and persecuted by ignorance, egotism and superstition. In the vicinity of every new thinker there exists an association that believes itself infallible;

every old prejudice feels itself wronged and wounded by a new idea, and hates it accordingly. Society is movement, but those who move it fall under the weight of its crushing wheels. Society is renovation, but those who renew it are slain by its old errors. The greater number of people believe you are tearing their souls from God if you endeavor to uproot one of the prejudices or errors under whose shadows their fathers have lived and died; by the side of each reformer is placed the eternal cup of hemlock. At least that is what Castelar says. Don't you think what he says is true?"

"It may be true; no doubt it is. But why need Truth care for the opinion of the world? He is a coward who cares, and he is a coward who is afraid to speak. A fine soul is ever indignant towards injustices. Truth ever has its reward. Invariably it rears its proud head to posterity. What one regrets is that there is need for reform," she replied, rather gloomily.

"What is the matter with you to-night?" asked Lester, in a lighter tone. "One would not know you; this afternoon you were sanguine in sorrow; to-night you are sorrowful in society."

"Society sometimes makes one sad, as music makes dogs howl," she replied, smilingly.

"But it has never made you sad before," he replied.

"Perhaps because I have never really thought of society's and sorrow's cruel contrasts before."

"And what makes you think of them to-night? Lennox and the old woman?"

"It certainly makes one think that we are like the Knights of the degenerating famous Table; during the next few months we will be following wandering fires, lost in the quagmire, while dormant lies strength and will to right the wrong."

"Your prey will be an easy mark. You will not have to waste much time over him," replied Lester, drily. "There is one coming in now who will be of much more use to you."

"Who is that?"

"Miss Austin, with the Seatons. She is from the South. She has suffered great reverses. She is going to make her home with Lady Seaton. Jack is going to meet her. Does he know her?"

"Has she come? Yes," replied Modena, her eyes brightening as they sought the newcomer. "They have a mutual friend—a Mr. Maxwell. He wrote Jack to try and make it pleasant for her," continued she, as she watched her cousin as he made his way towards the stranger.

"Miss Austin, Mr. Mainton would like the pleasure of your

acquaintance," their hostess was murmuring at the same moment in that low voice suitable for introduction.

Jack bowed low and warmly clasped the extended hand of the stranger.

"I heard from Maxwell to-day," he said, as he sat down by her side. "He asked me to call on you."

"How very kind he is," replied the stranger, feelingly and with a vague homesickness at hearing her friend's name in a distant land.

"He is a great friend of yours. You will miss him, but you will soon make many friends here. I hope you will like our country and our people. We will try to make you do so. I want you to know my cousin," continued Jack, with his usual abruptness. "She is the best one for that sort of thing."

"It is so different to our sunny South," she said, and her Creole eyes grew humid as she thought of all she had left in her far-away sunlit home.

"Yes, but you will find exceedingly warm hearts behind cold hand-shakes; we're slow and don't say much, but when you get us we stay by you," he said, with more earnestness and animation than he usually displayed. "But then Modena will tell you our charms better than I. That is she talking to Mr. Lester at the window."

"She is very beautiful. You must be very proud of her. And what a noble face her companion has."

"Yes, she is all right. Her companion's face is the mirror of his soul. I shall bring them to you," and he rose and made his way to his cousin and Mr. Lester and brought them to meet the stranger.

"You admire Miss Austin; not often you invite one to Apsley House without probation," he said to Modena some half hour later, when the Southerner had left with the Seatons to attend another reception the same evening.

"Miss Austin is a gentlewoman and possesses great talent. One must have an instinct like a dog, or some subtle magnetism must exist between some natures, which enables one to know one's friends," replied Modena.

"But usually you are not so generous and candid with our neighbors. Hitherto you have shown a decided antipathy towards them."

"You are as unjust to me as I to them. You would make me a second Mrs. Trollope. I have told you so often before that I do not dislike them, but if they persist in playing the eagle's part—and that does not express what I mean, but you know what I mean— surely you would not have one play the spaniel's?"

"It is only a certain class who do so. They do not all do so. If you go to the door on a calm summer night and hear the air vibrate with the hoarse ' go-roun ' of many frogs, while forty or fifty of the farmer's thoroughbred horses and cattle lie asleep in the same field, pray do not think that the frog is the only occupant of the field," replied Jack, smilingly.

His cousin smiled too.

"I wonder if Lennox will be a frog or a thoroughbred?" he continued, with a tinge of apprehensive incredulity in his query.

His cousin's face grew colder.

"That remains to be seen," she replied; "we have seen Miss Austin, and we feel sure she is a typical American, and one cannot help loving her as one does her works. She is going to make her home with the Seatons. She has originality and imagination. Doesn't some one of your great men say these two qualities cause all the great events of life? What a pleasant addition she will be to our party."

"Great events of life! Oh! Oh! that is too broad an assertion for one's poor brain to grasp. I'd rather look upon her as a fit mate for Lester than as a—a—what would you call it—reformer? crank? genius? goddess?"

"How intensely practical you are."

"Oh, no, I am only romantic."

"Why are you so anxious to see Lester married?" asked his cousin, abruptly, and with a tinge of resentment in her voice.

Her most intimate friend was Lester Lester, and she was very tenacious of her influence over him, and could not bear to see it shared by others or slip from her own grasp. She had known him as long as she could remember and she had always looked upon him as belonging to herself; whatever vanity existed in her nature sprang from a consciousness of her influence over others; she was as jealous of anything that served to lessen that influence as though love had been the source instead of vanity.

"You have Monteith and a half dozen others tied to your apron strings, and I don't see why you need to keep Lester, too, all his life," replied Jack, petulantly and perversely.

He possessed a great attachment for his friend Lester, and disliked and resented seeing the best years of his life spent in a hopeless attachment for his cousin.

"Don't be selfish and thoughtless. So long as you encourage him it prevents his caring for anyone else. Shake him loose," said he, as he rose and ceded his place to Carlton Monteith, who had come up.

Modena looked after her cousin in mute surprise, not comprehending what he meant. Her companion was telling her something, but she heard it not; she was thinking of the absurdity of what Jack had said. She knew many men had loved her, but Lester —absurd nonsense—and she banished the thought and did not allow it to disturb the serenity of their friendship or the sweetness and sympathy of their intercourse.

"What is love?" she thought, "what is there in it that makes the poets rave and men so passionate? Are they sincere in their expressions of adoration? If they are not, how can they simulate such sincerity? They must be, for I have seen their eyes burn with adoration; but why do I not feel like this towards Carlton?" and she raised her eyes to his as he spoke to her, and then unconsciously they wandered round the room and met those of Keith Kenyon, as he glanced at her for a moment from where he stood on the hearth rug, with his arm on the mantel—the central figure of a group of ladies. Her eyes fell; the mists of the last few hours rolled away; the gloom was dispelled, and her old world came back to her again.

A few hours afterwards she lay back in the depths of the warm robes of the sleigh and sighed a sigh of pure happiness.

"What was the cause of that sigh?" asked Keith Kenyon, who had walked up from the House to dinner and was returning home with them.

"I don't know. I suppose it is because one must give vent to one's thankfulness in some way."

"Thankful that the evening is gone?"

She smiled. "You must think one very ungrateful indeed to harbor such sentiments towards those who have so generously entertained us."

"A great many do, though."

"Oh, I dare say they do, but I pride myself on being an individual, and not a 'great many,' and go where I will, or when, or why. I always go for, as Jack says, 'a good time,' and I always have it."

"You have a happy heart. You are to be envied."

"Jack told me to-night it was vanity. A vain person is always happy, because she is perfectly satisfied with herself."

"Are you satisfied with yourself? Does your life not require some one else to complete your happiness?" he was about to ask her, but he checked himself. It was too bold a question to put to her, and then he realized he had no right to ask it.

But there are other ways of asking it than with the lips. By the fitful glare of the passing lamps she could feel his eyes seeking hers, and her eyes looked elsewhere.

"Parliament opens soon," she said, after a moment's silence, abruptly turning the conversation.

"Yes, you will be there?" he replied, recovering himself.

"Certainly. Is this the last session?"

"No, there will be another."

"I wish the contest were over, for father's sake. He cannot stand the cares and worries as he once could. Do you really think there is the danger he anticipates?"

"There is certainly cause for anxiety."

"I cannot see it. There is no disagreement or dissatisfaction in our own ranks."

"Oh, no, trust the chief for that; he possesses too much tact and diplomacy to allow any Jason's stones in his own camp."

"Ah, Keith, I did not know we were here!" exclaimed Mr. Wellington, who had been engaged in earnest conversation with Jack regarding the Lennoxes, as the horses stopped.

"I had a letter to-day from Mayne, asking for a change in seats this term. I want to see you regarding it." But the horses were champing and chafing to get away to their own warm stalls, which prevented any further conversation.

The younger man alighted and re-arranged the robes. "I shall see you in the morning," he said, and then he lifted his hat and ran lightly up the steps into his own home, Kenyon Court.

CHAPTER V.

KEITH KENYON, the youngest member in the Cabinet, and one of the rising lights of the day, was heir-apparent to one of the wealthiest estates in the country and possessor of another almost as great.

His father had been a man of high rank in colonial life—a man of great courage, stern integrity and brilliant intellect.

When he was but a young man finishing his education in Paris, he had there met Clare Arundel, the youngest daughter of an old English family. On the completion of his college courses he had gone to England and brought her a bride to his Western home.

Some years afterwards he had died, leaving her the sole guardian of his young children. Mrs. Kenyon was naturally brilliant, charming and popular. Her husband's early death had robbed

life of its joy and beauty; with great courage she had taken up the
threads of life, and had devoted herself to the care and education
of her children, and had resumed her old place in society, when
death once more robbed her of her only daughter.

She had never fully recovered from her second affliction, and
had continued to live retired as far as it was possible to do so in
public life. She had retained her most intimate friends; part of
her time she devoted to charitable work and the remainder of her
energies were given to the personal welfare and interests of her
son.

Keith had inherited from his father the integrity and intelligence for which he had been noted, and from his mother the
beauty and patrician looks, the natural tact, good taste and correct
intuitions of the Arundels.

His form was tall, squarely built and commanding; his hair
was dark and waving, his eyes deep and lustrous, while sincerity
and strong convictions had lent a shade of austerity and power to
a countenance which, without these, would have been almost too
classically regular.

He had been richly endowed with all the great qualities necessary for success in life. Fate had been extremely kind to him, and
even had not, like in the fairy tale of old, marred her gifts by the
malison of one godmother.

He was the most sought after and courted man of the day. He
knew this, but the knowledge had not made him vain. He was
too wise a man for this. But he did not disdain his popularity;
he was ambitious, and as his ambition tended towards the political
arena, his popularity aided him materially in his aspirations, but
he was never carried away by it.

He knew the world as Richard II. knew his greyhound.

He courted and valued its just praise at its true worth, but its
adulations and insincerities, its froths and inanities, he laid bare
to time-servers or enemies, or passed them over as the occasion
merited.

He was genial, generous and magnanimous, and possessed that
sense of humor which, when it is not an inheritance, invariably
comes from a deep knowledge of the world and a knowledge of
one's own powers.

His advantages had been many and great, his education
thorough; he had been an apt student and a deep thinker; he had
ever had an insatiable love for knowledge, and when he had penetrated the mysteries of the fabled well its treasures had not lost
their charm. It was a duty unfulfilled until they were applied

practically. His learning he would have counted of little value if it did not bear fruit for the public welfare.

From boyhood he had revelled in the lives of great men, but practical success cannot be gained by merely reading the lives of great men, but by daily intercourse, experience and personal contact with them. His father's home had been one of the favorite reception and dining rooms of a powerful political clique, and from boyhood he had had the advantage of personal contact with great statesmen. His family's influence might have gained position for him at a very early age, but the same instinct of his nature which had warned him it was not well to be carried away by the world's adulation, told him that it was wiser and better to proceed step by step, to fill menial places of office in order to study and comprehend the machinery of government, and that when merit, not prestige and patronage, wins the day the foundation is solid and enduring.

He had served in the City Council; he had made himself master of details and had risen step by step until he now held one of the most important portfolios in the Cabinet.

He had great application and endurance, and excellent method in work, and was progressive in spirit, but held himself well in reserve.

His knowledge of history, his keen insight and his logical mind would have made him an ardent advocate of many innovations, reforms and progressions, but his keen common sense had told him that the nation must be educated to those standards before it is ready or willing to accept them, and with this object in view he had taken much to the public platform, and his celebrity now was chiefly due to his oratorical powers.

As an orator he stood unrivalled in the House.

Beaconsfield, the silver-tongued orator, tells us that knowledge is the foundation and fundamental essence of eloquence; it may be of eloquence, but not of true oratory. One may be as learned as Socrates, and yet not be an orator; one may possess great brilliancy of rhetoric, great lucidity, logic and perfect diction, and yet not be an orator.

Oratory is the fruit of genius and of honest patriotism or honest altruistic convictions; and genius is a gift from the gods— the gift of an original, versatile, imaginative, passionate mind.

The gods had blessed Keith Kenyon with the mental aptitudes, and he himself had supplied the required data and diction; while his intense patriotism, honest convictions and enthusiasm gave to him that magnetic influence over the hearts and minds of men, that power of making soul move soul which is as necessary to oratory as the beating of the heart is to the life of the body.

In many a crisis his ability had served and saved his party, and his influence was beginning to be quietly but widely felt. He had travelled much and had tasted of the pleasures of life. He had been so accustomed to adulation from the fairer sex that he had grown indifferent to it and was looked upon by many as heartless and even self-centred, but when he had met the mistress of Apsley House he had been aroused from his apathy and indifference by that subtle magnetism which so instinctively draws two lives together, and which makes them realize that separation is imperfect happiness.

They had first met while the families were travelling abroad, Mr. Wellington with his daughter who was finishing her education, and Mrs. Kenyon with her invalided daughter who was seeking restoration, or at least a lengthening of life in warmer countries.

Clare Arundel had been in early years an intimate friend of Mrs. Wellington's, but having spent her later years travelling with her daughter in sunny lands or in foreign cities where her son was finishing his college courses, previous to this she had not met Modena. A few weeks after their meeting Mr. Wellington had been unexpectedly called home, and had departed leaving his daughter under Mrs. Kenyon's care.

They had remained in Florence for several months, but the invalid becoming much worse they had left to consult a specialist in Venice. The change seemed to strengthen her for a time, but as the days passed by the mother plainly saw that the soul of her young daughter was rapidly fleeing from its fragile tenement; at last the symptoms had become so alarming that she had cabled for her son.

One evening Mrs. Kenyon, being exhausted by nights of watchfulness and sleeplessness, lay down to rest, while Modena wheeled a low couch to the open window and placed the invalid upon it.

"Sing me something," said the sick girl, as she withdrew her eyes from watching the ripples of silver and amber and gold from the setting sun on the blue waters of the sea and fastened them upon her friend.

Modena had risen and gone to the grand piano in one corner of the room, but its magnificence jarred upon her, so she ran lightly up the stairs to her own room and brought down her guitar, and seating herself near the open window played and sang of things they knew and loved.

As the words, low and soft, fell on the darkening air, a form appeared in the shadows of the open doorway, and remained unnoticed for some time, dimly discerning his sister's face, holy in its calm resignation as the strains of music soothed her into a light slumber. When Modena saw that she slept she laid her guitar down gently and knelt by the couch, and gazed into the passing pallid face. " Oh, how young to die," she cried, overcome by the memories of her mother who had passed away at an early age.

The watching form advanced into the room to the couch. The footsteps aroused her; she arose, turned round in the dying light, and this is where she had first met Keith Kenyon.

"My darling sister! Poor Edna! How she has failed! God help poor mother!" he said, with a tremor, almost a sob, in his rich, deep voice. "You are the Miss Wellington, of whom they have written so much."

"Yes; and you are her brother?"

"Yes, Keith."

"Oh, how glad your mother will be that you have come. I shall tell her at once. She has had no rest for many nights. I persuaded her to lie down for a little while," she said, with a sad but glad tremor in her voice, as she thought of the mother's joy at seeing her son.

"No, do not disturb her, let her rest until Edna awakes." He drew a chair up for her, and then sat down on the side of the couch, and conversed in low tones until his sister awoke shortly after the lights were lit, and then Modena went away to send Mrs. Kenyon. Instinctively she felt a family reunion too sacred for other eyes.

The invalid seemed to rally somewhat after her brother's arrival, but the physicians gave them no hope; her one desire now was that she might live until spring so that she might return home and die in her own country. "Oh, mother," she would say, "to die here so far away from you; take me home."

They took her from one sunny land to another until the birds were singing and the trees blossoming in her own country, and then they took her home.

Mrs. Kenyon's country residence had at that time some imperfect drainage, and was undergoing repairs, so the mistress of Fernwylde had insisted on her being brought to Fernwylde.

The invalid was delighted with the natural beauty of the place, and insisted, when the days were warm and dry, on being carried or wheeled to the old Fernery. Here she would lie listening to the robin's song, or the bob-o-link's clarion call, or the soft murmur of many running and falling waters, or lie watching the deep blue sky with its fleecy garments of soft-tinted clouds; and it was here one summer day she passed away, passed so quietly away that her brother, who was reading to her, read on not knowing that she was gone. A cry from his mother startled him and Modena, and when they looked her spirit had fled.

They buried her under the green trees of Idlewylde in her own home, not far from where she died, and with her they buried the heart of her mother.

Attractions which had begun in sorrow and sympathy between the younger people, soon developed into deeper feelings. It was the same old story, old as the world but young as the morning dew; something which is felt but which cannot be defined. All one knows is that when one meets the love of one's life, there springs into life the knowledge of something long sought, some supplement of oneself long desired, and something without which one cannot rest.

He had felt this from their first meeting, and had drawn her to him, and it had been a great blow to him when they had returned, and he had learned of her relations to Carlton Monteith.

Her betrothal to Carlton Monteith had taken place when she was very young. He was an old friend of the family's, and had been much with Mrs. Wellington before her death. He was then a young man of twenty-two while Modena was but a child; he had loved her from childhood, and when she was grown had told her of his love, and of all that her mother had hoped and wished. As her father had done, so, too, had she made a cultus of her mother's memory, and she had been won more through her mother's memory than through any other sentiment. She had entered into the engagement with a sense of quiet peace, believing her affections and respect were love, and that if her mother had spoken she would have asked it.

She had not spoken of it in Italy, because she had not thought of it. It had come into her life as peaceful and with less emotion than her graduations at school, or her entrance into society, or a thousand other little things.

But when she met Keith Kenyon in Italy, her inner nature, which had hitherto lain dormant, began to awaken as the winter's earth awakens under the strong influence of spring's winds and warming sun's rays.

She knew that life had changed, but she had not stopped to ask herself the cause. It was only within the last few days that she was beginning to realize the cause, while he, now that he was aware of her betrothal, was troubled as he had never been before.

When he had learned of her betrothal his manner to her had changed. His " still small voice " told him it was not honorable to interfere or encroach on another man's rights; he would not do so; he would go on his way, and no one should know of his love. But good resolutions, where the heart is involved, are as brittle as glass. They may be kept in the letter, but not in the spirit. He kept his in the letter, but nature he could not conquer or control. His heart spoke every day, every hour, and it became a continuous conflict between logic and nature. The heart pleaded, " Love should be the Supreme Law." Logic said, " Another man's Love is her Law." Almost he said to himself he would go away while it was yet time, but his whole life and interests were centred in the Capital, and this prevented his leaving; he would see as little of her as possible, but the duties and social routines of life threw them together day after day and hour after hour, until at last he ceased to fight against fate, and took life as it came, and his daily conduct became a verification of the poet's words, " Love carves a portion from the solid present, and eats, and uses, careless of the rest."

In his youthful days he had built gorgeous castles, and had dreamed glorious dreams of power and honor; the maturer intelligence of manhood had cast a more prosaic aspect over his dreams, but since he had met her the fervent desire to prove himself worthy of the respect of mankind, and of her, awoke once more within him, and recalled all his boyhood's ambitions and renewed his love of power.

Malvolio says, " Some are born great, some achieve greatness, and others have greatness thrust upon them." If Keith Kenyon belonged to the first and to the last he dreamed of belonging to the second also, and his newly awakened emotions increased his dreams a hundred-fold.

CHAPTER VI.

IT was opening day at Parliament Hill.

The vice-regal party, gaily attired and with horses handsomely caparisoned, and carriages gorgeously bedecked, accompanied by a mounted escort from Rideau Hall, wended its way up Wellington Street and down the canal gorge, acknowledging at intervals the salute of the military bands, for the city at the present was in a state of martial furore, the Wimbletons clad in their red, grey and green having suspended operations for the day in honor of the opening.

The cortege slowly wended its way to the brow of the Hill, where they were received by a guard of honor at the precincts of the House.

The day was glorious; the air mild; towers and pinnacles shone in the sunlight, while the circle of smoke and boom of guns from Nepean Point circled the sky, and reverberated through the early afternoon air.

The precincts to the body of the chamber were brilliant with the blue and gold and red uniforms of militia, the crimson gowns of judges, the cordon collars and regalias of ministers, while the galleries were filled with ladies in their best, most conspicuous among them being the Wellington party.

"There they are," said Helen Lester, in a low voice, to the mistress of Apsley House as a rustle and stir in the gallery attracted their attention as the mace was brought down, and Mrs. Sangster and her party, accompanied by a middle-aged lady and a younger one, entered with great eclat and took the places in the gallery which had been reserved for them.

Modena noticed that many eyes were turned in that direction, but good breeding, as well as something else which she did not stop to define, restrained her from looking towards the newcomers who were attracting such general attention.

But soon the voice from the chair recalled attention to the House, and then she turned her eyes in cold scrutiny rather than in eager expectation to the opposite side of the gallery. "They have not overdrawn her; she is beautiful, but still—but still—" "There was something. What was it?"

She noticed the newcomer's eyes wander searchingly round the House until they rested on a familiar form in the ministers' row. At that moment Keith Kenyon happened to glance into the gallery and his eyes met those of the stranger's. He smiled rather with his eyes than with his lips, while those of the newcomer brightened and deepened in ready reply.

It was only a little thing, yet it had within it the power to increase the aversion which the mistress of Apsley House already felt towards the neophytes. She immediately withdrew her eyes and endeavored to turn her attention to what was going on, but despite her effort her thoughts wandered as the ceremonies proceeded with more than usual dignity and pomp.

In an interval of silence she noticed Mrs. Sangster lean towards her companion and say something, at which the stranger raised her eyes and looked in their direction, and as her keen, piercing, querulous eyes for an instant rested on the group, Modena drew back repelled.

An unerring instinct, with which prejudice had perhaps something to do, caused a repulsive coldness within her, and despite her usual good sense, a presentiment of hostility filled her mind as she thought of their advent into their society.

Verona Lennox, for it was she, had reached the age of fully developed womanhood. Her figure was tall and superb, her complexion perfect; her countenance a mirror of all inward impulses; her eyes were bright but not with that luminous light that comes from mellowness of heart and nobility of purpose, but the light of desire and determination, and although large and deep with interest and expectation yet possessed no magnetism or sympathy. She was elegantly dressed and carried herself with a supreme air of disdain.

"It was humiliating, really humiliating, from her point of view, to be forced to spend part of her young life in the wilderness and with such people, but then there was some compensation. Had there not been she would not have come."

They had arrived in the city some days previous to this, and were now domiciled in a modern mansion of great pretensions in the best part of the city.

Their first appearance in the political and social world had been looked forward to with great interest and anticipation.

"Which side?" in the political, and "Would they be taken up?" in the social world. The first problem in so far as opening day meant anything was solved; they had been secured by Mrs. Sangster, and although this did not commit them, yet to the uninitiated it meant something; and as for the second it was yet to be solved. Their receiving day was the following week; their surroundings were superb; their equipages the finest in the city; their servants many; but they were burdened with the greatest of all social crimes; no one knew them, that is, no one except Keith Kenyon, and would he be their sponsor?

It looked as though he would; at least so thought the mistress of Apsley House. When the ceremonies were over and the vice-regal party had taken their departure, she noticed the attention and courtesy extended to them by all parties, and her last glimpse of them, as their own carriage rolled away in the afternoon sunshine was the animated, flushed countenance of Miss Lennox as she conversed with the owner of Kenyon Court.

"What is between them?" wondered Modena as their carriage, drawn by its sleek bays with rattling chains, rolled on past the public gardens and over Dufferin Bridge. "Why should I care? It is nothing to me," she thought.

She was a very proud woman, and a very proud woman is very slow to admit, even to herself, that another is necessary to her happiness. She is so all-sufficient unto herself that to admit another is necessary is admitting that she fails to satisfy herself. She could not do this. She would dismiss it entirely from her mind. She turned to her father.

"What a beautiful day," she said; "I hope for your sake it may be a premonition of the coming session; the chief is failing and your duties are onerous."

"It is not the session one fears; it is the coming contest."

"Uncle is bound to conquer or die; conquer as did Wellington, or die as did Nelson," said Jack, as he whistled to his Scotch terrier, who was barking at a huge St. Bernard.

"One would rather die as did Nelson than live as did Wellington. Nelson died in his glory; Wellington outlived his. He undertook to do what he was not capable of doing; he was a general, but not a statesman; he did not know England as he knew his army," replied the elder man.

"Yet one is forced to admire him in his defeat. Even the most radical of the Populists let him die in peace in his bed. He had the courage to tackle a sleeping world. It is the lost causes, like the lost chord, which are so often the noble ones."

"Do you seriously think there is any danger now? There are no great issues at stake; everything is quiet," said Modena with a return to her usual manner. She was of too sanguine a disposition to see any danger in the false stillness of a seemingly harmonious atmosphere.

"Perfect stillness usually heralds a change of some kind! No great issues at stake, did you say? With a drought for five years. failure in potatoes, fly in wheat, cholera in swine, no prices, and no work, and the Government to blame for all these! It is useless to try and stave off defeat by sticking the 'Old Flag' behind caparisoned horses' ears; one might as well try to stop an avalanche with one's hand, or battered sluice-gates with a pailful of mud, or a burst thunder-cloud with your lace parasol. People can't live on sentiment," replied Jack, moodily.

"I have never yet doubted success," replied Modena, conscious of the difficulties but confident of their ability to overcome them. "The indomitable will which Mr. Kenyon possesses, your influence through the press; the excellent ability of the Cabinet, and the unsurpassable tact, and love of the people which the chief possesses, all combined cannot mean defeat."

"But it would take the d—— himself—I beg your pardon—to keep all races, religions and sectional differences in tune."

"But the chief does," replied Modena, smilingly.

"Then he possesses as much diplomacy as Mephistopheles himself," replied Jack, as the carriage stopped at Apsley House, and he stepped out, helping his cousin to alight.

"I wonder what they thought of us," said he, some half hour afterwards to an ex-minister and some others who had dropped in on their way home.

"They hadn't time to think anything; the speech from the Throne was too short to allow them time to descend from their high pedestal to our common level. I am afraid they will be disillusioned; postillions and powdered periwigs in lieu of birch-bark canoes and feathers must have been a pleasant surprise," said Mrs. Cecil, who had entered through a doorway leading from the gardens, and was now sipping some fragrant tea from a dainty Sevres cup.

"Here comes Keith; ask him. He'll tell you," continued she, as she helped herself to some dainty morsels of cake.

"What is it?" asked Keith Kenyon, as he came in through the open French window and joined the group.

"What do your proteges think of our council house and its chiefs?" asked Jack, as he took a rosebud from a bunch of flowers that Mrs. Cecil had brought in and pinned it on his coat.

"They hadn't time to form an opinion, but they seemed to be pleasantly surprised. It wasn't what they expected it to be," was the reply which caused the company to smile.

"They expected to see the wild and weird ceremonies of the Long House and the White Dog Feast," said someone drily.

"And to see us exchange wampums and chiefs as hostages, or kiss the hatchet and bury it as we spoke," added another.

5

"How ill-natured you are! You'll all end in adoring them!" said the young statesman, as he took his tea from his hostess's hand.

"She wasn't ill-natured. Her face was inspiring. It was as bright and happy as though she had found Kalevala, the happy hunting ground," said Mrs. Cecil, who had been aroused from her usual indifference by the mixture of force and fire and indolent contempt which she had seen portrayed on the face of the new-comer.

"Why waste all this time talking about them?" exclaimed Helen Lester, moving to the music stand. "We have heard nothing but 'Lennox' for months. Why make such a fuss over them? Sing us something, Modena."

"Sated people always make a fuss over any phenomenon," replied Mrs. Cecil.

"And play battledore and shuttlecock with the most sacred questions, and go into ecstasies over nothing," added Jack.

"But we are not sated people," replied his cousin, in her own serene, proud manner, as she placed some music upon the piano, taking part for the first time in the conversation, the air of contempt for her country being the sole thing which would arouse in her words of retaliation. "We are like Ovid and Pindar; we live in an unworn world. Sated people are unknown here, nor do we wish to know them; and no nation in the world has more respect for sacred things than our own, while we possess enough of Socrates and Solomon to enable us to be classed an educated people, and of St. Augustine and Epicurus to be perfectly happy. If it did not savor of braggadocio, one would say we are an ideal nation. We are Plato's garden."

"Bravo, my lady. But I am afraid the ideal nation is but an ideal state in your mind, and Plato's garden turned out to be a cave with people sitting at its entrance with backs to the light seeing only distorted figures of realities," said the ex-minister, gloomily, who had once dwelt within the holy of holies.

"Do not disillusion us. Things are as we believe them to be, not as they really are."

"Educated, you said. What did you mean?" asked her cousin, with doubt in his interrogation.

"What would anyone mean, but what Ruskin meant, when he said an educated man is one who has understanding of his own uses and duties in the world, and therefore of the general nature of the things done and existing in the world, and who has so trained himself or been trained as to turn to the best use whatever faculties or knowledge he may possess."

"If that's what you mean no doubt you are right, for that is synonymous with practical common sense, and no one can deny our matter-of-fact monotony," returned Jack.

"Our monotony will be relieved now," added the ex-minister in a lighter tone. "Mrs. Cecil said the Lennoxes were phenomena. The country will be indebted to them for taking us out of this common-place groove or rut, the abhorrence of all great minds."

"One fails to see why you should idolize him just because he has money. You don't want to borrow it, do you? If not, and he has no other qualifications, then one would consider him a bore. The money may alter the handle, but it doesn't alter the sauce-pan," said Modena, as she seated herself at the piano, while her hands strayed mechanically over the ivory keys in a soft and joyous strain.

"Yes, we do; we want both the man and his money. Money is the divine essence of this epoch. It is like the sacred fires of old, it purges all impurities. It is the only god we worship," said the ex-minister wondering at her antipathy, and wishing to enlist her sympathy in the matter.

"We will not admit that; one wants to look upon it as a useful accompaniment to merit, as oratory is to statesmanship," she replied, but unconsciously her hands strayed into a mournful andante. "We must prove their merits before we are willing to accept them."

If she called upon them she would be conscientious and fulfil the duties which a call entailed, and it was a concession she did not wish to grant. The city was becoming full of such people, and they went everywhere. Money was a door opener, but not with her. She had the right to say whom her hall porter should admit, and this right she exercised tenaciously.

"But while we are waiting to prove their merits the other party will be making hay while the sun shines," said the minister, as he left her in search of a more sympathetic audience.

"Does your new star possess merit?" she asked of Lester, who stood beside her turning over the sheets of music.

She had become conscious of the injustice and unworthiness of her prejudice and hostility towards them. "It was nothing personal," she had told herself. "It was only an irritability at the tendency of the world to run after something which was new and gilded." She had great respect for Lester's opinions.

Mr. Lester smiled.

"I scarcely know how to answer your question," he replied, and hesitated. "If he hasn't merit, at least he has influence," he said at last.

"Real influence?"

"When a man holds mortgages on a thousand houses to the last brick in the chimney, and on as many farms to the last leaf on the tree tops, and can foreclose these at any moment, and when work is scarce and labor plentiful, and when he employs thousands of men, I think one may be justified in calling his influence real, especially at the present time," he added.

"He wouldn't use his influence on the private rights of his men?" exclaimed Modena, in an incredulous voice.

Such a thing was beyond her comprehension.

Mr. Lester continued to smile.

"Why are you so prejudiced against them? Because they are new?"

"Am I prejudiced?"

"I heard Medway complaining of your exclusiveness. He's uneasy since he saw them with Mrs. Sangster.

"Am I exclusive? Perhaps so by instinct and desire, but exclusiveness is surely another name for selfishness and unkindness. I receive Mrs. Nairn, and she trims bonnets."

"One cannot hold her responsible for her husband's misfortune. She is to be pitied."

"She doesn't want people's pity. But she wants their kindness and remembrance."

"But you wouldn't receive her if she hadn't once dwelt within your circle. You don't receive Mrs. Beal, and she is covered with lace fine as cobwebs, and diamonds as big as a masher's plastron, and wears Mrs. Nairn's bonnets. She's new."

"I'll receive her in time if she is worthy."

"If you didn't receive any but those who attained to your standard you would receive no one but yourself. You are only satisfied with yourself."

"You mean I am vain and have no sympathy."

"You have a great deal of pride. You are too completely, too loftily above us. You should dwell with the immortals."

"Then I should be very unhappy because I would then be very dissatisfied with myself. When one dwells with them one realizes one's infinitesimal nothingness. No. I would rather dwell with humanity, with Mrs. Beal," she smiled.

"You dwell too much with the immortals."

"And one's daily calendar, one series of receptions, teas, musicals, eleven hours out of the twelve. Mayn't we have one hour's real enjoyment?"

" I suppose you have a date for Thursday. The Lennoxes?"

" Oh, please don't mention their names again. I am tired of the sound of it. You are going now? Will you have some tea? No! Yes, you and Mrs. Sangster may have them. Good-bye," she said to the last of her guests.

But she was to hear their name again.

" I want you to call on Miss Lennox at your earliest convenience. Will you?" asked Keith Kenyon of her a few minutes afterwards as they descended the mansion steps together for she had some late calls to make.

" Why are you so anxious about them?" almost coldly replied the mistress of Apsley Hall to his interrogation.

He noticed the intonation.

" For several reasons," he answered, as he contemplated the beauty of her profile in the early spring light, while the odor of the lily of the valley that she wore was wafted to him as he stood for a moment beside her waiting for the carriage to draw near. " You know we want him. You can help us."

" Is that all?"

" Oh, I knew them before, and they depend on me for a while. Will you take them up?"

" They cannot possess much merit in themselves when they, depend upon someone else for their acceptance," she thought to herself, but she did not say so aloud.

She was usually so generous and impulsive to do a kindness to anyone. She was well aware of the exclusive usages and habits of society, and she knew that many people of great worthiness were passing their lives in an uncongenial atmosphere because of birth and environments. Like her mother, she had been the sponsor of many of the middle classes to a more congenial atmosphere. Her lack of amiability now irritated her.

" What can I do?" she asked with no warmth of feeling.

" Place them under your ægis; take a few of the best to see them, and no doubt where you go the others will follow."

" You think they will appreciate a call?"

Her companion colored a little and then laughed.

" I didn't know you could be ill-natured."

" Mr. Medway and Mr. Lester have been using such epithets as exclusive, prejudiced and vanity, and now you say, ill-natured. I am not a Catholic, but I have great respect for the beauty of their religion, and when I go to Fernwylde I confess all my evil thoughts and evil doings to Father Jacques. What a burden of sins I shall have to carry this time, and all because I persist in not knowing people whom I do not want to know."

"That is what we cannot understand. You have always been so ready to help us. What was it that Radical from the West said about you? 'Your home reminds one of what Horace Walpole said of the Lady Grenville house-parties. They disturb the Pelhams infinitely more than any mysterious meetings of state.' Why do you refuse to help us when we require help so much? If they are once seen at Apsley House the Pelhams will weep."

"You mean to say they will come to us because they will derive more benefit by so doing? What has principle to do with party selection?"

"We'll give them the principles when we get them."

"You cannot; principles are things which must be inherited or acquired. The ptarmigan, that whitens ere his hour, wooes his own death. You would be doing them an unkindness. Let them go to the other party and acquire them, and then when they acquire them they will come to us of their own accord."

"You take one's breath away! What a sweeping distinction! What about Mr. Lester and others?"

"He is one of us."

Her companion looked at her.

"What do you mean by 'us'?"

"What anyone would mean. The people who are capable of ruling; those who would rule best for the common interest did it lie in their power to do so."

"You would do away with partyism?"

"Partyism, as you call it, should at all times be subservient to principles."

"What principles?"

"What a question to ask! The principles which would be the basis for the best system of government for the greatest number of people, of course."

"Those at one time belonged to us. Will you not help us redeem them?"

"How? By calling on the Lennoxes?"

"If you don't call the other party will win, and we don't want that just yet."

"Are you speaking seriously?"

"Never more so."

She hesitated a moment in doubt, then spoke.

"They will be seen at Kenyon Court. That will mean much

more than at Apsley House. You are worrying yourself need-lessly."

"You refuse to call?"

"With that object in view I most certainly do, but if you wish me to call because they are friends of yours I shall go."

Her companion again hesitated for some moments. The carriage drew up to the stone steps and the footman descended.

"I hope you will see your way clear to go," he said, as they went down the last steps together.

"You wish it?"

"I really think it would be better to do so."

"Then I shall go," she replied, as he handed her into the carriage. He lifted his hat and walked away down the avenue with its trees of swelling buds and early spring birds, with a light heart and quick firm step, and with a smile in his eyes, while Modena rode away irritated and lacking enthusiasm for the first time in her life in anything which would be for the welfare of her party's interest.

As her companion had but said, her party had depended upon her for much. She had always been of a keen, observing nature, and thoroughly understood the different interests, ambitions and fads of the different people with whom she came in contact, and like her father she possessed great tact. Instinctively she knew what to do, and what to say to win people and bind them when won. "Every man has a right to his own opinion," she was wont to say, "and one would be little worthy of respect should one change contrary to one's convictions, but if a man has no convictions one is justified in giving him some," and tactfully and unostentatiously into many a one she instilled her own convictions, and like her chief, when she won them she invariably kept them. Her influence was great, because her convictions were the fruits of wisdom, and she was honest and sincere, and practised in her daily life the principles which she upheld.

But as she drove along in the late afternoon with the faint perfume of early flowers and blossoms wafted to her on the spring air, she was not thinking so much of the Lennox adhesion to their cause, or his addition to their party, as she was of Keith Kenyon's anxiety and interest in their acceptance; and then she aroused herself. "What difference does it make to me?" she mentally exclaimed for the second time that day; and then she ordered the coachman to drive to Monteith House.

An hour afterwards Carlton Monteith returned with her to accompany her to the drawing-room that same evening.

CHAPTER VII.

" WILL you meet Mrs. Lennox and her daughter now?" asked
Keith Kenyon of her a few hours afterwards, as they were
gathered together at the Senate Chamber drawing-room.

" Yes, she would meet them. She had definitely said so in her
own mind. They were friends of Keith Kenyon's, and he was
anxious that their surroundings should be made pleasant for
them. Her duty was clear. She should do what she could. And
she never believed in doing things by halves. If she did it in the
letter, she would do it in the spirit, too."

" Will you come, too, Carlton?" she said, and she turned with
the two men to meet the newcomers with cordiality.

As she extended her hand to the Lennoxes she was conscious of
undergoing a searching scrutiny, and to her imagination there
was almost an insolence in their greeting, as if the strangers had
divined what was passing in her mind, and resented or ignored
her power. The same feeling which she had felt when first seeing
them came over her now. There was something. What was it?
She felt herself in the presence of some new force, some new
power.

For the first time in her life she was at a loss to become mistress of any situation; the common-place greetings refused to
come; she was too candid to simulate a cordiality, which, despite
her efforts to the contrary, she could not feel. She felt her face
grow warm with a confusion of feeling. Keith Kenyon saw her
embarrassment, but in the presence of the other man he could not
help her any; but happily at that moment Mrs. Sangster and her
party approached and diverted their attention, while Modena laid
her hand within the arm of Carlton Monteith, and moved on to
speak to her Excellency, and Keith Kenyon passed on and joined
Mr. Lester, leaving the strangers with Mrs. Sangster.

" I wonder how Modena will like her," said Mr. Lester; " she
is certainly beautiful."

" They are two beautiful women," replied the young minister,
little divining the important role he would play in their after lives.

" Yes, but there is a great difference," replied his friend, slowly.

" How is that?"

" One has splendor with poetry, the other splendor without distinction; the one pride with dignity, the other arrogance with pre-
tension. You know them both. They remind one of St.
Amand's description of Josephine the Queen, and Madame Roland,

the personification of that Third Estate, which having been nothing, wished to be something, and afterwards to be all—but there —I should not say that," continued Lester, as he recalled his friend's intimacy with the family. "Forget that I said it."

Keith Kenyon only smiled. "You, too, are prejudiced. Because one has had the fortune to be born within the pale, one must not exclude all outside its boundaries."

"Oh, no, it isn't that; it really isn't that," said Jack Mainton, who had joined them, and who mentally recalled the story Keith Kenyon had told him that afternoon.

In the days gone by, the Blains, the ancestors of Verona Lennox on the maternal side, had had good blood flowing within their veins, and great wealth within their possessions, but they had met with great reverses, and had been reduced almost to penury. With the tide of emigration from the East, they had gone to redeem their fortunes in the West, where Marene, the last of the Blains, had met and married Mr. Lennox.

Mr. Lennox had been a miner in a western town, but the mines had proved unproductive. He was by nature grasping, shrewd and adventurous. Money came too slowly in. Hearing of some rich discoveries on the shores of the northern lakes, he had left his native village and bought and staked claims which proved to be very rich in minerals. By dint of saving and judicious speculation he had grown to be very wealthy.

His wife and daughter had removed to a neighboring city, where Verona had been sent to a fashionable school, and having inherited many instincts from her mother she had quickly grown into a daughter of the fashionable world.

The last few years had been spent in London and Paris.

She was like her father, ambitious, grasping and arrogant in spirit, but she was also shrewd and had learnt many things during her sojourn abroad. Her sojourn there had shown her the vast difference between her western views of freedom and equality, and the views of the exclusive sets which reigned in eastern cities.

When their money had first come to them she had looked upon it as an open sesame to every door. She had used it as such, but she had been repulsed. She had profited by her solecisms, and their discomforting results, and was not prepared to make the same mistakes the second time. As time passed she had learnt there were many things which money could not buy, one of them being an entrance into the circles of the governing classes of the people. To a certain extent it had helped her into a circle of society which had at first charmed her, but she had soon tired of

its hollowness and fruitlessness. She was only one of the many.
Through Keith Kenyon's influence they had been admitted into
some inner circles of the governing class. She had there felt
near the centre of things, and she wanted to be the very centre.

Her father had but one god—gold; he had no tendency towards,
or ambition for, political life. His gold was too precious to be
spent in securing the suffrage of such people, and he was too self-
centred to try to win by popular favor. But such little things as
these would not have prevented Verona from accomplishing what
she wished to accomplish, if it were necessary to do it in this way.
This way took time, and she did not wish to waste life by waiting.
What she wanted she wanted at once, and at once she must have
it. There was but one way for her to obtain it. She must
marry. As Keith Kenyon's wife she would be all-powerful. His
talent would soon secure for him a high position in the Cabinet,
and, no doubt, in time title would follow.

The picture was alluring, and when love enters into cold calculation, the picture becomes doubly attractive and enticing, and
having once decided the matter in her own mind it was the same
as though it were accomplished.

Like all vain people she was intensely egotistical; all selfish
people are always positive as to their wants. This is in itself a
great force. She was positive as to what she wanted. On her
arrival in the city she had taken possession of what she wanted.

She was shrewd enough to grasp the existing state of affairs in
the political world, and to make the most of present opportunities.
She had sent for him and had laid claims upon his time, until he
was already beginning to feel that he would have to consult his
social calendar to see if the Lennox cross was before the date,
before accepting or refusing any invitation.

His people, he felt, were already beginning to notice it and
comment upon it. She possessed a faculty of giving the people
the impression that things were as she wanted them to be. She
had about her a certain air of mystery and reserve which suggested a thousand things which had not, and never would have, an
existence. Her present air now was that there was a mutual
understanding between her and the young statesman.

Jack Mainton had said to him: "It isn't that; it really isn't
that"; he hadn't said what it was, but some half hour afterwards,
as they were leaving the Senate Chamber for the opera, Jack had
offered him a seat in the box which Carlton Monteith had taken
for the evening.

He had hesitated for a moment, and had then declined the offer.

Miss Lennox had come up. She had arranged a theatre party. She had the faculty of arranging matters for other people without consulting their wishes. It was all arranged, and he had promised before he knew it.

At least so thought Miss Lennox, and so thought the world, "Who is all eye and ear, and such a stupid heart to interpret eye and ear, and such a tongue to blazon its interpretation."

But it takes two to make an engagement. This the young statesman knew, and he knew also his reason for joining the Lennox party was the instinct of a gentleman, or the spirit of the Arab, which dwelt within him, and which prevented him from accepting a seat in Carlton Monteith's box.

CHAPTER VIII.

IT was an ideal spring day.

Fernwylde robed in its fairest garments of green and with flags flying from the keep, and from every corner, presented an appearance of enchanted fairyland.

It was now some six weeks since opening day. The mistress of Apsley House had overcome her reluctance, and had done what she had promised to do, called on the neophytes at Lennox Court; and it had been as Keith Kenyon had predicted, others had followed like sheep, and they had become the fashion.

Their advent into society and the approaching contest had stirred the city to its depths. It had been the gayest winter the Capital had ever known. Almost every form of pleasure had been exhausted, and as the season had drawn to a close the ingenuity of minds had been taxed to their utmost to sustain the routine of pleasure by day and by night.

The advent of spring had found their interest unabated, but the bright warm sunshine, which crept in through open doorways and windows, sought out the dust and havoc of the winter's dissipation, and seemed to throw it up in strong relief and create a desire in each heart to go with the birds to the country, and therefore Fernwylde was en fete and wore her gayest dress. It was another temperature, another world, another mental atmosphere. Strife, formality and caste had given place to nature, full and free.

The infinite sense of peace and repose which nature invariably instils, and the sense of the possibility of noble efforts which it creates, had fallen upon the mistress of the place and inspired within her a desire to present to her friends something worthy of her surroundings, and so as a farewell to the season's festivities she had issued cards to a " Court of Inquiry."

On her mother's side, more than a century ago, one of her ancestors had been a titled lady of France. At the time of the Commune her father, the Duke, had been forced to seek refuge in a distant province of France. For several months he had lived in seclusion, ministering to the wants of the poor, sharing with them his dole of daily bread. The Communists had learned of his retreat, and had followed, hounded, and persecuted him, but had promised pardon if he would renounce his King and swear fealty to the Republic. He had kissed his sword, and died fighting with his King's name on his lips. His only daughter had escaped and fled to England, bringing with her many relics which her servants had secretly brought from their palace at Versailles to their chateau in the provinces. Among these relics were many memoirs of the time of the Valois and Bourbon. In the memoirs were, here and there, descriptions of those tournaments of tongues which had been the diversion of the France of that epoch.

From childhood the mistress of Apsley House had pored over these and had revived, in mental pictures, many of the pretty pageantries portrayed in the memoirs. " Why not revive and imitate them?" she thought on the first day of her arrival, as she stood on the uplands of Fernwylde watching the banquet of color on land and sky and sea, which was the glory of Fernwylde, while the little lake lay far down below, green and sparkling as emerald, bearing upon its waters the yellow willows of the lake-shore monastery.

Detaching a small key from a bracelet, which she ever wore, she dispatched a trusted servant to the city for a private cabinet, in which the memoirs were kept.

Later in the day she sat in the same place, awaiting her servant's return. She looked across the ravine towards Idlewylde, and as she looked Keith Kenyon came from out the gloom. In a few minutes he was by her side.

" They—all these great women and men were people of letters," she said to him on her servant's return, as she gave herself up to the fascination and charm of the contents of the casket. The words and wisdom of St. Amand, the child-like ennui of Sevigne, the intense melancholy of De Stael, the irony of Talleyrand, the religious fervor and the sensuality of the Sun-King, the pleasure, the pathos, the pageantries, the pains of that passionate playhouse, all seemed to pass in panorama before her mental vision from the pages which lay before her.

They sat on a seat overlooking the lake, and she felt the warmth of her companion's arm against her own. He spoke little, but the warmth from his touch permeated her whole being, and so vivid did her impressions become, that the present was forgotten, and her mind wandered away into the past, and the things about her partook of the past, and she dropped her eyes, and memory was lost in the land of Somewhere. When she again raised them, the moon, full and round as a golden bowl, was rising from behind the Siberian pines which lined the mountain sides, shedding its silvery lustre over Fernwylde, as the memoirs which lay in her lap, had said it had so often shone over Versailles and the Sun-King's Court and the Trianon, and it seemed to her that she could see their philanthropies, their puissance and their pageantries, and all the fair fruit of their fervor, and their faith, coming down to them through the stillness and silence of many long years, as the moon's rays came to them from the eternal silence of the mountain tops over the slumbering waters of the Idlewylde with the white swans floating peacefully away on its breast, and in one great longing and loneliness she mentally cried, "Where are they? Where are they? All these dead of long ago." And the echoes of her memoirs answered back, "They are not dead, they are not dead. All these great men and women of long ago, they are here, they are here." "And why are we here?" came some voice from within. "For the formation of character in yourself and in others. Knowledge is the only safe way, and from them we know. From the ideal comes the real," And slowly she raised her eyes to the ideal or to the real who was by her side. He looked up at her as she did so, and her eyes looked elsewhere, and she said, "Why not?" and a few days afterwards she issued her cards. "He at least will understand," she thought.

Her guests had come in the morning and had passed the early hours of the day in boating, riding, and on the links. The early afternoon had been spent on the green, where the children from the village, clad in the daintiest of white, to bands of music, had danced round the Maypole, gay and glad of heart as was Shenstone's lads and lasses in England when she was young and simple of heart. Their May Queen had been crowned, and they had been feted, and had returned to their homes, and for their elders the Court of Inquiry was now opened.

A dais had been erected in the upland glade overlooking the lake. On the dais was placed the throne, which was a carved oak chair, and on the throne sat its mistress, while around her were gathered many familiar faces from the city. She was robed in white and garlanded with chains of daisies interlaced with sprays of evergreen; her head was crowned by a circlet of roses, while in her hand she held a sceptre of ivory. On the throne lay a cloak of royal purple, and on a moss-grown boulder by her side was a fan of ivory, painted by a miniaturist, bearing her profile, her monogram, and the armorial bearings of her house. And though her dress was a mixture of simplicity and rusticity, in harmony with the scene around her, yet was there in her attire and her attitude a certain gravity and grandeur which were impressive.

Her guests were in a semicircle in front of her.

When the Court opened the music from the orchestra in the Fernery ceased, and a fanfare of trumpets proclaimed the Court opened.

The Queen in a low, clear voice then addressed her people:

"This beautiful world, in which we live and move and have our being, is ruled by Principles or Truths which were established in the beginning, exist now, and will endure to the end. To discover these Truths has been the aim and desire of all great minds of all ages. What the ancient Chaldean contemplated as he lay at night under the stars of the desert, so too do we. Modern philosophy is but ancient mythology grown old and wise. Science teaches us much, but yet it fails to solve the problems of old, and only does what its predecessors did, hands the insolvable over to the realms of faith and instinct. We may say now what Petronius said some twenty centuries ago, 'Truth dwells somewhere so high that even the gods on Olympus cannot see it"; but yet there are some axioms of life which have been accepted by the sages of every age, and one of these is, 'Nature's primary object was the happiness of man.' We have come prepared to accept this as true, and our object to-day is to inquire further into the nature of happiness."

"This Court would ask you, 'What is happiness, and what are its essentials?'"

"The rules guiding you are in your hands, their sacrilege a forfeit, their reward a crown of laurel; the Court is now open," said their Queen.

Mr. Lester was the first to speak.

"To win your favor we would quote your favorite's testimony. Aristotle said, 'Happiness is the highest good, being a realization and perfect practice of virtue!'" he said, and when he had ceased speaking, then came other answers, in rapid succession, from all parts of the lawn.

"Pope says, 'Reason's whole pleasure, all the joys of sense, Lie in three words, Health, Peace and Competence.'"

"Adam Smith says, 'Health, freedom from debt, and a clear conscience.'"

"George Sand: 'C'est un eclair qui traverse les brunes monotones de la vie.'"

"Epicurus: 'Be virtuous because it brings happiness.'"

"Madame Maintenon: 'There is no happiness but in serving God.'"

"Happiness is a chapter from the Symposium."

"Socrates said: 'Constant peace and tranquility of mind.'"

"The Decamerone said: 'Great appetite and great fruition.'"

The Queen interrupted the last speaker by a sharp tingle from the little silver bell at her side.

"We regret very much that our first words must be words of chastisement. If you are not breaking written laws, at least you are violating unwritten ones. Other men's testimonies are not taken in a Court of Inquiry. We may believe what they say to be true, but we do not know whether or not it is true. Speak from knowledge, not from belief. To quote other men's testimonies is the sign of a dearth of thought. Our own thoughts should afford material for discussion," she said with severity.

"We have enough humility to know we know nothing, and, therefore, have little prestige among our own people. To assert it as our own knowledge would be as a little drop of water falling upon a hard sea-washed rock. These people are immortals. To use them as our authority gives conviction. Socrates said to Crito what you have said to us. Had you quoted him as your authority it would have given weight to your chastisement," replied her cousin in extenuation of their conduct.

"If you know that you know nothing, then you know that you know something, and are the world's equal or its superior. And you must not use other people as your authority; if it is not true, do not tell it; if it is true, then truth requires no authority. Truth is the origin, essence and nature of things, and is independent. It stands on its own merits or basis. If you are the medium through which it is spoken, remember the little drop

dropping, at last wears away the solid rock. Had I used Socrates
as my authority it would have given greater weight, you said!
Not at all! Truth rules with the same power always, whether its
sceptre be swayed by a sage or by a queen, by the past or by the
present, by time or by eternity. When we use the poets we are too
apt to become like Hippias and the Schoolmen, full of vanity and
superficial knowledge—words without reality. Bacon taught us
the necessity of discarding syllogisms and of returning to nature.
Learning cannot replace forces which come from conviction.
The rules tell you to speak according to your light and your
convictions."

"If we have to do so, then mightest thou have chosen a
different subject. You have asked us to discuss, dissect and define
a subject with which we are very unfamiliar. Happiness is
archaic. It has been eliminated from the dictionary of our everyday lives. Like the sacred fires on Vesta's hearth, its last spark
has faded almost into grey. You cannot expect us to speak intelligibly on a subject we have never known, or if we have known
only remember it as a relic of youth. It belongs to the age when
the world was young and men were simple of heart. We can only
repeat their testimony," said Mrs. Cecil, with a sincerity of regret.

"What a doleful, doleful picture! You are not now speaking
from conviction, or if you are your vision is temporarily clouded.
Your words remind one of Southey, who, all the years he was
ranting atheism, was tipping his Prometheus with stolen fire."

"But, your Majesty," protested the Frenchwoman, divining
the inference in her words, "before one can judge of other's
feelings, one must enter into other's emotions. So long as one
can sit on a throne unsullied by the world, one can exercise pity,
charity and love, but let the mud of its miry labyrinth touch and
soil one, and one's glasses quickly change. With Virgil we may
truly say, 'A gate of ivory is indeed very stately, but true dreams
pass through the gate of horn.'"

"Perhaps you are right; we will concede that point. But it is
the law that is deciding the Court, and the law is impersonal; it
is reason unaffected by desire or emotion. You have made a statement which we will proceed to consider. Happiness is obsolete,
or if it exists, it is a relic of youth. If anyone will testify that
he.or she is happy, you will admit that it exists. The Throne
testifies, therefore the first part of your assertion is ruled out."

"But the Throne's testimony will not do. You are divine. It
is humanity's happiness we are discussing."

"I am happy, perfectly happy," exclaimed the Lady Greta,

who was curled up like a dormouse in an easy chair, munching
away at some bon-bons a page had brought her.

"But you are a child," replied the Frenchwoman, smilingly.

"Why do you say it belongs to youth?" asked the Throne.

"Happiness is mental and physical enjoyment. Its essentials
are health for bodily enjoyment, and simplicity, ignorance,
illusions, and the child-like faith of a St. Augustine for mental
enjoyment. These, inasmuch as they belong to our age, are
attributes of youth. Health is a relic of the Spartan age; we
know it by the name of dyspepsia, lumbago, and chronic ills, ad
infinitum. The faith of our fathers has slipped its cables, and
we are drifting. The modern world is a witches' cauldron, into
which has been thrown both cross and crown. The simplicity of
nature fails to satisfy us. We have left it in the ruder state, and
have not yet attained to it in the higher. We are too wise or too
indifferent to enjoy. We are like Childe Harold, we have lost
the simple faculty of enjoyment. It is only youth who cares and
enjoys. Youth has its ideals. Age has proved them illusions."

"Your picture grows more dismal. Your pessimism we cannot
pass without a criticism. Health, Faith, Illusions! This is the
scientific age. Science tells us our ills are products of the
imagination. You haven't really a heartache. You only think
you have. Faith and Simplicity!" said their Queen, in a low,
clear voice, and then hesitated, and then unconsciously her eyes
wandered down to the lake shore monastery where Father Jacques
had risen from his seat to go within to his orisons. He had
paused, leaning on his walking-stick, his head uncovered, while his
eyes looked out across the waters to where the intense depth of
color was deepening as the sun sank towards the Laurentide Hills.

The other eyes of the group followed those of their Queen, and
there was silence for a moment, most of those present knowing his
history. He had been a High Church dignitary in France. In
Paris he had once done the mistress of Apsley House a great
kindness. Years afterwards she had again met him in Montreal.
He had seen great trouble and great affliction. These had driven
him from the world of men. His life had been broken and he
was seeking a paraclete. Modena had not forgotten. She had
offered Fernwylde as his St. Bruno. He had become her almoner
and one of her most trusted friends. He had been a student and
scholar; he had taught learned men, he had taken part in masses
sung in Notre Dame, he had served his Master and his King, but
these were all things of the past. He was skilled in the sciences
and simples of the day. Part of his day and night was given

over to caring for the primitive people in the suburbs of the city and Fernwylde, to the sea-worn fishermen and foreign lumbermen. He had gathered about him a few faithful, and they were ever ready for any call. Their home was a hospice, their prayers a solace and sustenance to the needy and sorrowing. The remainder of his day he spent in erudition and art. "These never fail one," he was wont to think. "The world of men do not know," and yet he gave fully and freely of the best that was in him to the lowest of the world of men.

The stateliness and simplicity of his solitary life made him a solemn and sacred figure.

As the sun touched the top of the highest peak he turned, and, followed by the others, went within.

"Faith and Simplicity," repeated their Queen, with almost a touch of reverence in her voice. "A living commentary is the strongest proof of its existence."

"A commentary on Lost Illusions," said Mrs. Cecil, with a great regret.

"Disillusion is but disenchanted egotism," said Mr. Lester, delivering a great moral sermon in a few words.

Mr. Lester had been vested with vice-regal powers.

"Our vice-regent speaks beyond our intelligence. We cannot understand syllogisms. We must have nature. We insist on Mrs. Cecil telling us why we need lose our illusions."

"If we would retain them we would need keep out of the world and live alone with nature. Illusions are volatile substances and the world is a solvent in which they disappear. Youth is as plastic, sensitive and susceptible as the clay the brick-makers carry to the press. It receives, believes and enjoys. But maturer years are like these bricks, that have been pressed, hardened and burnt," she said, as she touched the smooth bricks of the Fernery with the point of her long walking-stick, making no impression whatever on the hardened surface. "This brick is the same hardened clay. It is the treatment it has received that has changed it."

"According to your theory, age is hardened brick, and the world is a disenchanting taskmaster. I am old and I am happy, as happy as Lady Greta. I both care and enjoy immensely and intensely," said Mr. Lester.

"Mrs. Cecil has disputed our first axiom; with nature we have refuted her scepticism. Nature's primary object was the happiness of man. She supplies the essentials. The essentials to-day are superabundant. Will you pardon your Queen for using an old homely adage, 'You may drive a horse to a trough, but you cannot make him drink.' The world enjoys as much to-day, if not more, than it ever did before. The immediate incidents of our life around us influence our feelings temporarily, but we are happy all the same, happy in the thousand little soulless trials and trivialities which occupy one's days. We do not know how much we have to enjoy until the loss of something is threatened. 'I wish some Frenchman would shoot off your leg, and compel you to stump through life on a peg.' These were words written by Lord Lytton, and are applicable to all of us. Aladdin's lamp is only old metal to those who do not know the secret. The point in dispute is settled; we will decide in favor of the Lady Greta and Mr. Lester; Mrs. Cecil will pay a forfeit and we shall then pass on."

"One moment, your Majesty! Youth cries while teething; age howls with the toothache. These are but imaginary ills; at least admit that one would require the imagination of the Golden Age to see any happiness in the toothache, or in stumping through life on a peg."

"We might admit this to some, but not to you. Your teeth are beautiful, and your feet fit for a Venus. Your forfeit! What is happiness? or will someone name some of its essentials, and perhaps in this way we may arrive at a definition of it."

"Happiness depends upon fame and position," said a young aspirant for office, stammering a little in his eagerness.

"Cleopatra and Catherine de Medicis were famous; and one poisoned herself with an asp, and the other carried a shagreen case with poisoned arrows."

"They were notorious, not famous."

"Alexander and Cæsar were famous, and they sighed for other worlds to conquer."

"Before deciding this point we will have to ask ourselves, 'What is fame?' Our vice-regent will tell us."

"Fame is the smiles and applause of the public. It is in itself, Disfame. It is shared with the pirouetting monkey, the waltzing bear and the flying acrobat. It is like a transitory star; it has no place in the heavens."

"Is it necessary to happiness?"

"If one's barometer is the frowns and smiles of simpletons, it is. But if one's barometer is the 'Sage's mystic voice,' then rank and distinction are pleasing adjuncts, but not essentials."

"But isn't there a fame justly won, the result of years or a lifetime of strenuous labor that is desirable and honorable? I mean the fame which comes from genius," asked Marion Clydene, her language somewhat confused as the thoughts she wished to express were vague and unshaped.

"There is; but a man's happiness does not depend upon the fame that comes from genius, but consists in the creation of a noble work. His happiness lies in his work and its accomplishments, not in what men say about it. He is the proud man," answered their vice-regent.

"Then we are all vain, Mr. Lester," said their Queen. "We do dearly want to be praised. We envy you your opportunities and regret it does not lie in our power to become famous."

"But it does. Your name will go down to posterity as one famous in the history of your country," replied he, gallantly, bowing in obeisance before the throne.

"On a May Day as your Queen!" she said; "but one would require the imagination, which Mrs. Cecil wished to borrow, to see any fame in such a plain, practical person as Modena Wellington. The only eulogy even a Boswell could write, would be, 'She has common-sense,' and common-sense in men's eyes is synonymous with monotony and boredom."

"Oh, no! He could truthfully quote of you what St. Amand said of Josephine: 'At every epoch in history there are certain women who become, as it were, living symbols, and sum up in their own person, the passions, prejudices and illusions of their time.' Your sincere devotion to your cause, your indomitable will-power to accomplish what you undertake, your success as a social and political leader, your silent influence over the people, your magnetism and individuality make you a striking figure of your epoch," replied Mr. Lester, in a low tone, his intimacy with her robbing his words of any flattery.

"And Mrs. Cecil has just said the present age is one of pessimism, irreverence and clay-idols. I represent those!" replied the Queen.

"The face is the mirror of the soul. Some souls show in the face what the modern world has discarded and outgrown, as that moss-covered abbey by the lake shore, with its still cloisters and lonely monks, may symbolize what the modern world has lost in silence, simplicity and faith," said Mrs. Cecil, with a deep tinge of regret in her voice.

"Mrs. Cecil has shown us that she has imagination, love and philosophy; having imagination, she might make life a pageant; having love, a poem; having philosophy, a passionless play-house: any one of these would insure happiness. Having these, and having not happiness, she will pay another forfeit," said the Queen.

"You are making your forfeits a reward," objected the Lady Greta.

"I rise to a point of order," interrupted Carlton Monteith. "We wander too far afield from our subject. We are here to discuss happiness, not persons. Our chief magistrate has broken her own laws. That is sacrilege."

"What is the use of having the power to make laws without the privilege of breaking them?" she contested.

"The force of example is contagious. In Homeric days, the only age of true heroism, kings were supposed to prove their right divine by courage, strength, wisdom, justice and eloquence; when they ceased to display these qualities the sceptre departed from them."

"I stand rebuked; to the abstract once more."

"Happiness depends upon a contented mind," suggested someone.

"But that does not enlighten us. What are the essentials of contentment?"

"Health, Peace and Plenty."

"That's what Smith says. The basis for these savors too much of the material. They are too passive. We want more activity. They approach the shoals of common-place. There are things higher and better in life than these. Surely someone will tell us what is the essential to happiness."

"Here comes Mr. Kenyon; ask him," said Verona Lennox, as the young statesman crossed the greensward and joined the group.

He had been recalled to town to an important Cabinet meeting, and had now returned.

"We are glad you have come," added Lester. "We want brains to solve the conundrum."

"What conundrum?" asked the newcomer, as he made his way into the midst of the group.

"What does happiness depend upon?" answered Verona Lennox.

"Mine, or happiness in general?"

"Both," replied Verona in a low tone.

"Mine depends upon the smiles and frowns of the fair ones, but I should say happiness in general depended upon a man's pocket, his digestion and his temper," replied he, who had been the inspiration of the Court.

"Ungrateful, but natural," growled Jack. "We were contending it depended upon fame and position, and because you possess both you do not appreciate either."

The young minister laughed outright at his friend's gloomy brow. "As if you cared a straw for either. What's fame and position compared with temperament and heart?"

"But one hasn't any disposition or heart any more. The world spoils the one and the other is never believed in."

"Yours depends upon smiles and frowns!" said Helen Lester quickly, as she handed the newcomer some cake and ices. "Have you ever lost one moment's sleep over the smiles or frowns of anyone? So long as you get your Waterloos, little you care whether one's face is like an Iceland or a Bermuda sun. Before you came someone compared you to Alexander. You have conquered all hearts and are sighing for others to subdue."

"And like Napoleon, as unfeeling and ungenerous to his captives as he was to his Josephine. You left us all morning," added Verona Lennox, archly and with animation.

"My country called me!" he replied with regret.

"You ever had the instinct of a Curtius, rather than of a Lovelace," said Helen.

"But there always comes a time in one's life when one does care for such things. I am not responsible that mine has not come until old age has laid its hands upon me. Nature will have to answer that charge."

A sharp tingle from the bell recalled their attention. "We have more trouble in keeping you to the question than in solving the question. This digression becomes personal. If we allow this to proceed, the Court will break up like an Italian village feast, in a free use of the knife all round. If we become personal we will all be revealing our secrets and that will be very bad manners," said her Majesty.

"Before we entered this temple of intimacy, we left our manners outside the door, as the Oriental leaves his slippers in Persia," said Jack.

"You told us to speak from conviction, then we must become personal."

"But you must reason from the concrete to the abstract. The world is based on principles. You must get abstract thoughts. Our remarks heretofore have been like American humor, savage with personalities. We want them like English humor, rich, mellow and impersonal."

"You cannot draw blood from a stone. Theory is as uninteresting as dry bones. Things which we admire in actual life only bore us in theory. It is much more interesting and amusing to pick one's neighbors to pieces than to theorize. Happiness is to be enjoyed, not dissected or defined. We would arrive at its meaning much quicker and much more easily, if you would dismiss the Court, and give us an Italian cotilion, or a cutlet, or one of Petronius' rose-water baths. Theorizing or self-analysis has the tendency to make one morbid. 'Know thyself,' said the sage of old, not knowing he was giving to man one of the most depressing and difficult of all tasks. Goethe's self-analysis no doubt was seductive and benefited the world greatly, but had he listened less to the immense Ego, and more to the beating of the sea on the shore, the singing of the birds and the growing grass, he would have been a much happier man. When a person begins to analyze and philosophize about life's happiness, it is the sign he has grown tired of it. The world is now as it always was and always will be; our thoughts and our works will never alter the evolution of history; 'che sara, sara,' despite all our little efforts," exclaimed Jack, depressingly.

"What a sermon!" exclaimed Mr. Lester. "You have uttered a sweeping condemnation against our Court, and turned it into a pulpit. What white-livered mortals you would make us all. Simmias, who loved an argument better than any other man living, admitted to his master that there was cowardice in not probing truth to the bottom. Courage is the greatest of the virtues. The courageous are the confident, and the confident are those who know, and how can we know without thinking and inquiring? Had not Goethe listened to the immense Ego the world would have been deprived of its greatest dramatization. You are looking at life with the same eyes as he possessed when he wrote the 'Sorrows of Werther.' His digestion was bad at that time. He found his footing afterwards, and exclaimed, 'Where did I get all that trash?' We are hunting for our footing, have patience with us and help us."

"We don't want to know our footing; we know that we stand and that's enough. Cuvier, no doubt, knew infinitely more than Adam. What was a science to Cuvier was an emotion to Adam; we only want to enjoy," persisted Mrs. Sangster.

"What an epicurean you are! If we don't know what we're standing on, life will make us fall."

"Epicureanism or egotism never yet produced any great people. We want to be great."

"Then be good," said Jack.

"We will, if you will tell us how," said her Majesty.

" Do your duty."

" What are our duties?" she persisted.

" Your duties, as ladies of light and leading, are to dress well, receive well, love well, amuse us well, and be admired and amused in return," said Keith Kenyon, lightly.

" What a category of duties. Do we fill the role? We certainly dress well and look well, that is, when domestic economy does not transform our clothes into rags and our paint and powder boxes fail us not. Receive well? What a heavy subject to weigh! Whom do you ask us to receive? Your friends and contemporaries. You are statesmen. A reception to men means logic, hard facts, sophistry, dry bones, death and decay, and then a great desire to return to nature. The inevitable result statesmen bring their wives with them. Women enter the political arena."

" D—— them, they do," muttered an ex-minister who was pleased to look upon his dismissal as the result of some social aspirant.

" Stop, Modena, or you will have them on the platform yet."

" Not necessarily so. The wisdom of all ages tells us the happy state is the mean state in life. We are searching for the mean state."

" Our ancestors did not allow their women to puddle in politics. They remained in their harem, or with jewelled fingers plied the distaff or disentangled the flax."

" And in a century or two the world degenerated into the Dark Ages of Misery and Pain."

" Your inference is that the world would go to sleep, if you did not stir it up. Women represent nature and keep the old world moving on. They feel," said Mr. Lester.

" That's the tragedy of their sex," said Mrs. Cecil.

" We cannot allow that word 'tragedy.' It only becomes a tragedy when men do not care," said their Queen.

" You live to please us. We're not worth it," said Jack, gloomily.

" What humility!"

" No; self-knowledge."

" Then we are glad we do not know you as you know yourselves."

" They weren't made to know, but to feel. It is their faculty of feeling which makes them the redressers of all evil."

" And it was their faculty for wanting to know, which made them the origin of all evil," said some ungallant one.

" Oh! oh! Isn't there a double forfeit for such a slander? Do the rules provide for a bill of attainder? At least ostracise him."

"Not without a hearing. What about that little story of Eve and the apple?" replied the wicked one.

"She could not have eaten without having first the desire to eat. The desire was given to her."

"You would infer that evil is an emanation from another source. You mean that Evil is a necessary evil."

"I do not admit its existence."

"You admit its results."

"It is a negation."

"You mean?"

"It is the absence of Good, as Darkness is the absence of Light."

"And what is Good?"

> "Where is He that knows?
> From the great deep to the great deep He goes."

"We have already spent some hour and a half in trying to define It. We must hasten. The sun has sunk behind the highest peak. I cannot dissolve this Court until the question is solved. Mr. Kenyon has said that happiness depends upon a man's temper, his pocket and his digestion. Each one has quoted health as an essential. Experience, which is the best teacher in life, has proved this to be true. We shall accept it and lay it aside from further discussion. To discuss one's temper would bring us into the realms of theology. This is too heavy a subject for a May afternoon; we will shun it. Does happiness depend upon one's pocket?" she asked, but continued before anyone replied: "If theology is too heavy, this is too gross a subject for a sacred court. To contend that happiness depends upon a piece of metal is an insult to the gods."

"Who will name some others?"

"Here is one," said Keith Kenyon, as his eyes wandered over the waving meadows, the woodland glades and the old mansion of Fernwylde, throned on its hill behind its screen of mantling vines, with the setting sun illumining its windows and gothics, making it a castle mate for that which Merlin built. "A home and Vera," he continued, taking in his arms a little child who had run daintily across the lawn and sought his side.

It was little Vera Gregory who had been with her mother to see an old nurse of the family's who now lived at Fernwylde.

Their Queen smiled as she watched Mrs. Gregory as she came across the lawn towards the Court.

"Mr. Kenyon has said 'a fireside and Vera;' we shall accept this statement and pass on. Any other essential?"

"Is it possible to generalize as to essentials?" asked Carlton

Monteith. " What is an essential to one's happiness may not be
to another's. We have the philosopher, the statesman, the poet and
the lover, each happy in his own way—the statesman in action,
the philosopher in thought, the poet in creation, the lover in
emotion. Pericles works while Pindar sings. Pericles made the
world infinitely better while he was here. Pindar sang of immortality and helped to brighten the world forever. Some are happy
in action, others in contemplation. Here is Miss Clydene, happy
with her German psychologists," continued Carlton Monteith, who
knew the tendency of his young friend was to draw back from the
world as a sea-anemone draws back from the human hand.

" Marion does not believe we know the meaning of happiness,"
added Jack; " continually in the midst of all this feverish fuss
and fiddle-faddle, with a daily almanac of receptions, teas, nerves,
pills and ennui, and one doubts if she is far wrong."

" Oh, Mr. Mainton, do not say so. Our cups and our chocolates
and our weather reports are quite harmless. Nothing more so!
And they really keep us out of mischief, from meddling in men's
affairs, and they help regulate political-domestic economy! Is
that what you call it?" exclaimed the Lady Greta.

" Haven't the philosophers of all ages decided that Lothario,
alone, could define happiness. Are not these birds much happier
and more to be envied than the beavers which have worked
unceasingly to build that dam which we see down by the monastery?" asked Verona Lennox. As she spoke she pointed her walking-stick towards the lawn where two stately peacocks were drawing their trains of purple and gold over the greensward.

" If one has to choose between Venus and Athene I'd prefer
Venus," continued Verona, getting her metaphors mixed.

" You mean you'd prefer the life of those turtle doves," said
Marion, pointing to a pair of doves which were cooing to each
other in the ivy covering of the Fernery. Opposite to where they
were seated was a large cedar tree, spreading its dark shadows
over the lawn; in and out of its boughs flew two mischievous
house-wrens chattering and pulling to pieces the nest of a song
sparrow, and carrying the hair and wool over to the eaves of the
Fernery to line their own mud nest.

" And yet the most of us pass life like these wrens," continued
Marion, smiling despite herself, as she watched the actions of the
sparrow and wrens.

" If we're not turtle doves, we needn't necessarily be wrens,"
said their Queen. The beaver leads his own life and lives on what
nature provides."

"But there are no clubs or newspapers or frills in beaverdom. It is easy for him to lead his own life."

"We're not responsible for our temperaments," continued Verona Lennox, who still continued to look at the turtle doves which had furnished them with their metaphors. "I was made to love the dove and the peacock. This is my ideal of happiness," she concluded, realizing that when once one has been a stray cur or a pack dog, and has been transferred into a kennel of thoroughbreds, petted and admired, one knows what life really is.

"'The pleasures of the world when they have become one's chief object in life are as empty as the left-hand sceptre,' so said Sevigne."

"Great men have always loved pleasure."

"As a pastime, not a pursuit; when it becomes one's pursuit it becomes one's dyspepsia, as Rome became the ulcer of the world."

"If one take life seriously, one will find it as Heraclitus found it—sad indeed, but if one take it as it comes and never worry over anything enough to let it worry one, one will find it as Democritus found it—no sadness whatever."

"If one would take life so, one would require the disposition of a Gui Patin, the famous Fronde physician, who remained unmoved and disinterested during all that reign of terror."

"Then according to Taine the modern world should be a world of merry-makers. He says we are ephemeral, our sorrows are trivial, we are worried by many things but pained by few."

"Then Taine slanders us, for we do care, we care very much. If we do not care, why this deep vein of melancholy beneath all our merry-making?"

"We have ideals. Our ideals are but a remembrance or a prevision. This melancholy is but the soul crying out in its strong desire to return, or to go on to better things."

"It's not the soul that's crying," interrupted Keith Kenyon. "It's the ninth muse, that baleful goddess of indigestion, who is responsible for much of the Wellschmerz and passionate unrest of to-day."

"Mr. Kenyon, don't be profane," rebuked their Queen. "This is a sacred court."

"Has the Court the power to chase away this melancholy?" asked Mrs. Cecil. "If it has it will become immortal."

"Melancholy is egotism," said their vice-regent, "and egotism is ourselves. To get rid of melancholy we must get rid of ourselves."

"That will never do!" exclaimed Keith Kenyon. "Life is too sweet to try the role of Romeo or Polyeute."

"That would be too theatrical. It would savor of poor taste; and as we are not a Lycidas, and cannot pass away a perfect youth, all there is left for us to do is to give ourselves away gracefully and æsthetically to someone else," said their Queen.

"You think marriage a cure for melancholy?" asked Jack, with doubt in his accents.

"That is too wide a subject to open. We are willing to accept it as another essential. We have now, I think, sufficient essentials to generalize. Who will define happiness?"

There was silence for some moments.

"The sun is going down. The odor from the kitchen is sacrilegious. I see Watkins with cutlets and cream, they would tempt even a goddess. Who will win the laurel crown? Is our Court to be fruitless?"

"The afternoon hasn't been wasted, Modena. Like Diderot's vagabond we have at least killed time," said Mrs. Cecil.

"But we're not living to kill time but to improve it. No cutlets until this is solved," said their Queen, who had the faculty of clinging tooth and nail to anything in life until she could bring order out of confusion. The confusion was dear and interesting to her, and gave a spice to life, but she did not wish the sun to go down without knowing that something had been accomplished throughout the day. Like her native beaver she had a great instinct for work, and when her house was pulled down, with courage she would go to work and rebuild it until she was pleased with the result.

"Mr. Lester, we are forced to appeal to you to solve the problem. We are very sorry that mortals have failed us. We are hungry and can wait no longer."

The Court laughed aloud, and then her Majesty smiled.

"Even goddesses may be tempted," someone was wicked enough to say.

"Mr. Lester, this Court is stupid, and it is also typical of the age; it refuses to believe in the divinity and infallibility of its Majesty. And yet she is wicked enough to wish to be revenged on them. Display the wisdom of the gods and enlighten them."

"But you are Queen."

"The goddesses receive their knowledge from the gods. It is your duty to know and mine to disseminate. All knowledge *must* come from the gods. What is it?"

"If it is a definition you want I cannot give you a better one than the one I gave you at the opening of the Court."

"What was that?"

"Happiness is the highest good, being a realization and perfect practice of virtue."

"That is Greek to the uninitiated. You will have to explain."

"The intellect is man's spiritual nature. It is the essence of Divinity. It is only a little spark at first, but it must be developed until it reaches the Ideal which is God or Truth. Knowledge is the first step to supreme good. The good of things is that which preserves them. The body is the receptacle of the soul and must be preserved, but it is perishable, and thought alone is eternal. The perfect intellect is the omega of life. It is attained by virtue. Virtues are purifications of the soul. Every time we gain a truth we are one step nearer the perfect intellect. As Pindar sang, 'Be that which thou wert made to be.' When the intellect is developed to simplicity and humility we know the true meaning of happiness," replied Mr. Lester, gravely and kindly, almost forgetting where he was while his eyes unconsciously sought the distant horizon where the sun was fast sinking from view, as if his thoughts, full of hope and trust, had gone to another world with the symbol of light

"We try to be that which we were made to be, but we can't," muttered Jack, moodily, with his usual abruptness.

"Pardon me, Jack, but we can," said his cousin, in her intense interest in Mr. Lester's philosophy, forgetting her role of May Queen. "I have never seen anything done yet, but I think I can do it a little better. I try, and I think it is wonderful. The world comes along like jack-daws, and picks me to pieces—behind my back, of course; I am too gilded a person for it to confront; but yet with inward eyes we see and feel those things. We do not allow the world to know we see them; our pride is too great. Somehow or other the good sifts out from the bad; we leave the bad as landmarks, and go on like Lucille, 'onward and upward.' The courageous do catch glimpses of real happiness," said their Queen, with a new-born wonder in her voice.

"And in the very midst of one's moments of happiness, one's liver gives a thump against one's shoulder blade, or lumbago a twinge in the back, or a tailor pokes an unpaid bill before one's nose, or a messenger arrives to inform one that five hundred employees have left one's works in sympathy with an uprising in Oklahoma, and one's happiness proves a mirage; and too," continued Jack, gloomily, " we have, as this same Lytton says, our devil-instinct moods, and when we would be happy we cannot be.

> "' We are what we must and not what we would be;
> The will and the power are diverse;
> We but catch at the skirts of the things we would be:
> And fall back on the lap of false destiny.'"

"What nonsense, Jack! Where's your will? One wills what one will be, and becomes that!" exclaimed Modena. "Any other spirit is the spirit of a coward."

"If you call that a cowardly spirit you will learn that sometime, either here or elsewhere, life makes cowards of us all," muttered Jack, almost sadly.

"Is the Court willing to accept Mr. Lester's definition for happiness and bestow upon him the laurel crown?"

"That the perfect intellect is the omega of life?" queried Mrs. Cecil.

"Yes."

"Then there is no such thing as happiness. The sages of all ages have told us that in much wisdom there is much sorrow. Goethe kicked despairingly against the bars of finite knowledge, and died, crying, 'More light, more light.' Mr. Lester cannot have the crown even if he has the wisdom of the gods."

"Will Mrs. Cecil enlighten us?"

"No, because she cannot. We are told to speak from conviction, and I do not know what it is."

"Periander cut off the tallest ears of corn until he brought the field to a level. We shall have to ostracise Mrs. Cecil, or we shall starve!" exclaimed Keith Kenyon.

"No, Mrs. Cecil must remain. Pyrrho doubted everything, but he shied before the concrete chariot wheel. Will you be the wheel, Mr. Kenyon?" asked their Queen in dismay.

"I said, 'Happiness depends upon the smiles and frowns of the fair ones.' My cause was strong, but my tongue lacked persuasiveness. Ask Helen and she will tell you the same thing in prettier words," replied the young statesman, who had seated himself near Helen Lester.

"What is the prettiest word in the English language, Helen? Name it, and you will receive the crown," said their Queen.

"Love is the Highest Good. Happiness is Love," replied Helen, lending to the old familiar word the charm of her own personality.

There was an expressive silence after she had spoken, the

group instinctively feeling that a deeper meaning lay beneath her words.

She had about her that air of rest and peace, which unconsciously transmits itself to its surroundings. One felt when in her presence what Petronius felt when he said, "I am considering in my soul how different this world of yours is from the world in which our Nero lives." Her countenance now was expressive of strong personal convictions.

The silence was broken by Mrs. Cecil; she knew that Helen had not referred to earthly love alone, but she preferred to think so.

"Love is perfect bliss while it lasts, but it is like a comet; in great brilliancy it mounts to its perihelion, and then disappears —elsewhere—and the aftermath tears the heart to pieces," she said.

"But love is eternal," replied Helen, gravely and quietly.

"In dreams only. That is one of youth's happy illusions."

"You will persist in destroying our illusions. We would rather come to you to have our wounds healed."

"If one possessed the power of curing you, one would soon grow wealthy, for the whole world would come for treatment. What the world wants is a physician for sick souls and weary spirits."

"We are hunting that physician. Are there no Romeos or Petrarchs to take up the cudgels for love and modernity?"

Voices in affirmation came from all parts of the lawn.

"Nature is stronger than philosophy. The mystic voice has spoken in her promptings. You will have to submit, and admit that love is eternal."

"How do you know?" persisted the Frenchwoman. "What law decreed it?"

"Nature's law. It is something felt, not seen. It is an emotion, not a science."

"Then it is physical, and happiness depends upon the physical alone," she said, and she smiled as she saw the consternation written on their Queen's face.

"Will you admit that love is perfect happiness while love lasts?"

"Yes."

"And if we can prove it is eternal you will admit we have found the true happiness?"

"Certainly."

"Who will unravel the mystery? We all believe our loves are true and eternal, but we will have to admit that Mrs. Cecil is right, we have not proved them. Will Œdipus not now appear in the form of a Montrose, and win the laurel crown?"

Protestations and assertions came from all parts of the lawn.

"Proof! Proof! Promises and assertions are not logic," exclaimed their Queen.

"Helen, this is your assertion. Prove it eternal, and we shall award you the crown."

Helen's eyes, as her brother's had done, sought the west, where the sun had now gone down, leaving behind it haloes of glowing fire, as if seeking inspiration from the great beyond. The shades of night were coming down slowly around them, like a benediction of peace on land and water, with no sound round them, save the rustling of the wind in the willows and the plunge of the beaver in the water, and the last faint notes of a Jubilate Deo on the pale blue air of a northern twilight.

Almost unconscious of her surroundings she said: "Man is powerless to obtain the highest knowledge through his own intellectual efforts; the human soul receives through a higher faculty than reason, revelations of divine and eternal truths. Plato says, 'The soul unblinded can see Truth.' When the soul dwells on truth and reaches the finite, if it be in earnest, unburdened by flesh, it soars beyond and sees Truth face to face, as Lancelot saw it in the enchanted Castle of Carbonek. Then it knows, and all the powers of darkness can never afterwards dim or blur this knowledge. It is instinctive faith made into a reality, it is knowledge transformed into emotion, and emotion into knowledge. Heart and mind become a synthesis. It is the strength of martyrs. It is the Light which dispels all darkness. It is a gift from the gods. It is Love Eternal, it is Happiness."

There was a silence when Helen ceased speaking, as if some angel had come with the haloes of light from the sunken sun over the waters and breathed a peace into each heart.

"Does Mrs. Cecil yet believe?" asked the Queen, almost in a hushed voice. Mrs. Cecil's voice was low as she replied, and she did not raise her eyes.

"We know Helen, and since she has proved it, and found it true, we must believe through faith, but yet it seems food fit only for goddesses. We are but mortal, and crave for something tangible."

"It has its reflex here," replied Helen, while her face grew grave.

"In man, you mean?" asked Mrs. Cecil, and in her interrogation, to those few who knew her history there was in her voice a pain which came from some wound which bled within, and then remembering it was a Mock Court, and that many eyes were upon them, she said, in a lighter vein. "Hunger is a more persuasive wheel than logic; I am hungry. I am convinced, your Majesty."

"Helen has proved that happiness is a gift from the gods, to be won in its perfection by warfare. It is embodied in the one little word Love. She has proved that the love of the gods is eternal, and has inferred that the love of mortals is also, if the mortals possess the attributes of the gods. As the mortals whom we love pretend to be gods, we shall take them in their vanities, and admit that Helen has justly won the laurel crown, and we shall bestow upon her all the honors, duties, pleasures and prerogatives of divinity," said their Queen, and rising from the throne she summoned her pages and courtiers to her, and taking from their hands a crown of laurel, placed it on the brow of the kneeling figure, while the music in the Fernery proclaimed the Court closed.

"What do you think about it all?" asked Keith Kenyon, of the mistress of the place, a few minutes afterwards, as they met in the library, when the other ladies had gone away to their rooms to dress for dinner.

"There is a great deal of truth in all that has been said, but it depends entirely on one's own disposition," she replied.

"But for your own part, what do you think happiness depends upon?"

She looked down at some violets which had been brought in from the Fernery before she replied, and as their sweet perfume reached her, where she stood, her face grew soft and illumined as she said, "I have never thought of it before. I have been happy all my life, and have never asked myself why, but since you persist, I should say, 'Happiness depends upon the possession of an inherited home, whether humble or grand, a mind at peace with itself and others, a soul-satisfying religion, a keen, healthy interest in one's work, and love with sympathy, confidence and respect.'"

It was one of those moments when his heart was stronger than his resolutions. Of late he had thought that she cared for himself. Love is such a blind thing. If he only knew, he could go on his way, and leave her to the other, happy in the knowledge.

So he told himself.

"Do you think love necessary to happiness? Isn't Marion happy in her art, and has she ever loved?" he said.

"There may be different degrees of happiness. If we are to believe what the poets tell us, we must believe that supreme happiness consists in supreme love. Marion, no doubt, is happy, but

7

there is yet a void in her life which we hope some day will be filled."

They were standing at some distance from the few remaining guests; the lights had not yet been lit, but the dying light from the sun's afterglow shone in through the western oriel window, and illumined her profile as she raised her eyes to his as she ceased speaking.

"And yours has been filled?" he asked, referring to her relations to Carlton Monteith for the first time. They were bold words to use, but his tone and the previous discussion robbed them of any offence or familiarity. He stood with his arm on the mantel and his hand partially shading his eyes as they gazed at her with warm admiration.

She felt the color rush to her brow and her eyes dropped, and then she remembered many things. "If there were not in her what would keep a man by her side and her side alone, she would not measure her strength with another, and with such as she," she felt rather than thought, and a darker look came over her face as she turned from him and went over to where Carlton Monteith was turning some music for Helen Lester, while he went out into the gloom, perplexed, towards Idlewylde.

CHAPTER IX.

"It appears to me like the glorious personification of that Right which we call Divine."—*St. Amand to his Sun-King.*

"HELEN said the prettiest word in the English language was Love. Perhaps it is to those who know it, but it is so exclusive, that to the most of us it is actually ugly. What little we know or see has become vulgarized. Music is much prettier. This would tempt even an Odyssey," said Marion Clydene the next afternoon in that dreamy, contemplative manner that bespoke the artist's soul.

They had gone out on the western terrace, facing the lake, to court the soft spring winds and warming sun rays, and had grouped themselves in little groups here and there.

In the early afternoon Grace Austin had made up a musical boating party, and had gone to a distant point up the river.

They were now returning. the music from the stringed instruments and their voices in some old folk-songs of the south and of the coureur-de-bois, floating faintly over the waters to the ears of those who listened from the bank.

Some of the party had returned from a fish-hunt and had not yet gone within, but had thrown themselves on the greensward to rest before going in to dress for dinner. Some of the men had come out from their duties in the city and had joined the others on the lawn.

A tea table sat under a spreading tent-like cedar. On it were Sevres cups and old Limoges china. Servants served from it tea and dainty morsels of cake or early fruit.

The music party neared the shore, and the mandolin melodies became more audible, and awakened in the woods all the old echoes which love to wander at eventide.

"But love is music," said Jack.

"I thought music was harmony."

"And love a discord?"

"It is an harmonious discord. It has infinite variety. It is this that makes it so alluring. No doubt Penelope was old and cross, yet she was more alluring to Odyssey than the sirens of Greece," said the mistress of the place.

"I prefer the harmony minus the discord," said Marion. "If I were her Excellency, the first thing I would do would be to petition the Government for a national band, and I would have music like this in the parks all the time."

"All the time?" interrogated Jack, with arched brows. "Wouldn't you save the Government extra fur expenses and limit your time to when the temperature was above zero?"

"You would limit us to five months in the year," added Mr. Lester.

"You are more liberal to us than foreign opinion," replied their hostess, as her eyes for a moment glanced towards the links, where the master of Idlewylde was making Miss Lennox familiar with the grounds for the game which was to be played the following day. "They would only allow us an Iceland sun and climate the year round. Would it be for pleasure or for education you would have it?" continued she, addressing her companion.

"If for pleasure, introduce the garden-system," interrupted Mr. Lennox in his hard, metallic-like voice.

He had not been invited to Fernwylde with his daughter, but had come out to see some of the members staying there.

"No, we will never introduce that system," replied Mrs. Cecil, abruptly, but with an air of grace and ease which robbed her abruptness of any rudeness. "Music must be associated with the purposes for which it was primarily intended. It is our medicine, and one might as well, with Hume, try to make a fine sauce out of a mixture of wormwood and aloes as a harmony by mixing the soul with beer-mugs."

Mr. Lennox was silenced, but inwardly rebellious.

"I would have everything done to music," continued Marion. "If I were a dressmaker I would not endeavor to drape a dress, or if a milliner arrange the plumes and shades on a bonnet, or a decorator or an architect, without music in the background."

"Or a sweep, or a plumber, or a rag-picker," added Jack. "Just fancy sorting rags to music!"

"And if an author or a poet," continued she, regardless of interruption, "I would not endeavor to compose or create unless I could go into the heart of nature, where myriads of birds would be singing, where there would be sounds of falling waters and trees whispering with wood-aged tongues. Then one could close one's eyes and compose."

"You would require a clairvoyant to accompany you with a shorthand typewriter. If you endeavored to portray your thoughts by the earthly use of pen and paper the spell would be broken," said Carlton Monteith.

"But the thoughts, the images, would not be ready for reproduction," said the mistress of the place. "They would only be present in one's mind as potentialities or phantoms; they would require to lie embedded there, to mingle and co-mingle with what was already there in order to be ready for reproduction. Thought is like food, it requires proper digestion. Undigested thought is similar to what Wordsworth said of Keats' first poetry, 'A pretty piece of paganism.'"

"It wouldn't be paganism if we were alone with nature, unless it were the paganism of Spinoza. Digested thought savors too much of realism, and we do not want that. The happiness which we were discussing yesterday is a vague, visionary thing in real life. It is like the hart with the golden horn which the knights chased, like a silver shadow it slips away into the dim land and vanishes at the fairy well that laughs at iron. It is only caught by such men as Richter and Rabelais, who have the amulet of imagination to transfigure life. The world is too full of prose. It is too small and too limited," contested Marion.

"Then there are only three classes of people who really live,

> "'The lunatic, the lover and the poet,
> Are of imagination all compact,'"

said Jack.

" Marion is out of place in this Iceland of ours. She should have
lived centuries ago with the sages of old. Their theory of music
would have satisfied her dreams. If they could, as they claimed
they could, settle the most subtle of law suits by music, surely
Marion could drape a dress or Jack pick rags by it," said Keith
Kenyon, who had returned from the links.

" Perhaps she did live then," suggested Carlton Monteith.

" She must be ' getting on ' by this time," replied Jack. " I am
surprised at your audacity in paying Miss Marion such a compliment."

" You are the only one who would interpret the compliment in
that way. Miss Clydene knows that I refer to the soul and not to
the body."

" If that's the case I'll drop out of the conversation. This life
is all I can manage, and more, too," added he, as he pulled his hat
down over his brow to protect himself from the sun's rays, and
turned his thoughts to the object of Mr. Lennox's visit and to how
he would reply to some political criticisms in the morning papers.

Although to outward appearances he was seemingly careless and
cynically indifferent, yet he was one of the hardest worked men of
the day. Even while talking nonsense or common sense to his
cousin's guests at Fernwylde, there was a continual undercurrent
of hard thought at work, which found its fruition in many hard
facts and lofty ideals in his morning edition.

Perhaps he would have been a more pleasing companion had he
considered Philantes' phlegm more preferable and more philosophical than Alceste's bile, but like Alceste his candid and ingenuous
mind was continually shocked and disgusted by the insincerities,
hypocrisies and injustices of the world, and he was wont to vent
his bile on his friends, while to the public he was endeavoring to
give some of the great truths of life.

" I wish we had some of the old conjurers here who lived then
to tell us our fortunes," said Marion.

" If we knew them, life would be very uninteresting. The spice
of life is the unseen and unknown."

" If the Fates would stop their spinning and weaving and leave
the warp and woof in our own hands, I wonder what we would
weave."

" Allow me to be your conjurer and tell yours," said Mr. Lester.
" Miss Clydene would live in a world a little above this one; she
would associate with Ovid and Pindar, revelling in Hera's jealousy
of Io, and of Io's transformation into the white cow, and of her
surveillance by the all-seeing Argus, and if she thought of us poor

mortals whatever, she would ostracise Hansard, and place in our hands Utopia and the Republic—"

"Oh, stop, Mr. Lester! A community of women and children! No doubt, like in Hamlet's brain, there are germs of madness in mine, but yet not so bad as that. You are slandering me."

"Theory and imagination unrestrained always end in—in—lunacy."

"Now I am going to talk about the weather, and a recipe for catsup, and May Laney's lack of taste in dress, and her horrid conduct with that young officer, while you tell Modena's fortune."

Mr. Lester smiled at Marion's pouting brow, and then good-naturedly turned his deep grey eyes towards his hostess.

"My lady here is like Marie Antoinette, fond of politics and pageantries, prejudiced towards prerogatives, and, like her, winning her way by philanthropy."

"Which is flattered, Marion? You are ideal and possess all the imaginative and creative faculties, while I am that which most men abhor, a cold, practical, common sense woman."

"You have read his readings wrong. Mr. Lester has paid you a subtle compliment," said Mrs. Cecil. "He has draped you with tact, diplomacy and beauty. You are competent to grace the Queen's drawing-room, or to stand on the street corner with white cap and apron, a board canopy over your head and a hot stove behind your back, giving out coffee and rolls over a pine counter to street waifs."

"And attractive in all forms. Could we but recall Kneller or Vandyke from their land of slumber, they would paint you as Cybelle, with a north star in your brow," said Mr. Lester, with tenderness and in a low voice.

"How nicely you say that! You must think we are yet in court and I your queen. Had you said it yesterday you would have received the laurel crown."

"I would rather be your knight than receive the crown of laurel," replied he, with a tinge of regret in his voice.

"You are becoming some other one's knight, and here she is!" she said, as Grace Austin and her party came up from the river. "You are just in time," she said to the newcomers.

"In time for something nice?"

"In time to have your fortune told. Mr. Lester is acting palmist. Hold out your hand to him."

Mr. Lester turned, bowed and rose, but the Southerner placed her hands behind her.

"Will it be something nice? Does he tell our frailties and

foibles. We do not want the world to know them. What did he give you, Modena? Some bon-bons?"

"Yes; he thought we had enough logic and hard facts yesterday to do for some time. So he gave us some nonsense as an antidote."

"What was your nonsense?"

"He told us what we are, rather than told our fortunes."

"How did he draw you?"

"Oh, he drew a picture of an ardent Loyalist with a deep shade of Toryism—this, and a little common sense—that was all."

"All! How much more would you want? Loyalty, Toryism and common sense are three big words. At one time they didn't mean nonsense."

"Nor do they yet. They mean more now than they ever did before. Don't they, Mr. Lester?"

"They do not mean now what they did under the ' Old Regime,' " said Mrs. Cecil.

"What did they mean then?" asked Grace Austin, who was hunting thoughts.

Mrs. Cecil's eyes wandered away down the river to where in the distance her own flags might be seen flying from the masts of the harbor boat, and her eyes deepened with many memories as she said, "They meant much; they meant prerogative and power, pageantries and powder, chivalry and honor and love; they meant life and joy and elegance and ease; they meant that life was then as it should be. We had courage and we had ideals," and her eyes softened and grew luminous, as all her youthful dreams came back to her.

"And vanished into autocracy. Why does history tell tales and disillusion us?" added Mr. Lester, not unkindly.

"And what arose from their ashes? What do they mean now?" persisted Miss Austin, interested in the evolution of history.

Mr. Lester smiled, but did not reply.

"We're waiting your answer, Lester," said Jack, as he picked up a pebble and sent it skimmering over the smooth surface of the little lake, startling some wild ducks that were concealed in the osier beds by the river's edge.

"A god yesterday and a clairvoyant to-day! You can surely answer the question," insisted Modena.

"No, I'm afraid it is even beyond the knowledge of the gods. You will have to solve the problem yourself. You are a political lady. You have knowledge and you have faith."

"But I'm not going to have them any more. Mrs. Cecil's dreams and retrospective visions have converted me."

"You would become a Madame McCarty, with her chaise and six-in-hand, with her cortége of liveried outriders, and with her beauty and grace and minuet steps," said Keith Kenyon, addressing her for the first time.

"I wish she had been Madame McCarty, or whatever they call her, and remained with her negroes and Frenchmen and court-revellers!" thought Verona Lennox, with a flash of resentment.

"The eminent Gayarri tells us she had beautiful arms, as white as snow, which she never covered in summer or winter," replied their hostess. "There is no comparison."

"And so has my Lady," said Carlton Monteith, as he handed her the zephyr shawl which had dropped from her arm, lightly touching her hand as he did so.

It was only a little word and a little act. So long as she could remember he had said and done the same, and she had received them gracefully. Now they had in them the power to irritate her—just a little. But she did not show it—only a little.

"Hers would certainly be as cold as snow, and one would need to carry rose-water and a naphtha stove around with one here," she replied, a little coldly.

"How ungrateful! This is a perfect May-day! and the place a veritable Arcadia."

"You believe in all those old things yet, Modena? Isn't this the land and age of—of—Equality? I detest that word—it is so common, but it is so expressive one is forced to use it," said the Lady Greta, with wide-open eyes, her English somewhat confused.

"So it is," answered Mr. Lester. "But yet in all ages that other spirit will appear. It is like the robins and the storks that return every year to rebuild in the shelter of the same eaves in the old Fernery. It is a spirit that was inculcated into man in the beginning and will endure to the end. It does not belong exclusively to any age, any person or any country."

"Hear! Hear! That coming from Mr. Lester! What heresy!"

"Mr. Lester is flying his colors under a wrong flag."

"There are others, too, doing the same thing. Time and Truth always make heretics of our cradle-creeds. This is the spirit that appears in all really great people."

"Oh! Oh! Mr. Lester, will you remember we are not in the Court! What flattery!" said Modena; "and a moment ago you were using such words as stagnation and tyranny."

Mr. Lester smiled.

"I did not mean to be personal. I was speaking in the abstract."

"We must learn to keep to the abstract," said their hostess, noticing she was monopolizing the conversation. "We require a Chesterfield here to teach us good manners and prevent us from bringing personalities into discussion."

"Personalities give spice and bristle to conversation, as onions give flavor to a dish," said Lester.

"But the flavor of the onion is disagreeable to those who do not eat it, and sometimes to those who do eat it."

"Your onion is surely not disagreeable?"

"I want you to go and see the onions—strawberries I mean. I have another engagement for a few minutes. Jack, will you go to the plantation? I promised the children we should visit them this evening," said Modena, referring to a number of plots of ground she had given to the children of her tenants as their own.

At their hostess's wish her guests rose, and grouping themselves in twos and threes, wended their way down the rose-bordered paths towards the tenants' quarters.

"I thought Miss Wellington too conservative to become an 'advanced woman,'" said Grace Austin to Jack Mainton as they walked side by side to the colony.

"What do you mean? How is she a 'new woman'?"

"I thought Mr. Lester said she was a political lady."

"She has been associated with politicians all her life and she has traditions and has read and thought and has views of her own, and has great faith in her party, but publicly she does not meddle in politics," answered Jack, who was always reticent in discussing his cousin in her absence.

"She is only a missionary," added Mrs. Cecil. "She doesn't want small game. She is going to convert the politicians and regenerate the science of politics."

"Your epithet is hardly appropriate," said Lester. "One could scarcely call her a missionary. She thinks the politicians are the elect and require no conversion. She is rather their patroness or mascot," continued he, as he whistled to his Scotch terrier, who was barking viciously at some hares in a clover field close by.

"The politicians the elect! Then God have mercy upon the sinners!" exclaimed Jack. "It is one's candid opinion that heaven will be as void of politicians as it will be of lawyers and—"

"And editors."

"Yes, and editors."

"At least, she is as enthusiastic in her cause as was Madame Junchereau in hers," added Mrs. Cecil.

"Would she employ the same means for the conversion of heretics as did our good Mother?" asked Lester.

"What were those?" asked Grace Austin, who was a foreigner and therefore unacquainted with the country's history.

"She ground to powder a small piece of bone taken from Brebeuf, one of the martyrs in their cause, and secretly mixed the sacred dust in the patient's gruel, whereupon an immediate conversion took place."

"Lord help the victim's digestion if he has to eat in his gruel the essence of some of the Tories of to-day; they are as tough and indigestible as old shoe-leather and as stale as hard-tack. He would need the vomitarium at the foot of the table, as they did in ancient times," said Jack, grimly.

"He could then uphold the party's principles with a clear stomach, if not with a clear conscience, as Petronius did Nero's poetry," returned Mr. Lester, as they reached the gardens.

"Sit down here and wait," said Jack to Keith Kenyon. "Let Lester act as gardener's guide. He hasn't told Miss Austin her fortune yet. I know he wants to tell it," and then they broke up into groups, some going one way and some another, while the two men seated themselves on some stone steps leading to the garden.

They were silent for some time.

"Lennox has come out," at last said Keith Kenyon.

"He came out to see Sangster."

"What does he want?"

"You," replied Jack, with brevity.

"If he want us, it's a funny way to get us by going to Sangster."

"When hunters stalk moose they go in the opposite direction. That's what Socrates did when he wanted to catch a fellow."

"What necessity for such circumvention?" said Keith, not wishing to admit the point.

"The straight and narrow way is like duty—dull. Some people could no more live without intrigue than they could live without salt and savory."

"Modena thinks we should let them go, and they will come to us in time. When they see as we see."

Jack laughed. "That would mean in centuries, if ever."

"To see as she sees! And yet she is an anomaly."

"What do you mean?" asked her cousin quickly, looking up at his companion in surprise.

"Instinct within her is the eupatrid, and yet she is a veritable St. Simon."

Jack's face flushed warm at such bold words of praise.

He remained silent for some time with bent head. He then rose and paced the stone terrace with quick steps, while his eyes deepened and brightened. In a few minutes he re-seated himself.

"You will never understand my cousin," he said gravely and with a depth of feeling and perception which greatly astonished his friend and in words which he never afterwards forgot. "You will never understand her unless you believe in a series of existence for the soul, and believe that the spirit of Maria Theresa or Queen Catherine has been transmitted to her. These may be strong words, but time will prove their truth. What Modena believes in is 'The principle of authority which is more precious than liberty.' She is a woman of light and leading, and believes that the government of a state is the highest good in which one can engage. The government must be founded on a basis of Good. Good is knowledge and the virtues. Justice is a virtue and implies all other virtues. It is the all-essential virtue in a person or in a state. The thoughts and actions of the just and wise are the realization of much that is good and true, and if generations of culture, authority and courtesy do not make a better product than generations of ignorance, servility and squalor, then let all law and learning, grace and manners die, for they are useless. She firmly believes that for this reason the 'Noblesse' have the right to govern and are more capable of governing than any other class of people. Could her heart, her instinct, her traditions be laid open to view they would tell us that our chief magistrate should be one typical of the Heart and Hand which is behind all, or as Balzac puts it, 'Were it possible to obtain king or governor who looked upon this office not as a trade, but as a priesthood, one wielded by the sublimest of royal dignity, one convinced that he is the living symbol and representative of authority and responsible to God alone for the sacred trust reposed in him, one sensible and above all things else solicitous for the welfare of his subjects, then we might have a just and impartial administration of justice; and she believes that this is the only true form of government; but seeing this is impossible, then perhaps the next best thing is representative government, and if party government, she thinks her party the most capable of ruling, because the fundamental principles and primary motives are patriotic and in a sense altruistic. She herself would render unquestioned obedience to a dignified authority, and would venerate and respect it as a parish priest does the Pontiff's of Rome. She possesses a strong sense of duty and keeps this before her as the chief axiom of life. It is these sentiments which build up a nation and which prove the greatness and stability of any nation. She is now being brought face to face with many rank injustices and cruel contrasts, the inevitable result of our own system. She is beginning to think, and when she thinks she will have the courage to speak. Reformations and revolutions are not the fruits of a moment, but they are the fruits of honest spirits seeking after what is just and true. She is honest "—and then he checked himself abruptly, realizing that he had laid bare his cousin's inmost nature and had laid bare himself by clothing her with many of his own regrets and longings. He was sensible of displaying feeling at all times, but his intuition told him that there was but one who would ever fill the need in his cousin's life, and he felt in speaking to his friend he was speaking to himself—herself.

His companion sat silent on the stone steps of the garden. From where they sat they could see, in the distance, the mistress of the place, accompanied by Carlton Monteith, extending the hospitalities of her home to a venerable bishop who was staying over night in the village, and who had now called at Fernwylde.

Many thoughts passed through the young statesman's mind. Almost he resolved to get up and go away from the country while there was yet time and his honor was left him unsullied.

During the last few weeks she had kept Carlton Monteith by her side. She would not hold out a hope to him to which she was not prepared to give full fruition, and yet man's intuitions are not easily deceived, and something told him that it was he, himself, for whom she cared. It was the possibility of what he saw which made him pause. Would he go on his way and allow her life to pass calm, full of the everyday interests of life, uneventful, or would he awaken within her the deeper joys of life? If he touched her life it would only bring her sorrow, for she was a woman, as her father had said, who was guided by the intelligence, not by emotion, and she would never break her pledge with Carlton Monteith. If he loved her he would do what was best for the peace of his beloved. He would sedulously shun her presence. Silence and absence was the only honorable course for him to pursue.

So he told himself.

But even as he said this to himself a restlessness like a great sea rolling on a lonely shore came over him. His mind was in a dual state. His reason told him one thing, his instincts another. He resisted his impulses, but all the while a subtler inner consciousness seemed to be driving him on.

An impulse came over him to speak of it to Jack, but he was not sure that she cared for him, and long habit had made him reticent, and silence always seemed such safety, so he resisted the impulse. He rose abruptly, and with hands deep in pockets and head bent, paced restlessly up and down the stone pavement, while his companion sat absently tapping the stone steps with his pocket-knife, until they noticed Mr. Lester and the Southerner approaching.

"Did you see the proofs of our Fernery picture?" at length said Jack, coming back to the scenes of everyday life. "They were sent out this afternoon. Here they are."

Keith extended his hand and took the proofs of the "Court of Inquiry," and looked at them.

"Did you mean anything about Lester and Miss Austin?" he asked, as he noticed where they had been grouped together in the picture.

"No," replied Jack; "Lester isn't a man to carry his heart on his coat sleeve for every daw to peck at. Disappointed in youth! Aunt? Yes. Between you and me he is hard hit the second time. This time the daughter."

His companion looked up at him in great surprise.

"Fact."

"And do you think she cares?"

"Cares! Yes. I don't think it, but I know she cares."

His friend's mouth set firm and he paled visibly, while he looked hard at the Fernery without seeing it. Mr. Lester was a man to be feared. He was of different calibre to Carlton Monteith.

"Cares for him as she does for her father!" and Jack Mainton looked straight into his companion's eyes and smiled.

His companion's eyes dropped and a warm color came to his face.

"You think he will find consolation in Miss Austin?"

"I do not know that it lies in his power to do so," replied Jack, as the boom of a silver-toned bell came over the gardens in great waves of sound calling them to dinner.

He arose and joined Miss Austin and Lester, while Keith Kenyon took the path which led to Idlewylde.

Nature had made him different to Mr. Lester. He could never have loved or served where he was not beloved. He might attain to any sacrifice where mutual love existed, but never otherwise. His absence and his silence was all he could offer her—unasked.

CHAPTER X.

"How tired I feel," said the mistress of Apsley House, as she ascended her own steps a few days after her party at Fernwylde had broken up, and they had returned to the city. "Will you come in and have some tea? It refreshes one. Jack is here, and no doubt others will come before the close of the evening."

"One would prefer an evening alone with you," answered her companion, Keith Kenyon, coming up the steps. "It is so seldom one ever sees you without a dozen people hanging round you. You might say 'not at home' for one evening."

He had not gone away, but he had left Fernwylde that evening and had not returned. His duties at the present time were many and exacting, and afforded ample plea for his absence. He had tried to fill his life with his work, but he owed duties to his order as well as to his position, and in fulfilling these it was impossible to avoid meeting her, when the changing scenes of a society are ever similar to those of a kaleidoscope invariably composed of the same pieces, and when he met her he could no more refrain from seeking her presence than he could stop the warm blood from flowing in his veins, that is, when she showed her preference for his presence. He had now met her on the street as he was returning from the House, and had walked home with her.

"Come in and we'll see," she said, as they entered the arched rotunda. "Richard, is Mr. Jack in his room? Take Mr. Kenyon there," she said to the hall servant.

Her companion turned from her light-hearted, and with a quick, firm step traversed the many halls, which were lined with statuary and with many passages leading to the other wings of the house, now dim and dusky in the twilight, until they reached the suite of rooms which were fitted up in every way suitable to Jack Mainton's taste, while the mistress of the house went to her own rooms to dress for dinner.

When she entered her rooms, with their fragrance of flowers and soft lights, she moved over to the glowing grate, with a soft look in her eyes and a tender smile on her proud face, and removed her street wraps, utterly forgetful for the time that their interests demanded their presence that evening at a reception Mrs. Sangster was giving for the Lennoxes.

Presently she turned and rang for her maid to dress her.

"Has Marion returned yet?" she asked.

"Yes, Miss Wellington. What dress?"

"It's only a house dinner, but one wants to look one's best. That old gold velvet and my pearls."

She lay back in the depths of an easy chair to rest for a few minutes. She had been down all afternoon in the vicinity of the large mills by the river, where many of their tenants lived. She was bodily tired, but she enjoyed it. It refreshed her so to be able to rest after the long walk.

She had gone to see Grace Vivien, who was ill, and had left as the street lamps were being lighted, and on her way home had met Keith Kenyon.

Cards lay on each of their tables for a reception in honor of Miss Lennox that evening at Mrs. Sangster's. She had not accepted, expecting to be at Fernwylde. If he wished to go there was nothing to prevent his going, either now or after dinner, so she said to herself, as she fastened some white roses in the old lace at her breast.

When she went down to dinner, which was served, when it was only a family dinner, in an oval room lined with mahogany and Venetian mirrors and hung with Flemish and Florentine tapestries and panels with gay shepherds and shepherdesses painted thereon, Jack, who was standing on a rug before the fireplace with hands plunged deep in pockets and his brows drawn together in a frown, was talking to his companion, who sat in the depth of the bay window which opened out into the gardens, with his profile dusky against the moonless night without.

The evening was humid and the air redolent with June blossoms and flowers; the casements were open, and the rose vines blew in and out on the wind which came up from the river; beyond the heavy embroidered curtains could be seen the swaying cypresses and the lights and shadows of the dark pines which lined the river's edge.

The two men had been speaking of the reception and of what it meant to them. They had made little progress with the Lennoxes. The Lennoxes had made more progress with them; each day something new had developed, which showed them the depths, subtlety and tenacity of the newcomers; the conviction had been brought forcibly home to them that they were in the presence of no mean power.

The two men's star was beginning to rise. They had tasted of the magic sweets of power, and they could not readily relinquish it. They knew their party's star was waning, almost on the horizon, and in their sanguine youth they had thought that by renewed exertion, inward reformation and inward life, they could make it return to its perihelion without going into darkness from sunset to sunrise. But since the Lennox advent the other's hopes had risen, and it almost seemed to the two men, to Jack Mainton especially, that they had become the loadstar to many of their own malcontents.

He was disgusted.

He was now grumblingly muttering to his companion about the reception.

"One would rather lose than kiss the coat-tails of one's own tailor or tumble over the cowhides of one's own butcher to make one's bow to them. The locals started this toadying, and we're giving them rope enough to hang themselves and ourselves. There is now no difference between the other ones and us, only the other ones are a little the worse; they resemble what Macaulay said about the philosophers, 'They are the same as the other people with the additional vice of hypocrisy.' Theirs is genuine hypocrisy. We are a little more genteel and call ours by the name of—diplomacy. I don't see that it matters one iota who gets there; the whole shibboleth is only a poppy-cock. It makes a candid soul sick when he has to go on the huskings every few years and scream rot by the hour to a gullible mass. For my own part I never attend a stump meeting but I feel like saying, 'You're a pack of fools for listening and believing what we tell you.' Ugh!"

"It is the thinking man the world now needs," said his companion, with his eyes on the gardens. "Carlyle knew what he was talking about when he told us that a thinking man is the worst enemy the Prince of Darkness can have. The Reform principles make our men, but what our country now requires is men with reaction principles. For want of courage we have allowed things to go too fast and too far. Like our own dignity and our own honor, we are making the suffrage too cheap. It's the world-old fable of too much freedom breeding contempt. Good government requires a happy mean in everything and, as you have said, while we have been spending our time pandering to the people, great evils have been creeping in, which will take the best of our years to again rid ourselves of. But there is no use kicking against the pricks; we can but do our best now."

"And our best now is the Lennoxes. What rot."

"What rot now?" queried the mistress of the house, as she entered the room and approached the open window, where the fragrance of the lily of the valley and the wild thorn was wafted to them on the humid air.

"That you are lacking in your duties to-night, or you would

be watching the Sangster clique," answered her cousin, gloomily, as he gazed into the dying embers in the grate and drearily con-templated the incongruities and grotesqueness of public life.

A shade passed over his cousin's face at the words.

"You are not helping us much. You do not care for them," said her guest, as he rose and looked at her as she stood beside him in the shadows of the draperies.

"Why do you say so? I have not shown it in any way. This is the second time you have said so. I invited her to Fernwylde at your request," she replied, rather coldly.

"In the letter but not in the spirit, as Cicero accused his brother of receiving the provincials with an open door and a locked-up countenance," smiled the young statesman.

"What would you have one do? I call upon them and receive them. What more do you want? Take them in as intimates? One cannot go against one's intuitions even to please you."

"Modena is only lukewarm in the matter. We will have to get Mrs. Cecil to take them in hand," said her father, who had come in.

"Mrs. Cecil!" exclaimed Jack, and he smiled. "She would do it, though, if she took it in hand," he thought to himself, but aloud he said, "Let us go into dinner, the whole question isn't worth a good dinner."

"Jack possesses the happy faculty of throwing care to the winds wherever his digestion is affected," said his uncle, as he led the way to the table.

When dinner was over and the others had taken their departure, Mr. Wellington rose and went across the hall to his library to work, while his daughter with her guest followed to the adjoining room, the one room in the house which was essentially her own. It had been the favorite of her mother's before her.

Her mother had chosen it in memory of her famous ancestress, the titled lady of France, this room being the one room of the French chateau which had remained wholly French. It was octagon in shape, and was called the white room because of the white marble columns supporting each corner, its white friezes, frescoes and cornices. It was panelled in white in Louis Seize style. In the centre of the panels were carved shields bearing the united arms of the Wellingtons and their famous ancestress. The walls were hung with white satin, silver fringed and heavily embroidered in white roses, the lilies of France and autumn maple leaves; the windows and ceiling had on them St. Cecilias and Loreleis and many mystic symbols done by the famous pupil of Lebrun. The mantelpiece was of carved ivory, and on it were Saxe plaques,

8

Watteau figures, old ivories and porcelain. In the fireplace were huge gilded andirons, and on them the servant had now placed some pine and maple knots, which were blazing cheerfully, sending their aromatic odor on the damp June air.

In the room was a Reisener cabinet filled with old silver, Watteau screens and figures of the same upholding vases of white lilies. There was an osier basket of white lilacs and bowls of white roses, and with these were always found the old-fashioned, homelike flowers, the white daisies from round the sun-dial near the Fernery, violets from Old Orchard, where the robins nested in spring, and the hepatica, tender and blue, from the shelter of the coppice which led to the lake.

Over the mantel hung a large painting of Fernwylde, with her father and herself near the Fernery. A life-sized portrait of her mother hung draped in white where the soft lights made her presence seem almost real; deep, easy chairs and soft rugs served to make the room comfortable and homelike, while her pet parrot, her grey Maltese and her dogs completed the family circle.

An open archway led into Mr. Wellington's private library. Heavy draperies hung in the archway. Modena now drew these aside to admit the warmth to her father, for the evenings were yet chilly and damp, and then seated herself in the depths of an easy chair before the grate fire, while her two dogs, Nell Gwynne and Cavall, stretched themselves on the white bear-skin at her feet.

"What shall we do?" she asked of her companion. "Cards, music or—?"

"Let us talk; we can have those any evening, but it is only once in a lifetime that one gets a moment alone with you," he said, as he seated himself not far from her.

"What shall we talk about?"

"About yourself."

"A very uninteresting subject! No, we do not want to pass a dull evening. The room is more interesting than its inmate. It was a whim of an ancestor of ours. The cold northern air chilled her veins. She wanted to remember France. This is her taste."

"One might well forget the outside world within its walls," replied he, as his eyes wandered over the harmonies of the room and rested on its present mistress as she sat, her face soft in shadow, the lights from the fireplace burnishing to gold the bronzes of her dress and lighting to splendor the many gems on her hand which lay lightly on the shaggy head of Nell Gwynne.

"You have never seen its secrets and its sacreds," she said, as she drew to his side a cabinet, and detaching a small key from a curiously wrought bracelet of gold which encircled her arm, she opened the drawers of the cabinet and took from their depths Jesuit missals, old MSS. of the early fathers, miniatures of herself and of her ancestors, of St. Ursula and the saints of Port Royal, done by the sisters of St. Ursula, and many memoirs brought from Marly and Versailles, and placed some on her knee and some on the table by her side.

"You are a connoisseur in art," she said. "You have been under the masters."

"Only in mind and memory; the world of to-day leaves little time for the arts;" but, little or no time, he took up one by one the missals, the miniatures and the memoirs, and discoursed upon them and discussed them with all the ready resources of a learned and cultured mind.

Although not naturally artistic, his great knowledge had made him sensitive to art of all kinds. As he had but said, the world of politics had left him little time for art, but in his wanderings he had picked up much, while his insight into the lives and his companionship with great artists and great masters of music enabled him to put into art and music what they had intended should be there.

With Jesuit missal or Ursuline miniature in hand, he spoke eloquently and with subdued enthusiasm of their own days, when the church was the "Portals of the Poor," and "Faith was Food," a subject which ever brought animation, interest and warmth to her features, and of that aid which art had given to faith; or with the firelight flickering on the memoirs of Marly and Versailles, with apt quotation from St. Amand or Sevigne, he pictured in passing panorama the many and varied, joyous and saddened scenes of the Sun-King's Court.

She was a woman capable of comprehending the intellectual movements of the day, and in her face was now pictured the pleasure which she derived from the companionship of a cultured and sympathetic mind.

His grace of manner, his felicity of expression, the versatility of his powers, the depth in his nature which she could not fathom, appealed strongly to her, and her heart sank within her as the sense of another's inferiority rose before her mental vision. It was the first time she had weighed him with the fine scales of her intelligence, and found him sadly wanting.

As her companion sat under the soft, shaded lights he looked handsomer than she had ever seen him before. From the memoirs in his hand he read to her extracts of verse, the suggestive and seductive intonation of his voice giving intensity and beauty to the melody of the verse, revealing to her the music and metaphors of the thoughts of master minds of that age. When they discussed it neither thought of its merits as a poem, but of the music which is so dear to the human heart.

A Latin extract had found its way into the memoirs. It was the story of Er, of how he had left the world for one thousand years, of his sojourn with the spirits of another world, of his passage through the Plains of Forgetfulness and the River of Unmindfulness, and of his return.

The mistress of Apsley House had read the story when she was but a child, and she had never forgotten, and now the melody and seduction of his voice lent to the familiar words the charm of some new, unknown, mysterious thing.

"Why does it sound so coming from him? What is there behind it all which makes one feel like this?" she dreamily wondered, realizing that within him lay a latent power, a great reserve, an isolation which made most women feel that they never really entered his life, and which attracted and attached them to him all the more because it was so. During the evening, as she had handed him a memoir or a missal, their hands had lightly touched and their eyes met. She now lay back, listening, in the depth of her easy chair, her face in shadow, moved as she had never been before; while he, when he had finished the story of many centuries ago, allowed it to drop idly upon her knee, as he thought in reverie, "Have we met in the centuries long, long ago." Almost it seemed to him that long, long ago she had been his lady and he had been her knight, and he had fought for her and died, and now they had met again. Although in him reason had always held sway, yet had he been emotional enough to believe in many old faiths and traditions. In the story which he had read, Er had not drunk of the waters of Forgetfulness which no vessel could hold, and he had remembered, and to-night it seemed to him that like Er they were stronger than the waters, and almost he believed that she had belonged to him before and his claim was prior to all others, and his honor ceased to strive against his desire, and the evening became one perfect page in his book of life.

"You play as well as you read," at last said Modena, coming back to the real scenes of life, as she rose and locked away her treasures in the cabinet and drew farther apart the draperies separating them from her father.

She placed some music upon the Erard piano as she spoke.

"Men weren't made to play; music was meant for women. We were made to listen and enjoy; the piano is not in harmony with its surroundings. Try this," he said, as he rose and took from an old ebony case inlaid with pearls, a lute whose chords had vibrated centuries before many mornings and many nights on the waters under the balconies of the Trianon.

He handed it to her as he spoke. She looked down on the strings and ran her fingers over them lightly, almost reverently, and as she did so all those women who had been dead long, long ago rose up before her as in a mist. "All those ladies who were dead and gone! They had been great women these! they had loved and they had been beloved!"

"I am really selfish to-night. It is so nice for once not to have to be amusing, but to be amused. I want to enjoy. You play," she said, as she handed him the lute, and seated herself again in the shadows of the windows overlooking her own private gardens.

He threw open the casement and seated himself in the deep embrasure, his profile clear against the moonless night without.

"On many a twilight air and at many a morning tryst had the lover wooed his lady love with song and serenade. Why not he? Why not she?"

Involuntarily came to his mind the old folk-lore songs of the habitant and coureur-de bois, as he had heard them from the river barges, or forest camp, or cottage door with their mournful, plaintive or glad refrain. They had in them all the mystery, the melancholy, the gay insouciance and the ideal of long ago. He touched the chords lightly, gladly, sadly, and played while she listened—played music without words, songs of a people who had lived and who had loved, who had fought and who had died for their faiths of throne and altar—played on and on, while her eyes grew moist as his music, dreamy, filled the room with the echoes of long ago. Hitherto the world had been her all, but to-night she realized that there was something sweeter and dearer in life than the unceasing treadmill of the busy world in which she lived and moved and had her being. Like Lygia, she felt that he was rousing in her something which had hitherto been sleeping, that a hazy dream was changing into a form more definite, more pleasing, more beautiful.

There were chords in her nature which had never been touched before, but now she felt that he was making them vibrate and thrill and tremble with sweet remembrance, as he was making the lute speak which had been silent since those other lovers had touched its chords so long ago.

He played on and on, unmindful of passing time, until a cuckoo-clock on the mantel chimed a late hour, and he ceased playing.

"I really must beg your pardon for remaining so long, but the evening has passed so quickly," he said, as he rose to go.

But yet he lingered by her side. loth to leave, looking out over the pine woods and dark waters to where a late moon was coming up like a great red ball of fire from behind the Laurentides, until Mr. Wellington asked him something from the library regarding the reply.

She went with him into the library, and when he bade her good-night if he held her hand longer than it was necessary she resented it not.

When he had gone she did not look at her father, but kissed him good-night.

"My dear," he said, "you must remember you are pledged to Monteith. I know you love him, but young girls are sometimes thoughtless. Keith is sterling stuff. Use him right."

"You heard all that passed to-night."

"Yes, my dear, but remember, Modena, that true women never play with men's best affections," he said, as he bade her good-night.

She went upstairs, and all night dreamed dreams of happy fairyland. Life was indeed beginning to wear its brightest colors; while Keith Kenyon, as he lay on his bed that night, lay long, dreamily awake, watching the now risen moon as it lighted the mountains, the pine woods and waters, and the stately turrets and towers of Apsley House. Soon it passed behind a heavy canopy of clouds which hid the house from his view, and as the darkness and the hush which precedes dawn came over the sleeping city, sleep came upon his heavy eyes, and he fell into the restlessness of an uneasy slumber.

<hr>

CHAPTER XI.

"WE'RE in it, and one might as well face the facts; things look blue. One doesn't mind being whipped so long as one feels one has done everything that can be done, but we haven't; we've been blundering. We must get them. She's no mean foe. She's a shrewd one and a fighter. She has the spirit of the bull-dog and the greyhound within her. She knows if Kenyon doesn't commit himself before then, she's gone, and she'll make him do it. If he doesn't, they'll throw their whole influence to the others, and that means much. Why doesn't he meet her with her own weapons and draw her on until the thing is over and then leave her? It wouldn't be honorable in private life, but this is war, and knife to knife. Modena is holding herself well within bounds, but she will not bend. She does not care for her. I wonder who told the Lennox one why he was absent from the Sangster reception last night. The very devil was in her eye to-day. She's ready for anything. The thing has to be smoothed over. I wonder if Mrs. Cecil could do anything," said Jack Mainton to himself, as he walked in the twilight from his office to call for his cousin at Monteith House.

"It will do no harm to touch her up, and it may do Mrs. Cecil some good," continued he in his meditations as he ascended the steps.

"You were at Mrs. Sangster's last evening?" said he, approaching Mrs. Cecil, who was standing with his cousin. "Which way are they going?" continued he, referring to the Lennoxes. "Mrs. Sangster should win. Her finesse and courage are great."

"Her finesse is too apparent," replied Mrs. Cecil. "You know the best way to stalk deer is to go in the opposite direction."

"Better to go in the same direction than in no direction at all. If the hound possesses enough grit and strength it runs its quarry down in time."

"What are you implying?"

"Whatever you wish to infer."

"You are accusing us of want of interest and application. Why don't you get your cousin to do it?" replied the Frenchwoman, looking over at Modena, who had moved away and was now conversing with Mrs. Monteith. "Her spirit is generally that of a Maisonneuve, who said he would go to Montreal if every tree was a Red Man, and in every hand were a tomahawk and scalp. Why doesn't she display that spirit now? She was born for that sort of thing. I wasn't. It's her forte, not mine. One must have faith in such things, and I have not."

"What were you born for? You are sceptical, but you have always admitted the truth of science. Science abhors a vacuum, and nothing is ever lost or destroyed. What is your object in life?"

"I haven't any," she replied, with infinite regret, and with the tone of one who, having no God and no home, realizes the emptiness and void of human life. "And if I had I would want something much higher and better than the securing of an egotist," she continued, with infinite scorn.

Jack looked up at her quickly, and for a moment allowed his eyes to dwell upon her with great meaning and earnestness. Her words and tone had touched him deeply. Although he was, like Dr. Johnson, a bear in skin, yet had he within him the sympathies of a George Sand, and he regretted seeing the Frenchwoman's brilliant talents wasted. His nature was similar to hers, and he could sympathize with her moods. But in his inner nature he had lifted himself above himself, while she was like a sick child tossing on a bed of fever, fancying now this side and now that will give it rest and ease, unconscious of the fact that there is no rest for it, because there is no rest within.

"We would all have higher objects if we could get them," continued he, earnestly and gravely. "Solon could not establish the best system of government because of prejudice and confirmed habits. Constitutions are not the result of creative genius or the fruits of happy inspirations, but circumstances are their real creators. It is the duty of statesmen to modify and shape already existing habits and customs into rule and law. What higher work can one engage in than the game of the gods? The Lennoxes are our present circumstances. We all want to do great things. These desires are our ideals and our illusions, and are but the precursors of great things. Once in youth I aspired to authorship. I wrote about the soul and the Renaissance and ethics and a thousand other things of which I knew nothing. I picked up Ruskin's 'Spirit of the Rock,' and Darwin's 'Earthworms,' and Burns' 'Field Mouse,' and then I crept back and burnt my soulwork. Life tells us that the ocean depends upon the little drops of water."

"If one could convince oneself that the Lennoxes are really little drops of water one might work from conviction. All other work is useless. But one doesn't feel like telling the whole world that there is only one fulcrum—gold and egotism."

"But then it's just the management of such little things as these that enables us to apply and rule logically and justly. One must have ideals and work towards them by dealing with existing circumstances. One always likes to remember Goethe's words, 'Faith is a question between man and his own heart, and immortality is not an inheritance but a greatness achieved like all other greatnesses by courage, self-denial and purity of purpose—a reward allotted to the just.' It is such a solacing and stimulating belief, and I feel confident that history and philosophy will tell you it is a true belief. Why not accept it? If the Ego within is numb, more reason we should strive for others. Gross things these are, but we are not accountable for their grossness. They are but the products of our age, an age that is not great. But let us strive to leave something better and higher for posterity," he continued, brokenly and brusquely and almost banteringly, as if ashamed of his preaching.

"I never looked at it in that light before," replied his companion, gravely. "Perhaps you are right. I would willingly assist you if any efforts of mine would be of any avail. But cannot you see for yourself, there is only one bait that is of any use on your hook. I saw it from the first," she said, as she smiled and bowed and turned away to bid her hostess good-night.

"I wonder if it will do any good," meditated Jack, as he remained standing in the shadows where Mrs. Cecil had left him. He watched her as she crossed the room, speaking to some late arrivals, bade her hostess good-night, and then pass out into the gloom of the streets. "I wonder what it is?" he thought, as he turned from the window and joined the others.

The Lady Greta had been staying for a few days at Monteith House, and its mistress had sent out cards for an afternoon. The most of the guests had now departed, and only a few remained as the twilight deepened. The servants had entered and quietly removed all traces of recent disorder; the doors which had been thrown open between the suite of rooms had not yet been closed, but the draperies had been dropped. The few remaining ladies had grouped themselves together and presented a pretty picture, with their jewels and laces and grace and laughter. The ceremonial restraint was gone, but the ceremonial splendor remained.

Keith Kenyon and Mr. Lester had come in on their way home.

"What a charming scene," said Keith Kenyon, as the hostess brought them some tea. "If numbers enhance the beauty we regret not being here sooner.

"We regret it also, and there were others who regretted it more than we," said Mrs. Sangster, who stood near him, and in her voice was a visible note of resentment. She was becoming discouraged from having to remain in the cold shades so long. Her reception last evening had not fulfilled her expectations. Keith Kenyon had not been there. She was clear-sighted, and despite her sanguine courage she saw the futility of their efforts in securing the neophytes so long as the master of Kenyon Court smiled upon them.

But the young statesman gave no sign of comprehending the inference contained in the words, and was saved from replying by Jack joining the group.

"Did you convince her?" asked his cousin.

"I tried, but failed."

"Were they quarreling?" asked Keith. "It must have been Greek meet Greek."

"Oh, they were talking soul and—and—"

And "Lennox," she was going to add, but checked herself.

"Does Mrs. Cecil admit there is such a thing?"

"Whether she admits it or not, one feels when in her presence that she is taking a mental analysis of one's own all the time. She gives one the blues," said Modena, who had been talking to Mrs. Cecil for some half hour that afternoon as they had wandered together through the grounds, trying to interest her in their work. Mrs. Cecil, who divined the truth of the situation, could not betray to her what she had to her cousin, and had treated many matters with good-natured cynicism and contempt, and this had jarred on her friend's conception of things.

"The world has been with Mrs. Cecil too early and too long. She is as one set before a banquet with cloyed appetite. It is only the young in heart, like my lady, who really cares so much," said Carlton Monteith, touching Modena's hand lightly as he came up.

The touch irritated her. It was so seldom he did such a thing. The afternoon had pleased him; the people had been the best in the city; the music had been choice and classical; his home had looked magnificent and stately. He was a young Senator, and could live his own life as he pleased. His entertainments were not prompted by political intrigues. It was only a little act of homage to her as the future mistress of his home, but it reminded her of her relationship to him. She thought of the previous evening. Night holds dreams and passions that fade and flee before the dawn of day, but who at noonday wishes not for night? Others had seen it, Keith Kenyon among the rest. Noonday to her was a stern reality, and she vented its reality in her tone when she spoke of her friend.

"People shouldn't come to a banquet with poor digestion. The world has taken infinite pains to give us the best that can be given. It is gross ingratitude to repay its trouble with chronic social dyspepsia."

"But one cannot help one's indigestion."

"Indigestion is almost always a result of indiscretion and intemperance. One must expect to suffer the consequences of one's own actions."

"My grandfather had heart-trouble. I have it, too," said Jack.

"But you don't tell it to the world. The world isn't interested in our ills."

"Mandeville and Rochefoucauld and—and—Mrs. Cecil say it is. It is interested insomuch as to rejoice in them. It only deplores our good fortune."

"What cynicism!"

"It's not what Mrs. Cecil says; it's the smile."

"Then it is a case of smile being the lady, as Buffon says style is the man."

"How ill-natured we all are in our fine clothes. Our style wouldn't please Buffon, venting our spleen on Mrs. Cecil. We are not doing her justice," said Mr. Lester, who ever sympathized with those susceptible natures whom the world as it is fails to satisfy. "She is like Mary Stuart, unfortunate to live in an uncongenial age and atmosphere. She wants things more artistic, more refined, more susceptible to poetry than she sees here. She is not irritable and satiated as are frivolous or vain people. She possesses a rich mind, and has read and thought and is dissatisfied because the world does not satisfy her expectations, not because she is not capable of apprehending the beautiful. Unless a person is dominated by imagination it is the finest temperaments that are dissatisfied.

> "'Humanity in fields and groves
> Pipe solitary anguish.'

As Petronius thought, so, too, does she think, that there are things in this world beautiful, but the people are so crude that life is scarcely worth a regret, that it would take tens of thousands of Arbitri Elegantiarium to polish the blockheads and buffoons into decent people."

"How rude you are, Mr. Lester! We all know we lack woefully in taste and temperament, but we do not care to be told it," exclaimed Modena.

"Your worst enemy couldn't dispute your taste, Modena," said her betrothed.

"And temperament?"

"I don't understand it to-night."

"One fails to understand Mrs. Cecil," said Modena, moving from the side of her betrothed nearer to Mr. Lester. "She is the soul of honor and kindness; why does she hide it? It irritates and depresses one to dwell forever under the shadows of grey skies."

"The great master minds of Goethe and Dante were portrayed in their own words, 'Men feel themselves oppressed and agitated by feelings and longings which have gathered until they assume forms of great moral uneasiness.' These moments are the most unhappy of men's lives, and these emotions cannot be appeased until they find their outlet. They poured theirs into 'Faust' and 'Inferno.' What Mrs. Cecil wants is an outlet. She wants to find her bearing, and this world is too small, too meagre for her," replied Mr. Lester.

"Her imagination should recompense her for the defects of the world. It does Marion."

"Marion is a child, she has also the faith of a child, whereas Mrs. Cecil, as she said to me one day, 'I don't know what science has taught me. I don't know what I believe. Nothing, perhaps, only that there is no such thing as happiness.' She hasn't yet reached the child-like faith of a St. Augustine. The road is long and rough. Will you not help her? The unconscious influence of a good woman is greater than all the powers of darkness and is sure to win in the end."

"There are no good women," replied Modena. "Unless it be Mrs. Gregory, or Helen, or the Ursulines."

"Yes, there are," replied Lester. "They are all good, and Mrs. Cecil among the best. I knew her in Paris. I have known her from childhood, and she is a lady whom I honor and respect, and no doubt when you come to know her and her history you will sympathize with her fully. She has had a sad life."

"You should enlighten one and let one judge for oneself," said Modena.

"Some day I shall, but not here, not now."

"Why are we lingering here; it must be nearly dinner-time. Are you ready, Modena?" interrupted Jack.

"Remain and dine with us; there is nothing to prevent your doing so," said Mrs. Monteith.

"Dine with these ladies in their best, and only this toggery on!" exclaimed Jack, referring to his street dress.

"What difference does it make about the dress?" persisted the Lady Greta, who disliked dining alone.

"That's so," replied Jack. "The sumptuary laws of our forefathers meted out to them a blanket. Then this should be good enough for us."

"That's so," repeated his cousin. "Your English is quite as provincial as your dress, and when you speak of your forefathers remember we are cousins."

"No, only seconds."

"We're blood related. Your grandfather was a cousin of the

hero of Waterloo. History doesn't say he wore a blanket to Windsor."

"Age gives precedence. Isn't that the rule? I was claiming a higher lineage than you. I went back to the Red Man, and if necessary I am willing to go back to the Mound Builders or the Stone Age, if procreation is going to add to our standing."

"Or to Darwin," added Keith Kenyon, turning the laugh on his friend.

"Very cleverly done; I wish I'd said that."

"The shade of your godfather, Dr. Johnson, once said the same thing to the shade of Shakespeare, whereat the Bard of Avon replied, 'Tell Boswell, he'll make you say it, and it will be all the same in one hundred years from now.' Tell some of those who are so fond of living on imagination, and when they're writing your biography they'll make you say it. It will sound good in memoirs," replied Keith.

"But I'm not living for the next century. I'm living for now, and now claims its own. Are you coming, Lester?"

"Yes, if Kenyon's ready; I came up with him."

"Mr. Kenyon is going home with us," said Verona Lennox, who had been out in the gardens with Mr. Patrie, and who had entered the room.

Mr. Kenyon had had no previous intention of going to Lennox Court, but at Verona's entrance the mistress of Apsley House had moved away with their host, and then he remembered the touch on the hand, which had been so apparent to all, and the comments which he felt were in the air regarding his absence the previous evening, and he changed his mind and thought it would be as well to walk home by Lennox Court.

CHAPTER XII.

A few days after this they attended a mass meeting held by the People's Rights Society, and addressed by a man named Stubs.

Their party hitherto had not been in sympathy with such meetings or such movements, but Parliament being on the eve of dissolution, it was absolutely necessary under the present circumstances that such meetings as these should be recognized, and their people represented at them.

The mistress of Apsley House had frequently noticed Stubs at social and civic receptions, but had not singled him out from the throng she continually met day after day, and night after night, until she began to hear his name mentioned so frequently by her friends and co-patriots.

Several evenings previous to this, as she was returning from taking some delicacies to little Lone Byers, she had seen him in earnest conversation with Mr. Sangster and some rough-looking miners in the vicinity of Pooley's Bridge. The group had melted away at her approach, the workmen walking quickly towards the works, while Mr. Sangster and Stubs returned to their city homes.

"Who is that man Stubs?" she asked of Keith Kenyon the next evening after the mass meeting, as a small party of them strolled around the winding walks of Parliament Hill.

"He is Mr. Lennox's nephew, and manages his business for him. Do you know him?"

"Not personally. I have seen him quite often. I saw him the other day in earnest conversation with Mr. Sangster."

"Oh!" exclaimed her companion, quickly. "Were they alone?"

"No; a number of workmen and miners were with them," she replied, looking at him with some surprise at his interest in such small details.

Keith remained silent for some moments with knitted brows.

"Has Stubs influence?" asked his mother, who was one of the party.

"Yes, great influence with the lower classes," he answered abstractedly, and then continued, "You don't want to offend him, Modena."

"I'm not in the habit of offending people; am I?"

"Oh, no, but you know what I mean. You are so particular as to whom you receive that he would never pass the lions guarding Apsley House if you did not know that we fear him."

"Do you wish to secure him?"

"I cannot say that we are so very anxious for him to enter the fold as his followers are antagonistic to us. If we received them, we would be in honor bound to uphold and sustain them, and we cannot do this, but we do not wish to needlessly displease him and rouse their influence against us at the present time. We cannot submit to their demands. We believe that ultimately it would not be for their good. The other people can do so. You know Whiggism is a scheme of practical expediency, a working policy with a chance of being realized, and they can do so without violating any principles. They are bringing it forward as a plank in their platform. It's a plank that reminds one of the little worm which was allowed to remain in the big plank used in a man-of-war. The worm was slow but sure, and in time scuttled the ship. How did you relish what he said last night?"

"His expressions were crude; his thoughts immature, but there was logic in some things. You remember his words, 'Were a man to lend you money and charge you one hundred per cent. you would call him a Shylock, a usurer, an extortioner, and yet you protect men who extort from the sweat of honest brows double that amount of usury. It is an injustice. It is one of the most glaring injustices which we suffer. Why don't you see this in time and pause? You are driving us with lightning rapidity to revolution, and when you see the blood-red banners you will repent, but it will then be too late.' A deputation of landed men waited on father last week. He required something and sent for me while they were in the library. They worded their wants differently but the thoughts were the same. They carried conviction in their words. Their pleas were earnest and courted sympathy and consideration. Stubs arouses a spirit of antagonism within one. Why cannot one sympathize with him?"

"Because he is not in earnest. He is the gangrene that grows on all democracy. He uses this as a hue and cry to gain popularity and notoriety. Chesterfield, who preached etiquette, was a bear in his own manners. Seneca, the moralist, 'a reprobate. Stubs is the same. He is seeking power and position and wants a hobby-horse which will carry him in on its back. He is like all other ranters; had he the power to-morrow, he would become a greater despot than those of Greece. It would then be a case of potter hate potter. Democracy has in it the essence of the worst kind of tyranny. Autocracy engenders despotism, but it is at least tyranny with clean hands and face. Democracy's tyranny means filth and the bottom of a beer-mug."

"Why don't you tell them so?" she asked, thinking because she was conscious of the integrity and honesty of their motives, that the world would accept them at their own valuation.

"It would be of no avail. People are not educated to it. They are influenced by what appeals directly to themselves or affects themselves. The tariff is affecting the landed man at the present time. He complains little but works the harder. He is lord of his own plot of ground; he lives with nature and grows up an honest and happy man. He is the sinew and backbone of any country. Ours is an intelligent class, and upon it depends to a great extent the future of our country. The increasing manufactures are enabling the laborer to eat butter, where a few years ago he ate dry bread, but his butter makes him want turkey. Stubs would eat turkey at other's expense," he said, and paused, and then continued as he saw his companion interested. "There are great principles underlying all thoughtful action, and in the application and execution of these, individuals for the time may have to suffer to benefit the majority. At the present time our landed men are suffering, but competition will soon regulate the prices, as it has done in every line of commerce. Yes, I know it is not protection that has caused this usury but its concomitant, the combine, the curse of all countries. This is the question which the country will have to confront, but our middle classes are slow and sure, and will gradually work reform. We are not frothy. It is these qualities of caution, carefulness, steadfastness and thrift which they possess, which will prove the greatness, stability and durability of our country. Mushroom growth and a nation given to speculation, graft, bubble-blowing, fads and froth, will be as transitory as a comet or a Napoleon—a brilliant bubble and then gone—an evolution of history in a few centuries. We are here to remain because we are building upon small things and real things. Everything means something; we are slow to accept the something, but when we accept it we are as slow to relinquish it. This spirit becomes inculcated into us as a nation, and the seed and fruit which come from it are the golden apples of Hesperides. Evils will creep in; these evils of which we were speaking a moment ago will be redressed by public opinion and public reform, or if the evil forces prove greater than the good, then history teaches us that the insatiable ambition of trade kings, sooner or later, brings about its own downfall as it did that of Rome."

"But why don't you lead and avoid those evils? You possess enough culture to look backwards, and intelligence to go forward and avoid the evils which degraded our predecessors.. Yes, I know our system forces us to a subterfuge and a pretence of appealing to the people, but the true leader should mould the people's views and lead them to his way of thinking. One wishes the world had but one mind. I would make it have, or die in the attempt."

"It is impossible to make it of one mind. It is the multitude, the numbers, which make intellectual government impossible. Law is order, and good law is good order. A very great multitude cannot be orderly. To introduce order into the unlimited is the work of a Divine Power, of such power as holds together the universe. This implies the great question which will soon confront our country—that of immigration. We do not want to over-populate our land with a conglomeration of the refuse and spawn of every land—better, far better, few and select and solid. We want to make the conditions so as to keep the masses on the land. We want to instil, as we go, into the people the spirit of the old landed gentry. We want to keep them simple of heart and life, by keeping them with nature, and yet place within their reach all the culture and advantages of civilization. There is an infinity of work before us; we regret our star is waning. We are going down and the other fellows are coming up. But perhaps it is better so for a time. The country is in a state of transition. It must have a period of steady growth and development, but cannot you see that at no distant day, we will, in the evolution of nations, come forward and take a foremost place in the eyes of the world? In a few years, a very few, our country will of itself send forth one great cry for men of knowledge, ability, courage, patriotism and purity of purpose. We are the men for that day. We must be ready with creeds and conditions, with men and a policy. Oh, no! I am not speaking in egotism or partyism, but with the humility of a patriotism founded upon knowledge. Knowledge gives confidence, and confidence gives courage and strength. We must be ready when the time comes. You see what I mean. You can do so much to help us, will you?" he said, with a personal ring in his voice and with a warmth in his words which made the blood flow warm in her veins.

Yes, she was beginning to see, and her awakened thoughts and visions attracted and attached her more to Keith Kenyon than any forces which had hitherto existed.

"I?" she repeated. "I thought so once, but that was one of youth's illusions. Life teaches us we are very small indeed," she said in a low voice.

"Do not say so. You have always been irresistible, and if you add humility to your virtues, you—"

"Hadn't we better rejoin the others?" she interrupted hastily. "I want to know what Mr. Lester thinks of Stubs."

They had been walking apart from the others and now joined Jack and Lester, who were engaged in discussing Stubs' address the previous evening and Jack's criticisms in the morning paper.

"It shows at least that men are thinking," Mr. Lester was saying.

"But barking up the wrong tree," replied Jack, who usually kept his English for his journal and vented his epithets on his friends.

"The expression of such sentiments as these only makes them dissatisfied with the bucking of wood and breaking of stone, and

9

generates socialism. A little learning is a dangerous thing. It makes a man wish to smash the plate glass windows in stone fronts and take the turkeys from the tables."

"It need not stop at a little learning. The education can become real."

"Education? That's a big word. We cannot build a house without a foundation and proper material. We must have brains furnished before we can educate people. What can one do with gin-soaked cells, chronic inertia, paralyzed faculties, ad infinitum."

"Nature must answer some of your charges," replied Lester.

"And yet these are your masters," said Mrs. Cecil. "Your logic shows us the fallacy and futility of our present system of government. Your logic shows us the necessity of being governed by the Senate alone, as Ruskin and Carlyle proved that the Lords were the only competent rulers."

"The Senate is a fat living, as was the Church in the beginning of the nineteenth century," said Patrie, who was like the dog in the manger. Because he could not get there he envied those who were there.

"It is a much slandered body, but it has the right to be so. It lacks the one essential necessary to its own existence, courage—the courage that scorns the voice of the mob. It is the fear of its own extinction that creates its cowardice. Were they a class of men capable of, conscious of and courageous in, the performance of their duties and responsibilities, history has taught us it would be better for the public good to do away with the House and rule by them alone," said Mrs. Cecil.

"You would have an oligarchy?"

"An oligarchy is preferable to a tyranny of bigotry, yellow journalism and gin-soaked cells."

"Hear, hear! do away with that for which our fathers fought and died."

"Why would you monarchise and centralise power like that?" asked Lester.

"Because dependence on the people for position tends to generate servility, grotesqueness and corruption, and it is only men of great positions who can govern without ulterior or personal motives. They must be men of wisdom and of honor. Honor is an impersonal, idealistic thing. It implies traditions, principles, duties, rights—and is synonymous with justice, the bond of union in any state—and is the product of culture and of generations of culture," replied the Frenchwoman.

"We're too young for that!"

"Time will awaken us to the necessity of it. They are the men who should be now thinking and creating."

"What rot!" interrupted Stubs, brusquely and rudely. He had joined the group with Miss Lennox, and met the mistress of Apsley House and others for the first time. He had a little learning and he wanted to pose; but Keith Kenyon did not think it wise to allow him to do so.

Miss Lennox had influence over Stubs, and the young minister was well aware that tact and diplomacy were more convincing than logic and hard facts; his co-patriot's sentiments were not in harmony with the newcomers'. The neighborhood was bad. Lover's Walk would be much more convincing and compromising; at least he had overheard Carlton Monteith trying to persuade the mistress of Apsley House that it was so. He rose at Miss Lennox's approach.

"What rank ingratitude to nature, to remain here criticising and condemning when we might be enjoying! Come, Miss Lennox, allow me to show you the beauties of nature!"

They turned from the others. Many eyes followed them as they went. The situation was becoming complicated, as complicated as the question they were discussing.

"Love is more powerful than logic. Keith is like Seneca, a philosophical moralist, yet in actual life as inconsistent. They are working at cross purposes," said Mrs. Cecil to Mr. Lester, as her eyes dwelt upon the flushed and happy face of the heiress of Lennox Court, and she mentally cast her horoscope.

"Will you cross the meadows with us? Modena and I are going out to see Mrs. Walters. She has gone on. We will overtake her. Come, the walk will be more refreshing than Stubs' logic."

Mrs. Cecil rose and joined Mr. Lester and Modena, her face grave as their words lingered in her ear.

She had lived in France, and from childhood had heard her grandfather rehearse the Terrors of the Tuilleries, and now for the first time she began to think. Jack Mainton's words, that "Immortality is gained by purity of purpose," had aroused within her many thoughts and desires which had long lain dormant. "It is no child's play to keep the helm of the ship of state in deep clear water," she thought. From having lived in France she knew much more about the deep unfathomed rocks, the shoals, the rough relentless waves that await on all sides to engulf an unpiloted ship. At the present time the labor world

was in a state of unrest. Stubs' words made her remember her
childhood's tales of the Commune.

"Do you seriously fear any trouble?" she asked of Lester, as
they left the walks and turned their faces towards the country.

"Oh, no! not at present, and our aim is to prevent its ever
occurring. Charlemagne wept when he saw the first of the pirate
Norsemen on his shores, not that he feared for himself but for
posterity," replied Mr. Lester.

"Stubs is a pirate Norseman," exclaimed Mrs. Cecil with
regret.

"It is not when one listens to Stubs, or when one reads Marx
or Lassale or Gregoire that one feels these things," said Modena.
"What do they know about the poor and needy? They only
arouse one's contempt; but it is when one goes down into the cottages by the river on a cold winter's day, or meets the cottager on
the street, it is then one feels. I was coming home from Mrs.
Byers' last evening; there was an ambulance at Mrs. Storms'
door and sobs came from within. I went in. Her only child
Edna was lying ill with the fever; there was no fire, little food
and every appearance of extreme poverty; unfinished sewing, the
price of their daily bread, wet with tears, lay there. They were
taking the little one to the hospital, its mother's heart was breaking. I turned away from the scene. I almost wished to die. I
hated my own fires, and furs, and a thousand needless luxuries.
It is then something arouses within one and makes one wish to
work a revolution if one could," continued Modena, while the
tears rushed to her eyes as she recalled the poor mother's misery.

"We all felt that way once," said Lester sadly.

"Once? What do you mean? Do not misery and heart-break
appeal to you yet?"

"Always. I meant that sometime in our lives we would all
work revolution if we could. In youth we would build Rome in a
day, but we cannot do it, and it is well we cannot. Any sudden
phenomenon is like the rattling of pease in a dry bladder, or the
passing of a comet across the sky. Experience has taught us there
is but one way to remedy the evil."

"How is that?"

"As you once said yourself, by individual effort. Good works
is a greater weapon than revolution or any social theory that may
be propounded. To theorize about Mrs. Storm and the New
Jerusalem, instead of sending her the comforts which I saw Jackson taking there late last night, would be to dream like Lisette, and
break all the eggs in the basket. But then the burden, if burden

you are pleased to call it, is greater on you than on the poor woman with the sick child. We are responsible for our light and our opportunities. Yours are great. In you lies the possibility of doing great good, but then," he continued, seeing his friend's great gravity, " the pleasure of helping, alone, is ours. You are a ministering angel."

" Oh, no," she said. " Where there is no sacrifice there is no merit. We are, alas, too much like Stubs; we can advance theories, but when it touches on self—"

" It does not need to touch on self. Self has its rights. If it is a sacrifice we should not give. Love alone is acceptable."

" And one does dearly love oneself," she said, brightening as they entered a meadow of new-mown hay, and forgetting Mrs. Storm.

" One would like to be a ministering angel. One would like to be a saint and canonized. Homage is the dearest tribute to the human heart."

" You would like to be Lady Bountiful?"

" Oh, no, I know my own weaknesses. I would want to be a Queen," and then she continued, regardless of the sequence of thought, " I can remember my grandmother telling us of the days gone by, when they rode in their carriage and four, and of how the school children courtesied, the women bent their knees, and grey-haired men doffed their caps as they passed by, while courtiers and lovers haunted their homes. I wish I had been she."

" You are a Queen—the Queen of Hearts. We worship willingly before you. They were forced to bend their knees. The stocks were before them. At least, we have something for which to be thankful. A stiff back and a surly brow do not ensure the pillory and lash. Nor do these things always ensure the Garden of Eden."

" One wishes they did. Then everything would be as smiling as this is," replied Modena, as they crossed the meadow, coming in sight of Mrs. Walters' farm house and its surroundings.

Mr. Walters had died several years previous to this, leaving behind him a widow and eight small children. They were tenants of Mr. Lester. The oldest boy, Morden, was now of age, and the younger ones being quite capable of taking his place with their mother on the farm, Mr. Lester proposed taking Morden and placing him with Mr. Byers, who was once more established in a shop of his own.

" This is surely one's ideal of happiness. If I were a Queen I would make the whole world like this," continued Modena, as they watched the two little boys and their little sister driving the cows homeward. The cattle were fat and glossy, and moved along lazily, the tinkle-tinkle of their bells floating in gentle rhythm across the meadow flats. The children were barefooted and hatless, but clean and neat, and laughed and sang, happy as the birds in the trees. The sun was going down in the west and hung like a great red ball of fire, as if bidding the scene good-night. Mrs. Walters, with sun-bonnet and apron and shining pails, stood waiting at the farther end of the lane. The elder boys were driving their work horses homeward. The smell of new-mown hay was over all.

"Oh, Mr. Lester! How can you think of taking Morden from this and shutting him up in a shop? This is surely a heaven on earth, leave him here!" exclaimed Modena, with more than usual animation and earnestness, which brought a warmth to her cheeks and moisture to her eyes.

A look almost of regret passed over Mr. Lester's face. "I wish I could, but there are Jack and Frank and three others. Morden will want a home of his own some day. Numbers force us to do these things."

"But, after the newly-turned furrows of the fallow-field, the waving grain, the golden corn, the blossoming trees, the pumpkin pies and autumn fruit, and nature in all its fullness and free-dom, how can one ever be contented with a plane and a board and a buzzing saw!" she exclaimed, the fullness of her emotion blurring her rhetoric.

"And yet when they are once there, they will not willingly give up the buzz of the saw and return to the boom of the bittern. It's where 'Bang, whang, whang goes the drum, and tootle-de-toot the fife,' that the densest crowds are to be found."

"And it's there we find the bitterest discontent, and envy, and hatred, and all the emblems of evil. Had we more naturalists we would have fewer Communists. Nature is a triple armor against self-love. Nature is the source and inspiration of all true great-ness. It is human nature to want to be lords and ladies. They are nobles on their own acre of land. If I were the chief, I would take every laborer from the city and place them in the meadows and in the gardens and orchards, and I would give them good books and music, and a pen and a brush, and some wood, and tell them to live and grow."

"You'd revise political economy by resurrecting the Garden of Eden. How would you look in homespun?"

"No, it would be sacrilege to resurrect the Garden of Eden. I would create a new one," she said, as they came up to Mrs. Walters.

"Don't do it, Lester! Leave him there. A cold potato and a clear brook, the sun on the hay by day, and the moon on the meadows by night are infinitely nearer nature's heart than wine and smoke and soot," said Modena, as she parted from Mr. Lester and Mrs. Cecil at Apsley House some two hours afterwards.

They had gone into the cool, clean kitchen with Mrs. Walters and the children, and had partaken of their simple hospitality of rich ripe strawberries and yellow cream and homemade cake, and had drunk from a clear spring not far from the door. The boys had come in with the smell of new-mown hay about them, tired but happy and contented with their hard day's labor in the hot sun, and had partaken of the late lunch of bread and cold rich milk which always awaited them at the close of a harvest day. The children were overflowing with mild mirth. It was an air of peace, frugality and simple content.

It had made Mrs. Cecil sigh.

"But the shops will lead to better things," continued Mr. Lester to his companion. "It doesn't mean buzzing saws forever."

"If it doesn't mean buzzing saws it means buzzing brains, and brains that buzz with inanities. Fate has been kind to them. It makes one wish one were a milk-maid," said Mrs. Cecil, thinking of Mrs. Storm and her own loneliness, and almost envying Mrs. Walters her family joys and peace. "When one thinks of it all," she continued, wearily, having heavily upon her the lonely sadness of a Solomon without the sanguine faith of a Job, "it makes one really wonder if human life is what someone has said it is, 'A game of cross purposes,' and one only wonders who first set the game going to amuse the gods, or make them weep."

"Nonsense," said Lester, sympathetically, taking her by the arm as they continued on their way through the gloom to Marly, the Frenchwoman's summer home. "Don't think, but work. Work and the open air are the very best antidotes for weak nerves. Mrs. Walters is happy, and she has found life, not a dream, but a stern reality."

"What's the use of working," she said, forgetting her late resolutions. "Nothing which we can do will alter things as they are."

"Pardon me, but isn't that a coward's philosophy? Men in every age have created the New Jerusalem here. They have written their names on history's pages."

"Is that why you work?"

"No, I work because I love it. I love everything on earth.

Life is very real," he smiled, "And there are those who do not love life, but they work to have their names written elsewhere."

"The beauty of faith and hope."

"No life can be pure in its purpose and strong in the strife, and all life not be stronger and better thereby, was the poet's talisman. It may be ours, too; it is only diseased nerves that have no hope."

"What you say may be true if one could only make oneself feel it, but when one cannot feel it, one cannot," she said, regretfully.

"You would feel it had you a real interest in a real work in life. You could go into the church."

"One must not empty ashes into a reliquary. I lack the one essential. I have not its faith."

"Your life is far from ashes yet, and your faith would come in time."

"No, it has gone. It was one of youth's illusions."

"What would Father Jacques say to that?"

"Father Jacques thinks so, too, or one is much mistaken in the depth of his intellect. But he is as the rest of us, he has not the courage to put the match to the tinder."

"What would you imply? Don't you think the Church plays an important part in the world's development and stability?"

"It should do so. It has done so in its day. It has been its salvation. But it has retained too much of the darkness which surrounded it in its infancy. It now fails to satisfy the learned who are honest."

"How will it end?"

"If the learned remain in it and work tactfully towards a higher ideal the reformation will be accomplished quietly and gradually. If the resistance which they encounter overcome them, it will end in revolution and upheaval."

"You would have?"

"One built upon knowledge."

"You mean to imply ours is built upon belief—faith. What wire-pulling! An intellectual age of hair-splitting!"

"Oh, no, it is only an egotism. I prefer to believe my own mind rather than the Schoolmen, traditions, myths—"

"A great lady and a good Catholic, a Quaker! What would Father Jacques say to that?"

"He would only smile kindly. Jesuit in name, he is, at heart, one himself."

"His life is a pastoral."

"Sorrow has made it so."

"Trials are so often the touch-stone of character. His life is given to the poor. If you lack his faith, why cannot you emulate his works? You have large estates in the southern provinces, you can devote yourself to them. The 'Noblesse oblige' instinct is an inheritance within you."

"What could I do for them? They lead simple lives. They do not murmur with their lot. I could only bring to them what the world invariably brings to solitude—discontent."

"Show yourself and let them love you. You think the game is not worth it. Really it is. When you look into human nature it is very similar all the world over. There is a difference in surroundings, environments and wealth. But these are only accidents, caprices of a day. The divinity is there in all; that is all that counts. It's as well to be loved by Lisette or Mascarille as by My Lord or My Lady. Better in your case for they will love you for yourself. Do try it. Your fathers fought for both throne and altar. They were sons of St. Louis. Your family has numbered themselves with the famous women of Port Royal. Many Ursuline cloisters owe their reliquaries to them. It is all these things that make a country."

"But I have no country and I have no convictions. I am an alien. I am one of those cross-bred hounds which we saw this evening chasing those sheep. Patriotism is an instinct and an inheritance. This country but reminds me of our fallen greatness. I love France."

"Then work for France."

"If France were here I might be a Lamartine, but being as she is, I am but a Sevigne. She does not need me."

"You were born under this flag. You have Saxon blood in your veins. Be your words as cynical as they are, your actions have invariably proved your love for your country. You have great talents. Many of them. Why not make your manner of life worthy of them? We need you now. If you apply yourself, convictions will come in time."

"But the feu sacre is wanting. I have not Modena's enthusiasm and earnestness."

"You have the advantage of her in many ways."

Mrs. Cecil's face was incredulous.

"You have ideals. Oh, yes, she has, too, but you know what I mean."

"Yes, I know, but we never reach our ideals. Nature did not endow us with dispositions to sacrifice present pleasures for ultimate good. We dream of the future but we live for the present.

Everything means something to Modena. She has the faculty of acquiring the ideals, of which we dream. We sigh for them and grasp at them but they elude us. I am afraid your patient is hopeless. You cannot put into a nature more than there is in it, and nature made me to care for myself alone."

"An excellent companion," smiled Lester.

"Oh, no, a very poor one. I am only happy when I can get away from it."

"Then lose yourself in others."

"I did once. My whole self! And it failed me," she replied, with infinite pathos in her voice.

"Forgive me, dear," said Mr. Lester, very quickly. "Have you heard from him lately?"

"No; have you?"

"Yes, to-day," and Mr. Lester was silent, and his silence told her more plainly than words could tell that there was nothing for her to hear.

"It will all come right some day," at last said Mr. Lester.

"Some day," said Mrs. Cecil, as they parted at the gates leading into Marly.

"Some day," repeated Mr. Lester to himself, as he walked on in the darkening streets towards his own home, Maple Hurst.

He walked along rapidly with bent head not noticing the passers-by. For many months he had been thinking deeply. His position and duties in life had caused him to do so. He was one of the leading men in the Opposition ranks, and they had been formulating a policy to give to the country, and the words of his friends during the afternoon had awakened a train of thoughts he could not banish, and fears he could not exorcise.

There are stages in a country's history when it is very easy to formulate a policy. Circumstances, which are the real creators of things, demand certain definite lines of action, and leaders can grant these demands and sail on in deep, clear water, and again there are stages when it is very difficult to formulate a policy, and these are eras when a country is in a state of transition. His country had seen great changes since '37. The men, who were now at the helm of state, were men who had been educated under masters of the old school, and many relics of the old regime yet lingered. They were honest men, influenced by a strong sense of duty, and with principles which, if it lay in their power to apply, would have given solidarity and continuity to their system of government. But the country had now reached another era, and the younger generation were coming forward with extreme policies.

Mr. Lester saw this, and was not prepared to adopt these extreme measures, and was much worried to know where Phocylides' happy mean lay. His Periclean policy he believed to be the only true one, the only one fostering development, but the wire-pulling, the trickery, the dishonesty, with which he hourly and daily came in contact, made him pause to reflect; and Stubs' words of the previous evening had made him see that the tendency of such a movement was to generate preaching without practice, froth without substance, words without works. "It's real work, work with an interest, work with a creation, work with a development, work with thought, which we require. It must be conditions which will give these. It must be as Modena says. We must keep them on the land. Morden must remain or go to wider fields," and then his mind reverted to those wider fields and what they meant.

The preceding week, the Government's attention being drawn to some important legislation, a committee had been dispatched to Montreal to interrogate and report regarding its necessity and advisability. After interviewing the leaders in the movement, for his own personal knowledge and benefit he had visited some of the slums and alleys and squalid tenement houses in the more wretched parts of the city. At the same time the Government was engaged in populating the prairie provinces, and while on the commission he had visited the docks and wharves, and watched the agents in their task of disembarking the masses as they reached port, and of preparing them for overland transportation. As the last consignment had come up from their slough in the steerage, in which they had been packed as tightly as sardines in a box, the women thinly clad and surrounded by a dozen tired, filthy children, the men vociferating and gesticulating, he had looked upon the illiterate, unregenerated mass of humanity, and then turned away. "One could make a citizen of Morden, but these—these—they are not the Greek's song of a model nation, 'Measure in everything,' 'A small city well governed is infinitely better than a Nineveh set upon a high hill.'"

And these were but one of the many things, and his mind once more reverted to Modena's words as she spoke of Mrs. Storm. "Cruel contrasts of civilization," she had said. Mammon and Fashion, Pomp and Pageantry, Idleness and Indulgence, Monopolists and Injustice against Poverty and Illiteracy and Socialism. Wealth playing with cold charity! Philanthropy striving to uproot the curses caused by civilization and manufacturing, and unconsciously sowing the seed of bitter discontent; and distilleries! and he clenched his teeth to keep back the oath which sprang to his lips, as he thought of the opulence coming from many a home that lacked its dole of daily bread.

"The poor, what do we know about them? There is no real intercourse or sympathy between us. We are as ignorant of each others' lives, habits, thoughts and feelings as if we were dwellers in different countries or inhabitants of different zones, fed by different food, clad with different raiment, judged by different standards and governed by different laws," he said, repeating some words he had once read.

It seemed to him they knew nothing at all about them, and as he thought of all he had met with in his recent visit to the larger cities, the woe and want, the filth and vice, the trials and temptations, the illiteracy and degeneracy, the deplorable struggle of the respectable poor and the arising spirit of the laboring classes against the rich—these all brought sadly home to him the almost utter impossibility of ever reforming and elevating the illiterate, or ever reconciling property and poverty.

It was after the labor hour. The streets were deserted by all save the hurrying wind. Thoughts flew through his mind, confused and presaging, like the straws in the eddying gusts in the streets.

The sun had gone down and night hung over the city. He had reached the avenue of maples leading into his private gardens. He paused in his rapid walk, took off his hat, and leaning against the low stone battlements looked back over the darkening city.

"God works from whole to parts, but man must work from parts to whole. And what is the whole?" he asked himself.

There was a vein of sadness in Mr. Lester's nature, that sadness of which Talleyrand had written to De Stael, "Having so superior a mind, do you not somehow recognize sorrow, as inseparable from all things?" He was a man with eyes which see, and ears which hear, of understanding and comprehension, and was trying to contemplate things in their entirety. In his thoughts he now removed himself, as it were, from the molecular movements of the world, and soared aloft, and looked down as other great men had done before him, on the endless passage of generation after generation, hurrying on in its course from the womb to the grave, each representative passing the torch from his dying hand to the living hand of the one who follows him, as represented in that fine figure of speech which Lucretius has made immortal, endeavoring to grasp from each torch all that was necessary to make a perfect whole, but his vision was not strong or clear enough to make up a perfect whole, and as he looked, more vividly was portrayed before him that endless succession of creation and annihilation, and then he realized his own infinitesimal nothingness, and he bowed his head, but not in sadness.

Other men greater than he had before this drunk of the fatal hemlock, for less than what he saw, what he felt.

Bacon, in concluding a chapter on science, closes with the remarks: " We see how necessary it is for men to be fully instructed in moral doctrines and religious duties before they proceed to politics. For these, bred up from their youth in the Courts of Princes and in the midst of civil affairs, can scarcely ever obtain a sincere and internal probity of manners."

Mr. Lester's ancestors had been Lutherans. Through their honesty, integrity and thrift, they had acquired immense wealth, then had come culture, refinement, traditions and honor, and all the concomitants of a high position, but the old Lutheran spirit had remained hid under the guise of a gentleman of the world. Politics might make him less scrupulous, and modern society make him lenient towards much laxity, but neither could move the probity of his manners.

He was a great man in his country, so great that position could scarcely make him greater, but yet he worked with unceasing effort, because his life had been based upon an instinctive hope, and his reflections to-day had aided in making his hope a rational reality.

He now replaced his hat, and was about to enter the grounds, when he noticed a poor woman whom he knew. Her head was without covering and in her arms she carried her little four-year-old boy. The little lad lay sound asleep with his head pressed close to his mother's breast, and as Mr. Lester stopped to speak to her, she pressed the little form closer and stooped to kiss the dirty tear-stained face, now smiling in happy security in his tired sleep. He had been blowing soap bubbles on the lawn, a pretty butterfly had attracted his attention, and he had chased it down the road. It had flown away, and he had wandered on gathering the dandelions by the wayside. He had made mud-pies and helped some workmen carry bricks, and had built castles in the air; he had been frightened by a dog, knocked down by a milkman's cart and almost trampled on by a carriage horse, and had grown hungry and dirty and tired, and was crying for home, when his mother found him, and was now bringing him happy and safe to his own crib and fireside.

" Some day," said Mr. Lester, and smiled as he went up his own doorsteps.

CHAPTER XIII.

THE next forenoon the mistress of Apsley House was alone in her octagon room in the chateau suite of rooms arranging in Watteau shells and Sevres bowls some flowers which had been sent in that morning from Fernwylde, when Keith Kenyon ran lightly up the steps and entered her presence.

"Is your father in?'" he asked, hurriedly, and with irritation visible in his tone and expression.

"No, he hasn't yet returned. Will you wait for luncheon if you wish to see him?" replied Modena, as she placed a vase of jasmines on the opposite table.

"I want to see him, but cannot very well remain. That Stubs is giving us so much trouble, and Patrie is not much better. I don't see why such men were made."

"You shouldn't criticize nature's handiwork irreverently," replied his companion, smilingly.

"Nature's handiwork is all right. I wasn't criticizing it. It is the Ego within that is wrong."

"No, the tone was more of a polite curse than a criticism," said Jack, who had come into luncheon. "What's the matter now? Anything fresh?"

"Yes, Stubs is considering holding a series of secret meetings. He intends communicating with the leaders of each union. He has secured a constituency for himself—a safe, one. He is espousing their cause."

"How do you know?" asked Jack, quickly.

"Don't be inquisitive, Jack," said his cousin, seeing he doubted the truth of what was said and wished for further proof.

He had not been at Lover's Walk the previous day, but his quick intuition came to his aid.

"Isn't he under Lennox?" he asked, after a moment's pause. "Can't he stop him?"

"Yes, if he will do so."

"And if he will not, you are the only one who can make him do so. It rests with you. I am sorry we can't help you."

"I fail to see that. I don't see why the responsibility rests with me."

"We did not say the responsibility. We said you could do it, if you would. If you opened your parlor door the fly would walk in."

"I don't know what you mean," replied the young minister, not admitting he saw the inference.

" Spiders are often caught in their own meshes," continued Jack. " The meshes here are of fine gold thread. They are very enticing."

" Not to me," returned the young minister abruptly, and for the moment off his guard.

He hadn't thought of the world looking at it in this light, and it annoyed him to think they were throwing a wrong light on his actions.

" Has he taken any action in the matter yet?" asked Jack.

" No, but their plans are matured, ready for execution."

" And what's preventing them from going on?" and his friend smiled, as he noticed the young minister's annoyance.

" There is no immediate danger; it is a ruse to hasten matters," concluded Jack Mainton to himself. Keith Kenyon could not see it in that light, and he was trying to make him see it.

There is an old homely adage that burnt children dread the fire. Jack had been burnt, and the burning had helped him to be wise for others. He knew that humanity, for want of proper knowledge, thought and decision, create for themselves most of the complexities of their lives. He had created for himself a situation which had become the bane of his life, and this fact made him desire to try to avert a similar evil from the lives of those whom he loved.

There had been a beautiful, high-spirited young girl who had married a colonel in the army. The union had proved unhappy. Youth, thoughtlessness and uncurbed desires had caused them to drift apart, and the Colonel had sought sympathy elsewhere. Fate had thrown Mrs. Deering and Jack Mainton together. Her heart had been piqued and lonely, and was in that state which craves sympathy and love. She had made him her confidant, and he had been thoughtless and had not resisted the temptations which arise from such intercourse, and awoke one day to the knowledge that she loved him, and him alone. There had been no visible disunion between the Colonel and his wife. Wisely they had kept it from the world. It was only a closet tragedy, but Jack Mainton had felt he had helped widen the gulf between them. It had been unintentional, but when too late he had realized the evil of his ways. He had used his uncle's influence in securing the Colonel an important commission in the far East, and he had prevailed upon her to go with her husband, and it was when she was away and he had thought himself free, entirely free, that he had taught Helen Lester the sweet lesson of love.

But Mrs. Deering had written from the East that she could not live without his presence, and had prevailed upon her husband to resign his position on the plea of climate and health and return home. The Colonel was only too willing to return to another and leave his wife free to her choice.

They had done so, and were now in the Capital. Her power over her old lover was gone, but as Jack had an abnormal sense of honor in such matters, he felt he owed her reparation and consolation; he could not undo the evil he had helped to do; he could not go to her as he had gone; there was a change in himself, but so long as she pressed her claims upon him in honor he felt he could go nowhere else. It was all he could do for her now.

No words had passed between him and Helen Lester on Mrs. Deering's return. Helen had seen it as it was, but she had not let the world see it; it had hurt, hurt so much that nothing could make her suffer now.

When the letter had come from the East he had shown it to Lester and told him all, or at least all that he could tell, and then had gone on his way not knowing how it would end.

He was very fond of his cousin. She had been more to him than a sister could be. He was very fond of Keith Kenyon. He was a good lover and a good hater. From the first moment he had seen Verona Lennox he had heartily disliked her. He was a keen, quick judge of human nature and he knew she would prove no mean foe. It hurt him now to see those whom he loved create for themselves complexities in life from which in honor they could not retreat. He could not intrude counsel on his friend, but he availed himself of suitable opportunities to awaken his mind to a knowledge of his danger.

"What about Patrie?" he asked, turning the conversation, not wishing to intrude any further in private matters.

Mr. Patrie represented to them the most objectionable person in their party.

"I saw him out driving this morning with Mrs. Sangster."

"What does that mean?"

"It means he has been wanting something he cannot have. The chief will not give him what he asks. He cannot. We might quiet him by—But the devil of it—I beg your pardon, Modena, but he does make a fellow swear."

"Why do you keep him? Why not let him go? He has very little influence," replied the mistress of the house. "He surely has enough intelligence to know right from wrong. If he does wrong, let him go."

"But if we allow all such fellows to go the other fellows will win. We want to die fighting hard."

"They would come back."

"In time! We're not quite ready to let them go, and we require him in our business to manage those who do not know what is right."

"He wouldn't make a very efficient teacher if he does not know how to act himself."

"We did not say teacher. We said manager. Can't you see the distinction?" and Jack smiled grimly, as he thought of many things.

"Then politics, instead of being a game for the gods, has degenerated into a matter of commerce," said Modena.

"We will turn Mr. Patrie over to you, Modena," said her father, who had entered in time to hear their troubles. "My child here calls herself our political whip. We will set her after him, and get her to exercise her sorcery over him until the crisis is past. But if she has to give a piece of her heart to each of our renegades there will not be much left for someone else," continued he, referring to Carlton Montcith.

Jack did not look up, but lighted his cigar as he drily remarked, "Not much left, anyway;" then he took a moss rosebud out of a bowl, and carelessly putting it in the buttonhole of his coat, lifted his hat good-naturedly and strolled out.

"Why did he espouse our cause, if he is not sincere?" asked Modena, quickly.

"You are going to Earnscliffe to-night; ask the chief, he will tell you." replied the young minister, as he replaced his hat and followed Mr. Wellington into the library to discuss in private the whys and wherefores of Mr. Patrie.

"Why did Mr. Patrie come to us in the first place?" asked the mistress of Apsley House that same evening, as she found herself seated alone by the chief for a few moments.

Mr. Patrie had been with them all profusion and servility, and had but left, but she had noticed the chief's coldness, almost cynicism towards him.

She was governed by high standards of action and was very generous, and people of generous natures very seldom doubt the sincerity of others. She had judged all by her own standards, but her instinct had made her doubt Mr. Patrie.

"What do you mean?" asked the chief, looking at her.

"Isn't he working with us from conviction alone? Isn't his primary object patriotism?"

Her chief smiled almost sadly.

"What a pity to disillusion her!" he thought. "If you define that as patriotism, how many of us are patriots? Some! No doubt

10

a great many, but of the majority how many men for one moment think why they belong to their party. Is it from principle, or because they are born so, or because circumstances have placed them there, or because they are selfishly benefited by espousing the cause? We have honest, capable men who would govern well, if it lay in their power to do so. But the great majority will not be governed; they want to govern. They will not think for themselves; they are becoming inebriated with our contemporaries' creeds, and cackle parrot-fashion what their chiefs and their clique assert, and they only assert policies that suit the hour and gain their immediate ends. Circumstances, or evolution, or the spirit of the age, or whatever you like to call it, has forced us from our pedestal, and forced us to resort to other means to retain power—to intrigue—to cabals—to office prizes—to manipulation. Men gain power to-day by unscrupulous trickery and by working on the baser side of human nature," and then he checked himself, remembering to whom he was speaking.

His guest looked at him in great surprise.

" Do we?" she asked; but her chief did not reply, but looked out through the open window into the gloom of the night, and his eyes darkened and saddened as if he beheld a world of woe into which he could bring no light.

" If it doesn't lie in one's power to do what is right, one should throw the whole thing down and start afresh. If one cannot win honestly, it is much more glorious to be beaten," she said, with decision and a faint tinge of derision.

" A true party man despises candor," said her chief, knowing how she despised a proselyte.

" One should fight for one's convictions. If one cannot do so, one should do nothing."

" But we have none left to uphold. We are flying our colors under a false name. What is there left to conserve? The prerogative of the Crown is conserved on condition that it remain a figurehead and pageantry; the Senate so long as it sleeps with folded wings. The faith of our fathers is an hallucination of the past. We are like Plato, we live in an unworn world, but even here plow-boys and milk-maids will soon be realities of the past."

But the mistress of Apsley House could not see this. She was judging her world by her home and by Fernwylde."

" Oh, no!" she said. " We have ideal ones at Fernwylde."

" That is only one place, an exception."

" You should make it the rule, not the exception. Our future great1ess depends upon it."

"You would make us all landed gentlemen. You would keep us with nature. Our land life has a foe as insidious as time and as cruel as envy in the modern craze and craving for excitement and for all the feverish fuss, stimulus and intrigue of city life. No one regrets seeing the boys leave the land more than I do. We are doing what we can to create conditions and open up new lands which will in time entice them to return. Out of all this chaff will come the real wheat. I am but the forerunner. There is one coming after me who will perfect and complete the work. Will you not help him when I am gone?" he said, lightly, to cover over the vein of sadness beneath it all.

"You are not gone yet," replied his young companion, while her eyes grew dim.

"Did you learn if Patrie was a good Tory?" asked Jack, who now joined them.

"We couldn't decide," answered their chief. "We have forgotten the essentials and are not competent to judge."

"Your people are like the lobster, the tarantula and the snake; they like to shed their old clothes once a year," said Mrs. Cecil, with a great regret.

"They are like the word 'hospital,' changed from a house of hospitality to one of disease," added Jack, with a greater regret.

"It's time we were going in for a bath again; the clothes Sir Robert Peel was accused of stealing from the Whigs while they were in bathing are getting dirty, and rather small and shabby," said Keith Kenyon.

"Dirty! did you say?" exclaimed Jack. "Filthy! and as for being small and shabby, why they're split to tatters long ago. Ugh!"

"If what you say is true, we are in a bad way, and it's one's own fault. We depend upon the mutation of the multitude, but the true leader bends that will to his own, and leads with a force and conviction and guidance, and the people follow." said Modena.

"Like sheep," added Lester, good-naturedly. "Would you allow no privileges to the people whatever?"

"All the freedom which comes from individual development and accomplishments, and this is the highest freedom. They are a law unto themselves, and until the proper time comes they must know and keep their place."

"It is so nice to advocate that when one dwells within the pale," said Lester, in the same tone.

Modena's brows drew together in deeper lines. She hadn't looked at it in that light. She had always belonged to the governing classes, and did not know what it was to be outside wishing to get in. She had always dwelt within the magic circle of power and patronage, and had ever tasted of its sweets. At many times she had been the power behind the throne, and had had the extreme pleasure of seeing her wishes and judgments carried into execution. She had not thought of those outside.

"If those outside the pale have anything better to offer than those within, then it becomes one's duty to step out and let the others step in."

"There must be a judge to decide which is the better."

"Public opinion does this."

"And public opinion has become a hydra-headed monster," said Jack, grimly, while Mr. Lester's face grew grave.

"Alas! alas!" said Mrs. Cecil. "Mr. Lester's frown tells us his Periclean Policy has degenerated into Jack's tactics, which have become but another name for Balzac's diplomacy of buying and selling, and keeping one's head above water, and pretending to look good and wise."

"Even to the selling of our own services to the state," added Jack.

"They should be sold. Sentiment should be laid aside and our state should be run upon a strictly business basis," said Mr. Sangster, abruptly and logically.

"What a basis!" exclaimed Modena. "You would make us a nation of shop-keepers and butchers. There is surely an infinitely higher basis, Love and Duty. That sounds priggish and prudish, but you force one to say it."

"You think all paid employments vulgar and degrading to the mind. You would revise political economy by making every man hoe his own hill of corn, and every woman weave her own home-spun," said Lester.

"No, I am too indolent to advocate that. I would have others do it for me—for the beauty that's in the hill and the homespun."

"And in yourself. I believe you could do it," said Mr. Lester, very tenderly. "You are too completely and too loftily above us all. We cannot grasp your dreams, but here is something we can do. Will you come?" he added, as the strains of one of Strauss' waltzes floated to them through the open door, and he led her away to join the gay throng of dancers, and forget Patrie and the strife and turmoil of the outside world.

CHAPTER XIV.

"Why is Modena so wrapped up in Fernwylde?" said Carlton Monteith, a few days after this, a little irritably, to Jack Mainton, as Jack was leaving the city to join the party which had preceded him to Fernwylde.

Parliament was dissolved, and the two parties were now touring the country. While speaking in that part of the country they had made their meeting-place at Fernwylde, and were never loth, when the opportunity presented itself, to mix a little private pleasure with the strifes and turmoils of public life.

The mistress of the place had gone down. It was impossible for her lover to leave the city at the present time. He had strongly hinted to her that it was his desire that she should remain in the city. She had not considered his wishes, but had expressed her longings to be in her country home, and accordingly had gone.

He was beginning to be impatient. He wanted her to come and live at Monteith House, but she was not willing to give up her homes and her many interests and live for him; she had not told him so, but he had felt it, and in his forebodings and longings he had expressed himself to her cousin.

"She has always loved Fernwylde, it is part of herself," replied her cousin, who fully understood what his companion felt. "I suppose, too, her duty demands her presence there at this time," he added, as he lit his cigarette before starting.

"Why does she bother her head about these things? There are better things in life for women. I wish you would tell her so," he stammered, in his confusion and irritation scarcely knowing how to express himself.

"What things do you mean?" asked his companion, looking up at him in surprise.

"Oh, politics, and the poor, and the country! All that continual worry is needless and useless."

"You mean my cousin is a ranter. You want her to stop ranting. I've never heard her rant. I admire her enthusiasm. It shows that she thinks, and it's only thinking people who will ever raise the standard of life. If people haven't the courage to express their honest convictions and opinions the world will never become any better. So long as there is a world, people will talk, and it is surely more profitable and much better to talk about something of universal interest than to be continually discussing trivialities, and self, and chronic dyspepsia. Yes, I know what you mean.

Melanchthon and St. John benefited the world while they were here. They lived their own lives of love and let the world alone; but St. Paul lives forever. Modena has lived in England. Its nobility, its grandeur, its durability, its traditions, that air which is over all, and round all, and in all, and which can be ever felt, and which permeates one's whole being to the core, all this has unconsciously sunk deep into her being. She has within her the instincts of a noblewoman. She is intensely patriotic, and if it please her to dream of a New England, we must admit they are noble and unselfish dreams, and if they don't help, at least they will not hurt anyone. For my own part, I think her life a very noble one," said Jack, rather coldly.

His companion looked at him in horror.

"You know I never meant that! Modena ranting! You might as well conceive of the Speaker dancing a minuet with the mace as associating her with preaching, but—but—nature never meant women to think—it meant them to feel. She thinks and works too much. I—I mean, I want her to feel more—that's what I mean. I wish you would tell her so."

Jack's face remained impassive.

"If nature meant them to feel, it also intended that man should teach them to feel; and I don't know about your theory of women not thinking. History tells us that when women stop thinking men soon stop too, and the world soon goes wrong. My cousin is a woman of great intelligence, and will remain mistress of her emotions until she finds a teacher with greater intelligence than her own, who will teach her to feel. Women of that calibre know how to love when they meet their master. It's a case of pull-devil, pull-baker. If you're her teacher you'll have to prove stronger than the devil. I can't do it for you. You'll have to do it yourself," replied Jack, as he took up the reins to drive off.

Carlton Monteith sighed and looked away. He was beginning to be afraid of her. He didn't care for all these things which were of so much interest to her, and of late he almost felt that she was weighing him with the fine scales of her own intelligence, and was finding him wanting. She was a woman of action, while he, like the hero of Lord Lytton, conceived of so much, and of so great, that he expended so much energy in conception that he had none left for execution.

He was more of a solitary, a visionary, a poet, than a statesman. Had he lived in other times than his own he might have become a Constantine, but as it was he preferred, like Diocletian at Salona, to remain with his cabbages and onions at Monteith House. He had tried to approach Modena several times of late to arrange for an early marriage, but she had avoided him. He had attributed it to her great love for her homes and to her intense interest in her world around her. He thought had he her in a different atmosphere, things would be different, that when she had once tasted of the fruits of Salona she would want, like Diocletian, to remain away from Empire and become happy in being his Empress.

His love for her was great enough to make him re-enter the political arena once more to please her, but he knew he could not work from conviction, and no other work would appeal to her. He was much worried as he turned and re-entered the gardens of Apsley House, where Marion Clydene was sketching the beauties of the river scenery.

"I saw Monteith as I was leaving the city, and he wanted me to persuade you to name an early day. He is getting impatient, and I think he is right. There's no use keeping him, like a worm, dangling at the end of your line any longer," said Jack Mainton to his cousin a few hours afterwards, as he stood beside her in the drawing-room at Fernwylde.

"Doesn't he think I know my own mind?" she replied, coldly.

"Oh, yes, you know it too much. He thinks you give too much of it to Fernwylde and your country and something else, and not enough of it to him. That's it."

"Something else?" she asked, looking up at him quickly. "What do you mean?"

"I suppose he meant your intrigues, and courtesying to place-seekers, and bending the knee to Baal. He wants you to think of measles and sock-mending and heart-warming. I told him to tell you these things himself, and he said you wouldn't listen. Of course, I tried to defend you, and told him you were interested in Fernwylde, and that he should be here and make himself its most interesting inmate. He didn't seem to realize that there are others only too willing to teach you these things. I had almost told him so."

"You would have displeased me greatly had you told him any such thing. Why do you say such things? I give you no cause to do so?"

"Don't you? If you don't, someone else does. Love is blind, you know. If you don't see it, there are many who do."

His cousin's face warmed, and she turned from him and crossed the room and raised a window embowered in ivy, where two turtle doves had made their nest under the casement.

"One can't help being what one is. I suppose nature never

intended me to be like those doves," she said, as she watched their fluttering over their little ones. "Perhaps I am, as he says, cold."

"Aphrodite was invulnerable until she met her Adonis; the lute is dumb until the chords are touched by a master hand," said Jack, as he crossed the room and stood by her side at the window and locked down upon her.

"If he isn't your Adonis, in justice to him you should let him go," he said.

She saw that her cousin knew more than she cared for him to know. She would not admit it, and she was too truthful to deny.

"I wish you would go over to Idlewylde and bring Mrs. Kenyon and Helen to dinner. They are alone. Mr. Linden speaks to-night at the Cathedral. We can go together from here," she said, in order to turn the conversation.

"Linden?" inquired her cousin, quickly. "Is he here?"

Mr. Linden was a celebrated divine, one of the most noted pulpit orators and philanthropic workers of the day. He came from a very wealthy family and was free to live his life as he pleased. Realizing his possibilities and opportunities, he had devoted his life to the pulpit and was loved and revered by all who knew him. He had met Helen Lester some two summers previous to this.

"Yes, it is their anniversary. They are fortunate in having him. I suppose he came to please Helen."

"Why should he come to please her?"

"Because he cares for her."

"And does she care for him?" he asked.

"I don't know. I hope she does."

"Why do you hope so?"

"I think everyone is happier when one feels and knows that she is living for someone and someone is living for her alone. Helen is worthy of the best. I think he would make her happy. We had intended her for you, but you don't seem to care."

Jack made no reply to his cousin, but stood for some moments gazing out through the green gloom of spreading maples, to where the shadows of evening were creeping down the hillside and over the little lake and ravine, and then he turned abruptly and left the room.

His cousin watched him from the window as he crossed the greensward towards the stables with quick steps and bent head.

He did not go to Idlewylde as his cousin had asked him to do, but instead he saddled the big black which was kept for his especial use, and rode away to a distant part of the estate to see a little blind boy in whom he was interested. The child's sight had for some time been failing. It had not been attended to in time, and when the case had fallen under his notice little hopes were held out for his recovery, but as the little fellow had been a special favorite of Jack's, he had now written to a specialist and was expecting him the next forenoon.

He returned as dinner was being served, and found Mr. Linden and the people from Idlewylde in the dining-room.

"Are you coming with us?" asked his cousin of him an hour afterwards, as the Cathedral bells rang out over the village, tolling the quarter hour. "We are going to walk through the park; the distance is short," she said.

"I am sorry I cannot go. I have to meet Kenyon in the village at nine. There are some things which require immediate attention. I may join you later," he replied, as they left the house, Mr. Linden and Helen Lester preceding the others. He didn't say so, but he was in no mood to go and hear Mr. Linden preach love for Helen Lester's benefit.

When the service was over and they had left the church by a side door, they met him with Keith Kenyon returning from the village, and they walked on together towards Fernwylde.

The night was clear and bright. A full moon swam high through fleecy cloud far above the Idlewylde.

Their pathway led through a maple grove. The stately Cathedral on the eminence, overlooking the river, threw its lights far out over the waters and into the shadows of the clustering trees and dense foliage by the river's side.

They passed on silent, impressed by the simple grandeur of nature, the beauty of repose, and the extensiveness of the view around them.

"How serene the night is! How majestic! As one gazes, one is lifted up into eternal greatness; the heart at sight of these goes out and up of itself, in peace and praise to its Creator," said Mr. Linden, who was returning home with Mrs. Kenyon and their Rector. "What a beautiful Cathedral! And placed in Arcadia! When one wearies of the world one could well come here and rest and grow," he continued.

"It was Modena's gift. She is fond of the beautiful," replied Mrs. Kenyon. "She recognizes and appreciates what art has done for faith. A rare thing to-day! Too rare!"

"You love a beautiful church in which to worship?" he said, turning and addressing the mistress of Apsley House. "One feels that beauty attracts and ennobles all the higher qualities of mankind. Architecture creates a worshipping, awe-inspiring attitude

of mind and leaves a more lasting impression. Like music, it aids
in the formation of character. Your choice was admirable."

"When one returns from abroad, one feels our primitiveness; it
is only a little thing—a little corner," replied Modena, while the
others laughed.

"Do you envy them their age?"

"Oh, no, I have too much vanity to envy anyone anything, but
their accomplishments and associations make one wish to excel—
to live. A thing of beauty is invariably a silent educator."

"Then the dwellers here should be in a high state of intellectual
development," returned Mr. Linden.

"They are very primitive and simple, I assure you," replied its
mistress.

"Simplicity is the highest state of development."

"We do not know the meaning of your words. They are beyond
us. All we can say is that we are happy. The soul of the Greek
dwells within us in so far as we do dearly love life and its beauties."

"The fruits of dwelling with nature."

They had walked on all together, and now paused by common
consent to gaze at the ruins of a moss-covered stone church that
had been built by the Ursuline sisters, and afterwards used by
the Jesuits, and now lay dark and slumberous in rank verdure in
the shadowed moonlight.

"When one looks at these ruins, and remembers what these brave
men suffered, and what they did for a young country, one could
almost agree with Mrs. Cecil that we have suffered greatly by the
change. It makes one wonder if the French had continued in
possession whether it would still be a country under the control of
the Church," mused Helen.

"No doubt it would," replied someone. "How can one read
the early history of the perseverance, consecration and martyrdom
of those early fathers and doubt it. Their handiwork still remains
in every village, town, hamlet and cottage, when almost every other
trace of early days has been obliterated."

Helen stooped and pushed the ivy back from a rude stone cross,
and by the bright moonlight read the inscription to one of the early
Jesuit martyrs.

"Any other age would honor these men," said Helen Lester, with
a sincerity of regret. "England honors her Cranmers, Germany her
Luthers, and the whole world its St. Paul. Why not we?"

"Their fruits are their monuments," said Mr. Linden. "If
you will notice, wherever they have worked and planted their seed
the people have never deviated from the truth, and have lived

happy and contented, if extremely simple and meagre lives. You will find neither schism or socialism abiding in their cottage homes. And where will you see so little crime and vice among so rough and illiterate a class of lumbermen and miners, as in the country to the north of us, the missionary field of the black-robed priest and grey-robed nun ?"

"They have enough of something else to make up for their lack of vice," muttered Jack in an aside to Keith Kenyon, with his usual irrelevancy. "The Jesuits always had keen scent. Their noses are sharp enough yet to ferret out what they earned and give us the devil of trouble," continued he, referring to their late trouble with the Government.

"When one thinks of the immense advantages of civilization and of science which we enjoy, and when one remembers that with all these this is an age of clay idols, one almost regrets one had not lived with Father Jogues and his sister saint, Marie de l'Incarnation," said Helen, venting her personal irritation on the age.

It was such an unusual thing for her to murmur or complain, that they looked at her in wonder, and thought for a moment that she was certainly espousing Mr. Linden's cause.

"I think you did live then. One could easily imagine the spirit of St. Ursula or Margaret de la Marguerite again living and breathing in you," said Jack to her in a low voice.

They were the first words containing any sentiment he had used to her in two years, and when he saw the cold, hurt look in her face he regretted very much that they had passed his lips.

He would atone.

"Let us walk on," said Keith Kenyon to their hostess. "That was surely a very clever speech of Jack's. She cannot help forgiving him after that.

They wended their way home slowly through the woods until the parting of their ways. To the left lay an avenue of maples, their boughs lacing and interlacing overhead, forming at the farther end an arch backed by the turrets and towers and metal roofs of Fernwylde on which the moonlight now shone, transforming them into dream edifices, fit for Merlin's castle. To the right a path led across the ravine to Idlewylde and the Rectory.

Mr. Linden was to be the guest of the Rector for the evening, and now, with Mrs. Kenyon and the Rector and some others, who were in advance, turned towards the Rectory and Idlewylde, while Mrs. Gwen, forgetful of her duties, passed on to the rotunda of Fernwylde.

It was such a relief to get away from the toil and strife for a few hours that Keith Kenyon, forgetful for the moment of proprieties and conscious only of the poet's theme that love lives for the present, drew his companion's arm within his own and wandered to the brow of the hill, overlooking the ravine and river, and looked over Fernwylde as it lay bathed in full moonlight.

"You love Fernwylde," he said, reiterating her betrothed's words, as the moon came out from behind some clouds and shed its lustre over the picturesque and imposing entrance to her ancestral home and over all the scene, making the gardens and fountains and statuary light as day, and leaving the pine forests which lined the river's edge in dense shadow.

"Yes," she replied, in a low voice. "One feels that a home cannot be bought. It must be made. Its life and fire must come from inheritance and tradition as the coals on the altar come from heaven," and her eyes grew deep and dark as they wandered over her old home.

And Fernwylde was a home of which she might well be proud. Tradition associated it, when it was but a French chateau, with the daring deeds of Champlain, with the martyrdom of the Jesuit enthusiasts, as the home of the most daring during the early warfare, and as the rendezvous of the United Empire Loyalists. It possessed its romantic as well as its historic spots. There was Laughing Eyes' Leap, where, up the stream where the rocks were rugged and steep and the waters black and hissing, the Huron brave had leaped from their heights to rescue his drowning sweetheart from her birch-bark canoe. Bleeding-Heart's Nook, where, in the treacherous past when white men's scalps hung from reeking tomahawks, the brave Charles De Bois stole out one night for a few short hours with her who was so dear to him, and where, by its old cave, not far from the Fernery, as he was returning home, his eyes watching the moonlit clouds pass over the Idlewylde, and softly whistling, "Then meet me, won't you meet me? Then meet me by the moonlight alone," the wily, catlike savages sprang upon him in numbers, and left his bleeding heart at his sweetheart's door. And far back in the distance were the deep pits and huts, where not more than a century ago dwelt the charcoal burners, busy during the calm, autumn days and nights, with their smothered, smouldering pits of pine, when the valley was filled with the mazes of Indian Summer and the nuts lay ripe upon the ground. Then there were the relics of one of the oldest churches in the country, the one they had now passed, built by an order of the Ursuline nuns, and now silent and covered with the lichens of age, its cloisters and choirs haunted only by the bats and owls, but a relic of the time when the church was the portals of the poor. Then there were many other landmarks: the stone cross where the martyr Beyou was supposed to be found kneeling; Frontenac Lodge, where on one of his northern trips he camped one silent summer night; West Wing Barracks, where the troops had mustered in '37; Duke's Saloon and the Princess's Bower, where royalty had been guests during the hunting days of an autumn season; while its museum was in itself like some black-letter record of the early history of the country, with its missals and tablets and memoirs, its arrow heads and ivory tusks, unbaked porcelains and images, its stags' heads and primitive armor, the building itself being a chronicle of the early architecture written in stone and wood and granite, while within its walls were many leather hangings, painted in mystic symbols, whose weird figures now seemed the phantoms of a spirit world. And the old Fernery, the present mistress's favorite spot—round it clustered the dearest memories of her childhood, for her mother had loved it before her. It was here her mother had spent the few blissful summers of nuptial happiness. It was here Modena, when a child, had played on the velvety grass and drank from the bubbling stream and gathered the peaches and nuts from Old Orchard near by.

She had been born at Fernwylde, and she had always looked upon it as her real home. It was her love for it, and her love for nature, which had aided in giving that restfulness, that steadfastness to her character. She was wont to say that " out here one has some tangible influence, one can do some real good, one's work is simple, solid, soul-satisfying. Here one's thoughts can rise above the sayings and doings of one's friends and one's foes. Here, when one's day's work is done, one's fancy can soar to the clouds."

Her fancy was now soaring to the clouds. In the presence of her companion, her betrothed's message to her in the afternoon had vanished from her mind. She was only conscious of his presence. He had said to her, " You love Fernwylde;" his words had awakened within her all that her home represented. All! No, not all, for no words could ever express what she saw, what she felt.

His presence and the surroundings had awakened within her some chords which had long been silent. Over the Idlewylde fleecy clouds met and mingled or passed over one another in hurrying billows, hiding at intervals the moon from view and leaving the woods in dusky darkness. But she, a daughter of the woodlands, loved the lights and shadows of the scene. Were they not the lights and shadows of the woods of Cameliard, where the knight of long ago had wooed his queen? She felt his hand, warm, touch hers, and as it did her eyes wandered out and upwards, past the clouds, past the orb in the sky, as though her mind was apart from her body, wandering in some unknown land, somewhere. Had she really lived in the days of long ago, and was her spirit striving to break the bonds which held it and soar away to fairer realms, or was it the inheritance of cumulated knowledge, together with the knowledge which comes from the possession of an active, versatile, imaginative mind, that had been working within her as potentialities wanting to find fruition in realities, or was it another soul whose insight into great things had made him see the infinity of life; was it this soul beside her, acting on hers and through the more imaginative, idealistic faculties of a woman bringing to light the dim, vague, visionary dreams of a New Empire?

At least, she found herself wandering in Unknown Realms, the many soft sounds around them lending to the scene the charm of some long-remembered, mysterious thing. From the monastery by the lake shore the monks were now passing to their late orisons. Soon the sound of chanting voices and the soft waves of the organ's melody came up to them on the still air, and in the stillness, when their voices ceased, there was no sound save the murmur of many waters round them, the river gurgling by the monastery, its voice low and soft and sweet, as the voices in the Sistine in Passion Week, and up above amidst the woods the rumbling and tumbling of many unseen brooks, and by their side the low moan of subterranean waters as they flowed from the upper heights and forced their way once more to the light of outer day.

The Present was forgotten and memory wandered into the Past. Almost in fancy, as the turrets of Fernwylde and the lights of the monastery cloisters loomed into view, could she see the pomps and pageantries, the fervor and faith of all these men and women of the " Old Regime "; or, as the Idlewylde murmured by, in fancy could see the white sails of St. Ursula with her eleven thousand virgins come floating up the moonlit waters; or, through break in foliage, the gleam of tomahawk, the fleet of moccasin, the white spirit of Manitou, the black-robed priest and grey-robed nun fleeing before the coming of civilization, as Tannhauser, the doomed knight, had fled through the gloom and snow; and then back, farther back, were the indefinite groups and forms of many banded bands, wild, indistinct, undisciplined as they had been before the coming of Arthur, and then a clearer vision of something that had been, of something with the form of Camelot, and " Why not?" memory murmured. Were not these western woods the land of sunset, the golden islands of Hesperides, the departed home of all

these great men of the world's age when the world was great? Might
they not have wandered here and lived and grown and flourished
for many Periclean summer days? "Why not? Why not?"

"You have dreams, like Marion's musical thoughts too vague
and visionary for production?" said her companion to her as he
gazed on her enraptured face.

"The product of the world's music," she murmured.

"No, your music comes from within. They would have to be
written in another key to be in harmony with the world's music.
What are they?"

"If I told you, you would only smile."

"If I did I should perhaps be smiling at myself."

"You, too, have visions. What are they?"

"Tell me yours. Women have finer harmonies within them than
men. I promise to become your knight."

"You promise before you know. How indiscreet!"

"By faith in things we know."

"How prettily you say that."

"Then repay the prettiness by telling us what you see."

"You want my Ideal Kingdom," she said, as she leaned over a
low stile. His arm yet held hers, while his hand lay warm on hers
as it rested on the wooden caps of the stile.

"A wise man's kingdom is his own heart."

"Yes! What is your heart? What did you see?"

"I am too practical to become poetical; my words would only
make it sound commonplace. I saw so great and so many things
that words of mine cannot portray what I saw, and I do not know
that they are intended to be portrayed. Ideals exist in the imagination alone. They are so familiar and yet so strange to one. When
one would give a name to them, they recede into the shadows of
some far-away past, so far away that one cannot follow them. My
version of the vision would only disappoint you."

"You are practical because the world is your all. It is the
practical the world wants. The imaginative may drape it with
poetry. What did you see?"

She was silent for some moments while the monastery bells
chimed out a Jubilate Deo; she felt his hand clasp hers more
closely, and then her eyes wandered away once more, and in a
far-away voice she said, "I saw a King and Queen come from
above, or perhaps they but came from the lily-vale of Avilion, for
hasn't Merlin said, 'They pass away but to return'?—come to a
country great and fair, a country so great that though they sailed
from morn to noon and from noon to dewy eve, yet could they not

compass it, and so fair in its virginal dress of white and green that the eye at eve sought rest in shade. And with them came great lights; and lesser lights grew up around them; and the people came from the mountains and from the forests and from the plains and became one with them, and although one, they were great and many in number.

"And the King held all land in trust to the Powers from whence they came.

"In the heart of this country was a palace such as Merlin built, and round about this palace a paradise of nature of great compass. In this palace dwelt the King and Queen and many of the greater lights. And this paradise stood in the centre of the world as the hub in the centre of a wheel, and from it radiated to all parts of this world lighted lines great and many in number. And in the centre of each of these lighted lines was placed a mansion, from which radiated many lesser lines; and in this mansion dwelt the Lord of the Manor with many of the lesser lights; and on the lesser lines were many lesser lights, and from the lesser lights many lesser lines, and so it was o'er all the land, and all the country grew and flourished.

"All land was held in trust to the Crown. The Lord of the Manor paid his tribute by his service to the Crown. His maintenance came from his land. The Landholders paid a nominal fee to the state and their maintenance came from the land. As Ulysses did, so too did they, swing their own scythe, hold their own plow and garner in their grain.

"Handicraft was honored and all men worked for the perfection of the beautiful, the useful and the good.

"Each Lord and Landholder held an hereditary title, forfeited only through mismanagement or misconduct.

"On each estate, on the outer circle of the Lord's Realm, in touch with the lesser lights, were depots for the exchange of products; many schools, and churches, and libraries, and museums, and dramas, and music, and flowers, and the finer arts. Each home was a Garden of Eden, with hedgerows and running waters and dim shadows, and twilight, and sunlight, and birds, and all things beautiful and useful and good. It was a Community with one purpose, a Community of association, a Community of heart to heart and hand to hand with man and nature."

"How did they till the soil?"

"In palace, mansion and home dwelt dim lights, many and great in number. Their sickles, their plows and their graffs were simple and many in number, and were made in a town by the state criminals."

"And did the youths not in time turn towards these cities?"

"No. Their life was a life of association, and the towns were to them what Siberia is to the Russian."

"But the land in time would become over-populated."

"This land was so great that countless new estates awaited the youths."

"That would have the tendency to separate families."

"No; when one generation became numerous the head of that family became Lord of a new manor, and his children and children's children Landholders about him. The building up of new families continually and continuously gave a stimulus to national growth. Each man might some day become a Lord, but like Gareth with his 'tilling of the soil and baking of his cake,' their name must be theirs because they have earned it."

"And who were your Lawmakers?"

"Their Lords gathered together in one place, and from their number the Crown called a few to his aid. The others, who kept heart to heart with their community, created and submitted all that would be for the welfare of all. Their sole maintenance came from their estates, their estates being sufficiently large to allow them to live temperately and liberally, but restricted, so as to prevent plutocracy and opulence."

"And were the Landholders silent?"

"They voiced their community."

"And was there no crime or strife?"

"Yes. Where there is human nature there will ever be crime and strife. There were state lawyers. Criminals were tried by their peers and sentenced by their Lords, and punished by being sent to the state manufactories. The Lords were tried by their peers and sentenced by the Crown, their punishment being for-feiture of titles and lands, and ostracism. But there was little strife. It was an age when knights rode abroad redressing human wrongs and led sweet lives in purest chastity."

"And Education?"

"It was a state affair."

"You saw a state Religion? Your imagination must have soared to the seventh heaven when you saw that."

"There should be but one religion."

"How did the state make the people believe so?"

"They believed it of themselves. They went to their own heart, life, nature and God, and only believed what they taught. Their

11

religion was their life. Their lives were happy and they praised.
Worship is an instinct. Their churches were kept for worship and
worship alone. Their religion taught them the five primitive virtues were the basis for the beautiful, the useful and good, and that
Duty, Trust and Love were the highest attributes of man, the
simplicity of the Soul's development."

"Your nation was built upon the land and upon the church.
'A city built to music, therefore never built at all; and therefore
built forever,'" said her companion, gazing intently at her enraptured face.

He was silent for some moments, and then as the last notes of
the monastery's Jubilate Deo echoed back from the lake-shore woods
he said with great tenderness:

"A daughter of a hundred earls advocating Communism!"

She had been gazing into the beyond, but her eyes now looked
at him, startled and round and dusky as the orb in the sky.

"I thought it the very essence of feudalism and responsible
authority?"

"And what did you call your Kingdom?" he asked, without
replying to her interrogative assertion.

"The gods of old gazed on the sun as it sank in the west. In
fancy it had gone to heaven. In honor of them I would call it—"

But her companion interrupted her before she completed her
sentence. "You said its Queen was a goddess dropped down from
the clouds. We shall call it Modena Land. For centuries the
world has been revelling in wise men's dreams. We will but add
another page—a page of Modenian Dreams.

"What presumption!"

"Perhaps so; perhaps not. Theirs were but Ideal Dreams. In
time we shall make ours real. From the Ideal ever comes the Real.
Pericles performed that of which the immortal Pindar sang in
song. Why not we?"

"Why not?"

"When had you those visions?" he asked, after a pause.

"What visions?"

"Your retrospective visions of an Ideal Land! Perspective!"

"Have I been talking nonsense?" she asked, as she seemed to
awaken slowly and to realize that she was standing by his side,
looking over Fernwylde in the moonlight, and that her hand lay
warm within his own.

A sweet thrill passed through her.

He felt it.

He had promised to be her knight; he was moved by the strongest emotion of his life. An almost uncontrollable desire passed through him to take her to him. She felt it and with great effort **recovered** her self-control, and then she remembered her betrothed's message to her that afternoon, and his phantom, which was stronger than his real presence, rose up before her, and her father's words to her in the library a few evenings previous came to her, and her manner changed and the change checked his words.

She withdrew her hand.

"You told me I was not fond of day dreaming. I am becoming even worse than Marion. Forget what I have said. It is nonsense."

"Forget! That would be an impossibility," he replied, again looking at her with great desire.

"It is late," she said, with a return to her habitual ease and grace, but, despite herself, with a new tenderness in her voice. "The monks are passing from the chapel to the cloisters from their late orisons. We must go within," and she turned towards the house.

CHAPTER XV.

The Lennoxes were coming down to Idlewylde for a few days. They must be secured and Stubs must be quieted. His invitation didn't mean any more than any other invitation; his attention to the heiress could not be misconstrued. So he told himself. He hadn't spoken of it to the mistress of Fernwylde. Somehow he couldn't. To discuss the propriety of it would be to admit there was something in it, so he remained silent; but he had asked her to join them, and this she had promised to do later on in the day.

She had been busy during the day with many matters in the interest of her tenants, and the early autumn twilight had deepened into night before she arrived at Idlewylde.

Carlton Monteith had written her that forenoon that he would join her at Fernwylde. She had at once sent him word of her intended departure, and he had replied he would meet her at Idlewylde. The message had brought her no pleasure. The urgent desires which she had read between the lines had made her think.

On her arrival at Idlewylde she entered one of the waiting rooms unannounced. As she passed the hall door, one quick glance showed her Carlton Monteith and the master of the house standing together under the crimson-shaded wax sconces, the former talking earnestly the latter with one hand in pocket, the other resting on his watch chain and with eyes bent on floor.

The few quiet days down at Fernwylde had given its mistress an opportunity to look into her own heart. She was beginning to realize she had made the first mistake of her life; but she would not admit it; she was slow to admit anything into her life, and slower to relinquish it.   She had admitted Carlton Monteith into her life. "Her mother had wished it, then it must be all right," she had concluded, "but why could she not make herself feel this sincerity?" she asked herself in her moment's pause.

Her quick glance caused varied and strong emotions within her breast; she waited a moment longer to recover her composure and then crossed the waiting room and entered the reception room.

As she approached the hearth and loosened the fur ruff from round her neck, for the weather was threatened with one of those early frosts so prevalent in northern climates, her host, who now noticed her entrance, approached and welcomed her; while her betrothed, who had not now seen her for some ten days, and who was anxiously awaiting her arrival, followed, and eagerly clasped her hand, holding it for some moments in his own, while his countenance showed the great joy he felt at once more seeing her.

A feeling almost of guilt stirred within her. Had she been doing what was wrong? She was attached to him by many memories. He had always trusted her, and those who trust us educate us. She would never betray a trust. He loved her tenderly, she knew, and yet he had never intruded or pressed his relations upon her. He had left her free, perfectly free. He did not now intrude. She was grateful to him for it, and she smiled sweetly and showed her gratitude.

The master of Idlewylde was almost glad he had invited the Lennoxes to his home.

"When you are ready I shall send a woman to show you to your room," he said, as he prepared to leave them together.

"I shall go now. I have been walking all day and feel a little tired. I shall rest until dinner time. Has Jack come yet?" she asked.

"I hear his voice in the hall now," and then the door opened, and her cousin, followed by some others, entered the room, cold and tired and mud-bespattered and grumbling, after a long country drive to a rural district, where they had been trying to convince the rustics that they were the salt of the earth. But for many reasons they had been unable to do so, and Jack was in an irritable mood.

"Such a country," growled he, as he approached the hearth.

" One cannot look outside the door without getting the point of one's nose or the tip of one's toes frozen. It's only in August we're sure of a Nor'-wester. Take a car or a cab and they're as slow as time."

Mr. Lennox had entered at the same time by an opposite door and was passing through to join the chief in the library.

" Yes," replied he, with a smile as soft as the south wind, but as cutting as the north, " the people here are rather slow, and their hacks and habits rather backwoodsey."

The slow, derisive smile served to add to Jack's already well-filled stock of ill-humor, and as he looked after Mr. Lennox as he passed through the doorway, he turned with the sombre anger of an ingenuous man, and with dislike bristling through every word and tone, muttered and mumbled anathemas and disgust against bubble-blowers, agitators, wheat-cornerers, jingoists, Sing-Sings of crime, Lynch laws, and then checked his torrent of words as he saw Miss Lennox approach, took a cigarette from his case and handed another to his host.

Mr. Lennox's supercilious tone of condescension had in it the power to irritate Jack's candid nature. He felt, as he had once said to Lester, that he would prefer kicking him downstairs and out of doors, and the servility, sycophancy and adulation accorded them by the whole of society disgusted his ingenuous temperament. Hitherto he had passed it over as unworthy of notice, but his ill-humor at the result of the afternoon, and his hearty dislike at seeing them made so much of at Idlewylde, caused him to temporarily forget his good manners.

The group looked guilty at Miss Lennox's approach, but their host advanced to meet her and claimed her attention.

" Why, Jack, what an orator! You missed your vocation. If the House heard you, they would present you with the mitre and the mace to-morrow," said his cousin from the midst of those surrounding her.

" But it is the Speaker's duty not to speak, and I couldn't do so," replied he.

" You are rather severe," said Grace Austin.

" I stand rebuked in Miss Austin's presence," returned Jack, " but one doesn't like to see a man pluck the beaver and continually hoot at, and hack, and hate the goose that lays his golden egg."

" You are not consistent. A moment ago you were anathematiz ing the climate."

" Who wouldn't condemn it, with a norther blowing twenty below zero, and it the middle of August? Were Dante here he would add another ice-bath to his 'Inferno.'   Dickens talks about people being saturated with thought.   We're frozen up in ours.   It's cold enough to freeze the words as they drop from one's mouth.   We're standing chin-deep half of the year round in our own conversation."

"The surroundings wouldn't be very wholesome or elevating sometimes," said their host, who had joined the group again for a moment.

"Our atmosphere is a very paradise of perfection," said Modena to her cousin.   "If we did not know you as we do, we would say 'snarling is self-love's little lap-dog.'"

"Momus was kicked out of heaven for grumbling," said Lester.

"This isn't heaven."

"It is the nearest spot to it.   It is Olympus."

"Minus a Queen," added Mrs. Cecil.

"It will not be minus long," said Jack, drily, allowing his eyes to meet those of his host's as they turned from the others.

"You should eat your bone of happiness and be done with it," returned he to Jack, as they went to their different rooms.

"What did you mean?" asked he of his host, as they stood together some hours afterwards where they had assembled for the evening.

"I mean you can have her for the asking."

"You are very much mistaken if you think so. These ones with consciences are the very devil to hang out."

"Speak plain English, Jack," said his cousin, overhearing the remark.

"I'm not speaking English.   I'm speaking facts."

"Then clothe them in conventional language."

"I beg your pardon, then.   I think I'll go over and make love to Verona Lennox and see what that will do."

"Don't, you'll spoil Keith's chances," said Mrs. Cecil, as she came up.

"Do you think so?   I don't think I could do so, but I'll try if it will make Lennox commit himself."

"Hasn't he decided yet?" asked the Lady Greta.   "I thought it was the—the—the—tariff—is that what you call the thing?—that brought him here.   I don't know much about those things, but I heard some great man say that is what he wanted, and that is what the others want.   Then he should espouse their cause openly and get it.   When I want a new dress, or a trip across the continent, I say so, and I cling to it, tooth and nail, until I get it."

"But if there are some things nearer your heart than a new

dress or a trip, you might forget these," said Mrs. Cecil, inadvertently.

The Lady Greta looked up in surprise. She was only a visitor at Government House.

"What do you mean?"

"Nothing; at least, I mean free trade is a phantom."

"What a fuss to make over one man! Have you no Walpoles to buy him up?"

"Plenty! But some ask too high a price. Civilization has taken rapid strides since Walpole's time. No doubt nothing less than a minister or the ministry would satisfy his ambitions."

"That man in the ministry! Then one does not wonder you resort to diplomacy!" exclaimed the Lady Greta, as someone came up to claim her for the set now forming in the grand saloon.

"If the game were only a worthy one, one might resort to diplomacy," said Mrs. Cecil, with some disgust.

"They are foreign affairs," replied Jack. "I heard you say the other day what Lady Montford said, ' Oh, bother finances! finances never yet ruined a nation. Real politics lie in foreign affairs.' You will have to admit they are more interesting subjects than the Lady Greta's taxation."

"Taxation! One grows tired of the sound. In the beginning of the eighteenth century they taxed people for being born. No doubt in the end of the nineteenth they'll be taxing them for dying. One's as logical as the other."

"It's the best we have," said Lester. "We're called upon to lay the foundation for better things. In every calling there is a vital trust, a sacred responsibility, and upon a consciousness of such a responsibility, together with its faithful fulfilment, depend the soundness and prosperity of all national life. The better things depend upon the foundation which we lay. Our calling now is a humble one, but our star is rising into view. A child must creep before it walks."

"We're not creeping," said Modena.

"No, we're walking with someone holding our hands."

"And our hearts, too."

"How loyal you are," smiled Lester.

"And hope to remain so. That is our privilege," replied the mistress of Fernwylde.

"If they'll only leave us that much," added Jack, and he went off again at another tangent.

Modena listened to her cousin's tirade with a rather cold smile.

She wasn't thinking so much of what he was saying as she was of the heiress of Lennox Court. Their host had passed with her to the music room. They had stood for a moment in the shadows of the arched draperies, Verona looking up into his face. The evening was given in her honor. She had made this mean volumes. She had contrived to keep her host by her side, and yet make it appear that his devotion was voluntary. She had about her a certain fascination which attracted, even while it repelled. She had a trick of appealing to men's baser natures and of alluring them on, even while they felt a certain amount of disdain and disgust for her. From their first meeting she had felt how almost impossible it was to enter Keith Kenyon's life. He didn't seem to have a baser side to his nature. The cultivation and development of the higher powers and mental faculties, to a certain extent, sap away the lower desires. Only a great love could touch his life. She had felt this, and this fact had enticed her on, and if it had made her careful of her actions, it had also made her more tenacious in her purpose. To-night she felt she was progressing. She knew that she was looking her best. In the coils of her waving black hair were many gems sparkling like sunbeams, her great luminous eyes had in them both coquetry and comprehension; her throat was as white as that of the wild swans on the Idlewylde, and had round it great strings of pearls matching its transparency; her superb figure was as bare as etiquette would permit, her dress was of some soft silky lace over an underdress of ivory satin. The sparkling rays from a brilliant sunburst of diamonds on her bosom pierced their way out like living tongues of fire through a great bunch of crimson roses, which nestled in her low corsage and which touched her bosom like flames lapping over the virginal whiteness of snow. "It is so easy to make men love one, if one will take the trouble to try," she thought, and she leaned towards him in her interest in what he was telling her.

Modena's glance, quick as lightning, swept over the two as they passed on conversing in low tones. She did not pause or betray any sign of emotion, but for the first time in her life she felt a great wave of emotion pass over her, emotions she had never felt before.

She did not believe he cared for the heiress, but womanlike she was intolerant and imperious where her love dwelt and would tolerate no dual submission. She was glad Carlton Monteith was by her side.

"Jack's tongue is like Sevigne's pen, it trots with bridle loose," she said, betraying no emotion.

“There is one article on which Kenyon will not have to pay a high tariff,” said Mr. Patrie.

Many eyes in the group followed the two.

“He might let us have her,” said Lester to Modena. “We are becoming discouraged.”

“What do you want?”

“It’s human nature to want to be great for a little time even while here.”

“Do you want praise? Are you a Mandeville?”

“No,” smiled Mr. Lester.

“What do you want?”

“The power to do good. Is that egotism?”

“If it is, it is a higher form than that which governs the majority of humanity to-day.”

“I want to be great,” said the Lady Greta, who had returned, flushed and happy, from the dancing room. “I want to become great, but I am like Poe, I want to be great to possess the right to despise a world that has ill-treated me and wounded my self-conceit.”

They all laughed aloud.

“You haven’t it in your heart to despise even a worm,” said Lester.

“Haven’t I? You don’t know me; I am a splendid hater.”

“There is a nicer way to become great than by securing—Miss Lennox—a more æsthetical way.”

“How? By keeping Ruskin’s two mirrors on one’s dressing table, and dressing the mind every morning as well as the body?”

“It would be as easy to make a silk purse out of a sow’s ear as to mix ethics and face powder.”

“If one took the ethics, one wouldn’t need the face powder. The face is the mirror of the soul.”

“Does the soul make the face beautiful?”

“Yes.”

“Then the links will be deserted for the libraries.”

“Don’t do so; there is nothing so detestable as blue-stockings.”

“Modena is the only one who reads the sciences.”

“They slander you, my lady, but like Maria Theresa you are long-suffering.”

“I am not like Maria. She was too modest. Had I been she I would have been Queen in reality, not in name only.”

“I wish you had been. You would have saved the Court,” said Mrs. Cecil.

“No doubt she would,” said Jack. “She would have shut up

poor Valliere in her Carmelite convent from the beginning, and have sent the elegant Montespan campaigning out here with Frontenac, and Maintenon back to her school-room and nursery, and have made Bossuet take the cowl from his head and dance a minuet with Colbert's mace, and ruled Old France in general as she does New France."

"How you flatter one! Is that the way you define love of country?"

"You see beauty here, Modena?"

"Some see beauty in everything because they carry beauty in their own eyes. They are like the glow-worm in the night-cold. grass."

"But the glow-worm can't glow unlesss the weather is favorable. And even if the weather is favorable we have no place in which to glow. We have no society," said Mrs. Cecil.

"We have our drawing rooms," said Modena.

"Where one is as likely to meet one's butcher, or baker, or candlestick maker as her Excellency herself. By Jove, I shall never forget the look of horror on her Excellency's face when she met her own butcher at her own ball at Rideau Hall some few years ago. When I saw the pallor of her face, I thought she had received word of a death in the Royal Family until I saw who was her opposite partner."

All laughed at Jack's moody brow but his cousin, who said, with annoyance, "You shouldn't say those things. You don't mean them. You do not say such nonsense in your paper. The aborigines beheaded the first invaders and hung their scalps on their wigwam doors as a warning to others. If I were the chief I would behead every Jeremiad and hang their scalps on the doors of their own narrow souls."

"Newspaper men are like Bentham's poets, they are privileged prevaricators," said Jack, in extenuation of his conduct.

"Then they should keep their prevarications for their newspapers."

"They do, but at the present time we have an over-supply."

"Then keep them for the savages."

"The savages would know better than to believe them."

"What a flattering estimate you have of us!"

"Oh! I don't know! I have a very high estimate of the savages. Some enthusiasts tell us that this continent was the cradle of civilization. Agassiz claims 'Les Savages' were the fathers of enlightenment, while Indians, according to Mather, are the descendants of the ten lost tribes of Israel, whom Satan inveigled hither to get them away from the tinkle of the Gospel."

"When one reads the early history of the country, one could easily believe he succeeded very well in his mission," said Lester. "But hush! Here comes Miss Lennox. If she hear us she will deny us the existence of a history."

"She might dispute its truth. History is but the product of imagination."

"It lacks imagination; it is very dry; real life is much more interesting," said Miss Lennox, who had come from the dancing room with her arm within that of her host's.

"That speaks of a happy heart," said their host, as he stepped aside.

"Life is what we make it, and what others make it for us. We may make it a poem, a pageant or a prison-house," she said, with a little pout. "He mightn't have made it so public."

"And you have made it a poem! You are wise. Let us make this a poem," said Mr. Lester to Miss Austin and Modena, who sat beside him. "It is a pity to waste all this nice music. Let us join the dancers."

"There is not enough pageantry in it for Grace to make it a poem," said Modena, as they rose. "It's the fault of Jack's atmosphere. In Grace's there is music, mellowness and romance in every breeze that blows. Ours died out with the Red Man and coureur-de bois."

"I am very sorry we cannot give you music from the breezes, but we're giving you the best we can. Will you come and try it?" said their host from where he stood by her chair.

"And revive romance again," thought some of those present, who were watching the drama. She felt there were many eyes upon her. There was within her enough of the "eternal feminine" to want to resent his conduct, but to do so was to admit that she had noticed it, so she laid her hand within his arm, and soon their steps in the dance and, it seemed to them, in life were one.

CHAPTER XVI.

" You have asked her to stay a week with you," said Jack Mainton to his cousin, the next evening as they stood together for a few moments in one of the open French windows leading from a suite of rooms to the gardens. " Was it wise to do so?" he continued, as his eyes followed the form of Verona Lennox, as she passed down the room by Keith Kenyon's side.

" We ask anybody and everybody at the present time," replied his cousin, evasively.

" But you don't ask everybody. You've always boasted that no rag-tag or bob-tail would ever pass your Cerebus. You are changing."

" I don't ever remember boasting to that effect."

" Oh, you never said much. You're not much on the talk, but you've always acted it. Why are you coming down to this?"

" She goes everywhere. Isn't she the most sought after person of the day? You asked Mrs. Cecil the other day to help us in securing them."

" Yes, but that was a public affair, not a private one."

" You would countenance doing things in public which you would frown upon in private?"

" Decidedly so ! We are forced to do so. That's the diplomacy Disraeli recommends—study men and nations, and when one meets subtlety and craft use the same weapons in return."

" One fails to see why there should be two standards of right and wrong."

" We'll not stop to discuss that. That isn't the point. I thought you didn't like her. Did you ever pause to think that when once a guest has crossed your threshold she becomes sacred property ?"

" What are you hinting at?"

" Can't you see Kenyon's getting himself into a box he can't get out of? You're helping it along. She was at the meeting this afternoon with him, and helped the League ladies serve tea with blue ribbons flying from her breastplate. It's becoming so public he cannot very well in honor retreat. He's not capable of a baseness."

" Perhaps he doesn't want to retreat. He asked me to invite her here."

" Oh, he did ! I thought so," replied her cousin in a tone which brought the color to her face, and they were both silent for some moments watching the two where they had seated themselves at a whist table.

Jack hadn't known of her coming, and on learning of her arrival he had been very much annoyed. From the beginning, between him and Verona Lennox there had been an enmity, veiled only under the polish and conventions of good society. Verona's intense selfishness, her bland air of assumption, her superior faculty of taking things to herself irrespective of the rights of others, were antagonistic to Jack's generous nature. On her arrival in the city all society, with the exception of the Wellingtons and a few others, had received her with open arms and paid homage to her to her heart's content; but the Wellingtons' air of being the very centre of things, their utter indifference to phenomena, their apparent disregard of her great importance had been a check and chill to her arrogant disdain. It had been a rebuff, and a rebuff was something which Verona Lennox could never forgive.

She had already shown her resentment in many a wary way. The mistress of Apsley House had gone on her way, indifferent as to their very existence, and had allowed the evil to pass her by or gather about her skirts as it would, but Jack Mainton's nature was to push the evil from his path as a man pushes a rock from a smooth wheel track and leaves a clean pathway. He had done it with Verona, but the rock had thorns and was not easily pushed; and it was the fact that he saw danger looming up in the distance, that she would in time prove no mean foe, which made Jack now so strongly object to her presence at Fernwylde.

"By some trick of the trade Stubs has caught the people's fancy. She influences Stubs. I suppose he wants to keep her away from the others. He might have sent her to Glenhurst or Earnscliffe."

"You would shift the sin to other shoulders."

"It would be no sin for them to do it."

"Your logic, like your English, is incomprehensible."

"In their case it would be a matter of diplomacy or political economy. Here it is a case of your eating Tantalus's apple."

"I fail to see why my sin should be greater than the sins of the ladies of other places."

"If you cannot see it now you will in time."

"How analytical you grow."

"If people were more analytical they would save themselves most of the troubles of their own lives."

"But logic and analysis spoil our illusions and leave us discontented."

"They are harmful—no, harmful is not strong enough. They are deadly when they spoil one's ideals and leave one without any others, but when they displace the old ones with brighter, and better, and higher, and more hopeful ones they have served the highest purpose in life."

"The wise sage's analysis didn't keep him from the fatal hemlock."

"The fatal hemlock was the result of bigotry, ignorance and prejudice. It was no trouble for the sage to meet it. It was rather a relief. It was only an entrance into a more congenial atmosphere, a place where he would be better understood and appreciated. His analysis helped him to look at it in that light, and made him take the hemlock rather than the open prison doors."

"You need not worry; we have no fatal hemlocks before us as a retributive incentive to our present actions."

"Haven't we? The world's full of them. The majority of its gods to-day are as false as when his persecutors worshipped the clay and molten images in the days when the smoke of sacrifice rose from the Parthenon, and lions and tigers bounded in the Flavian amphitheatre. But it's hemlock of our own making that hurts. You said so yourself the other day."

"How eloquent you grow! You can really use good English when you are interested."

"What is wrong with Hamlet to-night?" asked Grace Austin as she came in with Mrs. Cecil and Mr. Lester from a long walk in their favorite woods and dim green old gardens.

"He is giving me a lesson in political economy."

"Moral economy, you mean."

"The two are inseparable."

"In this case."

"In all cases."

"Was he objecting to all this?" asked Mrs. Cecil, as her eyes wandered over the suite of rooms, where many guests were engaged in varied amusements. "Surely this is a scene which would inspire a Watteau and charm even a Vandyke."

"As pretty as the one you have left?" asked Jack, as he drew a chair to the window for Miss Austin, and seated himself by her side, while his cousin moved away. "How could you leave the gardens for this?"

"This is beautiful, too. Plato loved his garden, but yet—like you—he was a veritable St. Simon in permitting his dramatic instinct to predominate, thereby deriving comfort and happiness in the cynic contemplation of the frailties and inconsistencies of human nature."

Jack looked at his companion in surprise. He hadn't looked for this in her.

"What did you bring in with you?"

"Moonlight."

"I thought so; the face is the mirror of the heart," he replied, while the Southerner's face grew warm.

"Not always," added Mrs. Cecil. "It may be in nature, but not in society. Society wears a mask."

"And this mask is the bunkum of our world. It's the bunkum that makes a candid soul sick. We're always saying things we don't mean and meaning things we don't say. One's ears are continually dinned with, 'How nice!' 'How lovely!' when it is really boredom. We simulate a sympathy with things we would like to kick out of existence. We drown all our likes and dislikes in one universal sea of whitewash. If society wears a mask, it is a mask of hypocrisy," said Jack, who was in one of his depressing moods.

"You would strip life of its illusions."

"I would strip it of its hypocrisies," replied he. venting his ill-humor at the Lennoxes' presence, in plain words, bristling with dislike.

"Are they hypocrisies? Hypocrisy intends to deceive; we don't," said his cousin, who had come for Grace Austin to join in a game of whist. "It is as easy to say the same thing gracefully as to say it rudely, to appear to be interested as to express boredom, to smile as to frown, to be pliable as to be stiff. If that's what you call whitewash it gives smoothness and amiability to our daily intercourse. and is as necessary to society as whitewash is to the walls of a hospital or oil to the wheels of a machine. Society reflects back ourselves as chameleons reflect the color of the substance on which they rest."

"Are there no forces outside ourselves which touch our lives— forces we cannot overcome?"

"Avoid them."

"That may be very good diplomacy, but yet there's a touch of the coward in it."

"You would knock them all down. Since pistols and swords have gone out of fashion it would only bring you to the police courts. That would only savor of poor taste. We are living in an age that says all those things without giving any very serious meaning to them. We are forced to do so. Custom and fashion influence our ideas of ethics and etiquette as they do of dress.

Ruskin looked upon dice as we look upon dynamite. The degree of politeness which might be thought effeminate adulation in Russia, would be regarded as barbarism in France. When one is in Rome one must do as the Romans do, even to the eating of abnormally sized geese livers. This is an age of enlightenment. You want one of Ruskin's cold mutton Sunday dinners to bring you to your senses."

"If all these things mean an age of enlightenment, one would prefer living with the savages where hands are not given to friend and foe alike, and where men eat bread with none but those they consider honorable and upright. As it is, one can never tell who are one's friends and who one's foes," continued Jack, venting his resentment in still plainer words as Verona Lennox's silvery laughter reached his ear.

"Do you think one can do that in any line of life? That power of distinction or selection is reserved for the dog," said Lester, as he reached his hand out through the open window and patted Nell Gwynne's head, and returned the affectionate glance of her great brown eyes. "To do so, we would have to accept of Momus the buffoon's suggestion, and have a door in the human heart."

"That would make us all modern Don Juans."

"Jack would have us all Dr. Johnsons," said his cousin. "His bad manners cling to him like Sinbad's burden. He would need the shade of Thackeray here to give him the lesson it gave to the company who suggested asking Adam himself as to his parentage, in order to decide the problem which has worried philosophers and scientists for twenty centuries. 'You'd look well going up to a man, and saying, Excuse me, sir, but—ah—was your father a monkey?' said he."

"Thackeray was a snob himself."

"His snobbery was certainly preferable to Dr. Johnson's unconventionality and bluntness. Good manners are to particular society what good morals are to society in general, their cement and security. If one doesn't like our society, one can make one for himself out of his own mind, conscience and heart, and be contented," said Modena.

"Then Mr. Mainton's enjoyment must be intense. His conscience is clear; his mind a veritable St. Simon's; his heart—" and the Southerner paused and looked down the long suite of rooms, to where in the distance Helen Lester was playing in minor chords to Mr. Linden.

"There is discord in Helen's music. It has been wailing for the last half hour. Go and see if you can put some harmony—some heart, into it. I want Grace," said his cousin.

"Can't do it," replied Jack, taking out his watch. "And I'm afraid I'll have to ask you to excuse me, too. My country calls me," and he arose and sauntered out through the open door and made his way round to his den, where out of the confusion of it all he hammered some hard facts and sound theories for his morning edition.

"Jack doesn't take very well to Verona's presence," said Mrs. Cecil to Lester, as the others moved away. "He doesn't care for her."

"She will make him. She has the faculty of making people do what she wants them to do. She is very far-seeing. She has the situation fixed before it arrives. One walks into it and doesn't see it until the trap is sprung. She is a very clever woman. She takes out of life all there is in it, and takes it for herself, too," replied Lester.

"Then she is an exception. She should be admired. Talleyrand says that no one born since the Commune can really know how sweet human life can become—that we do not know how to love. But yet it is better so. If we do, it tears the heart to pieces, and the aftermath—" and then she checked herself, and looked out through the green gloom of trees to where a full moon lay slumberous on the tops of the dense foliage bordering the Idlewylde.

"Love that is given in vain is yet lovely. Yours hasn't been given in vain. You wouldn't recall it if you could," he continued gently, as he drew forward the draperies a little to hide her from the strong lights of the room.

"I wonder if I would," she thought to herself, as she still continued to gaze out, and her mind went back into the past.

Her ancestor had been a titled officer in the Carignans. He had remained and had become Seigneur of one of the oldest French families in the country. Mrs. Cecil while very young had been sent to Paris, and had spent the greater part of her life in that city. On her mother's side her relatives were influential political people in France. She had made her home with them, and when young had married a man of high rank in military circles. They had loved each other with a great love, a love based on passion and mutual sympathies, and augmented by a similarity of taste and character. One child had been born to them, a child whom they both had idolized, but death had claimed it at five. Mrs. Cecil had been prostrated under the affliction, but with courage she had hidden her grief and had resumed all her old interests in her hus-

12

band's calling in life. He was an extremely handsome man, very popular, chivalrous and tender-hearted, but at times arrogant and exacting. He was a man of great firmness and decision in performing his duties, intellectual, and winning in manners but rather thoughtless and selfish in passions. His wife had been devoted to him and his interests, and their life together until the death of their child had been ideally happy, but after its death he had changed. He had grown morose and irritable and had absented himself from home as much as it was possible for him to do so. Then he had met a fascinating woman whom he had known in his younger days. She was a woman of high position, handsome, clever and unscrupulous. She had loved the handsome young soldier in youth, but through family interference had been forced to marry her cousin. He had lived but a year, and great wealth was now hers. She had never remarried, and when she had met her old lover once more, her slumbering passion had revived even stronger than it had been in youth. At first, Strath Cecil had not intended being unfaithful to his wife, but he had met his old love when his life seemed very empty and aimless, and he had lingered in her presence, at first because she made him forget himself, and latterly because he felt within himself a desire to do so. She had within her the power to rewaken some long slumbering chords of feeling within him. In her presence he began to feel a new life, a new interest, new desires, and as these grew in force willingly he lingered by her side. She was sought by men of high rank and position, and her preference for himself stimulated his vanity, while her fascination excited his fancy and her wit satisfied his intellect, and as day by day passed by his slumbering passions grew into great desires. But she was a very wise woman and knew the necessity of conciliating the comments of the world, not from any motive of morality, but because her happiness to a great extent depended upon the world's treatment of her, and she knew that the world does not easily forgive a continual breach of accepted modes of life.

She knew all the ways and the wiles of the women of her world, but on him she never exercised them. She saw he was surfeited with such, and that it was this surfeit that had caused his satiety and fatigue. He had but gone to La Trappe, and his heart was like a luxuriant weed or flower which had withered and frozen during the winter's snows, but with many wellsprings of life yet clinging close to the earth, ready to revive under the warming sun's rays of spring. But she knew that the sun's rays which would revive him must be young, virgin, fresh and simple, and she also knew they must be the simplicity of great knowledge. It must be a nature which had in it many resources which would hold his. So she buried all the ways of the present and appealed to him only through the long ago past. Without saying so, she made him feel that her married life had been a martyrdom, and that she had ever been true to him, and that he belonged to her first. It was this sophism which acted as chloral to his conscience in his treatment of his wife.

Mrs. Cecil had been intensely proud, and had gone on her way in silence and with great dignity. She had neither reasoned nor remonstrated with him, but had borne the many indignities to which she had been subjected with great fortitude and in quietude. She knew that remonstrances would be of no avail, and would only serve to lower herself in her husband's estimation. She knew that her husband was honorable, and she did not believe that he was really unfaithful to her. Had she believed so, she would have left him without a word. But she understood him well— knew him better than the other woman did, and acted according to her light. She continued in her devotion to his interests, and it was only when her pain became unbearable that she left his side and her duties to spend a few months in her native land, but invariably she returned and fulfilled her duties as his wife.

Her health had been impaired by the loss of her child. As the years passed her loss and her loneliness increased rather than grew less. She felt she could have borne and forgiven his indifference to herself, but his conduct seemed to her an immeasurable wrong to his child's memory. She had come from a family whose foundation had been faith. She had lost the simple faith of her fathers, but yet so instinct had it become within their blood that a broader, more visionary, more indefinite faith forever circled near her, though it forever eluded her grasp, and her broader views had made her look at death as only an invisible wall. Her child she believed to be living and growing in a fairer world, and that their spirits were ever with her. She would have sinned towards her more in life than in death. Her child had been one with her, and her heart was ever with it, often in loneliness and human weakness, crying out for its clinging touch, its lisping words, its infant caress. It was a holy thing, and she could not easily forgive its father's forgetfulness. She had suffered greatly and her suffering had hardened her in expression, but not in heart. She tried at times to make herself believe that his conduct had killed all the tender fibres of her heart, but she was jealous, and jealousy never exists where there is no love. Her husband's conduct had numbed much in her that had been amiable and loving; he had inflicted in her heart a rent into which the noblest of her nature, or at least its outward display, had sunk and lay buried, and had left her drifting in aimless indifference.

Mr. Lester had been an intimate friend of her husband and knew him as he was. She knew that Lester was aware of all her indignities, and her heart went out to him for sympathy, not that she wanted pity, for the pity of the world to a proud nature is more intolerable than the abandonment itself, but it was a relief to unburden her suppressed feelings to some one when her pain and loneliness became unbearable, and Mr. Lester was her only confidant and consoler.

It was very seldom that she unburdened her overwrought feelings to him, but when she did he was always extremely careful to impress upon her the one and only right course to pursue, that of fidelity and patience, but he learnt as he one day confided to Modena, who ever afterwards was kinder and more sympathetic with Mrs. Cecil, that no woman who loves a man with her whole heart can ever by any other means fill the void in her life caused by her loved one's desertion.

"When have you heard from France?" he now asked her after a short silence.

"A few days ago," she replied.

"I had a letter from Strath to-day. He spoke something of coming here."

"Of coming here!" she exclaimed in great surprise. "He said nothing in mine to that effect."

"No, he did not want to needlessly worry you."

"What do you mean?" she asked in alarm.

"Do not be alarmed," replied Lester, quickly. "He wished me to tell you. He expects there may be serious trouble in the army. He thought of coming here until it passes."

"Is his honor affected?" she asked, quickly, trying to conceal her emotion, but her heart beat so loudly that its pulsation was plainly audible by her friend.

"No, not his, but he is much worried."

An immense relief passed over her face. "He has been worried, and I have been here. What is the matter? Why didn't he tell me?"

"He could not. It would not have been safe to write to you regarding it. His letters might be intercepted. There are serious charges preferred against some officials in high rank. Strath possesses too much knowledge of their actions. When I was in

France he told me he feared it would come to this. He was troubled over it then but could do nothing. You know a man cannot inform; he couldn't resign without his actions being misinterpreted, and the only course left to him was to continue in silence. An investigation is impending."

"I shall go to him at once," she said.

"No, do not do so. At least, do not go to him until you hear from him, and be careful when you write not to say anything. His correspondence is watched."

"But how can I remain here and he in trouble? I could not bear the suspense. My duty is surely by his side."

"Perhaps you can serve his interests better by remaining here. Do not act hastily. He is well aware that you would have been there had you known it. He kept it from you purposely."

"Why should he do so? Does he want me to remain away? I have never complained to him. I have never interfered in his pursuits and pleasures. They displeased, they offended, they outraged me, yet he cannot say I retaliated or murmured."

"It wasn't that; you misjudge him. I am sure his only motive has been to spare you any unpleasantness. You know it's such things as these that bring men to their senses. Don't you see you must be very careful in your actions now? Take time and consider the matter well. Your own good sense will tell you how to act. Your future happiness may depend greatly on the wisdom of your actions now. We never understand each other in life until soul speaks to soul. Who knows but this may be your opportunity. Forgive me for speaking of it, but she is at the very height of power at the present time. The world is at her feet, yet she loves him alone. She cannot forgive you for being his wife. She will not accept him unless she can accept him with the world's favor and approval. She is implicated in this matter. You cannot tell what she might do to implicate him if he refuse her, or if you assert your rights. I would not speak of it, but one is forced to that you may act wisely and well."

"What would you have me do?" she asked, white with emotion. "I cannot sit idly by. It will kill me."

"But there are times in one's life when one is forced to do so. Have you ever had a very near and dear friend sick unto death? You have done all that human power can do. You have administered the strongest and best of medicines and as much as dare be given. You have then to fold your hands and leave the result in other Hands. Will you promise me you will do nothing hastily?"

"I cannot promise you anything to-night. I shall see you in

the morning. I shall go to my room now," she replied, rising, unable any longer to control her feelings, and passing out through the open window she reached her own room by another entrance.

CHAPTER XVII.

" You are going to the city this evening. Take me with you," said Verona Lennox to Keith Kenyon late the next afternoon as they came from off the waters and seated themselves on a rustic bench under a spreading maple tree near the lake shore monastery.

" You are Miss Wellington's guest for the week. She would not forgive me if I did so."

" She will not care. She doesn't care for me. She will be indebted to you if you relieve her of such a burden."

" Surely you wrong her. She would not ask you here if she did not want you."

" You say that as if one didn't know that you alone are responsible for my invitation. Do you think I would have accepted only to please you. The place has no attraction for me without you."

" There is Mr. Patrie."

" A pretty pastime."

" And Mr. Lester. He is surely more than a pastime. He will amuse you for the evening."

" Mr. Lester is very nice, but his amusement will keep."

" How ungrateful you are. There are few who would not remain when offered an evening with Mr. Lester."

But Verona only demurred.

A short time previous to this she would have done so in order to secure Mr. Lester, but she did not need to do so now. He was now hers, she had subdued him. On her first advent into the city she had felt that Lester Lester felt towards her much the same as did Jack Mainton. But this must not be. She had grown to hate Jack Mainton with a sound hatred, but Mr. Lester she needed. She needed him if only to further her purpose against the Wellingtons. She hated the Wellingtons with a hatred born out of antagonism of nature, and later on fostered by personal motives, rivalry and jealousy. Her antagonism sprang from the fact that the Wellingtons embodied that which she most loved and most abhorred. Her mother's blood, her environments and her education had made her patrician in instinct, and had instilled within her the consciousness that all these things were the real things of life, but she was a child of her father's, and her father's blood had in it all the germs of materialism, unrestraint, intrigue, strife, Nihilism, and it was this blood which had at first aroused her antagonism towards the Wellingtons.

They had been long in accepting her, and when they had accepted her, the atmosphere and the harmony of their circle had in it the power to annoy her. Its atmosphere was one of high-bred simplicty. She had felt she was not the central figure in it. Previous to this she had been in many circles which had only accorded her a cordial passing notice. She had accepted the notice, as all that was necessary, and had passed on amused, ephemeral, gay, like a butterfly flying from bower to bower, but here every little thing meant something and everyone was intensely interested in real things and she hadn't time, or will, or patience to grasp these little things and become one of them. Like Don Juan, she would have accorded herself all the privileges, laxities and pleasures of their order without acknowledging its duties and obligations.

Modena Wellington was to it what the lamp is to the moth. She would not be a moth. She would be the lamp, but would attain to the light by intrigue and by adroitness. Modena's work was uninteresting, monotonous, old-fashioned, thankless. Life was too short to be spent in living for others, in toiling and spinning and worrying over others' woes. She loved real life, and wanted all there was in it for herself. To dethrone Modena Wellington might be slow work, but it would be interesting work, and she did not doubt her powers to do it. To do it she must win people to her side. She had won Mr. Lester; but as the days passed by Verona had begun to feel that she was making little real progress with Keith Kenyon. His reserve, his indifference, his easy amiability had gradually awakened her from her security, and as time had passed her inability to secure him had been so forcibly brought home to her that her attentions to others had become less and less, and had become wholly centred upon him.

She saw his loyalty to and preference for Modena Wellington, but she did not fear her as a rival, as she was aware of her betrothal to Carlton Monteith, but with an unerring instinct she felt that it was her person which kept Keith Kenyon silent towards herself.

She was beginning to feel uneasy. The time was growing less day by day; he must be made to commit himself.

Their town-house was closed, but she could without any impropriety go up to the city with him. It would mean much.

"You must take me," she said. "Mr. Lester will keep."

"You would miss one day out of seven of this paradise?"

"Is it a paradise? Isn't that only a studied pose?"

"You want people," he replied.

"And the people don't want me to-night. Mr. Lester has Miss Austin, and when he hasn't her he has that Frenchwoman; Jack Mainton and Mr. Linden are quarreling over Helen Lester, and I am left as a burden on Miss Wellington, and she doesn't want me. She wants Carlton Monteith. She hasn't seen him now for some ten days. I know she is wishing we were all away. Have pity on him—on her—I hear he is pressing her to name the day. Three—four years—is it he has waited? He has been patient. She is going to reward his patience in the fall. No doubt the affair will be a brilliant one," continued Verona as she glanced up to the brow of the hill, where the mistress of the place and her betrothed were seated with others of their guests.

"No doubt," replied her companion, quietly, but without allowing his eyes to follow hers up the hill.

"Why has it been delayed so long? Is he never jealous?"

"Of whom should he be jealous?"

"Of Mr. Lester—of you," she replied.

"If one thought that he had any cause to be, there would be much in life for which to live," he replied, lightly.

She put little credence in his words, but she looked at him closely.

"Do you mean that?"

"Yes. We all worship her."

"Then he need not be jealous; his assurance will rest in numbers. Rumor says they are going to make their home at Apsley House. He will only be a Prince Consort. I would want a real prince."

"There are people for whom it is impossible to find a prince. Their natures are too great."

"Do you mean that she is one?" and she looked at him more closely.

"She is a noble woman."

"As some read nobility. She can sew, she can spin, she can milk her cows and make butter. So can Bridget. No doubt she possesses all the primitive virtues, but one cannot deny that she is narrow-minded, prejudiced and provincial. She has no chic, and she is neither amusing nor interesting. Are you in love with

her that you can see nothing but her virtues? I must tell Carlton
Monteith you want her."

"It would do no good. But let us talk of something else. Even
Arabs and Indians hold sacred the house that shelters them. Why
not we?"

He had spoken to her lightly, but yet she didn't like the tone
of his voice. She changed her tactics. It was not well to arouse
too much interest in this woman.

"Will you take me to the city with you?" she insisted.

"What attraction is there for you in the city? It is deserted
just now."

"I want to see Raynor."

"Is Mr. Stubs in the city?"

"Yes, I had a letter from him last evening."

"I shall bring him out with me in the morning. Will that not
do?"

"Perhaps he cannot come."

"You can write. I shall take your letter."

"But one cannot say all one wishes to say in a letter, and letters
are not safe things. It is very important that I should see him. It
is definitely settled that he secures the seat in the west, and there
are others about to be offered to his candidates."

"That means one against us and the prospect of more. That is
very discouraging."

"It needn't be if you will only take me with you."

"You think you could convince him otherwise?"

"I know it."

"The temptation is great. Almost you tempt me to speak to
your hostess. I am sure she will excuse you when she learns the
cause. Perhaps she could leave Helen in her place and come with
us."

A flush of anger passed over his companion's face, but she
checked the feeling.

"You think she would have influence over Raynor. I am afraid
not. And it wouldn't be fair to Carlton Monteith to take her away
from him."

"How would it do to compromise the matter? We shall go to
Idlewylde and drive back this way," he said, as he looked at his
watch and then rose. "I have an appointment at seven. I haven't
time to make my adieus. I must go. We can leave them with
Miss Austin and Lester."

She arose and put her arm within his.

"You always have your own way."

" Only by having the same way as women."

" This way is very pleasant."

" Especially so when the waters and woods are filled with naiads and hamadryads."

" But they only lived in classical days. The hamadryads were true to one tree. They gave their life to that tree and made a tree of it. I'm afraid most of us live for ourselves," she said, expecting at least a little compliment.

" Surely there are some who live for others."

" Like the mistletoe! They cling to it and sap its strength. Oh, yes! I know the kind you mean, I am not one of them. I am glad I am not. You mean the kind who go about fussing over their children's measles, and their calf's cough, and their husband's bedroom slippers, and the heathen in China, and the poor poor, and a thousand other trivialities, all for their own pleasure and glory, and forget there is a tree in the world. Had I a tree I would see nothing else in the whole world but this one, and I would only live to make it tower over every other one in the whole wide world. I would never rest until I saw him king over all men. I would live for and love only one," she said, with a force and warmth and passion like fire running through her veins, while her person clung close to him in her emotion.

He was surprised and uneasy, as though he had been tasting some unwholesome things. He flushed a little as he looked at her upturned face, and felt the alluring appeal in the depth of her deep grey eyes. He refrained from saying anything, and turned his head away and only said, " We must hurry. It is getting late!" She mistook the meaning of his color and motion, and did not notice the coldness in his words.

" What about Mr. Stubs?"

" What do you mean?"

" Shall I bring him with me, or will you write? There is pen and ink at Idlewylde."

" What would you have me do?"

" You know what we wish."

" What you wish. I care for no other wish but yours."

" Yes, what I want."

" Will it please you if I do?"

" Certainly."

" Then you know I shall do anything to please you. Since that day in Paris—you remember—your will is but mine," and she leaned a little closer on his arm as they came in full view of the people seated on the terrace, and then paused and abruptly withdrew her arm, as they met Grace Austin and Mr. Lester at a turn in the path.

"Will you take my regrets to Miss Wellington. I am due in town at seven. I shall drive Miss Lennox back on my way to town," said Keith Kenyon to Mr. Lester, and then he lifted his hat to the two and passed on to the road leading to Idlewylde.

"She has gone to Idlewylde," said Mr. Patrie, dolefully, to his hostess as his eyes followed Verona Lennox's figure.

From where they sat on the western terrace he could see the two by the water's edge. All afternoon he had watched them dismally, and could now no longer control his chagrin. "Is she coming back?" he asked.

"I do not know; I am not her keeper," answered his hostess.

"I thought you were. I thought she was your guest—not Kenyon's," he said, almost maliciously.

"She is, but guests are invariably allowed to follow their own pleasure. If Mr. Kenyon is her pleasure, we must make him ours also, but keep up your courage, Mr. Patrie; here come Grace and Lester; perhaps they will have a message for you. Patience and perseverance are invariably rewarded.

"I believe they are. The mills of the gods grind slowly and surely. It looks as if Lester is grinding his way to happiness," said Jack Mainton, as Mr. Patrie left them to join some others.

"Have you lost hope? Is he going to win at last?" asked Mrs. Cecil, thinking he referred to the coming contest.

"Oh, I don't mean that; those things do not count for much when the heart's at stake," replied Jack as he watched the two, who had been gathering nuts from a tree in the ravine, now ascend the hill laden with the fruit of their search.

"Is Mr. Lester's heart endangered?" asked the Frenchwoman, casually glancing at her hostess, and thinking what a queer world it was.

She looked pale and tired, while dark shadows showed beneath her eyes. She had not slept the night before. She had not lain down. So deeply moved had she been at what Mr. Lester had told her that she felt her husband's very presence near her. If she closed her eyes, so quickly did the blood flow within her veins that she started up thinking he touched her. In the intensity of her emotion a great remorse was in her for leaving him. It was now she was needed, and to be forced to remain away, and to remain inactive was more than her reason and her nervous system were able to bear. During the night, her one thought, her one desire had been to be by his side, to counsel, to support and to solace him.

After dawn she had fallen into an uneasy slumber, and had awakened late little refreshed, but when her reason and calmer judgments returned they told her she must not act hastily. In the light of day she reviewed her past conduct, and she could not see were all that time to be lived over again that she could have done otherwise. She had seen that Minon Barerre had possessed a potency over him, a great fascination for him. She had seen him seek her company continually. She had done her duties to him as a wife despite it all. She had done all she could, but there was one thing she could not do; she could not stoop to measure weapons with such as Minon Barerre. She was his wife. Their life together had been very happy until of late, and she could not debase herself by stooping to rivalry with another woman for her own husband's affections. She saw that he was, as Mr. Lester had said, a sick child with a disease which must run its course. Physicians, she knew, sometimes gave a poisonous drug to counteract the poison in some diseases, and thus bring their patient to a normal state with refreshed desires for healthy things. And this is what she had done. The one poison must counteract the other. Her health was shattered, and on this plea she had absented herself for a while. He had come with her to the sea-port, and had bade her good-bye on board the boat, and had then returned, and she had turned her face westward not knowing how it would end.

Mr. Lester's few words the previous evening had awakened her to a knowledge of their danger.

He had again sought her early in the morning, and she had told him that she would remain until she received further word from her husband.

She had then gone with her hostess to a distant part of the estate to take some delicacies to an old couple who were favorites of hers. On her return she had gone to the field sports, and had held her own with the best there. She had lunched with the others and been one of them, her companions little divining the great strain under which she was laboring. She was so exhausted that her one wish was that she might go to sleep and forget it all, but it seemed as if sleep had forsaken her.

"It is not my cousin's fault if Mr. Lester's heart is not endangered. He is as great a matchmaker as those people who lived in Rome," replied Modena in answer to her query.

"I think it is. The Southerner is doing him up."

"Then she is doing what many others have tried to do, but have failed to accomplish. His heart has been unresponsive. What sorcery has she used?"

"Love is a sorcerer. It is an alchemy. I suppose they were made for each other."

"He is worthy of the best," said Mrs. Cecil, with an accent of doubt in her tones.

"She is of the best. She has birth and is now famous. What more do you want?"

"Has she heart?"

"A creole heart! They're all heart."

"She doesn't show it in her face. She is very proud and cold."

"I knew Miss Austin when she wore the crown of Comus, and was bedecked and caparisoned with clothes of gold and jewels rare, and no sweeter or humbler heart beat or shone in the face in the whole pageant than hers," said Carlton Montcith, who sat near their hostess.

"What changed her?" asked Mrs. Cecil.

"During her father's troubles and losses she suffered much; she saw almost everything swept away, but that did not harden her until she saw the conduct of those who had been so servile to them in their prosperity. Her study of human nature embittered her against the world for a time. Desperation and resentment. as is so often the case, incited her to work. Her path was full of rocks and thorns for a while, but at last she succeeded. She.has the world once more at her feet, and her pride now is intellectual, which, even in its humility, is the stiffest kind, and mingled with that pride is contempt for those who would have trampled her in the dust had she proved a failure."

"That isn't very generous; since she is so great she can afford to be amiable."

"She couldn't be otherwise if she tried. She is like Josephine. She is too tender-hearted. But she loves the world; she is sensitive; she has been hurt; she has learned to keep herself in reserve so that it cannot hurt her again. Like Lucille, she has learned from the world to shield her own heart."

"Lester is thawing her out," said Jack, as he watched the rich color come and go in her expressive face, as she and her companion stood for some moments together on the brow of the hill, watching two red squirrels gathering beech nuts and stowing them away in their winter home. She carried in her hand her sunshade, which was decked with crimson maple leaves, and the breeze from the river played with the loose, dark ringlets on her brow.

Her countenance had in it that rich creole, creamy color. so delicate and susceptible to warm blushes and sparkles of animation and interest. Her intercourse with Mr. Lester had dispelled all memories of her unhappy past, and she was herself once more.

He had opened the beech nut burrs for her, and had taken out the fruit; he had been repartee and she had replied; he had said sweet nothings and in return she had let run riot that subtle charm which is so innate in creole blood.

When her mask of reserve was removed and her true self shone out, as it did in her intercourse with Mr. Lester, he caught glimpses of that sorcery, charm and passion which are almost obsolete relics of those southern Bourbon days when manners, and etiquette, and poetic love held sway; but yet there was something elusive within her which he could not fathom, and it was this charm within her which was drawing him on; this something within her which had the power to attract him more than he had thought it possible for anyone to do. Her intercourse and presence were beginning to give him consolation, and he was beginning to feel that she was filling a void which had hitherto existed in his life. He knew the memories of his early loves would always remain with him. He had tried to fill their places with other things, with his studies and his politics, but each day he was beginning to feel more and more that the joys of the intellect and the incense and excitation of the world were failing to satisfy all that was in his nature.

He contemplated her now as she stood facing the afternoon sun with a flush on her face. There was a poetic sentiment and passion within his nature which she was touching. The scene appealed to him. It was Indian summer. The dry leaves, crimson and amber, rustled at their feet, while a leaf drifted down from an over-hanging oak, and another and another, and played around them; the nuts from the nearby trees pattered down one by one into the rustling leaves. A thousand elusive perfumes of autumn rose to meet them. October, in all her gorgeous dress, sat upon her throne; dying daisies, paling golden-rod, wild rose thorn and luscious grapes hanging on dismantled vines were round about them. Wild ducks passed in dark flocks away down the Idlewylde. The lord-like pines bordering the ravine looked lordlier than ever towering above the dismantled oaks and maples, and seemed to touch the lowering clouds which hung over the river.

A little stream ran gurgling and plunging round the rocks at the foot of the ravine, anxious to rest itself in the Idlewylde.

"There are two kinds of strength," he said to himself, recalling the poet's words. "One the strength of the river which pushes its way through continents to rest in the sea, the other, the sea, self-sufficing and eternal. It must be so with love."

Almost he had spoken when the sound of music reached them.

Some of the guests, who had returned, had begged their hostess to permit a stray minstrel and a dog, who had found their way to Fernwylde that morning, to be brought around. The minstrel's music was played in minor chords, and was wild, and sad, and plaintive, and full of the love of early days and early loves, and as he drifted into old familiar folk-songs, songs which had been sung in the days of long ago by the coureur-de-bois, the miners coming from their winter camps, and the lumbermen on the river barges in these same woods, and on those same waters, the mistress of the place and some of her guests, moved by many memories, joined their voices in a closing chorus, and as her voice reached the lovers on the brow of the hill his heart beat quick and his blood flowed warmly, much more so than it had been when moved by his companion's wit and charm and the autumn scenery.

The spell was broken. He would not speak. He could not as yet; he turned with her and joined the others on the terrace.

At the same moment Keith Kenyon drove up the driveway to the lawn with Verona Lennox and diverted their attention to other matters.

CHAPTER XVIII.

"Why that frown upon your brow, Grace?" asked the mistress of Fernwylde as she entered the library from the rotunda late the same afternoon.

"I have been trying to write, to compose, to create, but I cannot without inspiration; it will not come. This should have been sent away a week ago, but here it lies waiting for the spirit to move me," replied the young authoress, rising from the ormolu table at which she had been writing. She was not in the mood for writing, but the publisher was depending upon it, and it must be sent at once. She had been in the mood in the afternoon, but her mood had changed. She had seen the change in her late companion and had divined the cause. It had made her sad, and she could not write when she was sad. She wanted all her work to be a work of art, and she knew that all art was revelation and all art was praise. There was something wrong somewhere; she could not praise.

"Cannot one write without inspiration?" asked Modena.

"If one is forced to do so, one may sit down and place words, polished phrases and hard facts together, but the essence, the beauty, the music is cold and unfeeling. Inspiration like enthusiasm is infectious. Only writers who write from inspiration are worthy of being read. All other writing is like the dull outlines of those rocks, where the rays from the setting sun fail to reach," replied the authoress, as she looked out to the northern slope of the Idlewylde.

"Then all knowledge comes from within, and one must have the sun in one's heart before one can become inspired," said her hostess, smilingly.

"Certainly."

. "And if it isn't there, you should put it there," said Jack Mainton. "It shone brightly this afternoon. I saw it shining. You were with it."

"Oh, I dare say it did, but one cannot put it there at will. It is a gift from the gods," replied the authoress, coloring slightly.

"Oh! oh! All our happiness depends upon something outside ourselves. What a melancholy thought!"

"We weren't speaking about happiness. We were speaking about genius," she replied quickly.

"Is it a gift from the gods? Philosophy tells us it is the product of education."

"How common-place you are, Jack! Do leave us our Cock-lane ghosts."

"Education may give us the embellishment, but it does not give us the foundation. This power to see and feel into the very heart of things, and make others see and feel it, is instinctive and cannot be manufactured.

"Bravo, Grace! We are so glad you said so. We have always believed in the existence of Dr. Johnson's ghosts; now we know it."

"All great minds have always believed it. No great work can be produced without this conviction."

"I was passing the dairy this morning. Bridget could not get the butter to come. The cream was in a froth. Instead of using a little warmth and giving us good butter for dinner, she was invoking all the saints in the calendar, begging of them to entice the witches from the churn. Methought at the time she could write better poetry than make good butter," said Jack, irrelevantly.

"Bridget is a nice girl," said the authoress, smilingly.

"You prefer her witches to good butter?"

"Certainly I do. They are my bread and butter."

"I am sorry I don't, most men do not."

"That shows the degeneracy of man. He thinks more of his bones and body than of his brain."

"I'm afraid we do. You may write good poetry as a pastime, but if you want to please us you must first learn to make good butter."

"Sappho or Hypatia at the churn! How incongruous the thought!"

"We used the churn metaphorically. Methinks they graced their position well."

"Then they were exceptions. Philosophy is not the heart's handmaiden," said Carlton Monteith.

"They were lovers of the humanities, not the sciences."

"You think logic and heart do not go hand in hand," said Modena, as she placed on a side table some luscious grapes which a servant had brought in. "You would advocate ignorance. I'm so sorry. I see a lonely future staring me in the face."

"You needn't be afraid," said her cousin, as he helped the ladies to some grapes. "You have enough heart to keep more than its share of blood from the brain and face."

"You are implying I am a blockhead and no beauty."

"Oh, no; your worst enemy would be forced to admit your intelligence and good looks."

"What a pretty compliment coming from the lips of a Gautier or Berlioz," said the Southerner. "A proper mixture of heart, mind and beauty. Prometheus gave us a perfect man; like the painter of Mona Lisa you have given us 'a perfect woman, nobly planned.'"

"An ideal one!" said their hostess. "It exists only in his imagination."

"That's all that counts. It's what people think we are, not what we are, that gives us standing in the world."

"What nonsense! It's the real John that's honored. The world isn't easily deceived."

"It all depends upon what you mean by the word world."

"What could one mean but what the wise bard meant? One's own still voice and the opinion of a select few. Any wise man makes this his world," answered Lester for his hostess.

"One would like to borrow your glasses of indifference and courage."

13

"They're glasses that cannot be borrowed. They are like the golden apples of Hesperides; they must be fought for and won."

"And the dragons guarding them wound, torture, murder the most of us before we win them," thought Mrs. Cecil, who sat silent, sunk so deep in retrospection that all that was said around her seemed but a dream, a far-away dream in which she took no part.

"Grace says there are ghosts or gods at the bottom of things, giving gifts."

"How analytical you are. You remind one of Diogenes with his lantern hunting for an honest man. Too much introspection is depressing. It made Goethe a Werther, Byron stand on a rocky precipice over hungry waves, and Dante look down into the fumes of an unfathomable gulf. Don't do it."

"The temptation to do it would be great, could one only see what they saw."

"Have you seen Miss Lennox? Where is she? I want her," asked Mr. Patrie, who was more interested in the heiress than in what the poets saw.

"She will be down in a few minutes. She is resting."

"Is Kenyon coming back to-night? Someone is here inquiring for him," asked Jack.

"I heard his mother say she expects him at Idlewylde, but it will be late."

"There is Verona now, Mr. Patrie. I heard her say she wanted to see the swans on the Idlewylde by moonlight. Take her out. Mrs. Sangster or Mr. Lester will go with you. Do you wish to go, too, Grace? You wanted the sun in your heart to aid you in your art; the moon is more inspiring.

"My poor piece is past the moonlit stage. I think I shall remain here and complete it with hard facts," said Grace. as she watched the others pass down the moonlit aisle of roses.

"Don't do so," said Mr. Lester, seating himself near her. "We really do not need hard facts. Life gives us a repletion of them. We want beautiful thoughts."

"They come from within, from knowing one's own mind, and the mind of those akin to ours, and Modena says this is depressing."

"One doesn't like to dispute such a great person as Modena, but in the interest of truth one must. The great Corinne says it is only depressing when one separates religion from philosophy. She says a synthesis of these two opens up infinite possibilities, and gives us the highest life," said Helen Lester, in the tone of one whose reason and religion ran together like warp and woof to weave the web of a holy life.

"But where can one get truth? When the gods on Olympus cannot see it, how can poor mortals pick it out of all the romanticism, relics of superstition, mysticism, hysteria and pretty paganisms which are continually dinned into one's ears to-day?" exclaimed Mrs. Cecil, interrogatively.

"Hush, here comes Mr. Linden; he will hear you."

The young minister smiled and seated himself beside Mrs. Cecil, while his clear, luminous, clairvoyant eyes dwelt upon her with extreme kindness and comprehension. "Have Augustine's child-like faith," said a modern teacher to a faithless world, but the young minister knew that in anyone whose intelligence was greater than the emotions, the intellect must be appeased and satisfied before one can return to or attain the highest state of development, that of simplicity. Mrs. Cecil's intelligence he knew was great. Her cradle creeds were gone, and she was without a rudder. Philosophy had brought her no peace, but he knew that peace must come through philosophy.

"One does not need to go to Olympus for truth," he said kindly and lightly, in order to dispel any sacerdotalism from his manner and give it the air of a logician. "Truth lies dormant in every human heart and mind. Nature placed it there when she made man. It is inherent and instinctive. We have only to open the doors and windows and let it come out.

> "'An honest man, through all his strivings dark,
> Finds the right way if led but by a spark.'"

The intellect is man's spiritual nature; he is created with infinite intuitions and with great desires for truth and knowledge as is so plainly evidenced in child life. He reflects, studies, learns, acts, observes and thinks, and in all his strivings he is led by this spark, and as he does so the scales and sloughs fall away, and the spark grows brighter and brighter until it becomes as bright as its source, the All-Ego. Ignorance is the only sin; we cannot sin if we know. There, what a sermon I have given you. I really didn't mean to, but these things creep out unawares sometimes," he said, kindly.

"I needlessly set foot upon a worm, I slander my dearest friend, I murder my enemy. I know these to be wrong, yet I do wrong."

"Ah, pardon me. You believe them to be wrong. We must learn to distinguish between belief and knowledge. If you knew them to be wrong, you could not do them. That would be an utter impossibility. All nature would revolt and betray you."

"What do you mean by nature?"

"Miss Lester's synthesis of heart and mind."

The Frenchwoman's eyes opened wide with wonder, and she remained silent, her mind working rapidly.

"Your point is very fine," she said at length. "It makes one wish for an Archimedes lens to develop this spark into a burning fire, a fire that would eat the world up, the whole world with all its injustices and cruelties and despairs. One really longs to hear the fire bells of peace and rest."

Mr. Linden's face grew very grave as his eyes dwelt upon his companion. During Mrs. Cecil's early married life he had known her for some years. He had left Paris before the death of her little child. He was aware there was something wrong, but what it was he did not know.

They were seated apart from the others.

"You are in trouble," he said, very gently. "Your trouble has warped your good sense, and clouded for a while your vision. When it clears away you will say that love is the origin and essence of all things. Human nature craves for it from birth to death. It's the only medicine which will soften. A woman's faith, hope and heaven is in her home. She can make it what she will; the home rules the world. It all depends upon one's self. Man is but clay in your hands. You can make him what you will." "The love of an honest man will make any woman believe in heaven," he was going to add, but he had heard faint rumors, and she had told him nothing, and he could give her no personal hope, and he only said:

"You won on the green this morning. What was your reward?"

"The joy and pride of winning, and the joy and pride of having won."

Mr. Linden was silent a moment, and then looked at her kindly and smiled.

She smiled, too.

"The true joy and the true pride. What was your reward, Miss Wellington? You won, too."

"Mine?" said Modena, "The clapping of the hands of this world which Jack and Mrs. Cecil deplores so much."

"You love its applause?" smiled Mr. Linden.

"Yes. I wish the gods had been as kind to me as they have been to Grace that I might do something to give me the right to sit on the house-tops, and listen to every street arab praising me."

"Even to the writing of a rag-time song," said Jack.

"Yes, even to a rag-time song if it touches our hearts and makes us happier; happiness is a better educator than the classics."

"Then people should be educated; they get nothing but rag-time tunes."

"That's rather severe on Miss Austin."

"Oh, there are a few exceptions."

"The world doesn't want to be educated; it wants to be amused. If one doesn't want to be relegated to the place described in Hume's letter to Adam Smith, one must write to amuse, not to instruct. Carlyle and Mill are left unread on the shelf, while every twopenny novelette is worn threadbare," said Jack from where he sat near the open window waiting anxiously for Keith Kenyon's return.

A disquieting message had come early in the evening. Stubs had succeeded in placing his candidates in several more safe constituencies, and in several others a third party was threatening the peace of the field. The matter was more serious than he anticipated, and he listened impatiently for the sound of carriage wheels.

"And yet one always feels that one might at least respect the intelligence of one's readers, and write something better," said the Southerner, who of late had been striving to do so.

She loved her work and was wholly interested in it. Her earlier works had been light. She possessed a fertile imagination and creative mind; her childhood's experience and the memories of her parent's tales of the Confederacy had furnished her with interesting themes. She had always loved the old Greek myths, and these had furnished her with beautiful metaphors and illustrations, and she had revelled more in love dreams, poetry, music in language, fascinating pictures and charming descriptions, and it was only in the book she had lately written that she had launched out into the questions which were absorbing the attention of the present age.

Of late she had studied history, and she had realized the demoralization which extreme doctrines and laxity of morals had caused in the cities of old, the homes of wits and philosophers, of casuists and rhetoricians, of poets and satirists. She had seen that it invariably leads to atheism and sensuality, and often to the confines of a strange credulity. The tendency of the world in which she had been reared had alarmed her, and she had lent herself to the accomplishment of a great work.

The knowledge had come home to her, that in her earlier works she had been surfeiting the fancy and feelings, and leaving the intellect empty. She felt in reviewing her books that there was nothing in them to which one might go for comfort and consolation when one's light was low. They were healthy, amusing and pleasant pictures, but in them was little food for growth, and she had resolved to do better. She felt her incompetency for the task. She knew how immature the very best that she would write would appear in the eyes of the learned and wise. At times she felt that all that was good and true had been said by the immortals of old, and had been written by their hands in music so heavenly that any product of the present age was as darkness is to light, as discord is to harmony, compared with those of the past.

At such times she would grow discouraged, and would lay aside her work. "Why should people read such trash?" she thought, judging the world by her own mind, when they may read the very souls of the immortals. But her inner voice was not to be quieted. Nature was strong; it would assert itself in expression. Individuality would seek an outlet and recognition. Many disappointments and discouragements had been hers, and she had almost despaired of success, but she had persevered to the end. Her southern nature had brought out the passion and poetry which were necessary to make it interesting and a work of art, while her northern had lent that energy for the great work of research, reflection and practical application which are necessary in such a work. She had been fearless, but charitable and optimistic in her parallelisms. She had possessed great hopes for its usefulness. It had become famous, and the author had felt it was worthy of its fame. She had felt when the last word had been written, and she had reviewed and revised it, the joy and pride of a creator in the creation of something of both use and beauty. With the proceeds of her work she had redeemed some of her old homes and repaired her fallen fortunes and was now resting, only writing at intervals for pleasure or from generosity, and a strong sense that it is not well to allow one's talents to remain folded in a napkin or sicken in a ball-room.

Her creole pride had at first strongly rebelled against the necessity of work but since she had tasted of the beauty, joys and freedom of an active, productive life, she could not readily relinquish it.

"But the average reader doesn't want knowledge. He doesn't want to be made to think; he only wants blood, thunder, murder, scandal, gossip. He doesn't want philosophy or internal history," insisted Jack, who had been trying to raise the standard of the press to that of journalism, but who had found it up-hill work.

"He is better without it," said Verona Lennox, who had returned from the waters. The swans in the moonlight were not interesting with Mr. Patrie as a companion, and on the still, clear night air she had heard in the distance the sound of carriage wheels.

"Philosophy in fiction spoils all our rose pinks and super-latives," said Mrs. Cecil.

"You are surfeited with the sciences. You want to return to superlatives. Then there is really hope awaiting you," said Jack to her.

"There is your hope coming now—or Miss Lennox's," replied Mrs. Cecil to him, as Keith Kenyon drove up to the door. "His brow is clouded. I'm afraid he hasn't brought much hope with him, but he has brought Mr. Stubs. Verona is claiming them. It looks as though they are her hopes. Grace has raised fiction to an art. She has clothed it with mental history and made it philo-sophy's handmaiden. We have raised politics to a science. We have draped it with keen calculation, a matter of an eye for an eye and a tooth for a tooth, and made it love's handmaiden. It is beginning to look real interesting. I wonder how people will take to it."

"Which? Grace's mixture, or politics and love?"

"Both."

"A mixture of metaphysics and romance is generally about as agreeable to the palate of the people as a fine sauce made up of wormwood and olive oil."

"And the other?"

"The mixture isn't made yet," said Jack as Mr. Stubs entered the room.

Their hostess advanced and greeted him, but despite her efforts to the contrary, with little warmth and enthusiasm. She was beginning to see things as her cousin saw them. Verona Lennox's arrogance of manner and her monopoly of Keith Kenyon were beginning to have in them the power to irritate her.

"You have come in time to help defend us against Jack's attacks," she said, with a faint tinge of irony in her voice. "He says things are in a bad way. You drove out? It has turned quite cold. Will you wait for some warm refreshments?"

"I cannot say. It rests with Kenyon. I am in his hands, and I suppose he is in my cousin's. I shall have to ask Verona. It all depends upon what she says. What's the matter with Mr.

Mainton now? Are not things going to please him. What a pretty room! What a pretty scene! Within its walls and with such fair ones, one might well forget all outside. If he murmur, how ungrateful to such a group. Discord should be unknown here," replied Mr. Stubs, in his own bland way.

"So it would be, if discord would only stay without, but invariably he's a sly god—goddess. Although Janus has two faces he isn't a good doorkeeper. He allows her to creep in, here, there and everywhere," said Jack, with a bluntness equal to Mr. Stubs' blandness.

But his bluntness was no daunt to Mr. Stubs' ubiquity.

"Yes, the evening is cold. It will take Verona some time to decide. Something warm? Thank you. May I sit here?" he said, as he seated himself by Grace Austin's side. "You remind one of civilization," he continued sententiously, as he took something warm which a servant had brought in.

Jack turned from him.

"According to your theory one would need to keep George Herbert's broom going continually to keep one's house clean," said Mrs. Cecil to him.

"Jack should use his own broom. The press is the most powerful of all modern weapons of warfare, more powerful than the surplice or the war office. It should mould our maxims and morals."

"Don't become personal," replied Jack, and then he smiled dubiously to himself, as he mentally recalled the words of Lord North, 'The press overflows the land with its black gall and poisons the mind of the people.' "If it tried to do so its back would break under the burden. It would die of starvation."

"You insist on saying there is no great demand for good reading."

"I mean to say there hasn't been, and I mean to say that those who have given it, have had to live like Marion, on the food which comes from above, and that isn't very fattening food, but I'm glad to say it's improving in quality."

"You mean there is an awakening and growing desire for better reading. You mean our newspapers are devoting their columns more to patriotism and less to partyism. Then there is hope for our country!"

"If women will only stay out, and not muddle up things again," muttered Jack as Verona Lennox's voice reached them from the doorway.

"How ungallant of you to say so! Blasphemy against the

gods was punished by stoning on the Acropolis. You should be banished from their presence. I am so glad Mr. Linden is here to take our part."

Jack refrained from taking up the cudgels against Mr. Linden who sat in the embrasure of an adjoining window with Helen Lester.

"If the part which Mr. Linden represents were played more perfectly, it would pave the way for a more perfect press," said Mrs. Cecil.

"Why did you write? Was fame your aspiration?" asked the young curate quickly, addressing the young authoress, anxious to turn the conversation, fearful of its turning upon the pulpit, for many of the politicians were his own adherents, and he had been too timid, and too sensitive to ridicule, to press his ideals, and his conscience was not at ease.

The young authoress smiled vaguely, almost sadly, as many and varied memories and emotions flashed through her mind. She forgot the young curate had asked her a question and failed for a moment to reply. Her creole blood was strong within her and she had many moods. This afternoon she had been bright and full of joy, but to-night she realized that life was passing away, leaving its shadows with her and allowing the substance to wander on. Yes, she had loved its shadows and its sunshine. In the days gone by, she had dreamed of fame and honor. At the publication of her last work she had received it. It was the reception of what she had so long desired, it was the homage of the people, some who had loved her and some who had forsaken her. It was one of those hours in life, when her heart had leaped with joy within her, that she had been able to demonstrate to her world that she was worthy of its homage; but even in that hour for which she had so passionately and so arduously striven, the fate of all genius was hers. There had crept into her an awakening sense of loneliness in life, and a knowledge of the necessity of keeping warm hearts near the human heart. She was beginning to feel that the praise from the lips of one would be infinitely dearer and sweeter than the praise from all others in the world. But the praise from the lips of this one was bestowed elsewhere, so she only said to the young curate—

"Why did I write? Fame? Oh, no, I think not. The glory isn't worth the game. One doesn't really care."

"You shouldn't say so," said Lester. "You do care. You really do care."

"We all care," said Modena, as her eyes met those of Keith

Kenyon's, as he stood in the lights which came from the open doorway. His brow was drawn together in deep lines and his face was dark as he discussed something rather warmly with his companion. "We care very much," continued Modena, lightly, as she felt his eyes follow her. "Nature made us to care. I am like Dean Swift. I would write my rag-time song as he wrote his book, that others might treat me as a lady as they treated him as a lord. I am like Nero. I would pipe simply that people might praise, or I would praise if people would only pipe."

"And are you like Racine and Gray? Would you drown yourself in a bath tub because of their censure?"

"Did they do so? History doesn't say so."

"Figuratively speaking."

"Then they were cowards; cowards, if they cared for the world's censure! Against public ignorance and stupidity the gods themselves are powerless. How funny to think that intelligence should care for ignorance and stupidity!"

All her guests laughed aloud.

"You would care for its praise but ignore its censure," said Lester, as those without attracted by their laughter came within.

"Oh, no; it isn't that. One would be happy with them in their happiness of praise, but one would deplore the lack of appreciation in their censure. One would pity, not ignore."

"You are infallible. You would require a Mandeville here for the vivisection of motive," smiled Lester, indulgently.

"One wonders at your caring for praise, Modena. Genius scorns it. Genius's true joy is the joy of a creator in his creation," said Carlton Monteith.

"But I am not a genius. I am only a very commonplace person. Yours is a beautiful theory, but rather a selfish one. Isn't it? God made the world. I speak with all reverence and respect. He rejoices in our praise of His wonderful work."

"That speaks of a happy heart," said her betrothed, while a great light leaped into his eyes, and he moved nearer her.

But she avoided him, rising and putting out some of the little dogs which had followed Verona Lennox within, finding them too troublesome for general comfort.

"If fame is a literary hack's ambition, he is to be pitied," said Jack. "It is like the devil's water in a desert—a mere mirage, leading one on, ever mocking, ever receding, and if one ever does reach the oasis, it is, as Johnson wrote to Chesterfield regarding his patronage, 'Until one has grown indifferent to it, and cannot enjoy it; solitary and cannot impart it; known and do not want it.'"

"What a Timon! You must think the world very unfeeling and very unkind," said his cousin.

"They are better without it," said Verona Lennox, smiling contemptuously. "It makes literary hacks autocratic and imperious. When they become famous they forget their place. They are now going about, here, there and everywhere. These quill-drivers!"

She was looking well. The light in her eyes was bright and she showed her pearly teeth as she spoke. It was so sweet to have within one's hands the power to do what one wants to do. She had compromised with him in the afternoon, because she saw that by so doing she would have it in her power to make her demands the greater and more forcible in the evening. He had tried to conciliate her and she had shown her teeth, as a cat shows its claws beneath the soft pads of its feet. This torture was sweet to her. She was conscious of her power, and from the height of her consciousness she could repay the rebuffs of a few of those people. Grace Austin was one of the few. She had been accepted into the very holy of holies, whereas Verona Lennox had only been received within the outer pale, so she nibbled at her bouquet and showed her teeth like a young fox-cub as she spoke with disdainful indifference about those people.

"Pardon me, but surely that would be an impossibility," said Mr. Linden, deferentially. "There is only one patriciate, the patriciate which Pericles in the Golden Age created, or, I should say, established."

"What was that?" asked the heiress, shortly, and showing her little teeth more contemptuously.

"The patriciate of genius and of character built up by virtuous activity."

The heiress's lips smiled scornfully.

"But we don't live in the Golden Age. Each age uses its own measure. When we are in Rome we must abide by the decisions of the Romans. This age pays the fiddler for fiddling, the piper for piping, and the scribbler for scribbling, and expects their innate sense will teach them their proper places," she said, with the same air of disdain for things so far beneath her notice.

"Beneath the salt at the table? Then it really is the Golden Age only vice versa. The inventor of a new beer is the arbiter of place. My Lord Maltby feeds the flesh and sits above the salt, while he who feeds the soul sits below. How funny! What snobbery!" said Lester, with good-natured cynicism.

The heiress felt the touch of satire, and her face flushed with annoyance at Mr. Lester's defence and espousal of the young Southerner's cause. Verona's gold was not far from nor free from beer-mugs, and she put Mr. Lester's remarks away in lavender for future reference and turned to a more congenial companion.

"How did you feel towards your critics, Miss Austin?" asked Mr. Linden. "Did they hurt?"

"Hurt!" repeated the young Southerner, while her eyes wandered out to the west, where in the evening she had watched the setting sun hang like a great red ball of fire on the border land of night and day. On its beaten path there were many clouds, small and great, blue and ominous, which had dimmed and darkened its passage of the day, but untouched and brilliant, it stood at the close of the day lord of all.

"Hurt!" she again repeated, while her mind recalled her many and varied emotions. "At first they hurt, you know; they hurt very much; they were so unkind, unjust, unsympathetic, untrue."

"Everyone?" interrupted Mr. Lester.

"Oh, no, no! The criticisms of the learned, of those who really did know, although they pointed out the most serious defects, were charitable, encouraging, almost inspiring; but these were the minority, a very small minority; and as for the majority, they —they—" and the young Southerner's lips curled with scorn. .

"They reminded you of Nero, the egotistical monstrosity, who was on the point of burning every copy of the Iliad and the Æneid because, he said, Homer had no taste and Virgil was without genius," said Mr. Lester.

"And yet the slave's thrust sent Nero to oblivion, while the poets are to-day as permanent, puissant and productive as the sun we watched set to-night," added Mr. Linden in that low, mellow voice, which was so suggestive of many higher and holier and happier things.

"Phocion always suspected himself of some great blunder when he won the applause of the populace," said Carlton Monteith.

"How cynical of you to say so!" exclaimed his betrothed.

"People who contemplate the vault of the Sistine Chapel, the masterpiece of Michael Angelo, draw away with no other result than a bad pain in the neck. Nothing is easier than to malign that which we cannot comprehend."

"We are more unjust than the people, and less comprehensive of them than they are of us," said Modena. "We have no Sistine Chapels. Our people are quite capable of appreciating, and do appreciate anything and all things that are worthy of appreciation. It's because we do not know how to touch their hearts and minds, that they remain passive. They know a good thing when they see it, and if one is clever enough to give it to them they both bite and sing. They are both generous and kind. One cannot stand idly by and hear them slandered," continued she, in her resentment forgetting her English.

"You would have us believe all they say to be true."

"Perhaps what they say is the truth. If it is not, doesn't the poet from the bottom of that fabled well tell us the only way ' is perfect stillness when they brawl'?"

"The same poet tells us, 'The vermin voices buzz so loud; we scorn them but they sting.'"-

"They sting, when and where there is guilt to sting," replied Modena in words which many long years afterwards she remembered.

"They sting often when there isn't guilt," said Jack, as he moved away with his cousin.

"You are too sensitive, too tender-hearted. Writing is only a trade. Writers are like turtles; they draw their head and feet in under a calloused shell of indifference and of gold, and allow the old world to beat and batter away; they know that when it is tired, or when some other attraction appears, it will pass on, and then they come out again as serene and smiling as any May morning, regardless of what all the wise heads have said about their shallowness, pedantry or plagiarism."

"I'm sorry, but Nature didn't make me a sloth, a stoic or a silent serf."

"And by not making you so, she is making your hair grey," said his cousin in a low voice from where she now stood by his side looking down at the dark waves of hair clustering around his temples. "Grace gave us a piece of art and the people were happy and praised. You give us art but you speak beyond us. We cannot comprehend or understand. You are sad, you are lonely, because we do not reach your standard."

"Oh, no, it isn't that; it really isn't that. One is sad because one's standard is so low. One is only dissatisfied with one's self."

"That cannot be true of you. You never think of yourself. Of whom are you thinking now?"

"Of you," he replied in a low voice, and he looked up at her. He sat in the shadows. She was standing between him and the lights of the room, turning over the leaves of " Phædo."

"Then your thoughts should be happy ones."

"You are happy?"

"Yes, perfectly so. I am satisfied with myself. You see what it is to possess vanity."

"Vanity alone wouldn't warm your heart and make it happy. You are quite confident that something more human than vanity dwells near it or you wouldn't be so happy."

A warmth came over her face.

"One only hopes it be allowed to remain there," he said in a voice which caused her to turn and look at him, and then she remembered a letter which had come out in the evening, a letter having upon it the same handwriting as she had once seen come from the far East, and she knew that things were not well with him. Faint rumors had reached her of the woman's struggles and loneliness and injured pride. In her heart she pitied her. She knew her cousin's sense of high, chivalrous honor, and a great wave of pity went over her for him, but it was something of which she could not speak; it was something the existence of which she could not admit. It was one of those situations which time alone could unravel; it was one of those situations, of which the remembrance and the landmarks could only be wiped out by a noble, courageous life. In the meantime one must live, and in the meantime in all his leisure moments she knew her cousin was concentrating the best energies of his life on the production of a noble work. The world was his Venusberg, and its conflicts and turmoils and troubles were distracting his mind and preventing him from the accomplishment of much. He was of the world; he could no more live without it than a naiad could live without water. It was his element, his love. He was worried over many things which dwelt within it, but yet he could not leave it to seek the shelter of solitude to complete his work, and his work was not progressing as he wished to see it.

His cousin was aware of this.

"You possess too lofty ideals, and because you do not attain to them you are dissatisfied with yourself. There is only one fame, one power you would wish—the power to move minds akin to yours. You would give us something like this," she said, as she turned over the pages of the book, "and because you think you fail, you are sad," she continued, wishing to detract his mind from the letter.

"One couldn't write so now," he said, the tone of his voice confirming the truth of her words.

"Why not? You have the same old material to work upon, and the cumulative knowledge of all intervening ages."

"But they, all these fellows, have said all that's worth saying. If we say anything, it's the same old thing over and over again, only draped differently, and we don't know how to drape. It isn't in us. We have even to use their drapings."

"You regret your inability to create. You are too modest. This knowledge is not theirs, no more than it is yours. It belongs to everybody. I heard Mr.— someone say the other day that all this which you are ascribing to all these great men was but a little spark which dwells in everyone, waiting to be fanned into a brilliant flame. All art is revelation; all art is praise. We worship before it and it becomes ours, and when it becomes ours we may do with it as we will. Your Venusberg is smothering your feu sacre. Tannhauser tore himself away for a year. Why do you not do so, too?"

His Venusberg was ruled over by a divine court. Stubs and his courtiers weren't there. He could get away. And he was tired of his court; I'm not. This game of the gods is too interesting. I want to see its finish. What is she after to-night? Does she want Kenyon to take her over to Idlewylde? Can't you get her away for a few moments? I want to speak to Kenyon. It is getting late. I must soon go."

"You are not going out again to-night."

"I must. I have no choice in the matter."

She remembered the letter, and she looked up at him once more; his eyes met hers.

"I have ordered refreshments. You will have something warm before you go."

"I would rather have a word with Kenyon. I want to know about those seats."

"If one may judge by his expression, he hasn't anything very favorable to report. There is the lunch bell. I shall send Lester to take her in. Then you may speak with him," said his cousin, and she went in search of Mr. Lester while Jack turned towards Keith Kenyon.

"Thank goodness! there is the bell," Verona Lennox said as he came up.

"Why? Are you hungry?" asked Jack.

"No, but your face is as dark as a thunder-cloud. You are not pleased about something, and one would prefer talking with the Lygians or the Yahoos than with you when you are in one of your moods," replied the heiress, as she put her hand within Keith Kenyon's arm and turned away to the lunch room.

"Take that, will you?" said Mr. Lester.

"Do you know what Momus, the buffoon, said to Minerva? He regretted that Vulcan had not made her house movable to avoid a bad neighborhood."

"Hospitable, by Jove! Kenyon had better take her to Idlewylde."

"He intends to, and the sooner the better for all people," replied Jack, as he left the room, and sought his cousin, leaving with her a message for Keith Kenyon, and then traversed the many great halls which led to the rear entrance to the house.

He stepped without and stood for some minutes looking away to where a ruddy glow on the horizon told of a sleeping city. It was almost midnight, and he was very tired. He had to meet a deputation of the Fernwylde villagers in the morning; he had to speak in a distant rural district in the afternoon, and in another in the evening; he had had little sleep or rest for weeks, and he hesitated. The night was very dark, so dark that the lights in the city shone brighter because of its darkness. Someone was in trouble there. The lights were dead lights to him, yet he descended the flight of steep stone steps to the path leading to the stables, saddled his big black, and rode away in the darkness towards the sleeping city.

CHAPTER XIX.

It was now some ten days later, and Fernwylde had been deserted, save for its mistress and Helen Lester and Mr. Linden, who had remained on at the Rectory. The gentlemen of their party had been touring the country, perching and cawing, here one afternoon, there the same evening, and some place else the next night. Their perching and cawing was the best they could do. Existing circumstances were preventing both parties from accomplishing anything tangible. The country was approaching a state of transition. Evils had crept in, and the party in power felt the impossibility of being consistent in the face of so many overwhelming, intangible forces, while the time was not quite ripe for the others, and the situation had simply developed itself into a warfare of personality and political trickery, which was neither inspiring nor encouraging to either party.

It was now Friday, and the men were returning one by one to their homes and to Fernwylde to rest until the following week.

Carlton Monteith was becoming very impatient and the mistress of Fernwylde was beginning to feel the situation very keenly. Her sojourn of serenity and seclusion at Fernwylde had made her think, and she knew now that she did not care for him, and she blamed herself for it, and she said she would return to her allegiance. Bringing all her will power to her aid, she tried to concentrate her mind and affections upon him. She took herself to task with all the self-censure of an ascetic. She recalled his associations with her mother, his patient years of waiting and of tenderness, his many kindnesses, his nobility of character, his purity of motives and the reserve and strength which lay behind his seeming lightness of disposition. She tried to make herself believe she yet cared for him; but when she would convince herself of this, then would her heart leap forth with a great cry, bringing more forcibly home to her than all her logic the impossibility of ignoring its secret. She might be conscious of her heart's cry, but she would not admit it; she could not. She was bound to him by pledge and by many memories; these were part of herself. Their betrothal was known to the world, and to break it was to admit to the world that she had made a mistake, and this she could not do. The world's censure and criticism were to her of no moment if there were no cause for it, but she loved her world and was intensely proud and sensitive towards giving it cause for comment. She valued the opinion of her world; she wanted to stand well in its eyes. She wanted her life to be such that it would command its respect, and she detested vacillation, froth, inconsistency and indecision. She had within her the instincts, habits, reserve, endurance and stability of the Englishwoman. She saw the necessity of formality, caste, forms and conventions in life, and was almost reverential in her respect of all unwritten laws of ethics and etiquette. She felt her position. She was a great lady in the eyes of the world. Could she not live her life as a life should be lived, then she was not capable of teaching others how to live. She was slow and deliberate in deciding any course or line of conduct in life, but having decided she was quick and resolute in action, and having once decided and acted she was as slow to relinquish as she had been to accept. She felt that her conduct, her character, was herself, and if she relinquished one line of conduct others would follow in quick succession until her individuality would have drifted away.

She had accepted Carlton Monteith into her life. It had been a mistake. She knew that great natures are great enough to acknowledge their mistakes, but if she acknowledged it the world would lose confidence in her judgments and she would forfeit its

14

respect. She would rather suffer in silence than do anything that would lower herself in the estimation of her world.

This might be a cowardly sentiment; her reason told her that it was so, but she couldn't act otherwise because she couldn't feel otherwise.

Then, too, she owed much to Carlton Monteith. Her first thought must be one of justice to him. It was now more than a year since she had felt that she did not love him, and during all that time she had kept him by her side. She had given him to understand that all was well; at least she had given him to understand this when he was absent from her. It was only when in his presence, under the pressure of his pleadings and his demands, that she had in any way resisted, and then she had not resisted, she had only evaded him. She had only filled her life more openly with the world that she might be freed from any intimacy with him.

She felt now that she had willingly and knowingly misled him. It hurt her to think so. She was generous and tender-hearted to an extreme degree. She would rather suffer than others should suffer through her. Her line of conduct must be consistent, and although she thought it out in every light she could not very well see how she could maintain her own character and traditions and break with Carlton Monteith.

Her heart might plead differently, but she was weak if she listened to the pleadings of her heart.

"Love," she told herself, "was an affair of the mind, not of the heart." If Carlton Monteith persisted, when he returned she would say the following spring.

So she told herself once more, as she stood alone in the great rotunda facing the public driveway, her hand resting on the stone columns of the portico, her form almost hidden from view by the columbine vines which twined round its pillars. And then she heard the quick trot of horses' feet and the sound of carriage wheels, and she looked up the driveway, and as she looked she saw in the distance Keith Kenyon driving towards Idlewylde. And then she was not so sure about the spring, and a smile came to her lips and a softness in her eyes that it was a pity he could not see; but as he approached nearer she caught glimpses of him as he passed the avenues of trees bordering the driveway, and she saw that Verona Lennox was by his side, and then she was glad she had made up her mind to say the spring.

But the joy which came of her decision was of short duration. Keith Kenyon's presence had in it the power to scatter to the winds all her logic and well-defined lines of conduct.

Nothing seemed very clear to her now—nothing but the sense that he was once more near her.

She hadn't seen him now for some ten days, and during that time everything round about her had worn an aspect of dull grey. Fernwylde had been cold and gloomy. She had been lonely, and she had wondered why this loneliness, almost a great longing, stole ever in upon her. She saw by the papers that he was now here, now there, and read of his successes, of the ovations given him by the people, and these places and these people had assumed to her the color of rose-pinks.

She knew that he was returning home, and something told her he would come out at once to Fernwylde; and then her country home had once more assumed its natural color of rose-pink; and she had wandered out the evening before, that morning, that afternoon almost thinking he would come; and he had come.

But he had brought Verona Lennox with him, and another note of discord had entered into the harmony of life, a note she did not wish to dwell upon, and to get rid of this note she turned and went into the house and sought Mr. Lester and took him to the gardens.

Some half hour afterwards, from the gardens she could see the master of Idlewylde and his companion rowing on the river. No doubt in an hour or two they would row over to Fernwylde and would join her house guests. She would give her hand to Verona Lennox and welcome her to her home, and then she would smile on Carlton Monteith. The thoughts irritated her. She was a child of nature and she hated the dissimulation.

Mr. Lester saw the rowers on the river, and saw her irritation.

She wouldn't deceive Mr. Lester and she did not wish to speak of it to him, so she sent him after Miss Austin, who was searching for autumn thoughts down by the river.

She wanted to be alone. But the hostess of a country house is allowed very few moments for solitude or reflection. Soon the others gathered about her.

"Mr. Lester has gone from you. You are always with him. You enjoy his company," said Mrs. Cecil, as she watched the two down by the river.

She was aware of Mr. Lester's attachment for their hostess, and she often wondered how it would end.

"We all enjoy Mr. Lester's company. He says something worth listening to, and knows how to say it, and when one replies he knows how to listen," replied Modena, evasively.

"It was only the other day you were wishing for rag-time music," said Jack, who had come in with some of the other men who had but returned from a fox-hunt. "How inconsistent!"

"One has many moods, and one soon tires of rag-time music and wishes for something better, and one gets it from Mr. Lester. Custom cannot stale his infinite variety," replied Modena, her eyes softening almost to dimness as she remembered his many kindnesses to and considerations for her.

As she spoke she patted the heads of two of her favorite hounds who were looking with great intelligence into her face, as if seeking some words of praise for their late successes.

"An Hypatia having moods! An unprecedented thing! What's the matter?" asked Jack.

"Nothing. We all have our likes and our dislikes and our moods. At the present my mood is common-sense. Tell us of your successes," she replied.

"At the fox-hunt or the man-hunt?"

"Both."

"At the fox-hunt they caught a silver grey and two reds. At our man-hunt, well, one never can tell what one's success is until their skins, or ours, are hung up, like the foxes', on the barn door."

"You should have taken Cavall and Ion with you on your man-hunt. The dog has unerring instinct. He can tell his friends. What bait did you use?"

"We suited our food to the eater. Those who wanted rag-time got it, and those who wanted good, sound philosophy got it."

"Were they like Mr. Lester? Did they listen, and did they reply?"

"Yes, but they will not think intelligently."

"Couldn't you supply brains as well as thoughts?" suggested Mrs. Cecil.

"We don't need to. The brains, the best in the world, are there, but they will not use them. That's what makes a fellow swear. We've got the people and the brains. Our country, our morals, our traditions, our blood breeds the right kind, then why in the name of heaven can't they realize this, and realize their opportunities and make something of themselves," replied Jack, with vehemence.

"They work intelligently, and surely that is better," said Mr. Linden.

"Do they work intelligently? Do they really bring thought into their work?" asked Marion Clydene, looking up from her sketching, while her eyes followed one of the farm laborers as he mechanically turned over the rich fallow lands of Fernwylde.

"You are wondering what thought Reuben is putting into the handles of his plow. These lines here are mechanical," continued Mr. Lindén, pointing to some perspective lines on the young artist's drawings. "So are some of Reuben's. Your details require talent, thought, a knowledge of nature. Reuben's details require the deepest study of nature. Nature is perfect. He is studying perfection and giving practical application to his thoughts. Reuben is really thinking; he sees the sky as well as the clod. He will yet make himself felt. The tilling of the soil is the only work which does not change with time. It is the only work which has not become vulgarized. It is the only work that remains natural, noble and beautiful in all its attitudes and in its simplicity."

"How refreshing to come out here, away from the dross of it all!" exclaimed Mr. Lester, as he ascended the hill with his companion and seated himself in a low lounging chair near their hostess. "It is like coming from the land of man to the land of God. I am like Cowley,

> "'Well, then, I now do plainly see,
> This world and I shall ne'er agree,'"

continued he, as he smiled and looked away over the landscape which lay before him.

It was Indian summer. In the early afternoon the air had been cooler and a white mist had hung over the valleys, hiding from view the Idlewylde, the distant spires of the city and the tall trees and mountain peaks surrounding Fernwylde, but later the air had warmed and the mists had lifted to the mountain side and a soft mellow haze now hung over the valleys, giving to the landscape before them a dreamy, sensuous sense of productiveness and peace. The scenes around them were the same. The orchard grass was covered with the late fruit of autumn; the fields were yellow and red with golden-rod and with mounds of golden-eared corn, which the huskers had left there to ripen and dry; children gathered nuts in the valley below; the famous Durhams roamed knee-deep in the rank grass bordering the Idlewylde, and from the fields far off the men were gathering in their winter store of roots, while here and there clouds of smoke circled to the sky from the busy barns where men were garnering in their grain. In the background lay Fernwylde, robed in all its autumn glory, the sun lighting up its towers and leaded windows with a mellow glow. Facing them on the far-away slopes of the mountain, white mists yet hung, but here and there where the air was warm a Siberian pine or a spruce tree loomed out, indistinct, on the breast of the mountain, like

Vivien veiled in grey vapor in Merlin's arms in the heart of the riven oak. Others, more indistinct, weird-like, now stood out suggestive or sombre-like, now disappeared into the nothingness of white vapor as the rain mists deepened or dispelled, while far above dark masses of rock towered towards and sometimes touched the lowering masses of deep grey clouds which drifted away in airy undulations from the bosom of the Idlewylde, while all around reigned the silence of the high hills.

The scene was peaceful exceedingly, more so to Mr. Lester, who, with the others, had been touring the country at intervals, expounding, gesticulating, attacking, defending. The people were apathetic and slow to move and slow to see. He was bodily and mentally tired, and in his leisure moments he had come out to Fernwylde to recuperate, and while surrounded by its simplicity and serenity, the grotesqueness of the political contest appealed to his common-sense and oftentimes made him almost resolve to leave it all and seek the repose, the serenity and the freedom of a private life.

But such moments as these came only when he was overtaxed or overworried, and when things went not well, or when sadly was brought home to him the knowledge that they had not done well in making illiteracy and improvidency their masters. At all other times the sacred fire of the political world burnt with a strong, sure, steady glow within his veins, but, like Jack Mainton, he was longing for more dignity, more real simplicity, more intelligence in the administration of the affairs of his country. He was only bodily tired now, and the relaxation was like a breath of peace and renewed vigor to him; it was like a draught of clear, cold water to a pilgrim travelling over a warm, wide plain, or the cool breath of morning air blowing over tired eyes.

He now sat in the depths of his easy-chair under the branches of a great spreading maple; the breezes from the Idlewylde blew the amber and russet leaves of autumn round them, while from a table near by a servant passed him some light refreshments.

"You would make this a retreat. Reuben will be your inspiration. He is the fruit of your labor," said his hostess.

"He doesn't think so."

"But he is. The Fates were all-wise when they spun you out a politician, not a plow-boy."

"You don't want to be a milk-maid. I thought you were a great lover of nature."

"I am, but I am like Horace; I want to admire it from the throne of Augustus, not from Lisette's."

"You would prefer being a queen. Perhaps Lisette would, too."

"Perhaps some day she will be, but not until her day comes. One has instincts, *a priori* knowledge, or whatever you wish to call it, that tells one that one has a certain vocation in life. Mine tells me that one time in my life I was born a slave—who knows, perhaps a black slave—and that all nature was my master, and that little by little I have served my apprenticeship, even to the vilest on earth. The time has been long, oh! so long and so hard to bear, but the term of serfdom is ended and now I want to be a queen. Lisette's time will come," said Modena, smiling humorously with all the humility of self-knowledge.

Mr. Lester looked at her with admiration.

She was seated on a high-backed chair of carved ivory, where the greensward caught the afternoon sunshine and the shadows of the clouds; her head was uncovered, save for the pearl combs which fastened the great coils of hair which circled her head; an open sunshade of white lace rested on the back of her chair. She wore a dress of soft white oriental stuff; white roses nestled in the laces at her bosom; round her waist was an old gold girdle with some miniature hunting horns and keys of gold hanging from it; her white shoes peeped out from beneath the laces of her skirts and rested on an ottoman of white morocco leather; her white hounds, Cavall and Ion, slumbered in the sunshine at her feet, while Nell Gwynne lay by her side.

"A veritable Semiramis of the West! Even to the hanging gardens!" said Mr. Lester, tenderly.

"You know how to turn a compliment so prettily."

"It is not a compliment; it is the truth."

"I'm afraid nature has had more to do with the gardens than I," she replied, as she looked towards the Idlewylde, where the great pine trees were mantled with luscious wild grapes and the many ivies and wild flowers and vines so prevalent in those parts.

"Nature has been kind to Fernwylde, as kind as she has been to you. It is a madrigal in scenic effect."

"It was the Lady of Orleans' choice. She lived at the Trianon. She knew what beauty was. She was an exile and a refugee."

"The inevitable fate of all divinity!"

"Catherine or Margaret, discrowned and homeless, in a garret, would still be a queen. A divine queen can be deposed by no one."

"But herself," said Jack.

"You believe in falling from grace!"

"By pride; even the angels in heaven have fallen."

"Herself!" repeated his cousin, raising her pretty eye-brows in astonishment, while she fed Nell Gwynne some crumbs of cake as she spoke. "If she isn't mistress of herself, she isn't capable of being mistress of anyone else. Did you find the people so obdurate? Couldn't you convince them as to our divinity and infallibility? Have you given up hopes?"

"The people are not troubling me," replied he, in a low voice.

"What is, then?"

"You are," he said, as the two from the river ascended the hill.

"Am I not looking well? I took particular pains with my appearance this afternoon. What would you have me do?"

"There is only one thing you can do," he said, and he rose with her to welcome the newcomers. But for the first time in her life there was a formality, a coldness, a distant politeness in her welcome to guests entering her home.

She was an uninvited guest, but for this very reason she felt that it entailed a warmer welcome, and her high sense of hospitality tried to impart it to her words, but she felt the candor, the warmth, the substance was lacking.

She greeted Verona first, but Verona was indifferent to such a small thing as this. She was indifferent because she did not notice it. At any other time this feeling of disfavor would have been as incense to her, but now her thoughts were occupied with Keith Kenyon alone. She wasn't quite so sure of him as she had been, and this uncertainty had been a stimulus, this indefiniteness had been an incentive and an anxiety. She had been playing her winning cards, but he had been wary and unsatisfactory, and she had made but little progress. Adroit, beguiling or threatening as she had been, she could not beguile him into any sort of declaration. It had almost come to an open war of words between them, but something within him had restrained her. She saw there were bounds which she could not pass, and she had changed her tactics. She must compromise him in the eyes of the world. She hadn't time to bother with those people now. They would keep. But in the eyes of those people she must make the most of the situation. It must be made to mean something definite, and she had smiled familiarly and intimately into his eyes as they had come up, and hesitated, and leaned a little towards him with a word of understanding, and then left him, and greeted their hostess with an apology for her presence and with words to the effect that Mr. Kenyon wouldn't come without her, and then seated herself and turned to Mr. Lester, while the mistress of the place turned to greet her companion.

She extended her hand to him without meeting his eyes. He

felt the coldness, and he made her eyes meet his. She flushed a little, and turned away to the table under the trees to send a servant to them with some tea, while he seated himself near Jack Mainton, sensitive to the presence of a wrong note somewhere. He had come and gone at will and wish to her many homes as though they were his own,. and he had come to-day with the same freedom of intimacy.

On his return to the city from touring the country, Verona had insisted on accompanying him to his country home. With Jack Mainton he had been to the constituencies claimed by Stubs. They had read his literature and heard his parrot-phrases repeated from lip to lip. They had counteracted much, but they had much yet to fear, and he thought it not wise to needlessly antagonize the Lennoxes, and had acceded to her wish.

But he had almost forgotten that she was with him.

He had been away for some ten days, and as his face had been turned from home they had seemed to him as so many long years.

When he had once more turned towards home a great happiness had dwelt within him and the expectation of he knew not what. He thought only of seeing the woman he loved; his eyes longed to look into hers, his hand to feel the warmth of hers; nor would this alone satisfy him ; he knew that these were only the precursors of greater desires. The sense of the dreariness, the emptiness, the loneliness of life without her seemed to come suddenly home to him. All the rest of the world had faded into nothingness as the knowledge of the need of her in his life had grown in upon him. He could no longer live without her, and some subtle intuition told him some hour of fate was soon to come. No trains could fly faster than his thoughts, his wishes, his desires had flown, but yet he had kept them in subjection, and outwardly had remained cool and calm, and had become master of each situation and each detail and had fulfilled each duty which had come from the demands of the people and his party, and it was only when the last had been fulfilled that he had turned towards Fernwylde.

He now took his tea from her hands and joined in the light discursive topics of the hour, but his eye followed her as she moved now here, now there, among her guests, a stately figure in white with her great white hounds following her.

Verona Lennox had taken the chair which the mistress of Fernwylde had used as a throne seat at her Court of Inquiry, and now sat upon it.

"That was our throne seat," said Mr. Lester to her.

" Jack has been giving us a depressing account of your kingdom."

" It was Athene's kingdom he was discussing. It was heads, not hearts," said Mrs. Cecil.

" Does he think the people stupid?" asked Miss Lennox, with a smile so innocent that it made Jack Mainton swear beneath his breath.

" Yes, real stupid, so stupid that they bit readily at bait which had been offered to them, bait as full of stimuli, froth and slow poison as a Chinese sugar-coated pill is full of opium," replied Jack.

" Raynor says the people are hopeless, but I'm afraid Mr. Mainton is more so. On our way here we wondered at the presence of the turnpike men, the stage coach and the ox-team, but now one wonders no more. I suppose you teach the children to sing psalms and say prayers," said Verona to him from the height of her throne seat.

" We don't need to do so. Nature teaches them herself."

" But it isn't quite the thing to listen to nature any more. Is it?" she asked, as she lifted her outer skirts a little and placed her feet on the ottoman of white morocco, leaned back indolently in her chair with her arm resting on its side and her hand pushing back the ringlets of hair which lay in studied disorder on her brow, and half closed her eyes, seeing all the while every glance, every motion of Keith Kenyon's.

" Listening to nature now would be of no avail; one could not hear for other noises." he said.

" The noises of civilization. They are nice noises! Interesting!"

" That is according to a person's taste," replied Jack, with a little offence in his voice.

Verona looked at him from the depths of her half-shut eyes.

Their hostess's duties at the tea table were done. Keith Kenyon had risen and found her a seat a little apart from the others, and had seated himself beside her, and had spoken to her in a low voice. The color had deepened in her face, and she had not replied, but had turned to Mrs. Gregory.

Verona had seen it. Jack Mainton had seen it, too.

" You don't like civilization?" said Verona, and her voice bristled with dislike as her eyes had sparkled with malice.

But Jack didn't reply. He could afford to be amiable, and only smiled as he watched the smoke curling from his favorite Havana.

" There is such a thing as being so satiated with civilization that this creates a tendency, almost a desire, to return to barbarism for a time," said Mr. Linden, and then he checked himself.

He wasn't aware that there had been an attachment between Jack Mainton and Helen Lester, but instinctively he felt that he was no favorite of Jack Mainton's. He had heard faint rumors of Jack's early life, and had thought that Jack had shunned him because of his gown, but his gown had only served to give him comprehension and great charity, and he had buried all the semblances of his surplice and had approached him in the circles of society, in the fields of manly sport and in the arena of politics, but it had proved of no avail. His presence was but a signal for Jack's silence or absence.

It was an unusual thing for him to reply to the divine as he now did.

"One has reasons to doubt very much whether civilization has done for us what men claim it has done," he said, rather coldly. "Our predecessors were the children of instinct and of nature. From whom they inherited these instincts, history fails to tell us, but they had within them the germs which would have made a better foundation for a better society than that which dwells within us. Knowledge, intuition, reflection tell us that they must have been the degenerate progeny of a very high civilization. We are the progeny of an uncouth, undignified, uncreative civilization."

"A Periclean age!" said Mrs. Cecil.

".Perhaps Jack's predecessors were the progeny of that age. Some historians claim, from a study of the Red Man's habits, religion, state relations and government that they were the descendants of the early Greeks. Many of their feasts were similar to those tendered to their ancient divinities, their names bear a close resemblance, while their games are the same as the games given in honor of their gods," said Grace Austin.

"You are saying the same thing as Mr. Linden, but phrasing it differently. He said the highest civilization borders on a strange credulity, and this creates a tendency to return to barbarism. From Pindar and Pericles to Blackfoot and Nighthawk! A parody on the Fall of Man!" said Mrs. Cecil.

"Perhaps there is much truth in the parody. The Greeks believed these western shores to be the blissful islands of everlasting spring; to them they contained the golden fruit of Hesperides; they were the Elysian abodes of the departed shades of all these great men. Perhaps, like Mr. Mainton, they wanted to know; they wanted to verify their faith, and set sail."

"With Homer as a sequel. Achilles went to Hades. He would willingly have returned to earth and lived on a crust of dry bread, but he couldn't return."

"The moral, that people should believe through faith and be

happy with heaven on earth. That's what Miss Lennox said a moment ago," said Mr. Lester.

"You are hinting at Psyche's lamp! Pandora's box! You mean Hamlet's ghost should be murdered. Talleyrand, Dante, even St. Paul tried to murder him, but they failed. I am afraid he is one of the immortals."

"He must be. Isn't he our own beloved Thor's Amleth, transported to Norway by Snorro, brought over to Denmark by Saxo, borrowed from there for England's use by Shakespeare, and now brought back to Thor's land again by Jack? An epitome on the pathos of life."

"Dante banished him to his own domains by the creation of Beatrice."

"Fortune hasn't favored me as it has Dante and—and—Miss Lennox."

"But the Fates have left you the bottom of Pandora's box—Hope. If you don't take it someone else will," said Mrs. Cecil, in an aside in a low voice, as she looked across the lawn to where Mr. Linden had gone to gather a cluster of grapes for Helen Lester.

But Jack Mainton didn't raise his eyes or reply.

"If the Greeks ever gazed on a sunset similar to this and refused to believe through faith, Achilles' Hades was but a merciful punishment for their disbelief," said Marion Clydene, who had been sketching the Idlewylde as it lay robed in its autumn glory.

From where they sat they could command an excellent view of the ravine, which was fringed with ferns and oaks and bedded by a clear, rippling, winding river, over which the monarch sun gleamed like sapphire and gold in the purplish autumn evening.

Beyond the river lay Idlewylde, indistinct to the naked eye behind its mantle of sunset brilliance; on this side the white mists, which had hung like a pall over the pine-covered mountains, had lifted, and their sombre peaks and plume-like summits and sides towered towards the sky as if to meet and greet the night now coming down; to the right the spires and steeples and shining metal roofs of the little village glistened like sapphires and sunlit sea-foam through the break in the Idlewylde foliage.

In the ravine the shadows were creeping round the farther shore; the Ave Maria bells in the monastery had ceased ringing, and the monks rested in the refectory which faced the waters; a hush and peace were over all below. In the sky the great orb was sinking slowly in all his majesty, but seemed to linger on the horizon as if loth to leave so fair a scene, a scene almost as beautiful in its aureoled transparency of crimson and gold and rose and amber as is seen in the sky behind the dome raised to appease the restless soul of Nero.

They one and all looked towards the setting sun, and an impressive silence like the hush of evening came upon them as they looked.

At length Modena broke the silence.

"Oh, how beautiful!" she breathed. "Whose pen could portray that? If one be disposed to be sad, surely the saddest of all sad things is to stand in the presence of a Sun-God, as Apuleius stood on the threshold of Proserpine, at the gates of the grave, with a Chaldean sun burning in its full glory at midnight, face to face with the gods of Hades and the gods of Heaven—to see and to feel, without the power of an Ovid or Pindar to pour out one's soul in praise. This was their god, and they sang. What a glorious temple in which to sing! How that cone-shaped cloud glitters like a golden spire! And there, naves of waves billow away to the east with azure blue aisles of air between; the air stirs among them; a bank of amber and crimson and purple is touched; and then another; they glide away into a mist of nebulæ, gleaming as they go like the many mystic symbols of an emblazoned lancet. They pause; the color deepens. A crimson transept, beautiful! A vein of vapor intervenes; a chiaro-oscuro of color! friezing the columns, fretting the cloisters and frescoing the walls; and there a billow of sea-foam floats to the feet of an amber bank like a vestal bent at a chancel step; its breath and glow breathes o'er her brow like the hush and shadows of sunset coming down on the virginal snows of a mountain side. How rare the air must be! Farther away the rays sweep zenithward, brightening to brilliance its mighty dome. A light comes from the north. An aureoled crescent surmounting an aulic pageantry! Nearer from the bosom of many waters veins of vapor sweep westward, a spectral army bearing upon their advancing spears the glorious rays of an upraised Host. They are praising Him. From the cloisters of the clouds white-robed cherubim pass to the choir steps and swell the chorus. A matin song of praise! The air pulses, the color deepens, the sea swells, the billows break into one great and glorious song of joy. Beautiful exceedingly! Ah, it is fading into a blessing, darkening into a requiem! Swan-like they sing their own death-song, the song of the death of the day," and her voice died away into silence as the monarch sun sank behind the line of trees and mountain peaks which bordered the Idlewylde, its trailing clouds of glory sinking into its arms, as the shadows of night came down, leaving the Idlewylde, the ravine and the upland glades of Fernwylde in dewy dimness, while it was yet day in the city beyond.

She sat on a rustic wicker seat; her arm brushed that of Keith Kenyon, who sat by her side. She was sensitive of the warmth from his arm. As she ceased speaking her voice was low and vibrating and seemed far away; her guests remained awed and silent, carried away by the emotion and the infinite suggestions which her personality and her words had given to the glorious splendor of the western sky.

"And then Mr. Lester once told us you had no imagination," at length said Grace Austin, breaking the silence.

"That was when the world was her all," replied Mr. Lester, in tender moodiness.

"And is it not her all now? What has supplanted it?" asked Grace.

"The touch of inspiration—invariably a human touch. Love is an alchemy; it changes the color of all things," replied Mr. Lester, in a voice intended only for his companion's ears; but low as it was it reached the two on the wicker seat.

Keith Kenyon had not seen the setting sun—only a glance at the first, then his arm imperceptibly had pressed hers; his eyes had been lowered all the while. At Mr. Lester's words he raised them to hers, but she did not meet them: there were too many present. The same sense of sweetness passed through her as she had felt the night of her vision. It was not for the eyes of the world, and she rose and joined the others.

"It is a very material all just now. I am hungry. It must be dinner-time," she said, with a return to her old manner.

"Your imagination is very vivid. Imagine you are eating it. That will do as well," said Jack.

"One doesn't fancy being a scarecrow. I know my own weaknesses. I am very fond of ortolans and truffles, the real ones."

"You are very human after all," he smiled.

"The imagination of most poets and artists is very human when there are truffles around. They are generally Bohemians and very big feeders. I have never yet seen one who looked at the truffles and passed them by."

"Their imagination isn't strong enough, and their works are in keeping with their imagination."

"You mean our mode of living has been the death-knell of great works. Diseased livers and not accomplishments is the order of the day. It isn't that; it's for lack of inspiration."

"Then Modena—" said Mrs. Cecil, and then paused.

There were too many near by, and she left the group and joined

Keith Kenyon as the tones of the great Ghirlandina bell came over the lawn in soft waves of sound, calling them to dinner.

"They are frying cutlets in the kitchen; the odor is tempting," said he to Mrs. Cecil, as they reached the portico together.

"More tempting than imagination? Inspiration?"

"I had a long drive. I am hungry."

"I am sorry you said so. We have always looked upon you as an oracle, and an oracle eating and drinking spoils one's ideals."

"One cannot help it, though; the sight of this dinner-table is too tempting to refrain even to preserve one's own self-adoration."

"How practical you are! Then you were not the inspiration we thought you were. We thought there was more poetry than prose within you. The sunset scene made one think so. But perhaps you reserve the poetry for the lake scenes."

. "The prose, you mean," replied the young statesman, slightly annoyed. "Politics and poetry cannot sail together in the same boat."

. "You surely cannot expect us to believe so. It looks very much as if Parsifal, sailing after the emerald cup of tradition, had turned into a Lancelot."

"What do you mean?" asked her companion.

Mrs. Cecil did not reply, but smiled vaguely and passed in to dinner with Mr. Lester, while Keith Kenyon followed, silent and absorbed.

Her words had touched him. He was beginning to realize that his actions were being wrongly construed. Slowly it began to dawn upon him that he was giving the Lennoxes and the world the right to believe that his conduct towards her had for its motive the affections, and not politics and social obligations. He had never looked at it in that light; he had never given her a moment's thought; he had been gracious to them because he had known them before. They had appealed to and deferred to him in every possible way, and he had been courteous. His acceptance of them had been an open sesame to every home in the city. He had done much for them, partly from kindliness of disposition, partly from his desire to secure them, and wholly from his consciousness that one is responsible only for one's own thoughts, words and actions, and that life is much more pleasant and peaceful passing through it with people than in going the opposite way. He was conscious of his own motives and he had thought that they were, too. He had judged them by the light of his own principles in life. The services which he had rendered them imposed upon them the greatest obligation of self-control, reticence and deference.

Since they had a right to his gratitude they should not presume on his indulgence; his service to them was a guarantee against any misconstruction of motive; but slowly his eyes were being opened. They were not seeing with the same eyes as he. They were looking at things from the standpoint of egotism. They were the people, the favored, the sought for. They had put much into his actions which had never been there. They had magnified their former slight acquaintance into the most intimate intercourse. They had put a wrong coloring on many matters. They were trying to compromise him in the eyes of the world. He had been slow to see it, but he saw it now. He saw now their aim and their object and how they had duped him. The thought irritated him exceedingly, and his features grew cold and he gave an impatient gesture like a thoroughbred shaking its head to rid itself of the sting of a poisonous fly; and as soon after dinner as courtesy would permit it, he arose and, unnoticed, went out into the gardens.

But the irritation which Mrs. Cecil's words had awakened within him soon faded away into the background of his thoughts before the forces of a stronger emotion which dwelt within him.

His absence from Modena Wellington had brought home to him the absolute need for her in his life. He could no longer live without her. Man's intuitions are not easily deceived, and he believed she loved him and him alone; but her relation to Carlton Monteith stood as an impalpable and impassable barrier between them.

He was not a man of impulse but of deliberation. He was a man with a great sense of honor; his honor was as dear to him as his life; a base action would be an impossibility to his nature, and whether or not he had a right to speak to her was the question which had been the subject of his contemplation for many weeks.

His actions in life must be based upon well-defined principles of conduct. He had inherited many principles. These he had verified in life and in his researches had acquired more. He had been born with a satisfied, scientific mind. He had often thought that his forefathers must have devoted themselves to the sciences, and that he had inherited the accumulation of their researches and reasonings, and in him had come a reaction to the humanities which had had the tendency to make him a happy, productive man. He had zealously striven to reach the fabled well of truth and generalize as to the real basis of conduct. Aware of the fact that knowledge is the only safe way to character, all his life he had been gathering data, and his generalization had brought him certain well-founded convictions, and some of these were a blending of Zenoism, self-advancement and altruism, and an instinct which had become a knowledge of responsibility to a Higher Power.

He had taken the world seriously, sometimes believing it to be the receptacle of an anterior life, but always believing it to be the anteroom to a posterior life. Love he believed to be the origin and essence of all things, and human love but the counterpart and reflex of divine love. This life he had looked upon as being too ephemeral, too fleeting, too short to be the all and end-all of great love. He saw how the world mistook passion and desire for love, and of how these were swept away by the great broom of destiny, as spiders are swept by housewives. Passion was of the senses; love a complex union of heart and mind. Every human soul is in a state of unrest until it finds rest in its own. When he had met Modena Wellington something long sought for, something long desired, had come into his life. Many times it had seemed to him that they had belonged to each other before, but for some reason they had been parted for a time, and like the birds of summer had gone to a sunnier clime to escape the severities of some cold, unfeeling wintry world, and by an unerring instinct had again sought each other, as the same birds return from the far south and mate and build beneath the same straw-built shed or eaves of last year's house. This love had come into their lives from somewhere else. He had not willingly or even knowingly tried to win her. Another Hand had been behind it.

Destiny had woven the web.

So it seemed to him.

He loved her. Hers was a strong nature. Carlton Monteith could not make her happy. He could. He knew that he was her master and he wanted her to love. He felt the need of her every day. Love was the only law. It was man's prerogative to speak.

So he told himself, but as he told himself this, all the conventions of life and certain instincts of honor rose up before him and forbade him to speak.

And these were stronger within him than his love.

So he felt in his calmer moments.

Silence was the only honorable course he could pursue. He could not speak, and he turned and re-entered the house.

But unless one has the strength or the cowardice of an Olivier to tear oneself away from what one loves but what one fears, in the presence of the heart's pleadings the strongest resolutions of the mind will soon fade into the semblance of a shadow.

When once again in the presence of the woman he loved he was

15

conscious only of one thing, her presence; but there was another also who was conscious of it.

As the evening advanced Carlton Monteith found himself alone with her for a moment in the music room. From here he led her to the portico on some slight pretext.

"Are you avoiding me?" asked he, with a great anxiety.

For some time he had felt the change in her manner, but his faith and trust in her had been so complete that he had not doubted her. He could not understand her moods.

"Why are you so cold?" he asked, earnestly.

"Avoiding you? Cold! I am occupied with the pleasure and comfort of my guests," she replied, despite herself a little impatiently.

"But you can spare me a few minutes. Sit down here. It is warm."

"But I cannot. I must not leave my guests. I must go. You will have to be content with this," she said, offering him her hand.

He seized it eagerly and raised it to his lips. He made a motion forward as if to draw her to him, when Keith Kenyon stepped out on the portico from an opposite door to light his cigarette.

Whatever surprise he may have felt, his countenance certainly betrayed none as he said, while Modena withdrew her hand in evident embarrassment:

"I beg your pardon. Do not let me disturb you. I only want to light my cigar."

As he struck the light he glanced into her face, but it was in shadow.

She turned from them to enter the house.

"Do not go in. I am going. Will you have a cigar, Monteith?" said he, as he raised his hat and retraced his steps into the house; while Modena for the remainder of the evening could not repress a feeling of irritable resentment as the scene ever stood before her. She felt as though she were being placed in a wrong light, and nothing hurt her more than having her actions misjudged.

It was so very seldom she allowed Carlton Monteith any familiarity, and then but the tips of her fingers; and to be caught in any weakness, and by Keith Kenyon!

It was only the tips of her fingers now, a caress born of her recent reflections and resolutions in solitude—one from her mind and one against which her nature rebelled.

For the remainder of the evening she noticed he did not once look her way, and she also noticed that a great change had come over his features.

Was it a look of pain, loss, blighted hopes? Or was it a look of disillusion? Did he think that she loved Carlton Monteith, or was it a regret that she was only as others? Was he disappointed in her? And the thought caused her the first bitter pang of her life.

She thought the evening would never end, but at last her guests from the village took their departure and her house guests sought their rooms.

As she was returning, before retiring, from giving the housekeeper orders regarding some changes she wished made, she noticed the library door leading to the rotunda had not been fastened. She entered the library and approached the door to repair the servants' neglect, when it opened and the master of Idlewylde and Jack entered from the rotunda.

She paused. "I did not know you were here. I was going to fasten the door," she faltered.

"I wanted Kenyon to remain all night, but he has to go to Idlewylde," said Jack, going on through the hall and out at the rear entrance to give the groom orders for his horse.

She made a motion to leave the room, but her companion detained her.

"He had been going home, going away," so he had told himself. "She would never, no never, allow Carlton Monteith any familiarity if she did not love him." He detained her to tell her he was going away. But as he looked down at her some power within her, within himself, made him speak otherwise.

"I could not help seeing that to-night, Modena. Do you mean it? Do you allow it? Do you love Monteith?" he asked, his voice low and tense from the strength of the emotion under which he was laboring.

The very thought that any other man should touch her hand, should caress her, should possess the right to look upon her with the eyes of passion, seemed to rouse that inherent demon of jealousy which lies dormant within all human nature, but which had never been touched in his before.

His face was colorless in his intense apprehension, while she was too moved to speak.

The color came and went in her face and her eyes bent under his at the passion in his voice. But she thought of her betrothal and what it entailed.

"Why shouldn't I?" she replied, but with little accent of truth in her tones.

"You have no right to ask me that," she was going to add, but she checked herself and hesitated. She could not say it.

But he felt the words which were checked on her lips, and it seemed to him that the whole tenets and all the unwritten laws of ethics and etiquette of the world had spoken to him, and he could not reply.

And he stood mute before her.

But the very greatness of emotion which beat within her own breast gave her comprehension, and having comprehension she had pity. "If this be love, then is the world well lost for it," she thought.

She heard the beating of his heart, and she looked up at him.

He stooped over and took her hand in his. The touch thrilled through her being. "I want to know the truth, Modena. Do you love Monteith?"

Her eyes fell and she could not look at him. A great wave of happiness passed through her being, as she felt his emotion gaining upon herself. "Or do you love someone else?" he continued, his voice dropping to a low note of passionate pleading.

She was now utterly oblivious to everything else but his presence and his passion, and she knew now that she loved him.

Life was perfect.

Her countenance became illumined by some great light from within. She had loved her world, but she had not known that the world could contain such emotions, such intense joy as now pervaded her being.

She was his and he knew it.

He was only taking what was his own, and with all the latent powers of his life in one great passionate gesture he stooped over and drew her to him, but at that moment Jack's low whistle was heard at the library door and the stamp of fretting horse's hoofs on the hard gravel walk without.

"Hurry up, Kenyon. The very devil's in him to-night," said Jack, as he opened the door. "You here yet, Modena! For heaven's sake let Keith go. You can have it out another time. I'm tired playing groom," he said.

The master of Idlewylde bade her good-night and turned and left the room, while Jack smiled, almost at peace with the world, as he went with him to his waiting horse, and the mistress of the house turned and went upstairs.

When she reached her room she turned off the lights and raised her window. That still, solemn hush which precedes dawn had fallen over the sleeping world; her whole being was aflame with emotions which the solemn stillness failed to calm or quiet. She watched the man she loved mount his horse, bid her cousin good-night and ride away down the avenue of trees until he was lost in the ravine which led to Idlewylde, the quick trot of the horse which he rode waking all the echoes hidden in the heart of her old home.

Over the Laurentide Hills far away a late moon was rising, casting its silvery lustre over the great pile which was her home, now slumbering in the midnight arms of the Idlewylde; in the northern heavens the stars shone bright as day; in the monastery down by the lake shore the monks were passing to their midnight orisons. Soon their words of praise and prayer were faintly audible on the still, clear air. She was much moved, and in the fulness of her emotion she bowed her head in her hands in great humility, asking herself what she had done that she should be thus blessed.

CHAPTER XX.

In the beginning of the week the party was suddenly broken up by an urgent call to Keith Kenyon from the city.

The chief was much worried.

The country was being agitated by questions and rights which had not yet risen to the surface, and which nothing but the chief's personal popularity and urbane tact could cover over with roses and sweetmeats until the crisis was past, and these he had been exercising to his utmost capacity and even beyond his physical strength, but even then the rose leaves and gloved hands did not conceal all the thorns and turmoil which eventually worked themselves to the surface.

There were low growls and grumblings to be heard; the majority ruled, but the minority clamored from the prairie provinces; there were sectional differences, racial and religious differences. If the wheat grew in the shock, or rusted in the field, or the potatoes rotted in the ground, or the cholera seized the cattle, the Government was to blame for it all; and the party being so long in power found its star waning and were often brought face to face with depressing circumstances, often the fruit of their own tactics. At the present time a serious disagreement had arisen in their own ranks. The Opposition had strenuously attacked part of their policy, and were steadily winning popular favor. Some of their own supporters, lukewarm, wavering, or personally antagonistic, had favored the Opposition, and the chief had hastily sent for Keith Kenyon to go upon the platform and restore order and unanimity in their own ranks.

It was difficult to do so, for the point in dispute was one which involved a principle, the establishing and execution of which would necessitate great sacrifice to many parties in their own rank. It would be for ultimate good and for the welfare of the majority, but not for the immediate welfare of many parties upon whom its execution depended.

The education of the present day is tainted with too much radicalism and provincialism to train pupils to sacrifice present opportunities for ultimate good. Principles are commendable things in the abstract, but when their application affects the coffers of the individual, the glasses through which the individual looks are apt to be very near-sighted.

The chief had hastily summoned his Cabinet together, outlined his policy, and arranged for a mass meeting the following week, at which Keith Kenyon was to be the orator of the hour.

"I don't see why the chief couldn't have sent for Clyte or Fitch or someone else, rather than Keith! Breaking up our party as we were beginning to enjoy ourselves! The summer will soon be past, and the long, cold winter is coming on! It is like going back to chaos and a chapter of Dante's 'Inferno' after the pumpkins and peaches and corn huskings of Fernwylde. Ouf!" said Mrs. Cecil, as she gazed out of the car window and watched the rustics piling the great red Spies in tempting heaps under the trees in the orchard as the train passed by.

She had really been tolerably happy for a few days at Fernwylde. She had received a letter from her husband, Strath Cecil. In it he had expressed a strong desire for her to remain where she was. She had shown the letter to Mr. Lester, and they had read between the lines, and it had breathed hope and an awakening light and a tender yearning for her. In it there had been a courage and a strength and a sense of honor which for a time had lain dormant or had been sullied. The tenor of the letter had awakened a new hope and a new tenderness in her heart.

She had also been charmed with the place. It was one of those places which possess the magic power of forcing one out of one's self and into a union with itself in its serenity and simplicity.

Its charms had really moved her: the cottages of the French habitants, the old Ursuline church, the cloisters, the monks at their prayers and their works, the feudal homage paid to its mistress, the minuets in the old halls and the serenades on the waters, all had in them the perfume of the "Old Regime" and "noblesse oblige," and had created within her a desire, which had almost become a resolution, to go away to her own estates in the southern provinces and take up life again, with its duties and hopes and loves.

But the call had come, and as they faced the city once more, with its intrigues and ceaseless strife and chatter and noise, the spell was broken, and the old life rolled over her again like the pall of mist rising over the valley through which the train was now passing.

"What a charming scene," said Modena. "One wishes one had the sympathies of a George Sand, that one might immortalize it."

"The sympathy!" and Mrs. Cecil laughed outright, her laugh expressing more than all spoken words could express.

"You know what I mean! My words are involved. The pen of a George Sand!"

"Inspiration makes the words flow faster than the pen can portray. Does the scene not inspire you? Is it too cold? Do you want something warmer? You were inspired the other day. Mr. Lester said inspiration came from a human touch, not from above. This serenity and peace might move you. How easy it would be to be happy there. I wish I were that girl driving the cows, or that squirrel stealing the nuts. I think I would be happy then."

"The girl has bare feet and the squirrel is a chipmunk," replied her late hostess, with a droll smile.

"You are not thinking of the girl or the squirrel. Your smile doesn't mean them," returned the Frenchwoman.

"What does it mean? Have you taken to mind-reading?" asked Modena.

"It meant that I, with my whining and continual fault-finding, reminded you of one of Gorky's or Tolstoi's novels, a chapter from Persæ, or a paragraph from a page of Herodotus. It meant to say, Why cannot you be happy as I am; as that girl is?"

"No, I wasn't thinking so; but to be candid, I was feeling glad that the girl with the bare feet was happy. Did you notice how Reuben's plow-horses were driverless while he crossed the upturned furrows of the fallow-field? Lisette was waiting for him. She wouldn't be anybody else but herself. I am glad I am not Lisette. I wouldn't want to be anybody else but myself. Now you see what you lack to make you happy—egotism, vanity and self-conceit."

"And Reuben!"

It was almost dark, and the twilight hid Modena's face. She leaned back in the cushions perfectly content with life as it was.

"You think love a panacea for all ills? I wish you would tell Kenyon so. It might help him cure our ills, at least it would give force to his convictions," said Jack, from his seat beside his cousin.

"Don't you think he is quite capable of accomplishing what he undertakes without help from anyone?"

"No doubt of it; but enthusiasm is like smallpox; it is contagious. A simulated enthusiasm is worse than none at all. It is always heart work which tells."

"Are you implying he is lukewarm?"

"Of late it looks as though something were nearer to his heart than his country is. Don't you think so?" he said, in a low voice as the train drew near the city.

"You mean Miss Lennox? Then, why don't you get her to inspire him if you are afraid of his failure?"

"No, I do not mean Miss Lennox; but since you have spoken of it, it is the general opinion that she has inspired him to a point from which he cannot very honorably retreat," replied Jack, who had been displeased with some of the proceedings of the preceding day.

"Perhaps he doesn't want to retreat."

"Doesn't he? You know best."

"What weapons will Keith use to-night?" asked Mrs. Cecil, as they left the car and entered the waiting carriage.

"Oratory," replied Jack.

"Will his subject admit of oratory?" asked Modena.

"Oh, yes, it is a principle and a precedent he is defending and establishing. It is not a concrete case."

"Will people know the meaning of it? I thought it disappeared with Laval's powdered periwigs. We have been taught to look upon it as a relic of the days of manners and madrigals. We have a little logic, a few hard facts and abundance of figures, but Oratory! Rhetoric! Melody! Diction! Ouf!" and the Frenchwoman shrugged her pretty shoulders disdainfully.

"But, my dear, the food must be suited to the eater. You cannot feed a grande dame on pork and beans or a ditch digger on venison and truffles. When Seneca and Cicero faced the forum, they gazed upon the upturned faces of wits and philosophers, rhetoricians and seers. When Burke and Pitt lauded Fox or ribalded the sycophants of the gentleman King in the Greek of Plato or the Latin of Cicero, they had for an audience an assembly of scholars and gentlemen whose ears were fine enough to enjoy the songs which they sang. But whom have we to sing to? And what themes have we to sing? Nothing but the commonplaces of a provincial life."

"You are slandering our countrymen and our country," said Modena. "We may not be an educated people, but we certainly are an intelligent people. Mrs. Cecil would have a universal culture. But our people are too busy with their agriculture and horticulture, and implement culture, to spare much time to the culture of the humanities. We must have our bread and butter."

Mrs. Cecil smiled. She was as sympathetic and generous with her fellow creatures in all their little cares and ills and duties of life as was her friend. Culture and knowledge are infinitely patient with infirmities and narrow minds; they are patient because they comprehend, but this patience has its own reaction in silent loneliness and lack of congeniality. She had been reared in the most select circles and schools in the French capital, and this had had the tendency to make her supersensitive to the grosser things of a provincial life, but it was only in the presence of her equals or her superiors that she gave vent to her desire for finer things.

"A universal culture would be an impossibility," replied she, in a lighter tone. "It would be impossible to permeate the world with intelligence, or with anything except it be with wickedness and stupidity. The majority will always remain blockheads, or apathetic, or at the very best mediocre. If all the scholars were here from Pliny, Petronius and Plato to Byron, Baur and Beaconsfield, they could not alter the present trend of events. They could not relieve the world of this lack of originality, the shallowness and inelegance, the crudity of it all."

"You would have us all Sapphos, and a moment ago you were wishing you were Phyllis or a squirrel, and all the while you are like Modena, you would not exchange places with anyone else in the world. I see it in your face."

Mrs. Cecil smiled, and then her face grew wistful.

"The inelegance and crudity of the world must be dear to you. It makes the world happy, and it throws up your own perfections in relief as the darker calyx of the lily enhances the purity of its whiteness," continued he.

"It is not to the stupidity of the world which one objects so much, but to the crudity of the leaders. One never enters the House of Commons but one wishes there would be an earthquake under the House and out of the bowels of the earth would step a—"

"Who?"

"Oh, a Pericles or a Pindar and—and Parsifal."

"Evolution has been kinder and more æsthetic than your dynamite or earthquake under the House and has given us the three in one for to-night," said Jack, as they arrived at Apsley House.

"This afternoon I was wishing for a statesman, a poet and a lover knight, and Jack Mainton told me we were to have the three in one to-night. What a treat!" said Mrs. Cecil to Mr. Lester, a few hours afterwards, as they stood together in Keith Kenyon's private waiting-room before entering the auditorium. "And a Hera inspiring him," continued she, looking over to where the mistress of Apsley House was conversing in low tones with the young minister for a few moments.

"Would you compare Modena to Hera? Hera inspired more admiration than love. Modena inspires love," replied Lester.

"And then ill-treats it."

"I don't know that she does. Monteith has a ticket on her, and it is one's own fault if one tries to steal the ticket."

"Don't you think the ticket has become a burden?"

"You think so? Perhaps so! But Parsifal will not win out. She will never sever the tie."

"But Fate will. Parsifal's mother hid him in the forest and reared him as a forester, but Destiny was stronger than even a mother's love. He wooed and won Queen Condwiramurs and afterwards became the Sovereign of the Holy Grail."

"His soul whitened ere its time, and he had to return to Hades until the real enchanted castle of Carbonek would come. Honor, in Modena's eyes, consists to a great extent in conformation to the conventions of her world. Her world and not her heart is her Holy Grail. I'm afraid she will be wiser than Parsifal's Queen and wait her time."

"You think all things come to those who wait, and the waiting time is a sort of patient penance? Modena would do her waiting with the patience of a Job, the humility of a Parsifal and the stoicism of a native; her only lamentation would be that she could not do Parsifal's penance, too."

"You mean there are some women who would die standing as the lace ruffles of '48. She is one of them. An Hypatia!"

"I wonder if Hypatia's ever-sustaining, ever-solacing, heaven-alluring philosophy and her standing death were ever glorified in other realms. They have never been glorified here."

"Perhaps her conduct and her creeds do not admit of justification. Perhaps it is a matter of penance."

Mrs. Cecil was silent for a moment and then said, slowly and gravely, "Her death stones had for their essence, mysticism, tradition, belief, faith. Her death had for its essence, philosophy, knowledge and direct revelation. Perhaps it was a penance. Perhaps it was a martyrdom. Who can tell?"

"Or perhaps it was the way of her sex, a determination to have her own way. Oh, no, I do not speak in a profane way. My words fail to express my thoughts, but you know what I mean."

"Yes, I understand. You think she would have displayed greater wisdom and tact had she buried her creeds in her heart, lived her own life, and let the world wander on into the dark days. But you overlook the fact that we were made with different natures to yours. We were made to feel. Suffering and misery and heart-aches come through feeling. Enid-like, we were made with finer instincts, a quicker and clearer insight, a keener penetration. You are smiling. Your smile means 'nerves.' Call it nerves if you will! But whatever it is, it is there, and we are not responsible for its being there. The ancients had three gods, Brahma the being, Vishnu the preserver or worker, and Shiva the destroyer. The Vishnu in some, in the majority, is dead, or if not dead is apathetic or indifferent. In others it predominates. It predominated in Hypatia; but you think her kicking against the pricks was of no avail."

"Oh, no, I do not mean so. Courage is one of the five virtues, and should receive all due honor. What I mean is that one should be sure one's cults are knowledge before one kicks against the pricks. One so often mistakes arrogance for knowledge."

"That is worse than being profane. You are ungallant. A woman's way is always the right way."

"You think Modena's way is the right way now?" said Lester, as he saw her pass in with Jack Mainton to the gallery.

"Remaining true to Carlton Monteith when she cares for some-one else? I—" said Mrs. Cecil, and then she checked herself as she saw Verona Lennox and Keith Kenyon approach them.

"Did you hear what Mrs. Cecil said?" asked Verona Lennox, who had taken her place at the young minister's side, silently exacting from him the courtesy of finding her a seat in the gallery.

"Yes," replied Keith, with his eyes on some notes in his hands, and his thoughts elsewhere.

"What did she mean?" asked his companion, with eyes of search-ing scrutiny, not alarmed, but somewhat disturbed.

He was ready for the scrutiny.

"Sir Colin Campbell, perhaps," he answered.

Sir Colin Campbell was an officer in command of Her Majesty's troops. It had been secretly whispered that the preference of the mistress of Apsley House lay towards him rather than towards Carlton Monteith.

A feeling of intense relief overspread Verona's face as she glanced across to where the Wellington party were seated on the opposite side of the gallery.

"Do you care to join them?" asked the young statesman, wishing to go, as his duties called him behind the scene. He led her across the floor of the house and ascended the steps to the gallery, and seated her beside the others.

The little incident was conspicuous, somewhat compromising, and disturbed his serenity, especially more so as he noticed the mistress of Apsley House leaning over the railing of the gallery in close proximity and in conversation with Carlton Monteith.

"Has Kenyon asked her yet?" he was saying to Modena, with more meaning in his voice than the little words expressed.

She noticed the intonation.

"They haven't made me their father confessor," she replied, without looking up.

"So soon as it happens she will make the whole world her father confessor," said Mrs. Cecil.

"The chief doesn't look well to-night," said Modena, wishing to turn the conversation.

She now realized the state of her own heart, and the realization made her feel that her friends knew it and were commenting upon it, and her nature forbade interrogation or comment.

"What would our country do if anything should happen to him?" she continued, as she leaned over the railing and looked down on the floor of the house, which was crowded in eager anticipation.

"Break its cane and cry, 'Le Roi est Mort,' and with its next breath wave a new one and shout and sing, 'Vive le Roi!' as they did after the Commune," replied Mrs. Cecil.

"What did Thackeray say about the time of the lace ruffles?" continued she, as she gazed down on the sea of upturned faces, the scene before her reminding her of many similar ones in her earlier life. "'What chopping and changing for almost a score of years; some of them dying and some of them getting their wishes and returning to their provinces to enjoy their plunder; some disgraced, and some going home to pine away out of the light of the sun, new ones perpetually arriving, pushing and squeezing for their places in this Galerie-des-Glaces.' Now I know what you're thinking, Modena; the world would have been much better had Thackeray been forced to earn his living at the wood-pile and I at the wash-tub."

Her friend smiled indulgently.

"If it is in I suppose it must come out. It would come out much more fluently at the wood-pile or the wash-tub. Action stimulates the brain."

"And much healthier," added Mrs. Cecil.

"The rest of his sentence would scarcely be applicable," said Lester. "'So many faces, oh, ye gods, and every one of them lies.'"

"How horrible to look at life through such glasses!"

"His glasses were his heart and mind. He was a real artist. He possessed the power of getting into the soul of things and portraying them as they were."

"How do you say that verse? 'The words of one's mouth are the promptings of one's heart.' What a deplorable heart!"

"How would you paint those down there, Modena? As Catos and Curtiuses?"

"Yes, every one of them."

"Lennox and all?"

"We were not speaking about Lennox; we were speaking of our chief. Biographers are comparing him with Beaconsfield. In many instances they are giving him the preference."

"Disraeli had talent, genius—"

"The men who have best served their country have not always been men of great talent. They have been men of high ideals, integrity, strong convictions, honesty, patriotism and progressive common-sense. As a statesman our chief is surely preferable."

"What unwarranted presumption!"

"Perhaps it is, but it is pardonable and palliative when based on honest convictions."

"What is the basis for your convictions?"

"An inherited love of country; the spirit of a Scipio or Curtius. Our chief is giving his life for his country. Disraeli used his country to build up his own life."

"Are you not afraid some Englishman will hear you?"

"If he did he would only smile pityingly and patronizingly and pass on like their poet laureate's poem, 'In perfect stillness when one brawls.'"

"You are only brawling! How relieved I am!"

"Oh, no, I mean what I say, but to them it would only appear brawling."

"You put the basis of their lives pretty strong. You said our chief's motive was love, the Jew's self-love. Your glasses are like Thackeray's. Isn't it your heart that's speaking? But I always thought you worshipped Disraeli."

"His genius."

"Not the man?"

"One doubts his sincerity, his honesty. Had he been in the Holy Land building up a New Jerusalem, we would have revered him and his memory—but in England— Well, it was the apex of civilization; it was the best field for sport. He was ambitious; he had genius; he loved caste and power. Destiny had placed him in a humbler position in life. Within him burnt the pride and power of some god of other days. He was conscious of this, and he resented the world because the caste and conventions of the world gave it the right to look down upon him. He was wise and subtle and suave and—and saucy. He piped to the Mob—to the People and to the Crown to gain his Throne, as Antony orated over Cæsar, and all the while he was silently laughing in his sleeve at the stupidity of a nation that could be blinded by such tinsel, and in his heart he scorned and ridiculed them when he attained to his throne. Can you doubt it when you read what he wrote? The one sentence is sufficient to convince: ' The Tories had now a great house in that of Imogen, the dressmaker's daughter.' He should have gone to Mount Ararat and remained there, and left England to a Mr. Pitt or a—"

" A Gladstone," supplied Jack.

" No," hesitated Modena. " England's need is not self-made men. She requires men who have been made before. She is built up. She needs handling. She wants a theorist."

" Then Balfour should fill the bill."

" You handle great men's names like battledore and shuttlecock. What presumption! Are you not afraid someone will hear you?"

" They are handling our chief's with Peel's just now."

" He possesses more tact than Peel. He is as the Princess Palatinate wrote of her King, ' He knows perfectly well how to content people even while refusing their request,' " said Mrs. Cecil, from behind the dainty piece of lace which she held before her to protect herself from the motes of dust and vapor of breath that rose from the crowded floor.

" They might better be compared to that illustration we saw in the paper to-day," said Jack to Lester.

" What was that?"

" Punch's picture of two penitent politicians going to do penance at Rome. They were to walk there with their boots full of peas; one is almost there, hopping and skipping joyfully along; the other, not far from home, sits by the roadside nursing his aching feet. The secret is, one boiled his peas before starting. That's what our chief does."

" That shows his good sense. Boiled peas is only politics' diplomacy."

" He might make a pot-pourri of—" and Mrs. Cecil hesitated

as she noticed Verona's proximity, and said, " He wouldn't do so if he were really going to Rome."

" That's what Disraeli did, and served them up with a glow and glamor on the outside."

" And when one broke them, as Modena has done just now, he found them filled with ice and Ego."

" You think if England's gulf had opened wide, to be appeased only by the warm blood of a human being, that the Jew would have stepped back and allowed a native to close the gap."

" No. He was no coward, and he also valued the praise of the people, as their praise was necessary to maintain his own existence. No doubt he would have stepped in, but his blood would not have closed the gap; it was too cold, cold as the scientific mixture of salt and snow."

" You mean he was an exiled shepherd to a stray flock of sheep on a far-away mountain side. He should have gathered the wandering Jews together into a New Zion. His blood would have closed that gap."

" Yes."

" Then there is no greater misfortune than to have no country."

" None. A love of country is only another synonym for a good man."

" He should have gone to Jerusalem. His blood is needed there."

" Had it been possible to re-establish the glories of his Old Jerusalem in one generation he would have gone and become its king. but he wasn't going to spend his life working for a mere ant-hill and have others come afterwards and enjoy the fruits of his labors. He wanted the best while here; he obtained it, and now the people honor and revere his memory."

Those near the mistress of Apsley House smiled, seeing more than she meant to imply.

" You think our chief is giving his blood to close the gulf?" asked Jack.

" There is no gulf to close."

" You think he is building an ant-hill, and we are too stupid to appreciate what he is doing."

" Yes, replied Modena, good-naturedly.

" The country *will* be in a box if he goes; but there's Kenyon! He is coming up with warm blood."

" I wonder what's keeping him now," said Mrs. Cecil.

" Perhaps Miss Lennox has forgotten her fan. He may have gone for it."

" A woman's fan between him and his country?"

"There always is. It's the fans that make the Curtiuses. Disraeli didn't care for fans; that's why Modena doesn't care for him."

"You think Keith would give his blood to close the gap if it were necessary," said Mrs. Cecil to Jack.

"Yes, I do, but he will be more æsthetic and more modern than your Curtius, or your earthquake under the House of Commons. He will close it with the fan," replied Jack, as the young statesman appeared on the platform, while he and Mr. Lester returned to their places in the auditorium.

A stillness came over the house as Keith Kenyon came from the back and stood in full view of the dense multitude awaiting him. What his thoughts were it would be difficult to tell, but to outward appearances he was calm and unmoved.

A deafening welcome greeted him from one side of the house and silence from the other.

He waited until the applause died away.

A division in their ranks at the present time meant defeat. He knew well what depended on his efforts of the evening. He did not doubt his powers, but his serenity for the last while had been disturbed, and the little scene at the beginning had irritated him. In the moment's interval he endeavored to regain his composure.

As he waited for silence he came forward and stood erect, one hand resting on his watch chain, the other on a table close by.

For a moment he raised his eyes to the gallery, and as he did so a light leaped into them, which the audience naturally interpreted as pride at his reception. But this was not so. A knowledge of his powers had come to him, and *she* was there. He would make her feel his powers.

He felt all the latent forces and acquirements of his life come to his aid. He had read much and deeply and he had remembered. From boyhood he had loved public work and public speaking, and nowhere was he more at ease, more master of the hearts of men, more powerful to sway the emotions at will than on the public platform. He had inherited the magnetism and the mental aptitudes, and had acquired the knowledge which gives confidence and fluency, and which are the requisites of oratory.

His preliminaries were cool and calm, but as he proceeded his voice gathered force and fire, and soon thrilled through the indifferent and sluggish pulses of the people, like inspiration in the veins of a genius—stirred them as they had never been stirred since the fiery eloquence of McGee rang through the same house and halls. His words flowed on, his voice now deep and thrilling, now sonorous and triumphant, now like Goethe's reading, 'deep-toned thunder blended with whispering raindrops,' and again vibrating with passionate eloquence which was so powerful to sway and convince. He was not trenchant, or prolix in denunciation; his subject did not require it, and he made it a point never under any provocation to lose his dignity. He was more suggestive than argumentative or logical; he was careful to allay rather than to arouse a spirit of antagonism. He would awaken a train of thought, give glimpses and pause, leaving the hearer with food for further thought. With a word, a phrase, he enlarged their vision, with a picture made the blood warm with new ideals, and with a few well-chosen words implanted some great vital truth. He had his subject well in hand and he kept well to his subject. He gave enough and not too much. He spoke for some two hours and ended with a peroration so powerful, so convincing, so magnetic, as to bring the audience as a unit to its feet.

He resumed his seat amid deafening applause, feeling confident that he had accomplished what he had undertaken to do.

His manner did not betray triumph, but an easy gracefulness and an almost imperceptible indifference characterized him now as his compatriots gathered round him in their enthusiasm.

As soon as it was possible he left the group and sought the Wellington party. He was thinking only of *her*.

He saw her at some distance, talking to his mother. He approached them. He smiled when he saw the look on the patrician face of his mother, but his eyes sought those of the woman he loved.

She knew it, and her eyes dropped under the fire and force of their appeal. She flushed warmly as her hand met his, but she said little, and soon turned and joined the group leaving for Apsley House, knowing that she had at least supplied the warmth to the blood required to close the gulf which had threatened their own party.

He joined her guests later on at Apsley House.

When they had all gone away she said to herself for the second time, " What have I done that I should merit such happiness "— she whom her world called so proud!

CHAPTER XXI.

Two mornings afterwards Mr. Wellington sat in his own private library at Apsley House.

It was a beautiful room, leading out from his daughter's favorite sitting-room. Its walls were panelled high in carved mahogany and lined with rich, dark book-cases which were filled with the thoughts of all the great men of all past known ages. The ceilings were deeply embossed and the windows deeply embeyed. The great leaded panes were clear to admit the western light, and opened out into Modena's favorite rose-garden. Transom panes of crimson surmounting these, and two oriel windows from the south flooded the room with a warmth of color. A crimson Persian rug covered the centre of the polished floor; the chairs and couches were soft and deep, and were lined with cordovan leather. A fire of maple knots burned on the gilded andirons beneath the great carved mantelpiece of mahogany and Viennese glass, for the morning was chilly; while the aromatic odor of the maple, the faint damp perfume of dead roses which came in through the open window, and the smoky haze of late Indian summer filled the room with a sensuous suggestion of a garnered harvest.

A huge polished table of mahogany, with massive pedestal and base, stood in the centre of the room, covered with piles of correspondence. Some half dozen letters had been singled out from the others, and lay near the master of the house.

He had been studying their contents, but had wheeled his chair of cordovan leather round to the fireplace, and now sat in its depths, his arm resting on its arm, his head bent in his hand. He was all alone, save for his daughter's two favorite dogs, the St. Bernard, Nell Gwynne, and the great white hound, Cavall, which lay on a white bearskin before the grate.

Everything in the room spoke of harmony and peace save its master.

He was silent, moody, taciturn. His eyes were partially closed, his eyebrows drawn together in deep thought, his one hand absently and irritably tapping the arm of the chair as the inner workings of his mind refused to formulate or take definite shape.

At length, not being able to bring order out of confusion, he arose abruptly and paced the floor with bent head. The great dogs looked up from their warm bed in wonder. Their instinct was very keen; there was something very wrong with their master.

Cavall raised himself on his forepaws and looked with almost human intelligence at his form as he paced the floor.

After several minutes in which no sound was heard, save his tread over the soft pile of the carpet and the clocks ticking one against the other on the mantels, Mr. Wellington once more approached the letters, and ran his eye over their contents, then touched a bell by his side with such force and decision as to bring Cavall to his feet with a deep baying sound.

A servant appeared at once at the door.

"Has Mr. Jack gone to his office yet?" asked the master of the house.

"Yes, Mr. Wellington, he went away early this morning, but he has returned for something. I saw him in the east library as I passed the door."

"Ask him to come here," said he, and then he seated himself once more before the pile of correspondence.

In a few minutes his nephew appeared at the door.

"There were parties here yesterday from three different constituencies. I have here correspondence from two more. Stubs has been in each. They are being caught by his tinsel; it is now too late to refute his arguments, but they each and all claim he must be quieted at once. He hasn't said much, but what he has said is ominous and presaging, and if allowed to develop means certain defeat in those places," said Mr. Wellingon, coming at once to the point without any preliminaries. "What are we to do?"

"Do you think it is going to be so serious that we may fear him? Don't you think you are exaggerating his importance and his influence?" asked Jack, weighing well his words.

His uncle handed him the letters. "Read those."

He seated himself at the opposite side of the table while Cavall came round and stood by his side. He rested his hand on the great head of the dog as he read.

"You are personally acquainted with these men?" he asked, when he had weighed their words well.

"I know them slightly, but their reputations are excellent. Majorities are often very small," continued the elder man. "Work is very scarce, labor is very plentiful. Machines have lightened labor and lessened its demands. The Lennox works give employment to a great many in each of those ridings."

"He is using his influence in that way?" asked Jack, without looking up.

"Yes, and his influence will certainly determine the result of those ridings," and Mr. Wellington's brow contracted into deep lines which were becoming more prominent and more permanent.

He was now plunged in gloomy contemplation.

"What are we to do?" he asked for the second time, after a pause.

"It is difficult to know what to do. Stubs' arguments, which are only tinsel, might easily be refuted, but cannot you see they are only a ruse to cover over this piece of private trickery? A man of honor cannot go up to a man devoid of honor and interfere in his private business. His own instincts tell him he is dishonorable in threatening his men with dismissal. He wants to stand well in the eyes of the public, and Stubs covers it over with a Marx mantle of philanthropy. It's their hypocrisy and audacity which makes a man swear. They'll come out of the fray as heroes, even in the eyes of the men they dismiss."

The elder man could not comprehend.

"I cannot see that we need care so much," continued Jack. "I would defy him, ignore him. I wouldn't pander to him. If we do secure him we cannot depend upon him. He's the kind that wants everything, and the kind that kicks over the traces when he doesn't get all he wants. I would let him go, and do his worst." concluded Jack with decision, while Cavall lay down at his feet to recover his disturbed slumbers.

"But if we allow all such men to go, we will go, too," replied his uncle.

"For a time perhaps; but give them rope enough and they'll hang themselves, and then they'll call us back."

"But we're not quite ready to go yet; there are some things which are not yet completed. I shall not be here when our day comes again. It is rather hard to see one's lifework left unfinished. One really wants to know he is leaving a tangible monument to his memory. If we could see it is for the best we would give up, but we cannot see it so—yet," said Mr. Wellington.

Yes, his nephew knew this and understood all the hopes and desires expressed in his uncle's words, and his nature was quick to respond.

"What would you advise us to do?" asked Jack, deferentially.

"One fails to understand the man. It seems so strange that he should work against Kenyon's interests."

"'Hell hath no fury like a woman scorned,'" said Jack.

"He hasn't scorned her, has he? What's all this talk in the clubs and in the lobbies? Is it true that he has spoken to Kenyon?"

"I don't know. Kenyon hasn't said anything about it, if he has."

"I am an old man and forget or fail to notice those things. In our day we were taught to believe that politics should be something more than getting down on one's knees to the froth and foam and scum. We were made to believe we had a calling, and that we were vice-regents and responsible to a higher power alone. The ancient heathen chose their rulers by clamor. Almost it seems that we have come to do so, too."

"Oh, no, they're not clamoring; she is working quietly and stealthily."

"Then there is a woman in it? It seems almost incredible. One is very strongly inclined to believe that women exist in politics, only in Disraeli's novels."

"But concrete cases disillusion one."

"Then you think she is really the cause of their indecision."

"Yes, I think she is," admitted Jack.

"It's too bad this has come up. Everything looked favorable since Kenyon cemented the break in our own ranks. It's a pity he couldn't cement this also. She wants position. Why doesn't he settle the matter? He has been going there long enough. He will surely satisfy her ambition; smartest man in the ranks, clever, handsome, best of families, minister, heart-whole— Going? Send Modena. Women know so much more about these things than men. I cannot reply to these letters until I learn something more definite."

Jack had risen; he was wanted at his office. He hesitated a moment, undecided what to say. In doubt do nothing, was a maxim which he had learned to respect. So he only said, "No one can dispute his beauty, his charm, his blue-blood or his standing, but one is not so sure about the wholeness of his heart, but I'll send Modena; she will know," and he went out, followed by Cavall.

Mr. Wellington pushed his chair back from the table, and once more leaned his head on his hands. He was yet little past the meridian of life, but the cares and worries of political life were beginning to weigh heavily upon him. His own portfolio was onerous and exacting, almost too great a responsibility at the present time for one man, while the chief's failing health, his frequent absence from the city, and the increasing demands of a growing nation caused many of his duties and obligations to devolve upon his first minister. Mr. Wellington was a man of the old school, imbued with a great consciousness of his responsibility, and hitherto what he had undertaken to do had received his undivided attention, and had invariably proved a success. Men had great confidence in his ability, his judgment and the wisdom

of his conduct; they invariably sought him when in any dilemma.
He had proved himself worthy of their confidence, but now he was
much worried; he could not become master of the situation. He
was not in touch with Mr. Lennox; he scarcely knew the man.
From their first appearance in the city, the new-comer had avoided
his presence; he had ignored him. He had made himself popular
with others and had won many to his way of thinking. Heretofore
Mr. Wellington hadn't noticed this; he had been so absorbed in his
work, so interested in the development of his country, so conscious
of the integrity of his own motives that he had had little time to
notice that many of his life-long friends were now seeking the
friendship of Lennox, and were becoming imbued with ephemeral
courses of conduct, laxity of administration and an infinitely
lower standard of honor.

His reflections, now as he realized that this was so, made him
bitter, but his bitterness soon softened into a regret.

" Jack would throw the whole thing down and start afresh, but
one cannot do so; if one did, it would only leave one all alone in
the world. One is forced to close one's eyes and look wise and
float with the tide. Isn't that what Balzac calls diplomacy? It
savors of cowardice, but it is the best one can do, and I suppose the
best now is to inspire Keith. Jack gave a queer smile as he left
the room, as expressive as Burleigh's historical nod. I wonder
what he meant! He said Modena would know. I wonder if he
told her," meditated he.

He turned to touch a bell, but as he did so he heard her footsteps in the hall without.

Her cousin had left the library with slow steps and had
traversed the many great halls which led to the conservatory,
where he knew Modena now was. He worshipped his cousin. She
had been kind to him, and he was extremely susceptible to any
kindness, and would repay it by a life-long devotion. By his own
thoughtlessness he had brought much trouble into his own life,
and through him trouble had come to others, and it now hurt him
to stand idly by and see those he loved do as he had done.

He had feared that it would end thus. Instinct is seldom in error
when it warns one of an enemy, and his had not been at fault
when it had told him that Verona Lennox was the one who would
bring trouble into his cousin's life. He did not for a moment
doubt what their reading of honor would be. "But one cannot
interfere," he said, as he opened the door leading into the conservatory.

His cousin was there sorting flowers from a great basket that had been sent in from Fernwylde that morning.

"Uncle wants you in the library. We're in a hole. We want to secure Lennox and quiet Stubs, and there is no way to do it but by Kenyon marrying her. Uncle wants you to help it along," he said to her abruptly and without any prelude.

Modena looked up but only smiled at the absurdity of his words. She did not for a moment credit the truth of Jack's tale or believe that he was speaking in earnest, and was expecting a denouement of some kind.

"We will have to rechristen you and father. What were the match-makers in Rome called? It is as cunning a plot as Hermes, the author of all artifices, could devise."

"It has been so far and it has now come to a climax, but there is no use wasting time over it, if you are going to discuss it in that way," said Jack, with a sternness in his voice.

Modena had resumed her work, but she now paused and looked at him.

"What do you mean?" she asked.

"I mean what I have said! What I have told you! Your father is planning to marry Keith Kenyon to Verona Lennox."

She couldn't refrain from smiling. Her father's interference seemed too preposterous to her to even consider it.

"Isn't your imagination far-stretched? From my knowledge of Mr. Kenyon I should judge he possesses a mind of his own, and could not be influenced by anyone."

"Yes, and I too know him. He is very susceptible to any appeal to his honor, and you know some men think it a point of honor to sacrifice their own pleasure, even their own convictions, for the good of their party. You will not uphold this, but it is a result of modern education. Acerbities, too, run high at election time, and a man is very apt to say and to do many things in the heat of passion and contest, that he would not do in calmer moments, and often lives to regret it. The party has appealed to him and to your father in all dilemmas. They would prove themselves worthy of the party's confidence. It will hurt their vanity, their pride, to admit they are now powerless. This, coupled with the fact that he has made his appearance with her very conspicuous of late, may induce and influence him to act unwisely."

"What a Curtius you would make him! And how would his sacrifice, if sacrifice you are pleased to call it, benefit his party?" asked Modena, with a little more credence in Jack's words.

"By securing Lennox."

"Oh, I see! But what do you want with me?" and through her mind ran the scene of a few nights ago which made her face warm and her pulse beat rapidly. "Do you want me to assist you in the matter. So far I have done all I can do. I have allowed no opportunity to pass without inviting them together to our social functions. What further can I do?"

Jack looked at his cousin closely and keenly.

"And would it please you to see him marry her?"

"Please me! What have I to say in the matter? What difference does it make to me?" she replied, in a tone which forbade any further interrogation.

"Then if it makes no difference to you, you had better go on in to uncle and assist him in the matter, but I am much mistaken if it doesn't matter to both of you," replied he, as he left the room with evident displeasure.

Modena remained for some time where he left her, too surprised to move. When he had opened the conversation, she had paid but little attention to it, thinking it some of his vagaries. She thought he was only bent on teasing her, and she did not wish to yet admit there was anything in it. She was not quite sure of the consistency of her own conduct. But as he proceeded she saw he was in earnest, and as she now thought of what his words implied about herself, a soft suppressed light came into her eyes, and she turned in sweet meditation to her flowers, and then she remembered that her father wished to speak to her.

She laid aside the apron of lawn which she had placed before her to protect her dainty swiss from the dew which was on the flowers, and traversed the great halls to her father's library, with her favorite dogs leaping and bounding before her.

Mr. Wellington looked up as his daughter entered, and took her hand, and drew her to a low ottoman by his side, and told her why he had sent for her. She listened to him with a growing apprehension. She knew her father would not lend himself to any scheme either ludicrous or foundationless, and slowly the seriousness of the situation began to unfold itself to her.

"Are you not allowing local circumstances to color your views? Yes, I know it is the minute details which make up the whole. Are they really of so much importance? Don't you think that much of it is braggadocio, and—and one must use the cant phrase, bluff. This chaff very quickly blows away, and the real wheat remains."

"Here is his wheat, men's bread and butter, read those," and he handed her the letters which he had received that morning.

The day was grey and dull but rainless. The library faced the west and was in shadow. She arose and took the letters to the leaded lights that she might see to read. She stood by the window and read. The casements were open and looked out into her own gardens. Beyond her gardens a path led down from Kenyon Court to the arm of the river at the foot of the terrace which bordered their home. As she read, Cavall bounded from her side through the open casement and bayed joyously. She raised her eyes, and as she looked she saw Keith Kenyon coming up the path towards Kenyon Court from the river's edge. The previous evening he had been called to a meeting at Idlewylde, and was now returning to his duties in town, having come up in his yacht from his country home.

He was walking very quickly. He saw her in the distance, raised his hat and slackened his pace. She smiled and bowed and then dropped her eyes to the letters in her hand. He stroked Cavall's head and passed on to Kenyon Court, while the words which she had read passed from her. The paper before her seemed one great blur. His face was ever between her and the words. She failed to concentrate her thoughts upon them, but mechanically her eyes followed the lines to their close, and then she turned once more to her seat beside her father. She returned the letters to Mr. Wellington, while in a few words he tried to impress upon her the importance of their contents.

But she heard not his words. She was thinking only of him. She thought of his love. She thought of him as she had seen him swaying vast audiences, of his integrity and honor, of his influence in his country and of the eulogy that had been given him. She thought of him as he was the evening they had spent in the room beside them, of his words in the library at Fernwylde, and of how his eyes had sought hers two nights previous, and as she thought her blood warmed within her in great passionate longing. She had forgotten her father's presence; her hand rested on his knee. He placed his on hers. "Has he said anything to you about it, my child?" her father asked.

"Spoken of—?" and she colored, warmly, thinking her father knew of what she was thinking.

"He has spoken to you of Miss Lennox?"

"No. Why should he speak to me of her?" she replied, recovering herself.

"I don't know why, only you seem to be the one round which everything revolves. He has always seemed one of ourselves. I thought perhaps he would tell you. I thought you would know if he really cared for her. If he speak to you, will you do what you can?"

A great desire to tell her father of her love almost overcame her for the moment, and then she recovered herself as she thought that he had not yet told her of his. She could not speak as yet.

"You would not think of interfering? Advising?" she asked her father.

"Oh, no; decidedly not, but the delay is hurting us."

His daughter remained silent.

"He cares for her; he must. He has made his attentions to her very public. He wouldn't wantonly trifle with the affections of one who loves him."

"I don't know that he has done so. If he has, that will be a matter which he alone must decide."

"You will not encourage it?"

"You say, they—these men say Mr. Lennox is threatening—no that is the wrong word—his men fear dismissal. Is there no law which will cover this?"

"You changed—checked your words; threatening and fearing are two different words. The law may reach the letter, but it cannot cover the spirit. There are so many intangible things which one cannot express, but which one feels, more powerful because of their indefiniteness and impalpability. Lennox imperceptibly has scattered these intangible things broadcast. The atmosphere is heavy and sultry and oppressive with them, like the air which presages a storm. One can feel them coming down on one like the stupor which creeps on men dying under the cold of falling snow. If it were only something one could touch, but it is evil in the form of a Calypso," and Mr. Wellington's brows drew together in deep lines, and he sighed.

Many times during his long career had he rejoiced to match himself against those intangible foes and to conquer, but now for the first time they were his master.

His sigh reached Modena, and touched her to the quick. She looked up quickly, and as she noticed how aged and careworn her father had grown she was moved to a great self-reproach.

"How intensely selfish I have been. I have been thinking only of myself. He has always known what is best. I must be guided by him," was her first impulse.

"What would you have me do, father?" she asked.

"Our work is not completed. You know how dear it is to me. One wants to leave it as a monument to one's memory. It would be an heirloom to you, one of which you may be justly proud.

Defeat means much to me. I thought—you know—that is—he cares for you; you know what I mean—and he will tell you about Lennox. If you understand how important it is to us you might do—say something to help us."

"What about Mr. Lennox?" asked his daughter in surprise, not having heard the rumors which were afloat.

"I don't exactly know. Report! Talk of clubs and lobbies! They say Lennox has spoken to Keith. Came from the auditorium to the Court after the meeting the other night; waited until Keith went from here. I don't know what passed between them, but it must come to a climax soon. Yes, I saw Keith last night; he said nothing, but he was very much annoyed. No, the newspapers haven't it, in respect to him they have kept silent. He cannot retreat without much talk; one doubts if he can retreat in honor. Why can't he see this and hurry it up, and settle the matter? That's what I mean. If he speak to you, you can tell him so."

Yes, she saw what her father meant, and she could not refuse his request; neither could she grant it—not yet.

"Is that all you want, father? If it is I shall go to my room. I feel rather weary to-day."

"Yes, my dear."

She kissed her father and went to her room.

"I knew it was not to be," she felt rather than said as she went. "I have never done anything to merit such happiness."

She stood long by the open casement, which looked over the gardens. It was late autumn; the skies earlier in the day had hung heavy with storm-clouds, but later on the sun had come out and now shone through the watery pall of mist overhanging the river, shedding its rays over the amber, russet-brown and golden glow of the many maples which dotted the garden and lined the water's edge, the darkness of the intervening cedars and firs making their ruddy glow seem brighter still. Late asters and dahlias yet reared their heads. The earlier flowers had drooped at the touch of the first frost, and were now being swept away with the autumn leaves by the gardeners at work beneath the great spreading trees. The air had in its breath the first premonition of a long cold winter; the scent of the wet earth and fallen leaves and dead roses and ripened fruit came into the room, bringing in its odor the same feeling of voluptuousness and sensuousness which one feels when reading a poem from the pen of a Keats. Something of this feeling stirred within Modena now. At no other time of the year would she, or could she, have felt with the same intensity with which she now felt.

All through the long gorgeous golden summer of a northern clime its people live in the open air, happy as the birds in the trees in the very happiness which comes from living. Doubly gorgeous does the summer seem, after the severities of the long cold winter, and a new life pulses and throbs within one's veins, as it does in all nature, but when "the melancholy days have come, the saddest of the year," one shivers and turns to the fireside with a great intuitive longing for the faces which they feel should be there, the faces which are necessary to their happiness in life.

Modena felt this now as she turned from the landscape to the fireside; his face dark-splendid rose before her, pleading for its place by her hearth. Could she let it come in? Almost it seemed to her that she was called upon to shut it out, as she had closed the casement barring out all sunshine and all nature.

All the blessings which life could bestow had been given to her. She had accepted them as things which had rightly belonged to her, but when her love had come into her life it seemed too great a blessing for her to accept.

"Love must be like Pindar's immortality; it must not be an inheritance; it must be a greatness achieved like all other greatnesses by purity of purpose—a reward allotted to the brave. I must not murmur. I have not merited it," she said again and again within her own mind. But yet some subtler inner sense told her that she had, but as it told her this, all the conventions of life rose up in array before her love, and she arose and paced the floor in the strongest disquietude which she had ever felt.

Over her life for the first time had come a cloud, bringing with it the sombre shadows of a moonless night.

CHAPTER XXII.

"But can Cæsar himself or can any god ever experience greater delight or be happier than a simple mortal at the moment when at his breast there is breathing another dear breast, or when he kisses beloved lips? Hence love makes us equal to the gods, Oh, Lygia!"

Modena sat long by the fireside that day. Outwardly she had regained her calm, but inwardly her mind and heart had yet to become mistress of themselves.

She felt a reluctance towards going out, fearing that she migh meet him, and yet was she ever troubled at the force of the desire which she ever felt to see him and to be near him. To a person who has been born with a spiritual nature and who has lived a life removed from the senses or any sensual indulgences, the first impulse of passion to such must be in a certain sense humiliating. The emotion in itself creates a feeling of lost confidence, of lost sovereignty and of lack of power to resist. Although she was all alone the blood warmed her face when she thought of the intense emotion which penetrated and pervaded her being at a mere touch from his hand, a glance from his eyes. The power had gone from herself to resist this.

She could not trust herself.

He was coming to Apsley House that evening to meet some men from the continent who were touring the country in the interests of immigration. No doubt he would remain afterwards, but she feared to meet him.

Late in the afternoon, she rose, rang for her maid, dressed herself in a street costume of dark-blue trimmed in sable, with sable hat to match, and went for a long walk to a little cottage in the outskirts of the city, where lived a little invalid, Grace Vivian, a grandchild of her old nurse. From here she went to Maple Hurst. She went with the Lesters to an opera, and later in the evening Mr. Lester brought her home.

She went at once to her own room. From here she heard the strangers take their departure, and then Keith Kenyon and her father came into the old English hall which extended from the front of the house to the centre, forming the donjon keep of their old home. She could hear the murmur of their voices, and as they approached the spiral stairway she heard Keith's voice asking for herself, but she did not appear.

The two men, turning from the main entrance, passed through her suite of rooms, which lay on the first floor, to the French door leading to the gardens. From here a side path led to the grounds surrounding Kenyon Court.

At the door her father bade him good-night, and he went across the rotunda with her dogs leaping about him. Their noise attracted the attention of Nell Gwynne, who was asleep on the upper portico. The dog arose, stretched herself, and with a few short cries begged to join them. Her mistress rose to release the dog, and as she did so, her form stood out, distinct, in the clear moonlight.

Keith Kenyon turned, raised his hat and paused, but as she made no movement to descend, nor gave any encouragement to invite his presence, he replaced his hat, and for the second time that day went on his way without seeing her.

During the next few days, several times she saw him pass along the street, walking with quick step and with bent head and dark, moody brow.

He did not again approach the house, and she went out little. She felt a reluctance towards meeting him or towards meeting anyone. Until she could become mistress of herself she doubted her ability to preserve a mask of indifference before her world, and she did not wish to have her world connect her name even in thought with that of Verona Lennox. Through that subtle intuition which tells us more plainly than spoken words, she felt what was going on around her.

A stormy interview had taken place between Mr. Lennox and the young statesman. Keith Kenyon had not spoken of it, but the Lennoxes had hinted at something. Then they had smiled and looked wise, and spoke of some nobleman whom Verona had discarded while travelling abroad. "How unwise she was to persist in her fidelity to Keith Kenyon; his reluctance to release her; love laughs at locks and at wisdom."

Idle rumors floated over the city like the crowd of carrion crows which hung over the gateway of the castle to carry off the carcasses of those who failed in their quest for the charm. No one spoke of it openly, but there was a strong undercurrent of feeling that an acute climax had come. A mystery surrounded the affair.

These rumors did not pierce the walls surrounding Apsley House. No one spoke of them in its mistress's presence, but its mistress felt them without being told.

The third evening after this her cousin came up to her boudoir, "Are you going to Idlewylde on Monday?" he asked her.

"I sent a note over to Mrs. Kenyon asking if she would excuse me. In her reply she insisted on my going if possible. The weather has turned warm again; it is depressing. I am surprised at their going down now. They are so busy."

"It is the English party; they cannot exist without the sound of the hunter's horn and the hound's bay. The hunting is excellent now. Keith cannot go. He was forced to go north for a week, but he asked Mayne to take them out for a few days. Mrs. Kenyon isn't very well."

"If I can be of any service to her I shall certainly go to-morrow," replied Modena at once, on learning of the absence of the master of the place. "Are you going?" she asked her cousin.

"I may run out for a few hours, but I cannot remain. Did Helen come in to-day?"

"Yes, but she returns to-morrow. How is father to-night?" she asked, changing the subject.

"He is very tired. He isn't looking well. St. Amand says the world of nature consoles, calms and does not betray, but the world of politics spoils and embitters the most beautiful of souls. If we cannot persuade him to leave it all and go to Fernwylde or abroad, I fear for him."

Modena looked up quickly. "Have you noticed it, too?"

"Yes, for some time. He takes life too seriously. Everything means something to him, and everything with the exception of intrigue means little to many of the men with whom he now comes in contact. Until recently he has taken this sudden transition in men's morals and manners and management very philosophically, but his failing health and our loss of prestige are making him irritable. This levity and laxity has so lowered our standard that he fails to know himself, measured by the rules which he once used. He has been forced to submit his superior judgments to the sovereign will of the masses, and submit to their tactics until he has lost his own self-respect. History testifies that it has ever been thus, and the men who try to keep breath in a dying government invariably become tainted by the dirt which gathers there. Couldn't you persuade him to retire or rest?"

"I don't think it would be wise for him to do so. Life without work would be unbearable. He will die in the work."

"No; perhaps it would not be wise for him to retire into private life, but there are offices of honor which he might accept, offices independent of the will of the mob. He could make himself felt there."

"I am afraid these offices are too far removed from the heart of the people. It is the people he really cares for. I am quite confident he will do his best to the end, whether it be for good or for ill."

"But he has never yet suffered defeat; defeat now will kill him. If he would only retire before it comes!"

"And leave the party in a crisis. You surely wouldn't wish that."

Jack frowned and remained silent, gloomily gazing out of the window.

"Has anything occurred of late to worry him? Since the mass meeting everything looks very favorable."

"Nothing, but this affair of Kenyon's. I thought—" said Jack, and then he hesitated and spoke of other matters, and soon afterwards left the room.

"He thinks that father is encouraging Keith, and that if he would retire he would read the situation with different glasses and discourage it. Jack would sacrifice his own interests for my happiness. I wonder what has passed between father and Keith," meditated Modena, as her women prepared her for the night. "Surely father is unwise! How strange of him to say anything! He has always been so careful to inculcate into us the knowledge that it is wrong to proffer advice, or interfere in other people's affairs. He has never done so before. He is surely blinded as to the consequences, but then, no doubt, he is looking at it as it affects the public welfare, and private feelings should not be considered," she thought as she fell into a troubled sleep.

She slept ill and awoke unrefreshed with the knowledge of what lay before her vividly on her mind.

The previous evening she had learnt that Verona Lennox was at Idlewylde, and she did not care to meet her—to meet him. Her reflections and her judgments had told her that it was a situation which they had created for themselves, and they should be left free to decide for themselves. To her, justice was the world's greatest attribute, and she wished to be just, even to Verona Lennox, and she knew that her presence would blind the scales of justice.

It might break her heart to do so, but Keith Kenyon must be left free to decide.

She would break the law much quicker in the letter than in the spirit. To break it in the letter would be to have the world as her accuser and judge, to break it in the spirit would be to have her own conscience. And her own conscience was a much sterner judge than the world.

She was afraid of herself. The intensity of her love had taught her that in his presence she could not withstand his pleadings, and should she willingly do an act of injustice to another she would forever afterwards scorn herself as a coward, therefore she wished to sedulously avoid his presence.

But Mrs. Kenyon had sent a second message to her insisting on her coming. The party included some Englishmen of high rank, and Modena was one of those people who make a place or a gathering dull or interesting by her absence or presence.

On learning of Keith's absence she went the next day to Idlewylde, and assisted Mrs. Kenyon and Mr. Mayne in their task of entertaining nobility for two days.

Their visit was a success; the old place with its servants in state liveries, its banners and flags floating on lake shore and from tree top, and from the pinnacles and towers, never looked brighter before. The woods had on their full autumn dress of gold and crimson, and resounded for two days with hunter's horn and hound's bay. In the evening the old theatre room was thrown open to a troupe of travelling players, and afterwards the long ball room was filled with music and dancers and gatherings gay.

They spent two days at Idlewylde, and late in the evening of the second day they returned to the city, but the mistress of Apsley House remained with Mrs. Kenyon to attend, the next day, an amateur performance at some distant school, in which both parties at the present time were very much interested.

It was late when they returned. A message was awaiting the mistress of Fernwylde, informing her that her father and Carlton Monteith had come out for the evening. Mrs. Kenyon at once ordered the carriage to take her to Fernwylde, but she insisted on walking, as the evening was beautiful and the distance by the ravine and meadows very short.

"You will let Helen come with me? I shall send her back in the morning," she said.

"Yes, but where is she?" replied Mrs. Kenyon.

"I saw Mr. Linden join her at the fish pond," answered Verona Lennox, who had spent the day at home not caring to listen to the rustic songs of the school children.

"Then I shall meet them," said Modena. "No, thank you, Mrs. Kenyon, you needn't send Holmes. Mr. Linden will walk over with us."

She turned, and in a few minutes after she had passed the turn in the path which hid her from the view of Idlewylde, she met Helen and Mr. Linden.

They were accompanied by the master of Idlewylde who had returned unexpectedly, and who had joined them as he walked over from the evening train. He had come direct to Idlewylde, not knowing that his guests had limited their stay to two days. On learning of their departure he turned and walked towards Fernwylde. As the foot-path narrowed he laid his hand on Modena's arm and detained her, allowing the others to proceed.

It was the first time she had been alone with him since the night in the library some two weeks previous. "Was it only two weeks?" Almost it seemed like ages, but the ages were forgotten; she was now only conscious of the warm touch upon her arm;

17

she was glad that the twilight had deepened into night to hide her emotion.

The evening was beautiful; the moon, which had just made its appearance as a great red ball on the horizon when they had left Idlewylde, now shone clear on the shimmering waters of the river by their pathway. The ravine and the woods were dusky with fleeting shadows.

He spoke of indifferent topics while Helen and her companion were near, but perceptibly slackened his footsteps that he might speak alone to the woman whom for days he had been longing to see.

But how to speak to her he did not know. He could have breasted a line of spears with less effort or courage than it took to speak of this to her. No man can go to another, whether it be to man or to woman, and say, as the father of men said, "She tempted me and I did eat." His honor forbids his doing so.

He could say nothing and the time was passing.

They had now reached the Fernery; their companions had gone across the lawn by Maple Grove. Fernwylde loomed out distinct in the clear moonlight. He had said too much to her the other night not to say more, and how was he to say more until she knew the position in which he was placed!

He paused abruptly by the Fernery stile which hid them from view, and stimulated by desperation said as abruptly, " Modena, you see the position in which I am placed."

He felt in having to say this he had lowered himself immeasurably in her estimation, and under his breath he uttered a good round English oath to relieve his indignant disgust at all things past, present and to come, but herself.

Yes, she understood the position, but she could not speak or help him. She knew nothing definite. She could only remain silent until he enlightened her.

" I cannot marry her!" he exclaimed at length.

" Marry whom? You are speaking in enigmas."

" You know whom I mean. Verona Lennox!"

" Must you marry her? You are master of your own actions surely."

" No, I must not, and will not," he ejaculated, bitterly.

" Then why do you speak of it? Who wants you to marry her?"

" Can't you see how it has been! How it is now! Her father! Herself! The interests of the party! I didn't mean anything. She knows I didn't," exclaimed he.

"But you needn't marry her because they wish it. You are only responsible for your own actions," she replied.

"But that is the basis of the trouble. I didn't mean anything. You know I didn't. But they—and the world have given a wrong meaning to my actions. They claim—" and he hesitated, too full of honest indignation at the intangibility, misrepresentations and myths of their claims, to speak. "The publicity!" and "One's honor," was all he could say, which told Modena little.

"Do you consider, yourself, that you have compromised her?" she asked, speaking in her usual way direct to the point, and she waited with intense apprehension for his reply.

It seemed to her that her whole life depended upon his reply.

"I—I—I have been to blame," he admitted, feeling how unwise he had been to have allowed himself to have been drawn into such a position.

"Then, if you have been to blame, you should marry her. It is not right or honorable to trifle with anyone's affections," she replied very coldly.

All the light seemed to have gone out of her life. She had thought him so different from all others. "To have loved her, and at the same time gone to others—to Verona Lennox." The thought was repulsive to her and she turned towards the house. He detained her.

"How can you reason so coldly?"

"Because I am reasoning for other people."

"If you were reasoning for yourself, would you admit what you have now admitted?"

"I do not think I would allow myself to be drawn into such a position," and then she remembered her own position. "That is—" and she paused. She could not say what she was about to say—"after she had once met him."

"You know why I did it."

"How do I know? What have I to do with it?" she said, as coldly as before.

"You have all to do with it. I did it because I loved you," and he made a motion towards her, but she drew away.

"It was an unprecedented way to show your love for me—to go to another—it was at least peculiar."

"I thought at times you loved Monteith, and I did it to hide my love from the world. It wasn't a noble act, but—my God, Modena! You don't for one moment think that I have ever thought of her, spoken to her, that I even as much as touched her hand. You didn't think so—"

A weight as of a mountain of lead seemed to roll away. What she suffered at the thought of having to live all her life without him was as nothing to what she suffered when she thought him to be lower than her ideal of him had been.

"How could you think so? I would no more doubt you than I would doubt heaven. That night—you remember—I even doubted my own eyes," and his voice had in it a tenderness and a pleading pathos which spoke more constancy and love and trust than all spoken words could express.

She felt it, and she again knew him as he was, and her whole heart went out to him but she could not speak. She could not admit anything; not until after he had decided.

He felt the change in her manner; he felt her form relax, and he knew she had thought thus, and stooping over he drew her to his breast in one passionate embrace, and for the first time in her life she felt the sweetness of kisses on her lips, her cheek, and her hair.

All the passion in her nature rushed into her blood and veins at his thrilling words and close embrace, while his hot, labored breath on her face and brow caused the blood to course through her veins with greater warmth than she had ever known.

In his arms she was powerless to resist.

"Will you tell me you love me? I want to hear it from your lips," he said, and he raised her face to his.

She opened her lips twice for her heart to speak, but words refused to come.

Was it some Unseen Power which held her back, or was it only her pride, which in all its glory is but a bondage of weakness, and which invariably holds back human souls from their own deliverance? Which was it? She could not tell. Nor could she ever afterwards in the course of her long life tell.

With great effort she recovered her self-control and drew herself away.

"You have forgotten my position and your own for the moment, Keith. Forget what has passed between us."

It cost her much to say these words. They seemed so cold and commonplace, but it is only with the most commonplace words one can express the deepest feelings of one's life. All words seemed too feeble to express what she felt. She could only express it in the simplest of words.

He felt it and he replied to her in the same way.

"Forget what has passed between us! Forget! I cannot and will not as long as life shall last. Do you think since my lips

have touched yours they can ever touch another's? Do you think
I could live and see another man's touch yours? You are mine.
I want you. I want you," he cried.

She felt herself yielding before this great love, and she feared
herself.

There was an appeal in her voice when she next spoke.

He felt it and felt for her.

"We must go in," she said.

It would have been unmanly to have made her bear more.

"When shall I see you again?" he pleaded.

"To-morrow—the next day—when you will, but I must think,"
she said. "No, do not come any farther. I am tired. Helen is
waiting for me. You see how it all is. Good-night."

He raised his hat, and watched her as she passed over the greensward in the moonlight, Cavall and Nell Gwynne coming to meet
her. She joined Helen and Mr. Linden at the avenue leading to
the rotunda. He saw her kiss her father and greet Carlton Monteith, and then he turned and retraced his steps towards Idlewylde.

CHAPTER XXIII.

The following morning the men returned to their respective
duties, while the mistress of Fernwylde, who had promised to
return to Idlewylde in the morning, sent a servant over with a
note asking its mistress to excuse her for the day.

She sent Helen back and spent the day alone. There were
some things which must be hid from the common light of day;
things which must be felt, not seen. Love was one of these. She
wanted to be alone with it. All was confusion, but the intense
intoxication of happiness which pervaded her being dominated
the confusion.

She would do what was right when the time came, but in the
meantime she wanted to live the happiness. He was coming to
her again. There was intense joy in the thought.

In the first intoxication of her love she had felt herself not
worthy of such blessing, but as her calmer moments came, her
confidence in herself came with them, and she began to feel more
assurance that this great love would one day be hers. It might
not be hers now, not yet. She could promise him nothing nor give

him hope, until he could in honor speak to her, and she could in honor listen and reply. All her life she had acted wisely and well, and she could wait. She would do the same now, and all would be well.

So she felt and waited for his coming.

Early in the evening Helen returned and later on they were joined by Jack, who had come over from an adjoining town.

After dinner as they sat out on the western terrace her cousin turned to her.

"I am tired, very tired; this is an evening in which ghosts and goblins love to wander; bring your guitar and play us something. Music lulls the soul to sleep."

"Is your conscience so uneasy that you seek oblivion?" inquired his cousin, as she looked at him and noticed how tired was his appearance.

"Not so very uneasy. You know a person has two consciences,—a private one and a political one. My private one is tired from the uphill strife of the other. This is fairyland; all it lacks is the music," replied he, as his eyes wandered over the magnificent view which unfolded itself before them, now softened and tinted by late autumn.

"Then why not listen to nature's music? It is sweeter by far than any I can give you. The whip-poor-will is calling to his spouse in Maple Grove; the owl is murmuring to the moon; the chimes from the monastery echo back the notes from the clock tower; Reuben's whistle is in harmony with Lisette's song, and the wraiths, which you say love to wander in our western woods, are telling strange stories to one another had we ears fine enough to hear or eyes fine enough to see," said Modena.

"You would have us Grays!"

"To write elegies!"

"This scene doesn't inspire elegies," said Marion. "It suggests love lyrics. The rising moon is claiming its own, not listening to the moping owl's complaint. Reuben's walk tells us that his way is not weary. It is like the voices in the woods, and the notes in the water. It is pulsing with joy. One can feel it in the air."

"Love tragedies, you mean. We take life too seriously for lyrics. Lyrics are relics of the days of Montespan, Juliet and Marguerite. We only know them by the name of 'Mariage de Convenance,'" said Jack.

"It's one's own fault if life is a love tragedy," said Marion, warmly, with a personal ring in her voice.

She had known what had been in the air around her, and her heart had sung with joy. She had no patience with people who mistook the meaning of life's philosophy of present pleasure. "How stupid of them not to eat their apple when it is placed before them! What a funny conception of life they possess! They should be made to suffer to bring them to their senses," she thought.

"But destiny, that uncouth master of ceremonies, often diverts himself by making a tragedy out of it, despite our best efforts to the contrary," said Jack.

"Oh, don't say so! You remind one of the Persæ, or a chapter from Euripides."

"And they are continually reminding one of the Devil."

"We are speaking of the classics," said his cousin. "At least you might be musical enough to use their language."

"Those are things in retrospective, and may be expressed by the classics, but we are talking English facts and require the force and crudity of the English language to express the facts."

"One fails to see where you can get any such facts out of this scene. Any scene suggests what dwells in one's own mind," said Marion.

"Then love lyrics dwell in yours. How nice to be a poet and a lover!"

"Oh, I wasn't thinking of anything so prosaic as the present," said Marion, quickly and coloring slightly. "I was thinking of the past. I was thinking of the only classical age our country has ever known, of the days of Vaudreuil and Sevigne, of Frontenac and Montespan, of their courtiers and pageants and minuets and elegance out here in these old halls. How gay and grand life must have been then!"

"You would go back to the minuet and the distaff instead of to the galop and plush. You think those people understood the moon and Reuben's whistle and the whispering of the trees. Perhaps we do, too!"

"What a funny way you have of showing it!"

"But an Englishman doesn't show it. He only feels it."

"You would run the gauntlet without a groan? The stoicism of the aborigines! You would eliminate human nature altogether."

"Oh, no, we're not quite so bad. We only lack courage. Other people's smiles or frowns are our barometer, and we cover up our real feelings afraid of their laughter at our little weaknesses and humanities."

"You mean the conventions of life," said his cousin, quickly,

"You would place no restriction on love? In time you would have no love."

"Oh, no, I do not mean its conventions. I would place a very strict one upon love, but it wouldn't be one of other people's frowns."

"Our own frowns are our restrictions."

"Then your frowns are like your tree whisperings; they are too fine for our minds to comprehend. Is your music as fine? Here comes Kenyon. He has a fine ear for music. At least, he will be able to appreciate your frowns and your music. Will you not give us some?"

"Which? Frowns or music?"

"Oh, music. You may keep the frowns for him. If he cannot clear them away, no one else can."

She sent a servant for her guitar as Keith Kenyon came up the walk and joined them.

The previous evening he had not returned to Idlewylde, but in reply to a message he had received earlier in the day he had taken a late train to a nearby town. Mr. Stubs had passed through the town. In the morning a deputation had waited upon the young minister. Their words had but increased his confusion. On his return to the city he had met his chief, who had expressed a desire that he would show himself in the districts through which Stubs was now touring. He had promised to do so the following day, and had then left for Fernwylde.

He now greeted them and seated himself near her, as the servant returned with the guitar and handed it to his mistress.

She was seated near a trellis covered with passion flowers and clematis vines, where the breezes from the Idlewylde rippled her hair back from her brow, and the dying light shone on her profile.

When the servant handed it to her, she took it and laid it down by her side, but her cousin insisted upon her playing. To please him and to compose herself for what she knew must soon follow, she once more took up her guitar and ran her fingers lightly over its chords.

She was dressed in white with old lace at her bosom and arms. Crimson beauty roses nestled in the lace and circled the dark masses of hair which were coiled low on her neck. Over her shoulders, for the evening was chilly, she had thrown a wrap of crimson lined with sable, and her feet rested on white bearskins which covered the floors of the rotunda. Her dogs lay at her feet. As she raised the guitar and paused for a moment, wondering what she would play, she made a figure, simple, stately, patrician, in keeping with the background of great leaded lights with their mystic symbols, the spacious halls with their statues of bronzes and terra cottas in their niches, their spiral stairways leading to the famous Ghirlandina Tower with its flower-like openings, where hung the famous chime of bells which had been brought by some of her ancestors from the Campanile of Modena Castle, and which had rung out over the lands of Fernwylde now for some two centuries.

She possessed a touch which had in it a great tenderness of interpretation. From the time she had been able to lisp a few words until the present, she had taken much pleasure and pride in music, and although a natural-born musician she played with great precision, which was the result of application and pains-taking study. But to-night she chose something simple. Her heart, her life was full to overflowing. It was a relief to give vent to her tension of feeling, and she did so in an outburst of melody —melody full of strength and weakness, love and pathos and plead-ing. In the hush of the evening the notes of her guitar echoed through the twilight air in that sensuous and suggestive inter-pretation of the passions which string music alone can give. There was now no other sound on the night save the ripple of the gliding dusky waters of the river and the far-away rumbling of many waters falling from the mountain sides. She played on and on, songs without words, drifting into many old airs which she had heard some wandering minstrels play, now in one land, now in another, and now in her own, when the winter was white on all the land, airs having within their notes the echoes of Goethe's Lehrjahre, its lost wanderings, its mysticism and Mignon's longing for light.

They listened as they had never listened before, and he, listening, understood, and his heart sank within him.

As the last notes vibrated through the darkening air she arose and handed her guitar to Jack. "Let us go in," she said. "The dew is falling."

They rose, but as they came to the doorway Keith Kenyon laid his hand upon her arm. "I would speak with you," he said.

He drew her arm within his own and turned towards the Fern-ery. He paused at the edge of the terrace overlooking the river and took her hand in his.

"I want your answer," he said, without any prelude.

"My answer?" she asked in a low voice, and with a tremor in it.

"Do you love me? Will you marry me?" he replied as briefly.

She had thought all night. She had thought all day. She had

thought until it seemed that her head as well as her heart was in one confusion.

When it comes to the crucial test of one's life, action is not the result of impulse, or if it be, then impulse is that which has in it the concentration of all one's previous life, theories and actions.

So it was with hers.

Her whole life and theories seemed to pass before her mental vision. She thought of all the theories she had advanced regarding consistency in life, of all the privileges and duties she had claimed for her order, and of how she had scorned a moral coward. For people to be governed by consistency, abnegation and a strong sense of duty seemed to her the chief axiom of life. "If one cannot carry into practice what one has advocated all one's life, then one is a traitor to oneself." Death would be preferable to her before a betrayal of self.

She thought of how he himself had pleaded the spiritual nature against the sensual in the advancement of the higher life; and now when it was brought home to themselves!

They must be consistent.

Her reflection, introspection and reasonings had brought some facts very vividly before her. She felt that if he had by his own actions or thoughtlessness enlisted or encouraged the affections of another, he must be left free to decide his course of action in the future. Her love and her happiness must not stand between him, or influence him, in his sense of duty or conduct in life.

And there was her father. Any gentlewoman would suffer rather than see others suffer through her. Her father had consulted with her in many matters, and her fine insight and quick perceptions had aided him in many a sore strait, but in her intercourse with him she had also learned how immature were her judgments, and from prejudice and tradition how narrow were her views, and she had come to accept his judgments more so of late. She knew now that he believed that the Lennox adhesion was an absolute necessity to success. She couldn't see it herself, but since he had said so, it must be so, and she knew that defeat at the present time would mean much to her father. He must not suffer through her.

Nothing could alter her decision.

The circumstances and situations of life, however crooked or contrary, the courageous may change; but character the gods themselves cannot alter.

Self-abnegation and justice were integral parts of her nature and made her act thus.

"If he married the other she would live it out as it was, but if he did not, in time—" and her whole being warmed at the thought. She now turned to her companion.

"You asked me, if I would marry you. My answer can only be, No."

For some moments he was too overcome to speak, and then he asked her, "Why?"

"From what you admitted last night you have no right to ask me. It is not honorable."

"What did I admit?"

"You admitted that by your actions you had compromised another woman."

"Do you love me, Modena?"

A spasm of pain passed over her face. He saw it.

"I love only you. Is it honorable after these words to go to another and ask her to be my wife?" he said, and he could say no further.

There was only one law and that was love. So his whole nature told him.

He knew the only way possible to persuade her to retract her words and alter her decision would be to appeal to her reason, and convince her that love was infinitely greater than sacrifice or duty, but he was governed too much by the same principles as she herself was, to use what was to him a false logic.

Like Goethe before the bars of finite knowledge, he stood helpless and hopeless before the bars of his own actions. But he wanted her so much that his love became greater than himself. His passion grew in upon her and he felt her form relax, and then in lieu of words he allowed human nature its sway and drew her to him.

Her closeness seemed to fill his veins with fire and passionate words came to him, and he pleaded as only a great love can plead.

A weakness stole in upon her, sweet and insidious as the lulling charm left by opiates. "It was so sweet to be loved," she thought. "I cannot give him up. I cannot give him up," and for a moment the strongest temptation of her life assailed her, a temptation to tell him so. But yet she could not tell him. There are some things one cannot do. Why, one cannot tell. And it now seemed to her that this was one of them. But she could not wholly refuse him.

"I can say nothing now," she said, at length. "I shall go down to the city in the morning and see father, and then you may come," she replied, indirectly admitting her love for him.

He knew her so well that he knew what was passing in her mind. He knew that these moments were the first in her life in which she had shown any weakness, and he hesitated in pressing his love upon her.

With her words he was forced to be content, and then he went with her to the house.

He did not go in, but returned to the city, while Modena did not retire that night but sat at her window going over once more the battle of her life.

Before dawn she laid her head back in the chair and fell into an uneasy slumber, and was awakened at daybreak by Nell Gwynne baying beneath her window. She rang for her maid, bathed and dressed herself, and went to seek Jack, asking him to bring Helen and Mrs. Gwen up to the city during the day, and telling him that she was forced to take an early train.

As she stood on the velvety lawn wet with dew, waiting for the carriage, she looked away to the east where the first rays of the rising sun had not yet made their appearance, as if seeking guidance from the great golden dawn.

She stood for some moments, and at any other time the peaceful calm of the late autumn morning and the great love that would have been awakened in her young heart for her old home as the sun, now rising in blinding radiance on the horizon, dispelled the lingering mists and made the dew-drops on the maples and ivy glisten like diamonds, would have moved her to tender emotions, but she was utterly oblivious of it all, and round her mouth were new lines of care as she turned and entered the carriage. The glory of living seemed to have passed away. To her, stern duty had stretched forth its grim hand in irony and smote her in the very morning of life. But she did not murmur. She was no fair-weather woman, and she was too young, and too strong, and too courageous to doubt for one moment the path of duty.

She only wondered which way it lay.

She was disposed to think the whole affair a hideous dream that would pass away with the morning light, but as she sat in the coach, unavoidably she overheard the conversation of two workers in the contest regarding the importance of the Lennox adhesion, and this recalled it as a vivid reality to her mind.

It was a strange ride for her that morning from Fernwylde to Apsley House.

All her life long this ride had been one of the pleasures of her life. To her it had been a path of roses lying between two beloved homes. It was all so familiar to her, the birds chirping to each other in the trees at the little wayside station, the sparrows hopping after the crumbs, the peaceful busy milkmaids and plowboys, with sunbonnets and broad-brimmed hats, singing or whistling softly as they went to their morning tasks, so free from care and so happy, the late marguerites and golden-rod by the roadside, the children on their way to school, the hurrying milk carts, and the barking dogs. All these had seemed to be her own and part of herself. They had all been associated with her young life. Now her nervous system, strung to severe tension, was more than ever susceptible to impressions, and this morning they marked themselves on her memory with that cruel distinctness with which scenes and places associate themselves, and paint themselves in undying colors of red and black on one's memory with great mental conflicts or great sorrows. They were never to her the same again.

He had taken a red rose from those which she wore in her bosom the night before. The others she now carried in her hand. They were some of the last late roses of summer. These she kept with her always, but she could never bear to look upon the last roses of summer again.

CHAPTER XXIV.

When Modena reached Apsley House her father was in the library, and she went direct to him and told him all. When she saw by the early morning light how grey and aged he had grown her heart ached in pity for him.

When he heard what she had to tell him he was silent. Of late it had come home to him that things were not well; he had done what he could to keep her true to Carlton Monteith, and now it grieved him greatly when he learned what his daughter had to tell.

Local circumstances and situations invariably color one's views and warp one's judgment, and he had always allowed minute details to move him; he allowed them to move him much more so than generalizations. His own business affairs and his household were ever kept in the strictest order. As his daughter had grown to womanhood he had had great confidence in her and had entrusted much to her management. She had devoted herself to their care and had brought to bear in their administration a skill and judgment which had added materially to the already immense revenues of Apsley House. To all her dependents she was kind, generous, and thoughtful of their welfare and quick to reward merit, but she would never countenance the waste of the smallest thing nor the loss of any power. She was strict and firm, and her servants feared as well as loved her. "Wilful waste makes woeful want," was a maxim which had been inculcated in her. She was acquainted with the smallest details of their many large interests, and the smallest details had invariably received her closest attention.

So it was with Mr. Wellington in the government of his country. Had he had his way he would have ruled disinterestedly and justly by great vital principles, but since the ruling depended upon the will and pleasure of the individual, the securing of this individual will became of as much importance as the ruling. In his ruling he had always believed that if he allowed one vital principle to slip from his grasp others would follow in rapid succession until one's own individuality would have slipped from oneself; and so, too, with the loss of the individual. He could not willingly see one slip from him.

In his imagination now he allowed the Lennox adhesion to appear of infinitely more importance than it really was. The constituencies most affected had so persistently sought his advice and assistance that this had caused him to dwell upon it and exaggerate it to such an extent that he had almost come to believe the fate of the whole country depended upon it.

But his daughter's happiness and conduct were dearer to him than his ambition, and he was greatly moved when he heard her confession, and bowed his head on his hands.

He was doubly worried, worried over the situation and the publicity which would be given to it, and vexed over his daughter's inconsistency and inconstancy. He thought she was pleading for herself, and he had scarcely looked for selfishness in her nature.

At length he raised his head and looking at her said, "Modena, if your happiness depend upon him, I would not ask you to sacrifice it for either power or prestige, but young girls often mistake a passing fancy for love. I wish you would reconsider the matter for a few days before you decide. It has been the first effort of my life to make you a noble woman, and I believe the care and culture bestowed upon you have not been given in vain. I feel there is something better and nobler within you than in most women. I trust, my dear, you are a gentlewoman, then your instincts and your intelligence will guide you in your decision."

It hurt him to think she was selfish, and his voice contained an accent of sternness.

She looked out through the window to where the sun was shining so brightly. Two birds were sitting in a peach tree top near the window, and the brightness and serene happiness of all nature seemed to mock the conflicting emotions within her breast.

She turned her eyes to her father where he sat at his desk, and her heart melted as she saw the change which the last few weeks had wrought in him, and as she mentally reviewed all that he had done for her, and how careful he had been with her education and her morals, she was moved to a great self-reproach, and her resolution returned to her in all its confidence and strength.

"Father," she said, " I am strong; I shall do it," and to comfort him she continued, "It will not be hard," and she was going to add, " Carlton Monteith is a noble man," but she could not say the words, and only said, " Time will change it all. Do not think of it any more."

He looked at her gravely and intently.

"Do you think, my child, that you really love Keith best? Do you think your happiness depends upon him?" he asked.

"I did not know the meaning of love until I met him," she replied.

Mr. Wellington looked at her and sighed as he saw the tender look in her eyes and the fleeting softness in her face which told more than all words could tell.

He was proud that she had decided to sacrifice herself; he was proud that the instincts of a gentlewoman had predominated; but he would be as generous as she, and her happiness was dear to him.

He seemed to realize the depths of her nature and her love for Keith Kenyon. Memories of his only love came to him with a force so great in all its past sweetness that he quailed before its living presence.

He had loved one; another had loved her, too. He had wooed and won her, and she had been taken from him so soon, so soon. He had murmured not. He had always felt that his happiness was so great that he had not merited it, and he looked upon his waiting-time here as a probation, a battlefield where he might win his reward, her love eternal. This very thought made him careful in what he would say to his daughter. He could only place the facts before her. It must be something which she must decide for herself.

"No, my darling child, I cannot ask you to do it. It pleases me more than I can tell that you are willing to do so. I am sorry, under the present circumstances, that you love him. But for that man, and your relations to Carlton Monteith, nothing could have pleased me better than to see you marry him. Next to Lester I respect him above all other men, but you must consider your conduct towards Carlton, and you must remember what defeat will mean to us, and what gratitude we owe the chief, and Keith's prospects in the event of success—but there, those are nothing. What am I saying?" and he checked himself. "Your happiness comes first, my dear."

"Then, father, I shall be happy in comforting you," she replied, with that instinct of self-abnegation so great within her. "I shall see him and send him to you," and she kissed her father and turned to leave him.

"No, my child, do not do anything to cause yourself one moment's pain; think well before you decide, and only remember I love you better than anything else on earth."

She left him with these words ringing in her ears.

"How cowardly and self-centred I should be if I could not repay him for his life's devotion; and success to Keith means title, honors, distinction. What is love, true love in true womanhood, but complete self-abnegation, self-control, self-effacement?" she thought to herself as she traversed the great hall to her own rooms.

She had left orders with the head servant that when Mr. Kenyon came to show him to her private room.

He was waiting her now.

He had been pacing the floor. His face was very pale. When she entered the room he paused by a small table, but he did not approach her.

She went up to the table and stood beside him. She knew by his appearance that he had not rested since they had parted, and his suspense now was plainly evident.

When he looked into her face he knew his fate and moved nearer her.

"Can nothing I say change your decision?" he asked, with incredulity and despair.

"No," was her only reply.

A chill ran through him like the cold of death.

"My dear, you have willed it. Don't you think that in time you will regret it?" he asked, his mind trying to comprehend what her one little word entailed.

"Remorse would be infinitely worse than regret."

"Why remorse?"

"The loss of one's self-respect."

"But our self-respect is too often our prejudices and our pride. There is nothing perfect or eternal but love. Why do you ignore t? It is all there is in life. If I go to her and speak, that closes my lips forever. Why do you will an eternal separation?" he pleaded.

A spasm of pain crept through her veins at his words. "Why need he go to her? Why cannot he wait?" was her one thought, but she could not say so; and the word eternal rang in her ear like a death-knell.

No facile love could ever have any abiding-place in her life, in his life. Theirs was a great love. He was a bold, brave man, but his heart quailed and quivered within him as a sense of the loneliness of a long life-time without her took its root there. Events, emotions, decisions came but slowly into his life, but when they came, they came to remain forever, and were as much to his life as the red corpuscles were to his blood.

As he looked at her his brow contracted and his face grew colorless as though he suffered from some inward pain.

" Can you not see how it will be, Modena? You are young and have your illusions, but in time these illusions will be usurped by the real passions of life, and one will have many dark moments and hours of temptation," he said to her, in the words of a man who had learned some of the bitter lessons of life, and one who knew that the sensual too often proves stronger than the spiritual. He had been unaccustomed to weakness, because he was neither sensual nor licentious from inclination, but he knew that great loves like theirs had within them the germs of great dangers.

But this was something she could not understand. The will ruled the passions. She would be weak indeed were it otherwise.

"Then you still persist in refusing?"

"There is no other course open to me."

He was silent for some moments, trying to realize what it meant.

"You would advise me to marry her?" he said, in despair.

" I never advise. Your own sense of honor must decide your actions."

He was exasperated; his actions had rendered him powerless to defend. He felt there was nothing to do but accept the fate destiny had willed for him.

His senses were not normal, and he felt he was being driven by a fate he was powerless to resist.

He almost felt that she was implying by her words and actions and her reserve that his spirit was weak in being unwilling to suffer the result of his own actions.

He seemed to realize her great courage.

18

He could not bear to have her think him cowardly. He was not a man of impulse, but under the impulse of this thought he said he would do it.

"Then I shall marry her," he said, almost bitterly, and without any further words she allowed him to go from her.

When he left the room she seated herself in a low chair. The strain had been so great that her mind was dazed, and she remained passive.

Her father came to her, but she said little.

He went away, and she remained in her own room until the following morning, and what she suffered that day and that night left an indelible mark on all the after days that she lived.

She appeared the next morning as though it had not happened, but there were lines on her face and an expression round her mouth which are the fruits only of the tragedies of life.

Her father, who loved her so dearly, was too much absorbed in the turmoil of the strife to notice the change, but change there was, a change impalpable, intangible, but as great as the change from the noontide of a summer day to a midnight of winter. There was no physical alteration perceptible, but in her eye was a look, to those who loved her, painful to behold. Her cousin Jack was the only one who saw it, and when he saw it he went at once away from her presence, away from the city. He was afraid of the forces which warred within himself.

She was conscious of it herself. She felt years older than she had felt a few short weeks before, but she went about her duties as usual. She went to a church meeting in the morning and then to a musical in the afternoon, and appeared at two teas afterwards, and then returned home to dress for a Cabinet dinner that evening.

She dreaded going to the dinner. "If he has spoken to her the world will know it," she thought, as her women dressed her. She was physically exhausted and felt unequal to the strain of a simulated serenity and self-command. But her world must not know it. So she gathered together her little reserve of strength and went to the dinner, and heard what she expected but dreaded to hear.

CHAPTER XXV.

WHEN Keith Kenyon left Apsley House that morning he did so as in a dream. He was like a traveller who had been walking all his life, as it were, on one of Turner's shining plains beside a sunlit sea, but now a great cloud had darkened the sky, and he had fallen from the high cliff into a yawning gulf below. He could see the rocks and shoals as they passed by, he could feel the treacherous sand sliding with him at his touch and hear the rushing, angry waters below, but yet he was powerless to resist.

He walked along the street with head bent and brows dark and lowering. He raised not his head nor spoke to anyone, but went direct to Lennox Court. When he reached the threshold of the door he shook himself like a great mastiff that had been swimming shakes itself, as if to rid himself of the ludicrousness of the whole affair.

He saw that he had made a mistake in allowing himself to drift into such a position. His conduct towards her had been as open as the day. No words of endearment or even of intimacy or confidence had passed his lips. She had occupied no thoughts in his life. He had not realized that they were putting a wrong meaning upon his words or actions until a few days previous, when Mr. Lennox had spoken to him.

Then he had been rudely awakened.

Any publicity or scandal was abhorrent to his fine instincts. Closet tragedies were permissible and endurable, but to give one's finer feelings and inner life to the scrutiny and comment of the common world was a lack of good taste and a vulgar display of all the finer things which men of his order tenaciously hold in reserve.

He was to the very heart a man of the world, and was morbidly sensitive to any such display or comments. He had come from a line of men who had been for centuries proud of their honor, integrity and stern sense of justice. His race had been unsullied. The thought of any public scandal was unbearable, detestable, revolting, and yet to marry her was more so.

He would see Mr. Lennox and speak to him as he would to a man of honor.

He rang imperiously and harshly, and asked to see the master of the house. He was ushered obsequiously into the library, and in a few minutes Mr. Lennox made his appearance, smiling and affable.

Keith Kenyon was a man of few words, but his words were

invariably very expressive. His words now were brief, and their brevity was to the point and very forcible.

But they were no more pointed or no more expressive than his opponent's. He had met his master.

All his life long the young statesman in his many conflicts had avoided argument and gained his point by escaping through the side door of tact, but as he made his exit now his opponent appeared through the front door of subtlety.

Mr. Lennox was blandly civil, urbane and polite, but assertive. His strength lay in his assertions, and his assertions were all true. "Mr. Lennox regretted it very much, more so than did he, but he shouldn't have spoken so in Paris. On the strength of his words Verona had refused and discarded a man of title. This was very regrettable, but Verona was obdurate. Her whole happiness depended upon her love. They were forced to submit. It was indeed regrettable, but his daughter must be humored. She might have done so much better. It was really too bad."

An accomplished prevaricator and egotist has the knack of getting himself believed in, even by those to whom his artificiality is most fully known.

Mr. Lennox was an accomplished prevaricator and egotist. He merely gave his companion his assertions. His companion might take them or leave them as he pleased; the fabled sword hung there. His power to choose was his own and the decision of little moment to the master of Lennox Court. And his assertions all tended to convince Keith Kenyon that his intentions had really been premeditated, misleading and compromising. It was only a matter of honor—or—or—exposure. Just as the young statesman wished! The neophyte was in the right and blandly indifferent as to the result. There was but one thing he would exact, the decision must be immediate. Both parties were pressing him, and he must know. If Keith Kenyon wanted his daughter he did not want to go against his interests.

So he made the young statesman believe. It pleased him to make him believe this. Mr. Lennox had been an adept in such tactics in the accumulation of his many millions of money. It had now become second nature to him, but it had palled on him a little of late; now a fresh zest was added to it by its transference to the realms of love and politics. From out of the scheming and manipulation of many a business transaction he had invariably come with clean hands and full coffers. The slough and dirt and loss had invariably gone elsewhere. He had an innate skill in placing others in a dilemma and of shifting a false position from his own shoulders to those of others. It was more natural to him than candor or straightforwardness. He was even enamored of his own skill in doing it, and when done he had within him enough humor to enjoy his companion's discomfiture.

His companion's discomfiture at the present time was complete. For the first time in his life he understood the impulse which forces ungoverned natures to use the weapons with which nature has endowed them. His impulse was to put Mr. Lennox out of his own library with his foot or a horsewhip. But to do so would be to insult his own dignity, and it would also for the moment raise the man before him to the same level as himself. With great self-restraint he forbore.

Before such an antagonist he felt helpless and hopeless. His candor, arrogance and honesty could not cope with his opponent in the duel of duplicity, dissimulation and deception in which it pleased him to engage.

So crafty did the master of Lennox Court prove himself in the manipulation of the situation that had it been anything else but an affair of heart and honor his opponent would have allowed enough of the St. Simon spirit to predominate within him to admire his ingenuity and craft, but as it was he was angered and depressed beyond all words or power to express.

He knew he had been duped; he knew he was now being duped. This knowledge is irritating to anyone, and to a man of great ability and fine intelligence it is intensely mortifying and humiliating. But he was face to face with the stone wall of his own actions, and could but submit and surrender.

He hated himself for doing it but it had to be done.

Miss Lennox was waiting him in her room, and Mr. Lennox blandly bowed him out of the library.

He left the room with a feeling akin to that of a thoroughbred that had been whipped by a brutal groom with lashes made from the silken threads of its own mane.

He made his way across the hall, wretched and vanquished, and with as great a distaste within him as if he had been eating some bitter, unwholesome thing. He was too irritated, worried and feverishly depressed to stop and reflect on the grotesqueness of the situation, no more than do statesmen who have for their ideal, Utopia, stop to reflect on all the incongruities, ludicrousness and grotesqueness to which they must submit themselves under a system of bribery and beer.

A man may be a Solomon or an Aristides, but if he wish to become a statesman the extent of the franchise forces him to become a fool, a trickster and in later days a buffoon. In his soul he despises it, and yet he is forced to stoop to it. A game which in his youth he thought fit for the gods proves to be, alas! too often, but a matter of manipulation and an appeal to, and a revelation of, man's baser attributes, with a reward for such merit and such manœuvres. But activity banishes the sense of the ludicrous, and ambition and the desire to win forces one on.

The descent from the sublime to the ridiculous is nearly always but a step. Keith Kenyon was in such a position now, but he was too engrossed to apprehend the truth, and even had he stopped to reflect it would have been so easy for him to find sophisms to cover over any sensitiveness in the matter in the fact that marriages of convenience in high life were now more the rule than the exception.

He paused as he went across the hall and hesitated. "If I refuse to marry her, what is there left to live for? She will marry Carlton Monteith. To see her Monteith's wife!" It was this thought which decided him the second time, and he turned his steps towards the other woman's apartments.

Although irritated, impatient and disgusted with the whole matter and in no mood to take any notice of his surroundings, he could not but contrast the ostentatious display of gilded furniture, plush-covered panels, highly-colored pictures, massive silverware and glaring bronzes of the rooms, especially Verona's own private room, with the refined and subdued taste of the rooms he had traversed but yesterday.

At the threshold he even yet paused and hesitated, but before he had time to think or act the door opened unexpectedly.

The heiress was in her room reclining indolently in a low chair by the window. She wore a dress of pale-green silk with much lace; her hands and her hair were shining with gems. She arose at his entrance. A poodle dog, which had been sleeping in the depths of a chair beside her, awakened and barked angrily at being disturbed. She paused, and patting it fondly succeeded in quieting it, and then returned it to its warm bed and disturbed slumbers, glad of the respite to recover her equanimity.

She had been expecting him. For the last hour she had paced the floor, laboring under the strongest emotions and the greatest apprehensions which she had ever felt during the twenty-six years of her life. It was only when she had heard his footsteps coming down the corridor that she had thrown herself into an assumed, indifferent attitude of ease.

The shades of evening were coming on, and she had closed the shutters and turned on the lights.

A great bunch of yellow roses nestled in the lace at her bosom; the pale gas jets of the room reflected the yellow of the roses and the green of her dress upon her countenance. The intensity of her emotion made her cheeks warm, while she could not repress the lurid fire which burned within her great grey eyes.

The room was close and heavy with the odor of many damp vines which hung round the casements of the window, and with the odor of many flowers and the perfume of lavender which she had ever about her.

She knew he would not have come had he not been prepared to say something which she had been longing for many years to hear.

She had dressed early for the evening; her arms were bare to the shoulders save for some puffs of lace and bands of gold set with glittering gems.

She made a striking figure as she now approached the young statesman. The room was sensuous, her manner enticing. She looked at him with burning, alluring eyes and extended her hand to him with a happy, self-satisfied smile.

He merely touched the tips of her fingers. He knew not how to approach her, but desperation as well as disdain for himself spurred him on.

"Has your father spoken to you, Miss Lennox?" he asked, abruptly and very coldly.

Her quick ear detected the very unloverlike tone, and she grew a trifle more reserved.

"Yes," she replied.

"Has he told you why I am doing this?"

"No," she answered, with a fear beginning to awaken within her breast.

The task before him seemed almost impossible, and he scorned himself for his part in it.

Although all his life he had ever been in the strifes of the world with his fellow men, yet had he always treated the opposite sex with the kindliness, the courtesy, the chivalry of a knight. It was natural for him to do so. Like the knights of old, he had ever been a kindly man moving among them, and he could do naught else, and it had been this which had endeared him so to women.

The words which he had now to utter, to him seemed almost brutal. But justice and honesty were greater forces within him than chivalry, and called for their own.

"There must be no misunderstanding," he said. "I shall be candid with you. May I speak plainly?"

A great fear rose within her, and her face hardened at his words and tone, and she said, " Proceed."

" I cannot offer you an affection I cannot feel. It is so hard to say what I wish to say—"

" Say on," she said, as she moved nearer him in her apprehension.

" It is your father's desire that I should marry you. He thinks I should. He thinks I have led you to expect it. I fail to see how you could have interpreted any words or actions of mine to mean so. But if you have, if you also think so—then—"

" Then you do not love me!" she exclaimed, bitterly, her bland bearing of superiority disappearing for the moment before the force of her disappointed hopes.

" No," he said, quietly and very coldly, and his heart, which would have softened at the sorrow of a noble woman, had he been forced to admit so to one, only hardened as he noticed the selfish passion and resentment which darkened her whole features.

She was silent for some moments, convulsed with an agitation she could not conceal and a mortifying incredulity she could not conquer. Unable longer to control herself, she cried bitterly, " And you know I love you!"

Yes, he knew it, and although it failed to touch him, it was this fact which made the task before him seem almost impossible.

" I—I cannot profess or proffer an affection I cannot feel," he said, slowly, " but if a marriage with me is your desire—"

" Why did you make me love you?" she asked, with a whole world of craving, challenge and resentment in her voice and mien.

It was this he dreaded hearing her say.

" Did I? Then it was my misfortune. I did not intend to. All I can do now is to pay the penalty of my perversity."

Her face had grown pale, but callous and self-centred as she was it flushed warm at the irony and disdain, so unusual to him, which were in his words.

He was silent for some moments, too downcast to care to speak. " And you know that I love you," rang in his ears.

Then suddenly a thought came to him and for a moment a ray of hope lighted his countenance as the sun's ray may fitfully play on a thundercloud.

" Was it for love alone she wished to marry him?" He had not looked at it in that light. From the first day he had known them he had been their sponsor. Through his efforts and influence they had made their way into the inner circles in several cities. He knew them to be ambitious, intriguing and audacious, and he had thought that she wished to marry well—marry for assured position.

But if it were for love alone!   His whole nature rebelled at the thought.

"Why do you wish to marry me?" he asked, clinging to this one little ray of hope.

She looked at him with incredulity.   "Hadn't she told him? What was his object in ignoring what was so obvious?"   Her nostrils dilated, her eyes glittered, her whole form distended from the force of her growing indignation.

"You ask me why?   Because you made me love you," and she believed what she said.

Like her father, she had the faculty of seeing things as she wished to see them.   She had seen in Keith Kenyon's actions and heard in his words many things which had no existence save in her own wishes and in her own imaginations.   Her vanity had blinded and misled her.   She had thought she had but to smile on him and he would fall at her feet.   Her humiliation and disillusion would now have been complete, but her indignant passion was too great to allow her to become conscious of any humiliation.

"You made me love you," she repeated again, seeing he did not speak.

He could not refute her argument, but he could refuse his love.

"I—I didn't think that was the reason you wished it.   I thought it was only for—   I cannot render you any affection or any personal attention.   I am not responsible for nature.   You must know that love is not of the senses alone.   It is a union of all the abstracts which make one's individuality and one's personality. After what has passed one cannot force one's feelings into the matter.   If I pretended to do so I should be betraying myself and yourself, and this I cannot do.   I cannot promise that now or at any time I can render you any affection whatever.   You will not accept these conditions," he said, his ray of hope growing brighter.

Her face had grown harsh and dark, and she did not reply.   She could not, so great was the emotion within her.

"I am waiting your answer," he said.

For a moment she was thrown off her guard.   Her mind was quick enough to grasp that he was beyond all allurement, all entreaty, and that she must resort to other means.   But to what means?   "Give me time," she said.

She moved from him to the one unshuttered window which looked out into the streets.   Some poet has said, "A whole world lies cryptic in each human breast."   Within her breast during the next few minutes raged all the passions and unrestrained desires of a passionate and unrestrained life.

Her very bosom heaved and swelled from the forces of concentrated rage as a volcano from the strength of the lava burning within its bowels.

"She—she, Verona Lennox, had been spoken to thus. She could not believe her own ears." That any man should be allowed to insult her with impunity, was something inconceivable. All the egotism and evil-temper which had been in her nature from birth, but which of late years her surroundings and her society had forced her to control and conceal, welled up in her for utterance now, but yet she was silent. She was silent because for the moment, in the intensity of her wrath and in the disappointment of her most cherished hopes, all language seemed too poor and too feeble to express what she felt. She was silent, also, because her heart was speaking very loudly to her, warning her to restrain the flow of passionate words which were burning for utterance. But her vanity was ever greater than love, and wounded vanity is even more vindictive and tenacious than the jealousy of love. Love may relent, but rebuffed vanity will never pardon. In her own mind, so great was the injury done to her, so uncalled-for the insult, so bitter her resentment, that her love was momentarily turned into hate and her desires into a thirst for revenge.

"That he should dare to insult her with impunity. What would she do? What could she do? She might open her lips in invectives, in derision, in denial. She might pour the vials of her wrath upon him. She might turn him from her with scorn and abuse, but of what avail? It would be but what he wanted. What could she do?" Her impotence overpowered her. She stood by the window, silent, with a grey pallor on her face, the light green of her dress and the yellow of her roses giving to her features the face of a Messalina. Her eyes had in them the glitter of the gems which sparkled on her bosom and on her arms; her whole form dilated with the intensity of her passion.

"That he should dare to say this to her! And she could neither retort nor retaliate—at present. But she could wait. Yes, she knew how to wait. It was all she could do—now. Her hour would come some day. She would make him love her yet."

That she desired it was sufficient reason in her own mind to fill her with an immediate knowledge that her desires would some day be gratified, and at the present aided her in regaining, if not composure, at least a rational control of her thoughts.

"He has offered me an insult, to-day! He shall be made to relent and repent and some day sue for pardon and for love. I shall live for that day. It will come. It must come. I shall make it come," and so great was her confidence in her own indomitable will power to accomplish what she wished that she could already feel herself towering over him, looking down upon him in scorn, deriding him, denying him, hounding him from her presence, craven and disgraced—and all because he had not loved her when she had desired it.

"But how to do so? Could she accept him in the light of what he had told her? She could ignore almost all things, but there were some, a few things, which lay beyond her power to ignore. This was one of the few. She could not do it," she thought, but at that moment the mistress of Apsley House, who was returning from a late tea, ordered the driver to pause, until she spoke to Carlton Monteith, who was passing in an opposite direction. The very sight of her sent the blood beating and tingling to Verona's cheek and brow, causing a revulsion of feeling and relieving her pent-up emotions as the eruption of the lava relieves the volcano.

Keith Kenyon, too, saw her, and only smiled bitterly at the scene before him.

"Accept him! Yes, I shall accept him if he ask me to be his slave! Refuse him, and allow him to marry that woman!"

The mistress of Apsley House had slighted her, injured her, insulted her, wronged her infinitely more than had Keith Kenyon. Her suitor's insults were to her rival's as love is to hate. She would consent to become anything in the world to him that it might lie in her power to humble the woman who had just passed. It was she who had tried to win him from her. She wouldn't admit that her rival had won him. But in her innermost heart she knew it, and this knowledge had within it the power to arouse all the latent vindictiveness of her nature. She was the cause of it all, and her resentment towards Keith Kenyon faded into nothingness before the greater truth.

In the light of the other he became her knight, her champion, her redresser.

She turned to him and said, "Yes, I shall accept your offer. When will the ceremony take place?"

For a moment he couldn't comprehend what it meant. He felt as though he had reached the bottom of an abyss by the angry crawling waters, stunned and sore.

The little ray of hope had disappeared, leaving the thunder-cloud black and sullen and silent. But the reality came to him slowly and menacingly, awakening him to a knowledge of his position, as the treacherous waves crept inch by inch over the stunned stroller, wakening him to action.

"When you will," he replied, and then without further words, or without even touching her hand, he turned and left the room.

She listened as the echo of his footsteps resounded through the halls. She heard the door open and close, and then she saw him pass down the street walking with quick step and bent head. Soon the trees of the avenue hid him from view.

"A strange wooing," she said, as he passed from her sight. She turned from the window and, seating herself by a small table of bronze, buried her head in her hands.

Beneath all her assumption and audacity she possessed a mind and heart ever ready to grasp the truth in its nakedness. She grasped it now. There was but one thing she would not admit, that he loved elsewhere. That could not be so, and she banished it from her mind. But he did not love her! But this thought had lost its bitterness. Her jealousy of and hatred for another woman had consumed it. But if the bitterness had passed away the longing for his love remained. It must be hers. She had never yet failed in all her life in anything she had undertaken to do. She had never failed because she knew what she wanted, and what she wanted was invariably something for herself, and all her whole energies and strength had been brought to bear upon her desires. She was very assertive and decisive in her ways and words, and possessed great strength, a sensuous nature, unimpaired health and nerves of steel, and brought into all her relations of life an unceasing and rapacious zest. She had immense confidence in her own powers. She could not now fail. She could scarcely believe that she had failed.

"She must have been dreaming, and his words must have been a delusion. All but his promising to marry her. The rest must be forgotten. If not a delusion, they must be ignored," and she banished them with her bitterness. "She only remembered he was going to marry her. If she wished to recall the others there was plenty of time when he was hers. Now she would treat the whole matter as if it were an ordinary affair of the heart. There was no need for the world to know otherwise. Not even her parents need know. When one gains nothing by making the world one's confidante one is unwise to do so. She could gain nothing now, and time would decide her future conduct."

Having decided her present course she at once began to believe in it, and she soon became her old self once more. "When one has gained the greater point, why worry over the loss of the lesser," she said very philosophically to herself and to her poodle, whom she had now taken upon her knee.

But the poodle was indifferent, and waddled back into the depths
of his easy chair, and curled himself up once more in its depths
and went to sleep like a dormouse. The soft plushes of his present
bed were preferable to the cordovan leather and carved rosewoods
of Kenyon Court, and Verona patted his head and went in search
of more sympathetic ears.

Her betrothed had said, " When you will," and with these words,
and these words alone, she went down the stairway to the library,
where she knew her parents were anxiously awaiting her.

Mr. Lennox had remained in the library, waiting for the younger
man's return, but Keith Kenyon had not approached the door, but
had gone on his way home. He was in no mood to see anyone. He
hated himself for the part which he had that day played. But they
had thrust it upon him, and he could not see how he could have
done otherwise.

He knew that he was leaving the woman he loved with a heart
utterly dead to any and every other love, and was binding to him
that of another whom he could never love; but they had both willed
it, and his heart ached at the thought.

When he arrived at Kenyon Court he threw himself in profound
despair into a low lounging chair on the western terrace, where
the dusky shadows of evening were creeping round the eaves and
shrubs and rose-gardens of his beautiful home.

He had dreamed of what would be, and it had ended thus.

" Was it only that morning he had gone to the house of the
woman he loved?" As he went he had thought of her words to him
the day they had discussed happiness in her Court of Inquiry, and
his heart had leaped within him. And now! It had been indeed
but a Mock Court. Another woman was to rule and reign in his
homes. " It could not be! It could not be!" he yet said to himself, as he looked down the river towards Idlewylde. " But what
could he do?" Almost it seemed to him that he was as a man in
a boat in the circling waves of a maelstrom, driven to his fate,
utterly powerless to stop or prevent it.

CHAPTER XXVI.

"I KNOW he is ours! At least, last evening he gave Mr. Sangster to understand he was coming to us," and Mrs. Sangster smiled knowingly at Helen Lester as she told her this, as they were returning from the same tea late that same evening.

"Do not grow too sanguine, Lilian. He hasn't committed himself yet," replied Helen, who had learned from experience the truth of the old adage, "There's many a slip 'twixt the cup and the lip," and who never allowed herself to become sanguine over uncertainties.

"No, not publicly, but he has privately. No, not confidentially. He rather seemed to wish to have it known at last. You know his interests here are intimately connected with his interests in his former home and abroad, and our policy is certainly the best for him. He realizes this and admits it is the best for the country at large, but for some reason he has hesitated; but to-morrow he will have to decide, and I am quite confident he will be ours, for we are certain to win this time," said Mrs. Sangster, in the tone of a woman who was about to attain that for which she had fervently wished and for which she had long and tenaciously struggled.

Mr. Lester, who had joined them on their way home, smiled pityingly and incredulously. "I doubt it," he said.

"You doubt it! Doubt his joining us, or doubt our winning?"

"Both," he replied.

But Mrs. Sangster still persisted in smiling triumphantly.

For many months she had known more than she thought it wise to tell. She had been the one confidante of Verona Lennox, and Verona had told her much. She had rigidly kept these things to herself—only now and again a word, a look, a smile, which Verona had seemed to wish her to say or give, and which had told those about her that she knew much and was doing more, and now all these things had gathered together in her mind until it was almost impossible to refrain longer from speaking. Their espousal of their cause seemed to Mrs. Sangster to be almost a personal achievement, and she wished to be the one to make the denouement. Of course, Mr. Lester was only speaking according to his light, and her smile of triumph had in it all the pleasure of an anticipated surprise and the joy of "I told you so," "I knew it." Mixed with this also was the thrilling sensation of pleasure that she had for once outwitted Modena Wellington.

She had done much for her party, but this would be the climax.

"Time will tell," she said, confident of victory.

"And that right soon," replied Lester.

"How southern you grow in your expressions," said his sister.

"And in his affections," added her friend, as they parted at her home.

At the dinner that same evening at Clarian Hall, Mrs. Sangster smiled bitterly as she met Helen Lester, but no more bitterly than did Modena Wellington.

"Have you heard the news?" she asked of Helen, or rather snapped spitefully. For many years position had sat there throned on its height, tempting, delicious, alluring. like the apple before Tantalus, and now to have the golden apple of position touching her very finger tips and to have it snatched away like this! It was really too bad! She must give vent to her disgust to someone.

"No," replied Helen. "What is it now? Who is dead, or rather, judging from your expression, who has turned traitor or proselyte?"

"We have lost that Lennox. Keith Kenyon and Verona Lennox are engaged to be married," replied Mrs. Sangster, with a whole world of defeat and disgusted disappointment bristling through her words and tone.

"Impossible!" exclaimed Helen, turning white with consternation and emotion. "I cannot believe it," she almost gasped.

"But she wasn't thinking of that Lennox and his partisanship. She shrewdly suspected, from her intimacy with the Wellington family, that Keith Kenyon was very dear to the mistress of Apsley House.

Mrs. Sangster for a moment forgot her own disgust as she looked at the white face of her friend. She knew that Helen Lester's heart was not interested in their political cause as was her own, and she wondered at her consternation. She couldn't understand. She was thinking only of her party. The betrothal was of no moment. It was not unexpected. She had known of it. Verona had told her of it many months previous to this. But their espousal of the other's cause after all their hinted and implied adherence to theirs was too much for her nerves or her powers of comprehension! But the Lesters hadn't known this!

"Why so impossible?" she asked, thinking that her friend was speaking of the loss to their party.

Habitual good-breeding and reserve soon made Helen recover her outward composure.

"Oh, it may be probable, but I am very much surprised," she replied, with evident disbelief yet in her tones.

"So am I, and disgusted, too. How pleased Modena Wellington will be when she hears it!" said Mrs. Sangster, glad to have some-one upon whom to vent her ill-humor and resentment.

"No doubt he will be a great addition to their party in the crisis," returned Helen, as the Wellington and the Lennox parties entered the room almost simultaneously, but she had grave doubts regarding the pleasure of the mistress of Apsley House, although she did not say so to Mrs. Sangster.

As the others entered the room she turned from Mrs. Sangster to her brother. "Did you know of it, Lester?" she asked, in a tone of despair, and with almost an appeal in her voice that he would refute the truth of the report.

It had come upon her with a shock so great that she couldn't grasp it. She had shared the Wellingtons' antipathy for Verona Lennox. And Keith Kenyon had been one of them. Their families were the oldest in the city. Their intimacy had been great, their intercourse one long summer dream. And to have to admit Verona Lennox into the holy of holies! And Modena! Modena! There was something very wrong somewhere. It couldn't be true. Her brother would deny it.

"I heard it but a moment ago," answered Lester, very gravely.

"But it isn't true?" she pleaded.

"I am afraid it is."

Helen was silent from sheer grief.

"And what do you think of it?" she asked, after a pause.

"I am very much surprised and shocked. Kenyon is so honor-able, cool and level-headed, one cannot understand his being carried away by any gross motive. There must be something else behind it."

"And Jack never told us! I cannot yet believe it!"

"Why should Jack know?" asked Lester, and the little mono-syllable contained a world of apprehension, for he well knew that the mistress of Apsley House did not care for the man to whom she was plighted, and suspected but dreaded hearing Helen confirm his own suspicions.

"Because it may not have been so, but I thought he cared for Modena."

"Perhaps he does, but perhaps she does not care for him. It may be this that is making him marry the other."

"Oh, I know she cares. I know he is the only one whom she has ever loved."

Lester knew this, too, and he grew grave and then depressed as if some great woe overhung the ones he so dearly loved. He was a noble and generous man, and Modena's happiness was dear to

him. His feelings for her had grown into more of a tender regard
than a passion for possession, and he would have been passively
content to have gone through life as her dearest and most intimate
friend if she were only happy. He knew he held a place in her
heart which no one else could ever fill and which no man could ever
usurp. It was not love, but sympathy, regard, comprehension,
esteem, trust. Love might rule over these, but love could never
usurp their place. They would always rule with love. All the
years that he had loved her he had been strong enough to stifle
the passion and not allow it to interfere with her happiness. Her
happiness was yet as dear to him as it had ever been.

He valued her trust more than he valued anything else in life,
and to keep it he knew he must keep his soul pure towards her.
It had always seemed to him that had she lost faith in him, had he
lost faith in her, then was there nothing in life worthy of trust.
And he would sooner have died than to have believed this.

His love for her was the love of a Bors for his Lancelot, a love
that would have relinquished his sight of the Holy Grail that his
brother might win.

He looked across at her now with a grief equal to his sister's at
his heart.

She had greeted their hostess, and as she noticed the entrance
of the other party she had passed down the room with her usual
proud carriage and smiling mien.

Lester's eyes followed her. "She does care." Even at a distance, like her cousin Jack's, his eyes were quick to note the change
within her.

He rose and made his way to her. She was as usual the centre
of a group, and she was smiling and interested, and with the
others was commenting on the topics of the day, but all eyes were
on the group at the door. She was glad of this, as it detracted
attention from herself.

She looked up and smiled as Mr. Lester approached her. He
was shocked when he looked at her, and unconsciously he
retained her hand, while his dismay was plainly evident on his
face. "Why are you doing this?" his eyes asked, as plainly as
though his lips had spoken.

She looked away from his appeal, and he stood by her silent.

Others had come in, and the Lennox party were moving their
way. They would be forced to say something.

It was a trying moment, and he saw Jack's brows knit together.

Jack had had another very pressing engagement for the evening, but since his cousin insisted on appearing at the dinner he

19

had waived his engagement to accompany her. He knew that the parties would meet and that they would be forced to say something. He knew his cousin was too candid to express any delight at their adhesion to their party when she felt only displeasure, and was too sincere to offer any congratulations to the heiress of Lennox Court. But something would have to be said, so he thought it wiser for him to come. It was as foreign to his nature as it was to his cousin's to speak the polished phrases which would have to be spoken, but he was very sensitive towards giving the world cause for comment, and he did not wish the world to connect his cousin's name with the Lennox and Kenyon nuptials.

What he had expected had happened. From the first he had known Verona Lennox to be a foe of no mean mettle. She had won out against him and now held the winning card. Had she won in an open, clear, clean fight he would have extended his hand generously and magnanimously, but her ways and means he hated with a good, sound hatred. Her hypocrisy and her duplicity were detestable to him and would have been unworthy of notice but for the way the world accepted and countenanced them. It was this fact which depressed Jack Mainton and made him disgusted. But he would not show his disgust. He might stamp and fume and fret over public matters, but where private matters were involved he was too polished a gentleman to show any irritation or display any feeling. He could hold himself well in reserve.

He knew that Verona Lennox hated his cousin, and that she would now carry the situation with great eclat, even, by one of her expressive words, a hint or a smile, making it appear that she was the sought-for and that Modena Wellington was the rejected and was dying of love for him. But not if he were near. He knew she feared him. He had the faculty of stripping her words of their air of indefiniteness and suggestions and showing them up in their nakedness and true light.

He was now prepared, but fate intervened in the form of Mr. Patrie and smoothed the way from any unpleasantness which might have arisen. Mr. Patrie had lost her, but she had retained him. In the future he might prove a very useful appanage, and it was as well to have him by her, and she had taken pains with him and made him believe that he was as near and dear to her, or even nearer and dearer, than Keith Kenyon. As the wife of Keith Kenyon she could do much for him, more than if she were his wife, and he had believed her, in so far and in so much as it had suited his purpose to do so, and had remained her friend and knight.

He was now standing with the Wellington group, and at the

Lennoxes' approach extended his hand with effusion, and was so profuse with his congratulations and felicitations that it was unnecessary for the others of the party to speak. They had merely to bow and acquiesce or tone down the temper, the quality and the quantity of Mr. Patrie's effulgence.

Keith Kenyon could have sworn at him, at all of them, and more so at himself. But Mr. Patrie gave him no time to swear. Mr. Patrie had received too many rebuffs from Keith Kenyon and from his colleagues, and now Verona had been the proverbial straw which had broken the camel's back. Dinner would soon be announced, and it must also be made known that Mr. Lennox had publicly promised his support to their party.

"Your father is coming to us! How kind of him!" he continued, with the faintest tinge of cynicism mingled with his suavity.

But Verona only saw the servility.

She was a little irritated at Mr. Patrie's lack of good taste in speaking of public matters here and now, but she was prepared. "Oh, no, not kind at all," she replied, blandly. "It was only a question of duty; he did not wish to act hastily and repent afterwards; he took time to consider well which was the best for the general welfare of the people. Conditions are so different, and one has to study people as well as policies. Raynor is so enthusiastic over the poor workingman; he is quite crestfallen, and our private interests pointed that way. With such forces as these arrayed against one it was very difficult, I assure you, to rise above all things and espouse the cause of those who will eventually accomplish the greater and ultimate good of the people," continued Verona, hesitatingly and modestly, and she looked at Mrs. Sangster with the air of a martyr.

"Yes, he did! Were the Socialists swinging the chief from the gable peaks of Earnscliffe, or the Royalists pelting his Excellency with rotten eggs and paving stones or ducking him in Government Pond as they did Elgin, or the Annexationists holding the country in mid-air over Niagara Falls, and if the Lennox adhesion to the party could have saved the neck of the first, the dignity of the second and the fate of the last, his promise would not have been secured until his daughter had weighed the matter well and counterbalanced such insignificant things as these with her own exaltation and interests," replied Jack Mainton with his eyes, but aloud he only said:

"It's too bad, really too bad, the way politics makes Curtiuses of public men!"

Keith Kenyon felt the warm blood mount to his face; his ear

was sensitive to the ring of true manhood within Jack's voice, and nothing else could have hurt him quite so much, but Verona looked at him with composure. She knew he was not approving her, but ridiculing her, and hate rankled in her heart, but to-night she could afford to be amiable, and instead of replying to Jack she asked Keith Kenyon if he would bring her fan, she had forgotten it in the waiting room.

"I knew from the first time I saw Miss Lennox that she would join your party," said Mr. Lester, speaking for the first time, as the group dispersed and they were left alone.

"Then if you knew, why didn't you tell us so, and save us all this manœuvring and wire-pulling and brain-worrying?" replied Jack. "But what made you so certain?" he asked.

"Keith Kenyon."

Lester's two little words contained so much meaning that Verona colored vividly, and almost hated Mr. Lester as much as she did Jack Mainton.

"Then you doubt Miss Lennox's reasons for delay?" asked Jack.

"It would be ungentlemanly to do so," replied Lester, as the young statesman appeared with the fan, and Verona passed from their side to meet him.

"Yes, I doubt her reasons very much," said Lester, gravely, to Jack, when she had left them. "Lennox is like Buridan's proverbial ass. He stood on the bridge with the hay at both ends. He has verified Buridan's assertion that it is external circumstances that control will power."

"You mean Kenyon was the sweeter hay. She might have failed in bagging her bird. You know that little rhyme, 'A woman's love that has been spurned'; there always lurks such a danger as this, and if Miss Lennox had proved unsuccessful revenge would have been sweet."

"Would to God she had failed," replied Lester, abruptly.

"Why? Were you so anxious to secure them?"

"No, you know I do not mean that! But what does Kenyon mean? He, of all men living, to do this! Does he realize what he is doing? Can't he see how it will all end? Yes, I know well it's none of our business, but why can't he see?"

"Love is blind, you know," said Jack, with cynical brevity.

"It certainly is in this case," replied Lester, desperately and dejectedly, knowing well that both their minds were dwelling upon the one and same person.

"To marry a Medusa with such a goddess in sight," he thought, as the soft waves of sound of a distant bell came to them, and he turned and took the mistress of Apsley House into dinner.

They sat opposite Keith Kenyon and his affianced bride, and Lester's quick intuition soon saw the restraint beneath his companion's words and manner.

He noticed how unconsciously Keith Kenyon's eyes came their way and how she sedulously avoided meeting their appeal. He saw the great strain under which she was laboring, and he endeavored to divert the conversation to foreign topics and protect her as best he could. Despite the effort of the host and hostess to the contrary, the dinner was long, tedious and heavy, and the guests left soon afterwards, each going to fulfil some evening engagement, while the mistress of Apsley House appeared at two other evening parties and then returned home, having heard but the one topic of conversation discussed the entire evening.

CHAPTER XXVII.

"You are not going to ask her here?" said Jack Mainton a few weeks after this to his cousin, as he entered the library of Apsley House one cold October morning.

Autumn had deepened into winter; the waters of the rivers were now frozen from shore to shore; a white mantle of snow covered the earth and hung heavy on the naked boughs of the many trees of the city. The merry ting-a-ling of winter bells floated joyfully on the frosty air, and the passing people, under the tonic and stimulus of the clear, cold northern air, were hurrying to and fro. Afar off the morning sun shone with a ruddy glow on the virginal snows of the mountain side; its rays slanted westward over the broad sheet of gleaming water which ran up to the foot of the terrace surrounding Apsley House and shone through the great wheel window of the library, which had been copied from those famous in the Modena Castle on the Æmelian Way.

The mistress of the house sat on a high, straight-backed chair of carved leather, at her writing table, where the morning rays touched her profile and warmed and lighted all around her. Great knots of maple blazed on the andirons in the fireplace and lighted up the shadows of the room. Her dogs were with her, asleep before the fire.

She had been preparing, for her secretary, a list of those whom she wished to invite to her annual Thanksgiving Reception.

Her cousin had come in, and she had placed the list before him, asking for any addition or omission which he wished.

She sat erect in her chair; her hands with their many rings lay on the table. Her face was pale and grave; she wore her great pearls at her throat and had on a morning dress of pearl-grey serge with old gold girdle. Her hair lay low on her head in shining coils and was fastened by a pearl comb. The glow through the painted panes of the great wheel window warmed the color of her face, but her cousin was quick to see the change which was in it, and when he had come to the name of Verona Lennox he had vented his resentment in his words and tone.

During the last few weeks they had met the Lennoxes, accompanied by Keith Kenyon, everywhere. Their betrothal had been the one topic of comment and criticism. Even politics had paled and become a secondary consideration in the city before the glow and glamor and air of mystery which surrounded the affair.

The Lennoxes had carried the situation with great eclat. Announcements had been made and extensive preparations had been begun for the coming nuptials.

During the days which followed Verona had been seen in a new light, and had been viewed with different sentiment. Since her coming to the city she had never been very popular with the most exclusive set, but now since Keith Kenyon had chosen her, whether willingly or with reluctance, it was forced to open wide its arms to her.

"What think you of Keith's choice?" the chief had said to Mr. Lester on hearing of it, and Mr. Lester had replied:

"She is beautiful, wealthy and capable of accomplishing much. She has chic, facility and fair intellectual ability. She has done wonders."

"I mean her moral worth."

"The people here are taking to her, and our people have enough English blood within them to be slow in seeing merit in strangers, and surely Kenyon would satisfy himself as to that before making her the mistress of his home and the mother of his children."

"In short she is a paragon of perfection. He is to be envied," concluded the chief, with a little cynical smile of incredulity. "But we may as well believe so since she is to be one of us."

"It has been generally conceded that Kenyon has had good taste in his choice of things in life, then one would expect that his taste in the choice of a wife would be perfect," said Lester, with as queer a smile as the chief's and a curious intonation in his voice.

"You are implying that had he been free to choose he would

have chosen someone else. It is a very regrettable thing. His position is not an invidious one, but he carries himself well through it. She will make life interesting for him.”

“Interesting! Already she has gathered about her people—” and then Mr. Lester had checked himself, not thinking it quite honorable to discuss further Keith Kenyon’s private affairs, even with the chief who loved him so well and who had felt, when he had heard of it, a pang almost as bitter as if he had been his own son.

It was not what he had wanted and hoped for.

And it was these people, of whom Mr. Lester had been about to speak, who were proving Verona’s strength and stability. Since coming to the city she had gathered about her a powerful clique, as anyone with great audacity and strong will can quickly do—a clique who had never been accepted by the exclusive sets of the city, but who had wished and striven to be accepted, and whose failure had made them very bitter to the best. They had called upon Verona, and, being congenial to her taste and temperament, she had accepted them.

“With our superiors we are ill at ease, with our equals we derive pleasure, and with our inferiors we become the lowest of the low,” someone has truly said. They were her equals, and with them she was happy. In their presence and their pleasures she had felt as much in her element as Undine in the water. Their sympathies, their comprehensions, their joys, their aspirations were hers; their hatreds, envies and jealousies were hers also. These other people were a people apart from them, a people of pride and privileges and prerogatives, and had no right to be such. In their presence she was forever sensible of their impatience of her as a stranger and of their feelings that she was unworthy of them. She hated them, with their insane idolatry of what their grandfathers had been, and done, and said, and worn.

Her grandfather had worn corduroys and carried the coal hod and pick in the lower regions. She wanted to trample in the dust a world that would hold her responsible for the sins of her grandfather. She did not want to become one of these people, but she wanted to take her own and place them in their places, and put such people as these out of existence. She only wanted a pivot. She had now obtained her pivot, and her new power had made her a queen in the eyes of her people, and they had clung to her with increased servility and tenacity. They flattered her vanity to her heart’s content, and she was ever glad to have them about her. She had always wanted to be a queen. She was a queen now over her own kingdom. The rise and fall of dynasties was interesting work.

Her kingdom would yet rule. She had wished it, and willed it, and that was sufficient reason why it should succeed.

Coupled with this desire and resolution was the spur and stimulus of a vehement and unrequited passion and a personal hatred towards another which made her doubly zealous in her cause. During the last few weeks she had succeeded in making things intensely interesting.

Her friends were beginning to be powerful, and having had to confine their powers within their own narrow souls for so long, it was an immensity of relief and gratification to be allowed to now expend them on foes worthy of their steel.

Verona's manner and assumption had been almost insolent, but had been cloaked with sufficient insouciance, modesty and deference to conceal her real motive and rob one of reprisal. Her future husband was the most sought-after man in the city. Already to the Wellingtons her air had in it the shade and suggestion, faint and illusive, but ever there, of patronage and power. But vague and fleeting as it was, it had been patent and powerful enough to ruffle Jack Mainton's feathers the wrong way several times, and his desire now was simply to ignore her existence.

"Why do you ask her?" he continued, as he stood by his cousin's side at the table, looking down on her.

There was something almost stately and regal in her attitude, as if she had been fighting a great battle with great powers and had come out conqueror in the warfare. It had cost her much to write the name, but now it was done, and she felt more at peace with herself."

"Society forces one to do so," she said.

Her cousin made an impatient gesture of denial.

"Haven't you sufficient courage to live your own life regardless of society?" he asked, forgetting for the minute that her society was her life, and was no more to be separated from her than the blood from her body or the white cells from her brain.

"Oh, by society I mean our social relations. Our communal, our state relations, the duties which we owe to ourselves and to our state. Our world is a neutral meeting ground where people of the most diverse, difficult and diffident dispositions come together. Harmony is the chief essential of a good society. A display of likes and dislikes tends towards discord and dispute. Self-control is an absolute necessity. It is a duty we owe to the state."

"Our state commands us to smile and make believe we adore people whom we hate. What hypocrisy! The savages wouldn't do so. Their worst foe is sacred to them when he once crosses their threshold. If she once eat your bread you are in honor bound to treat her as something sacred. Can you do it?"

"You have the faculty of putting truth in a funny light."

"What other light could anyone put it in?"

"Be charitable to those who dislike us so."

"She doesn't like you. She cannot forgive you for being It. The Third Estate never will forgive."

"If I am It, I have a right to be," replied Modena, as she looked down on the many heirlooms shining on her fingers.

"What about the accidents of birth and wealth?"

"If they are mine now I won them elsewhere."

"What a theology!"

"Philosophy, you mean."

"Why would you be charitable to her?"

"Charity should be the basis of everyone's conduct. Everything should be based on charity. Even Bacon admits the sciences are based on charity."

"Don't you think it is because of another It she hates you?"

"A personal matter?"

"Yes."

"Perhaps so."

"Would your philosophy extend to that, also?"

"Decidedly so."

"Then you think love is preordained?"

"Yes."

"Then the fellows down there make a bad mess of it, sometimes; but the Fates are women, aren't they? That accounts for it. They make a mess of everything they touch."

Modena smiled. "Except men. You'll surely have to admit we manage them wonderfully well."

"To get your own way, but you don't always know what is best for yourselves. You should let the men manage you."

"What have we done wrong?"

"You are doing a great wrong now by sending her this," he said, abruptly pushing the unsealed invitation from him. "Why are you so considerate of her? Is she worth your treatment?"

"One is forced to do it. If we notice anything it will make it very awkward and unpleasant for others. We accepted her invitation the evening of their announcement. We move in the same set, and we cannot avoid her. There is always some good in everyone. Perhaps it will develop in her. We can look for it and close our eyes to the other. These things come in, I suppose, as the necessary evils of life. We have to take life as it comes," she said, regardless of sequence of thought, while her eyes wandered away and rested on the still, white world without.

"She is a cruel woman. She will be vindictive, relentless."

"You flatter her too much. Is there so much as that in her? I thought her very shallow."

"You have been misled. The candor of your nature cannot comprehend the intrigue of hers. She will never forgive. She will never forget or pardon."

"I have done her no wrong."

"The greatest wrong one woman can do to another! In her eyes and estimation! She will yet bring great trouble to you."

"You exaggerate. Are you not a little unjust?"

"You would condone and uphold evil-doing."

"I would try to be charitable."

"But cowardice and carelessness and conventionalism too often clothe themselves with the cloak of charity. It is cowardly to condone and not kick against evil."

"We may hate the evil, but love the evil-doer. Isn't that true charity?"

"You cannot separate the two. The one, without the other, is a negation and therefore there is nothing to hate. The other, without the one, is a goddess, and is indifferent to our love. It is cowardly to take life as it comes without slapping back."

"Evil is its own slayer."

"But it does a lot of mischief before it slays, and makes life very unpleasant."

She was silent for some mements, so was he; then he said:

"According to your theory one goes on growing until one becomes a goddess. I think you are one now."

"Far from it. I am intensely human and weak."

"You don't know yourself. I wish, dear, you were weak enough to let your heart speak."

"I am," she said, and despite herself her eyes filled with tears which did not flow.

"Then he is a fool if he cannot see it. He deserves to suffer when he takes life so. It is more than regrettable that others should suffer through him."

She owed her cousin an explanation. He loved her and had done what he could.

"Oh, no, Jack, you misjudge him. He wanted me—he wants me—he implored—but—but—there is Carlton Monteith and father and his own actions towards her, and—and—I can't see my way clear to speak. It must be as it is. One cannot help it," she said, brokenly.

"The heart is the best guide. Let it speak."

"Not with me."

"Yes, with everyone."

He approached nearer her and laid his hand on her arm and looked down on her, and in his voice was a tenderness and an earnestness. "Dear," he said, "I am older, much older, than you, and have seen life in its many phases and forms; it is from experience we learn the bitter lessons of life. What is experience but a statue carved by the weapons which have hurt us most? It is something built upon our dead selves. Why cannot we learn from the gravestones of others? You are young, and you are misjudging the meaning and value of life. The wisdom of all ages has ever told us that the only true happiness lies in the home. You do not love Carlton Monteith. You will never marry him. You love another. You are great, but your very greatness will only make you more lonely. It is well, Modena, to keep human love near your heart. Why will you not be warned in time? You are young and actuated by noble motives, but you are not capable of acting wisely in this matter. You possess high ideals, and now the opportunity presents itself for you to do in your own sight an heroic action, but wisdom teaches us that forethought, prudence and discretion are the better part of valor. Fervor and impetuosity are counsellors not to be relied upon. False sentiment is infinitely worse than no sentiment at all. They are stimuli which will keep you alive for a while on their excitation, but like all other stimuli they will soon pass away, and what will become of your life? Others will suffer with you. You have always been so considerate for and indulgent to others. Why should you now cause those who love you so much sorrow? One cannot find words forcible enough to impress upon you the folly of your decision. I do beg of you, dear, to reconsider it, and remember you are willing the severance of your life from his forever."

A spasm of pain passed over her face at his words, but she spoke not. What she was thinking he could not tell, and as she said nothing he despaired.

"Do you never think how it will be afterwards? Do you never fear your own strength?" he asked, oppressed by his prescience.

She looked at him with disquietude, and he felt he had touched a wrong chord.

No, she could not comprehend weakness in this form. Having within her the instincts of a Lucretia, the weakness of a Guinevere or an Eleanora of Toledo was something which her mind could not grasp.

"Cannot you see why I speak?" he continued, quickly. "Cannot you see how through thoughtlessness I have ruined my own life?"

"Your life need not be ruined. Helen is free if you would speak."

"But I cannot speak."

"Perhaps your sense of honor is abnormal, supersensitive, morbid."

"No, I think not. And even if I spoke she wouldn't listen. I couldn't speak," he said, sadly, in after reflection. "One feels that when one has sinned one must expiate and do penance before one can ask or merit forgiveness."

"Cannot you see how it is with him?"

Her cousin looked surprised, and remained silent for some time.

"Is he doing it because of his conduct towards her? You have nothing to do with his marrying her?"

"Nothing whatever. It is his own choice. It is his sense of honor."

Jack was again silent for some time, his brows drawn together, his mind working rapidly, and then he said:

"He isn't marrying her for that. His actions have not misled her. He hasn't compromised her in any way. She thrust herself upon him. She has misrepresented, miscolored, misconstrued his words and actions. He's not made of such namby-pamby stuff as all that to be hoodwinked by such duplicity."

"Then why is he marrying her?"

"Because he cannot tell you this about another woman. No man can. And he fears that you will think him cowardly in shunning the seeming consequences of his own actions. Why can't you advise him to wait? It is only a misunderstanding between you two."

But there are some things which one cannot do. Why one cannot do them, one cannot tell; and this seemed another of those things to her. If this were true, and she believed it was, his mute homage moved her much. He must indeed love her to care so much for her good opinion. She could not do so for him. She could not betray herself for anyone. She wondered if she were harsh or cruel. What was it that prevented her from speaking? Was it pride or was it humility? Was it self-love or was it another will controlling hers? She could not tell, but speak she could not.

"I cannot do it," she said to her cousin. "And it is now too late. One does not want one's inner life and finer feelings torn to shreds by the whole world; as wolves tear offal," she continued, a little bitterly, for she was already beginning to realize what life was without him.

"The wolves will tear them in time. We let such people in· among us and they wreck hearts, lives. homes as ruthlessly as a child pulls a rose to pieces. They hate, and when they hate they are as insatiable and vindictive as Phædra was to her stepson. They should be shut up in some madhouse, where they could harm no one but themselves. And yet we continue to ask them as though they were our friends. At least you can refuse to do so. You can save yourself further trouble. Cannot you find any excuse to avoid her?"

"I can scarcely see how one can. unless one goes to South Africa or Japan, and I suppose that is what she wishes one would do, but I don't feel like doing it. And if one remains here one meets them at every house, and since we have accepted them we cannot very well drop them without comment," and as she said this she thought of how she had strenuously tried to avoid them on their first arrival, and they had insisted on her receiving them, but she did not say so.

"I wouldn't eat her bread," persisted Jack.

"If we would refuse to eat the bread of all those who do not love us, I'm afraid we would often go hungry."

"Oh, I don't know. I think we would have a loaf for every day in the week and some to spare. And if not, I would stay at home and eat our own, rather than eat sugar-coated dates, prawns and ortolans with senna, aloes and poison within."

"You would soon become a Timon with your spade and pick on a lonely island."

"One would rather spend life on a lonely island than spend much of it with her. She isn't worth a minute of your life."

"That is why I am asking her. I do not want to needlessly make an enemy. Her tactics are not worthy of notice. One lowers oneself to her level by noticing them. In time she will know better."

"Never," said Jack, abruptly. "Character the gods themselves cannot alter. One cannot put into one's nature what is not in it. It is not in hers. The Messalina and Borgia spirit does not sleep for aye. It comes back every now and then, and it does much mischief while it is here. If she would only leave you alone. But she will not."

"She cannot hurt me. Nothing but my own actions can do so," said Modena, as she sealed the invitation and rose from her chair.

"I do not fear her in the least, and do not let us waste any more time talking of her. Are you going with us to-night?" she asked, changing the subject.

"Are you going alone?"

"No, Lady Greta is going with me."

"Then I shall call for you. We are very busy now," he said, as he turned slowly, and moodily left the library.

On his departure his cousin remained standing for some time looking down upon the great pile of sealed invitations. Then she gathered them together and put them in a leather bag to be mailed. Verona Lennox's she kept in her hand and looked at it for some time. Then she laid it on the table and turned to the window. The sun had come out from behind its bank of snow-clouds and now shone brilliantly; the mantle of snow and frost, which had been one of those early October ones so prevalent in northern climates, was fast disappearing. The trees were once more naked; through the break in their overhanging branches she could see the terraces of Kenyon Court. As she looked she saw its master come down the great stone steps which led up to the Court and enter his waiting sleigh. She saw the horses stop before the gates of Apsley House; then her cousin stepped within the sleigh and the two men rode away together. She watched them as they disappeared in the distance, and she still remained standing.

"If one drop her it means the dropping of him also," she thought. "Could she drop him? Oh, yes." She was sufficient unto herself, and for a moment, in the resentment of her feelings towards him, she felt it would be a very easy matter for her to do so.

She was stronger than all forces together, and if in time she lent her countenance to their exclusion it meant their relegation to the outer circles.

Her world to her was her own heart, and her heart was her world.

"But if he were relegated to the outer circles, what was there left to live for within the inner circles? Was she doing right in severing his life from hers. She loved him, and do we trample in the dust that which we love? Verona Lennox's nature, instincts, motives, were antagonistic to his. She was audacious, strong-willed, assertive, Napoleonic. No doubt her vitality would aid him in reaching his Austerlitz. But, like its hero, she did not know the foundation of things, and their power would undoubtedly end in a St. Helena. It couldn't be otherwise. He was to the core a man of the world, and his home and honor would be sacred in his sight. He would have to give his life up to his wife's, and live her life. She would dwarf and chill and blunt the nobility within him with the petty acerbities and animosities and inanities of life. His life would dwarf and dwindle and die as a noble oak withers and dies from a canker-worm eating at its heart. She, Verona Lennox, had within her too much vitality, vindictiveness and vanity to allow him to lead his own life. Her will would be law and his powers would be wasted. Could she, the woman he loved, stand idly by and see his powers wasted?"

"Was living and loving so slight a thing as this? Was there not such a thing as communion of spirits?"

She did not doubt for one moment that her spirit was the only one which could perfect his. Hers would not have been love had she doubted it. This knowledge is in the nature of love.

"It would be intensely selfish on her part to remain passive to his welfare and happiness. He would know that his interests were always hers. Prayer was to her the thoughts of each moment of one's life; her presence and her prayers would sustain and stimulate him to his best. It would be cowardly and craven to avoid them."

So she told herself, and turned and put the invitation in the post bag with the others.

She went that evening to where she knew that she would meet them. It was almost a self-inflicted torture to do so, but her suffering would have been infinitely greater than her torture had her courage failed her. There was in her what has been in all great women. If necessary she could have sent the man she loved to the block, but in so doing she would have suffered more than he, but the world would never have known of her sorrow. Like the Lady of the Lake in her white samite, it lay within her to dwell in a deep calm whatsoever storms bestirred the earth.

She felt that his eyes were on her the entire evening, but he did not approach her. He had not spoken to her since she had sent him to another.

She noticed how he was courted and honored, and how noble and deferential he bore himself, but she saw the lines deepen in his brow and the curves of his mouth harden as everyone, or almost everyone, flattered and congratulated Miss Lennox to her heart's content.

He and his betrothed were the cynosure of all eyes. She was supremely happy. Her face was expressive of every inward impulse and pictured joy, triumph and unalloyed enjoyment, while his was a mask. What his thoughts were his world did not know.

Nor was he very sure that he knew himself. Arrangements for their union had progressed so rapidly and elaborately, and his time had been so fully occupied, that it had afforded him little opportunity or time to reflect or retract, but there was one thing of which he was conscious and that was, that regrets and remorse, neither vague nor visionary, had filled every moment of his life, whether waking or sleeping, since the day of his betrothal.

His knowledge of the world told him that somehow the world was aware of his love for another. Although no one hinted of it to him or spoke of it or betrayed it by a glance, yet some subtle sense told him that the world knew of his dislike for his future wife and his love for another, and this knowledge humiliated him so in his own sight that it created within his own dead self a tendency to treat his future wife with a marked courtesy, but a courtesy having within it so much coldness that the eyes of the world invariably turned to the other, and this made him very careful in his conduct towards the other. He had no right to place her in a trying position before her world.

He did not approach her, but as the evening drew to a close he descended the stairs with Jack Mainton to the waiting carriage. He opened the door for her to pass in. A fine misty rain was now falling and the driveway was very wet with melting snow, but he stood at the carriage heedless of it, with his hand on the open door, until Mr. Wellington would come.

"Ah, there is Miss Lennox. How well she looked to-night! You are to be envied, Mr. Kenyon," said the Lady Greta, who accompanied the Wellington party.

They looked towards the stairway, and through the misty rain saw the Lennox party descending the steps.

"We do envy him. We all adore her," said Jack, briefly, with a little laugh.

The Lady Greta looked surprised.

"This is not an age of adoration," said Keith Kenyon, as he replaced his hat, murmured a good-night, and walked away into the gloom of the night.

The Lady Greta looked more surprised, while her companion leaned back in the shadows of the carriage, every chord in her nature responsive to the feelings expressed in the departed one's accents.

That same night as Keith Kenyon walked home through the deserted streets he seemed to realize what he was about to do, and so bitterly did he repent of what he had done that his courage failed him. "He couldn't do it. Would he buy a weapon and end it all? No, that would be the last act of cowardice. Would he go away and leave it all? He couldn't live without her. Could he not persuade her to go with him? The world would be well lost for love. At least he could try once more to persuade her to relent. There was yet a little time left, and while there was life there was hope; he would do what he could. Although there was no palpable, perceptible change in her, yet his eye had seen it. Perhaps her suffering and separation would weaken and lessen her sense of duty and make her more susceptible to sentiment." This thought gave him courage, and with a ray of hope shining in his heart like the sun shining for a moment between passing thunderstorms, early the next morning he made his way to Apsley House, only to learn on his arrival there that she had gone to Fernwylde for the day.

He could not leave the city until late in the afternoon, but that was of no moment. A new joy was in him. He attended to his duties during the day, the many calls receiving his attention and advice, but his heart was with his memories and his hopes. No word or look had passed between them the previous evening, yet was he conscious of a yielding within her. He felt happier than he had felt in many weeks. He had no definite hope, yet, being of a sanguine and happy temperament, he felt the future held within its lap great possibilities and great joys for him, and these could only come through her.

He took an afternoon train, and when he arrived at Fernwylde went in search of her. It was almost evening, but the sun was yet shining brightly. The great white mantle, which yesterday had covered the earth and bent beneath its weight the naked boughs of the trees, had disappeared as if by magic, leaving behind it a robe of brown and green. The waters had once more broken their bands and flowed away past the bends and curves of their fir-lined shore. He found her down by the river, leaning against the bent bough of an old elm tree, with her dogs by her side. She had been for a long walk to a distant part of the estate, where an old nurse of hers lay dying, and was returning home. The snows and glaciers on the mountain side had melted and were coming down, rumbling and murmuring in their hurry to join the streams below. She had paused by the river to watch the great masses of ice and snow whirl round the rugged rocks and pass over the swollen waters of the many cascades which intersected the river. Father Jacques had been with her, but as it was vesper hour he had left her at the lake-shore monastery. The chimes of the monastery bells now rang clear upon the evening air.

She did not see him coming. Her eyes were on the farther shore, where the shadows were fast creeping round the distant hills and lake and ravine. A flock of wild geese, in their V-shaped course, darkened the sky as they made their way southward.

20

As he came across the brownsward the dogs saw him and ran joyfully to meet him.

She turned, and as she saw who it was all the blood in her body, for a moment, rushed into her face. She had been thinking of him, and it seemed to her he had but risen out of the mists of her thoughts. He was by her side before she could regain her composure.

"I came down on purpose to see you, Modena," he said, as he stood beside her, but he did not touch her. "We are doing wrong; we will live to regret it. You are my only love, and I cannot live without you. I will not give you up," he breathed, with intense passion in every word and hunger in every tone and ardent accent, while his eyes sought hers with language more powerful than any words of lip.

There is no passion so magnetic and irresistible as the submission of one who has never been known to submit. He had never been known to submit until he had met her, and now his obedient adoration moved her as no other power could have done.

She had learned in her short separation from him how absolutely necessary was his companionship to her happiness, his presence to her interest in life and his love to her life. She knew this now. All day she had thought of nothing else. All night she had lain sleepless and worn from her mental exhaustion. The actions, attributes and honor of man were more to her than man himself. The vision of his doing it because she had implied that he should do so, which her cousin's words had opened up before her, had moved her profoundly. But it was now too late to speak. She had come to her country home to detract her mind from it. Like Coppee's Olivier, she had felt her own weakness, and she had fled from it. "Why had he followed her? Why did he torture her thus? Of what use was it? Her own pleadings and her pain were greater than her strength, without his prayers."

She turned her face away to hide her emotion, but he could see how she was moved by the violent throbbing of her pulses and the beating of her temples, but she replied almost coldly:

"Why do you reopen the subject? It is surely too late now. Why cause us both pain?"

"It is not too late. I want only you," and then he pleaded with her, not with the words of reason, for he knew that now it did not lie within his power to use such words, but with the words of the heart, the language of the lips, and the pleadings of a close embrace, until she grew weak and almost felt she could give it all up and go away with him forever and forever.

But she did not wholly relinquish herself. She drew herself away. She did not raise her eyes to his, for they were moist, and she was bracing herself to conquer her cravings and conceal the reciprocal pleadings of her own heart.

"She could not treat another person thus," and her world rolled over her again. "She could do nothing that would cause her to lose the respect of her world or her own self-respect. To submit now would be almost a baseness." Her form quivered with suppressed emotion.

He looked at her.

"You love me?" he said.

"You want the truth. Yes, I love you. But I could not love dishonor."

Her words fell on him like the cold of death, and his soul swooned within him.

"You have strength to say that I should do penance for my thoughtlessness. Love makes cowards of the most courageous. To-night my love is greater than yours? I have not the strength to say it. I am weak in your presence. What if some day I should prove stronger with you than yourself?"

But this was something beyond her conception. He, too, had touched a wrong chord.

"It is useless to discuss it further. How can you ask or expect it on the eve of your marriage to another woman?" she replied.

"Spare me that," he said.

"But I cannot. It is all that separates us." He knew this, and remained mute and motionless for some time from the intensity of his anguish.

"There is no use trying to reason with you?" he asked, not knowing what else to say.

"None," was the reply.

He bowed his head in despair; his despair moved her—moved her more than all his pleadings and passions had done. She could never suffer more than she did at this moment. But one thought dwelt within her, "Could she only bear it all?" She was very weak under the thought. She must go away while she had yet strength to go.

"You must go now," she said, and her voice seemed very far away.

"You wish me to go?"

"Yes."

He stood for some moments looking down upon her, thinking he could never again care for anything; then the world and its ways rolled over him once more, and without further words he turned and passed from her sight over the brownsward into the gloom of the ravine.

CHAPTER XXVIII.

The following week he received a message, which was almost an urgent command, to call at Lennox Court.

When he obeyed the summons and made his appearance at the Court, Verona awaited him in the library.

Since the day of their betrothal she had treated him as if their alliance were one of ordinary love. She never admitted that there was anything peculiar in their relations, or referred to them to anyone, least of all to himself. It was not her way to do so. She must first bag her bird before betraying any of her motives or desires. She knew that one is never sure of anything until it lies within the palm of one's hand, and she was very careful in her management of him. She knew that a false step might yet mean disappointment to her. It was absolutely necessary that his most intimate friends must be consulted and interested in their marriage. They must be with them now. Afterwards it didn't matter. Modena Wellington must be her first bridesmaid. She had set her heart upon this. For many reasons! It was impossible for her to be married without the leading lady in the city being present. Without her presence the affair would be robbed of half its prestige. And Modena Wellington, above all others, must be made to feel her triumph! There was intense joy in the thought of her rival's chagrin and defeat. She, Verona, must not be robbed of the pleasure of seeing it. This was half the joy of her marriage. She would be her maid of honor, and the matter had been settled— in her mind. And the invitation had been sent. She had received her reply that morning. It was a note of regret. Mrs. Monteith was ill at the seashore. She was going to the seashore, and would not return in time. "How mean of Mrs. Monteith to be ill at this time, and how base of Modena Wellington to go off when she wanted her! She didn't believe Mrs. Monteith was ill; it was only an excuse of Modena Wellington to escape witnessing her triumph. But she wasn't going to get away so easily. She would circumvent her, even if she had to resort to dynamite on the track, or call up a plague by incantation down by the seashore." But she knew that a word from Keith Kenyon would be more powerful to convince than either dynamite or plagues, and she was too wise a woman to waste her energies and time in straining and pulling when a lever would accomplish the same result with infinitely less labor. Keith Kenyon must make her remain or return.

On receiving the note she had sent for him at once.

"Modena Wellington cannot be my maid of honor; I have received a note of regret. How thoughtless and selfish of her! To disarrange one's plans at the last minute! Of course it is of no moment. But having asked her one cannot now ask someone else. Can't you persuade her to come?" she said, coaxingly and caressingly, and a little petulantly to hide her chagrin, and she looked at him closely as she spoke.

He was glad the library shutters were closed, and it was twilight, for he felt the blood leave his face. He had only seen her at a distance since he had parted with her at Fernwylde. He had noticed that she had sedulously absented herself from all functions at which he had officiated, or from all meetings at which he had spoken. Several times he had been forced to call at Apsley House, but she had invariably absented herself from the room while he was there.

He now recovered himself and asked "Why?" with as much indifference as possible, but anxiously awaited the reply.

"Mr. Monteith's mother is ill at the seashore. They have telegraphed for her to come at once. She leaves to-night."

"Leaves to-night," was all that he heard.

"Will you call on your way home and try to persuade her to return in time?" she asked, with a little more command in her voice.

Her companion failed to reply. He hadn't heard what she was saying.

"Will you call?" she asked again, with the command a little more in evidence.

He awoke from his meditation and answered quickly and almost with aversion.

"Call, yes, but I think I know Miss Wellington well enough to inform you that when she has once made up her mind to do anything she cannot be persuaded to do otherwise, especially when she considers it her duty," and he smiled bitterly. "But I shall call and see her," he added, turning and leaving the room.

He returned home with bent head and darkened brow, not noticing those of his acquaintances whom he met on the street.

"Kenyon looks as though he were going to his grave rather than to the altar," said an ex-minister to one of his colleagues, as they passed him.

"He's getting wealth and beauty and youth. Does he want a Diana or a Venus de Medici? Or what does he want?" replied his colleague.

"Love," said the other, with a queer little laugh.

"Don't you think she's capable of loving?"

"Yes, and of hating, too."

"*He* wasn't made to be hated. *He* was made to be loved. The gods have given him all the graces. What's his doubled rose-leaf?"

"Modena Wellington leaves to-night for the coast. Mrs. Monteith is seriously ill."

"Humph!" said the other, as he looked back at the young statesman who was now ascending the steps which led into Kenyon Court, with the same words ringing in his ears.

"Leaves to-night," was all of which he was conscious. As he went to his room to dress for dinner the words kept ringing like a death-knell within his confused mind, chilling him to the heart, as a deathbell tortures the most sensitive nerves of a mourner. He couldn't go to her again. It would be useless. No doubt she would refuse to see him. He could bid her a formal good-bye, and offer his condolence on her friend's illness. This courtesy would be extended to him, and he rose, and going out of a side door, made his way across the grounds to Apsley House. He entered by the door leading from her private gardens. She was not in her sitting-room, and he asked for Mr. Wellington.

The servant ushered him into the library.

The master of Apsley House was looking well. He was quite confident of success. His daughter was happy, at least she was his same girl, loving, thoughtful, interested, and cheerful. Life looked very bright to him.

He turned with a smile to his young friend, and drew a chair for him before the glowing hearth-fire. He was always pleased to see Keith Kenyon.

The younger man remained standing.

"Mr. Wellington," he said, and his voice was low and strained. "I have learned that Modena leaves town to-night. I shall not see her again. I would bid her good-bye."

A change came over the elder man's face. It grew grave and a little troubled. The memories of his only love had not lessened with his years, and he was quick to sympathize. But he regretted that the subject had been reopened.

"Do you think it wise?" asked the elder man, a shadow passing over his face as he spoke.

"Wise or unwise, I want to bid her good-bye," replied the younger man, with an accent of command in his voice.

But Mr. Wellington hesitated and lingered, undecided what to say or what to do. At length he said, "Very well. I shall send her here."

He went himself to her room. Servants are curious and given to comment.

Her train did not leave until midnight. The Lady Greta was staying with her. They had dressed early for an opera. Then the telegram had come. She was taking the Lady Greta over to join Lady Seaton's party.

Her father told her she was wanted in the library, and then left the room by a side door.

She rose, picked up her cloak, and went down and entered the library where he was.

She had grown quieter and much graver, but she never looked more beautiful in her life than she did now, with the magnificent Wellington diamonds shimmering in her hair and on her bosom.

He advanced to meet her, but at the same moment the Lady Greta and Jack entered the library by another door, ready for the opera.

The Lady Greta looked surprised, and then she began to see, and her little mouth closed in hard lines, while Jack frowned heavily.

"Are you ready, Modena? We are late now. Cannot you come with us, Kenyon?" he asked.

"I—I was going—I was to go—I forgot all about it. You are going away to-night, Modena. I called to say good-bye."

"You need not accompany me to Lady Seaton's, Modena. Mrs. Gwen will come," said the Lady Greta, very quickly.

"What would her Excellency say to such a lack of courtesy? We do not treat our guests thus."

"'Say,' be bothered!" exclaimed the Lady Greta, "I can go alone. I would rather walk than take you away. Your sense of hospitality is that of a chatelaine of the Middle Ages. We don't mind those things now. They died out with—with—love. You haven't time to come. You have to dress for the train. I shall not see you again, good-bye."

"Her ladyship would not lend you to me again if I treated you thus. The train does not leave until midnight," said Modena, as she took up her cloak.

The Lady Greta pouted, and remained silent, while Keith Kenyon took the wrap from her hands and placed it round her shoulders, and then walked with her to the waiting carriage.

He bade her good-bye, and stood on the pavement until the carriage disappeared from sight.

He then turned and went home.

She returned to Apsley House some half hour afterwards, and a few minutes before midnight left for the late express. It was now raining heavily. Her father and Jack went with her to her own private compartment, and then returned to the waiting carriage. The train left a few minutes afterwards. As it passed out over the iron girders, there was a continual sound of splashing water audible above the noise and scream of the engines and the throb of their great wheels. The water beat against the panes and ran down into the darkness of the night. She sat at the one window of her compartment, looking out into the inky blackness of midnight. She felt the affinity between the night and herself.

In some half hour the train pulled slowly into the little flag station at Fernwylde. It slackened its pace, but it did not stop. The lights of the little wayside station were almost hidden from view by the heavy pall of misty rain which hung over the valley, but in their dimness a figure, lonely and alone, loomed out of the darkness of the night. It was strangely familiar. Her compartment was lighted and its one window open.

She drew back quickly into the shadows of the car.

She had seen him; he had seen her.

The train quickened its pace. The far-away lights of her country home and of his loomed out of the darkness and disappeared like weird will-o'-the-wisps. The express rolled faster on its way. Soon its oscillations and speed shook the surrounding hills, and in a few minutes Fernwylde and its lonely knight were left far behind in the darkness of the moonless night.

Two days after this she arrived at the seashore and found Mrs. Monteith very ill indeed, so ill that no one but the nurse and physician were allowed in her chamber. This relieved her of the sick-room duties and prevented her from mingling in any society. She was free to wander through the private grounds all alone, with the pale sunbeams and hazy mists of the south her only companions. For a few days, perhaps weeks, if the patient did not recover, she might live as she pleased, unfettered by duties and position. She was glad of her freedom, and willingly shirked the strain of keeping up a simulated interest in the joyous festivities of the season and of the coming marriage.

Solitude was what she wanted, and yet there were times when solitude became unbearable to her. There were times that the remembrance of what she had loved and what she had lost came to her with such great force and with such poignant pain that she would willingly have sought the world to escape from herself.

"If it were only over, and beyond her power to relent, then all would be well," she said to herself, and she waited with almost as much impatience as did Verona Lennox for the day to come and go.

Before leaving home she had searched her private rooms and secretary for every note, every token, every faded flower from his hand, and locked them away in a secret compartment of the private safe in a vault known only to her father, herself, and the family solicitor, for although she possessed the most trusted of servants yet are they often careless and curious, and she wished her past life to be hidden from the outside world; but she could not bring herself to destroy those links which bound him to her life.

There were some pages in her life sealed away, too sacred for the common light of day, pages illumined and thoroughly happy, reflecting the innermost thoughts and emotions, and written with all that was best and noblest in Keith Kenyon. These she told herself she would keep with her forever.

As soon as she was gone, Keith regretted letting her go. After his interview with her at Fernwylde he had resolved he would never address her again, and he had not; but she had been near him, and her presence had filled his life. His body might have been walking, moving, acting, living the movements and life of the world around him, but his inner life was ever with her. But now that she was gone, life was one hopeless void. As he had stood upon the platform and watched the train disappear into the inky darkness, it had seemed to him that his life was as the night. His last hope had disappeared with her departure as the lights of the train had vanished in the blackness of the night. He had turned towards Idlewylde, and he had felt as Menelaus had felt without his Helen. Almost he made up his mind to follow her, but after-thought and reflection told him that such action would cause comment, perhaps without altering her purpose; and he had no right to compromise her in the sight of her world. "I shall write to her and try once more," he resolved, as he walked home late one night from the village through his own woods to Idlewylde.

Her presence was with him, each step of the way was fraught with memories of her, and burning words came to him for utterance. When he reached his own room he drew his table to the eastern window, where the wind rustled in as it came over the pines from Fernwylde, and the moon shone down from its place over the Idlewylde. His eyes rested on the ravine and river, and on the spires and turrets and towers of the Fernery and Fernwylde. All the memories and joys of life haunted the scene which lay before

him in the stillness and serenity of midnight, and moved him to
the deepest emotions of life. His past, present and future rose
up before him. He seemed to be brought to a knowledge that
within him lay great powers, which as yet had lain dormant and
undeveloped, and which her presence alone could ever bring to
perfection. Life and love were something sacred. His life was yet
on the morning side of its meridian, and his country might yet
crown him as Rome crowned Petrarch before his shadows length-
ened into night.

With her his life might be made the triumphant poem of a
Solomon. Without her it might become the Dead March of a
Saul.

How could he tell to her all his ambitions and hopes and fears
and loves? Inspired by all which tortured him, the genius within
him made him a poet in impression and expression, and thoughts
flowed from his heart in burning words from his pen. Under the
stimulus and spur of the one passion of his life, a passion which
now seemed almost hopeless, he poured out his last prayer, as the
wild swan dying among the frozen rushes pours out its plaintive
reprisals of life in one outburst of melancholy song.

All that was in him he put on paper; he wrote as he felt, and
he felt that she must read as he wrote. By the light of the rising
sun he read again what he had written, and it seemed to him that
if she loved him it could not fail to make even a heart of stone
relent. "If this does not move her, I shall never look upon her
face again," he said, as he walked over to the early mail and himself posted it while the town yet slept.

He remained down at Idlewylde for the day, full of renewed
hope and courage and life. There could be but one reply to such
an appeal. Even an Hypatia, Polyeute or Pauline would succumb
to such a prayer. He had won her in time. He wanted to remain
at Idlewylde until her answer would come, but calls, urgent and
pressing, came down upon him, and towards evening he was forced
to turn his face once more towards the city.

Here the pillory of the press, the platform, and many public
functions awaited him and awakened him from his midnight
dreams and hopes, and brought him face to face once more with
the conventions of life. And the world and its ways came to him
once again, and as they did he began to doubt, and then he grew
feverish and restless and impatient and anxious for, yet dreading
her reply.

CHAPTER XXIX.

THE physicians had said that Mrs. Monteith would live, at least for a while. They had ordered her removal to the South for the winter. They had cabled for her son who had been called to the continent. On his return the mistress of Apsley House would be free to return home. She had now been some two weeks at the seashore. Her health, which had been impaired by the severe mental strain under which she had been laboring, had been, restored, and as her strength had returned her old courage had come back with it, and she had been anxious to return and take up the duties of life once more with renewed vitality.

She would put behind her the past. Regrets were useless. A person of sanguine disposition is not given much to retrospection. She would waste no time thus. To do so would be dreaming, not living, and her nature was one which must live. Every moment meant something. All her life long she had been careful in word, wise in judgment, and resolute and serene in action, and there was little in her life to cause her regret, but what little there was she was quick to redeem by wise and serene activity. She was a woman of action and a fortnight of inactivity was sufficient for her.

The place at which Mrs. Monteith had been staying was a secluded summer resort. The place was utterly unattractive and uninviting. It had been chosen for its seclusion, its air, and some mineral springs. It was barren, bleak and lonely without the compensating grandeurs of nature which are so often the chief attraction in such places. It possessed nothing which would restore one's hopes or revive one's ambitions. It was one of those places which take upon itself the character and coloring of the crowd who frequent it.

All summer it had been gay and glad with the many butterflies who had flown from the heat and noise and dust and teeming life of far-away cities, but now they were gone, the only occupants of the place being Mrs. Monteith and her servants, she being too ill to be removed.

Even to those who care nothing about the multitude, there is still a vague sense of depression in the dispersion of any gathering. The few big houses standing where the sea washed their base, now shuttered and barred, seemed so silent. The little cottages, facing each other in a double hedge with a lane of sand between, were closed and deserted. The one lonely, little, weatherbeaten church on the bare rocks looked grey and forsaken. Fragments of boxes, cans, papers, littered the ground and blew here and there in the eddying gusts which came in from the lake; broken toys, a summer novelette, an old awning, a faded sunshade, were all that were left from the gay, glad gathering here but a short time ago. Though they are nothing to one, yet is there a certain sadness and depression in their departure.

The place palled upon Modena. There was nothing to do. There was no one to whom to talk. The few peasant folk and fishermen were taciturn, dull, stupid. They were happy and contented and didn't need her, and she spent most of her time sitting silent on the big bare rocks which overhung the seashore, simply waiting, her mind passive and resigned.

One day she had gone down as usual. The air was cold; she took with her a heavy wrap and found a seat on a sheltered rock on the seashore. All was dull and bleak and sombre. The dispersion of the crowd had left upon her a saddened, forsaken sense.

She sat watching the afternoon fade into twilight. No sound stirred the stillness, save the sound of the sea surging among the rocks at the base of the church tower and the cry of the wild heron among the rushes and osier beds in the marshes.

Farther down the shore a few old women dried and mended the fishermen's nets; a few old men did the same. Out on the sand some children were playing; out on the waters some fishermen were bringing in the last of their fishing boats before the setting of the summer sun.

A west wind came from the sea bringing with it fine rain mists, and rustled among the tall reeds and larches farther up the shore. All was melancholy, lonely and cold. It depressed her exceedingly. She was anxious to get away from it, but she could not go until Carlton Monteith's return. She would not go until after the day of Keith Kenyon's marriage. Carlton Monteith would return in three days. She would go home the day after the other's marriage. The threads of her life had been weakened, but they had not been broken. She had repaired them once more. They were not quite so strong as they had been, but they would strengthen and harden in time, and she began to formulate in her own mind many things she would do.

A noise from the house dog attracted her attention. It was only the post-boy. She would go up and read her mail. But he was coming down. She watched him as he descended the winding path. In his hand he held a letter with a special stamp upon it. Her other letters he had left at the house. He crossed the sands and handed it to her. Before looking at it she gave him some silver, and he went his way. She then took it up. It was sealed with armorial bearings which she well knew. She recognized the handwriting, and all the blood in her body surged to her face, while a thrill like fire and a chill like ice ran side by side through her veins.

He had written.

In a moment of time the whole coloring of the place had changed. Her self-control and serenity had vanished; and life once more was one troubled bitter sweetness, one alluring sweet bitterness, and all by the mere sight of a handwriting—she, who had been planning what she would do!

She kept the letter unopened in her hand for some time.

"Would she open it? Had she strength to do so? Or would she return it unopened? Would this be unkind?" She was all alone and she bowed her head upon it. Had even his handwriting the power to move her thus? She moved her head until her lips touched the cold paper.

When she had again regained her self-command she raised her head, and then opened the letter and read, and as she read the first tears which she had shed since childhood, since she had stood by the death-bed of her mother, coursed down her cheeks.

She read it but once, and then sat very silent and still with her eyes on the sea, but seeing it not.

After some half hour she took the letter and tore it into minute fragments as it had torn her life, and walking to the edge of the surf cast its shreds upon the waters.

She could not reread it, nor could she keep it. It was beyond her strength to do so.

She made her way slowly up the steep hill-side to the house. She went to her room which looked out over the sea towards the land of the setting sun, and there made answer to the letter.

The third day came, and with it came Carlton Monteith. The next day was Keith Kenyon's wedding day. At four of the clock she sat in the same place as she had sat when she had read his letter. She sat silent, her eyes on the sands of the shore. The surf had already washed the last fragment of the letter far beneath the sands of the sea. She wondered if time would do the same in her heart. The half-hour chimed out over the waters from the old clock tower. She raised her eyes and said, "It is over now." But this did not bring her the relief that she had thought it would bring. The letter had left her profoundly dejected and depressed.

Evening was creeping over the waters. She tried to tell herself that all was well, that life was very short, and that each moment, Time's last ambassador, would claim its own. But already the shadows seemed very grey and the day seemed over long.

She rose and went slowly back to the house.

He received the letter the next day, and when he read it he knew his fears were realized, and in the bitterness of his disappointment his first impulse was to cry out, " She is unworthy of any man's love." But he could not do so. It was this very unworthiness within her which drew him and bound him to her. There was something within her which he could not reach and subdue, and it was this unattainable something which was the secret of her power over him, and which made him want her the more.

" What was this something? Was it only a woman's obstinacy and pride, or was it the one quality which the world lacks, Creeds and Courage? If it were obstinacy it was the obstinacy which makes Marguerites de la Marguerite, De Reccis and Semiramises and was a quality worthy of worship."

But the words of the letter were not the words of a woman of little comprehension or of little feeling. He read it again, and he did not need to read between the lines to see that they were words written by self-abnegation, by one who owed allegiance to her own conscience alone, by one who yet believed self-sacrifice to be a principle of life instead of the means to a principle. Its lofty tone, its suggestions of spiritual fidelity and its undercurrent of pathos moved him to opposite emotions. They were the words of a woman who was writing with a breaking heart. It is the courage of an Hypatia to die for her creeds. She is an angel in exile, he said to himself, while a great calm came over his soul. Deep and vivid impressions play an important part in forming man's character and conduct in life. Her letter moved him to submission and subjection. " Lucius had recovered his manhood by eating a crown of roses. He would have to be a Donatoillo and regain his, by throwing his crown away. I shall do it," he said for the last time.

He took up the letter and read it again until the words were his. The letter had in it the odor of dead roses, and they seemed to him like the perfume of flowers which lie on the grave of one's beloved. He folded it, and taking the last red rose which he had taken from her at Fernwylde, he locked them away in his own private room in a secret drawer in an antique carved cabinet, belonging to the family for many generations, where he kept those treasures and heirlooms which he held sacred, the most precious among them being notes and mementos from her, and little did he dream the important part it would play in his life's drama.

From this time forward he had no further time for reflection. He held himself well in reserve and wore a mask of cold serenity that the world knew not what he thought or how he felt.

The invitations had been extensive; the ceremony, which was elaborate, took place at four in the afternoon. The festivities which followed were lavish and extravagant, but the weather proved dull, grey and depressing.

They left Lennox Court as the lamps were being lighted. In the streets a dreary rain began to fall. People were hurrying home with bent heads from their day's labor to a warm fireside. A strong west wind swept up in great gusts from the river, bringing with it a spray of falling waters, and the smell of gas and smoke from the many works, while the water poured off the carriage-tops, and ran down the waterproof coats and helmets of the coachman and policeman. Nothing more dismal can be imagined than the scenes round a railway station during a driving storm, but they were in perfect keeping with Keith Kenyon's feelings and temper.

When they left the carriage, by the aid of the footman's umbrellas and waterproofs they made their way over the dirty platform, oily sleepers and greasy girders, with the rain, laden with smoke and the coal dust, sweeping in their faces, to the coach at the rear end of the train.

After what seemed to him an endless time, the train lumbered heavily out from the station, with the discordant jarring noises of heavy drays, shunting engines and screaming whistles lingering in their ears, as they passed out of the city in the moving coach.

Soon the train's speed quickened, the lights of the suburbs passed from view, the trainmen passed through and they were left alone. And then he realized what he had done, and what she was to him. A feeling of repulsion came over him. He smiled bitterly but he said nothing. He did not know what to say. Light talk was foreign to his nature, and his instincts refused intimacy, so he remained silent, only answering her queries or replying to her remarks in monosyllables.

It seemed to him that it must be some hideous dream, something without any reality. She was nothing to him. She could never be more than she was.

The one cold kiss of the clergyman's command, the first he had ever given her, was yet frozen on his lips like a kiss of death.

He shuddered, and soon afterwards rose, and sending her maid to minister to her wants, passed to his own compartments.

He had limited their honeymoon to a very short distance and a very short period of time on the plea of important public matters. He took her to the public places of amusement during the day, and to the operas and musicals during the evening, and when he had bade her good-night went his way to one of the many clubs which gladly welcomed him, and where he had many aquaintances. He was glad when the fortnight was over, and he had returned home and had resumed his busy life once more.

The day after his marriage the mistress of Apsley House returned home. As she approached the house her feelings were as those of one who had returned from a lately closed grave of a loved and lost one. She felt as Orpheus might have felt when he returned without his Eurydice, or Persephone when she was forced to return to the bowels of the earth.

The house seemed so still and quiet and empty. Everything was as it had been a few short months before, but to her it was changed. As the carriage drew up to the grand entrance she looked up into her home. When absent from any of her homes for a few days she had invariably returned to them as a lover returns to his beloved, but to-day it failed to move her. The evening sun illumined the massive pile of gothics and towers and emblazoned windows. An infinite peace seemed to rest like a benediction on the great home in its silence. It was the symbol, and suggestive of all her pleasures of her former life, but to-day it hurt her to look upon it.

The members of the family and the old servants met and welcomed her, and then she left them and traversed the great halls, with the men in armor in their stalls looking down upon her, past the dim corridors leading away to the several wings of the house, to her own room, Nell Gwynne and the other dogs following her and leaping about her in their joy at her return.

The late sun still streamed through the stained windows across the soft rugs of her room. The room was warm with hearth fires and filled with the fragrance of many flowers and the harmonies of soft colors. In a little while the servants came in with her tea, some anchovy sandwiches and some deviled biscuits, placed them on the table, and then crossed over to light the wax candles in the sconces and chandeliers in her suite of rooms, but she bade them go away for a while. She was tired and the lights hurt her eyes. She would rest.

In the gloaming she sat gloomy; the clocks on the mantel

ticked softly one against the other. She looked at one to see if she must dress for dinner. On the mantel by its side rested a portrait of Keith Kenyon which she had failed to remove. She looked at it from where she sat in a deep chair by the fire, and it seemed to gaze down on her with eyes muttering an eternal farewell. She had thought that they would meet as friends, that they would ever be near each other, but now she knew that this could not be so.

As she had sat by the seashore that day watching the shadows stealing over the waters, sadly had come home to her what the word marriage entailed. She had always held that high and spiritual view of marriage, that it was a union of souls and that this life was but a preparation for eternity. Another had now a claim upon his thoughts, his moments, his love. To think of him now would be sacrilege.

She must banish him from her life, and as one step towards doing so she arose and took from its place the portrait, which had been one he had given to her father, and locked it away with her other treasures, but her resolution left as great a void in her life and heart as the removal of the portrait had left on the mantel where it had stood for so long.

Her past life must become the reliquary of her love as the antique cabinet had become the urn of all that was his. So she told herself as she stood looking down into the glowing coals on the hearth with the empty space in front of her. She had her old duties and interests and pleasures. She would take them up with courage. Any form of cowardice in her sight was almost a sin, and now to become pale in spirit or apathetic or cynical or self-centred would seem to her cowardly, and if she would have become thus she would have become, in her own sight, as the modern world, and although she loved the world, yet its insincerity, its apathy and frothy vacuum she scorned. She had taken life seriously, and the instincts within her were strong that the greater the opportunities, the greater the responsibilities, and that some day, somewhere, she would be held responsible for all that she had done or left undone while here. She was like a high-blooded, mettled thoroughbred. She would win in the race or die in the attempt. Her old duties were as interesting, as important, as dear to her as ever. She would enter into them and she would banish Keith Kenyon from her mind. To sin towards him in spirit was infinitely greater in her sight than to sin towards him in the letter. She would not do so and she turned to dress for dinner, and as she dressed she wondered where she would first

21

see him. She could see the glad light which would leap to his eyes when they would meet hers, and her cheeks grew warm and she wished that time were here, and then she checked herself.

And so the struggle with her inner life began.

She must get away from herself, and to get away from herself she went down to meet the bevy of friends who had come to call as soon as they had learned of her return, but when she met them it was only to hear of him, the one topic of conversation being the wedding the previous day.

The evening's conversation was but a harbinger of others which followed during the next fortnight. The mistress of Apsley House wondered as she went from house to house or received her own friends at home, if they would ever cease talking about the Lennoxes and their merits or demerits. She possessed too much delicacy and good-breeding to discuss personalities, and especially more so since they were now connected with the Kenyons, and was at most times at a loss what to say.

At last she heard that they were home. She knew that the bride's reception day would soon be announced, and she wasn't prepared to meet them. The words of his letter had burnt into her life. She could never forget them. Time alone could put upon them a covering of serenity. He now belonged to another. She could not meet him—her, honestly, and until she could do so she wished to avoid them, so she went out to Fernwylde for the week.

"Am I to spend my life running away from them?" she thought as the train bore her towards Fernwylde, and her actions to herself seemed almost cowardly, but she could see no way out of it. She could not of her own free will go to Kenyon Court and extend her hand in friendship to its mistress. She could not be a traitor to her own feelings. All she could do was to avoid them and govern her own actions by tact and prudence. To meet them on neutral ground would be of no moment, but she could not meet them in their home—in her own home. She would refrain from entertaining, and in time they would drift apart. She could fill her life with her own interests. She had her homes and her farms and her thoroughbreds, which she dearly loved. She had her interest in her people's many schools. She had her people on her land who depended upon her for much. She had many unfortunates and poor in life whom she succored. These were all the real things of life, and among them she felt that her manner of life was worthy of her. Among them she felt that life was a sacred trust, and that she was fulfilling that trust. " These things would console and sustain her," she said as she stepped out on the little wayside platform at Fernwylde.

The carriage was waiting her. The way was fraught with many memories, but she put them from her, and on her arrival entered with all the ardor and vitality of former days into the many interests surrounding her country home. Her time was wholly occupied. The early fall of snow had cleared the first frost from the air, and the autumn season had lingered late. She rose early and spent the day out of doors. The little village was becoming gay with its season's festivities of simple pleasures. She graced many of them by her presence. She spent the mornings at the more distant parts of her estates, the afternoons with the fishermen's and lumbermen's wives, aiding and suggesting to them in their work for the coming winter, while her evenings were eagerly sought for by more congenial friends. Each night she retired physically tired, slept well and awoke refreshed.

In time Helen Lester wrote her that the reception was a thing of the past. "Kenyon Court saw many new faces to-day," wrote Helen. "Verona is going to establish a new era; her ambition is to become a social leader. Hitherto her entertainments have been costly, lavish, heterogeneous, but there has been method in her madness. No time or money has been wasted. She is too shrewd for this. She has gathered about her a powerful social and political clique, a phalanx which can no longer be ignored. Will it be a real commonwealth, or will it be only the Tyrannus to which all republics succumb? Everything seemed so strange, so unfamiliar, one might say so sacrilegious. She and her friends in Kenyon Court drawing-rooms reminded one of a cheap edition of a sensational summer novelette pasted on a poem of Pindar, or a bust of Madame Roland beside that of Maria Theresa. Keith's mother was there, and she reminded one of Marie Antoinette in the arms of the mob. I went late and I saw Keith as he returned in the evening. He looked as Lancelot might have looked by the lonely shores of the Usk. No; this parallel is inappropriate, he looked like Dante going through Inferno with Beatrice awaiting him at the pearly gates. When do you return to the city? The town is dull and grey without your presence. At least, everyone says so. Do come soon."

She returned to Apsley House the next day. As she had been out of town her absence from the reception would not be commented upon, and as she had not called they could not invite her to their home. Their friends had now become so numerous and their entertainments would become so frequent that her absence would be unnoticed, and she could continue her even course of life.

But she had reckoned without her host.

The next morning the master of Kenyon Court sat in his library, polishing and perfecting an address he was to deliver that same evening, when his wife came in with some invitations in her hand.

"Keith," she said, "shall I send Modena Wellington an invitation to our dinner?"

"Why not?" he asked quickly, and then checked himself. He had been deeply engaged all morning with his notes and had finished them, and having laid them aside had leaned his arm on the table and bowed his head in his hands. He had not seen her since his marriage, and he was wondering if she would be in the audience that evening.

His wife noticed the intonation and immediately a cloud passed over her face.

"You ask 'Why!' She treated us shabbily. Mrs. Monteith was not so ill but she could have returned in time for our wedding, if it were her desire to do so. She came back the next day."

Her husband did not know how to reply to her, so he remained silent while she continued, "It was a public slight. We can afford to know her or know her not. What do you say?"

Keith resumed his notes. "I should think if she is what I believe her to be, that the sending or the withholding of your invitation would be of no moment to her. She knows herself. The eupatride spirit is predominant within her, so that anything we can do cannot hurt her feelings or her position. But I should think for your own sake it would be best to forget her absence at the wedding and send her an invitation, but, however, please yourself."

He was cautious in his careless reply. He did not want any open hostility between them. The conventionalities of life would force him to uphold his wife, and he knew that it would be an impossibility for him to do so.

"But she might again refuse," said Verona.

It was of this she was afraid. In life she had received few rebukes or rebuffs; the givers of the few which she had received she hated with an intense hatred. Modena Wellington's refusal to be present at her wedding and her husband's reserve and coldness in persuading her to come when she had so insistently persisted, had aroused within her the most embittered resentment of her life, and now she did not want to needlessly lay herself open to another from Modena Wellington, but yet she must have her rival present. The whole joy of her triumph lay, not in her accomplishments, but in her rival being a witness to them, and how to gain her presence without her husband's aid she did not know. When she had asked his aid before, she had allowed him to see a little too plainly that she wanted her presence. She would be a little more wary this time and a little more indifferent, so she only said a little more carelessly, "You think she would not refuse?"

"She will not refuse unless she has some reason for doing so. She called of course?" he replied.

His wife affected not to hear his interrogative assertion.

"If I drop her now we need not renew any intimacy. What do you wish?"

"I have no wish in the matter," he replied, restraining himself with difficulty.

The conversation was unpleasant to him. To be forced to discuss such a person as Modena Wellington, without daring to vindicate or repudiate and not arouse his wife's suspicions, was distasteful to him, and he wished to end the discussion.

"If that is all, you will have to excuse me, I am busy this morning," and he turned to his notes.

But it was not all. She had gained nothing. He was as cold about her as one of Pygmalion's marble statues, and the invitation must be accepted.

"Perhaps it might be better to invite her. If we do not, it will make it unpleasant for others. She has been such an old friend of your family, she might resent my invitation as coming from a stranger. She might misunderstand my motives. How would it do for you to write a little note with it? You could word it tactfully. You do those things so nicely. Will you?"

"I fail to see the necessity of my doing so. It is customary for the woman of the house to invite her women. If you send her one you have done your duty. Then the choice is hers. Why need you worry?"

"If I send it you think she will come?"

"Why shouldn't she? What have you done to her that she should refuse?"

"Oh, nothing—nothing, I suppose, but rob her of you," she said, lightly, but she watched him closely.

But her husband was impassive, and continued gathering together his notes.

"You couldn't rob her of something which she never possessed. You flatter one exceedingly."

"You are sure, quite sure, she never possessed you?" she asked, lightly and carelessly, but looking at him all the while with fire fairly sparkling from the depths of her deep grey eyes.

The master of the house took out his watch and gathered up his notes. "I should be at the House now," he said, and left her without further words, while his wife remained for some time looking down on the sealed invitation which she held in her hand, as if she would wrench from it the secret which she had told herself she would ignore, but which she had already found to lie beyond her power to do.

The same afternoon the invitation went to Apsley House, and its mistress had perforce to accept it. She could do naught else.

The day of the dinner arrived; the new mistress of Kenyon Court was very nervous. Mrs. Kenyon's atmosphere was already telling her that she was not one of them. Her egotism was being disillusioned. She was beginning to be not quite so sure about her powers, and she was losing some of her assertiveness. She hated them for making her feel thus, but her hatred only made her wish the more to be as they were. His own friends were coming to-night, and she wished to do well. She went from room to room, giving and revising orders, impeding old servants more experienced than herself in those matters, arranging and rearranging what expert decorators had considered perfection, seeking her husband, and worrying him over trivialities until he, trying to maintain a cheerful aspect, but feeling irritable and ill at ease, persuaded her to go and rest for the evening.

Modena, as she dressed for the dinner, thought of a little story she had read in one of her school-books, when a child, about the bad boy who would not go to school, and his mother told him he would either have to go or take a whipping, whereat he promptly replied, "I'll take the whipping, mother." But the world is a stepmother, and its whippings are more hateful and harder to bear than the severities of the rules of its school, especially so to those with a courage and a conscience. Her courage would not let her shirk the severity of the rules of her own world, while her conscience had once more come under her self-command.

"To meet him in his own home!" she had said on the receipt of the invitation. There is something in the home which makes one true to one's conscience. "Can I do so?" Yes, she thought she could do so.

She went to the dinner with her father, and met him for the first time, standing with his wife, as they received the guests of the evening together.

He received them with that supreme deference, kindliness and dignity, which were so admirably blent in him, while his guest greeted them with unassumed amiability and easy indifference. She spoke briefly on the common topics of the day, and there was no consciousness or embarrassment in her mien or bearing as she cast her train of richest white velvet in all its array of golden leaves and lilies and ostrich binding on the soft carpet, and moved to the centre of the room where the light from the golden candelabras shone full on the tiara of diamonds gleaming in her hair, and on her shoulders and on her proud calm face.

She was soon the centre of a group. She was one of those people whose presence was to others as light is to the moths of summer. Her friends were glad to see her again; their pleasure shone in their faces. Their host's eyes had followed her. It had cost him much to greet her with the serenity with which he had received her. He had been able to do so because into his love he had poured his pride, his self-respect, his moral sense, and it had sustained him as fluid poured into soulless bodies makes the faces animate, the lips speak.

Others had come in at the same time as they, and this had given her an opportunity to avoid his extended hand. She had not met his eyes. He had not even received a glance from her, but her very presence in the room had made the blood flow like streams of fire through his veins, but he was very careful and to all outward appearance remained calm and self-possessed. His eyes followed and lingered on her for but a moment, while in the return and the effulgence of all his pent-up emotions he thought, " As if anyone could compare with her," while his wife, who, too, was watching her, thought with rising bitterness, " She is mistress even in my own home," and she said that this must not be so.

She could not go up to her guest, and say, " I am mistress here. I should receive this homage." She could not do this, but she could say, " I am his wife," and within these words lay more power than in all other written or spoken words. She said them now with her eyes, her lips and her actions—a word of command to him, a light familiar touch on the arm, a " dear " thrown adroitly in, a fond glance, these carefully managed as she sent them to the dining hall. And although the mistress of Apsley House looked not, yet did she see it all.

She went down to dinner by the side of the British Commissioner. The dinner was magnificent and sumptuous. She thought it would never end. At her other side sat Mr. Lester. In former days Lester's proximity comforted and pleased her, but to-night her conversation with him seemed commonplace and forced.

She was glad when the evening was over. Despite her better judgments she went home with a cold, resentful heart. All the natural nobility of her nature recognized the nobility of his actions, but her heart had spoken so loudly that womanlike she would fain have had him think more of her than to marry another. "He might have waited," she said, as she entered her room, with a little anger and hardness at her heart, but before she slept it softened and relented, as she felt the mesmerism of those eyes which had pleaded all evening for one kind glance.

CHAPTER XXX.

As the days passed by she met the Kenyons everywhere. But many events, neither gay nor agreeable, were occurring in the world about them which kept her mind from dwelling altogether on her separation from Keith Kenyon.

She had sedulously taken up her old routine of duties and entered into the old life once more, but she could not force her heart into the matter in the same spirit as it had been, for it seemed to her that her heart had grown cold in many matters.

During the days which followed she caught glimpses of much which had hitherto failed to attract her attention, or if attracted had been covered over with pleasing sophisms, or the sanguine credulity of youth. She was daily and hourly brought into contact with unpleasant circumstances, the inevitable concomitants of the coming contest, and the inconsistencies of the life began slowly to unfold itself to her, and caused her courage to waver.

These awakenings were only the inevitable disillusions and disenchantments which invariably accompany life, and which are but the precursors of better things, but in her present state of heart they took upon themselves the colorings of doubts and despairs, and caused life to wear a very different aspect from that which it had ever worn before.

To all outward appearance her life continued its even tenor, but the serenity of her inner life was much disturbed, and it was this which hurt and humiliated her more than anything else. She, who had always been so calm, resolute and sanguine! Now she was not always sure of herself. Her moods were beginning to be variable, even irritable. Sometimes she wanted solitude, but she soon learned that solitude, which is so often the begetter and fertilizer of great thoughts and lofty desires, may also in a morbid state of mind become the hot-bed of unholy desires, and that it were much better to allow even the trivialities and frivolities of the world to detract and distract one's thoughts and desires; then would she seek the world and its ways. Sometimes she even craved for excitement, but she soon learned that excitement was but a stimulus whose power was soon exhausted, and whose aftermath was but a hot-bed for a greater discontent than ever before.

For some days she was very unhappy. She was unhappy because she could not control her own thoughts, her own desires, and regulate her life according to her better judgments.

As an antidote to her restlessness and disquietude she sought much the open air.

One forenoon she took a book and a wrap, and going out through her own private garden she descended the brow of the hill to the river, which ran past the foot of the terraced grounds of Apsley House.

She seated herself in a low lounging chair in the shade of the boat-house where the warm rays from the sun pierced through the dismantled maples, and began to read. But her reading had been woven into her life, and the lines of the book brought with them so many memories that she allowed it to drop into her lap, while her eyes absently followed the flight of a crane that had started from the brake at the side of the water and was now vanishing in the illimitable air beyond.

"I wonder if I shall ever cease caring for him?" she was thinking. "I could banish him from my thoughts if I should cease meeting them. But I cannot avoid them. I believe I am beginning to hate her, and how vulgar and ill-bred it is to hate! How insanely jealous she is of my influence, and how she tries to assert herself through him! He is hers. How she makes one feel this. Her manner has in it the power to irritate, antagonize, rouse all the inherent evil which is in one. She arouses in one the temptation to take him from her," thought Modena, and then she checked herself. "Have I stooped to such thoughts as these?" she asked herself, impatiently, and with despair. "I shall not, I shall not. I shall never notice them. But they intrude—they intrude. The crane has gone! Lost in the horizon! I wonder what there is beyond. Will there be such thoughts as these over there? There need not be here," and she picked up her book once more.

Jack's voice broke in on her reading.

"Will you come with us, Modena? Watson sent in a message this morning, inquiring why we hadn't been out for our winter's store of nuts. I have ordered the big boat. We have this afternoon and evening free. I thought we would row down for them."

"So late in the season? The water will be very cold."

"It is very late and the weather is very chilly, but he will be very much disappointed if we omit our annual visit and order. It is his only means of support. Oh, yes, we could send for them, but he has always taken so much pride in his little home, and his humble surroundings, and the method and exactness of his supplies. Our visit to him has been the chief pleasure of the year. It would be almost cruel to omit it."

"Why, certainly, I shall be delighted to go!" replied Modena, her heart responding to the appeal in her cousin's voice.

She arose at once and followed her cousin to the carriage. When they arrived at the boat-house she was surprised to see the Kenyons among a party of people already there. She thought they were at Idlewylde, as it was only a few days previous to the elections, and their duties there were onerous, exacting and imperative.

She greeted the people and took her place in the boat by the side of Sir Colin Campbell.

The hermit lived on the bank of the river on one of their distant estates.

They now went to the distant point, partook of some lunch which their manservant had brought, gave the hermit pleasing words of praise on the beauty and taste of his surroundings, bought their supply of nuts, and then prepared to return.

As they returned they passed by a deserted, untenanted, dilapidated hut, standing in a little space, which had been cleared near the river's edge at a point where one of the many rivulets flowed down to join the parent stream. The hut was almost hidden from view by the reeds and willows which lined the water's edge. As they approached it, the sound of uproar, hilarious mirth and fierce dispute fell upon their ears.

The Lady Greta, whose young mind had been filled at home with weird tales of the wild West, looked startled, and turned pale as they came opposite the place.

A motley group of ten or a dozen men were lying or sprawling around on the ground, or swaying on wooden benches outside the door, while in the centre of the group was the well-known, dark-brown, black-lettered cask over which Bacchus loves to dwell. The group consisted of black and white promiscuously mixed in the flow of wine and feast of reason.

"Who are they? What is it?" gasped the Lady Greta, white with fear. "We have passed here quite often, and we have never seen anyone here before. Will they hurt? I wish I had remained in London," and she rose and seated herself like a dormouse between Modena and Sir Colin Campbell.

Modena noticed her cousin's and Keith Kenyon's quick glance at Mr. Lester, who only smiled sadly, divining the situation.

But Mrs. Cecil came to the rescue of the Lady Greta.

"Don't be afraid, Greta!" she said. "It is not Blackfoot, or Robin Hood and his merry men, or Faust's midnight orgies. This is not an age of tomahawks, robbery or romance. It is the age of reform and civilization. They are only a few of our street waifs spirited away for a few days. Bacchus is a more convincing god than Logic, and I am sure Mr. Lester is inwardly exclaiming, 'God bless the Conservative Government for making such men as these our masters,'" continued the Frenchwoman, smiling at the grotesqueness of the situation.

"Oh, is that all!" exclaimed the Lady Greta, a little disappointed and a little disgusted. "We can have such commonplace things as these at home. Why wasn't it Cameliard, the lily-isle of Avilion or Carbonek? You said these western woods were the homes of all these great people, Modena. You remember! The day of the sunset scene!" And then continued as she again took her place by Mr. Lester's side, "Do you wonder I'm disgusted, Mr. Lester?"

But Mr. Lester answered never a word, and his face grew grave as the boat glided on, and the distant echo of hilarity reached them on the clear, cold air, for he was much in earnest and was greatly grieved over many matters.

They were now passing Montebello, Papineau's home, and they all looked at it as it lay slumberous in the deepening twilight.

And then Mrs. Cecil smiled again and said, as the faint sounds died away as the boat turned the curve in the river:

"Papineau's music of '37! Its crescendo would surely exceed his wildest and most sanguine expectation. Pan's piping made the dry bones dance. This should make Papineau groan and turn over in his grave."

"'37 was much needed," replied Mr. Lester, briefly. "But men have forgotten Aristides' happy mean."

"One could forgive it under Radical rule, but when one remembers that this is the result of our so-called Conservatism, one may well pause, and ask one's self to what depths are we drifting. You should put on the brakes, Keith," said Mrs. Cecil.

But Keith Kenyon was not thinking of the brakes or the depths to which they were drifting. These had become a secondary consideration in the presence of another and greater fear which had within the last few days assailed him, and which was now before him.

They had been away longer than they had intended to be, and were later than usual in returning, and the sun had sunk for some time behind the distant hill-tops. The splendor of the night was around them; in its stillness there arose the boom of the bittern, the human-like whistle of the plover and the harsh cry of some stray wild lynx. As they glided down the stream, ever and anon meeting the lumber barges with their cargoes and singing rowers, the lovely, clear moonlight of the north shone brightly upon the turrets and towers and glittering spires of the sleeping city, and on the broad, shimmering surface of the water by their side.

The mistress of Apsley House leaned back in the boat, with a large bunch of golden-rod in one hand while the other lay idly on her knee. Sir Colin Campbell, a British officer, was by her side.

Keith Kenyon had said little during the entire evening, but he had been quick to see. He feared Sir Colin, as he had never feared Carlton Monteith. He knew that Sir Colin was a man of sterling qualities and great talents and that he would appeal to her as Carlton Montcith had never done. Of late she had been seen little with her betrothed, but had appeared continually by the side of the officer. He now conversed with her in low tones.

Keith, who was seated with some others, now replied to Mrs. Cecil lightly and discursively, but soon after becoming annoyed at, and tired of, his wife's incessant chatter, rose and moved away to where Jack Mainton was seated in the shadow of some awnings near his cousin and her companion. He stood leaning against the boat's railing by Jack's side in shadow. He drew his broad-rimmed hat over his face, and unseen by anyone but Jack Mainton looked at the woman before him as the lights and shadows from the moon and trees fell upon her profile.

The night, the scene, their voices in chorus, the Lady Greta's lately spoken words, had awakened again within him the chords which he had tried to silence. He realized now what he had done, and loathed himself for doing it.

"What were her thoughts?" he wondered. She had never once looked at him or spoken to him since his marriage, only when forced to do so through the common courtesies of everyday life.

"Was she thinking of Sir Colin Campbell?" He moved farther back into the shadow. His companion said nothing and he remained silent, so deeply absorbed in his meditations that the voices, the sounds, the scenes around him seemed something far away, something in which he took no part. His wife spoke to him twice and he had replied. Sir Colin's light laughter and his companion's low voice fell upon his ear. He remained where he was until the lights of the city began to appear one by one. Soon the boat stopped at the landing. Their carriages were awaiting them. He stepped out and handed the ladies from the boat, but when it came her time she stepped back and allowed Sir Colin to precede her, and then took his hand and went with him to her carriage, but in the moonlight he caught a glimpse of her face as she passed, and something he saw there told him his fears regarding the officer were groundless.

The greatness of his relief made the world seem very fair.

He went over to his wife and took her to her carriage; then he turned and walked away to one of his many clubs.

His home to him had already become detestable.

As the Wellington group entered Apsley House that night, Jack said to his cousin as they parted, "You should go away for a few months."

She looked at him in surprise.

"Why?" she interrogated.

"You do not look well, and the change will do you good," he said with partial truth, but with suggestions in his tone.

"I am feeling quite well," she replied coldly, but a little wearily.

"You could go away after Friday," he insisted.

"I shall be at home Friday evening," she said, changing the subject. "Do you think you will be able to get away from the office early?"

"It depends altogether on the returns," he replied, as they parted.

Friday evening came, and with it the tidings that they had won.

The mistress of Apsley House held a brilliant reception the same evening in honor of the results. All the notables of the city were present, while telegrams rained in from all parts in congratulation.

The chief himself called on his way home from the public speaking room, and the smile on her father's face as he clasped his chief's hand repaid her for much that had been done.

She stood by the tea table as parties came and went. Verona Kenyon sat near her on a couch piled high with soft cushions, receiving homage from all who came.

Among the last to arrive was her husband with Jack Mainton. As her husband approached she noticed him, and rose flushed and happy, and extended her hands in a joyful enthusiasm.

"I am glad, oh, so glad, you have won!" she said, giving vent to the anxiety which she had not been able to control, until she had heard the results.

"Don't you think he has merited much praise, Miss Wellington?" she asked, as she put her arm in his and laid her hand familiarly on his, with a proud air of proprietorship, and turned to their hostess at the tea table.

"Will you have another cup of tea, Mr. Patrie? Warm! Try some of those ices," she said before replying to Mrs. Kenyon.

"Oh, I am not surprised. I never once doubted our winning," she said quietly.

"But you haven't congratulated my husband yet," insisted the proud wife, maliciously. The moment was sweet.

Her husband dropped her arm.

"Oh, Mr. Kenyon knows he has the best wishes of our family," replied their hostess, with an air which, intentional or unintentional, conveyed to Verona Kenyon the inference, "How bourgeois to display such feeling. We take those things quietly, and send the bill in to the ratepayers to-morrow."

It was a rebuff given in public and couldn't be resented in public. It had to be borne. It stung to the quick and sent the warm blood mounting to her face. The joy of the moment was numbed and chilled by the calm indifference of this woman and her air which had alone implied, "Keith Kenyon is one of us."

But she smiled and passed on to a more sympathetic audience.

"What can I do for you, Mrs. Cecil?" asked their hostess, wishing to avoid further conversation with the Kenyons. "You look infinitely bored. What is the matter?"

"Nothing, my dear," she answered. "Only rid the house of such a chattering pack of blue-jays and—and—geese."

Their hostess smiled at Mrs. Cecil's expression of disgust.

"I am surprised at your caring so much, Modena," continued the Frenchwoman. "It surely isn't such a great honor to learn that we have the permission of those—what shall I call them?— those we saw the other day down by the river—their permission to rule a little longer. One would infer from all this fuss and, hubbub that we had driven the Russians out of Asia, or the Boxers out of China."

"Well, you see, someone must lead, and I think we are the best qualified to lead. One feels it is one's duty to do what one can," she replied in an apologetic tone, and she was humiliated in herself that she could not force herself to put more sincerity into her words and tone.

"But what difference does it make? With such men as these as our masters, intellectual, patriotic government is an impossibility. Then what's the use of working one's self into a political fever over it?"

"Why don't you care, Mrs. Cecil?" asked the Lady Greta, as she nibbled away like a mouse at some bon-bons. "I'm an alien, and yet I care. I was told to keep quiet and look dignified and uninterested, or interested in everyone—in no one more so than in another—but yet the other day I fought when I heard someone slandering Mr. Kenyon for something he had done. They were saying such horrid things about him. I fought like a fox-cub, though really I thought some of the things were, alas, only too true," and she bit her little white teeth deep into a chocolate.

They were alone by the table; their hostess had seated herself by the Lady Greta's side. Keith Kenyon stood with his hand resting on the back of the Lady Greta's chair looking down upon her.

"How kind of you," he said. "One's reputation is in no danger when the Lady Greta is near."

"Not among foes."

"What would you infer by that dark saying? What have I to fear among friends?"

"Oh, nothing, I suppose. Perhaps it's men's way of doing things—taking things so cool—but—but—if I started out after Jason's golden fleece I would get it, and when I got it I would have cannons and fire-works and set the town wild. You don't seem to care much more than Mrs. Cecil," said the Lady Greta, and then innocently looking up into his face she continued in an aside, "Modena doesn't seem to care either."

Keith Kenyon's face remained perfectly impassive.

"Oh, yes, we care. I am sure we care very, very much, but like Virgil, perhaps she believes 'Silence is a woman's glory,'" smiled her companion.

"How mean of you to say so, after I have been wanting cannons and fire-works! How does one know you feel joy unless you show it? 'We dream of glory and honor, but the fulfillment of a

dream is never quite the dream itself. It has always some glory
wanting,' said some wisehead. Almost you make one think
there's some glory wanting in your dream. Perhaps the dragon
defending the fleece bit you. I thought, perhaps, by what they
were saying the other day, that it did!" she said, with innocent
malice.

But her companion was wary and avoided the sharp little
tongue by smiling kindly at her. He had spoken little since his
entrance. He now looked closely at the mistress of the house, and
noticed the weary lines around her mouth.

His wife was coming towards him. He had stood long enough by
the tea-table.

"You must be tired, Miss Wellington," he said, addressing her
for the first time, since his marriage. "I think we should go,"
he said to his wife. "No, I am not going. I have to go down
with Mainton, and compile returns for the morning's paper."

Verona's manner changed at his words, but he did not seem to
notice it, but handed her to her carriage, bade her good-night, and
returned to the library where the mistress of the house had gone
to serve her father and Jack with some tea and some light
refreshments.

The remainder of the guests having taken their departure, he
joined the group in the library, and in the confidence and intimacy of the circle entered into an animated discussion of the
results, in which they were soon joined by Modena, who displayed enthusiasm for the first time.

The hour seemed their own.

As they sat round the glowing hearth fire and spoke of this constituency won, that one lost, some old enemy vanquished, some
friend triumphant or some friend left behind in the race, and
entered into the details of their own constituencies, almost they
forgot the outside world, and Modena began to feel that her heart
was once more the heart of the people at large. Everything
seemed as it once had been, and her blood flowed as of old. As
she fearlessly met Keith Kenyon's eyes as they warmed in their
subject, once more she wished that the great, big world had but
one heart and one body that she might warm and feed and make
it happy. Now she felt sure of herself, and at peace with herself
and her world, and she could scarcely wait until morning to put
into execution many plans she had formed months previous to
this, plans which had lain dormant for days and days because of
her inability to put her heart into the work.

For an hour the old world was itself again. Life was full of intense interest. What more interesting game than the game of politics and—hearts!

She smiled as she bade her guest good-night.

As Jack Mainton and his friend walked back to the office that night Jack said to his companion: "I was wanting Modena to go away for a while. It will be better." His voice had in it the note of a warning. He did not wish to interfere, but he wished his words to be marked and emphatic.

His companion looked at him and colored warmly, but spoke of other matters.

CHAPTER XXXI.

It was Christmas time.

The gaieties of the social world had been suspended for the home festivities of the Christmas season, and for the many acts of remembrances and of charity which come perforce at this time of glad tidings and great joy.

"Jackson, have the sleigh ready at four this afternoon," said the mistress of Apsley House to her footman some few days previous to Christmas. "The Avernons and the Owenses are leaving town to-morrow morning," she continued, turning to her father. "I must call and see them. I am sorry, as I have to go out to Mrs. Black's to make arrangements about little Mirah, and it will make it rather late."

"Cannot you go before you call, or wait until to-morrow? I do not care for your being down in that part of the city so late. Since that foreign element has come, it is not very safe," replied Mr. Wellington.

"I cannot go before. I meet the architect from Fernwylde at two, and I cannot very well leave it off until to-morrow. Dr. Bruce told me this morning, the sooner the child received attention the more hope there is for a permanent cure. I have already telegraphed Dr. West to meet us there to-morrow. Mrs. Black isn't aware of this, and there is much to be done."

"Then I wish you would call at the office and Jack will go with you after five."

"Do you think it is necessary? He is very busy at this season of the year. I have been down there almost every week for many months, and they are perfectly harmless. Our presence rather

22

amuses them. When we pass they pause and admire. The Lady Greta startled them the other day by driving four-in-hand," and Modena smiled as she thought of how the Lady Greta had enjoyed her popularity. "But I shall call and take Helen with me to-night," she said as she rose, and gathered up her embroideries, and then went away to order the necessary linens and nourishment which the physician had prescribed for a poor little patient in the outskirts of the city.

In the afternoon, after she had given final instructions to the architect, and had bidden adieu to the wives of some of the ministers who were leaving town, she ordered the coachman to drive to Maple Hurst, only to learn on her arrival there that its mistress had gone to the west end to meet with the ladies of a committee who were providing supplies for the newsboys' annual dinner. So, alone, she turned her horses' heads towards Beaver's Dam, the place where the little invalid lived.

The air towards evening had become very cold, so she buttoned up her warm sables about her throat, and ordered the coachman to quicken the horses' speed as the lights began to appear on the street corners as they passed by.

The streets were all aglow with life and preparations for the coming Christmas season. The Fair windows filled with dolls and toys and cotton men, the butcher shops with rose-papered, fattened fowls and meats, the fruit stands with their tempting hot-house fruits and sweet-meats, gave an air of festivity and joyousness to the surroundings, while laden omnibuses, flying cabs, jingling bells, laughing children, flying snow-balls, all bespoke the hurry and interest and happiness which spring into life in the veins of the people at this time of the year, as surely as the sap pulses through the native maple in spring.

But as she left the thoroughfares and turned her horses' heads towards the outskirts of the city, the streets became quieter and darker and the houses more thinly placed, with here and there on a corner a little outlying store with shantymen's jerseys and flaring red scarfs flying like banners on the night breezes, from where they hung outside the store door.

In a little while the last house was passed, but her destination was yet a mile and a half further away on a winding, unfrequented river road, which led down to an old saw-mill.

Soon the city was left behind, and as the horses flew over the lone country road, the bells floating their music on the clear cold air, she looked out over nature in all its frozen stillness and whiteness and at the lights gleaming on an eminence far away across the river. All was still and cold and lonely. To her it seemed as if the whole world had grown suddenly silent, and she was left all alone in it. It was so like her life. Over there the lights were burning. Ovid's Hero had kept the lights burning across the river for Leander. No lights burned for her. They had burned in the darkness of one night, but they had dimmed and deadened under the strong, fierce light of the day's realities, and the real day had seemed the darker because of their burning and fading. Out here, all alone with the virgin snows of heaven, she felt her loneliness more keenly than she had ever felt it before. Not that she was sad or that she murmured. These had been conquered and had passed away with the first intensity of her bereavement.

She was but lonely. She drew the warm robes about her with a shudder.

Her horses flew on, turning out of the broad level road to pass by some peasants and lumbermen who were swaying their arms from side to side to warm their tingling fingers, as they wended their way homeward with empty sledges and white-frosted horses.

On the long stretch of lonely road a deserted hut, which had once been, in the days gone by, an hostelry at a wayside inn, loomed into view.

As they neared it, she noticed that the snow, which had fallen early the previous evening, was much trodden and blood-stained, and in the deepening twilight she saw a suspicious-looking sleigh turn from the road and seek the shelter of the shed.

"What has happened here?" she asked of the footman.

"I do not know, Miss Wellington," and his imperturbable visage betrayed no knowledge of the cause of the disorder.

"Has some animal cut its foot in the deep snow, I wonder? How it must have suffered!" she thought as they passed on.

Very soon they arrived at the old mill and then at Mrs. Black's as the evening bells ceased tolling in the city.

In an hour's time, after having arranged for the operation the next morning, she emerged from the house.

"I think we will return home by the highway," said Williams, the coachman, to her. "It is two miles farther, but the river road is not always safe."

"Why? What nonsense, Williams! No, indeed, we are very much later now than I intended to be. Father will be very uneasy. Hasten as much as possible," she replied, as she seated herself amidst the robes of the sleigh.

"We will arrive home much sooner by going the other way," persisted Williams.

"What do you mean?" she asked, rather coldly. She was not accustomed to having her orders disobeyed, or to have to repeat an order. Both her servants were tried and trusted, and she could not understand their persistence.

"I have never yet gone the other way. Go home the way we came, and as quickly as possible," she repeated, and then lay back in her seat facing the cold, west wind, now filled with heavy flakes of snow which had begun to fall shortly after her entrance to the house.

There was no other course open to them but to obey; so he once more mounted his seat, while the coachman drove up the river road, and his mistress leaned back and closed her eyes against the blinding flakes of snow which were now coming so rapidly and so plentifully that it almost seemed that the heavens had of a sudden opened wide their doors and poured out their effulgence on the earth below, as they had poured the manna on the pilgrims' way. Her mind dwelt upon the little child, and the success of the operation. She was almost as anxious as was the mother, and she went over and over again in her mind the minutest details which were necessary for the morning's work. Her physician had explained to her the cause of the suffering, and had held out great hopes of recovery. Already she could see the child well, playing about in her home. She would clothe and educate and provide for her. "It is not well to take them out of their own sphere in life," she said. "The others must be cared for and educated. They must be kept together," and her mind ran riot in planning for the several boys, and she was not aware that they had reached the lonely shed, until she was rudely awakened from her dreams of the future by the sudden stopping of the sleigh, and by a confused noise and clamor from rough voices, clinking steel and flashing lights peering out of the darkness directly in their way.

"What is it?" she asked, quickly starting up and laying her hand on Williams' arm. "What does it mean?" she asked again, beginning to wish she had taken her father's advice and brought Jack, or Williams' advice and gone home the other way.

"Oh, nothing," replied the coachman. "Sit down, ma'am, and we will clear the way in a few minutes. It's nothing, do not be afraid. Sit down or you will be thrown out!" he exclaimed, as the horses began to shy and plunge at the sudden noise and confusion.

It was seldom Modena lost her presence of mind, but her eyes had been closed, her mind far away; the fall of snow had been so great that even the coachman was scarcely discernible. She had been rudely awakened. It had been so sudden that it almost seemed that the noise and lights had come out of the heavens with the snow. In a moment she regained her presence of mind and resumed her seat, but leaned out to learn the cause of delay.

Many dark objects, looking like Esquimaux huts, loomed out of the gloom, but which on closer inspection proved to be sledges and horses with coverings of blankets and snow. They stood by the roadside and on the roadway barring their progress. Through the weird gloom she could see an excited, circled, serried mass, with heavily darkened lanterns, now moving this way and now that way as something in their midst changed its vantage ground; while deep muttered curses, sharp exclamations, loud angry altercations, and the noise of clinking steel fell upon her ears.

"Do not fear. It is only a game-bird fight," said the footman to her.

"What is that?" she asked.

"They are only fighting birds, ma'am. They fought here last night, and there was some talk of foul play, and their blood is up to-night. They are a rough lot. But do not fear. This pair is nearly finished. In a moment we may pass," he replied, as he caught sight of a bird struggling and spluttering in its death throes, and heard the victorious crowing of the other one, as triumphant as the Roman general's "Veni, vidi, vici."

"If you will step out and let Jackson guide you through those sleighs to the other side, I shall drive round the shed and meet you there," said Williams from his seat, trying hard to keep in check his thoroughbreds, who now had scented the blood, and who were trying to flee from the flitting shadows which the darkened lanterns cast upon the snow.

"No, I shall not; they are law-breakers and I shall not leave my carriage for them. They must clear the way."

But almost before she ceased speaking the choice was not left her. Fierce and angry altercations had taken place between the owners of the combatants; the circle had parted; the dying bird, with its last angry, agonized flap, flap, and spurt, and followed by its assailant, who strutted and crowed and flapped, threw itself into the midst of the now frenzied horses' feet, causing a stampede and panic.

In the presence of the panic no choice was left her but to obey. Her horses had become frantic and had reared and plunged, upsetting the sleigh. By her suppleness and strength alone she was enabled to step out into their midst and avoid the stampede. Her horses now flew down the road with Williams vainly trying to get them under control. Jackson was thrown from his seat, and lay smothered and stunned in the snow by the roadside, while confusion reigned in the motley mass around them.

The pickets having wagered on the birds, in their interest and anxiety had deserted their posts; the snow had muffled the Wellington bells. Their approach had been unnoticed. Had an angel dropped down from the clouds in the fast falling snow into their midst, as Aphrodite had risen from the deep in a shower of sea-foam, their surprise could not have been greater than it was at her presence, while Modena was too bewildered for the moment to speak. Some of the other horses having also become panic-stricken, had overturned another cage of birds which were already spurred, awaiting their time and turn. The released birds, not waiting the word of command, flew at each other's heads in deadly earnest.

The crowd at its best was a motley conglomeration of humanity, and the sight of the ferocity, vindictiveness and brutality of the birds had aroused the brute in man. When Modena had entered their midst she thought at first that she recognized several well-known faces, but if so they had quickly withdrawn into the gloom.

"I must be mistaken," she thought. "Law-makers would never become law-breakers," and she banished the thought.

For a moment, as she saw the black, angry, scowling faces around her, a fear came upon her, but at that moment the two fresh birds approached her.

She had heard of such things being done, but not here, never here, within the very lights of the town and limits of its law, and with spurs—spurs—and the sight of the angry birds as they strutted and flew at each other's throats and heads, the sharp prong of steel piercing eye and flesh, banished the momentary fear and roused all the latent anger and courage within her. They were only dumb birds, but yet had they feeling, and her womanly instinct was aroused within her. There was so much suffering and injustice in the world which could not be avoided. But deliberate, premeditated cruelty! It was only a little thing, but it had invariably been the little things which had appealed to Modena in life. She had always said, that if the little things were overcome there would be no big, intangible, world-degrading injustices to overcome, and at the sight of any cruelty, however small, or any injustice, however veiled or golden or purple-draped, her indignation had ever burnt with a great force within her. The sight before her made the blood flow warm within her now. She forgot her fear. She felt her form dilating, her nostrils quivering

in her indignation. Words welled up within her for utterance,
but she refrained from interference. The sport was theirs; the
way was hers. But her way was barred. She could not proceed.

She saw the crowd begin to waver, and soon one after another
passed into the gloom. But the owners and abettors of the beaten
birds were not to be deprived of their opportunity of retrieving
what they had lost. Their blood was afire, and like the Spartan
spectators of old nothing but gladiatorial blood would satisfy and
satiate the demon running riot within.

She was to blame, and one rough stepped forward and seized
her tightly by the wrist. " Git out of this and mind yer own
bizness. We don't come meddlin' in yer affers. Git out of this, I
say, or I will mak ye go, ye spy," he fairly hissed.

She flung him from her with more than human strength, and
never once lost her courage or self-control.

" I shall not. I shall not leave the road for you. I do not fear
you. You are cowards. Your conduct is disgraceful. It is cruel.
It is inhuman," and she quivered inwardly as the blood from the
bird spurted and stained the sable which bound her dress.

" Ye'll not! We'll see! Here, Limbers, lend a hand. We'll
teach her to cum spying round here. That's what we will. They
kin hev their sports jist as they lik, and we or the law don't meddle
with them; we've a right to ours. Here, Limbers, help me make
her mind her own bizness."

Outwardly she remained calm and immovable. She saw Limbers
put down his lantern to join his comrade, and she also saw the
attention of the others was being withdrawn from the birds and
centred upon herself and the two ruffians. She feared from them
no bodily harm, but she would submit to no indignity. Williams
would soon return, and remain she would where she was until his
return. These ruffians were impeding the traffic of the Queen's
highway. They would not force her to leave the road. She stood
still and never once took her eyes, cool and calm, from their faces.
" Will Williams not soon come?" she was thinking.

" Steady, Limbers. She's a beauty,' called out a rough from
the background.

" Fair play," said another, " she's a brave one."

They were now close to her, but seemed to waver; even the most
brutal and cowardly admire courage; but a hoarse, derisive laugh
from someone in the rear, who had lost on the birds, spurred them
on. Their faces were dark and scowling; their mien brutal; their
whole appearance repulsive. A quiver passed over her. They had
reached her. They put out their hands to seize her and force her

on her way, but like a thunder-bolt from the clouds, or the aveng-
ing hand of the statue in "Don Giovanni," a hand stretched out
of the darkness, and with the heavy end of a rawhide riding-whip
struck their hands to the ground. And before anyone there was
aware of his presence, Keith Kenyon sprang from his foam-flecked
horse and stood by her side.

He was muffled in a great coat, while the peak of his seal cap
concealed his face. He was recognized by no one present, but the
ruffians, fearing the law and thinking the police were in pursuit,
with their vans and birds in a few seconds vanished as if by magic,
leaving them the sole occupants of the battlefield.

For a moment they were alone together, in the deserted road, in
the darkness of night.

"Thank God that I was in time," were the first words that he
uttered.

For a moment she was unable to realize that it was he who was
there. His presence seemed as unreal to her as her presence a
moment ago had been to the roughs. She felt dazed; she could
not believe, but the knowledge came to her when he again repeated
his words, but with this knowledge came also a greater one. With
the ready intuition of a woman of the world she knew the world
and her people would blame her for subjecting herself to this, if
they knew it. They must not know of it.

"We've had a little accident. Our horses took fright at the
birds and the blood. Did you meet Williams? Are you going to
Idlewylde?" she only said, her voice shaking a little as she spoke.

"No, I am not going to Idlewylde. I came on purpose to meet
you."

She didn't understand.

"Why need you have done so?" she asked, coldly.

"Williams is coming with the sleigh. Here they are," he said,
before replying to her, and then he helped her in, and after putting a warm blanket from her sleigh on his own hot horse and
sending Jackson with him, took his place by her side.

"I saw your father at the House at seven," he then told her.
"He is detained there until late this evening with a deputation
from the north. He had called up to learn if you were home. He
was anxious about you then. I promised him I would send someone to meet you. I called at the house. Some of the stablemen
had known of this affair out here and had communicated the
knowledge to your maid, who had told Marion. I went to the
office to tell Jack, but he had left town to remain away until late
this evening. I rode out. I met Williams as he had quieted and

turned the horses. Jackson had thought that you were in the
sleigh and had followed on. They are bad ones. The police have
been after them for weeks, but have failed to locate them. You
shouldn't run these risks. Don't you see how others suffer who—
who—care for you? Thank God, you are safe," he said again, and
he leaned towards her and brushed the great flakes of snow off her
seals and drew the robes in around her. It was all he could do
or say, but he had the faculty of expressing much in his least act
or word.

She felt what was expressed.

She knew what she owed him, but to admit it would be to admit
that she had acted unwisely. She dreaded the affair becoming
known and commented upon in the papers or among her friends,
and since it was he who had come to her rescue it was doubly
necessary that it should not be known. She quickly saw the only
way to repair what she had done was to make light of it.

"It was nothing," she said. "A runaway, a few roughs like
yours by the river, with Mars in the battlefield in lieu of Bacchus.
They would not have touched me. Had they insisted, no doubt I
would have walked on and met Williams. The other day we were
lamenting that the world was full of mole-hills and pinpricks,
and were wishing for great opportunities. The Lady Greta and
I wanted to become heroines. I have become the heroine of the
rostrum of a few roughs and the arena of some bantam birds.
You must not tell the Lady Greta, she will envy me my greatness,"
she said, lightly, but despite her efforts of light-heartedness her
voice shook.

He knew what she meant to imply, but his heart was too full to
ignore the late danger or to speak of other matters, and yet he
could not discuss what he saw was her wish to ignore; he could
but remain silent.

There are times when people understand each other better by
silence than by words. It was thus with them now.

The snow still continued to fall in great flakes, making the
roads heavy and their progress slow. He knew that she must be
cold, and tired, and hungry, and yet he wished it were miles and
miles into the city. He wished it were forever. To be beside her,
to feel the warmth from her presence, to have the great coat on
his arm touch hers, was the nearest approach to happiness which
he had felt since his separation from her, while she for a few
moments forgot there was another in his life. It would be a
base ingratitude and a cowardice in the light and presence of the

present circumstances to resent his present or his past conduct, and she gave herself up to the sweetness of the moment.

She spoke not, nor moved, yet he felt the change within her, and was quick to recognize the nobility and tenderness in her character which caused her to feel and act thus.

But if he loved her he must think first of her. He, too, knew that her encounter and his appearance must be kept from the world's knowledge. He knew the greatest kindness he could do her would be to leave her, silent and unrecognized. He would leave her sleigh at the outskirts of the city. The roughs had not recognized him, or if they had, the road led to Idlewylde and his presence there would be attributed to this. Her servants were tried and trusted and silent as the grave. He had nothing to fear from them.

They were now nearing the city and she, too, was thinking the same. Conscience makes cowards of the most courageous, and the sweetness which she felt made hers not quite clear. She could do no less than silently acknowledge his act, but the sweetness which came with the acknowledgment made her feel guilty in her own sight. Had her conscience been quite clear, fearlessly would she have driven through the lighted, crowded streets with him at her side, indifferent to any comment which might be placed upon their actions, but this feeling of guilt made her uneasy, and she was glad when they reached the outskirts, to learn that the heavy fall of snow had so crippled the several lighting plants of the city as to cause it to be in total darkness. The fall of snow was yet very heavy. The streets were deserted. He left her as they reached the curb stone at the side entrance to Apsley House. She entered the house by a side door, and emerged from her rooms as her father and Jack came into the house by the front door. She joined them and the other members of the family in the library, and asked about the wants of the deputation, the day's voting, and of some protests which were now pending, and delivered to them the Avernons' and Owenses' messages of leave. She left the room for a few minutes to give orders to the house-keeper to have ready, early in the morning, some nourishment and more linen for the little patient, and on her return she told them of the child's fever and suffering, and spoke for some time of her hopes for a permanent cure, but of the birds and the roughs said never a word.

CHAPTER XXXII.

"How is the little Mirah? Was your operation successful?" queried the Lady Greta, as child-like she placed herself on the low, broad arm of a great easy chair, and caressingly put her little arms on those of the mistress of Apsley House.

They were all seated in the spacious, hearth-lighted parlors of Apsley House. It was the afternoon of their weekly literary club. During the afternoon they had been discussing Tennyson, but had put him aside as the men came in on their way home, and were now enjoying cups of fragrant tea and talking of current matters.

They were gathered in little groups; the mistress of the house and the Lady Greta were apart from the others.

"She is much better; we hope for a permanent cure," replied Modena, wondering at the new and sudden interest of the Lady Greta in her little patient. She hadn't spoken of her to anyone. "How did the Lady Greta know anything about her?" she wondered.

"Will you take me out to see her? I want so much to see her." Her hostess looked at her in greater surprise.

"There is nothing very unusual in her case. Why are you so interested in her?"

"Oh, I want to see the little sick child," persisted the Lady Greta.

"You told us a few moments ago, you could not endure the sight of sickness. You said you loved joy, and beauty, and life. Why this fad?"

"But she possesses a peculiar charm. I want to see her. Why will you not take me?"

"Oh, I shall certainly take you, if you care to go," Modena was forced to admit.

"Is it far?" queried the English girl.

"Yes, quite a long way."

"Is the road lonely? Will anything hurt us? Since the day we saw Papineau's progeny, her ladyship has been like—like—Maud's Sultan."

"Then don't go," replied Modena, who began to suspect danger.

"But I want to go. You monopolize all the opportunities of becoming great. Your heroic courage will go down as one of the great traditions of your family. I want to become great. When Helen and Lilian returned from Africa they made our hair stand on end with the recital of their adventures and hairbreadth escapes. I want to make theirs stand, too, and things here are really so commonplace. Do take me," she coaxed.

"And you think going out to see a little sick child—what shall I call it? A hair-raiser?"

"No, but I might meet Sir Lancelot coming back," replied the Lady Greta, very innocently, in a whisper.

Modena continued sipping her tea, but the hand that held the cup trembled although she remained calm and collected.

"Oh, that's why you want to go! Is it? Why did you feign philanthropy? I am afraid your reading of Tennyson this afternoon has turned your little brain. You have woven a romance. You think the old mill Merlin's Castle, with domes and peaks, dazzling and clear, towering to our snow-laden sky. You had better remain away and keep your illusions. And Lancelots do not flourish on highways. Mine proved to be lumbermen and peasants with empty sledges and horses covered with frozen foam-flakes. It was cold and cheerless, and very real and prosaic. Perhaps we could get you a knight nearer home."

"Oh, bother the knights! They only bring great big heart-breaks. We do not want them. I only want an opportunity to become great. I envy you your greatness."

"I don't know what you mean! There is no greatness in me, except it be the little there was in your hero-knight: In me there dwells no greatness, save it be some far off touch of greatness, to know well I am not great."

"I often wonder what you really are. It makes my poor brain whirl to think it out. With your mixture of pride and humility, your spirit of the eupatrid and the St. Simon, you are an anomaly beyond one's conception. You must be Aristotle's— Shelley's—whose is it? How do you say those things? Morally— metaphorically—black and white joined together and divided by two? Do you wonder my brain whirls when you hear how I express myself? But whatever you may be I wish I were like you. When I look at you I always think of what that other poet said about 'Truth being at the bottom of some fabled well, and the world might find the spring by following his lady,' " said the Lady Greta, caressingly.

"Have you turned a De Stael? What have I done that merits such praise? It was Dr. West and Dr. Bruce who did it, not I."

"You don't need to do things to be great. Destiny made you so."

"Oh, oh! Lady Greta! Hush! The others will hear your nonsense. You've been eating too many chocolates and have had sweet dreams."

"Weren't you sorry this afternoon for our knight and his Queen. When he had her, why didn't he take her away to his castle and keep her there forever and ever? I would never have left his side for a nunnery. She was a coward to care for the world's opinion. When he loved her and she loved him, what else mattered? How they must have suffered! Their greatness made their suffering the greater. What did Chateaubriand say about De Stael? 'The souls of greatness have great suffering. They are solitary in the world like Mount Blanc.' Do you ever feel that way? You always remind me of Psyche."

"It is only a Psyche or a Sappho who feels that way," said Modena, despite her efforts to the contrary, with a note of sadness in her voice as she thought of how she had felt when she had looked out over the hushed, white world, which had stretched away over the vast plains into the gloom of night. "One would be very unwise to allow one's self to feel that way. Your Queen was a very unwise woman to have gone to the knight's side. De Stael found repose in Rocca her husband."

"But she loved the knight before she loved the King. Was she to live her life loverless? There is only one law, love, and had I loved as they loved, I would have had the courage to live for him."

"Then she should have wedded the knight, not the King."

"But she had no choice in the matter. Fate willed it otherwise."

"You believe in fate and disbelieve in God?"

"What had God to do with it? Oh, do not look so grave. I speak in all reverence. By fate I meant—the conventions of the world."

"The conventions of the world are its necessities. They are evolved from the very nature of things and must be respected. There, what a sermon I have given you, while the others are eating bon-bons and talking Dolly Varden or Mrs. Grundy."

"Oh, yes, I know, we must respect them; something within us makes us do so, and if we don't do so, something outside of us slaps us and makes us do so. But you cannot deny the fact that all these things bear with them endless suffering and cruel injustices, and all one can do is to suffer and smile and make believe one is happy."

The Lady Greta and her lover and her people were not all of one accord, and the young girl's heart was aching and lonely. In her desire to extend sympathy she was almost cruel. But her hostess saw nothing.

"Are you not exaggerating? You have allowed your sympathy and your love for your knight to run riot with your better judgment. Had he not dallied with his Delilah, in time he would have recognized the beauty of Elaine. And when your Queen had married her King she should have learned to love him. He loved her."

"What did her knight say? 'Yet to be loved makes not to love again.' Perhaps she couldn't love him. Her knight was one of those men God made to love and to be loved. He was all humanity. The King was all divinity. You know women love a little—what do you call it?—in men, especially if it be mixed up with courage, and courtesy, and chivalry, and honor, and loyalty, and blood. It gives a relish to things, like onions in an exquisite dish of soup."

"But, my dear, in time she learned to love her King, and then life was only one long atonement. How sad! How unwise!"

"Do you think she did? Do you end the story that way? Does Tennyson tell us that? I always like to end it my own way. When Dante had gone through all those horrid places he found Beatrice at the pearly gates as Faust found Marguerite. I cannot but think, that when our knight arrived at the Castle of Carbonek he saw the Queen at the aureoled end of the beam of light awaiting the return of the Holy Grail."

"And where was the King?"

"Oh, he was there, happy, living on the essence of his own divinity. He was a god. He didn't need love to sustain him. One of those lonely ones, you know, beyond our conception, beyond our human heart! There to be worshipped! No doubt in time he hardened up into Reason, Hard Facts, Philosophy and all that stuff—Thought, Shelley calls it. You are shocked. You think I should reverence him. So I do, but I love Lancelot. You ask me why I do? Why do you love—love—Carlton Monteith?" she hesitated, and said drolly. "I love Lancelot, I don't know why, just because he was a man, a kindly man moving among his kind; he felt, he had heart, a heart like—like—Keith Kenyon's. And he was always doing things. The King was always saying things. Oh, yes, I suppose he had done his things before and had the right to say, but somehow women love men who *do;* they don't care for drones. It was Lancelot who fought the fights, tilted in the tournaments, won the diamonds from worthy foes, championed the weak, redressed their wrongs. Oh! all those things which have within them the ring of true manhood. The Queen loved him. We all love him. Something within us makes us love him. That is the only reason I can give you for loving him, and having once loved him thus, I shall continue to love him for aye. If I didn't know he was at the end of my Holy Grail, I would go and make my bow with the Big Falls."

Despite the air of pathos underlying it all, Modena laughed outright at her friend's funny way of putting things.

"You are getting your metaphors mixed. Do you mean your knight—or—Keith Kenyon?"

"Both, they are inseparable."

"I am afraid that disillusion awaits you. When you come to know him as—as—well as—as I do, you will learn he is more like your King, your—your Hard Facts—Fate—Cold Logic, and Conventions, than he is like your knight."

"You are very wise, my dear, as wise as your Socrates or your Solomon, but like Plato your sky-gazing prevents you from seeing events which are tumbling about at your feet. A child so often sees what a seer fails to see. Would you call that an irony of life, or would you call it a little justice, evening things up a little? We wander from our subject. Your wisdom blinds you. You are the King, and you are clothing him with your own clothes. You'll harden up into a goddess if you don't keep human love close to you. He is really Lancelot with—with—unstained honor. How lonely his life must be!"

"You must cease reading Tennyson. He is pleasant as a pastime, but you require something more substantial. Your imagination is running away with you. You mustn't read romances. We haven't time for them. Life is too full of realities. When shall I take you to see Mirah?" said Modena, as she rose to join the others.

"I don't weave romances. Life weaves them for us. I don't want to go to see Mirah, that is, unless I might have an opportunity of—"

"Becoming great," added Modena, while her mind was working hurriedly and rapidly within her. Somehow or other her Ladyship had learned of her encounter with the roughs. "Was it generally known? Did her friends know of it? There was but one way to render the affair harmless—make light of it publicly."

"The vermin voices buzz so loud, we scorn them but they sting," wasn't written for the Queen alone. She remembered what she had said about these lines in the library at Fernwylde. Although guilt did not lie beneath the sting, she thought it wise to prevent any " vermin voices from buzzing."

She put her arm within that of her young friend's, and approached the others.

"The Lady Greta has been wanting an opportunity to become great. Some few roughs monopolized the Queen's highway the other evening. I disputed their right of way. She envies me my greatness. She wants to meet the mob and play the role of Princess de Lamballe or Hypatia," she said, lightly.

The words made the Lady Greta's heart beat quickly. She hadn't looked for this as a result of her words. The encounter and the rescue were but surmises of her own. She had called late at Apsley House, and had learned that Modena was in the country. She had made some other calls, and had met Keith Kenyon going that way. She had been out with Verona to Idlewylde the following day, and when passing the place had overheard a remark of the groom's to the coachman. She had woven her little romance, not knowing that truth lay beneath it, and teasingly had spoken. If it were true she regretted very much having spoken.

She turned the conversation very abruptly, and moved over to the window.

Through the frosted snow-hung trees they could catch a glimpse of a side street leading down to the river's edge. A feeble old woman, carrying a heavy basket of fishermen's nets, was going down the street with tottering steps, her body bent under the heavy weight. "Who is it, Modena? I thought that was a private way!" she said.

The mistress of the house drew aside the heavy, crimson satin draperies, and looked out after the drooping form.

"It is a private way," she said. "It is only old Susan. We found her one day by the roadside. They had put her in a Home, but the Home to her was a charnel-house, and she refused to remain. Her freedom and her independence were dear to her. Father gave her that little cottage by the river. She gathers firewood from the shore. She mends the fishermen's nets. She is perfectly happy," and the mistress of the house continued to gaze out through the leaded panes upon the frozen world and on the old woman in the lane.

Almost at the present moment she wished that she were the old woman, or that Merlin's chair would appear by magic, and she could sit in it and lose herself. Keith Kenyon had come in, in the twilight, and had taken tea from her hand and had looked into her eyes, and his presence had filled the room, had made concrete

every abstract thought which her clearer vision and deeper powers
of thought and feeling had that afternoon taken from the love of
the poet.

> "He saw thro' life and death; thro' good and ill.
>   He saw through his own soul.
>   The marvel of the everlasting will
>   An open scroll
>   Before him lay."

Her own heart lay an open scroll before her—his, too. In his
she saw both the knight's and the King's. In her own was mir-
rored the guilty heart of the Queen. What right had she to use
such harsh words towards the Queen and her knight? His appearance out in the wild storm of the night on the lonely moor, his
few words and the sweetness of his presence had opened anew the
lately closed wound. The afternoon's reading had awakened her
to a knowledge of her danger. With a firmness she had striven
to right her spirit, but like the Queen,

> "The Powers that tend the soul to help it from the death that
>   cannot die
>   And save it in extremes, began to vex and plague her."

But where Verona Kenyon was she had the power of making
one feel there was flesh as well as spirit, and she was now in the
room, and her heart, which had been deeply stirred in the reading
that afternoon by a sense of unseen danger, had also leaped at her
husband's entrance, and cat-like, like Mark through his wife's
halls, she approached his side.

"Miss Wellington met some roughs and ordered them out of
her way. Lady Greta has been envying her her greatness, and has
been wishing for an opportunity to distinguish herself. For her
benefit, cannot you suggest something more artistic or—or—
romantic than a—a street brawl?" she said, with an unpleasant
derision in her voice.

Keith Kenyon gave one quick, fleeting glance towards the mistress of the house, but her face was impassive.

"There is no necessity for your doing so, Mr. Kenyon!"
exclaimed the Lady Greta. quickly. "Nature made me idealistic,
and endowed me with a vivid imagination. It supplies all the
defects of realities. Modena's roughs existed in my imagination
alone. One couldn't become great even if one wanted to. It is
impossible to leave the impress of one's personality on this age,"
she continued. "We are all so great that greatness doesn't show.

23

One must have dark backgrounds, contrasts, to throw out the greatness. Something like this," she said, pointing to a portrait of Modena, painted by a famous artist when she was but eight years old. It was a profile in soft relief with a halo crowning her head on a burnt umber and siennese background.

They all looked towards the picture, and then at their hostess, who said, smilingly:

"The painter wasn't a clairvoyant. My backgrounds have been dull greys. Your imagination has been running away with you, Greta, if you have been painting me white and my backgrounds black. They have only been prosaic country greys, with a touch of rose-pinks, the touch which comes from the air of the meadows and orchards and waters."

"I am so glad. Black and white tears one's life to tatters so."

"What do you know about life's tatters? No more than does your butterfly. Your cynic to-day said the same about the world, and a few weeks afterwards when Maud appeared he called it a rose-garden. You only want a Lancelot to make it a garden of rose-pinks," said Lester, lightly.

"That's what I was telling Modena a moment ago, only I phrased it differently."

"And from among her many friends could she not get you one?"

"Not the one I wanted, and I would have none other."

"How sad!"

"Greta says our backgrounds are so golden that no one is more noticeable than another. Even with our golden settings, surely we have some whose brilliance makes the background dim!"

"Generalizations are never convincing. Be more specific and name one, Modena," said Lester.

"Goldwin Smith."

"Why do you say so? In what role is he great?"

"As an original thinker, as a man with clairvoyant insight, judicious reasoning powers, and conservative and sound judgments: one with the desire and the courage to defend the oppressed and champion the weaker cause."

"We have others, too," said Verona, from the other side of the tea table.

"Who?"

"My husband," she said, blandly, as she helped him to a second lump of sugar.

She said it almost jestingly, as she was well aware it would have been very bad taste to have said it otherwise, but yet the assertion had within it enough truth, and the expression of her voice enough boastfulness to make the moment very unpleasant.

"You are making him blush, Verona," said Mrs. Sangster.

"A prophet is never a prophet in his own country."

"A man is never a hero to his own valet-de-chambre," added Lester, lightly, in order to bridge over the awkwardness of the moment.

"What are you wanting, Keith? The sugar tongs? Modena has them," said Helen Lester.

"I gave you the second lump," interrupted his wife. "You do not want to spoil your tea."

Tutored by the ways of the world, as he was, he replied courteously, without looking at her, "Thank you," while he felt the opposite. The two little words which she had uttered were ringing in his ears, stinging him like a child that had been stung by a honey-bee. He saw the hand which played with the sugar tongs twitch, and noticed the lines deepen around her mouth, and he hated himself for what he had done. Almost he felt he could have given the rest of his life—all but a few moments in which to speak to her—to undo what he had done. But it could not be undone thus; he couldn't even speak to her. He could do nothing but go away with his wife, who was now ready to go.

"We will judge of your greatness to-night. We are looking forward to a great pleasure," said Mrs. Sangster, who was leaving with them.

"What are we to have to-night?" asked the Lady Greta. "Oh, yes, I had almost forgotten. You are going to talk about 'Imagination.' No doubt it will be interesting. Mr. Lester and I were making out a list of things this afternoon for a New Jerusalem. We forgot oratory. Will you add it to the list, Mr. Lester? My imagination is vivid. Mr. Kenyon, can I not help you with some picturesque suggestions? Do take an ideal and centre your thoughts around it. Abstract thoughts are so dry and preachy-like. Passionless oratory is like a beautiful queen without a soul."

"I shall make the Lady Greta my queen. The success of the evening is already assured," replied he, quietly and gravely, but gallantly.

"Oh, no, I am only your Elaine," she said, as he went alone with her to her carriage. "I was telling Modena this afternoon that I always ended that story my own way. I am quite sure that the Queen was at the aureoled end of the knight's Holy Grail, or

—or—with some roughs on the road," she could not refrain from adding, smilingly.

But her companion knew as little about the roughs as her hostess had known.

"I am afraid you are ending another story your own way, too. I shall ask her Excellency to hide Tennyson and your chocolates. You are dreaming too much."

"What else can one do when the reality is denied one? Her Excellency is coming to hear you to-night. May I tell her I am to be your ideal?"

"I am much honored," he said, and he smiled as her carriage drove away.

That same evening he spoke in the Grand Auditorium to a crowded house, on "The Power of the Imagination," a subject more suited to a poet than to a philosopher or statesman, but of late it had been in harmony with his moods. He had been born with the blood of generations of statesmen within his veins. It had been his native air. In his youth he had dreamt of a Periclean Age, which meant the highest state of culture to the lowest person, but, as Matthew Arnold says, "The highest person is yet in the lowest state of education." As the years had passed he had realized that education was too big a word for the world to grasp. He had recognized its impossibilities, and he had ceased to be a dreamer and had become a practical man, grasping the necessities of his age. He had been conservative from tradition, and had remained so from intelligence. He had learnt how youth, full of vigor, philanthropy and egotism, was too apt to be led away by the principles of liberalism. History had taught him that liberalism, unrestrained and unintelligent, invariably leads to Socialism, anarchism and blood-red banners. Conservatism, as stagnation or autocracy, was more abhorrent to him than blood-red banners, and his desire had been to find the Greek's maxim of measure in all things, and nothing in excess. He had creeds and codes dear to himself, but he saw that the country was not yet ready for them, and although his ingenious candor rebelled against many prevailing things, he had, with all the powers within him, fought for what he considered best; but within the last few months since these things had touched his own life, the inconsistencies of the life, its incongruities and its forced servility were driving him more and more from the field of statesmanship to seek solace in that of the philosopher and poet. His ideals were higher than the standards of his age, and like many great men had done before his age, he was drawing more and more to the closet and platform, and in other forms giving to the world at large his ideals under the guise of poetic fiction, and his hidden passion now lent force to his genius and power.

He had smiled that afternoon when the Lady Greta had asked him to concentrate his thoughts around an ideal, as if it were possible to create anything without either an imaginary or a real ideal in one's mind and heart! Until these last few years, his had been an imaginary one, but it had ceased to be so, and had become real; and as she listened to his voice to-night, now low and deep, now full and resonant, now tremulous in cadences, and noticed the breathless, enraptured audience, or saw the expressions of vague desires, or mingled regrets for something lacking in one's own mind and life, in the upturned faces, the two little words she had heard Verona Kenyon utter that afternoon came to her mind and dwelt there like a heavy weight of lead, reawakening regrets and longings she was powerless to assuage or dismiss.

He did not once look her way, but she knew he was speaking to her. As she listened to him she knew that passage after passage was inspired by herself and addressed to herself alone.

The words of his wife had also awakened within him a great remorse and an uncontrollable desire to cherish the woman he loved. He dare not speak to her, but he could sustain her through the well-concealed guise of poetic oratory. She would see it, feel it and understand. He had only intended to assure her, he had not intended to arouse any agitation of feeling, but as he progressed, inspired by all that tortured him, his talents became the genius of a lyric poet who drew his inspiration from his own heart alone, and the fire and force of his own words grew in upon him and gave out an intensity, a passion, a pathos, a power, far beyond that which he had premeditated or conceived, and moved her until her emotion became almost in itself a pain.

Homage is at all times dear to the human heart. She knew he was speaking to her alone, and her pulse throbbed until she felt that her cousin, who sat near her, could hear it, and her heart swelled with unspeakable emotion as the hope, which he had portrayed in his peroration, grew in upon her.

But outwardly she remained calm, and remained seated for a few minutes after he had finished, until the way should clear.

"Kenyon will have to stop that, or she will find out, and there will be trouble," her cousin Jack said to her, crossly and irritably, while his brows drew together in deep lines.

Her heart seemed to stand still. She hadn't thought of others seeing what she had seen. "Had others seen it?"

The thought caused her the strongest emotion of her life. The intensity of her emotion kept her mute and motionless.

"Let us get out of this," continued her cousin, impatiently and moodily.

She arose, took the arm of her companion, Sir Colin Campbell, and passed out by a private door to a room leading to the main entrance.

She felt that she must be alone, but yet she was forced to offer Sir Colin Campbell a seat by her side to avoid being alone with her cousin, whose manner plainly indicated, "I shall publicly thrash him if he draw any injurious comment on your name," and her own conscience must again become clear before she could admit him to her presence.

On reaching Apsley House she went direct to her own apartments, and shortly afterwards to rest, but she could not sleep. It seemed to her that although her body lay on its bed, her soul was apart from it, wandering in some far away, unknown world. She had never known the meaning of nerves. She had never taken an opiate in her life, but it seemed to her now that she must do so to quiet the strange feeling which permeated her whole being, but she resisted the impulse, until at last when it was almost morning her heavy lids closed over her tired eyes, and she fell into the indifference of slumber.

CHAPTER XXXIII.

MODENA slept ill and awoke little refreshed.

The Lady Greta had the previous day compared her to Psyche. Keith Kenyon, with a word, a suggestion, had brought home to her the sweet, sad story in all its pathos and depth of meaning.

The allusion had been unfortunate. All night long she had dwelt in the Dream Valley as Psyche had done with her Unseen, and awakening, as she did now in the dim lights of morning, with her night lamp still burning in her apartments, where Cupids, painted by the famous pupil of Lebrun, wantoned in a scroll-work round the ceiling of the room, and Psyche hung in shadow on tapestries brought from cities of the East, it was with difficulty she disentangled the realities of the past night from the dreams which had haunted her all night in the unknown world. Was it her story—Psyche's story—that had been beneath all his words? So vivid and realistic was the impression made upon her that she believed it was, and a chill of despair ran through her as in the dim lights the pathos on the Soul's face peered out from its background of old gold and crimson tapestries.

Her maid entered the room, extinguished the night lights and raised the window. The chill, cold air of morning stirred among and rippled the hangings on the wall. A sudden gust, and the heavy cloth unloosed its fastenings, and the face of the redeemed daughter of Venus, in all its chastened hope and happiness, rippled out on the breezes of the morning.

"Was this what he meant?" she thought, as she rose, bathed and dressed herself. "A story pretty in legend and on tapestries, but, as Greta says, 'In real life.' My brown cloth," she said to her maid. "I am going for a walk. The cold air and a long walk is the best antidote for nerves," and she called Nell Gwynne and Cavall to her side, and crossed the frosty lawn towards the water's edge.

At nine her cousin sought her, but she avoided any allusion to the previous evening. She perceived that he was much annoyed and worried, and that his desire was to censure, console, admonish; but she did not choose that he should refer to it in any way. She could not admit there was anything in it. To admit it was to become a party to it; or to take any solace from it was equally as deteriorating. She could only ignore anything personal in the words. Every word was burnt into her brain as aqua fortis eats into metal. She knew them all, and knew the story, and if it were referred to in her presence and any personality attached or attributed to it, why, the Lady Greta had been his avowed Ideal! She had Sir Colin by her side, and his presence would aid her in passing off any allusion as intended for the Lady Greta.

For the next two weeks she appeared constantly in public, and quite often by the side of Sir Colin Campbell. No one spoke of it in her presence, but her knowledge of the world and her instinct, which is more subtle than reason, told her that it was being commented upon. It irritated her exceedingly, but she carried herself well through it all. She avoided meeting the Kenyons, and gave her days and her nights unceasingly and unremittingly to her friends and acquaintances.

The following week she accepted a long-standing invitation from a college friend of her mother's in a neighboring city. She spent with her a fortnight, and it seemed to her that the time was very long and very dreary. At the end of the fortnight she returned home.

The day of her return the chief sent out a slogan cry. The majority was not as large as desirable, and some were wavering, too. It was a toss-up which way some of them would go, and the chief, not wishing to show the white feather or any sign of uneasiness or weakness to that element in every party which makes things troublesome and unpleasant, and who invariably go with the stronger section, had sent out cards to gather them into the fold, to demonstrate to the Opposition the harmonious union of his own party.

But at the last moment there was illness at the chief's home, which necessitated the reception being held at Apsley House. The mistress of the house stood with her chief and her father, with their grand Cordon collars on their breasts, and received the throngs of guests as they came, among them Keith (now Sir Keith) Kenyon, and his wife, Lady Kenyon.

For her own peace of mind, from prudence, and from her sense of justice, the mistress of the house had avoided meeting them. Since their marriage she had purposely refrained from entertaining. She looked upon hospitality, given and received, as something sacred. She knew what an invitation entailed, and her instincts refused intimacy with Verona Kenyon. The laws of the land and the church, which she held sacred, had given Verona a claim on the man she loved, and this made it doubly hard for her to receive them as her guests.

Since her moments of weakness she had also begun to fear herself, and then her conscience had become guilty, and she had suffered more from her feeling of guilt than from her separation.

She had been humiliated in her own sight; but she could suffer anything rather than her world should see her humiliation, and thus her pride became greater than her candor and sincerity, and supported her in the ordeal, and enabled her to greet her now with conventional cordiality, while to Sir Keith she was again cold. "He must be made to feel that there must now be nothing between them," she said to herself on their entrance, remembering her conflict the night of his oration, and what she had suffered when she knew that the world was commenting upon it afterwards.

"She made me do it, and now she is resenting it, and making me feel as if I were a cad for submitting," thought he, as he listened to the kind and sympathetic words which she bestowed upon her guests, and contrasted them with the indifferent monosyllables with which she answered or addressed himself. The thoughts made him moody and morose, and strengthened the desire which was now ever present with him to assure her by word or tone that his whole being was hers. "She must doubt me, or why should she act thus? Why should she doubt me?" he said, time and again to himself, forgetting the existence of his wife in his life.

But where Verona was she was not to be forgotten.

She was now by his side where he stood silent in the embrasure of a window, sunk so deeply in a despair of remembrance that the room seemed to him a stage, and the life and light and joy a drama in which he took no part.

"I don't think we should allow Modena Wellington to monopolize all the chief's receptions. Our position is equal to hers, and we should gradually assert our rights. We are as competent to lead as she," she was saying to him.

"I am afraid you would become discouraged if you tried," he answered her, briefly.

"Why?" she asked, her eyebrows drawing together in a frown.

"Because receiving is an art, and receiving in a case similar to this requires tact and experience, and one must possess the faculty of doing it before one can do it successfully."

"I may not have had the experience, but don't you think I have the ability?"

"We shall see, but you cannot be too careful at first. I am afraid you will find it burdensome and tire of the responsibility."

"Don't you think I could do it as well as Modena Wellington?" she asked, and she watched him closely as she spoke.

"You have had your dinners and your crushes, and I expect you will have innumerable more, and you have been successful. What more do you want?" he replied, evasively, trying hard to conceal his impatience.

She noticed the evasion and the intonation.

"That is not what I want. Dozens of others have the same," she said. "What I mean is that we want to lead. When the chief is in a dilemma he goes to her. I want him to come to us. That's what I mean, and I want you to help me. It is our right," she continued, with as much innocence and candor as she could bring to her aid.

"But one cannot do it unless one is born to it. It is an instinct given only to great ambassadresses or great queens. There are few who possess the gift," he replied, and as he spoke he thought to himself, "She is one," but he did not say so to his wife.

But he had touched the skeleton within her closet, and her face grew dark as the night without, as she said with vehemence:

"We will lead yet."

Sir Keith looked at her quickly, but before he had time to reply their hostess approached with Carlton Monteith.

"Will you join Mr. Patrie in a duet?" asked Carlton Monteith of her, as he bowed low before her. "The chief has asked for it. Mr. Patrie will sing it only with you."

"How I am honored! How can one refuse after that!" she said, as she moved away with Carlton Monteith, leaving her hostess alone by the side of Keith Kenyon.

As they stood alone for a moment, but for a moment only, for the demands upon her were incessant and her duties as hostess exacting, her companion looked at her warmly as the shaded lights cast a mellow glow over her face and form. There must be some subtle magnetism between two kindred souls, for, despite her inner self, all her late resolutions vanished, and her face softened as she felt his gaze upon her. He saw it, and all else was forgotten. "If life could only be even like this," he thought. It was happiness to be alone in her presence, even were it in a crowded drawing-room. Dare he but reach out and touch the hem of her garment he thought it would comfort and sustain him, and yet he dare not do so.

His wife's voice was wafted to them from an adjoining room, where she was singing with Mr. Patrie.

As Modena heard the gay, glad notes her countenance changed, and she gave her companion an almost imperceptible bow of courtesy, and moved on to her other guests.

She would never, no, never, she told herself, either by glance or word, permit one message from him.

He noticed the change and divined the cause; unnoticed he stepped out through the open French window into a small conservatory.

From here he could see the bright, flushed face of his wife as she turned round when the song was sung. Carlton Monteith and others were chatting gaily with her, and he noticed the deference paid her. He did not care for her. He had never cared for her. She was no more to him than the housekeeper or the butler's wife. Not as much, for his servants were old family servants and seemed a part of his home. But she had never really entered his home. He felt she never would. He felt his indifference was growing into active dislike, and his one desire now was to avoid her as much as possible. Never before was he so glad of the distractions and onerous duties of public life as he was now. They occupied almost wholly his time and his attention. Gradually he would break away from the social engagements at which he was forced to appear at her side. He drew back in the shadows that she might not see him now.

As he lingered outside Lester came out through the open doorway.

"What, Kenyon, mooning and moping here alone! You don't seem to be very enthusiastic over the gathering of the Tory clan."

Sir Keith only smiled, and the two men lighted their cigars and leaned back against the casement of the conservatory, watching the passing panorama within.

"It must have been a general call. One notices many new faces here to-night," said Lester.

"Yes, one is forced to do it. It reminds one of what Byron said regarding De Stael's English society, 'It is like the grave, where all distinctions are levelled,'" he said, moodily, his pain lending to his voice a touch of the English bard's cynicism.

"Perhaps it is better so; extremes need to meet to produce the happy medium. Coppet and Ferney are possibilities in other ages only. Coppet's daily mind expenditure far exceeded our yearly expenditure. A universal cultured society is an impossibility, and, as you say, one is forced to make the best of what there is. But what can she have in common with many present? The smallness of their minds must weary her infinitely," replied Lester, referring to the mistress of the house, and the eyes of both men involuntarily followed her as she moved through the rooms with simple, stately grace and sympathetic words, the many lights shining on the tiara of diamonds that crowned her shapely head, and on the tissues of her train as it rippled over the floor.

Sir Keith dropped his cynicism and said, with the same vein of sadness in which the woman of whom he had been speaking had written to Talleyrand:

"No, I don't think they weary her. Her politics are to her her life and religion, as they were to De Stael; and like Sismondi, her religion is essentially morality, which is but another synonym for the laws which give the best conditions in life, laws which evolve themselves from the nature of things, and which are generalized, specified, defined through reason and by reasoning; otherwise it would rest only in feeling, and, having no principle, it would become isolated and therefore fanciful and fanatical. Religion requires firmness. The understanding alone can give this, and therefore she controls her heart by her will," he continued, his own feelings entering into his words, causing him to wander somewhat. "No, do not misunderstand me! I do not mean to say she is a moralist and lacks spiritualism. She is essentially spiritual. She has the heart and enthusiasm of a De Stael, which, one of her late French admirers has said, is the incense of earth ascending to heaven, inviting both. Corinne's heart was nature, full, free and spontaneous. She possessed the esprit of a Frenchwoman and the vein of sadness, the inevitable concomitant and fruit of genius, whereas Modena is essentially an Englishwoman of position. Her dignity, her self-command, her reserve, are immense within her. She may feel as intensely as a Corinne, but to display it to the world would be a lack of good taste. She is the sum incarnate of self-abnegation, and yet, without being aware of it, it is herself she deifies. The world is her god, and she would go to the block rather than do anything that would humiliate her in the eyes of the world. She might love one deeply, but were it not a legitimate love she would never betray it. No, it is not a cowardice, it is a pride based on knowledge. She may suffer, feel, but no one will know of it. She has been strong, her strength has arisen from a strange mixture of self-love and self-knowledge. Duty, heretofore, has been her god. Her sense of duty has been stronger than her emotions. Her sense of duty arises from her family traditions, which are instinctive rather than volitional. Joined to her family tradition is a deep knowledge in herself of the basis of things and the necessity of things, which has but served to verify and strengthen the traditions of her forefathers. Her reason and religion teach her the possibility and perfectibility of the human race through right and justice, and it is for this she is striving. She feels profoundly, and this inspires great kindness. She comprehends, and this grants indulgence. One might say of her what Chateaubriand said of Corinne, 'I know of no woman more convinced of her own immense superiority over all the world, and who makes others feel the weight of that conviction less.' No, I don't think they weary her. I don't think she is lonely, or if she be, it is when she is alone, for she feels for all but herself."

Mr. Lester listened, understanding his friend's mood, and having full comprehension of his meaning. He was silent for some moments, and then said, " She is changing. Corinne admonished Lucille not to permit her superiority to show itself in pride and coldness. Modena has grown colder and quieter of late."

" Ambition and enthusiasm, like love, have their seasons of strife and lassitude."

Mr. Lester well knew that satisfied ambition was not the cause of her lassitude, but he also knew it was one of the laws of good society never to intrude in any personal matters, and refrained from making any comment, and only looked at his companion and wondered how he could ever have placed himself in such a position.

His companion felt the scrutiny, and he also felt that his misery had made him say something unjust.

He knew what was dwelling in Mr. Lester's mind, and he valued Mr. Lester's opinion.

"Life holds many ironies. We do things, why we do them we cannot tell, and then when they are done we must stand for their having been done. Our own actions too often become our own pillory. One can but do penance, but one regrets that others suffer through us. If one could only bear it all oneself, but one cannot. One can only repent and live," said Sir Keith, and the pale gas jets shining through the window shone on a countenance where remorse had already stamped its signet.

He was glad Mr. Lester had spoken of her. He felt it an immensity of relief to unburden his feelings to someone, and he was glad of an opportunity to vindicate himself in Mr. Lester's sight, even if it were by unspoken words.

"You said a moment ago that her sense of duty was stronger within her than her emotions. It would be a pity to disillusion her," said Mr. Lester, who felt himself justified in speaking, once his friend had spoken.

"It would be a crime," replied Sir Keith.

"Then why—" and Mr. Lester checked himself.

"You were going to say, why does one do it? One does not: something outside oneself does this."

"Isn't this something only one's own weakness rising up and confronting one, as one's shadow confronts one on a clear day."

"Is it? You mean it is one's weakness which makes one love."

Mr. Lester did not reply, and they both remained silent, Sir Keith pitying Lester's hopeless attachment, but admiring his strong, manly fortitude and fidelity, and Mr. Lester mentally exclaiming, "She loves him. That is the cause of his weakness. His strength is his weakness."

Lady Kenyon's voice interrupted their meditations.

"Lord Glaston and Sir Kenneth Malcolm are coming to the chief's next month. Matters of diplomacy, you know. He has asked me to show them the beauties of Idlewylde while they are here. I told you I would do it," she said to her husband, with exaltation in her voice. "It will have to be a party. Ah, Mr. Lester, you here! I did not see you. You'll come, too," she said, as she noticed them.

"I'm afraid I cannot be of any service to you," he answered her.

"We do not ask only those who can be of service to us. We find plenty of those, but very few who are interesting. You always

bring your welcome. No party is perfect without your presence.
Remember to come. We must go now," she said to her husband.
" We have to show up at Lady Delaney's and at Merta's afterwards.
Are you ready?"

She went in, and in a few minutes he met her at the carriage
and accompanied her to another reception, and then to Merta's,
but refrained from going in with her, and after leaving orders
with his servant to call for her, retraced his steps towards Apsley
House. He was in no mood to listen to the frivolous chatter of
those whom he knew he would meet where his wife now was.

He was well acquainted with the grounds and the private gardens
of Apsley House, and unconsciously his footsteps wandered there.
He did not stop to think how injudicious his actions were, and
how his presence would be misconstrued if he were seen there. He
only thought

> " Of Love.
> For love himself took part against himself
> To warn us off, and Duty—loved of love,
> O, the world's curse—beloved, but hated—came
> Like Death between thy dear embrace and mine,
> And crying, Who is this? beloved thy bride,
> She pushed me from thee."

Something, Duty or Destiny, had pushed him out of her life.
Although it was yet early spring, he sat down on a seat under a
spreading maple in a secluded spot and bowed his head in his hands,
and remained there alone with his regrets and his longings, and
with an anguish as great as that of Faust's in the solitude of the
mountains, accompanied by Mephistopheles, and tortured by his
desire for his Helen.

After some time he noticed the carriages drive up to the entrance,
and then he realized he was acting very injudiciously, and also that
he was allowing himself to drift into a very unhealthy state of mind.

His manhood was dear to him. He would go home. Home?
No, he had no home. He would go away. He would go down to
Idlewylde and rest for a week or two. The place would require
some alterations and preparation for the coming guests. It would
take him out of this unhealthy mood. " It will at least be a
respite," he said, as he arose, buttoned his great coat around him,
for the air had yet enough cold in it to frighten the early prim-
roses nestling at his feet back under their leafy covering; and then
he wended his way to his favorite club, where he remained until
morning.

CHAPTER XXXIV.

> "And may there not be
> A friendship yet hallowed, between you and me?
> May we not be yet friends, friends the dearest? Alas!
> She replied, for one moment perchance did it pass
> Through my heart, that dream, which forever hath brought
> To those who indulge in it, in innocent thought
> So fatal and evil an awakening. But no,
> For in loves such as ours are the Dream Tree would grow
> On the border of Hades; beyond it what lies?
> The wheel of Ixion. Alas! And the cries
> Of the lost and tormented. Departed for us
> Are the days when innocence could discuss
> Dreams like these."

Jack Mainton again suggested to his cousin the advisability of a trip to the Continent, to Paris, or to Japan. His cousin did not act upon the suggestion. She could not leave her homes at the present time. Much work awaited her at Fernwylde. "One has duties due to one's order as well as to one's position," she was wont to say. Like in the ladies of old, the "noblesse oblige" instinct was predominant within her. Her responsibilities she held as a trust and never allowed idleness or pleasure, self-indulgence or self-depression to interfere with the duties which she considered she owed to her landed people. It was now the time of their church anniversary, and they had sent for her.

She left the city quietly, as the shadows were lengthening into afternoon, leaving orders with the hall porter that she was not at home.

Keith Kenyon had gone to Idlewylde by an earlier train. Since the night of the reception it had come home to him that he must with a firmness break away from the memories of the past. He was not acting a man's part. Mr. Lester's words had made him realize his weakness.

The amorousness of a Gawain he had always looked upon as unmanly. What were such thoughts but the precursors and the germs of the sensual loves of the Heptameron or the Decameron of Bocaccio, or the idlers of Venusberg? He would crush the seed before it had yet begun to germinate, and to help himself do so he went down to Idlewylde.

On his arrival he sent for an architect, some workmen and gardeners, and spent the day discussing plans with the architect and in giving instructions to the workmen, but with the day's work he was little pleased. A place or work invariably takes upon itself the character and coloring of one's own thoughts and feelings, and his were colorless and motiveless.

Towards evening he ordered his hansom and thoroughbred and drove to the village to meet the evening mail. He received his mail, selected from it those letters which required his immediate personal attention, returned the others to his manservant and ordered the coachman to drive home, telling him he would walk home through the woods later in the evening.

He went to a reading-room close by and perused his letters; then to the telegraph office; from here he despatched replies to the city to those which were urgent, and then turned his steps towards home.

His way lay through the woods of Fernwylde. The weather had turned warm, the trees were in full leaf, the breath of spring was pulsing in all nature. He walked along with bent head, his mind dwelling upon the contents of his letters and on his replies, but the surroundings and their associations were stronger than his will power and made his mind wander.

He had left the town to escape from his memories and his desires, but he had only left the land of prose to enter into the land of poetry. He paused in his walk and, leaning against a stone balustrade, the ruins of an old Ursuline convent, which bordered the path, looked out over their homes as they lay bathed and verdant in the glories of a spring sunset.

It was all so familiar to him. Wherever his eye turned, what he saw was fraught with memories of her. How often had they wandered down the honeysuckle-edged path by the clear trout stream, lingering to catch the crimson and gold of the fish at play, or angled for trout in the shade of the overhanging elms. How often had they ridden on errands of mercy, she on her favorite steed, Zenobia, he on big black Ali, through the meadowlands, over the turnpike road which led through the heavy forests flanking the mountain sides, to the hamlets which lay scattered on the outskirts of their lands, and returned at peace with themselves and with the world, when the shades of evening were coming down on the great Siberian pines which lined their way, with no sound about them save the rippling and rumbling of the many waters which flowed from the mountain side to swell the waters of the Idlewylde. It all came back to him now, all the pleasures he had felt; but somehow out here it was mingled with less pain and less desire. Out here, alone with nature, he felt refreshed, invigorated, infinitely stronger, imbued with a strong sense of manhood's duties, conscious of the possibilities of noble efforts, courageous to meet the truth and do justice to the situation.

They had been friends for many years. Why should he relinquish this friendship? Not to be able to meet her honestly was a sign of weakness within himself. To avoid her was a sign of cowardice.

They could be friends. Could he only see her and tell her this. The impulse was strong upon him to return to the city and tell her this, but he was sadly in need of a rest; he would remain at Idlewylde for the fortnight, and on his return he would be able to meet her as a friend.

So he told himself, and went on his way.

His path lay by the little church, the pride of the village and country round. The church had been built by the mistress of Fernwylde, who was a strong believer in the elevating effect of architecture on the spiritual nature of man. Its situation was picturesque exceedingly.

As he now passed it, his attention was attracted by strains of music from within, as Faust in his wanderings had been many years before. It was a selection from one of the great master's oratorios adapted to stringed instrumentation, and a full, rich soprano, which he instantly recognized, took the solo part, while many young voices rolled out on the clear northern air, pure and simple as the notes of their native meadow-lark.

"It is Modena!" he exclaimed to himself. "I did not know she was here," and the whole nature of things changed in a moment.

When Sir Keith recognized the voice he hesitated, stopped and listened, as Ulysses had done when he had heard Calypso's voice. Soon the last notes vibrated on the air. Then he heard a stir, and presently Modena, with her violin in her hand and surrounded by a score of children, appeared in the arched doorway.

A summer house covered with vines hid him from their view.

He hesitated a moment, in doubt what to do. To proceed would be to expose himself to full view, and his presence might be misunderstood. He knew the children's way lay towards the village, only she would take the path to Fernwylde. There was only one course left open to him.

He had been wishing to see her. The woodland fairies (?) have their way of granting wishes, and they had granted his.

He stepped within until they should pass on their way. They emerged from the doorway, and Modena crossed the grass-plot to a stone stile on the terrace overlooking the waters, where her cousin was boating with Helen Lester and Mrs. Gwen, the children

24

following, loth to leave and depart to their different homes. They each and all loved the great lady who was so kind to and so considerate with them.

"The sun is sinking fast. Should we not hurry home?" she said to the group, but seeing them yet hesitate and linger, she asked:

"What is it, my children?"

"Oh, Miss Wellington!" cried one little bright-eyed child of eight, "the music is so beautiful, it makes us think of heaven and the angels. Will you not sing us something out here before we go?"

"Do you wish me to sing, my dears?" she asked, quietly, the gift of generosity being strongly instinct within her.

In an instant the group closed round her, with shining eyes and pleased, pleading looks.

"Oh, please! It is so beautiful here! The sun is lingering to listen," said a grave-eyed little boy.

"What a pretty thing you have said! One cannot refuse after that. Shall we sing him to rest?"

She seated herself on the stone stile, with the last slanting rays of the dying sun playing on her figure and graceful position. Her profile stood out in soft relief with a background of evergreen arches and purple clematis, with the children grouped with upturned faces.

"St. Cecilia and the angels!" thought he who watched.

She thought a moment with her violin poised against her shoulder, her right hand curved and held partly aloft, with bow suspended, and then began to tune her chords, and soon passed on into a favorite old air, low and soft and sweet, but oftentimes weird and sad, that she had heard the choir boys sing in distant Italy ere they went to their night's repose.

Her voice was exquisitely trained and of the sweetest melody, and she sang to her audience with as much precision and feeling as if she had been singing in the state drawing-room of Rideau Hall. The lingering rays of the slanting sun shone on her face, and showed there that consecrated, rapt look that is seen on the faces of great singers when they give themselves up completely to the emotions which alone can inspire a perfect piece.

The children stood hushed and awed as the beauty of the music grew in upon them, their eyes softening at the pattering of the rain-drops on the thatched roofs and gentle breezes whispering through the trees, but melted to tears when she came to the orphan's prayer and lonely vigils which the monk's prayer of praise failed to console.

When the last notes had died away on the darkening air, the

children spoke or moved not, but wistfully looked at the coming stars and at Modena.

"What does it all mean, Miss Wellington?" asked one little child, gravely, with humid eyes.

She arose and said gently, "It means, my little dears, that we must go home at once, or mamma will scold. I shall tell you all about it some other time."

The children turned homewards, silently wondering what were these vague longings, these half-awakened desires and glimpses of finer things than they had ever seen before, which they felt stirring within their childish hearts.

They wended their way silent for some time, and then one little girl murmured, "Mamma was telling me last night about a sweet, sad lady who found a chord which the great people of old had long been trying to find, a chord, oh! so grand and strong, like God, but sweet and soft like the angels, but she lost it almost ere she had found it, and she says it has gone to heaven and is waiting for her there. Don't you think that might be it Miss Wellington sang to-night?"

"Perhaps it was," said another; "but why does it make us feel like this? I am going home to my room to pray to God to make all the people in the world good and happy, and to be kind to our dear lady. Isn't her face sad, like that picture of the angel kneeling by the tomb which is painted on our pew window?"

"But she is seldom sad. I never saw her sad before. I shall gather her some flowers for Wednesday," said another.

"She is so fond of them. I shall take her some, too," said others, as they separated, almost in silence, at the parting of their ways, for their different homes.

When they left her Modena remained for a few moments with her fingers absently passing over the strings of her instrument. It was the same one which had lain for many long years in the chateau apartments of Apsley House. It had come down to her family from a French ancestress, who had dwelt midst the glories of the Sun-King's Court.

She ran her fingers lightly over its chords, and they seemed to sigh and sob with remembrance. He had touched its notes long, long ago. He had made music for her, music dreamy, which had carried her soul from earth to heaven. Beneath his touch the dumb notes had pulsed and vibrated anew with the long-forgotten refrains of the lovers of long ago.

"How many fair lovers had touched its chords? How many

tender ballads had been sung to its sounds? How many fair hearts had leaped responsive to its call?"

He had made the dumb notes speak to her as they had spoken to all these fair men and women of long ago. All these fair men and fair women! Dead, dead, so long, long ago! and the dumb notes answering to the same old pains and the same old passions. Ah, me! Ah, me! How would it end? Where would it end?

She arose and handed her violin to her footman, who was waiting for her. "Jackson," she said, "I see my cousin rowing into the boat-house. Tell Williams to drive down and take Mrs. Gwen home with you. I shall walk home with Jack."

When the carriage drove away she crossed the grass-plot to the round-house for her wrap, which she had left there, and met Sir Keith emerging from the summer-house.

She was for the moment so surprised that words refused to come. Had he stepped out of her reveries? So vivid had been his presence that for a moment she failed to disentangle his actual presence from the dreams she had been dreaming.

The sound of the carriage wheels on the hard, gravelly road leading to the river brought her to a realization of the presence of others. With an effort she recovered herself. The music had left her impressionable, and for a moment she colored warmly as she realized his presence, and then the next moment she remembered how it all was.

"Had he followed her here?" and at the thought her face grew very cold.

He noticed the change.

"I did not know you were here until I heard your voice in the church. I came down for a few days' rest and quietness," he said; and, unconsciously and unintentionally, his voice had in it a note of pathos and pleading which no woman could altogether resist.

It was with difficulty she recovered her habitual composure.

"You will grace the children's fete," she replied, to cover her inward confusion.

"To hear you sing?"

"Oh, I do not sing at it. I am only helping train them. Midian takes the solo on Wednesday."

"After hearing it sung by an angel, one would not care to hear it sung by the common clay. It would spoil one's illusions and one's ideals."

"Her voice is really good."

"It's not the voice. It is what is behind the voice. It's the soul in the voice. Those things were composed by great souls, and can only be interpreted by souls who have felt as they have felt. Passions cannot be portrayed unless they have been felt. One cannot interpret unless one understands. One has one's conceptions of those things. One wishes to retain them."

"You mean we are presumptuous. Poor Midian! I'm glad she doesn't hear you. Don't you think you are harsh? Cannot she understand in the abstract? Poetry and music may be imitative, as prescribed by Aristotle, or imaginative, as represented by Bacon. We have Keats and Shelley discarding materialism, rising to the extreme of idealism and descending to the world with faith and knowledge. Thought alone is eternal."

"But Dante with his Beatrice and Petrarch with his Laura are infinitely more appealing, suggestive and touching. We are intensely human. We weren't made to live on thought alone."

He was looking at her with as much hunger in his heart as was in that of Dante's or Petrarch's.

She knew it, and she was touched to her woman's heart, but she could not permit even an undercurrent of meaning.

"You are unkind to Midian," she continued. "I think she has a Reuben, but if not, your presence might inspire her. You could do this for your country. They worship you here. Why not let them see that you appreciate it?"

"Do you always appreciate the worship bestowed upon yourself?" he asked her, abruptly.

She wished Jack would come. "Why did they linger?" She felt a great weakness coming upon her. He was awaiting her reply.

"You think I am ungrateful and heartless? I am sorry. I thought I was doing my duty towards them," she said, looking away from him.

"You know I wasn't thinking of them. I didn't mean them," he said, and his voice had in it the power to unnerve her much.

She couldn't trust herself to reply further, and stood silent, with dimmed eyes gazing out over the soft, spring, wind-blown river, with its drifting canopy of pale blue clouds, to where the softness and radiance of the sun's afterglow was giving place to night and darkness. The music, the memories, the surroundings had moved them greatly.

"Oh, Modena! Why did you do it? What is it all worth? I cannot! I cannot live without you," he said, with a great wail in his voice, as from some noble animal that had received a mortal wound.

She noticed his blame of her, but took no exception to it. "What did it matter now who was to blame? It was done and irrevocable."

"Oh, hush, Keith!" she murmured, but with little expression or emphasis in her rebuke and tone. "You have no right to say those things to me now."

"I know it, and it is this thought which maddens one. I long for you by night and by day, and yet I dare not insult you by telling you so. But when you know this, why are you so cold? Why can we not be friends?"

He knew as well as she that this was now an utter impossibility. "If love be not all in all, it is not love at all." Sadly had come home to him the force and truth of this couplet, and so, perforce, friendship was the only plea he could utter. But it was an empty plea to her. Enid-like, her instincts were more subtle and more sensitive to danger than were his. She had felt the truth of Corinne's words, "Alas, what a conflict goes on in a soul susceptible at once of great passions and of great conscience!" This conflict had taught her to fear her strength. She dare not grant it in the way in which he had asked it. The time had long since gone by in which they could talk in innocence of friendship. Their relations must be limited to mere acquaintanceship.

So her reason told her, but her heart pleaded otherwise.

He saw her wavering; he saw the soft light which was in her face. He heard Helen Lester's voice in the distance. His wretchedness made him momentarily forget his manhood. He felt within him a great, uncontrollable desire to take her to him, despite all the laws of God and man. He took a step nearer, and then he checked himself.

She seemed to divine what was passing in his mind, and moved from him, and her face changed.

"You must not say those things. I cannot even admit that you have said them. Until you refrain from doing so, we must meet as strangers. They are calling me," she said, in a far-away voice, and almost before he was aware of it she had gone from him.

He watched her form as it passed from sight. His blood coursed through his veins until the throbbing of his pulse became almost painful. "Had he offended her? She must pardon him. He could not rest until he knew it. He would follow and seek her pardon."

But he must not compromise her.

He knew the woods well. He stepped into a side-path which led towards Idlewylde, and walked quickly away, and was emerging from the Idlewylde grove, carelessly smoking his favorite Havana, as the trio came along.

"How are you, Kenyon? When did you come down?" exclaimed Jack, in a surprise which had in it a tinge of displeasure.

Sir Keith withdrew his cigar, raised his hat to the ladies, and bowed.

"This morning," he answered. "I was tired and thought I would run out for a day or two to freshen up. I wasn't aware you were coming. You said nothing of it yesterday."

"We only decided this morning," replied Jack, whose mind was working rapidly.

He could only do what courtesy and their intimacy necessitated his doing.

"You are alone? You will dine with us?"

"One is like Horace. Solitude is enticing in perspective, but yet one prefers the company of Augustus. With pleasure," he replied.

"How unwise," said Modena, very coldly. She was forced to say something.

"To dine with you?"

"Oh, no, we are not inhospitable. I meant, how unwise to prefer the company of the crowd to one's own mind."

"But one's own mind is, alas! too often, so poor a companion that one is glad to escape from it," he said, and then turned and walked with them down the rose-edged path which led to Fernwylde, conversing with Jack upon the current topics of the day, while the ladies lingered behind.

Soon they emerged from the woods to the open green which surrounded the house. Evening had spread over all the land; a west wind rustled among the trees; the moon's rays swept across the darkened sward and lit up the great pile of turrets and towers of Fernwylde, as it lay slumberous in the arms of its own wooded hills and many waters. Here the path led to the ravine, there a path led to the old Fernery, and farther away to the westward, across the waters, dark as iron, glittering as steel now that the sun had gone down, lay Idlewylde, peaceful and imposing as the scene before them. Its master shuddered as his eyes fell upon it, and he turned towards Fernwylde.

"Horace hadn't seen Fernwylde when he sighed for the palace of Augustus," he said, and they paused by common consent, overcome and awed for the moment by the solemnity, the peacefulness and silent grandeur of the scene before them.

"Dinner will be waiting," said Jack, abruptly and a little irritably, and they went on.

Dinner was served when only the family were present in the

white room off the gardens, so called from its white pillars, friezes and satin hangings with their gold embroideries and bullion. It was such a cosy room and so home-like. Almost it seemed to them, as they lingered at the table, that there was no other world but the world within its walls. So much so did it seem that Jack took his guest out on the portico on the plea of smoking.

The ladies remained alone, and the mistress of the house crossed over to the grand piano in one corner of the room, and seated herself before its keys. She had been as silent as courtesy would permit her to be, and she was now glad of the majesty of music which would supplant and silence speech. She turned wholly to the piano and played without prelude some of the wanderings of Parsifal, the grave and tender sonatas of Schubert and the struggles and the triumphs of Tannhauser, and then, as the majesty of the music soothed and calmed her into peace, old airs, long forgotten, came back, other airs which came from she knew not where, airs without words but full of feeling, chords which came responsive to some inward call, and her hands wandered on over the ivory keys, making the music speak with a melancholy pathos which brought a dimness to the eyes of those who listened.

She played on and on, unmindful of time, until Keith Kenyon came in, bringing with him the wild-rose-scented air from the moonlit gardens. It was clear almost as day without, but swiftly passing fleecy clouds sped across the skies, and the air though balmy had in it strong suggestions of a coming storm, while an angry line of yellow, surmounting inky clouds in the western sky-line, boded ill for the night. It was one of those nights in which the atmosphere plays upon the chords of sympathetic nerves.

His entrance recalled her from dreamland. Orpheus-like, she seemed to return from the land of struggle and shadow, and, like him, found herself on the brink of a pit with the person dearest on earth.

She looked up as he entered, and smiled, but there was a dimness in her eyes as she smiled. It seemed so natural to see him come in thus, that for the moment the past few months and the past evening were forgotten. He stood for some few moments until the last chords died away in their echo. Then she rose from her seat, and began rearranging the music.

"Hadn't we better rejoin the others?" she said.

"No, I am going home," and his voice had in it the echo of the music as it lingered on the last word. "But I cannot rest until I know that you forgive me the words I spoke to you this evening. I only came to tell you so."

"I shall if you promise not to repeat them," she replied, touched by the melancholy in his voice.

"I am sorry for uttering them, but I cannot promise as to their repetition. There are moments when the soul is full to repletion, when the heart is hungry for love. You are my only love, I—"

"Oh, hush, hush! I will not listen to such words. Leave me—"

"Are you ready, Kenyon? I shall walk as far as the Fernery with you," said Jack, as he, Helen and Mrs. Gwen came in through the open doorway.

A gust of wind from the lake blew out some of the lights and left the room in partial darkness, while Sir Keith stooped to replace some of the music which the wind had blown down, and so hid the passion and pallor of his face.

"Yes," he replied. "I think we shall soon have that storm. Good-night, Miss Wellington," he said, as he extended his hand.

In the semi-darkness, unnoticed, she avoided the extended hand, and said good-night, and turning, went upstairs with Helen Lester.

She bade her guest good-night, and went to her own room, locked the door, and stood silent in the strongest disquietude of her life.

She heard the two men leave the portico, accompanied by Nell Gwynne and her two favorite hounds. Her room overlooked the Fernery. She turned out the lights and seated herself in the deep bay window.

Silence and serenity brooded over the sleeping world; not a sound, save the drowsy tinkling of the sheep-bells in the glen, and the faint rumbling and murmuring of the many waters among the distant hills stirred the stillness. The air was oppressive, the spring breezes had rocked themselves to sleep in the heaving swells of the little lake and in the arms of the old oak trees. Dark clouds now drifted up from the westward and passed swiftly over a waning moon, causing alternate lights and shadows over the lake and ravine.

She watched the two men as they crossed the greensward to the brow of the hill overlooking the waters. Jack threw himself down on the ground, with his eyes on the distant sky-line, where a ruddy glow, midst the blackness of the night, told of a sleeping city, while his companion seated himself on a bench, with the two hounds at his feet and Nell Gwynne at his side.

She looked at the man she loved as he sat in the lights and shadows with bent head, and her heart longed and pleaded for him. It was a moment of weakness, one of those moments which he had told her would come, a moment of pain, so poignant that she seemed to lose the power to strive or struggle.

She could only feel. All through the days she had gone on her way serene; her pride and her work had sustained her, and it was only when the night was down that she let grief have way. She looked at the stars. "Were these the same stars that had looked down on her, on him, the night his hand had lain on hers, as they stood not far from where he now sat, and she had told him things which had been with her always, things which had come from Somewhere, and he had called her his Queen?" It all seemed so long, long ago, and now it all rose up in all the fullness of its past strength and mocked her past joys, as the carcanet of rubies had mocked the past joys of the sad Queen; and now he sat there, with a great barrier between them, a barrier which death only could sever. At the thought she shuddered, and, as there was no one to see her but the stars, she laid her head down on the cold casement of the window in an utter abandonment of grief and weakness.

When it is very cold the skies cannot rain.

From the monastery by the lake shore came faintly on her ears, like the sound of the heaving waves of their own troubled lake rolling on the Idlewylde shore, the echoes of the priest's words of prayer and praise, as they passed from the monastery to the little chapel to their midnight orisons.

Almost it seemed to her that her life stood still, while these holy men prayed for her. She herself could not pray. She could only live.

How long she remained thus she could not tell. The deep baying of the hounds and a short, sharp cry from Nell Gwynne, with the distant rumbling of thunder, awakened her from her lethargy, and, looking up, she saw that the world was one mass of darkness, save for the blinding flashes of lightning which illumined at intervals the mere and ravine and Idlewylde. The storm was yet distant and the flashes of light yet broad. She looked towards where the men had been, and in the light she saw the master of Idlewylde rise, pass his hand wearily over his brow and through his hair and then replace his hat, and, accompanied by Jack, walk over to the stile, where the groom had left his saddle-horse, Ali.

She saw him mount, bid her cousin good-night, and ride away into the darkness of the ravine, while Jack recrossed the sward towards the stables, and disappeared in an opposite direction.

"The storm will break before he reaches Idlewylde," she said, and almost before she had said it, from out the inky blackness in the west came a sound as of the rushing of many winds in another land. Nearer and nearer it circled and came on the darkness of the night, and then, with a suddenness almost appalling, it seemed to sweep and wrap the great timbers and eaves of Idlewylde in mighty embrace within the folds of its power, and then cast them from it in fury and rush to meet the mighty oaks of the ravine.

"He would be in their midst. Would their strength resist the maddened fury of the hurricane?" She sat spell-bound, power-less to act. Against the angry sky she saw the mighty oaks stand, towering towards, daringly defying the very thunder-bolts which heaven now seemed to open and send. Now they are caught in the arms of the blast; they laugh, they weep, they sigh, they bow, they bend, but they do not break; they lash, they leap, they writhe, they wriggle, and at last rear their proud heads aloft, like a thoroughbred which had been unjustly struck by the silken lashes of a corded whip, and the storm, as though now chastened and beaten in its maddened course, swept northward with sullen moanings down the river, and lost itself in the mountain fastnesses beyond.

But the tension of her nerves did not relax. The last echo of the hurricane had not yet died on the northern air when the heavens became one vein of forked fire, and the air filled with peals and crashes of thunder, which seemed to shake the earth to its centre.

From her room, whose windows looked over the Idlewylde, she watched the tempest, straining her eyes to discern his form, but the dense foliage hid him from view. The sight which she saw was weird exceedingly. Ever and anon, at the lightning's whim and play, the fishermen's huts nestling along the shore, the sleeping vil-lage, the cathedral's shining steeple, the Ursuline cloisters, the monastery by the lake shore with a beacon light in its turrets, flashed strangely into view, and again were swallowed up in the inky blackness of the night. The turrets and pinnacles and long lancet windows of Idlewylde came and went like some weird ball of fire or elusive will-o'-the-wisp, while the great Siberian pines, which flanked the mountain side, seemed to sigh and sob and tremble and bow their proud heads to those on the Idlewylde shore.

For a moment the storm seemed to cease and the earth to tremble, and then the heavens opened in one great vein of forked light, and the earth quivered from the forces of the mighty crash which followed.

Modena sprang erect with white face. In the moment's stillness she had seen big black Ali emerge from the woods to an open space under a great giant oak. Then had come the flash of light, blind-ing the horse and stunning the rider. She had seen Ali fall, rise, rear and then plunge, riderless.

For one short moment she remained spell-bound, and then in the next her mind began to work. The rain was now coming down in torrents, which seemed to somewhat clear the air and relax the tension of her nerves. "What should she do?" She had seen Jack go towards the city. It would be unwise to perhaps needlessly alarm the menservants of the house and furnish food for comment. She could but go herself. All her life she had been quick to decide and resolute in action. She went quietly and quickly to a closet near by and clad herself in a hooded waterproof, and then passed down a private stairway to the store-room, secured some stimulants, and let herself out through a side door to the western terrace. She paused but a moment to call to her side Nell Gwynne and her hounds, but no answer coming to her call she crossed the lawn to their kennels. They were empty. She knew they had not followed Jack, and her heart contracted with fear. "They must have gone with Keith," and she turned towards the ravine. At the stile she paused and listened. In the lull of the tempest of sound it seemed to her that she heard some other cry than that of the storm. "It is the distant baying of the hounds," she said. She paused yet as she heard a rustle and pant in the pathway, and in a moment Nell Gwynne leaped whining to her side. "What is it, Nell? Where is he?" she said, and the great dog looked with human intelligence into her face, cried loudly, and then turned and hurried down the pathway.

She followed, making her way as quickly as possible through and over the debris which lay piled in her path, down past the monastery to the edge of the bridge. Here her way was barred by Nell Gwynne.

She paused, waiting for another flash of light; and when it came she saw many of its timbers had been rent from their fastenings and were now floating down the swollen waters. The boat was on the other shore. There was but one other way—over the bridge, which lay some half mile away in the village. Her course this way would expose her to the view of the village, and would cause her to lose much time. "What shall I do, Nell Gwynne?" she asked, and at the sound of her voice the dog gave a short leap and bark. "Perhaps it is but the railings," she said. "I shall wait and see," but in the next glare a dark abyss yawned before her. "It must be but one board or Nell could not leap it. I shall see," and she knelt in the rain and darkness and groped beyond. Her hands rested on the firm planks on the other side. She passed over. "I can trust you, Nell," she said. "Go on," and the dog moved on before her footsteps, pausing and remaining firm at each riven plank. She knew that a false step meant the seething waters below, but she felt no fear. When the fissure meant more than she could span, she looked beyond and in the darkness in fancy saw the form of him she loved so well, and the vision gave her more than human power, and she passed on. "We shall soon be there. I see the stone stile on the other side," she said, her heart beating hard with gratitude to the faithful friend by her side.

"Ah, here we are! Where is he?" she cried, and Nell Gwynne left the main road for the open space where the great oak stood. The hounds leaped to her side. "He is dead!" she cried, as she saw his form senseless on the wet earth.

He lay still and lifeless on his back, with his face, dark-splendid even in its pallor, turned to the sky, one arm across his broad chest, the other outstretched on the greensward. His hat lay back, and his hair fell over his broad brow.

There was no sign of life. She knelt by his side with one great, silent cry and supplication, but she knew it was no moment for hesitation or lamentation, but for action. She passed her hand over his face. It was cold. A spasm of fear and despair contracted her heart. She quickly unbuttoned his great coat and laid her head to his breast. The beating of her own pulse was so great that for a moment she could distinguish nothing. Soon she thought she could discern a faint throb, and her heart swelled with unspeakable emotion. He lived, and all else was forgotten.

She sought the stimulants which she had brought, and with them she moistened his lips and bathed his brow and pulse, but there were yet no signs of life or warmth. "What shall I do?" she thought. "I cannot leave him here to seek help," and in her despair she stooped over, pressed her lips to his and breathed great breaths of life into him. In a moment he breathed faintly. She placed her arms beneath his head, raised it slightly, and again applied lightly the stimulants which she had brought. Very soon he sighed and shuddered, and then she spoke to him.

"Keith," she said, in a tense voice. "You have been stunned by the lightning. I saw you from the window and have come to help you. You must rouse yourself; there is danger here beneath this tree. The storm is not yet past. You must go home," and even as she yet spoke, great flashes of light, followed by greater darkness, blinded him from her sight, and her voice was faint in the many noises of the tempest, while the rain came down in torrents. "It is I, Modena."

He heard her voice, but knew not what she said. He tried to rise, but sank back in her arms.

"You must come to the open space, Keith," and centring all her latent will power and strength in her efforts, she forced him to the open space, and even as she did, out of the heavens came a bolt

cleaving the giant oak to the ground and javelling with darted
spikes and splinters the dark earth round. The terrific force of
the shock seemed to relax the tension within him, and soon he
roused himself to a knowledge of where he was and what had
happened.

"I have been stunned," he said, weakly. "Is it you, Modena?
How did you come? You are drenched. Take my great coat; you
will take cold."

"No," she replied, quickly. "I am strong; nothing can harm
me. You must go home. You have lain some time on the cold
ground. You are weak yet," she said, as she saw him quiver and
raise his hand to his brow.

"Rest on this fallen trunk for a moment. The rain has ceased.
The storm will soon be over. That bolt has cleared the air," and
she quivered and shuddered as she looked towards the riven oak.

He sat down on the fallen trunk to recover himself. The rain
had ceased, and the storm, having spent its passion, rolled slowly
northward, moaning and calling out of other lands, and leaving
the ravished woodlands to peace once more.

She stood by his side until he should recover somewhat, and
then she said, "You must go home now, Keith. It is almost morning. They will miss you. I shall remain here until I see you enter
your home."

"And what of you?" he said.

"You must not think of me. I am safe. I have the dogs. I
shall be in my room in a few minutes. Please go."

"And leave you here! I shall be better soon, and then I shall
take you home."

"It is almost morning. There is already a faint line of light in
the east. They must not know I have been out. Jack was away.
From my window I saw you fall. There was no other resource left
me. You are very weak. Please go," she said, her voice quivering
somewhat, the strain now beginning to tell upon her.

He rose slowly. The exertion brought him to a knowledge of
his bodily weakness, and he said, "Then come with me. My man
Matthews is old and trustworthy. He will take you home."

"No, no! No one must know," she pleaded. They were losing
much time. She realized she must compromise with him, so she
said: "The monastery chapel is close by. Father Jacques is cross-
ing the river to matins. I see the light at the prow of his boat.
Come and remain there until you see a light in my window. You
are very weak. Father Jacques can be trusted. He will take
you home."

He turned and walked with her to the river's edge. Here their path divided, one leading to the bridge, the other to the chapel.

"I want to thank you for saving my life. Will you take my hand now?" he said.

She could not do so. She hadn't strength to do so. She wanted to tell him what the world had seemed when she had thought him dead, and what it had seemed when she knew he lived, but she could only say: "It is only a step to the chapel. Father Jacques is mooring his boat. You are safe now. Good-bye," and she passed from him in the pallid light of the risen day.

Soon she reached the bridge. In the grey light the black fissures yawned before her, and she shuddered and turned aside to the boat.

She had now no strength to brave their danger.

In a few minutes she was in her own room. In a moment a light burned in her window, as Ovid's Hero's had burned for her Leander. The lantern from the monastery chapel swung thrice, and she knew that all was well.

She extinguished her light, had yet enough strength and presence of mind to divest herself of her wet garments, place them away, and put on a warm robe, and then she threw herself on her bed in a mental and bodily exhaustion which was almost a prostration.

It was now four of the clock in the morning of a beautiful June day.

CHAPTER XXXV.

It was Modena's custom to arise at six. Her maids came to her at that hour, but she bade them draw the blinds and go away. Her head ached and fever burned on her brow. But on their departure she could neither rest nor sleep. If she knew that he were now uninjured and well, she could rest, but she would have to wait until some stray tidings would tell her how he was. If he lived and were well she would never again murmur or regret. "We do not realize or appreciate our blessings until their loss is threatened. I have been dowered with all that this world can give, and because of one affliction I have murmured. Have I murmured? If not, at least my heart has been hard. Has it been hard? At least it has ached. This I cannot help, but thoughts of him I must not harbor. If I knew he were well I think I could rest," she said again to herself, suffering greatly in the confusion of a fevered brain.

At nine she arose and, putting on a dressing-robe, went to her boudoir. From its window she viewed the results of the night's tempest. Seldom, if ever, had such a storm visited her lands. Wherever her eyes rested were visible great ravages of the storm, and the beauty and serenity of the June morning threw out in greater contrast the disorder and confusion of disordered nature.

The sun was shining brightly. The early roses were all aglow. The sunbeams were dancing on the blue surface of the water. The grass was green as emerald. The leaves on the trees had swelled and were pulsing with life. The orchard ground was covered with millions of blossoms. Myriads of song-birds sang in the woods. But in the songs of the birds she thought she could distinguish a faint tinge of lament. Their nests had been many, their young had been more, and many of them were now no more. Already she could see many of the birds gathering straws and soft wool to replace what nature had given and what nature had taken so ruthlessly away.

Out on the flat-lands, which had escaped the severity of the storm, the men were busy with their seeding and planting. Down by the lake shore the monastery stood, serene in the midst of the desolation around. The monks were at work among the ruins. She looked towards the ravine. Many trees, which had braved the battle of the winds for centuries, now stood white-listed or lay prostrate upon the ground. At the sight her heart was touched, as at the loss of something personal. The broken bridge stood out distinct in the clear sunlight, and she shuddered.

Farther on, in the open space, the great oak lay riven, and for a moment she covered her eyes to hide it from view. When she looked again her eyes sought Idlewylde, but it told her nothing.

She touched a bell by her side.

" Will you ask my cousin to come to me?" she said to the woman who came in response to her call.

Soon her cousin was by her side. He was startled when he saw how she looked, but he refrained from making any comment.

" It was a terrible storm," she said to him, when he had greeted her. " It unnerved me, and my head aches this morning. I think I shall remain in my room and rest for the day. Have you been out over the lands? Is the damage great? Is there any loss of life?"

" Yes, I have been out. No loss of life has been reported, but the damage to property is great."

He wondered at the great change which came over her face.
"The lower lands escaped the severity of the storm."

"Yes, I see the men at work. It seems to have spent its force
on Idlewylde and the ravine."

"Yes. I was with the monks. Keith saw me and came down.
The new wing which he has been adding to Idlewylde has been
demolished. I left him looking at the bridge. He says the storm
broke in all its fury as I left him last night. I suppose he is
thinking, a few minutes later and the bridge would have meant a
broken neck. He looks this morning as if something had been
broken."

"Is he not well? I thought he looked well last night."

"Oh, yes, I suppose he is well, but he looked pale, weary,
exhausted. Will you return to the city soon?"

"The children's fete is to-morrow evening. I shall go to the
city Thursday morning. Will you ask Helen if she will attend
the rehearsals to-day?"

"Shall I give orders regarding the removal of the wreckage?"

"Can you remain here to-day?"

"If I can be of any service to you."

"If you will. Yes, see that everything is removed. What has
been destroyed must be rebuilt. Have the fishermen and cottagers
suffered much? Is their personal loss great?"

"A little loss is a great loss to them. Yes, they have suffered
much."

"How can one reach them?"

"I would suggest through Father Jacques. It is easy to be
generous; to be just is much more difficult. He is a just and wise
man. In his hands charity will serve its proper purpose."

The mistress of Fernwylde rose and went to a cabinet near by,
and from one of its drawers drew forth her cheque book, and after
affixing her signature to some, returned to her cousin's side.

"I have left them blank. He may fill in the required amount.
Helen will be engaged with the children until evening. She will
excuse me, and I shall rest," she said, as her cousin left her.

She returned to her room, and in a few minutes her heavy lids
fell over her eyes, and her exhaustion soon lulled her into the
indifference of slumber. She slept well and long, awakening at
five in the afternoon. She arose refreshed and strengthened, and
soon afterwards resumed her place among her household.

The following day she spent with her cousin on her farms and
among her tenants, receiving information, inspecting the ruins,
giving orders and bringing order out of confusion.

25

In the evening she attended the children's fete. Sir Keith, with some of the magnates of the village, was there, but he did not approach her, nor did she speak to him during the entire evening.

The following morning she returned to the city.

Keith Kenyon had said of her that her politics was her religion. Religion is like Merlin's chair; to dwell in it is to lose oneself, and, like Sir Galahad, by losing oneself, find oneself.

On her return to the city her religion or her politics served its highest purpose—that of taking her out of herself and of causing her to enter into the hearts of the people for a short time.

There was trouble in the labor world.

The leaders of the labor party had long been agitating for many matters of much-needed reform, and some months previous had availed themselves of this propitious time to demand their rights and justice, and had sought the intervention and assistance of some of the leading members of the government.

Fair promises had been given, but as no action had yet been taken to redress their wrongs, the laborers had now ceased work. The doors were guarded, and the mob had become troublesome. All night long the alleys and avenues and public parks were one seething mass of embittered humanity. All places of business were closed, the windows shuttered and barred, and trade for the time paralyzed.

Verona Kenyon had sent out invitations for a two weeks' visit to Idlewylde, to meet a party then staying at Rideau Hall, but the mistress of Apsley House had remained in the city, an impassive eye-witness of the turbulent scenes around her.

During her week's sojourn in the city her mind was awakened to many truths. The cruel contrasts, the rank injustices, the heartrending privations with which she came in contact, made an impression upon her mind which never afterwards left her during all her life. At Fernwylde no one was ever destitute. She had never been so near to helpless, human misery before.

Mrs. Cecil, the Lady Greta and many of her intimate friends had said to her, " With your mixture of cupatrid and St. Simon spirit, you are an anomaly," but during the week her insight into many matters had had the tendency to make her wholly a St. Simon.

" But it would be of no avail to speak to them," she said. " To put a little learning on their lips would only be putting blood-red banners in their hands. One can only work any radical and permanent change through one's own order," she said, " and at the present time one can only do the little which lies within one's power." And so she went amongst them. She did what she could to relieve their present distress, but to her it seemed so little in comparison with the mighty forces which were ever at work.

The words, which her father had said during troubles of his own, " They have no grievances; they have only gone out in sympathy. Where will it end?" she knew did not refer to his own trouble but to the world at large. But what irritated her most now was their inability to deal with many questions which in future years would cause great trouble.

In her perplexity she spoke to her father. She saw that he, too, was much worried. He, too, realized the justice of the laborers' demands, and was keenly sensitive to the need for reform.

" Reform must come from us," he said to his daughter, when she spoke to him.

" But we don't think nor care. We are careless, cruel, unkind. Pleasure and gold are our only gods. Oh, yes, we have our missionaries and our charity balls and our charity bazaars. Some of us are in earnest, but more are merely actuated by the desire to be ' in it.' And of what avail are our little efforts. It is like unto the wiping of the mouth of a volcano with a lace handkerchief while the lava seethes and boils within its bowels, or the drying up of a cough while the germs feed on the lungs of life. The true physician will reach and remove the source of the disease. Then health depends upon nature and the patient. There is disease here. Why not remove it?"

" All you say is true, but one can do so little. We want more men of thought. Keith seems apathetic of late," he was going to say, and then he checked himself and said, " I sincerely wish Monteith would take more interest in the matter."

" He has the ideas and the ideals, but he lacks adaptability, ambition. He must become more practical and patriotic. I shall speak to him and tell him so," said his daughter; and so, when they went down to Fernwylde, when the disturbance had been allayed, she spoke to her betrothed.

" It is not woman's work. Why do you bother about it? Your estates are model ones. You have granted co-operation to the greatest extent possible. One's duty in life is to keep one's own doorstep clean. Yours is spotless. Example is as contagious as smallpox. You have everything this world can give. Why don't you live and enjoy it? Of course, if you insist I shall do it to please you, but the life is not congenial," he had said to her, as a party of them left the house to join the Idlewylde party at an illumination on the lake.

She was irritated, almost angered.

"To look at life so! What does he think we are? Sloths? Drones? How selfish," she thought, warmly, to herself, but she replied, with calmness and composure, "Women were made to be ministering angels to the world. Their capacity for suffering incites them to be the instigators of their—their friends to make the world better. We are responsible for our moments and our talents. A woman can only work through her—her—" "husband," she was about to say, but she hesitated and said, "friends," and then she continued, her manner somewhat disturbed, "I could never marry any man who had not the interest of the people at heart. For some time, Carlton, I have been thinking we are not congenial to each other. I have long been intending to speak to you about it. I was led into this before I knew its meaning. I think it is best that we should part," and she faltered, seeing the great look of pain on his face.

It had come to it. He was not so much surprised. He had almost expected it. He had loved her so, but he had seen it coming, and was almost prepared for it.

"But I love you so," he cried, realizing that the best part of his life had slipped from him, and that his hopes had vanished as suddenly as a ship which sinks in the dead of night. "Cannot I make my love so great that you will forget all else?" he asked, with great humility.

"I am afraid not, dear," she said, gently. "My decision is not from impulse. I have thought long and earnestly over the matter. I am sorry to give you pain, but I am afraid it cannot be. It must be for the best. There are others so much better suited to you than I am. They will make you happier than I can."

"Stop, don't say so! Spare me that. Do you realize what it means to me? Oh, Modena!" he cried, his eyes darkening with pain.

It hurt her to say what she had said. He was dear to her through many memories, and she would not willingly pain him. But she could not marry him, and she thought it best to make him understand so, now that the subject had been opened.

"It must be, Carlton. Do not think me without feeling, or unkind. I feel it very much, but I cannot help it. One cannot love where one will," she said, and for some moments they walked on in silence.

"Would you love me, if you could?" he asked her, with a sudden abruptness, the question prompted by a fear and doubt which had come to him for the first time.

She couldn't reply, and her silence told him that it was as he had feared and doubted.

"Do not let us part in anger," she said. "The world need never know why our relations have been severed. Let us yet be friends."

"I cannot say. I must think," he faltered.

"There is Marion; she is alone. Go to her; I must join the others," and she walked slowly away and joined Sir Colin and Mrs. Cecil.

Almost mechanically he did what she had ordered him to do. He was depressed and dejected. Life had changed from sunshine to darkness, from hope to apathy, from substance to shadow.

But yet, despite the pain there was a certain sense of relief in his freedom. He had loved her, but she had seemed so far away from him. She had left his heart lonely and cold.

He turned with a little pique and a forlorn smile to Marion.

"Why are you alone?" he said to her, as he joined her in the wooded walk.

"One is never alone when one is with one's thoughts. One would not care to admit that one was lonely with one's own mind as a companion," she replied, her countenance lighting up at his presence.

"Then our happiness depends upon nature; what has nature been telling you to make you look so happy?" he asked, brightening under her influence.

"On such a night as this, and amid such surroundings, one is incapable of expressing one's thoughts in words. One feels they should be embodied in music, and yet they are too fleeting, too visionary to be embodied at all. They can only be felt and enjoyed," she said, with that dreamy look which was so instinct within her.

"I know what you mean," he replied, as he heard his own sentiments voiced. "For the power to express what he felt, portray what he saw on a night like this, Othmar would have given all his millions of gold. We cannot help those vague longings. To me it has always been an assurance of something within us which has come from a fairer realm and is ever longing and striving to return. We miss something in life, what it is we cannot tell. When we hear a poem, see a picture, listen to a song, or when one is alone with the beauties and grandeurs of nature, one catches glimpses of the purer life one so longs for," he continued, as the faint, far-away sound of many cataracts fell on his ear, and the moon swam high over the Idlewylde, making it shimmer in the gloom, and the church spires glisten in the distance. "But it does not last, and one grows weary of the dross of it all," he said, giving vent to his personal feelings.

Marion's dreamy eyes deepened and brightened at hearing thoughts and feelings which she had deemed too strange for any kindred sympathy shared by others.

She was under the charm of nature in its most seductive and suggestive mood, that charm, voluptuous, yet poetic, which no artistic nature can resist. She had always loved to dwell with the thoughts of all those men who had lived and were now dead and gone, and on nights like this, " When the moors were dark beneath the moon," vague creations would fill her mind, but the meagreness and mediocrity of her productions saddened her when she thought of the beauty and the force of those whom she had studied and whom she had loved.

"You should not grieve over your life. It has been a noble one," she replied, softly, to her companion, as she watched a night-hawk circling over the Idlewylde.

"But I do not care for it. I have no affinity for it whatever."

"You would prefer the life of the poet or philosopher to that of the statesman?"

"No, but I would prefer a life of action based upon thought. But that is an utter impossibility. This age will not permit it. Other ages would, but not this. Our ancestors lived quiet, happy, peaceful lives. Why is it?" asked he, as he continued to gaze at the Idlewylde, as it flowed on in the clear, silver light, through rich meadows, narrowing into a woody ravine, and at the Fernery dimly outlined in the distance, while all around a perfect serenity enveloped them, save for the whir and hoarse croak of some north-ern-bound fowl and the singing of the water-frogs in the air. "How is it we have lost our fathers' simple content and power to enjoy? Why do we want all this stir and bustle and tittle-tattle in order to make existence endurable? This cancer of civilization and centralization is eating the heart and nerves out of man. What the modern world wants are physicians for sick souls and weary spirits," he said, as his eyes gazed into the gloom.

"You are depressed to-night. What is the matter with you?" asked his companion, looking up at him.

"Matter! Everything! Modena wants me to enter public life," he said, evasively.

"Altruism is the physician you have been seeking. Your country needs you. If you wish to please her, now is your opportunity."

"But I cannot please her any more. She has ceased caring for me."

" Ceased caring for you!" exclaimed his companion, as some others passed them by.

His heart was too much at war within him to notice the glad surprise in his companion's voice, or to reply further, and he remained silent. Soon they reached the Idlewylde party. After greeting their host and hostess and their guests, he led his companion to a seat under an overhanging cedar. From where he sat he could see the mistress of Fernwylde. " Could he give her up so easily? Would he yet enter the fray and make a name for himself and hold her to him?" She had said, " It must be a man who loves the people whom I shall marry," and unconsciously his eyes followed Keith Kenyon, and he sighed.

" How blind I have been. No, it can never be now! It is now too late! It will have to be someone else. A new nature will have to win her now. Why did I not see it before? Why not? Why not?" he cried to himself, as he watched her as she moved about with the Lady Greta and an English lord.

It was the first time she had been in Sir Keith's presence since they had parted at the bridge at the grey dawn of day. He had remained at Idlewylde until he had regained his strength, and then had gone about his duties as usual. At the chief's request he had gone west with the English party for several weeks. He had remained with them and represented his chief in other cities as they passed through, and on their return had taken them to Idlewylde. The party had been charmed. His presence always seemed to bring peace, harmony and vitality into any assembly. Never before had he been so popular or courted as he was now, the host of a great house and a great party. His grace of manner, his polish, his deference and respect to people, his broad and charitable view of men and things which invariably mark a gentleman, these all were his, and were quick to be acknowledged by the men of his party; while his easy grace, the winning tact with which nature had endowed him, his mixture of seeming nonchalance and deep instinct of sincerity, and the great beauty of his person enhanced him in the sight of all women. The world knew that he cared not for his wife, and the world of women were not slow in taking advantage of this fact, and accordingly were never loth in approaching him, but although he was invariably gallant and courteous and paid tribute where homage was due, yet they one and all felt they never really entered his life. Instinctively they knew that, in so far as love touched his life, his heart was as a stone to all women save one. His wife alone was the only woman who refused to realize this. So blind is love and egotism.

He had made extensive preparations for his guests' visit to Idlewylde. He had filled the old halls with music and artists and actors. He had provided them with hunting and out-door sports, and not for many years had Idlewylde been so gay. Flags and banners flew from keep and tree-top. Pavilions dotted the grounds, little tents nestled along the shore, while canoes continually plied up and down the waters to the city and return. He had military bands in attendance, and the air was full of festivity and joyousness, but until the present moment the party to him had seemed soulless. He knew it was perfect, but to him it had seemed as cold and lifeless as the white marble had seemed to Pygmalion.

But with her advent everything had changed. The music meant what it said, the moonlight was magic, the myriads of lights in the canoes on the lake, flitting like will-o'-the-wisps, now in and now out among the cedars and pines fringing the shore, at once ceased to be "wandering fires lost in the quagmire." The very atmosphere was pulsing with a new life.

She had gone and spoken to their hostess and his Excellency's wife and her guests, and had then joined the others, but he had not approached her.

He had noticed his wife's mood change. For some few weeks his wife had been passively happy. She had been a great lady at the head of a great party and a great house, courted and deferred to by all. The world had been at her feet. With the advent of the mistress of Fernwylde all things seemed to change. Her prestige seemed to fade into the background.

"Why is it she makes one feel so small even in one's own home, on one's own ground?" she mentally exclaimed, as she saw the best of her people gradually draw towards the mistress of Fernwylde. "My own people following her here—here, under my very eyes," she said, in growing anger, and again she at once began to assert her rights as the wife of Keith Kenyon, and the mistress of Fernwylde began to feel them.

Modena had heard of the growing popularity of Lady Kenyon, and, being of a magnanimous nature, she had been pleased that it was so. The knowledge had failed to arouse any jealous sentiment within her breast, but when Verona's rights as the wife of Keith Kenyon began to grow in upon her, this knowledge had within it the power to touch chords in her nature which had never been touched before.

She had not been long at Idlewylde before she felt that she was between two fires. She felt Verona's eyes dwell upon her with "Envy, eldest born of hell," and she noticed that several times their host withdrew himself from the others and made his way to where she was alone for the moment.

To Verona's displeasure she was seemingly utterly indifferent, and her host she avoided, and gave herself up to where the lights were the brightest and the people the most joyous. If he would receive any kindness from her it would be before the public gaze of her whole world.

The evening had been ideal, the fireworks beautiful, the illuminations magnificent. Each of the canoes had worn the colors of a lady, and the rivalries had been keen. Before entering the pavilion for refreshments it had fallen to the lot of their host to award the prizes and choose the Queen of the Regatta.

The canoes had drawn up in a semicircle, a dozen deep at the entrance to the grounds. A canopied platform, with a dais for the Queen, had been erected at one end of the pavilion, almost touching the water's edge. A band was stationed at the other, while side doors led into the supper tents.

The guests had repaired to the amphitheatre of the pavilion, when Sir Keith, accompanied by a herald of trumpets and pages bearing the prizes, entered and made the tour of the pavilion, then paused before the wearers of the colors.

Modena had avoided him all evening. He understood her motives. It was his whole world which was gathered here. An impulse and a desire came to him to render unto her, in the presence of his world, the homage of a knight to his queen.

A great fear seized her that he was going to do so.

The stillness was intense; the music had ceased; hundreds of faces she knew best in the world looked down into the arena; the occupants of the canoes leaned out on their paddles and peered in from the darkness. The spectators, instinctively aware of some personal undercurrent, drew their breath almost with oppression, anxiously awaiting, yet dreading, what was to come.

He had almost done so, when his wife, Mark-like, approached from behind and begged of him the honor of giving the laurel wreath to his choice, and he named the Lady Greta; and then the band burst into applause and there was commotion everywhere, while their host turned, ascended the steps, and asked permission to take the mistress of Fernwylde out to supper.

"I have promised Sir Colin and the Lady Greta," she replied, without meeting his gaze.

"Sir Colin may take the Lady Greta. Come with me."

The Lady Greta stood by their side. "Pardon me! But you have the greatest faculty of arranging things to gratify your own wishes. Sometimes someone else has something to say in those matters. Modena may go with Sir Colin. I am the Queen, you are my Knight. I shall go into supper with you," said the Lady Greta, who beneath her child-like innocence possessed the wisdom of a woman of the world, and at the present time she did not think it very wise of Sir Keith to make his attentions to the mistress of Apsley House either marked or conspicuous.

Sir Keith noticed the intonation.

"If my Lady call me, I must obey," he said, as he turned with the Lady Greta.

"I am sorry to intrude myself upon you against your will or wishes, but sometimes it is necessary."

"When one's duty and one's pleasure point the same way, it is easy to follow them in action," he smiled.

"That is why you were so anxious to take in Modena! You have a funny reading of duty."

"I meant you, and even if I did mean Modena, she is my honored guest and my dearest friend."

"Your reading of friendship is as funny as your reading of duty. You know she has severed her relations with Carlton Monteith. She is going to marry Sir Colin. Leave her alone," she said, as abruptly as was her nature impulsive.

He drew a quick breath as if he had been struck a blow, and paused, gazing at his companion.

For a moment she was afraid that she had wounded him. Merely by accident had she learned of Carlton Monteith's dismissal, and her quick intuition had told her that Sir Colin had within him much that would appeal to and please the mistress of Fernwylde as never Carlton Monteith had done. The Lady Greta's was a loyal heart, and she feared that in time Sir Colin might win.

It was only her way of venting her resentment.

"Come in. I am hungry," she said, and he drew himself together and took her to the table which had been prepared for their Excellencies and the English party.

From where he sat he could see Sir Colin as he led his companion to a seat in the centre of the room. But after the first glance he did not again look that way. A new fear had entered his heart, the strongest fear he had felt in all the long years of his life.

Modena returned to Fernwylde that same night. The two following days she spent at intervals at Idlewylde, and returned home the third day. In a few days the party were to become her guests for a week's time.

She was glad of the next day's quietness. In the forenoon she rested and in the afternoon went for a long walk over her lands. Her mental strain during the labor trouble and the ordeal to which she had been subjected during her two days' sojourn under Verona Kenyon's roof, had once more disturbed the even tenor of her life.

Someone has very aptly said there is no loss from which one cannot recover except it be the loss of one's illusions. During the labor trouble she had become conscious of many weaknesses, many insincerities, many injustices, much inability in their administration, and the knowledge had led her to see that things were not as she had always thought them to be. It was only another of the disillusions which lead to the realities of life, but somehow they had now the power to chill her enthusiasm and discourage her somewhat. Despite her desire and will to the contrary, there were now many interests and people and things and beliefs which had been all in all in the world to her, and which had filled her life with sanguine enthusiasm, but which were now gradually becoming paler and losing their power to interest and please her. She was becoming conscious of a loss within her life as deep and regrettable as the loss of a loved one. She regretted exceedingly that it was so, but she could not help it.

During her stay at Idlewylde, Verona Kenyon's rights as his wife had been brought home so forcibly to her that she was humiliated in her own sight for even allowing her mind to wander his way. Carlton Monteith had gone out of her life. As yet she had not seriously thought of Sir Colin, and her life to-day for the first time seemed to have within it a great void.

She had always loved Fernwylde, but to-day its magnificent extent and beauty seemed to mock her drooping spirits; its associations only served to deepen her dejection.

"Life is not complete without love! Mine is dead, a living death, a bitter sweetness, a sweet bitterness. It is as the perfume of dead roses. No one can ever take his place," she thought, as the loss of his love came home to her, leaving her, like Lucille, on her way onward and upward, with a sense of "Weird desolation, in her self-perceived isolation of soul."

There is no sorrow, no matter how poignant, which time and nature fails to mitigate or make endurable. The little pleasures, the obligations and environments of everyday life, all tend to wean the afflicted away from their affliction. But such moments as these, when great regret assails one, for the joys which were theirs, for the love which has been lost, for the ideals which have vanished, such moments as these renew the poignant suffering and dejection, and seem to tinge the after life with sadness and lack of interest and warmth, and rob life of its power to care, to accomplish, to enjoy.

She sat down on a fallen tree, with Nell Gwynne at her feet, and as she sat there among the russet leaves and leafless vines, a silent, unexpressed regret overcame her, a regret for what might have been. She leaned her head in her hand as her arm rested on the fallen trunk of a tree.

As she sat thus the loud clarion call from a hunting-horn fell upon her ears. The Idlewylde party had spent the day hunting, and were now stragglingly returning home. She could see them as they wound their way over the clear, rippling stream, down by the lake and up the ravine, past the old Fernery and on through the elms.

Nell Gwynne was by her side. She had also seen them. She arose and called loudly for Cavall and Ion. Her cry attracted the attention of the hounds, and they came towards her with great leaps and deep bayings.

The noise startled a fox concealed in the green foliage by her side. Slyly and swiftly the silver-grey fox stole in and out of the sylvan glades, over the brownsward, stopped and sniffed the air with startled nostrils and eyes gleaming, and then crouched in a coppice close to where Modena was seated.

The hounds were between it and its home. With great leaps and bounds they quickly approached the place, then paused, sniffed the air, and hoarsely bayed to the hunters.

With one wild bound past Modena, the victim fled from its pursuers.

Sir Keith, who led the chase, was the first to see it. He raised his gun and took steady aim at the game.

"For God's sake stop, Kenyon! There is Modena!" cried Sir Colin Campbell, in intense excitement, as he sprang forward and knocked the gun upward.

As Sir Keith saw the close proximity of the mistress of the place he dropped his gun to the ground in consternation, while the game doubled away in an opposite direction and was bagged by Jack.

When the men reached her she noticed the extreme pallor of Sir Keith's face, but he did not speak.

"This would remind one of the famous White Lady in German Fairyland, when her knight came to carry off the lady he loved," said the English lord, who had been in the rear and had not seen or known of the danger.

"Kenyon was about to carry her off in a rather barbaric way," said Sir Colin. "He had that fox sure, Jack, but your cousin was so near he was afraid of startling her day-dreams."

"You were not always so considerate of her day-dreams," muttered Jack (who had noticed his cousin's languor of late) to his friend, as they walked back together to the parting of their ways. His friend did not answer, but in silence went his way with his guests to Idlewylde.

CHAPTER XXXVI

MODENA returned home to Fernwylde, and a few hours later was forced to receive the mistress of Idlewylde and her house guests. Her Fernwylde parties had always represented to her all that was simple, homelike and intimate. But the advent of Lady Kenyon into the circle seemed to bring with it a disquieting element, as one false note brings discord into the harmony of a perfect piece of music. The week following was the most trying of her life.

That "ill weeds grow apace," is a wise old saw, never truer than of jealous, vindictive and suspicious passions and desires. The mistress of Fernwylde had always been aware of Verona's passive dislike for herself, and she felt that this dislike was now growing into an active, almost morbid, hatred, and she knew that her own mortification, humiliation or dethronement would be the sweetest triumph for one of whose latent envy and jealousy she had long been conscious. She said nothing, however, but went her way, preserving to her guest, so far as it lay in her power to do so, a perfect courtesy of manner.

She was a just woman, and she knew that Keith Kenyon had of his own free will made Verona his wife. As his wife, both homage and respect were due to her, and these she in justice tried to render unto her.

But such a course of conduct had in it only the power to increase Verona's vindictiveness. It had only in it the power to make her feel as she had felt at Idlewylde, and it robbed her of the joys of reprisal. "She is so great in herself that she cares not for the opinion or conduct of the whole world," she said in bitter passion to herself, when she was brought to a realization that all her many acts of assumption were devoid of fruit. "One can only reach her through Keith," she was forced to admit, and she began to subject her hostess to a series of petty annoyances—a word of endearment to him, an adoring look, a familiar touch of the hand; a command when in his presence, or in his absence a reference to his tenderness and solicitude for her, an expressed longing for his company—all of which had within them the power to bring the warmth to the face of the mistress of Fernwylde; and it was this feeling which alone had the power to irritate Modena.

She was well aware of the insincerity, the lack of truth, the assumption, which lay beneath each word and act, but yet nature had endowed Verona with such a supreme faculty of assumption and of the power to convey to others that things were in reality what she portrayed them to be, that one was forced to believe even while one's reason and one's knowledge were cognizant of the falsities of the situation. Yet so supreme was her egotism that in her own sight her conduct became the convictions of honesty, and had in them the power to make others believe in their honesty. It was Verona's ability to make people believe in her deception which had in it the power, more than anything else, to arouse within Modena the evil which is inherent in all human nature, but which, through inherited nobility of disposition, great self-knowledge and strong purity of motive, had never before become dominant in hers.

It was not jealousy which she felt. Jealousy was as foreign to her nature as lament to the Spartans. Hers would not have been love or self-knowledge had she admitted her dethronement possible. "No one can be to him what I am. No one can be anything to him while I live." She knew this, but yet, knowing it, Verona's little acts at times aroused within her a desire to retort or retaliate. "How is it she has the faculty of arousing one's lower instincts? Modena would sometimes ask herself, in the solitude of the few moments which now and again were allowed to her. "She arouses all the hatred within one, and hatred lowers one to her level. One should not care for these mere externals of life, and yet she makes one care." But, although she cared, she said little; she held herself well in reserve, and continued to treat Verona with cold courtesy, and Sir Keith she avoided as much as it was possible to do.

These mere externals of life were much to her—much more to her than to most women—but she was too great a woman to allow any of these to come between him and her. A smaller woman might have done so, but not she. Whether or not he had done wrong in marrying Verona she did not know, but the evil was done and the act irrevocable, and since it was done its results could only be borne in dignity and silence. "He sees them and can say nothing;" and she did justice to the motives actuating his conduct.

But if he were an impassive eye-w ness to his wife's conduct, it was because his code of honor bade him be so. There were times, however, when he was not wholly impassive. There were times when the lines of his brow grew deep, and the sterner, colder, harsher look came upon his face—the look which had daunted many brave, bold men, and which his wife was already beginning to know and fear.

It was at such times as these that Modena feared him. She knew him well, and knew that beneath the reserve of his temperament, his courteous and habitual grace, his easy nonchalance, there dwelt a code of honor, a sternness of justice, and an innate hatred of all things ignoble, which when roused were apt to rule with an iron will and an ungloved hand. She valued public opinion, and she did not wish to be even distantly the cause of any "scene." At such times she avoided him.

So unpleasant, annoying and humiliating had the situation become to her that she almost decided that at the end of the week, when the party had made their departure, she would act upon her cousin's advice and go away for some time.

But she could not make up her mind wholly, to do so. Although she was wholly her own mistress, far more so than most women, there were some things she could not do. To leave her homes and her country at the present time seemed one of these. To do so seemed to her a form of cowardice, and cowardice was an impossibility to her nature. Her own personality was dear to her, and she was aware that one's personality depends to a great extent upon the rightful conceptions of the principles underlying the actions of life, and upon the positive and definite hold one has taken upon life in some particular place. She knew that the basis of all things must rest upon the home life. It is these facts which have been the basis of English social life. It is these facts which make one feel, when in England, that one is near the very centre of things, and it is this feeling which is the lodestar of democracy and republicanism in their higher moods.

Modena was intensely English in her conception of life. Her hold on life was in her own home, in her country and its people. They were the integral part of herself. She had within her the feeling of the Parisian that all outside one's own asphalt was darkness. Instinct within her was a patriotism and a hope similar to that which the Greek in olden times had within him for the land of the Hellenes. To become a wanderer now was to relinquish her hold on the very centre of life. Her duties demanded her presence in her own home. "Why should I break up my life because of one woman's aversion towards me? I am sufficient unto myself, and will live my own life. I cannot see why I should leave my home because others interfere in my life," so she told herself at the times when reason and justice held sway, and at the times when Verona Kenyon failed to stir within her the baser leaven of human nature.

She would be glad when the week was over and life had once more resumed its simpler and plainer duties, which ever filled her hours when she was with her own people and her own lands.

It was the last day but one of their stay. Despite the many things which had disturbed her peace of mind she had brought all her latent powers to the fore, and, ably assisted by Helen Lester and Mrs. Cecil, had succeeded in making the week a brilliant one. If the week at Idlewylde had been a chapter from Versailles, then the week at Fernwylde was its sequel, with the more subtle and seductive air of Coppet and Ferney as its atmosphere.

Their Excellencies and their guests had been delighted. The English nobility had lingered, loth to leave, charmed with the intellect and simple splendor and pastimes of the circle, and with its surroundings.

The Lady Greta had been in her element. She had had hair-breadth escapes while following the hounds. She had succeeded in capturing a wild lynx. She had shot the falls, masqueraded in Indian costume, ridden, golfed, danced and flirted to her heart's content, and through it all had persisted in wearing her crown of laurel.

It was now late in the afternoon of the early autumn day. They were seated in groups under the great cedars of the lawn. Some of the men were returning from the hunt. Others had returned, and were within changing their clothes before appearing in the presence of the ladies.

Carlton Monteith had returned to the city. It had now become known that her relations with him were severed. The world was not surprised. It was whispered that there was a new light in Sir Colin Campbell's eyes, and the world was much interested.

The Lady Greta sat on a low ottoman, a little apart from the others, at the feet of her hostess. Her arms rested on Modena's knees, her head was in her hands. She had been silent, her eyes dwelling upon Sir Colin as he conversed with one of his country-women.

After some time Lady Greta withdrew her eyes, took from her head her wreath of laurel, and slowly began rearranging its leaves. "They're fading," she said regretfully; "but they have served me well. For one whole week I have kept him by my side. Have you ever read the Italian tale of the evil eye? By keeping him by my side I have foiled the evil eye. I shall press these leaves and leave them as a memento to you, as the diamond the knight went in quest of for his lady-love," she said to Modena.

"Why to me? Why don't you take them with you to remind you of past glories, and of the fealty of a loyal love? You said once you loved your knight. Would you give away his crown?"

"Stolen fruit is sweet, you know, but when it has lost its flavor I always make a point of returning it to its rightful owner. They were meant for you. They weren't meant for me. That is why they have faded. Had you received them they would have remained green forever. You knew all this time that he wanted you to have them. My heart stood still when he paused before you. I thought he was going to give you them. I hated him when he gave them to me. I wanted to tell him he was a coward, he cared for what the world would say. You once said your backgrounds were all dull greys. For the moment it almost seemed that your background was black as the night without, and in the foreground he was writing something with letters of blood. Ugh!" and the Lady Greta shuddered. "Don't you want these?" she continued. "But perhaps you don't want to keep faded leaves around? They tell tales, and Sir Colin might see them, and if he saw them he might turn into Psyche's lamp. I burn all my faded leaves and use the ashes to fertilize the next ones."

"And do you never find any leaves you cannot burn?" asked her hostess, very quietly.

"Oh, the unburnable ones! Oh, yes, but we do not speak of these! You're smiling. You think I should not speak of them now, but there are times when one becomes tired of keeping one's heart locked up, and one would rather give it to daws to peck at than be so lonely. Misery likes company. But you know to others I do not speak of *the* leaves. They are locked away from the common light of day. They have been dipped in some elixir and remain evergreen. Only one of those is given in each one's life."

"You have so many, how can you tell which is the evergreen one?"

26

"Oh, one can easily tell that. Something inside tells one so at once—the ego, I guess! They are only half leaves, and they fit perfectly into the other ego's half leaves and make a perfect whole. But I have always thought they were a perfect whole somewhere else, and got broken somehow. Doesn't your Plato, about whom you are always talking, say so? But we do not speak of those leaves—we feel them."

"And if the one half leaf is lost somewhere, or wanders off to another world and one doesn't find one's complement, what then?"

"Oh, one will sometime. If not here one will somewhere else. If you have ever truly loved you know that this is true.   One could live a lifetime in the hope built upon that knowledge.   I would not patch my life up with a misfit. I don't know that Sir Colin would be much of a misfit, though. I have been sounding him, and he rings true."

"How changeable you are! Are you transferring your affections to Sir Colin next?"

"No, I am not, but you are," said the Lady Greta. "At least, you are trying to, I mean. No doubt it is the next best, but somehow or other if it were my doubled roseleaf that was missing, I think I'd wait for—" and the Lady Greta hummed "The Beautiful Isle of Somewhere," as she childishly held her crown up to view it.

Her hostess's face grew a little grave.

"No, I do not think I shall give you this crown, Modena! My allusion to the diamond was unfortunate. You know when it was all over, the diamond lay as a restless heart in the carven flower of the dragon's chair. That is why I made him take me in to supper," said the Lady Greta, in a very low voice. "I don't know that this crown entitles me to much honor. Anyone could have decked a canoe. One doesn't wonder its leaves are fading. I envy Helen Lester her crown. It was worth winning. It's an evergreen one," she continued at intervals, as she rearranged the leaves.

"What crown do you mean?" asked Mrs. Cecil, who with some of the others now joined them.

"The crown which Helen won here two years ago. Was it only two years ago, Modena? It seems like ages. At the Court of Inquiry which we held here! Don't you remember, Mr. Lester defined happiness for us, and Helen told us its essentials? We all talked a lot of rubbish. We quoted things which other men had said, and said we believed this, that, and the other thing;

but Helen spoke of things she knew, and as knowledge is truth, and truth is evergreen, she received the crown."

"But how did she know that she knew? Psychologists tell us we know nothing. Socrates tells us we know nothing. What to-day is, to-morrow is not," said one of the English party.

"Marphurius denied the presence of Saganarelli. To convince him of his presence Saganarelli caned him. The doubter knew because he felt. When we know that we know nothing, then we know something, because we feel it," said the Lady Greta.

"Our Lady Greta turning theologian! What next?" exclaimed an English friend.

"Miss Lester told you the all-essential to happiness!" said the English lord. "I wish I had been here. One wishes the whole world had been here. Miss Wellington, you have given us Coppet. Your genius makes us thirsty, and your generosity makes us bold to ask for more. Will you not reopen the Court of Inquiry? Our forefathers believed the West the fabled Hesperides. To return with the golden apple of happiness would be to bestow upon England her greatest need. Will you react the Court for our pleasure and our profit?" persisted he, pleadingly.

His hostess smiled good-humoredly. "How kind of you to say we have given you Coppet! You make one think that the cynicism of Byron yet dwells within his countrymen. To react the Court in your presence would be but giving you a chapter from Molière's Precieuses or Trissotin. It would be Corinne playing Phædre at Vienna with Benjamin Constant acting as Hippolyte. Sismondi was *gauche*, but his self-knowledge was great enough to restrain him from taking the part of Talma, or, at least, if he did so, he did it in the privacy of his own room. We are Sismondis, not De Staels. Ours is presumption, not lights hidden beneath a bushel."

"Then if yours is presumption, one wishes all lights were such," said his Lordship.

"Cannot you see what it is? We are only Herrick's dairymaids and shepherds, Shenstone's May-day lads and lasses. We are green and gay and simple of heart. A little pleases and amuses. A Molière or a Talma would be Greek to us."

"Your humility comes from self-knowledge—then it is the simplicity of greatness. It is refreshing after the surfeit of egotism one encounters. How fortunate the country which possesses such children," said his Lordship, gravely.

"Do you really realize that it is the humility of a self-knowledge, and that our loyalty is the yoke of a great love and

respect? You do not look upon us as—as—Esquimaux or Iro-
quois?" interrogated his hostess, as quietly and as gravely.

The Lady Greta had succeeded in arranging her leaves to suit
her taste, and she rose abruptly and placed the crown upon
Modena's brow. She had been seemingly engrossed upon her
crown, but her mind had been deeply alert to what was being said.

"There you may wear it! I am your mother, you are my daughter, the fairest daughter in my household. I place my diadem
upon your brow. You are simple of heart. Simplicity's highest
attributes are love and trust—the love of a mother for a child, the
love of a child for its mother—a bond of nature, therefore, of the
highest and holiest kind. My blood is in your veins; the bonds
of birth are strong. You wear your crown well. Modena is a
worthy child," she continued, turning to her countryman. "She
is a good worshipper, but her god must be a good one, a great
one, a noble one, a just one. I was going to tell you this when
I returned home. I am so glad you have come and learned it for
yourself. This crown is yet soft, like the padded feet of our own
lion. Beneath the soft pads there are sharp claws. These
leaves may wither and become thorns. Sir Keith, why did you
give me a crown of thorns? I shall take it off. Modena, you must
have an evergreen one—one which has been steeped in the real
elixir of love. My metaphors, like my leaves and my thoughts, are
mixed, but you understand what I mean, Lord Averton?" she said,
as she took her crown and resumed her former position at
Modena's feet.

His Lordship smiled. "You do not want us to prove unworthy
of worship? As the individual is, so is the state. The best state
is the state built upon virtuous activity. Knowledge is virtue.
Happiness is the best educator. Will Miss Lester not enlighten
us? We want to prove worthy of trust."

"Helen, Lord Averton wishes to know what was your thesis of
happiness."

"The Lady Greta has already told him—your attributes of
simplicity—Corinne's last chant, 'love and trust.' Lord Averton
would make knowledge or virtue his basis, as Lester would have
done. But we are poor, weak creatures, we would make love the
basis," replied Helen.

"Dreams, dreams, all dreams! Dreams of the cloisters, the
paraclete and the acolyte! Food for the saints! We are only the
common clay, ever pursued by the spirit of Persæ. There is no
evergreen crown for happiness, because all our loves are febrile,
fluctuating, fanciful and ephemeral," said Mrs. Cecil, but with

less emphasis and conviction than she had once used at the Court of Inquiry.

"Oh! oh! Mrs. Cecil!" came from many parts of the lawn.

"Love is eternal," said Verona Kenyon, as she had once said before, but this time touching her husband's hand lightly with her own.

"In youth's dreams only! There is no love eternal but love nipped in the blossom. Then it remains as a memory for ever," said the Frenchwoman.

"Modena, you were Queen of the Court, you will have to decide," said the Lady Greta.

"What do you wish me to decide?" she asked, turning from Mrs. Gregory, and smiling at the Lady Greta's animated face.

"The fate of England!" replied Greta, genially. "What is love? Where did it come from? Is it eternal? Is it the essential to happiness? The Court said it was. Have you proved it so? Lord Averton wants to know, that he may take the apple and the doubled rose-leaf back to England."

"Oh! oh! You might with as much wisdom ask, 'What is life?' 'Where did it come from?' These questions are too weighty for simple heads. They have bothered the philosophers and scientists of all ages. I do not possess the intellect of a Corinne, a Sevigne or a Rambouillet to answer them."

"But we do not want an intellectual answer. We want a heart answer. They insist it is heart which the world wants," said the Lady Greta.

"A chief magistrate must be consistent and must uphold her decisions. The Court decided that it was so."

"There, I told you so!" womanlike, exclaimed the Lady Greta. "Mrs. Cecil, I have won the evergreen crown!"

"Beautiful theories," replied Mrs. Cecil; "but one is forced to say to you, what Chevalier said to Lycidas, 'You overwhelm us with fine words. Humanize your discourse a little and speak intelligibly.'"

Their hostess smiled. "We are idealists. This Court would insist on making us as realistic and personal as Molière, who wrote and acted parodies on his own plays, analysed and dissected until all emotions had become dry bones of contention, and then took a seat on the stage and laughed at the picture drawn of himself by his own enemies. Pardon us the presumption of saying so, but we always thought Molière rather commonplace. He resorted to personalities. He dealt in the concrete, not in the abstract. Oh, yes! I am aware he said he portrayed passions and emotions so true to life that he could not help if men saw themselves in them. It is his realism to which we take exception. We want to think that our loves are what we believe them to be, not what they really are. This Court would not ask us to pick our emotions and our loves to pieces and sit and laugh at them as Molière did," she said, lightly and impassively.

"Oh, no, it only insists on human theories," persisted Mrs. Cecil. "We are very weak creatures."

"But love is strong. True love is a supreme self-abnegation," Modena said.

"There, Greta, you will have to concede the crown to me!" exclaimed Mrs. Cecil. "According to Modena's theory, there is no love to-day, because the world is ruled by the god of self."

"What a Mandeville! You would make self-love the basis of all actions!" said the Lady Greta, with a little contemptuous derision in her voice.

"You will yet require a philosopher or a statesman to decide the question. Sir Keith, you are both. Is the world ruled by love or self-love?" asked Lord Averton.

Sir Keith, who had been in the city all day, had joined them at a late hour on the terrace. On his arrival his wife had asked him to bring her a wrap, and had succeeded in keeping him by her side. But her touch on his hand had irritated him so, that soon afterwards he had risen, and had shaken himself as impatiently as he had seen Nell Gwynne shake herself the day previous, when she had disturbed a nest of hornets in the woods while they were hunting. The note of light-heartedness in Sir Colin's words and laugh also irritated him exceedingly. It had in it the hope of the joys, the lack of which was making his life miserable. For some moments he had paced the stone terrace and had then seated himself in her chair of carved oak, which had been her throne. From where he sat he could see the Fernery, the ravine and the riven oak. Unobserved he could also see the face of the woman he loved as she spoke. He had seen in her eyes what he wanted to know, and his eyes had said, "There is one who knows how to love," but with his lips he answered Lord Averton.

"I have never dissected or analysed other people's motives, nor generalized from any data which have come before my notice, and so am not in a position to speak from experience; but as I am an optimist, and a Sir Gawain, I shall have to decide in favor of the Lady Greta. No doubt there is a certain amount of egotism in all personal loves, but even if there be, it is only nature and therefore excusable. There are other than personal loves. There are love of country, love of right, love of principles and creeds, and love of truth and consistency. The women of Rome sacrificed the glory of their heads to make bow-strings to defend their city. No doubt ours, if occasion necessitated it, would do the same. History gives us our Boadiceas, women of Port Royal, Maria Theresas, Penelopes, Heros and Hypatias, and history ever repeats itself. One could easily imagine amid such surroundings, and amid such fair forms as these, that here might yet linger those who possess enough self-abnegation to sacrifice their own lives and loves, and send their loved ones to the salvation of their country, their creeds, and their consistency, as the woman of Ancona gave to a starving soldier the milk that her half-famished babe required, and sent him refreshed and strengthened to defend the walls of his beleaguered city," he said, quietly and gallantly, his hand carelessly dangling his watch-chain, and his eyes smiling benignly on the Lady Greta.

Jack's back was turned to the others, and as Sir Keith ceased speaking he raised his eyes in profound astonishment, and looked his friend straight in the face, and was about to speak, then checked himself, and said nothing, but looked at his cousin, who had turned her face aside in the gloom to Helen Lester to hide her consternation, while the doubts regarding his marriage were realized in every mind present.

"I should say, Kenyon, you deserve no better fate than Socrates with his Xantippe. Any other man in your place could have turned his wife such a pretty compliment there," said Lester, endeavoring to break the awkwardness of the situation, but only succeeding in making it worse.

"It is you who are the blockhead! Kenyon was comparing his wife to the women of history!" exclaimed Jack, venting the ill-humor he felt towards Sir Keith on his friend Lester.

Sir Keith's ear was sensitive to the note of displeasure within Jack's words. He looked up quickly. He hadn't thought of them attaching any personal meaning to his lightly spoken words. He hadn't intended any, and he was annoyed that they had done so, but he said nothing; and at that moment the boom of the first dinner-bell came to them over the greensward in great waves of sound.

"Wasn't that splendid? I can forgive him now for not giving you the crown," said the Lady Greta to their hostess, as they went in together. "I knew you were his doubled rose-leaf."

"Are you not fanciful? Where did you see any such infer-

ence in his words? I assure you his women were purely ideal, or
if not, you are his Queen, and he may with perfect propriety
render you the homage of his knightly love."

"You tempt me to steal him away from you."

"You cannot steal from me something which I do not
possess."

"No, I suppose you do not. You said love was the union of
the human and the divine. You have the divine, but you lack
the human, and the void makes life lonely," said the young girl,
kissing her friend as they parted at the threshold of her room.

<hr>

CHAPTER XXXVII.

It was seven of the clock the following evening, and the mistress of Fernwylde was in her own room. The last twenty-four
hours had taxed her strength to its utmost, and she had sought a
few minutes' rest and quietness before going down for the evening.

She stood by her window looking out over her lands. The day
was closing in. Some rooks were hoarsely cawing in an old elm
tree at the edge of the ravine; the night was bleak and dreary; the
golden and russet leaves were being whirled in eddying gusts, while
the hoarse whistling of the wind round the eaves was monotonous
and depressing.

"Why did he say it?" she was thinking. "He meant nothing,
but yet others have put a meaning in his words. He holds high
the value of silence. He has scarcely spoken to me since his marriage, and yet the world knows. What can one do? I cannot
spend my life running away from them. I can only remain here
and avoid them." And yet to remain at Fernwylde seemed to her
almost as cowardly as to go abroad. The spirit of progression had
been born within her. A life of activity was in harmony with the
desires and instincts of her temperament. The busy world was
her element, and she could not well live without it. "We have
great powers within us, why should they remain here undeveloped?"
she thought as she continued to gaze out of the window. "How
misguided and misdirected we are. We can only work through
them. Our powers should be lost completely in theirs, our love
and our life one long self-immolation, stimulus, sympathy, solace,
soul-communion with theirs, as Greta says, the lost half of their
being. How many powers, oh, how many, lie dormant and unde-

veloped, or are frittered away on the inanities of life! Why
should mine be?" And her memory wandered back to dreams
which she had dreamt, and then, like Elaine and her beloved's face,
his face dark-splendid speaking in the silence, full of noble things,
ever rose before her. Were his powers being developed, or were
they dwarfing in the sight of man? She was sensible that he was
changing with these years of pain. His ability, his bearing, his
ambition were unaltered, but yet there was a change. The elas-
ticity, the love-light, the innate, sanguine hope, the joy which comes
alone from living, were changing into sombre shadows, and an
austerity which at times became almost an asceticism; and as the
lineaments of the knight of Camelot's face were marred by the
strife between his unholy love and his moral sense, making it aged
ere its time, so, too, she felt, were his.

To the world and to other women these qualities only made him
the more attractive, the more sought after, because they had in
them the suggestion of a mystery and of unseen power; but to her
they brought only remorse, because she knew they were but the
progenies of a lost love and the companions of unlawful desires.

There is no more melancholy sight than the abuse or waste of
power. Why should his be wasted? He had pleaded for a friendship. "Why cannot I give him that solace which will stimulate
and sustain? I cannot, because I am so weak," she cried, as she
realized how hard it was to guard the gates of the soul against its
tempters; having learnt, as Molière had learnt, that honor and
will power are of little avail when passion has assumed that
ascendancy of which temperament is usually the cause. "I can
only shield myself by losing myself in another," she said, as the
door opened and Jack entered her apartments.

He did not approach her, but stood by the table, silent. She
turned from the window and greeted him, and then spoke of the
contents of the evening papers; but his replies were brief, and
then he said to her, without any prelude, "I wanted to tell you
that Kenyon will have to be more careful, and not say such
things as he said last evening."

The color deepened in his cousin's face, as he spoke.

"Verona Kenyon is a dangerous woman," he continued,
impressively, before she had time to reply. "Last night she did
not hear his words, or if she heard she did not realize their meaning, but this forenoon Patric was dilating upon his words.
Mrs. Sangster checked him. They were not aware that Verona
was on the other side of the shrubbery. I did not hear what was
being said. I could only infer from their looks and actions. A

change passed over Verona's face, horrible to see," and he paused, as he remembered her face as he had seen it.

Verona had not heard her husband's words, but the previous evening she had felt that things were not well. The morning had found her fears unallayed, and then she had overheard Mr. Patrie's words of reprisal. As the force and the meaning of the words came home to her, for a moment all the evil passions of her nature had become portrayed in her face. Her nostrils had quivered and distended, her brows had drawn together in deep, dark lines, and as her eyes followed the mistress of the place they had grown black as sloes, and had glittered with the fires of a great, unspeakable anger. Unable longer to control herself, she had risen and passed swiftly down the avenue to the lake. When she returned she was calm and smiling, but her face had in it the semblance of much that was evil. "I am quite convinced that her suspicions are at last confirmed," said Jack, after a moment's pause.

His cousin listened as he spoke, and paled, but not with fear. Her conscience was clear, but before this she had felt the force of Lady Kenyon's malignity, and she had been humiliated in her own sight in being made the target of her world. She was a very proud person and valued highly public opinion. She did not want her private life and sentiments held up to public view.

"What am I to do?" she asked her cousin. "His words were spoken in the abstract and addressed to the Lady Greta. I cannot help if people attribute to them a personal meaning. He has scarcely spoken to me since his marriage. I cannot discuss it with him. To discuss it would be to admit there is something in it, and this I cannot do. Her actions I cannot help. I cannot warn him because I cannot discuss her with him."

"I know that, and that is the reason I wanted you to go away for a while."

"I shall think about it," she replied, wearily. "The party breaks up to-morrow. I shall then be free. Thank you, Jack. You will have to go now, I must dress."

Her cousin hesitated and lingered, and then left the room, moodily.

"He wanted to tell me it is myself I need fear. I am afraid it is," she said, as she dressed for dinner, and before her mental vision rose the struggles of the wife of Cleander with her passion for Lysander, and she shuddered as the sense of their fatality came home to her. "Rather the fate of Lucretia," she said, as the last bell rang, and she went down the stairs.

In the corridor she met Sir Colin Campbell, and she smiled, her resolution being taken. She would accord him a greater degree of intimacy. She knew what it meant if she did so. She would not wantonly trifle with any man's affections. She had long seen that he loved her, but he had refrained from speaking because of her relations with Carlton Monteith. But now she was free to be wooed and won. He had been her shadow for a week. Previous to this she had not permitted herself to be alone with him. She went in with him now, and afterwards, during the evening, she allowed him to lead her away for a few minutes from the gay, glad gathering to a pretty blue room, leading from the room in which they were gathered.

The door to the central hall was partly ajar. She stood on the hearth with her arm resting on the mantelpiece, her other hand by her side. The lights from the fireplace shone upon its many gems, and burnished to gold the soft tints of her dress.

Sir Colin bent over her with a warm but grave look on his bronzed face.

"Is it true your relations with Monteith are broken?" he was asking.

"Yes," she replied, and her voice seemed to her to have in it the echo of all the past years of her life.

"You are free now. You know I have loved you long. This week I have almost hoped. Is it so?" he asked with great humility and deference.

His eyes deepened and brightened, and his voice had in it great earnestness, but he did not approach nearer her.

There was something in her which held men at bay. They felt as Luvois felt towards Lucille, that there was something lofty and lonely in her which held them in check. Bold man though he was, he could not approach her without her permission.

For some moments she did not reply, but looked past him. Her person to her was sacred. It was hard for her to give it up to any man. She had given herself up to one man. These relations were sacred. It was not easy to turn to another.

A great desire to tell him all came to her, and almost overcame her. He was a man of the world and would understand, and having comprehension he would be magnanimous, and would shield her from herself in his great love, and yet she thought, what if it lay beyond herself to sever her life from the life of the man she loved. That afternoon, when she had sent them all away to the hunt, she had spent a few moments with Heine, who had said, "For a woman there is no second love, her nature is too delicate to withstand a second time that most terrible convulsion of the soul." She loved Sir Keith Kenyon. A soulless body was a mockery. It would be unjust to Sir Colin. She would wait awhile and see if she herself would change.

"No, Sir Colin, I do not love you. You say you have hoped. Have I given you cause? Then forgive me, for I do not know myself," she replied, almost tenderly, her suffering having taught her tenderness to others.

He was much touched by her words and manner, but not discouraged or dismayed.

Her voice had in it a faint suggestion of hope. He approached nearer. "Modena! May I call you that? I had not hoped that yours was love. Nature made you to feel deeply. Your heart is not touched. I had only hoped a permission, a tender regard, which in time would develop into sympathy, solace and perhaps love. I know what your life needs. You love your world, and it pleases you now, but you have great powers within you which the world in time will fail to satisfy. You will then be very unhappy and very lonely unless you lose yourself in the love of a warm, human heart. I can make my love great enough to shield you. May I hope?"

"I do not deny your presence is pleasing, but further than that I cannot bid you hope."

"Then I have your permission to try to please," he said, with a certain amount of masterfulness in his voice and mien, and he raised her hand to his lips.

At that moment Sir Keith Kenyon was passing the open door with Mr. Lester, who had gone in search of him to join in a game of whist, and his quick eye swept over the two as they stood on the hearth rug with their images reflected in the glass, while the softened light from the gas jets shone on her face, making it tender and soft in the subdued light.

It was the first time in his life Sir Keith had seen her show any sign of love, or even tenderness, to the opposite sex, and the sight roused all the latent passion and jealousy which exists in all human nature, but which had seldom been touched in his before. The thought of her union with another had never come home to him. He expected life to go on as it was, and the sight now sent a chill of despair to his heart, and made it ache as if from some wound which bled within. A spasm as of physical pain passed through him, and he paused for a moment, and then passed on. He knew that Mr. Lester, too, had seen it, and tutored by the ways of the world as he was, he controlled any visible sign of emotion and proceeded to the whist table, but his thoughts were not on the cards, and he who was invariably so cool and deliberate now played absently and feverishly, until Lester proposed a smoke on the portico to which he at once gladly agreed, his one desire being to get away from all restraint and all forced appearances, and to be alone, and yet to be alone was but to be with remorse and forbidden memories.

Unobserved he left the others, and knowing the rooms and grounds so well made his way to the western gardens which were her own private grounds.

A great remorse was upon him. Why did he do it? he asked himself, and he could not tell why he had done such a thing.

Byron regretted having made up his mind to ask Miss Milbanke, but after having written the letter it appeared to him so beautifully worded, and such a perfect composition, that he could not bear to see it wasted without effect. He had often wondered at, and blamed Byron for his insouciance, but yet he had done likewise. But lament was foreign to him. It was done and could not be undone. What must he now do? Philosophy told him to go away while it was yet time, but as Aristotle said, " Youths are poor hearers of moral philosophy because their desires are not yet allayed and tempered by time and experience." He wondered if his would ever be. He did not think they would. He knew his desires were not the desires of youth. The desires of youth had their origin in passion. His were based in love. She was his, and no other man had any right to look upon her. He could not rest until he had told her so.

He was in that mood in which a man feels that all other things may perish if his love is left him. Under the stimulus of remorse and the first stings of jealousy, his love took unto itself the semblance of that of a Faust, which was almost that of a Don Juan when he cried, " I give my soul forever that this woman may be mine."

But he was not a man of impulse. He had within himself the power to hold himself well in reserve. A display of emotion to the world was a sign of weakness. He did not go in, but continued to pace the stone terrace which fronted the water's edge until he should regain command of himself.

Out here alone with nature he soon became himself once more. " Could Sir Colin make her happy?" was the thought which came with his noblest mood. " If he, Sir Keith, thought that it lay within Sir Colin's power to make her happy, then he would go from her. Could he do so? Would he do so?" A wise man is

never very sure of his strength. He believed he could, and he
retraced his steps towards the house.

The lights were disappearing one by one in the house, and he
knew the guests were retiring or departing. He entered by a side
door, and made his way to where he knew he would find her.

She had bade each of her guests good-night, and had left them
as they repaired to their different rooms. Lady Kenyon was
inquiring for her husband, and had sent a servant in search of
him.

The mistress of the house had noticed her eyes follow her the
entire evening, and knew that what Jack had told her was only
too true.

"How unwise of her to act thus! Why does she notice it?" she
thought, as she traversed the hall towards the blue room where
she had left a jeweled bracelet whose clasp had become unsafe.
"Her mind seemed to grow easier, and her manner less strained,
as she noticed Sir Colin's attentions to me. What did I promise
Sir Colin? I wonder if I shall ever be able to bid him hope," and
her face grew grave as she thought of what it meant. His words
to her had reopened the old wound. "It must be," she said, as
she turned to the blue room.

At the door she met Sir Keith. By common consent they
paused. All day she had been wishing to speak to him of many
things, and he to her, and yet she knew it was of things of which
they could not speak.

When she met him she could but bid him good-night, and was
about to pass on, but he detained her.

"Will you spare me a moment, Modéna? I would speak with
you. I was passing the door an hour ago when you and Campbell stood there," and then he paused; he could say no further.
Twice his lips parted to speak, but no words came, and she could
not help him.

He was very pale, and he thought that she must hear the beating of his heart. His eyes were on her, hungry with their long
denial, and hers did not dare meet his.

But he was not a man who, having once said to himself that he
would do a thing, would leave it undone.

"He is a noble man! He loves you! Do you think he could
make you happy?"

She looked up at him, and so looking understood, and she knew
now that she could never marry Sir Colin Campbell.

"There is only one thing I can do, Keith. I shall go away."

And he knew what she meant, and some great strength seemed to come into his life once more.

"You think we cannot be friends? We could live above the world."

"It is not the world I fear. It is ourselves. We are not strong enough. A person's strength is like a gold piece; break it and spend it in small pieces, and it is soon gone. Oh, no, ours would not be love were it otherwise!"

He grew very weak before her words, so weak that he grew deadly pale and laid his hand on the open door for support.

But she continued, without looking at him, "There are other reasons, too, why we must part."

"What are they?" he asked, quickly.

"We cannot discuss them," she said, and he knew what she meant. "Your wife." These words had never yet passed between them. She was as a dead letter to them, and nothing but her actual presence or command had ever intruded into their relationship.

"There is something I wish to tell you. May I, Modena?" he said, but before she could reply a servant approached, and informed Sir Keith that Lady Kenyon was awaiting him in the hall below.

"Good-night," he murmured.

"It must be good-bye," she said, meeting his eyes in farewell, and she passed on.

He turned and went down the corridor, his face deadly pale and his soul at war within him. When he said that he would do it, he had overrated his own strength and underrated the powers and memories of the past.

"The blame is wholly mine," he said. "Why do they have to suffer so through us?" Could he only have borne it all himself he would have done penance for life. "She would not be herself could she find happiness in another. And she never doubts my love!" And her absolute trust in him made her dearer to him than she had ever been before.

The lights in the hall had grown dim. The guests were all gone but a few who were waiting for their carriages to draw near. He buttoned his great coat, and replaced his hat to shield the pallor of his face from their view. He approached his wife, took her to her carriage, spoke to the footman, and then turned to the stables where his saddle-horse stood ready for use. He took him from his stall, mounted him, and looked towards Idlewylde. He shuddered, and turned his horse's head the other way. It was now past midnight, and he rode long and fast on big, black Ali over the green glades of Idlewylde, through the heavy Siberian pine forest, past many streams fed by the snows and glaciers and springs of the mountain side, and did not return until the woods and moors were dim and dusky in that darkness which comes before the pallid light of coming day.

On his return he passed Fernwylde. In the west a waning moon hung over the mountain tops, pale and spectral through the river mists, and against it there rose squarely and darkly the mansion of Fernwylde, dim and shadowy as the home of the Sleeping Beauty.

In the shadows of the forest he dismounted. His horse, tired with his long, hard run, hung his head and cropped the rank grass at his feet. He looked up at the house, and something which was almost a sob came into his throat.

He had been fighting a battle bitterer than death with his own soul, and had conquered.

Long had he felt towards her as the king of the Golden Age had felt towards his only love.

> For saving I be joined
> To her that is the fairest under heaven,
> I seem as nothing in this mighty world,
> And cannot will my will, nor work my work
> Wholly, nor make myself in mine own realm
> Victor and lord. But, were I joined with her,
> Then might we live together as one life;
> And, reigning with one will in everything,
> Have power on this dark land to lighten it,
> And power on this dead world to make it live.

But now had she become to him more than the woman he loved and wanted. She had become unto him his religion.

In his childhood days for special lessons in the classics his parents had secured for him the services of a Jesuit monk, who had received his education from the most studious, most superstitious and most ascetic order then in France. He was a visionary, and a devotee to the cause of religion, and had ever before him the part that art had played in faith. He had with him several miniatures of the Madonna from different masters' hands, and when his day's work was done, with his pupil he would invariably dilate with picturesque, mystical and often melancholy suggestions upon his favorite subject. His pupil's young mind at the time was plastic, pregnant with the emotions of youth, and filled with the weird tales of the martyrdom of the early fathers whom his old teacher looked upon as saints, and his young mind had gone out in instinctive supplication to the Unseen. But when he had left the cloisters for the schools, and the world and politics, all mysticism had vanished, and its place had been usurped by keen common-sense, ambition, pleasure and power. But now since these things had proved so unsatisfactory and unsatisfying, his mind had gone out once more in the same old instinctive worship and need to the woman he loved.

His conflict of the night had made him look upon her as something holy, had helped him banish the carnal, enabled him to see only the divine, and had given him strength to do what his manhood told him he must do.

"We are heirs of the flesh, the flesh is weak, and he is weaker who tempts it," he said, as the waning moon dropped behind the hill-tops, and the river mists ascended and hid the house from view.

"Farewell," he said to his vanished Castle of Camelot, and the same sob rose once more in his throat as he turned his face towards Idlewylde.

CHAPTER XXXVIII.

MODENA'S party broke up the next morning. Her English guests were loth to leave. As they were not remaining for any time in the city she bade them good-bye on the threshold of her country home, promising that she would spend some time with them on her visit to their land in a few weeks' time.

To her cousin and to her friends she had intimated her intention of spending the winter abroad.

"Sir Colin is being sent to represent his country at some military manœuvres during the Christmas festivities at home. She wishes to be near him," said Verona Kenyon, in her husband's hearing, on learning of the mistress of Fernwylde's intended departure, as they sat in the library at Kenyon Court.

"A worthy pair of representatives! Our country will be much honored," said Mrs. Sangster. "When does she go, Helen?"

"Not for some few weeks."

"Meanwhile she remains at Fernwylde."

"Yes; a severe storm in the spring did much damage there.

27

She wishes to see the buildings made ready for the winter's use before she leaves. Her time is fully occupied."

"From the calf's cough and the swine-sty to Windsor Castle! It is a leap requiring at least much agility in social gymnastics," said Verona.

"I believe Modena's dairies and day-schools are ever dearer to her than the pleasures of Piccadilly or the pomps of the purple pale," said Mrs. Sangster.

"Then why does she go?"

"I thought you said Sir Colin!"

"I had forgotten," said Verona. "The transfer of her affections was so sudden that one fails to grasp it. I wonder who it will be next. Are you going down to Idlewylde soon?" she asked, turning to her husband.

"I am going west in a few days," he replied, briefly, without raising his eyes from the many papers which lay before him.

He knew that his wife's eyes were upon him, as they had been for many weeks, but from his countenance she learned nothing. His face was impassive, almost cold. He had put the memories of the past away from him with the firmness of a great will power. He had resumed all his arduous duties, and had filled his life with them. He knew that the woman he loved was there in his life, the motive power behind it all, but he never allowed her to come into his thoughts any more than she came into his actual presence, or if she came it was but for a moment when the past became stronger than he, and then it was but a fear which was full of infinite pain that she was unhappy.

Sometimes, suddenly, such thoughts would come to him. Sometimes when his mind was wholly centred on the affairs of state, sometimes when waking suddenly in the dead of night, sometimes when all alone, and sometimes when in the midst of the gaieties of his world, this fear would come to him bringing with it such an intensity of emotion that for the moment he feared himself; but he put it behind him, and turned with a greater application to the many duties which ever awaited him.

Meanwhile the object of his thoughts was passing her time at Fernwylde in very much the same frame of mind, but with less strength to endure.

"I am so glad to be alone," she had said, as she had stood on the threshold, and watched the last of her guests pass from sight down the green defile which led to the outer world, the sound of the horses' hoofs wakening the echoes of the hills as they passed by; "but yet"—As she turned within a great sense of loneliness and dreariness weighed heavily upon her, made lonelier and more drearisome by the deserted rooms and gardens which had so lately been filled with life and laughter.

She had said she would go abroad in a month's time, and in the interval her time would be fully occupied with the many improvements which were now nearing their completion, and the many duties and social obligations which ever awaited her at her country home.

She went at once out amongst them, to the fishermen's cottages, with Father Jacques on his visits to the foreign element in the lumber district, to the autumn festivities in the village, and to the men on her lands where they were garnering in their winter's supply of fruits and other produce. She spent some time at a domestic and manual training school which they were establishing in the village, and discussed with the architect the plans for an art room. These were all much to her, and she neglected none of her duties towards them.

All her life she had taken as her guide Prince Metternich's motto of " Right," and these to her had ever seemed among the vital principles of " Right." The smallest details in life had made her great in the great things of life. Fate had been kind to her, yet had she built a stronger fortress upon Fate. But as she went amongst them now she felt they were not to her what they had once been. Somehow they had lost the power to please and fill her life.

At all times she did what she wished to do, what she thought it right to do, but she could not force her heart into the work, for it seemed to her that her heart had refused to remain any longer in submission to her will.

After Sir Keith's marriage, when she had seen his wife's many acts of reprisals, she had passed them over with silent contempt, the contempt of a proud nature for a parvenue; but as time passed and Verona's position had become more stable, and she had begun to draw to her side a powerful clique, she began to feel the force of her designs. She knew that she should not let them affect her, but she had loved her world so well, and to see the world she had so dearly loved, swayed by such sordid motives, so thoughtless, so ephemeral, so prone to ingratitude, had moved her to a disdain and exclusiveness which were only the precursors of discontent and loneliness.

In her leisure moments she went much to her libraries. She shunned the scientists; they were cold comfort when one's lights are low, and she sought the humanities, but their words had only in them the power to touch the vital pain, and bring sadly home to her the knowledge of the truth of the German philosopher's words, that "a soul in disorder is its own torment." Then would she close her books and shun them, and wander out over her lands, but their extent and beauty, which had ever before been a joy to her, now seemed to mock her drooping spirits, as the Orangery, the Swiss Lakes and the Hills of Sartory must have mocked the heart of the deserted Queen Louise.

There were times now when she would ask herself had she done well to refrain from speaking. For many long months she had gone her way with courage, seldom doubting that her course was right. It had seemed to her that if she wished to be consistent there was no other way possible, but sometimes when she was very lonely she told herself, were that time of temptation to be lived over again she would not send him from her; and sometimes yet, when the echo of his words lingered in her ear, she would feel a vague, unexpressed desire to stretch out her hand to him and draw him to herself for evermore, but it was a desire which she never allowed to find expression in thought. Had she done so she would have felt herself humiliated beyond all hope.

He had pleaded lately for a renewal of friendship. At one time she had thought they could be friends, but not now. She had prided herself on her idealism. Within her had dwelt the belief that all the sensual phenomena of our world are but unsubstantial shadows of the eternal and divine realities. With Shelley she had believed that "thought is love; thought is infinite; thought is independent of gross material conduct. One is capable of more real, lasting love, of seeing more, of knowing more of the divine in one hour of thought than in a lifetime of the senses." But this was before love had touched her life, and now since love had touched it, the shadows alone she found to be but poor food for the human side of life.

In the society in which she moved she had been accustomed to seeing much that was sensual and deteriorating, but it had only possessed a repugnance for her. Without any effort of her own she had walked immeasurably aloof and distinct from it, even while it had touched her senses. To her it had been sacrilegious and abhorrent, but she knew what the world smiles upon and accepts as correct, every day becomes more plausible and seemingly less sinful, and that it would be very easy to allow herself to drift into its ways. She would have chosen death rather than have done so,

He was only asking that they be friends. She felt it was her all in life, and yet she dare not grant it. Could she only by any act of her own, any sacrifice, any suffering, have rendered him happy, she would willingly have done so.

When a child she had read of how in the time of war a Spanish lady had loved her lord so well that she had entered a condemned cell and changed clothes with the woman who was beloved by her lord, that she might free the woman from death by dying in her stead, and restore her rival to the man she loved. This had been her ideal of love. Was it not the ideal of supreme love? Tradition said that supreme love had renounced all that was best and dearest in itself to humiliation and death for the eternal good of those whom it loved. A beautiful theory! A theory which in childhood she had accepted as essential, and in maturity had left unmolested, because it exalted love to its highest degree.

And there was in her what was in the woman of Spain. Could she have secured his happiness by renunciation she would willingly have done so and gone her way with courage to the end.

But his happiness depended not upon renunciation but upon possession, and this knowledge caused her the greatest joy and the greatest pain of her life, but it was a gladness and a sorrow she was striving hard to banish from her life, but of no avail.

The three weeks she spent at Fernwylde were the unhappiest weeks of her life. She had said she would go abroad in the course of a month's time, and because she had said so she did not wish to go an hour before the time in which she had said she would go. Had she gone it would have seemed to her that she was fleeing from her own weakness. And she would not go where she would meet him, and she learnt that the solitude into which she had placed herself had only the tendency to foster great passions. She knew that she should banish him from her thoughts, as she had banished him from her actual presence, and day after day she said that she would do so; but even as the unhappy queen in the silence and seclusion of the cloisters, in her repentance resolved not even in her innermost thoughts to think again the things that made the past so pleasant, even while in her meditations moving through the past, unconsciously grew half-guilty in her thoughts again, so, too, Modena, in the silence and seclusion of her country home, even while she was resolving never to think of him again, found her thoughts forever with him.

It was now the end of the third week. The work on the new buildings had been completed, and her other duties having been fulfilled she was at liberty to return to the city, but her health had become so impaired for the time that she refrained from going. She had told her household that she would remain the fourth week, and then leave for the Continent, when a message came from the city calling her in haste to the side of her father who had taken suddenly ill.

The call for action roused her from her mental conflicts to a knowledge of danger, as a trumpet sounding rouses a troubled nation to a sense of war.

In a few moments after the receipt of the message she was on her way to the city, and in a few hours she stood by the bedside of her father, whom she found very ill indeed.

CHAPTER XXXIX.

A FEW days after Sir Keith's return to the city from Idlewylde his ministerial duties called him out West for several weeks' time.

He was glad of the change and the rest which would give him time and strength to once more take up life and live it as it should be lived.

The instinct of patriotism was strong within him, and while west he was awakened to an immense consciousness of the vast resources and possibilities of his own country.

His country was now in its embryo state, and had within it the possibilities of one day becoming the light of the world.

All which he had seen, all which he had felt, all which he had known, and all which he had dreamed, seemed suddenly to come home to him and tell him that she was a child of destiny, and his heart once more beat within him with all the patriotism and pride of his youth.

The advent of the foreign element, the growing need for great enterprises and the immense possibilities reawakened within him the knowledge of the necessity of wise and capable government.

History had taught him the great necessity for a proper foundation. Rome had at one time been a model nation. She had attained to the apex of civilization. Her foundation had been virtue, integrity, patriotism and fear of and faith in the gods. Her citizens had been men of culture. As the individual is, so is the state, but the state makes the individual. At the present time the character, the kind, the ability of the individual was a matter of the greatest moment. The advent of the foreign element was a question which could not be lightly dealt with. The necessity of highways to the north and to the west appealed strongly to the progressive spirit within him. The fusion of sectional, racial and religious differences was work worthy of a statesman. The great gardens and garner fields were sending forth a cry which could no longer be ignored.

Evolution in Rome had generated its "Trade Trusts." As a result of their own policy many combines, which would in time threaten the general welfare of many, were springing into existence. Study, reflection, generalization had taught him the immense evil, injustice and cruel contrasts which would invariably develop from such a course and conduct in commerce. Labor is the source of all wealth, and labor must be protected, recompensed, ennobled. Manipulation must be condemned, not encouraged and condoned, were the St. Simon instincts which sprang up within him crying for utterance, and creating within him an immense consciousness of the great responsibility of their own positions, and filling his life with a new hope and peace which comes from the desire to live for others.

The hopeful, buoyant spirit of the West, too, was inspiring. He caught glimpses of a life of freedom with nature, a life untrammelled by the conventions and etiquette of a state society, a broader, kinder, manlier life. He felt his old ambitions stir within him once more. His ideals reappeared in more definite and tangible form.

They had already accomplished much in the development of their young country. Encouraged and inspired by what had already been done, new and greater visions rose before him; the unlimited resources of the West now revealed to him their opportunities, and it was with new resolutions and renewed vigor and vitality when his work was done he once more turned his face towards home.

On his return he found the Capital gay with life. The notables of the country had returned, and the House had settled down to business, while the social world had once more entered into its winter's routine of pleasure and gaiety.

He was but a short time in his own home when the even tenor of his life began once more to be seriously disturbed. He had returned home fully determined to make the best of his home life, but his environments were stronger than his power to do what he had said he would strive to do.

During the weeks which followed, his wife's whole nature seemed to. be brought to the surface.

She had known neither peace nor pleasure since he had uttered those words on the terrace at Fernwylde. Her suspicions aroused had neither slumbered nor slept, but the announcement of her rival's departure had somewhat allayed her injured passions. But now, although Mr. Wellington had resumed his duties at the House he was far from well, and his daughter had said that she would not leave his side. She had accordingly remained in the city, and was going her old familiar ways, and they were meeting again as of old.

There is no blinder thing than hate, wounded love and jealousy, and Verona had now grown to hate her with a hatred born of these, and her nature was one which could hate well and forcibly.

Until the last few months she had been hopeful and sanguine of winning her husband's love. In private she had been too shrewd to harass him for affections he did not bestow, or render to him those he was unwilling to receive, but in public she had sought him and monopolized him with an espionage which had become both irritating and irksome, but all to no avail; he did not turn to her, and she blamed her rival for it all and hated her accordingly.

The words which she had heard them utter made her rival's very presence a menace to her happiness. Under their sting the meats of her home life became as wormwood to her, as they had centuries before to the jealous Queen in her rage. In her presence all the little pleasures of everyday life became as bitter to her as the apples and the water had been to Sir Percival in the land of sand and thorns. Sir Keith saw the change, but as he had forgotten his words he did not attribute them as the cause, but ascribed it to his wife's disposition and temperament, and his heart once more became heavy within him.

Each day as he was made an eye-witness of some petty action, or the subject or object of some innuendo, the instincts of the gentleman rose up in arms within him, rendering his home-life detestable to him, and day by day as his wife's nature was more openly revealed to him, the contrast of the moral loveliness of the woman he loved, in her life of high-bred serenity, her innate sense of justice, her devotion to the simple duties of life and natural abhorrence of all things base or unjust, enhanced her in his sight many times over.

He had avoided meeting her. He had seen her but he had not spoken to her. She had said to him that it must be good-bye, and he had striven to make it so. While west his separation from her had increased his gratitude for her near presence, and he was

passively content to pass his life near hers, but for his wife's
constant espionage and interference. He felt that his wife's eyes
were ever on him—on her, but from their conduct she learned
nothing.

"Am I mistaken?" she at last asked herself. "Did I hear
aright? If I only knew; uncertainty is worse than knowledge.
I cannot rest until I know. Should I ask him he would but deny
it. He could do naught else;" and then a thought came to her,
"I shall ask some of his former friends; they will know."

Of all his friends who were now her friends she preferred Mrs.
Sangster most. Mrs. Sangster was a woman of wide experience and generous disposition, and possessed great tact in adapt-
ing herself to any circumstances. Verona felt more at her ease
with her than with any others in her circle, and in the misery of
her jealousy and unrequited love she made a partial confidante of
her.

"You have known my husband all his life. Did he ever love
anyone very much?" she asked her one day, as they sat together
in the library at Kenyon Court.

"Isn't he one of the favored of the gods? Surely women
would burn incense at his shrine. You do not appreciate him or
you would not ask such a question," replied Mrs. Sangster, lightly.

She was well aware of Verona's disturbed peace of mind, and
when she replied she spoke with well-bred assumed indifference,
not wishing to enter into any serious discussion.

"I did not ask you about women worshipping at his shrine.
You evaded the question. I asked you, did he ever worship at
any shrine?" replied Verona, almost irritably.

"What a question to ask! What difference does it make to whom
he has been Lovelace, so long as he is Montrose to you? Almost
all men have passing fancies, transitory as comets, forgotten when
their fixed star appears. You are his star. His comets have
faded."

"To whom has he been Lovelace? Name me one," urged
Lady Kenyon, with ill-concealed apprehension.

But that was what Mrs. Sangster had no notion of doing. When
she had said "many," she had only thought of "one," but she
was a woman of honor, and had no intention of speaking of
"one" or of discussing the matter whatever, and replied in a
voice intended to close the conversation.

"But, my dear, that is not a question for you to ask. Any
woman who is wise will not seek to unravel her husband's past.
A wife's duty is to burn incense blindly and reverentially at a

husband's shrine. This incense of reverential trust and love in woman soon becomes in man his conscience. Opening old urns will not aid her any. That she has now the right to his love, and that he has voluntarily given her that right, should be sufficient proof of his love. It is unwise to resurrect old deadened fires; it is even unwise to think of them. They are not a subject for discussion, Verona."

"Ah, but the fires may not be dead, only smouldering, and may be rekindled at any moment!" Lady Kenyon replied, very quickly.

"Has he ever given you reason to think so?" asked her friend, rather coldly.

"You heard what he said that day. I overheard Mr. Patrie and yourself discuss it afterwards," replied Verona, in justification of her assertion and conduct.

"How? Where?" asked Mrs. Sangster, in great surprise and consternation.

"I was behind the shrubbery when you and he were discussing it and heard your words. Whom did you mean?" she insisted, with a tinge of defiance in her voice.

"We had no right to mean or to say anyone. He has given you—no one—no cause to think there was anything personal in his remark. He is certainly too well-bred and too reserved to offer up his heart at a feast of logic, as the gods did the boy Itys," replied Mrs. Sangster, as she moved from the light.

"But you admit yourself that he has cared very much for some."

"I admitted it in general. If in particular, do you think, my dear, I would condescend to tell you anything? No one would be a friend to you who would do so. Marriage with us is the most sacred ceremonial. I think you are certainly annoying yourself unnecessarily. The fact that he married you should make you believe in the sincerity of his motives. Take my advice, Verona, and if you doubt his love make yours so great, so patient, so infinite that he cannot live without it. Rise above the present and be a noble woman. Live for his interests alone. True love is self-abnegation, and true love will always in time be appreciated. Forget yourself and live for him alone."

"If he does not love you, do not dwell on your wrongs or supposed injustices," continued her friend, earnestly. "It will only cause you to grow morbid and distasteful to him. He has given you no reason to think that he does not love you, and one fact is certain he goes nowhere else with his love."

"How do you know that?" asked Verona, very quickly.

"How do I know! Why, if he did the world would soon know it! It is impossible to keep such a thing as that from the world. Everyone who knows Sir Keith is well aware that he is honorable and worthy of trust."

"Then if he has not been unfaithful, why is he so indifferent?"

"If you will not enlighten me, I shall ask himself," she pleaded, as her friend rose to go.

"Be careful, Verona," her friend replied. "I have known Sir Keith from boyhood. He will brook no interference. He interferes not in other people's line of conduct, and he will allow no one to dictate to him. You may utter words which he will not soon forgive or forget. It will be much better for you to take the nobler course, and live a life that will command respect from him and from the world. All women cannot be clever or charming, great or accomplished, but all women can be good and loving. That is all men care for. They are our gods, and they want to be worshipped. Life teaches them that we alone are to be relied upon, and in time if we only love them truly they learn to lean wholly upon us. We can make of them what we will. Now think over this, Verona, and for your own sake try to act wisely, and all will be well."

"You would make me a Griselda," replied Verona, sullenly.

"There is no more comparison between you and Griselda than there is between the frigid zone and the tropics. Griselda was beaten, bruised, deserted and deprived of her children. Your injustices exist in your imagination alone. You are growing morbid from dwelling on your supposed wrongs. Forget yourself by living for his interests, and in time he will recognize your true worth," she said, as she bade her hostess good-night.

But this was what Verona was not capable of doing. It was what she was not even capable of understanding. It was not in her nature to do so. Nature had made her to look upon the world as being made for herself and for herself alone, and when her wishes were denied, she could not easily brook their denial.

She sat in the darkness when Mrs. Sangster had gone, looking out into the gloom of night. The servants came in to light the lamps, but she bade them go away. Her mind was in confusion, and the darkness was more in keeping with her mood. Nothing which her friend had said was very vividly impressed upon her mind, but yet the general impression, that her suspicions were verified, had taken root there. She felt that others knew what she did not know. She felt that there was a mutual understanding between her husband and her whom she considered her rival, and that their friends were cognizant of this, and that this understanding was greater in the sight of the world than was her rights as his wife. As this consciousness grew upon her, all the evil passions of her nature rose up within her, and were portrayed on her face in a silent, cold bitterness. That the world should know of her indignities and injustices wounded her vanity, and wounded vanity is often more vindictive than the jealousy of love. "I hate her! I hate her!" she thought within herself. "But I have nothing with which to accuse her. I can wait, there is always time, my day will come. I have been blind, stupid, but I shall be so no more. I shall ask him the meaning of his words. I am his wife. I have a right to know," and having once decided on this course she became calmer and more rational but none the less apprehensive.

She went to her room, dressed for dinner, dined alone, and went alone to fulfil several engagements of the evening. She returned at midnight more than ever determined to know, many events of the evening having added fresh fuel to the burning fire within her.

She learned that her husband was in his library still at work. She went to the library, and without any prelude asked him to explain the words which he had uttered on the terrace at Fern-wylde. "They are being made the subject of comment. It is said they emanated from a personal feeling. What do you say?"

Sir Keith sat at his desk, his head bent over his papers. He had spoken on her entrance but he had not raised his eyes. As his wife spoke his face grew very cold and impassive, and he still kept his eyes on his papers, but his mind was working rapidly. He had not intended them as personal. He had not even intended that there should be an undercurrent of meaning within them. It was the world, having knowledge of his love, that had put this meaning upon them. But no doubt they had been prompted by his own personal feelings, and he could not reply. He was too truthful to prevaricate or dissimulate, and could offer no explanation of their meaning, whereat his wife's face grew cold and harsh, and she accused him of seeking solace elsewhere, but she refrained from using her rival's name.

She wished to cheat herself into the belief that it was not so. She could not, even to him, connect their names together; the very sound of her name coupled with his sent a chill to her heart. She longed to hear him deny it, but he only remained silent.

His silence exasperated her. Her bitterness overcame her, and
in her injured passion she uttered innuendoes he could no longer
ignore, and gave vent to threats of retaliation which he could not
fail to understand.

He rose from his chair, and the colder, darker look which
many men, but few women, had seen there and had learnt to fear,
came upon his face, and in words which were few but forcible he
spoke to her. He was a man who believed it was not wise to make
one one's enemy, when one might be made one's friend, and he
was a just man. He did not wish to needlessly antagonize his
wife, and he recognized her rights, and spoke in a forcible and
firm but kind tone. His voice had ever in it that power to allay
and to silence.

She knew so little that she was silenced. She left him subdued
but sullen and with a sense of failure upon her. " I have spoken
too soon," she said, as she went to her own apartments. " He
denied nothing," she thought, as she tried to recall what he had said,
and as this truth came forcibly home to her her heart rose once
more in passionate anger within her. It was some hours before
she retired, and when she retired she could not easily sleep.
" There is always time," she said over and over again to herself,
until she fell into an uneasy slumber.

Sir Keith, when she left him, seated himself once more and
bowed his head in his hands. He was beginning to fear for the
honor of his name.

His wife was asking for love. Before his marriage he had
promised her none, and he could give her none. He had been
married only a few short hours when he had seen the fatal mistake he had made both for himself and his wife. Why did he
ever do it? he asked himself again and again as he sat with
bowed head. Perhaps, like Zola's Jean, one does so many things
not knowing why, when one has said to one's self that one
would do them. He saw that he had done wrong in binding
to himself a young girl in a loveless marriage. The temptations
and seductions of society were overwhelmingly strong on such
natures as hers, and he knew that if her love for himself became
less or grew into indifference, she would seek consolation elsewhere, and could he blame her? He thought of Helen of Troy
and her fate, and of what Ovid had written regarding her infi-
delity. He could blame his wife no more than Ovid had blamed
Helen. He had no cause for a separation, and even if he had he
would have shunned doing so, owing to the publicity and scandal
of such proceedings and the obloquy on both parties involved.

He knew so long as she loved him she would remain faithful to him, but if her love failed she had been brought up in a society that thought lightly of marriage fidelity, and he had strong apprehensions that she would yet stain his honor and bring scandal on his fair name.

His wife had been too wary to bring her rival's name into the discussion. She knew so little that she did not wish to alarm her quarry until she knew more. She was but pleading her own cause, and his mind for the time but dwelt upon her.

"What should he do?" His instincts rebelled against going to her, and on reflection he said to himself that when she would become calm she would see the error of her way and apologize for her words, so he did what was best under the circumstances— allowed matters to remain as they were and trusted to time to heal the break and solve the problem.

CHAPTER XL.

For several weeks after the open rupture Verona was sullen and miserable. The thoughts awakened never slept, and as far as it lay in her power to do so she kept a strict surveillance on his every movement. Sir Keith realized this and chafed under the espionage, but did not approach her.

But Verona's nature was one that could not endure long any denial. She was longing intensely for his presence again. She knew she would have to retract or rather condone the words she had uttered before he would accord her any degree of friendliness. It was difficult for her to do so. Her temperament would have made it an impossibility for her to do so, but for the one ray of magnanimity which her love for him had brought into her life; but the rancor which she bore in her heart was so great that it had the power to minimize this ray, so much so that when she approached him, it was in a spirit which had in it the power to increase rather than retract her words. He was wise enough to accept them at their literal meaning, and once more accord her the kindly treatment she had hitherto received from him because she bore his name.

For several weeks after this their life resumed its old routine, and they continued to go out, meeting the mistress of Apsley House wherever they went.

Modena had dreaded meeting Sir Keith, because she feared the force of their love, but when she had met him he had said to himself that he would devote what was left of his years to the simple duties of life. The first time that she was in his presence she had felt that this was so, and a peace had entered her own life, and very soon its interests had again become to her what they once had been.

She knew that the eyes of the world were upon them, but she tried to put this knowledge from her, as the sense of it had a tendency to make her assume a part which was not in harmony with her nature. The world is not long or easily deceived, and as her own spirit righted itself, and her life once more became serene and sanguine, her own people were quick to feel and to recognize that it was so, and to gather about her as of old.

Verona Kenyon was the first to feel that this was so, and the only one to resent it.

"How is it?" she asked herself again and again. "How is it she has the power to make one feel as Jean felt towards Francoise and her people—an alien? Although I wear the crown, yet she is queen," she was forced to admit, as Napoleon was forced to admit to his unconquerable, unquenchable rival, De Stael.

Napoleon had hated his fair enemy with a sound hatred. And for what reason? Because within De Stael had dwelt that passionate, patriotic pride, that hatred of democratic tyranny which is the worst of all tyrannies, that accurate knowledge of the foundation of things which is the requisite of all character, that Periclean desire to uplift the self-respect, the self-control and the self-culture of the common clay. Within her dwelt the self-abnegatory instincts of a noble woman and that inborn consciousness of prerogative which made her of the elect. She was the product of principles, while Napoleon was a man born of the moment, the product of circumstances, and was devoid of true moral and religious sense. He lacked the doctrinal integrity and knowledge of the fundamental essence of things. He had ambition, genius and audacity sublime, but the nature and the genius of a Pisistratus, who publicly scourged himself to secure the popular favor of the mob because through the mob alone could he rule. His feelings were vanity not pride, self-love not self-knowledge. His was an empire built in a day and it vanished in a day, but while the day was at its zenith, and its fairest, it was ever made dark by the presence of the eupatrid.

And so, too, with Verona. She was but the product of circumstances, and by the sheer force of her audacity she had won the day. Within her dwelt the same instincts, feelings and insatiable desire to dominate, but her day was ever made dark by the presence of the mistress of Apsley House and her husband, and her inability to reach her rival—much darker than the despot's day because within its darkness lay the jealousy of an unrequited love.

Before many days had passed Modena became conscious of this, but being at peace with herself she was able to go her way as Corinne had gone. She neither noticed nor resented. To have done so would have been to lower her dignity, and dignity she considered the safeguard of a woman of position. She accordingly went her way, and lived her own life, and this habitual indifference and the disregard which she invariably displayed towards her enemy's actions, were the most bitter and most exasperating of all things which her enemy had to bear. Verona could have forgiven their mutual love sooner than she could forgive this. Their conduct irritated her almost past all endurance. She knew that her grievances existed, but she could not reach an impalpable, intangible thing.

The conduct of the mistress of Apsley House had at last brought brought her to a knowledge of her own impotence.

"Nothing can dethrone her but her own actions," Verona was at last forced to admit. "She must be made to compromise herself. She is not made of stone. In time she will seek him. I have been a fool to thwart them. They must meet." And so she changed her tactics.

As Mark had done to his wife Isolt and her lover Tristram, so, too, would she do to her husband and Modena Wellington. She would allow her husband perfect freedom. She would do her utmost to increase their intimacy. She would thwart his plans only when she knew interference would irritate and drive him on. All that intrigue could accomplish she would accomplish with it. It was all she could do.

Could she have had her wish, she would have done it as quickly and as forcibly as the hand in Don Giovanni had touched its victims. But seeing she could not, she could wait with as much courage and cruelty and patience as the women of the age when the dagger and poison had become a fine art. The thunderbolt would have been more preferable and more pungent to her nature than the slow, insidious poison of the Mediceans, but failure and rebuff had taught her to be patient.

She would give them rope enough now, and when he had hung her he would leave her. Modred-like, she would wait and watch, and when the time would come, Modred-like, she would cry it from the house-tops.

On the discovery of the knight's passion for his queen, the gallant knight had given his life, his honor, his castles, his all to protect his queen. She could not imagine this. This might be possible in an ideal world, but not in a real world. Her conception of a man's love was that of a Don Juan. He wanted it so long as it was denied him. Possession robbed it of its flavor, and when he wearied of it he soon cast it aside. She was only capable of judging love through passion and the senses. She knew nothing of the force of that magnetism which makes two lives one.

After having decided on her course of action, she became more at her ease than she had been in many long weeks. She saw she had made a mistake in committing herself before she had anything tangible upon which to work. She had lacked in finesse and adroitness. She had acted as any child of nature might have done. Straight ways were not the ways of her temperament, but she had been carried away by impulse. All her life long she had loved intrigue. She had lived in it. Without it life would be devoid of pungency and flavor, and now to the lesser intrigues of her life was added a great passion which had the power to make her malignant and insatiable.

The season was now at its height, and this afforded ample opportunity to do what she said she would do, and for a few short weeks the mistress of Apsley House was deceived by her change of manner, and felt almost kindly towards her.

The candor and trust Lady Kenyon was displaying towards Sir Keith and herself made her feel quite guilty and ill at ease.

One evening as they had gathered at the home of a mutual friend she had expressed a wish to see some paintings on exhibition in the city at a friend of Sir Keith's.

"Keith, cannot you take Miss Wellington to see them this evening? I am sorry I have another engagement and cannot go, but you are at liberty. Do take her," his wife had said.

At another time she had insisted on his going with Modena to collect antiques for a church bazaar; several times she had suggested their names as deputations on different committees, and at many social functions she had endeavored to keep him by her side. At their country home there were many social, charitable and political functions which must be attended, and she had insisted on Sir Keith calling and taking with him the mistress of Fernwylde. "I am busy. I cannot go. I do not care for those

28

things. She does. I do not care for bare feet and homespun. She worships them. I cannot simulate an interest I cannot feel. She can. Take her, she will represent both of our interests," she had said at many times, and at all times with such candor and frankness that the mistress of Apsley House was carried away by the deception. She had not at any time accepted their proffered service. She had tactfully refused it, but she had been won by Verona's manner. She had suspected nothing.

People of a generous nature are slow in suspecting the duplicity of others. Tartuffe and Ornupre might walk by their side, but they would see in them only Alceste and Melanchthon.

She thought Lady Kenyon was beginning to realize that she had judged her wrongly, and her great comprehension made her lenient and forgiving towards previous injustices and unpleasantnesses. She thought she was beginning to appreciate her at her true worth, and she was touched. Since her fear had grown upon her she had felt guilty, and this secret consciousness had humiliated herself in her own sight, and made Verona's actions appear doubly magnanimous.

" She is trusting me now," she thought to herself, and her heart turned cold to Sir Keith, so willing was she to believe in other people's motives.

" Why did he place us in such a position? And to have to admit even to herself that there was anything unusual in their relations made her resent his conduct more and more.

" I believe I should hate anyone who would compromise me in the eyes of the world," she said, and her resentment changed her carefulness to coldness, and as her chilliness towards Sir Keith increased, her kindness towards Sir Colin Campbell became more marked, and as her intimacy with Sir Colin became more apparent, Sir Keith excluded himself from her presence more and more until at last they rarely, if ever, met, and as this was not what Verona wished or wanted she became very impatient, and in her impatience she betrayed herself.

In the latter part of January the chief, who was desirous of extending hospitality to some visiting notables, asked her to take them down to Idlewylde for a few days. This was the second time he had shown his preference for her. It was what she had long desired. It had pleased her once, but it had lost its power to please her now. She had expected that the mistress of Fernwylde would have shown her displeasure at the chief's preference for herself, but she had not.

She had not even noticed it, so there was no pleasure in doing it to outrival her, and it was quite a bother to entertain all these people. They were, no doubt, cultured people, but they were not English lords. No doubt, they were great, they were self-made men and clever men, but she could not be bothered with self-made men and with artists and literati. They were generally opinionated, vain and unpolished, and would be of no use to her when she went abroad, and she was about to offer some plausible excuse when a subtler thought came to her like an inspiration. Perhaps it would afford her husband and her rival an opportunity to commit themselves.

It would only be a small, select party, and amid old scenes and surroundings and in the solitude which the country affords and the emotions it creates, they might forget themselves in so far as to betray themselves.

She would not ask Sir Colin. She would leave them to themselves, but on further reflection she decided to ask Sir Colin. His presence would stimulate Sir Keith to action. And so she prepared her list for her party.

On Wednesday evening their party arrived from the city. When Modena had received her invitation she had hesitated some time before accepting. She did not wish to enter their home, but some of the visiting tourists had extended great kindnesses to her when abroad. She had expressed a desire to have them with her for a few days, but their time was limited and the chief had arranged otherwise, so she had no choice but to meet them at Idlewylde. She compromised the matter with herself by going to Fernwylde. She could make this her home and from here spend a few hours at intervals with the Idlewylde party.

On Thursday evening she joined the house-party. As she stepped from her sleigh at the door, Sir Keith, who had been out adding a new pack of hounds to his kennel, joined her, and they entered the reception-room together. The twilight had deepened almost into night, and the lamps had not been lighted. The guests were in their different rooms dressing for dinner, and the hall servants had gone to the rear of the house. No one came to take her to her room, and Sir Keith did not ring for a servant. She crossed the room, and stood for some moments warming her hands before the glowing fire, which burned on the hearth.

Sir Keith laid aside his riding-whip and gloves, and approached the hearth. It was the first time he had been in her presence in many long months. For an instant his eyes met hers, and hers dropped. He did not speak; he did not need to speak. There are moments which come into persons' lives when silence expresses more than all written or spoken words, moments when all outside one's self is as forgotten as though it existed not. At the present moment it was so with them.

The French Court had banished the brilliant Montespan from the Court of the Sun-King, because of the love of its god for her. On her exile he had given his heart and soul to the church. On her return one moment of her presence was more powerful than all the creeds of throne and altar.

Sir Keith had said that he would give his life to his duties. Modena had said once again that she would turn to Sir Colin Campbell. One glance had in it the power to undo all that they had said they would do. At the present moment Modena was oblivious of all else but his presence. She knew Sir Keith was much moved, but she knew that in his own home she need fear no words from him. She passively wondered why a servant did not come, or why he did not ring for one. She knew that she was playing with fire, but this knowledge was away in the background of her thoughts. All she was aware of was that for many months the world had been very cold, but that now the very nature of things had changed. Sometimes a whole lifetime of suffering or joy is crowded into a few moments. These few moments seemed that to them now. They had not spoken since entering the room; their faces were in shadow; their thoughts one. All that had been pent up in his heart through these long lonely months found expression now in silent messages, whose warmth seemed to change the wintry eve into the lulling, dreamy sensuousness of a tropical day. Like the knight's love of old, his love had wrought through all his flesh into his life, and it was impossible for her to be in his presence without being submissive and responsive to it. He wished to speak to her, to tell it all to her, but he dare not. She knew this and she wished to hear it, but she dare not. She dare be with him no longer alone. She raised her eyes, looked past him, and asked him to ring for a servant.

He saw and felt the change within her, and did not resent it. It would not have been she, had she been a weaker woman and responded.

He drew himself together, turned from her and crossed the room to touch the bell, but as he turned, his wife, who, having heard their voices in the hall, had come down, and stood concealed by the draperies, now parted the hangings and entered the room.

As she had watched them her heart had leaped within her with jealous rage.

She had given them opportunity to commit themselves, and

when they had not hung themselves with the rope she had meted
out to them, she had been indignant and impatient, and had felt
herself outwitted, and now when through mere accident they had
lived three minutes of time together, she felt she was being outraged; but as she had watched and listened she had seen and heard
nothing tangible with which to accuse them. There had been no
words, not even an eye-message, and soul-messages are invisible,
inaudible, intangible things, and she could but meet her guest with
words suitable to the occasion, but her voice had in it an accent
which awakened Modena to the knowledge that she was being
placed in a wrong position.

"She trusted me, and she thinks I have been untrue to her
trust," she thought in her confusion of feeling. She did not wish
to have her motives and actions misjudged. Deceit was abhorrent
to her nature. It humiliated and hurt her greatly to think of how
Lady Kenyon would judge her. But her humiliation and her grief
were of short duration.

"Ah, you here, Modena!" exclaimed Mrs. Sangster, entering
the room at the same moment. "When did you come?"

"Yes, when?" repeated Verona. "I happened to come down
and found her and my husband mooning by the hearth," she said,
in a tone of light badinage, but with the slightest suggestion in
her accent and words.

Instinctively Modena felt that her actions were being misrepresented, but the suggestion was so slight that she wondered if it
were really meant.

"I arrived some three minutes ago. I met Sir Keith at the
door," she replied, irritated at herself for stooping to defend
herself.

"Did you walk or ride over?" asked Lady Kenyon, picking up
Sir Keith's gloves and whip, and addressing her husband.

Her words implied directly "I do not believe you. You have
met somewhere. You have been together."

She was fingering the little whip with a slow smile on her face.
She knew her rival was embarrassed, and she was thoroughly
enjoying her discomfiture.

Sir Keith, who all along had known the meaning of his wife's
candor, came to her rescue.

"I shall take these," he said, quietly to his wife, and then
turned to Mrs. Sangster and Modena. "I was out this evening
and bought a new thoroughbred. She's a beauty. I want you to
see her. Will you come now or wait until morning?" he said,

handling the whip as if he would like to use it—on the thorough-bred or on something else.

But his wife was equal to the occasion.

"Oh, I am sure Mrs. Sangster doesn't care to go, but perhaps Miss Wellington would care to go," she replied, and to Modena's ears the words contained a covert insolence which she felt she could not resent.

"Will you go, Modena?" asked Sir Keith, turning to her.

But Modena felt that Lady Kenyon wished her to go. "Why did she wish her to go?" And then it dawned upon her. She had been duped.

The apparent candor of Lady Kenyon had been a blind to draw her on. She wished to invite comment upon her conduct. She saw it all now, and the knowledge roused all her latent courage and honest indignation. Her words were a menace to her courage and her honor. Certainly she would go; but she was a wise woman, and knew the value of discretion and restrained herself from acting on impulse, and addressed Lady Kenyon with as much and as sincere candor as her own.

"I am at your disposal. If you wish us to go I shall enjoy going," she said.

"It is almost dinner-time. You must dress," interrupted Mrs. Sangster, who understood the undercurrent of meaning and motive, and who realized Modena's danger. "I think you had better defer it until morning."

"Very well," replied Modena, and she turned and ascended the stairs to her room.

"Why did I come? How can I eat her bread?" she asked herself as she dressed for dinner, while the blood coursed hotly through her veins as she thought of how she had been duped.

She had been humiliated and she had been duped. Although her conscience was clear, yet she felt guilty in her own sight and deceitful towards the woman whose bread she was eating. This was precisely how Verona Kenyon wished her to feel, and she had been blindly led into this. "Why should we meet such people?" In all these past months she had been blind and deaf to all Verona's rudeness, envy and misrepresentations. She had been so from wisdom, dignity and contempt for such conduct. She had invariably remembered the words of her favorite Greek sage, that "Contempt was a sentiment which would in time overthrow the tyranny of ignorance and injustice."

Her conduct had been a mixture of instinct and philosophy. Hume's philosophy of conduct, that resentment was given to man by nature for defence as the safeguard of justice and security of innocence, had always seemed to her so low, but it almost seemed to her now that her silence and forbearance verged on ignominy; it almost seemed to her that there comes a time when forbearance becomes a cowardice and an admission of guilt.

She had been extremely kind, considerate and magnanimous; and she had been duped! She was very slow to believe it, but when she did believe it she could not easily forgive or forget it. She had never before known that there were both cruelty and revenge within her nature. She would resent such conduct, and her countenance grew cold while her nostrils dilated and quivered like those of a blooded mare under a curb. "Why shouldn't I publicly take him from her?" she thought, and then she checked herself. "Have I stooped to this? To enter into a rivalry with another woman and for that woman's husband! Have I fallen so low?" She couldn't believe her own senses. But what was she to do? She couldn't avoid them, and so long as she met them things would be as they were now, or perhaps much worse.

At the present moment had she followed her impulse she would have left the house, but to do so would be to invite comment upon her conduct, and to render an act of disrespect and discourtesy to the tourist guests. She could but remain. In a few weeks' time, for his sake and for her own, if her father were well, she might yet go abroad. What would she do while away? She might exist but she could not live. She could not live without real work, and there was no work to be done abroad. She might go under some of the great masters for a year and improve herself, but this was such a selfish life when there was so much to be done at home. Opportunities had been hers to ally herself with some of the leading families of England. She might yet do so. The age, traditions, the feeling that one is very near to the centre of things, which the Old World gives and inspires, possessed for her a great fascination, a fascination so dangerous that she never allowed herself to dwell upon it.

She might yet ally herself with some of these families, and by this means be enabled to enjoy life at its highest and best. But no, she could not do so. Hadn't he said to her, oh! so long ago, that their country was yet in a comatose, chrysalis state, but that the day was fast approaching when they might, if they would, place themselves in a foremost place among the leading lights of the world? She knew that there comes a time in the history of every nation when its most urgent need is a man, a man born of the moment yet the product of the virtues, the man of the occasion, the man of destiny, the man whose spirit attracts, creates, uplifts, inspires, performs. They were the people for that time, and they must be ready. She could not go. Her every interest in life was centred in her homes. There was so much to be done. Life was altogether too fleeting, too short to accomplish what she had always wished to do. There were dozens, scores, hundreds of people depending upon her for the little ray of sunshine in their everyday life. New visions and luring ideals had opened up every day to her view, and although she was the soul of humility, yet so interested was she in the things which surrounded her life, that she felt that if she absented herself for any time, the world would stand still.

Only a few weeks ago all these things had failed to interest her, and she had wished to go, but that was when she was weak and her health broken. She was well and strong now, and she would remain with her duties and interests in life. "Matters must go on as they were. Her innate sense would tell her how to act in any emergency," she concluded, as the last bell rang.

She went downstairs to dinner, but she ate little. She made herself pleasant to the tourists, and during the evening and next forenoon accorded Sir Keith a greater degree of intimacy than she had given him since his marriage.

The subtlest poisons are those which enter the system we know not how, and permeate it before we are aware of it. She knew that Verona Kenyon was infusing her surroundings with an air of suspicion and mistrust.

"She wants me to compromise myself," she thought, as she wended her way with the others to the ice that afternoon. "Compromise myself! I would die sooner than do so." And new lines formed round her mouth as she joined the skaters on the ice and faced the cold northern air. "She is even making this place and this pastime, which has been one of the greatest pleasures in life, distasteful," she thought, as she adjusted her skates and paused for a moment before joining the others, looking upon the scene around her.

On the borderland, between the two estates, lay the Idlewylde, one of the many rivulets which fed the Outaouais. For many years it had been the favorite resort for parties staying at either house, in the summer for boating, in winter for skating. It was now fast bound by nature's bands. The ice was one shimmering sheet, while all around the surroundings were in keeping with the scene.

Nowhere in the world, except it be in far-away Russia, can one

behold a scene so grand, so imposing by nature, as in the wilds of
our own northern woods. The glassy sheets of ice; the leafless
trees drooping with massive icicles which glitter like jewels in a
December sun; the fringing needle-like pines waving in the wind,
like plumes on a funereal bier; the snow-laden firs reminding one,
with their many fantastic shapes, of old Kriss Kringle and his
pack; the deer, so plentiful in these parts, browsing on the green
spruce edging the stream; the naked boughs with their sunlit
frozen diamonds, the distant peaks of the snow-capped Laurentides, the king-fishers' nests in the banks, the rooks in the old elm
trees, the sombre forests sloping from its banks, the frowning
slide on the mountain slope, and the cozy little tents on the shore
with their warm fires and tea and biscuits—these all combined to
form a scene as simply grand and fascinating as nature holds
within her lap.

It was here the ladies, warmly clad in sealskins and sables,
delighted to spend the afternoon, gliding swiftly over the frozen
surface, courting the clear, stinging northern air, and then, when
the snow-laden clouds darkened the sky and the day waned, they
were joined by the men returning with their hounds and guns and
game-laden bags from beaver's dam, martin's haunt and silver-
grey fox's trail, and when twilight deepened they would wend
their way home to dress for a warm dinner and the pleasures of
the evening.

To-day, as the mistress of Fernwylde stood for a moment alone,
all that the scene had represented to her in the past came up
before her. What had gone out of her life, and what had come
in? She did not know what had gone out, but she knew that the
pebbles which had come in were changing to a great weight like a
stone over her life.

She was aroused from her moment's reverie and retrospection
by the others calling to her to join them. She turned from the
scene and was soon among them, but she wished she could avoid
them. The visiting tourists were congenial to her, but the few
Verona Kenyon had asked to meet them were not. Their incessant chatter and loud mirth grated on her overwrought nerves
and irritated her. For some time she glided in and out with
those gathered there, but as the day waned and the groups
gathered around the warm fires in the tents on the shore, unnoticed she glided away up one of the little streams which fed the
lake.

She longed to be alone, to be free from simulated appearances, to be herself once more, and she sped on and on, regardless of time or distance.

Every spot, every tree was familiar to her from childhood. The ice was like glass; the woods were sombre, solitary, still, almost melancholy, wrapt in that winter whiteness and stillness which had been so dear to her from childhood; the keen northern air stung her face, invigorated her nerves and quieted the irritation which had lately dwelt within her. This was what the world should be. This was nature full and free, and her spirits became almost joyous. She went on and on; here paths led to the village, there to the mountains; and ever and anon she passed the favorite drinking places of the forest animals. She knew no fear. How many times had she been here with her friends! And her eyes softened and darkened with many memories.

At length she came to where the stream branched into several rivulets which led away into the forest wilds, and she followed the one which skirted the mountain side. In the foreground the stream narrowed, and the shadows deepened from the closeness of the overhanging cedars.

She paused for a moment, poised on her skate as an ibis on its wing, to regain her breath before returning.

In the moment's stillness she was startled by the close baying of hounds and a noise in the underbrush bordering the banks. She passed between the trees in the dusky shadows, and was emerging into the open space beyond, when she saw an immense wild lynx, at these times rare in those parts, but now driven down from the northern woods by the severity of the winter and the scarcity of food.

The dogs had infuriated the naturally fierce animal and had at last driven him to bay by surrounding him. With lightning rapidity he sped up the overhanging cedar, and for the first time caught sight of Modena.

For one short instant he glared at her with gleaming, dilated eyes, mouth foaming and teeth gnashing.

At that instant Sir Keith, with gun on shoulder, appeared on the shore, but a dead limb intervened between him and the desperate animal. In a moment he divined the situation and the murderous beast's intent. "For God's sake, Modena, drop flat on the ice," she heard him cry in a hoarse, deep voice.

She was a brave woman, possessed of great presence of mind, and at once did as she was told. At that instant she saw the infuriated animal make one great leap towards her. Her heart seemed to cease beating as she felt it pass over to the edge, a few feet beyond. The ice was smooth as glass, and the lynx glided on for some distance. She well knew the murderous nature of the beast, and knew that it would immediately turn upon her. When she saw it pass she rose, and with great rapidity made for the shore.

She saw Sir Keith aim, but her body intervened and she could feel the hot breath from the beast behind her and hear his labored pant.

"Swerve to the right," she heard Sir Keith cry, in an intense voice, and as she did so she felt the sharp whiz of the bullet to her left, and immediately the great beast with one agonized cry and bound rolled in death a few feet from her.

When she reached the shore she was as pale as death, and caught the boughs of the overhanging cedars to balance herself on her skates, but otherwise she was calm and collected.

By this time her cousin and Carlton Monteith, who were also in pursuit of the beast, had reached the stream and divined the situation. As Jack unloosed her skates the situation in all its peril dawned upon her. She trembled visibly, and was forced to seat herself on a fallen tree trunk.

Sir Keith had had no time to address her before the others had come up. His eye had been sure, and his hands firm while the danger lasted, but now, strong man though he was, he shuddered when he thought of what might have been.

"They will miss me, and come in search of me. Will you go back by the river and tell them I have gone home with Jack, but say nothing of this," she said to Carlton Monteith, when she recovered herself.

As the three walked back together she did not thank Sir Keith for what he had done. She knew that she need say no words. She remembered what she had felt on the night of the storm, and she knew that no words were needed.

"You will make some excuse for our absence to-night," she said as she removed her seal gauntlet and placed her hand in his warm clasp, which had in it the power to wake any human heart to an echo, as she bade him good-night at her own door.

He turned away and walked back home. It was the first time he had touched her hand since his marriage, and the touch made the blood flow like fire in his veins and made his heart ache with a great passionate pain during all the long hours of the night.

CHAPTER XLI.

But cautious and careful as had been the participants in the accident, the knowledge of such things as these will creep out.

Sir Keith's servant, whose duty it was to bag the game, had been an eye-witness of the accident, and like fog rising from a malarial marsh to the heights above, from the servants' hall the incidents of the afternoon gradually ascended and reached the fine ear of society, foremost among those to hear it being Lady Kenyon herself, her maid having learnt it from some of the upper servants, and possessing to a certain extent the confidence of her mistress, and loving sensation as an epicure loves dram-drinking and curry eating, imparted the information to her as she was about to retire for the night.

When Verona heard it, for some moments she remained silent and very still, moved to intense emotion. It had come upon her so suddenly that for some moments she was not prepared how to receive it. The first feeling which sprang up within her was one of great bitterness towards the mistress of Fernwylde, and of anger towards her husband for saving the life of her rival and being associated with her in such a thrilling scene, her mingled emotions causing her eyes to gleam with as much brutality and uncurbed desire as the wild beast's had done towards its innocent victim.

But the next moment her heart beat with joy. "Now I have her in my power," she thought. "Why did she leave us? Why did she go away alone? She had an appointment with him. He was with her." But as these thoughts dwelt in her mind, her injured passions once more became greater than her gratified designs, and abruptly she dismissed her maid for the night, not wishing an eye-witness of her misery and humiliation.

For some moments she paced the floor, incapable of intelligent thought. Not for a moment did she doubt Modena's motive in leaving the party, or her husband's appearance at the river's edge.

"She would have no leniency towards them." It was impossible for her to do so. It was as impossible for magnanimity and charity to spring from a nature rooted in narrowness and selfishness as it was impossible for blood to come from a stone, or warm milk from an ice floe. Culture and discipline might train such natures to become generous, but the sympathies and the animosities, the calumnies and the charities of the present world, have their mainspring in nature rather than in the mind.

"She stole away to meet him," kept ringing in her ears, as in that state of mind which Horace describes as "Anger unbridled becomes the violent tyrant of the soul," she paced the floor of her room. "She will live to regret that the wild-cat did not tear her to pieces. Before one week from to-day the whole world shall know it."

Her head ached, her temples throbbed, while the blood coursed like living fire through her veins from the intensity of her emotion. At length, overcome by exhaustion, she threw herself on a couch in her dressing-room, where she fell into a feverish sleep until morning; but the morning sun, which rose late over the Idlewylde, brought her no peace or rest.

To-day was the last day of their stay at Idlewylde. She dressed herself feverishly, debating within her own mind all the while as to how she would best betray them. Her desire was to spring upon them at once with as much ferocity as the wild-cat had displayed the previous day; but her previous experience had taught her to be cautious, and very soon the subtlety and intrigue of her own mind asserted itself, and became greater than her wounded feelings, and she went down to the breakfast table with an outward air of composure, but with a hardness of heart so plainly visible that her guests were soon aware that some unpleasantness had occurred. They noticed the absence of the mistress of Fernwylde, and wisely refrained from making any comment, and no opportunity presented itself to Lady Kenyon during the morning hours to refer to the matter.

She was beginning to be very impatient and irritable, when a messenger arrived from Fernwylde with its mistress's regrets for her absence on the plea of indisposition.

They were assembled at the lunch table when the messenger arrived. Lady Kenyon took the message, excused herself, and after reading it handed it to Sir Keith with much the same spirit as the Courts of the People might have handed the scaffold document to Marie Antoinette or Eugenie Montijo.

Sir Keith felt that all eyes were upon him, and as he read, despite his every effort, his face flushed warmly. His wife noticed the warmth. It was what she wanted.

"Miss Wellington is indisposed," she said, turning to her guests with a slight, fleeting smile, but a smile containing a world of meaning.

"Where did Modena disappear to so suddenly last evening?" asked Mrs. Gregory. She was all unconscious of the accident by the river, or of there being anything wrong in their surroundings.

"She had a rendezvous up the river," answered their hostess with the same smile and a meaning glance of triumph towards her husband. "But the meeting proved rather unfortunate, I understand. Sir Keith will tell you all about it. Ask him," she added, and then, knowing full well that she had sown seeds of mistrust which would grow and ripen, and which like one grain of mustard seed would pollute a whole field with its noxious weed, she turned from Mrs. Gregory and resumed conversation with some of her guests, as if the subject were of no interest to her whatever, while Sir Keith's face darkened, and his brow knit into sombre lines. It was not the first time he had felt the force of his wife's malignant and implacable mind.

He knew that she possessed that faculty of throwing lights, by a meaning smile or a slow soft word, on words and actions, harmless and innocent in themselves, which made them appear offensive and compromising, as certain lights thrown on a clear wall transforms a mole-hill into a mountain or a line into a landscape. He felt that she was now intentionally misrepresenting the situation, and intuitively he felt that his guests were also conscious of her purpose.

He left the lunch table as soon as courtesy would permit, and went out into the grounds with his friends. During the afternoon he felt that while his friends were ignoring the inferences in his wife's words, her friends were freely commenting upon the situation.

It was what they wanted. It was what they had long wished for. Not that Modena had ever done them any harm. To some, a great many of them, she had been extremely kind, but they were like the illiterate peasant writing Aristides' name upon the ostracised tablet, "I have nothing against him, but I am tired of hearing him called the Just." They had nothing against her, but she had carried herself a little too loftily and completely above them. To take a place side by side with her was an impossibility; but, like all small natures they thought that by pulling her down it raised themselves to a higher level.

Sir Keith saw this and perceived their malignity, and the knowledge served to awaken all his latent courage for what was just, and disdain for what was contemptible, and caused him to treat his wife for the remainder of the day with ill-concealed contempt and coldness.

He was glad when the party broke up next morning, and they had returned once more to the city and duty.

Instinctively he felt that the visit to Idlewylde had been productive of great mischief, the more apprehensive and baneful because of its indefiniteness. No one spoke of it in his presence. No one even hinted at it either by word or glance, but he was as well aware of what they were saying as though he heard it all. They even refrained from speaking of the accident, and their silence on the subject told him that their conduct was being maligned. He chafed and rebelled under it, but he could say nothing, so went his way.

He had heard his wife say nothing further than the few words at the lunch table, but many times when the air around him seemed suffused with it, he had met her eyes, and her eyes had in them a little derision, a subdued triumph, a satisfied reprisal, which told him that the moments to her were very sweet, and which roused within him a desire, almost a resolution, to show his contempt of their conduct by publicly appearing with Modena, but for her sake he refrained.

For the next few months, through prudence, he avoided the mistress of Apsley House, and this lull in the drama was not what his wife wished for or wanted, and it caused her to again become incautious in her impatience.

Towards the end of the second month they went to a French reading at Maple Hurst. For several winters these readings had become very popular, and had proved both interesting and instructive. Lady Kenyon had been for the most part a silent member, but to-day the subject under discussion attracted her attention.

They were discussing the writers of the Louis XIV. epoch, St. Amand and Molière being congenial to Modena's and Mrs. Cecil's taste; they had warmed in their debate and discussion, and had now moved to a western window, where the lights were bright, to examine some famous paintings of that period, that had been presented to their society by one of the recent French tourists. Sir Keith had come in and joined them at the window, and had entered into the discussion, favoring the idealism of the mistress of Apsley House in preference to the realism of Molière and his admirer, Mrs. Cecil.

Lady Kenyon, who was standing by the side of Mr. Patrie, holding in her hand a " Serenade at the Petit Trianon," where the Sun-King was doing homage to the brilliant Montespan, noticed her husband's attitude, and made some comparison between the scene in her hand and the scene up the river.

The remark was uncalled-for, and was intended for Mr. Patrie alone, but the conversation in the room having ceased for a moment the words were audible to many others.

Mr. Lester looked up quickly at his guest, and his eyes grew sombre with anger at the inference, and his gentlemanly instincts recoiled at the coarseness of her revenge.

Respect for Sir Keith bound him to silence, while contempt for her conduct made warm words strive for utterance.

His sister Helen was no less indignant, and for the remainder of the afternoon was not slow in letting her guest feel the onus of her displeasure. Her knowledge of the purity and unselfishness of her friend's motives and conduct made her quick to resent the vague uneasiness which Lady Kenyon's words were arousing in the breasts of her friends. True, no one doubted for a moment the situation, but as a drop of wine in a glass of spring water robs it forever of its purity, or one drop of venom from the fangs of an adder poisons the whole system, so words of aspersion and calumny tend to injure the character attacked.

Her answers and remarks were rather vague and desultory to her guests as she was debating within herself whether it were better to treat the remarks with indifference as unworthy of notice, or repudiate them in justice to her friend.

She noticed her brother's face lowering, and she knew that his mind, too, was dwelling upon what had been said, and she deemed silence best until she could speak to him alone.

When they were gone Lester stood for some time in the gloom, in gloomy silence, debating within himself what he should do. He had heard of the Idlewylde accident, and of Lady Kenyon's version of it. He realized that the reports must be checked at once. He began to fear for Modena. He knew, so long as she remained unconscious of them, that she would treat Sir Keith discreetly, if not coldly, but he also knew that she was a proud and courageous woman, and if she heard of Lady Kenyon's words she would consider them a menace to her honor and courage, and as insults only act on proud people as water on burning oil, he knew it would arouse all her latent contempt for such things, and that she would accord Sir Keith a greater degree of intimacy than prudence would allow. She was as dear to him almost as Helen. He knew it was the first rule of good society not to interfere in other people's affairs, but there comes a time in one's life when not to do so is cowardly. Should he tell Jack? But Jack was abrupt, and at times lacking in tact, and his interference might cause it to become more public. Sir Keith was the one who should know and act, but Sir Keith, he knew, was one who lived his own

life, took things as they came, and allowed evil to be its own
slayer. But evil too often slays its victim before it hangs itself
with its own rope. What should he do?

"I do not know what to do," he said, and as he said it the door
opened abruptly and Sir Keith entered the room.

He had learnt of her words from another source, and wished to
verify them, and, if true, apologize to Mr. Lester for their utterance in his home.

When Sir Keith heard what his friend had to say his face grew
harsh, but after his apology his lips remained mute and motionless.
He could not discuss his wife with another, the truth of the
meeting it was needless to tell, but he must shield the honor of
his own name which his wife's mad passion was now endangering.
He loathed the publicity she was giving the affair. It was like
throwing offal to a pack of hungry wolves. What was he to do?

Few words passed between the two men, each understanding the
other, and in parting they clasped hands in silent sympathy.

Sir Keith returned home in the gloom with bent head and
drawn brows, not noticing the many friends he met on his way,
thereby increasing the vague, involuntary doubts in each mind.

On reaching his home he went direct to his own room, and
paced its length with a greater disquietude than he had ever felt
in his public career. Mingled with his agitation was a just indignation and contempt for the coarseness of her revenge.

He would have to speak to his wife. His whole nature
rebelled at the thought of his having to do so, but he would have
to do it if he wished to keep unsullied the honor of his own name.

He touched a bell, and when a servant appeared sent him to see
if his wife would accord him a few minutes' interview.

He found her in full evening dress about to leave for a late
reception.

She stood under the gas jets with her hands resting on a small
oval table, her ermine-lined wrap lying ready by her side.

When he entered the room he almost regretted having come. To
be forced to notice such words and such conduct seemed to him
so degrading, and the thought of discussing the matter with her
was repulsive to him. He hesitated for some moments while she
bent her steel grey eyes in interrogation upon him.

"What is it?" she at length asked. "I am surely honored by
your presence. What can I do for you?"

It was the first time he had been in her apartments. Her tone
touched him, and he answered in a stern voice:

"I was informed this afternoon that there were some reports

29

being circulated in our social circle in which there is no truth. Do you know anything about them?"

"Reports?" she asked, with uplifted brows. "You are very indefinite. About whom?"

"About myself."

She laughed lightly, with a certain tinge of derision, and replied, "Oh, a man cannot expect to lead a public life without being slandered! Isn't there an old saying, 'If you wish to know your pedigree from tip of root to blush of fruit, enter the political arena'? You are becoming very sensitive to reports. You cannot be a good Tory, because I heard your chief say yesterday that Tory consciences were as tough as old shoe leather. But you will have to excuse my remaining to discuss them as the carriage is waiting, and Mr. Patrie promised to accompany me," she added, as she moved from the table with her wraps.

He knew that she was aware of what he meant, and her tone exasperated him.

He pushed an ottoman aside and approached her. "I will not detain you long," he said, in a very firm voice. "The discussion contains no pleasure for me, but in a few words I shall tell you a few truths. I did not say 'political reports,' I said 'slander,' and you need not try to evade the question. You started them. They have not yet gone outside our immediate circle. You know what I mean; you must stop them."

But his audience was bland and smiling. She had at last made him come to her. She had waited long, but she was reaching him at last.

"*I* started them! *I* know anything about them! You know I do not discuss such things as these with my friends," she replied with indifference.

"Don't you!" despite himself he replied, with infinite scorn in his two little words.

"I am surprised at your listening to them," she said, indifferently.

"So am I. They are unworthy of notice. But yet one respects the honor of one's name."

"You must care very much for the honor of her name, or you would not worry over it. And if you care so much, why do you give people cause to talk?"

"I am not worrying over any other name, but my own. Her name—if there is a woman in the matter—her name, I say, is nothing to us. She is only answerable to herself. It is the honor of my own name I am defending. It is endangered."

"Then why do you endanger it, if it is so dear to you?"

"I am not endangering it."

"Then, who in the world is endangering it?"

"You are."

"What do you mean?" she asked, losing her bland smile and self-command at the thought of his defence of the woman she hated, and his condemnation of herself.

"I mean that you have been making injudicious remarks and insinuations which you must retract."

"There is no need to retract the truth."

"What have you been accusing me of? I wish to know the truth."

"And I wish to say that I do not think you need ask me," she replied, offensively.

Sir Keith went white in a mute wrath. Could he have stricken to earth with a sword of scorn the woman who stood before him, as Perseus had slain the Medusa, she would have dropped dead before him. His face went cold as the faces of those who had once looked upon the Medusa. It was some moments before he could recover himself.

"You know the meeting was accidental. You do not yourself believe it otherwise," he at length managed to say.

But his wife only smiled still more offensively.

"If any other person should say such a thing she would publicly retract it or prove it, or I should shoot her nearest male relative like a dog. You say it. You are my wife in name. Almost it tempts one to play the coward's part and put an end to this state of affairs."

He turned to leave the room, but hesitated as he realized the futility of his coming, and the danger which menaced all parties. Then, too, he was a just and kind man. He had of his own free will married her, and this had given her claims upon his affections which he had not rendered unto her, and he knew that it was her jealousy of his love that was bringing out all the evil in her nature. He knew it would be of no avail to enter into an explanation with her. She was incapable of rising above the common, and of admiring heroic conduct. He was conscious of the obligations he owed her, and he wanted to end the discussion, so he turned again to her, and said in a gentler tone:

"You are acting very unwisely, Verona. Your actions will cause great trouble. Will you take my word for it if I swear to you that your suspicions are groundless?"

"No, I shall not unless you deny your love also."

With great difficulty he controlled an oath.

"I have never had my bare word doubted before, and I offer it to you now on oath, and you doubt it."

He offered her no denial of his love, and the omission caused her to look at him with cold, chilly eyes of revenge.

"It is not I alone who doubt it; the whole world will soon doubt it. You may condemn me for saying so. You may loathe me, as in time you will loathe the whole world for misbelieving you; but you know yourself you could not tell the truth if you would. Your honor would forbid your telling the truth about a woman, and even if you did, the world would not believe you."

His eyes again grew very sombre and deep lines formed between his brows.

"Your world might not. I know very little about your world," he said, with a whole world of disdain bristling through his tone and accent, and then once more checking himself for descending to the tu quoque form of dispute, he repeated, in a milder tone, "You are doing wrong, Verona, you will live to regret it. Your thoughts and suspicions are only hallucinations of your own mad passions, and you knew I did not love you when I married you."

"Then if you loved another, why did you marry me?"

"I told your father and yourself why I married you. I was perfectly honest with both of you. I did not feign a love for you, nor did I tell you I had never loved another. I gave you your choice. You were free to accept or reject."

"Do you love Modena Wellington?" she asked him, abruptly, with a world of apprehension in her voice and mien.

"You have no right to ask that question," he answered, very coldly.

"I have a right. I am your wife."

He could not answer her, and so remained silent, and his silence told her what she dreaded knowing.

Had she been a noble woman it would have pained him to hurt her thus, but he knew these embittered scenes were caused by her own words and actions, and he was wearying of them. He had been strictly candid and honest with her. He had never intentionally uttered one unkind or discourteous word. He had given her everything, and every honor he could bestow, but his love he could not give.

"I think if you are wise, Verona, you will not repeat these scenes. Since we have been married, had you lived an open, upright life one might have learned to respect you."

"*Love* you, why don't you say?"

"Man's feelings are beyond his control. One cannot love at will. It depends altogether on yourself what I prove to you. I think it is better we should not quarrel. If you force it on me you will live to regret it, for when words are uttered I do not quickly forget them. Until lately we have lived in harmony; it is better that we should continue to do so. You have started reports which are both false and foundationless. You may take your choice. You must either retract them or henceforth we meet as strangers."

It was foreign to Verona's nature to curb her words or restrain her temper. Instinctively she felt that with him there were limits she could not pass if she wished to be again reconciled to him. With the greatest effort of her life she now restrained herself. Her heart swelled and burned within her with unspeakable anger and jealous rage, a rage so great that she found it once more overcoming her, so she turned from him, white with suppressed passion, and without further word entered an inner room, while Sir Keith turned and left the room, and soon after the house.

The next morning he left early on some ministerial matters which required his attention for several days, and when he returned he learnt that through the other members of the hunting party the truth of the details of their meeting by the river had been made clear, and that their world was quick to resent his wife's coloring of the matter. His wife had been quick to feel, to see this, and had, with great tact and skill, passed the circumstances over with light badinage, and had greeted her husband on his return with a cordiality which made him regret that he had spoken; not that he was deceived by her apparent cordiality; he knew that this was but a cloak and that his words, although they had served to check her for a time, had but added to the intensity of her anger. He was well aware that the desire for revenge remained as imperative and impregnable as in the first stages of discovery, and the rancor at her heart as deep-rooted and insatiable as Phædra's for her stepson.

CHAPTER XLII.

"My dear Modena, we are delighted to see you home again," said her many friends, as they gathered at Apsley House to welcome its mistress home after a three months' sojourn abroad.

For some months after the Idlewylde incident, Modena had gone her way with a calm demeanor and a seeming indifference to the many conjectures and vague unexpressed doubts which she felt Verona Kenyon had caused to be aroused in the breast of her friends and in the community at large, but at heart she was bitterly angered and deeply offended and humiliated.

She had heard nothing. No one had spoken of it to her. No one had even spoken of the accident, but to her, as it had been to Sir Keith, their silence had been more expressive than many spoken words. But although she heard nothing, by that intuition which some women possess and which knowledge of the world increases, she was sensible that Verona Kenyon, by her subtlety, suspicion and insane jealousy, was causing doubts to be raised in the breasts of all but her immediate circle, as Modred, all for hate of the gallant knight, had by silent smiles of slow disparagement made disruption in the Table Round, and the knowledge was humiliating in the extreme to her. It seemed to drop her conduct to the level of all, which all her life she had held in cold contempt, or had abhorred.

She was not to blame for the accident by the river. She had been the victim of unfortunate circumstances. She had regretted the incident very much. She had always very wisely considered that social approval is a very necessary appenage to position, and invariably had been careful to give her world no cause for comment, and now when she felt its attitude, she was deeply incensed at the callousness, misconstruction and enmity of the world she had so dearly loved.

She had not thought that it would treat her so. Hitherto she had judged it by the feelings which dwelt within her own breast. It had been perfect, and her all. Like the Homeric poets of old, "The varied pageantry of earthly existence did not pall upon her, but seemed more fair than any casual hope of being elsewhere blest." Within her had dwelt the same sentiments and ambitions as had dwelt within the noble king of the Golden Age. Dagonet had said of his king, when the king's Excalibur had proved a straw, "He is a fool, because he conceits himself as God, that he can make figs out of thistles, silk from bristles, milk from burning spurge, honey from hornet-combs and men from beasts." To her there had been no thistles, bristles, spurge, hornet-combs or beasts in the whole wide world. Her milk had been cream, her honey the purest and sweetest, her men angels. She had treated them as such; and to be treated thus in return made her soul writhe within her with just indignation, and aroused a feeling of contempt for the world's base ingratitude.

Had she allowed herself to act on impulse she would have gone away, but under the circumstances, to absent herself at the present, she thought, would be a very unwise course of action.

The novice had said to the unhappy queen, " I am not great, I cry my cry in silence, and have done, but the great cannot weep behind a cloud." Silence and seclusion were not for her. She was great and could not weep behind a cloud. She must be forever before the footlights, so accordingly she gave her time, her words and actions more openly to the public. She hinted to her father the propriety of going to Sir Keith, and openly thanking him for the great service rendered her, and she herself continued to publicly treat Sir Keith, the few times which she met him, with greater kindness and consideration than she had accorded him since his marriage.

In the course of time the rumors had come to the ears of the men who had formed the hunting party, and they had spoken with a vehemence which had silenced the lady of Kenyon Court and had sent the world once more, humiliated and repentant, to the feet of the mistress of Apsley House.

Modena was quick to realize this, and the generosity within her was quick to respond. She knew that Sir Keith, too, saw it, but he was not quite so quick to respond. She saw that it had had the tendency to make him a little contemptuous, and a little cynically indifferent to the opinions of those whom before he had respected, and that he sought her company more openly, and more often, and this she feared. Under the circumstances she thought it best that she should go away for a while.

She realized that the situation was sapping away what was best in both their lives. Their physical health was being impaired, their spirits were being weakened, and this was preventing them from performing the higher and nobler duties of life. He was young yet; his country needed him; his life lay in his hands and in hers, like potter's clay, to be moulded into an imperishable statue or to be wasted on illegitimate longings, as they willed.

The highest test of love is the obliteration of self. She would go away while it was yet time. She had heard of a party en route to Italy and decided to join it.

She had done so, and had remained away for some three months. She had thought by going away that she could learn to forget him. She had striven to do so, but had learnt that passion cannot be uprooted when it has grown to maturity. As Castelar said of Byron and his love, "Separation may be a remedy for passing fancies, but it is a stimulant for deep sentiments," so it was with hers. In the midnight stillness of the ocean waters, with no sound but the throb, throb, of the mighty engines and the swish of the waters against the ship's bulwarks; in the stir of great cities; as she drove through the vine-clad hills of France, or wandered over the sunny plains of Italy, in all her journeyings his presence was ever with her by day and by night.

"One is not responsible for one's thoughts. Thought is some power outside one's self. One is only responsible for harboring them. My thoughts I cannot help, but I shall not harbor them," she said, time and again to herself in her quiet wanderings, in a vain effort to justify her conscience; but as the days passed by she realized he had become part of herself, and she could no more separate him from her life than she could her own ego. Other women might, but not she. She had in her what was in Heloise an infinite capacity for loving. Heloise would never have been known to posterity had she harbored other thoughts than those she entertained of Abelard. Modena had within her the feeling that if she resigned part of herself she was giving up what was immortal. She could not forget him; and so much so did she feel this that her philosophy or religion became almost as fatalistic as that of Œdipus. So, resigning herself to the inevitable, she ceased to strive, simply saying, "What must be, must be." And when she had admitted this she became more reconciled to things as they were, and more at peace and rest with herself than she had been in many long months.

Modena was glad when the limit of her time had expired and she had turned her face homeward. A greater sense of joy pervaded her being than she had felt in many months, and a feeling almost of light-heartedness dwelt within her as she had driven through the familiar streets the previous day and recognized familiar faces as she approached Apsley House. As her many friends came in bringing with them kindly welcomes, she wondered if he would call, when she heard his voice in the hall with her cousin Jack's. Had his voice yet the power to move her so? He did not enter the room, but went down the hall with Jack to Mr. Wellington's library to discuss with him some matters of state.

At the same moment the Lady Greta entered the room and impulsively threw her arms about her. "The place has been so lonely without you; we cannot live without you; you will never go away again!" she said.

"To hear such welcomes as these makes one think of Farmer John—the best of the journey is getting home," she replied, with unmistakable warmth in her words.

When they all went away Modena went to her sitting-room. In a few minutes Sir Keith came in with her cousin to welcome her home. She turned to meet him, but the words which she was about to say faltered on her lips when she saw the great change in him. He was worn and haggard and had aged greatly. She was painfully startled. "Has he been ill?" she asked herself, in great solicitude, not willing to admit that her absence had anything to do with the change. So intense and varied for the moment were her emotions that she failed to control her surprise and solicitude.

Sir Keith saw this, and a great wave of feeling came over him. He had missed her so much; he had thought that the winter would never end and that she would never return. The days seemed so long and dreary and the nights so lonely and without end. But he said little to her now, and soon afterwards went away.

When he was gone, the mistress of the house stood for some minutes looking out of the window, her eyes on old Susan, who was hobbling down the side street to her hut by the river-side. "How happy she is!" she said for the second time. Then she turned, and as an antidote for what had come to her, she rang, and although late, ordered her carriage, and went to see an old servant of the family who, she was told, would pass away before morning. On her return she called at the House for her father, and Sir Keith rode home with them. Some division of great importance was pending in the House. His words to her father were audible to her as their carriage rolled home. His views were concise, clear, forcible and full of sanguine hope. She felt better on her return.

For many days after this Modena remained at home to meet her innumerable friends who came to welcome her. She was now glad she had gone away. The change and the rest had done her good. "My life has crept so long on a broken wing that I come to be grateful at last for a little thing," sang the English bard. In her sojourn she had missed everything which had been so near and dear to her; so much so that she felt it was now a joy and privilege to perform the simplest duties of everyday life, knowing that they were ever near her now. Like Castelar, she had felt that exile is a mortal malady of the heart, that we anxiously desire to live among people with whom we have a community of origin, of blood, of life, and of interest. As he felt, so, too, did she feel, that these sentiments constitute the being of one's country, the happiness of one's existence, and that after having seen all the greatness and glory and wonders of other countries, we turn our eyes longingly to our home, so thankful for the privileges of freedom and of liberty that we are content to become the least among the greatest.

When Modena returned to Apsley House she felt she was once more in her own element. Her old interests in life had returned, and she had again resumed her many duties, meditating within herself what she would do or originate to please, instruct, develop or amuse her immediate world. Although her life was calm and serene, yet her nature was one of those which are forever generating and emitting something new and interesting, a nature upon which one might feed and be ever satisfied.

"They have missed me! What shall I do to prove myself worthy of their expectations?" she wondered, as she went about her duties as usual. She thought long over the matter, and at length resolved what it should be. That same afternoon, as they walked over the upland glades of Fernwylde, an opportunity presented itself to confide her plans to her compatriots.

"You said the other day you felt like Farmer John. Did your travels not furnish you with something more poetical than this to relieve the monotony of this humdrum life of ours?" queried Mrs. Cecil.

"What would you have one think of, if not of Farmer John? Ulysses or Agamemnon? These are visions which dwell in Etruria. They are not in harmony with these scenes," replied Modena, as the humble music of belled flocks rose faintly to their ears from the flats on the opposite shore.

"If we had any imagination or originality we would make them into harmony. If there be such a thing as a series of existences for the soul, one wishes that the soul of a Molière or a Racine would spring forth now," insisted Mrs. Cecil.

"Imagination is all that is required to make it spring forth. We possess it. We have also the ability, the material and the opportunities. All we lack is what the sage of Solon called the charioteers. Will you co-operate?" asked Modena, who had unbounded confidence in herself and her companions.

"What will it be?" asked the Frenchwoman, with little credence but some interest in her accents.

"A week in the Queen's City! Tournaments, jousts, dramas, fireworks, processions, masquerades and music. We have a common humanity. Let it be a saturnalian feast!"

"Would that be wise? Would we do well to admit humanity within the pale for a week and then deny them the sacraments afterwards, as Pitt did to the Jesuits and Sulpicians, and Louis XV. to artists?" said Mrs. Cecil.

"What nonsense!" replied Modena. "One's good sense should teach one her proper place, and one's tastes and mind should form one's society. Merit and true worth are the arbiters of place. The world so often has talent, even genius, hidden within its womb, continually crying out for the light of day, undeveloped for want of opportunities. We shall give it an opportunity to distinguish itself. What we can accomplish will reveal us to ourselves as Marathon revealed the Athenian to himself. We are living in an age when, to be appreciated, we must be known. It will help bring us before the eyes of the world."

The Lady Greta was all excitement. "Superb!" she cried.

"It will require an immense amount of work and great executive abilty," observed Mrs. Sangster, who was naturally inclined to suggest prudence in such matters.

"That will be the beauty of it," replied Modena, who was by nature a modern Mascarille, believing that the greater the obstacles the greater the glory, and that the difficulties which beset us are but a kind of tire-woman to deck and adorn virtue.

And so it took the form which the mistress of Apsley House suggested. The greatest care was taken in choosing the executive, and when once chosen, it was given autocratic power. Each committee was given its day, and for weeks and weeks they worked laboriously, unceasingly and indefatigably. Only those who have undertaken such things can comprehend the difficulties to be overcome.

They decided to hold the pageant in June, when the city was looking its best.

The guests began to arrive from all parts of the provinces towards the end of the preceding week, and the city became theirs. In the beginning of the following week the tournament opened in earnest.

But whose pen is to describe the pleasures enjoyed, the pæans sung, the pageantries performed in the Queen's City during the week? Not ours! Words fail us, but it lives in our memory as one long, sweet, passing dream, a dream of other days than these, a dream of the days of masquerades and serenades, chivalry and poetry, of the Valois and Bourbon and Medici, of the days when Osiris and Isis were worshipped in all their mystical and amorous rites, of the days when men lived a life of the soul and the senses, when women kissed their lovers and husbands and bade them slay.

The city and waters were gorgeously bedecked with holiday attire. The weather was warm but otherwise ideal. A soft haze pervaded the air, giving a mellow tint to nature in its effulgence. There was music always, and music everywhere. When the pastime depended on music it was gay, joyous and exhilarating; but when there were other diversions, it was low and inspiring rather than diverting. There were fireworks in profusion, nothing being more pleasing to a multitude.

The city, with its fragrance of flowers, its lights and life, its chiming bells and fresh voices of children, its leaping waters, its gaily floating flags and banners, and its immense multitude of animated beings passing to and fro, seemed like an enchanted isle which had dropped from some visionary realm.

The scene had its origin in a single mind, but in it was the product of many minds, the voluptuary, the visionary, the poet and painter, the lord and the laborer, the soldier and statesman, contributing to its success.

The fete opened with an immense procession, headed by his Excellency and her Ladyship in state, followed by those who were to take part in the week's programme.

The first day was given over to a tournament of tilting, archery and chariot-racing. The many knights in costumes of centuries ago, with their plumed helmets, grim visors, steel corselets, shining shields, and the gorgeous trappings of their thoroughbreds, passed to and fro from the city and suburbs in splendid panorama to the palestra in the valley of the Rideau.

They had erected for their Aphesis, as the ancients did for the tomb of Endymion, a bronze dolphin on an altar of unbaked brick, and surmounting this an eagle, which, when the spring was touched, soared aloft as a signal for starting.

The procession formed in the city, and was headed by a troop of cavalry, mounted on white steeds with crimson and velvet trappings; then came the trumpeters and regimental bands and banner-bearers, followed by the heralds. Then there was more music and a body of stalwart men-of-arms preceding the King of the Tournament. The latter was followed by the famous knight of the Round Table, who wore his sleeve of scarlet seeded with pearls; then Percival with his monk's cowl, Galahad the Good, and Gawain, who ever tarried with the fair. After these came the knights of the Dragon, Ram's Horn, St. John, and White Rose, clad in armor of polished steel inlaced with gold and silver or black, as the character required, and mounted on steeds caparisoned in crimson and gold.

The knights were followed by their outriders, who were forced to be ever on the alert to avoid the jesters, who followed on their gaudily-decked mules with flaring ears hung with bells, and who ever kept the good-natured spectators merry with their impromptus.

Then came admirable representatives of Champlain, Frontenac and Vaudreuil, and many more of the early, fathers of the country, in carriages emblazoned with the arms of France, and having their postillions and powdered lackeys.

The procession was of an immense length and passed through the main part of the city to the jousting valley in the suburbs. The jousting, which was one of the principal features of the day, was keenly contested, the excitement and interest being intense.

The next morning the tournament was followed by an immense trades' procession, representing labor from ocean to ocean. In some instances the representations were unique, in others artistic; some diverting and amusing, and in many instances showing the immense progress which science and invention have made in the industrial arts.

In the afternoon followed the saturnalia of Olympian games, while all gathered together at the close of the day in the Prytaneum, to see the victors crowned with ivy and olive wreaths, which were to be worn during the remainder of the festival.

Then there was Children's Day, when the white-robed girls and boys danced round the May-pole, as joyous and simple of heart as were Shenstone's lads and lasses when England was as simple and gay of heart as is her daughter now. The evening of the same day was given over to a banquet to statesmen, when the city resounded in "a feast of reason and a flow of soul."

Under the supervision of Grace Austin and the Lady Greta came a miniature Mardi Gras Carnival, with its pageantry and crown of Comus and Twelfth Night Revellers, which proved one of the successes of the week; while the last day of the week was given over to " A la France," under the supervision of Mrs. Cecil and the mistress of Apsley House, aided by an excellent cortege of kindred spirits. And what more appropriate programme could they choose than " A day at Versailles with the Sun-King "?

Mrs. Cecil, who had entered heartily into the spirit of the undertaking from the beginning, during the weeks of preparation had received a stimulus which served to ensure the success of her part of the proceedings. Unexpectedly she had been joined in the city by her husband.

Why Strath Cecil had left Paris and joined his wife had been a matter of conjecture for many days. It was known that his life and prospects there were brilliant, and that the woman who had fascinated him was now in the very zenith of power and popularity; so that his publicly forsaking her and joining his wife was freely commented upon on all sides. But his wife said never a word. She had borne his desertion in dignity and in silence; she bore his return in the same spirit. Her husband's life had been filled with the great things of life. He had lived and enjoyed before and beyond his time. The star had appeared in his life at a time when pleasure and passion had been exhausted. The woman had loved him passionately and unrestrainedly. She had exhausted all her wiles and powers to have him commit himself, but without avail; and then she had tried other means, very daring ones, to bring him within her power. He was a man high in military office in France. Some of his superior officers had become implicated in matters of a very serious nature. He had been aware of their actions, and he was in great danger of being made an accomplice. Letters, innocent in themselves when explained, but having on the surface a coloring of intrigue, were stolen from his private rooms and forwarded to the Department. He had intercepted them in time. The whole thing had been polished up, glossed over for the time, but he realized the danger which still threatened him.

His temptress would have sold him had he not sworn allegiance to her. It had awakened him to a knowledge of his precarious situation. It hurt him more than he had thought it would, this sense of degradation. He would dally no longer with this Delilah. He knew that, even from the first moment he had met her, his soul had been crying out for that peace and consolation which comes from the sympathy of two kindred natures; and his intimacy with her had but aided in the reaction towards his wife. He was wanting her, and he knew there was but one way to merit her forgiveness. His acceptance by the star had been public; his desertion must be as public. He owed it to his wife.

On his return Lilian Cecil asked no questions. She knew her husband was a man of honor, and knew he would not approach her were he not justified in doing so. On his arrival he was charmed with the high-bred simplicity, the fine tastes, the progressive aspirations and healthy enjoyments of her circle of friends, and entered into their plans with the ardor of youth; and from his genius, knowledge, and experience sprang many of the best things of the day. He had sent direct to his home in France for armor, swords, relics and costumes of the Valois and the Bourbon period, and no one who came under the ægis of his power and personality but felt the magnetism of his presence, and the power of that indefinable charm which attracts and attaches, of which he possessed so much. As the days passed by they each and all understood the gulf which had hitherto existed in Mrs. Cecil's life, and rejoiced that it was now closed by a warm human heart.

During the weeks of preparation he was the inseparable companion of his wife and the mistress of Apsley House, and while they had, with the gentlemen, the supervision of the whole, their attention was specially devoted to the proceedings of the last day. These were held in the grounds belonging to Apsley House, which were decorated in the Florentine fashion. The terraced lawns were outlined with double rows of stars of light; triumphant arches, gay with bunting and flags, led to the grounds; lanterns hung from boughs, while electric lights nestled in the foliage of the trees.

In the morning they had a serenade at the Petit Trianon. Then came the parade. In the procession the Court ladies came first, Mrs. Cecil as Maria Theresa leading on a magnificent steed with trappings of gold cloth, heavily broidered in crimson spangled with white lilies and bullioned with silver; then abreast came Grace Austin as Henrietta in crimson and blue, and Lady Greta as Sevigne on a steed as spirited as herself; then d'Alencon and Frontenac in Amazonian costumes; then Montespan as brilliant as of old, and Valicre when she was young and innocent of heart. These were followed by many more in costumes suitable to the personages represented, and then came Marie Antoinette, in the person of the mistress of Apsley House, on a magnificent black charger with trappings of white velvet brocade, with the lilies of France outlined in crimson broideries, crimson facings and gold bullion. Immediately following the Court ladies came the Sun-King with his many courtiers on gaily caparisoned horses and wearing plumed helmets, gorgeous armor and shining spears.

The procession was of huge length, but not nearly long enough to satisfy the tens of thousands of spectators who witnessed it from every available place.

In the afternoon a dramatic company gave as a matinee Molière's " Impromptu " in the music room.   This room had once been the French chateau, and contained the famous paintings of the pupil of Lebrun of that period. A miniature gallery of mirrors lined the wall, and the Salon de Beuf led from the chambers, while the famous paintings of the ceiling and walls represented noted personages of that day.

The gondola illumination in the early evening, as viewed from the shore, was brilliant. Marie Antoinette and the Sun-King headed the procession, while sail-boats and flat boats with music glided in and out, distant Nepean Point and Major's Hill echoing and re-echoing the sounds as from some other land.

But the main event of the week was a drama which was to be given that evening, followed by a masquerade.

Two years previous to this, the Wellington party, while travelling in France, had spent several days with distant relatives of Racine, and had been shown fragments of a manuscript composed by the great dramatist, which were instinct with genius but had never been united into one play. The different parts had been copied by Marion Clydene, and on her return home she had sought a playwright, and in conjunction with him had been engaged during the last two years in compiling, revising and making perfect this piece of art.   It had been submitted to the inspection of some of the leading artists of the day, who had at once become enthusiastic in their endeavors, to have it presented in Apsley House that evening.

The play was under the direction of Marion Clydene and Carlton Monteith, and the mistress of the place was well aware of the immense amount of thought, arduous labor and perseverance which had been put into the work, and of how their aspirations were centred in its success. This was their first public presentation of the work, and she knew what it meant to them.

The story was founded on Greek mythology and was written in verse. In composition and dramatization it was a work of art, and its success depended upon the rendition being a perfect impersonation. Eastern in its lore and superstition, Greek in its classical beauty and mythology, monasterial in its asceticism and altruism, and modern in its pessimism and psychology, it could only be interpreted by people of culture, and by people who in actual life would be capable of comprehending and performing what was portrayed in ideal life.

The dramatists of the play were well aware of this, and had exercised the greatest care in choosing and assigning parts. Artists from a distance had been engaged; only a few of their own people were to take part.

The role of the Grecian princess had been assigned to the mistress of Apsley House, and that of the scholar and knight to Sir Keith Kenyon.

When Modena had read the play she had been carried away by its beauty, force, perfected love and mysticism, but when she had seen the part assigned to her, she had sought the dramatists and refused the part, suggesting the Lady Greta in her place. "I cannot take a prominent part as an individual," she said. "It would be poor taste. One should avoid any prominence, rather than monopolise it. It is the part the Lady Greta has asked for. Give it to her."

But the Lady Greta was a very wise woman, despite her youth and vivacity. "Oh, I know I'm quite capable of acting the part," she had said; "but the world does not know that I am, and I shall not pipe to a people who patronize but do not pay. They think I am a butterfly," she maintained, when Modena had insisted. "Genius wants to be great and to assert her rights. Public opinion is her arbiter—a senseless one, but the one to whom we must bow. A butterfly acting the part of a Greek goddess would be more like a chapter from Aristophanes' Clouds than from Racine. It would be unfair to Marion. It's not what we are, but what people think we are, that counts. They know you and believe in you. The part is part of yourself. Some other time, when they know me better, I shall do it, but this time I shall play Lisette, Toinette or Dorine."

"You have professionals; they will take the part much better than I," Modena said, later, when the committee further insisted.

"No doubt they can; but we want you, Sir Keith and the Lady Greta to accept those parts, to invite, enlist and ensure a warm, personal community interest and pride in the performance. Their acting, no doubt, would be perfect acting. Yours will be, too. The people worship you. You belong to them, and each heart will glow with the knowledge that some one very near and dear to them has done well."

"How prettily you plead, but—"

"But! You think it lowering to your dignity. Isn't there such

30

a thing as pride being prudishness?" Carlton Monteith was about to say, but these were words which no one would dare say to the mistress of Apsley House, and he only said: "Isn't your conduct very unkind to Marion and myself?"

When Modena recalled his great forbearance and his continued kindness, it seemed such a small concession for her to grant, that for his sake and for Marion's sake she consented. But her consent had been given with many misgivings as to the wisdom of her actions.

The preparations in this, as well as in the other arrangements, had brought her continually into the presence of Sir Keith Kenyon, but she had done very little rehearsing. She was very busy. Innumerable demands were made upon her time and strength. In the earlier rehearsals she had sent her substitute, only taking part in the finals, telling them that she was reserving her strength, and that when the time came she would be ready.

During the weeks which preceded the performances, Modena had been so engrossed with the many demands upon her time that she had had very little time for reflection; but during the week of the performance, in the isolation of the immense crowds which thronged every thoroughfare and every function, she had felt the eyes of Keith Kenyon dwell upon her with such latent desire that she had become unnerved.

She had said that genius lies undeveloped for want of opportunities. The week had given her scope for her powers; she had been the central figure in this magnificent pageantry, and as he had seen all that was best in her brought out to the admiration of their world, it was with difficulty he refrained from crying aloud to her, "You are mine! all mine—mine alone!" and such a desire for possession dwelt within him that she felt its force in full and feared the coming play.

The theatre in which the drama was to be enacted, and which its mistress had improvised out of the French chateau, was the largest and most beautiful in the city. The house was crowded, the assemblage being the most select the country could offer. Their Excellencies, with the chief and his party, occupied seats reserved for them in the centre of the auditorium.

The play was founded on Greek mythology, and offered scope for pageantries, masques, tragedy, love-verse and passion. Pages dressed in Greek costumes passed noiselessly through the vast audience with illuminated programmes. A soft, subdued light pervaded the scene, while an orchestra filled the air with music. The curtain was one of the famous paintings by the pupil of

Lebrun, whose people had built the French chateau, and was a beautifully painted view of the Athens of classical days.

The first scene opened with a background composed of a Greek palace with its marble colonnades, fountains, courts and rotundas, in the midst of groves, tropical flowers and laughing sunlit waters. The King, surrounded by his ministers and courtiers, sat in state, while before them appeared the lovely form of his daughter the Princess, the foreign Prince who was seeking her for his bride, and the lover, who was a scholar and knight.

The plot of the play consisted in the King and his ministers, in order to preserve peace within their realm and strengthen their kingdom abroad, sacrificing their Princess to the foreign Prince, as her namesake, the Greek goddess, had been sacrificed to appease the anger of the gods; while her lover, who is a genius as well as a knight, and who is worshipped as such, pleads his cause at the very foot of the throne. But the King and the Court appeal to the patriotism, the martyrdom, so instinct within the Greek maiden, and so the struggle goes on.

During the first scene, the Princess, her lover (who was clad in his knight's clothes, with his scholarship badges worked in crimson and gold on his breast and shield), the crafty Prince, soldiers, courtiers, pages and Greek maidens, passed to and fro in panorama amid classical scenes, while the presence of veiled and unveiled gods and goddesses lent a subtle charm to the scene.

Sir Keith had stood many times before immense audiences and swayed them at will by the power of his words, but at no time in his life had he been more master of his audience than during the play. As he pleaded before the King in glowing verse his great love for the Princess, his voice was sombre and sonorous in defiance to the King in his sternness; tender and thrilling as some joyous lied as he saw the King change to the father; tense with passion as he gazed on the woman he loved, or tremulous in its pathos and triumphant in its sublimity as he pleaded the supremacy of love.

But the King's fear of the gods was greater than the love of the father for the child, and the curtain dropped on the first act with the inexorable decree that she must submit to the will of the gods.

When the curtain rose upon the second act it displayed a midnight scene, with the full moon shining down on palm-groves, marble terraces and the low, deep waters flowing past the sleeping city.

Sir Knight stood in the shadow of an orange grove in the

outer courts of the palace, pleading with the Princess to flee. He was a scholar, and therefore did not believe in the gods, but in the supremacy of nature and love; and as Sir Keith realized that the end of the night's performance would again send them back into the cold, conventional world (for two months they had been revelling on the border land of Ixion, giving vent to true passions through the medium of the drama), he became reckless and threw so much vehemence into his passion, so much seductiveness into his pleading, so much truth, beauty and force into his acting, that the woman who stood encircled by his arm lost in herself the part she was playing, while the heart of his wife, who sat in the audience, seemed turned to stone.

Low, soft, tremulous music from maidens dressed as Greek sirens, filled the air, and the lovely Princess, with his hot breath on her hair and brow, his passionate words burning within her, seemed as though they were alone in some voluptuous land where heavenly music lulled their souls to sleep.

Then came a pause in his torrent of words, and, propelled by some power outside of herself, she moved from him to the low stone window overlooking the deep, black waters of the castle, and dropped her eyes, that he might not read what was written there. The moon shone down clear and pale upon her face, revealing a countenance illumined by the great joy which came from within.

The stillness and suspense in the audience were oppressive. A subtle sense of personal woe and danger hung over all. For one brief, fleeting moment the Princess felt it was beyond her power to proceed. Had she at length overrated her powers? As the peril of the situation came to her with lightning rapidity, her heart seemed to stand still, and then resumed its beating to suffocation. But the world and its ways were strong within her. With the greatest effort of her life she recovered herself. For one brief moment she paused, and then drawing all her latent courage and command to her aid, she resumed the soliloquy in which she fought her deadly battle.

The work here was heavy, the heaviest which fell to the part of the Princess; Greek in her being moved by her belief in Fate and her fear of the vengeance of the gods who protected her country, yet modern in her psychological analysis of the motives of consistency and duty which prompted her to do it. But the acting, after she recovered herself, was perfect.

"She will never send him from her. She cannot. She is not strong enough to do so," breathed the heart of every woman there, carried away by the realities of the situations. An intense stillness pervaded the audience, each being afraid almost to breathe for fear of losing one look, one word, one tone.

Without motion or gesture, simply by modulation and expression, the Princess carried the vast audience with her to the climax. As she had spoken her monologue, the illumination of her features had changed to a doubt, a perplexity, mingled with a shade of weariness and melancholy; then to woe, despair and desperation; then gradually they cleared and became supreme, resolute and resigned. She turned from the waters to her waiting lover. "Duty, destiny and the gods are greater than love, and must be feared and obeyed," she said.

But her lover refused to hear, and again pleaded with her.

In return she appealed to his sense of patriotism, which is an instinct with great and good men, and more so with a Grecian, and to his honor and his courage. But, being a scholar, he could not view the world as she viewed it. Within him dwelt a touch of Ibsen, that the state is the curse of the individual, and that free-will and spiritual affinity should be the only basis of union.

For some moments, as the knight gazed upon her upturned face in the pallid moonlight, with silence and serenity all round them, and looked into those eyes which in other days had moved men to madness, he was torn between a sense of sensual and voluptuous passion and the nobleman's instinct of altruism. He read her as he would an open book whose pages lay in blood-red letters before him; and, knowing her so well, his nobler instincts prevailed and he bade her go.

Then followed the wedding festivities. The play was staged during the time of the Renaissance, and the gorgeousness, wit, poetry, masques and carnivals of that time were brought out in such splendor that the audience at times seemed wafted away to the real abode of the gods and goddesses who were the patrons of the play.

The scene in the third act changed to the Italian Court, and here the inherent subtlety and cruelty of the Prince to his lonely bride lent tragedy to the drama. Reports of her indignities and injustices, faint at first but soon assuming vividness and reality, reached the Grecian Court, where the knight and his followers begged leave of their King for a commission to the foreign Court in order to be near and protect her.

Then followed the persecution and tyranny of the foreign Prince, who was only kept in subjection by his fear of the people, who worshipped and feared the genius and, to them, sorcery of the knight. When at last, after many weary months of cruel indignities and almost inconceivable suffering, she met her lover once more at midnight, and gave herself into the keeping of the gods, he bade her go within until he would gather his followers together; he would send her under escort of a trusted band to a strong castle in the mountains, while he would remain and wage war for her against the kingdom, as Menelaus had done for Helen of Troy.

But his bravery was no match for the subtlety and cruelty of the King. They were driven at the point of the sword, wounded and undone, to their mountain fastnesses. Here the play by subtle degrees led itself up to the climax at the close, where the knight, after first casting his eyes up in one long supplication, which despite himself had in it a note almost of defiance to Fate, took in his arms the woman whom he loved, and who was now kneeling in submission and supplication at the feet of the gods, and calmly, coldly, courageously met the doom which the cruelty of the Court meted out to them.

For some moments after the drop of the curtain there was deep silence, the audience having been so carried away as seemingly to believe in the reality of the scenes and surroundings, unable to separate the fictitious from the real.

On the whole the audience was cultured, young of heart, unsatiated, and as capable of appreciation and enjoyment as in the days when Talma first moved the hearts and minds of men. When they came back from the realms of fiction to the knowledge of realities, and realized that for three hours they had been living a life of the soul and the senses, they burst into one immense ovation, calling and recalling the actors before the curtain. Seldom had the city the privilege of listening to such a production, and even the most critical and satiated among the audience were profuse with their applause and appreciation. The gentlemen gave vent to their enthusiasm and admiration, while the ladies forgot propriety and, rising from their seats, showered the platform and performers with their bouquets of roses and lilies-of-the-valley.

But the persons most moved were Marion Clydene and Carlton Monteith. All their lives long they had dreamed of fame, but fame had been as illusive as their dreams, and now their emotion of intense joy was almost a bewilderment. The play had not seemed so when they had compiled it. Its power to move had deepened; its passions had become more sensuous, its love more purified and powerful, its beauty more spirituelle, its harmony more ethereal, its genius supreme. Things which to them had been mere dead letters and dry bones, had become instinct with living fire and torn lives. The verses had been Racine's, they had but clothed the piece with their own sentiments and motives, yet failed to recognize these in the play. They had not known that Racine had meant so much. They had known he was a genius, and that he had lived when the intellectual life of man was at its height, but they had not known he was capable of this. It was something beyond their comprehension. It had exceeded their most sanguine expectations.

They had said to Modena, "You *must* take the part; the praise will be heart-praise, for they will feel someone very near and dear to them has done well." "They had done well in assigning the parts."

But Jack Mainton and Mr. Lester, who had been unacquainted with the purport of the play, and who had listened and watched spellbound as it progressed, were moved by different emotions. A sense of the undercurrent and of a personal tragedy within the play was stronger within them than their appreciation of a display of power and talent. They had noticed Verona Kenyon's attitude and feared a scene.

"How indiscreet of Modena to place herself in such a position," thought both men, not knowing how she had come to do so. "Why did she ever do so?"

They left the audience immediately on the drop of the curtain, and making their way to the wings, sought Marion Clydene and Carlton Monteith. Very adroitly conducting them to the front of the platform, they conferred upon them the honors for the success of the play, while Jack led his cousin away to her own room on the plea of dressing hastily to receive her guests to supper afterwards.

Jack said nothing to Modena. He had learned the value of silence, and its effectiveness. But his cousin felt the chilliness, austerity and censure within his manner. "It is always thus one is misunderstood," she thought. "I was weak enough to want to do an act of kindness to Marion. I did it for her sake, and no doubt the world will censure me." But as a consciousness of the purity of her motives grew upon her, her old courage returned, and she dressed hastily and went down to meet her guests, while Jack left her without a word and went to seek Sir Keith. He found him in the dressing-room and, looking him straight in the face, informed him rather coldly but markedly that his wife was waiting him in the octagon room, where they were gathering for supper.

Sir Keith met his friend's eye frankly and honestly. The part had been forced upon him despite his better judgment. He had but done it to further and ensure the success of the play. He had acted his part, and had acted it well, and that was all there was to it. If others put more in it, he could not help it, and was indifferent to it. Surely the world would learn in time to mind its own business. He dressed himself and joined the guests in the rooms below.

The drama was followed by supper, and then by a grand ball in the state salon, the guests remaining hour after hour, lingering loth to leave, charmed and fascinated, until the sky began to whiten in the east and the first rays of the rising sun warned them of the approach of day. A great regret was filling each heart and mind that the week was nearing an end. So grand had been the pageantry, so immense the success, so fascinating the surroundings, and above all and over all such a charm of good fellowship and perfect understanding, and of developed and acknowledged powers, that it made each heart feel that with the end of the week something had passed out of their lives, leaving behind it a great void surrounded by sweet memories.

CHAPTER XLIII.

FROM the moment the mistress of Apsley House placed her hands in those of her lover and succumbed to his pleadings in the play, she knew no peace. So completely had she entered into her part that the feelings of the Princess had become her own. When she had consented to the part she had not doubted her strength nor feared herself, but she had doubted the wisdom of her actions. The accident on the Idlewylde was yet fresh in the world's mind. It had been unfortunate, and had taught her the value of discretion, and when they had approached her to take the part of the Princess she had thought it very unwise for Sir Keith and herself to place themselves in any position which would connect their names before the public. She had resisted their pleadings until she had seen that her resistance was giving the impression that there was something in it, and was causing more comment than her acceptance; and Carlton Monteith had pressed his claims

upon her until she felt that it was almost ingratitude on her part
to refuse any longer.

It had been one of the chief traits of Modena's character to
sacrifice her own pleasures and interests for the pleasures and
profit of others. Perhaps this was the secret of her great popularity. And then, too, since her sojourn abroad and her restoration to health, she had laughed at her former weakness. She was
a woman over whom the passions had little power. It had been
her great sympathy for him, rather than any impulses of nature,
which had made her weak. When she had promised to play the
part it had not been themselves she had feared. But the week
had proved the words of her favorite author to be true, that
"even the most spiritual and most dutiful of characters cannot
wholly resist the impulses of nature." In the play she had
passed the borderland and had tasted of the sweets of surrender,
and they had permeated her being. This was the only thought,
feeling and consciousness which had followed her from the stage.

She was young and sanguine of heart, and dearly and honestly
loved applause. The bursts of applause had penetrated even to
her own room as she hastily changed her robes, but the applause
was nothing to her now. In all her life before she had never
felt so helpless. She dressed hastily when her cousin left her,
and had her woman servant bathe her brow, all the while regretting exceedingly that she had listened to their pleadings.

But her regret was of short duration. When she descended
the stairs and saw the supreme joy on Marion Clydene's face, as
she stood side by side with Carlton Monteith receiving ovations
from her whole world, she was glad she had done so. She saw
the best possible course for her to pursue was to join in the
ovation and distract all possible attention from herself; so she
conducted them to the seat of honor at the supper table, with the
representatives of royalty, and, approaching Sir Colin Campbell,
remained by his side the greater part of the evening.

Sir Keith did not again approach her that night. He had
gone to his wife and had taken her into supper. He had talked
with those near and discussed the merits of the play, had spoken
lightly of his part in the performance; he had gone to the ball-
room afterwards, and had left immediately after the departure
of their Excellencies, his wife and her cousin, pleading fatigue,
having already returned home.

Since their last open rupture, months previous to this, Lady
Kenyon had been more careful regarding her words and actions.
Her rival's absence on the Continent had caused a lull in the

drama, and during the preparations which followed they had met but seldom, Lady Kenyon having worked entirely under Mrs. Sangster's supervision. But during the week of presentation her old animosity had re-awakened when she had seen the popularity and puissance of the woman she hated, while every word and every act of the last day's performance had become a menace to her happiness.

She had known of the play but she had known nothing of its purport, and as it had progressed she had become incapable of either thought or action. But she had now dwelt long enough in the world to realize the absolute necessity of preserving an outward appearance of composure, so she had smiled and applauded with the rest, while her heart was heavy and cold within her as stone.

She had left early, unable longer to maintain her composure and had remained in the library at Kenyon Court awaiting her husband's return. A great loathing towards her rival filled her whole being, and this must be dispelled in some way. But when Sir Keith came he passed on into his own apartments, locking the door behind him. She sent a servant to his room to see if he would accord her an interview. His reply was that he was very tired and would see her early in the morning.

Sir Keith now locked his door and threw himself into a chair. He had been intensely moved. He had held her in his arms, and his blood ran fire at the remembrance of it. He had not betrayed himself to the public, but he had to himself. A sense of fear and guilt beat angrily at his conscience, as a child beats at a door which has hitherto never been closed to it. Jack Mainton's tone had touched him to the quick. He would take a sword and run his body through sooner than not be able to meet Jack Mainton's eye honestly.

He was exhausted, and prepared to retire, but he could not rest. In his bed, as he lay, he could see the towers and turrets of Apsley House, like the pinnacles of the citadel of the Sleeping Beauty. He wondered what she was thinking of—feeling— dreaming. He knew it was wrong for him to dwell upon her memory, but knowledge is powerless where love is dominant. Had she been a weaker woman her power over him would have waned before the force and necessity of conventional laws; but she was not a weak woman, and she had for him that puissance which the almost unattainable has for all humanity. He had the power to move women easily, and he had thought all women facile, but in the mistress of Apsley House he had found his previous psychology of women at fault. There was something within her which he could not master, and this something, though opposed by his better judgments, ever led him on. At last exhaustion overcame him and he fell into an uneasy slumber, the slumber of a knight with darkened soul and tarnished honor.

His wife, meanwhile, had gone to her own room, but not to rest. Jealousy, that corrosive vitriol of the soul, was rendering her life one long burden to herself as well as to others. She sat by the window thinking and planning as she watched the sun's first faint rays creeping over the river. As the words and actions of the play came to her memory her face grew dark, and her nostrils dilated when she realized her impotence before them. Modred had waited and watched long and patiently. He had climbed the casement to the latticed window, and had brought his followers to spy and cry aloud. The whole world had seen her lord and his lady, but yet the whole world had praised and applauded again and again. O that the world had but one neck, that she might trample upon it for doing so! She had been injured and outraged; every word, every phrase, had been an insult and menace to her rights; but no one—not one—had avenged her.

"What power has she over men?" she thought, as her wrath spent itself in silent rage, and she returned to a calmer mood. "If she offered them alloy of the basest metal and called it gold, they would accept it as a sacred coin. Her morals are like the metals —they are mixed with alloy. The words of the play hid the alloy, and they could see only the fine gold," she thought, as she remembered the applause of the people. It was this thought which annoyed, irritated, almost drove her mad.

Again, there was nothing tangible of which she could accuse her husband. Her calmer mood told her the words which were burning for utterance upon her lips led to no purpose. They were only invectives, abuse, words of vengeance, bitterness, loathing, ferocity, cruelty and slander. They had failed to move him before; would they be of any avail now? She felt as if she were against an unyielding wall of iron, that the wall was hemming her in, smothering her, and she lay back in her chair physically and mentally exhausted. Mists rose from the river and penetrated her room. Stiff with the cold, she arose and threw herself as she was on a couch, and fell into a sleep which was almost the stupor of exhaustion.

She awoke late, ill and unrefreshed, dressed hastily, and descended to the breakfast-room, where she found her husband had been waiting some time for the interview he had promised her. But her cousin entered the room by an opposite door at the same moment, and then the servants announced breakfast. Her rage had spent itself in silence, leaving her in a stupor of silent vindictiveness. She addressed her cousin in the customary way and without looking at her husband, and almost with a savage sullenness took her place at the table.

As the meal progressed and her cousin's attention was distracted from them, she glanced up at her husband with a cold, meaning look; but despite her intense egotism and anger, she was moved to awe at the change in his features.

Her cousin, who had been reared in a society whose chief cult was not that of God or king, was passing some cynical criticisms on the motives in the play, while her husband was apparently listening, with eyes bent upon the table. His face was dark, stern and weary, almost melancholy. He looked as though he might have come from the battleground where his country and his hopes had been blighted and blasted, and all his loved ones lost.

And so he felt. He had gone to sleep with darkened soul, but the morning light had brought him back from the land of love and poetry into the realm of prose, calm, cold reason, and inexorable conventions. He had gone to sleep thinking of her. With the dawn of morning the danger which menaced him, if he allowed his mind to dwell upon her, came home to him once more as it had done in the woods of Idlewylde. He had pulled himself together in all his manhood and strength, and had unflinchingly faced the future. As he dressed he recalled the knight's words by the running stream:

> "What profits me my name
> Of greatest knight? I fought for it, and have it:
> Pleasure to have it, none; to lose it, pain;
> Now grown a part of me: but what use in it?
> To make men worse by making my sin known?
> Or sin seem less, the sinner seeming great?
> Alas for Arthur's greatest knight, a man
> Not after Arthur's heart!"

No, he said to himself, he would never allow such words as these to become his. He would make the manner of his life worthy of the little greatness which his name implied. He knew he had great talent and greater opportunities. A virgin world lay before him to be moulded by intelligence and integrity. Alexander, by the force of his genius, had conquered a world; but Alexander had had more genius than character, and his glory was as transitory as a passing star. His character would supersede his genius.

He loved a woman whom the ethical side of his nature told him he must cease loving. His heart and life were full to repletion with her. Could he banish her from his life? He could not forget, *tout casse, tout lasse, tout passe* was not written for strong natures. But by the force of this same strength he thought he might, if not efface, at least assuage her presence in his life; at least he would try. He knew that the best way to do so was to fill his life with another. By his own free will he had bound one woman to him. This fact entailed many duties and many obligations. He was not insensible of duty. He had never taken her into his life. He would try to do so. He could not take her in yet, but he would as soon as there was a little empty corner in his heart and life. From his suffering and strife he would carry into life the sense of duty as supreme over all emotions, and his comprehension would make him merciful and lenient to the frailties, follies and falsities of his wife.

He had risen early and had stood by the window waiting for the breakfast-bell to ring. He looked out over the city in its morning robe of peace and life and strife. The morning had been misty, but the mists had risen and floated away to the hills beyond. The sun in all its June glory shone out, lighting to soft brightness the turrets, gothics and lancet windows of Apsley House.

He looked long and earnestly, and a great change passed over his face. His features became almost worn and haggard, and then settled into a resolute resignation. He had turned from the window and, remembering his wife's request, had gone down to the breakfast room. He listened now to her cousin's tirade, which to him was like a draught of absinthe after drinking pure, clear spring water. Somewhere back in his mind came Pope's old saying, "A little learning is a dangerous thing." It is apt to make men morose, discontented, Nihilistic, Bakounistic, while it takes a very deep and even life-long devotion to study to make a man content with life.

His guest had a superficial knowledge of many things, which is a cryptogram of the rankest sort, and was airing it in her criticisms, in the spirit of the modern world's cynicism and ridicule of all things sacred.

The gods had never been abstract things—symbols of the greatest of all religious emotions. They were only concrete relics of paganism. Religious emotions were imbecile caprices.

Science dissected its own origin, and philosophy resolved all creation into a germ, but with Macaulay she agreed that scientists and philosophers were only intelligent children and half-civilized men. These teachers of virtue were worse than other men, for they had all the vice of other men with the additional vice of hypocrisy. Psychology was a modern humbug. Yes, no doubt, Bacon had said, "Clothes cannot be cut to fit a body without taking a measure of the body; in the cultivation of the mind it is necessary to know the mind," but all these things which he said were so simple. Everyone knew them without dissection. As if the world could be run on first principles! England had tried to do so, was trying to do so, but England was in a deplorable state. She would adjust all contradictions by dynamite. The Grecian princess, with all her psychological analysis, had acted so foolishly. She had lacked decision. She should have known what she wanted and obtained it in spite of everything and everybody. Cicero had never conceived of any point of view but his own, and Cicero's name had become immortal in history. The play was not a success. Its glaring fault was the lack of realism.

Sir Keith listened, replying in kindly, courteous monosyllables.

The monosyllables irritated his wife. "Lena thinks he is agreeing with her. Cannot she see he is rendering her ridiculous? How is it he has the power of making all our cults seem ridiculous? He doesn't say anything, but one feels it. Why cannot Lena see this and shut up?" she was irritably thinking to herself.

Lady Kenyon had come down undecided as to what course to pursue. She had never learned the value of silence. She could not allow her wrongs and injustices to pass unrebuked, unvindicated. But her cousin's tirade turned the current of her feelings and thoughts. She had now for some time dwelt within the inner circle, and its elegance, refinement, mellowness, deference and grace, although they had not permeated her being, were yet casting their subtle charm around her. Her cousin's criticisms were coarse, crude, plebeian, and by the sheer perverseness of human nature she was almost tempted to take the Princess's part. Why did she say such things? She must learn to keep these theories to herself. She couldn't abruptly tell her so, but she would go with her to her room and delicately hint the propriety of her doing so.

Sir Keith left the house soon after breakfast and did not return for luncheon. Dinner time brought its usual quota of guests. This relieved him from any private scenes with his wife. He was glad of the respite. He was ill prepared for any onset or any promises. His mind and his will were willing, but it required time to make himself willing. He realized his wife's grievances, and he thought well of her for refraining. He felt kinder to her than he had ever felt before. He gave her credit for the highest motives, not knowing it was her cousin's conduct which was distracting her mind.

At the end of the second week her cousin returned home, and Lady Kenyon resumed her old routine of life, and her thoughts once 'more became centred upon her husband and his love. But as the days passed and the scenes of the play began to grow dim in her vision, and as she noticed her rival's intimacy with Sir Colin Campbell, and her husband's reticence, she began to wonder if she had been wrong after all. "Perhaps it was only acting," she said to herself. She had heard no comments upon it. People only praised it as a perfect piece of art. But if it were only this, what was the cause of his continued coldness to herself? He was kinder, but why did he never allow her to enter his life? Always the same courtesy, deference and respect. Her footman gave her these. Almost she came to hate them more than she would have hated disrespect.

At the time of their marriage she had blinded her eyes to the cause of his marrying her. Now, when she saw it with all its nakedness made hideous by the burning light of wounded passion, she made herself believe she had been duped. No doubt that woman had aided and abetted him in duping her. They had won, and now he regretted his marriage and was yearning for her love. If only she could expose her to the ridicule, the scorn, the calumny of the world, nothing else would matter. Was Sir Colin only a blind, and was her husband meeting her in secret? Was his kindness a blind towards her? she wondered. Her broodings made her once again grow morbid and suspicious. Sir Keith again began to feel her espionage, and he also began to realize that there was a new air of masterfulness in Sir Colin Campbell's manner. Sir Colin had boldly worn her colors at the tournament, and had not been rebuked. She had appeared with him openly ever since. She was a woman of honor and was aware what this entailed. Was she filling the void in her life with him? He had resolved to put her out of his life, but before this fear his resolutions had vanished into a more ardent longing than ever before, as water in a kettle evaporates into burning vapor, leaving his heart parched and burning as the burnt-out cauldron.

He had said he would turn to his wife, but his desires left him in no mood to do so. His wife was quick to feel this. She watched their every movement, her one desire being to find something tangible on which to work; but her efforts proved fruitless until one day, when Sir Keith had been suddenly called east on some urgent ministerial business, she went to his private room bent on searching his letters and papers.

She had often noticed a small key he had worn on his watch-chain, and several times had asked him about it, but he had invariably evaded reply. She noticed when he entered the break-fast room that morning that in his haste he had forgotten this chain and key, and she believed that if he possessed anything this key held the secret. When he left she availed herself of it, and went to his private cabinet, and after hours of laborious search at last discovered the secret drawer which contained his hidden treasures.

When she found the letter, for fear of interruption she carefully replaced the other papers and carried it to her room for perusal and contemplation. When she read the sentences and learned the truth of the drama, saw it stripped of the false clothing with which she had clad it, and knew that the persistent love of her husband had been repeatedly refused by Modena Wellington, and that even after their own betrothal, her rage knew no bounds.

For some moments, spell-bound, she held the letter before her, looking at the paper with its odor of dead roses—the odor which had reminded him of dead one's graves—as if she would wrench all her wrongs out of it. But when she recovered herself she spent few minutes in contemplation. She grasped the situation only too quickly and too clearly. She cast the letter from her as she would some loathsome thing, and paced the length of her boudoir in the strongest passion of an over-passionate life. In the heat of passion her love for him had become transformed into hate, and it was with impatience she awaited his return to confront him and expose what she had learnt. She did not stop to consider the appearance in his sight of her own conduct in tampering with his private correspondence.

When he returned she did not send to him to see if he would accord her a few minutes' audience, but went direct to his rooms with the open letter in her hand, and without any preface or preliminaries proceeded to pour her invectives upon him.

He was almost too surprised to speak. "I thought, Verona, that these scenes were ended. I told you the last time that their repetition was both wearisome and vulgar. I shall not tolerate them," he answered her, coldly and slowly, and rose as though to leave the room.

"Then do not cause them," she replied.

"What am I doing to merit this? My life is open to the public. What am I doing to displease you so?"

"You loved Modena Wellington when you married me. You love her now, although she now loves another," she replied, scarcely able to utter her words intelligibly from the intensity of her emotion.

He could neither deny nor affirm, and remained silent.

"Ah, you do love her!" she cried, white with rage and wounded love. "I knew it! Read that!" and she handed him the letter which the mistress of Apsley House had written him from the seashore in reply to his own a few days previous to his marriage.

"Where did you get this?" he asked her, with a whole world of cold scorn and indignation in his voice as he recognized the letter.

The enormity of her offence had not as yet dawned upon her, her anger being too great to allow of calm judgment as to her actions. "You would not tell me," she answered, warmly. "You denied my right to know. I only did what anyone else in my place would have done. I found out for myself."

"Then you now know the truth. I did love her. I do love her now better than life, God help me!" and the infinite pathos and loneliness in his voice bore witness to the unvarnished truth of his assertion, and pierced like a poisoned dagger the heart of the woman before him. He knew it and felt for her.

At his words she turned pale as death with anger and agony. The mask was now cast aside and she was reckless as to what she said to him, reckless as to how she wounded, stabbed, maddened him. She was now hopeless of winning his love, and she had forfeited his respect. She was now actuated by one desire and one motive alone, to bring disgrace and obloquy on the name of the woman he loved. "Then you did serve your heart up in the play!" she said, as she grew a little calmer. "The love of a Lancelot for his Lady! The unholy love of a traitor knight!" she continued, with so much covert insolence and innuendo that he was forced to reply.

"In a certain sense, yes. But a lady with the beauty of the Queen, the chastity of an Elaine, the soul of an Hypatia, and if there were more like my lady, knighthood might revive on other scenes than those of Camelot and Lyonesse."

31

The calmness of his tone and his fidelity and homage touched her to her last resort. "The world shall know the true version of the story. It shall again witness and enjoy the sequel to the play. But our world strikes otherwise than with our hands. I shall seek a divorce, and she shall be the co-respondent."

At her words he turned deadly pale and his face went cold. She had never seen his countenance more attractive than in this intense mute wrath, which was like the frozen lake of his own land. He felt helpless, powerless, paralyzed; but it was not of himself he was thinking, but of *her*. To spare her he would have undergone any torture; he would have welcomed death for her with relief. He had taken a false step in life. It was irremediable. It could not be expiated, effaced, retrieved thus. It, and the fate it brings, must be faced and borne to the bitter end. His face still remained cold and white in mute wrath, but he remained master of himself. He knew that she had no grounds for her assertions, not one tittle of evidence or proof. Their words and actions had been as open as the day, but he dreaded the publicity of the affair. At all costs he must compromise; anything to quiet her.

"Verona," he said, very quietly, his tone changing from anger and outraged indignation to one of weariness, for he had not been well of late. "We have discussed this subject once before. I do not wish to reopen it; your assertions are insulting to me, calumnious to another, derogatory to yourself, and indicative of great meanness and suspicion in your own nature; but your words and actions force me to reply. I shall tell you what you must do, or what I shall do. You must see you cannot hurt or harm Miss Wellington. It does not lie in your power to do so. Her own actions alone can do so. Her conduct, like her love, is of a high order. Her kingdom is her own heart, mind and conscience. Her conscience is her god; therefore, she is responsible only to her own conscience, and it is such that it would be an impossibility for her to do wrong. Then you would be wise to leave her alone. Myself you cannot harm only in so far as you bear my name. Now, I do not wish to see our name made a by-word in men's mouths. It is a name which has remained unsullied for centuries. I owe it to the memory of my forefathers to keep it so. I am a public man preaching principles, veracity and honor. I am responsible to my country to practise what I preach. I cannot afford any scandal. For my past and present thoughts and feelings I am not responsible. They have been products of nature; for my future ones, time alone can tell what they will be;

but for my words and actions I am responsible. If I willingly give you any cause for complaint you are justified in your line of conduct. I have seldom done so. What my life proves, to you depends wholly upon yourself. You must learn that a man loves a woman for what she is. A noble life bends all hatreds and hardened hearts to it, as the cross in Faust drew the fiend to his knees. Any woman may make her life noble. Great possibilities lie before you yet. You are now at a crisis in your life; you have acted very unwisely, but if you will pause and reflect and pursue the nobler course in life, no doubt in time things will all come right. But if you continue your maddened course and utter one word without just cause which will bring our names before the public, I shall never look upon your face again. Now, for your own sake think seriously over what I have said. I have been far from well for some time. When the session closes I purpose going abroad for a year. It is not well that we should part in anger," he said, more kindly, as he saw her relenting; and then, thinking she would see the folly of her ways much more quickly if left to reflect in silence, he turned and left the room.

CHAPTER XLIV.

WITH the open letter still in his hand he went into his private room and locked the door behind him, leaving his wife standing in his dressing-room. Dazed and sick at heart, he sat at his desk and bowed his head in the open letter in his hands. His wife's words hung over him like a pall; nothing seemed clear but the significant words his wife had uttered, "although she now loves another." Were the words true? Was she learning to love Sir Colin Campbell? Then he suddenly checked himself. For some time he had harbored the thought. Now the mental strain through which he had passed, as is so often the case, awakened him to a knowledge of the truth. The supposition was derogatory to him and unworthy of her. She had not once doubted him. Why should he doubt her? It was now some three months since the play, and he had not spoken to her in that time, no more than the common courtesies of everyday life, but he had seen that she was looking far from well. She was but shielding herself in Sir Colin Campbell. Perhaps it would be better were she to learn to care for him. He knew her to be a woman of great thought and feeling. Her interest in life had been intense and sincere. She had had her prejudices and illusions and convictions. Experience and the world disenchants and disillusions. When these would come to her, like Lucille, she would want a warm human heart in which to seek solace.

In his sight hers was a soul apart from the rest of the world. It loved the world because it comprehended the nature of things, but in the affections of its own soul it was as of the soul of genius, apart from the common clay, an angel in exile with infinite longings for higher and holier things.

All great souls have felt this isolation—Virgil, Dante, Byron, Angelo! It was this isolation which caused these great souls to seek solace in great works.

Modena, he knew, was too practical to turn her powers to any other source than the world. When she became disillusioned, her life would be a void unless she could bury her infinite desires in the depths of a warm human heart, as Sappho had appeased hers in the waters of Leucadia. "If she were only happy he would make the best of life yet. If she accepted Sir Colin he might in time make her happy. Then perhaps he could accept his wife into his life. Would he see Modena and tell her all, and then separate his life from hers forever?" he said, as he had once said before. He resolved that he would do so, but somehow he could not. "Was this all there was in life? Was living and loving so slight a thing as this, that their souls should live and love as theirs had done and their bodies be united to an alien soul?" The very thought was repulsive to him. "No, it could never be," and he banished the thought.

What could he do? Nothing save that which is hardest in life to do, to pick up the threads of everyday life and go on; and this reminded him that he was due that evening at a convention. It was almost the hour now at which he was to speak, so rising hurriedly and putting the letter in an inner pocket, he rang for the carriage and left the house.

The next morning he met his wife at the breakfast table, but he could not tell from her manner what she purposed doing. Yet he feared her. Of late he had not cared for her conduct with Mr. Patrie. He knew that for many reasons Mr. Patrie bore to the Wellingtons or Kenyons no good-will, and that in him they had an enemy as subtle as was his wife. He could not tell what they might do, and he feared for the honor of his name.

The same day he had to meet and confer with several delegations. The session was nearing an end, and his duties were onerous.

The third evening after this, Mr. Wellington gave a full Cabinet dinner in honor of some eminent diplomats who were in the city for the day. The time of these gentlemen was limited, and they left immediately after dinner to catch the midnight express for Washington. After their departure the other guests remained, free to pursue their own pleasure, and had formed in groups, some at whist, some at cribbage, and some discussing the current topics of the day.

There being no ladies present, Modena had gone to her own suite of rooms, when her cousin and Keith Kenyon came in from the gardens. They spoke of nothing but the current topics of the day, the diplomats' diplomacy, the bye-elections, some immigration restrictions which were then occupying their time and attention, and some minor appointments before the House.

Nell Gwynne had immediately joined her old friend, looked into his face as if to ask the cause of his continued absence, and had then lain at his feet during the evening.

Jack had taken up the evening paper and there was silence for a moment, and in the moment's silence Sir Keith's eyes had met Modena's with that gaze which strips bare the heart and reveals the inner soul. And her eyes had dropped.

The next moment a servant summoned Jack in haste from the room, and Sir Keith had risen and gone with him, leaving the mistress of the house alone. She sat motionless and looked after him, her eyes wistfully searching the vacant air after he had passed from sight. Withdrawing them, she sat gazing into the glowing embers in the grate, but seeing them not. She was looking past them into the beyond. But no light burned in the beyond.

Nell Gwynne had risen on the men's departure and had nestled her big, brown nose in her mistress's hands, and had looked with almost human intelligence into her face. His hands had caressed that head all evening, and the mistress of the house bent her head in great despair and loneliness over the big, brown head of the dog.

How long Modena sat thus she did not know, but she was aroused from her abandonment by the entrance of a maid, looking very pale and with traces of recent tears on her cheeks.

"What is the matter, Jean?" she asked.

"Oh, Miss Wellington, the iron steam-pipe in the farthest conservatory broke and scalded John badly! I am afraid he will die."

John was her sweetheart.

"Why did you not tell me at once? Where is he now?"

"Mr. Jack and the doctors are with him. They carried him to his room," she said, giving fresh vent to her grief.

Modena rose and made her way to the conservatory. "What

could have caused it?" she thought. She was always solicitous regarding the welfare of her lowest menial, and to have one injured through any neglect or carelessness was almost an unpardonable offence.

She had to pass the conservatory before reaching the servants' quarters. On nearing the door her foot caught in a projecting piece of the broken pipe that lay concealed by some trailing vines, and she fell forward, striking her head against the door and momentarily stunning herself. She was unnerved and would have fallen, but Sir Keith, who had returned to see that the steam was not escaping, was standing by the open door, and caught her as she fell. The shock lasted for a moment only, but it was a moment in his arms.

Sir Keith gazed into her face as he thus held her, with a strange look on his face, a look of fear for her suffering yet of joy at holding her so close; of madness and self-surrender to clasp her closer, and yet almost a look of coldness which came from his honor and his instincts. The next moment she roused herself. One thought alone flashed through her mind, " to live one moment thus and then to die," but the consciousness of her position and what it entailed, seen or unseen by human eyes, recurred to her, and instantly she recovered herself, and, trembling and undone, she arose and moved to a seat in the hot-house.

Sir Keith followed her. He had felt her weakness and it had unnerved him.

"Are you hurt, Modena?" he asked, with a great longing he could no longer conquer.

He knew the force of the fall could not hurt her; his agony was not caused by the fear of any bodily pain, but he had held her to him, and it and her yielding had undone him; it had exhausted and scattered to the winds his little reserve of self-willed strength. He was now completely powerless before his passion as he knelt at her knee.

"No, but leave me; oh, leave me at once," she cried, in great distress.

"I cannot, Modena. I will not."

"You must, you must!" And she buried her face in her hands.

He rose and looked down on her. It was the first time he had seen her in an abandonment of grief. She had borne their separation with a courage and fortitude worthy of her, and her suffering now moved him as no other forces could have done. His heart was beating to suffocation. He forgot everything in heaven and on earth but his longing to have her forever. His blood coursed through his veins like streams of molten fire, while all the suppressed passion of years burnt for utterance.

The strongest desire of his life seized him. He would ask her to leave it all and go with him to foreign lands. He felt that life with its ambitions, successes and honors were but dross, mere bottomless vessels, without her presence, her love, her sympathy, her solace and her support. He was weary of it all, weary of the farce of his married life. His indifference for his wife had grown into distrust, then into dislike and discord, and now into detestation. His contempt for her conduct, his hopelessness, his longing, overcame him, and he was about to ask her to go with him. " Other lands were far and fair," he argued to himself. " There was but one marriage, the marriage of love. What a hideous farce! What a rank, inexorable injustice, this institution that binds two uncongenial temperaments together for life! It might be a necessity for morality—for the weak—but for those who were a law unto themselves it was an unnecessary institution. A supreme courage was all that was required. It was only the cowardly who would care. Their courage was great. He would do it."

But yet he paused. Why he did this he did not know, but in the moment's hesitation, a moment which seemed to him ages, a change took place within himself. Without any effort of will of his own, but at the command of some Unseen Power, as the Holy Grail had come to the knight of Camelot, all his former life and theories, knowledge and hopes and intuitions, came to him, centred themselves in himself, and acted of their own free will.

He was a just man and he was a wise man, and a just and wise man becomes a law unto himself, his conscience becomes his king. He would have to answer to it for the step he was about to take. Could he honestly do so?

He had said to himself that courage was all that was necessary. To the cruel calumnies, conventional canons and cold charities of the world he was deaf and indifferent. But was this all? Would his honor permit him to do so?

He had willingly bound one woman to him. Her happiness and position in life depended upon him. Justice and honor demanded that he should continue to render unto her what he had promised to bestow upon her. He had no right to place her in a humiliating or degrading position before her world. It would be a base action, and meanness was an impossibility to his nature. His honor forbade his doing so.

And there were duties which he owed to his fellow-men. He had spoken of marriage as a necessity for the weak. If he ignored it, in time the weak would follow in the footsteps of the mighty. He was conscious of his duties to others. It would be a cowardly and selfish act towards his fellow-men.

And would he be acting wisely towards the other woman? He knew that the woman he loved loved her own world. It was as much her element as the water was to Undine. She could not live without it. It would be a very unwise act to place her in a false position before her world.

What was true love but the renunciation of all that is dearest and best in one's self for the welfare of one's beloved. No, he could not do it. He would tell her so.

He looked down upon her, but as he did so he faltered and quivered; he could not tell her. He dare no longer be with her alone. He feared himself, as the best and strongest among us need do in those great hours of weakness when there stands nothing between us and some great temptation over which we have no control. His lips paled to ashy grey and his form quivered. He did not look at her again, nor did he speak, but something which was almost a sob rose in his throat, and he turned and left her.

Modena remained where he left her for some time in great distress and weakness, and then she rose wearily and dejectedly and went back to her sitting-room. The servants had come in and turned down the lights. In the dim shadows she saw the deserted room as in a dream. Her piano stood mute, with its music lying on the ebony case; the book which she had been reading lay open; the Fernwylde flowers sent their odor out on the air; Nell Gwynne came to meet her. The room seemed to mock her. One hour before she had sat here with him passively strong; now she was undone, and the knowledge caused her the greatest pain of her life. As Tolstoi believed, so, too, did she believe, that to have desired in thought to go away with him was the same as in act.

"I cannot endure it," she moaned, and the blackness and blankness of the long life before her weighed heavily upon her.

She went up to her own apartments, but she could not rest. Dismissing her maids, she turned out the lights and passed the hours of the night walking to and fro in the room where she had slept since childhood, hearing the hoarse notes of the town clock recording the dreary passing of time. Hitherto she had met the complexities of life with a great courage and quietude, but now she had no more strength to do so.

At last, exhausted, she sank into a chair. "I wish I could go to sleep and forget it all," she said, as if suffering from some great physical pain, but sleep had forsaken her eyes.

She looked out over the city. Myriads of stars watched over the sleeping city, and the pale moon looked down at its own image in the gurgling river at the foot of the gardens. All was still save for the heavy tramp of the policeman on his beat and the clocks chiming the hours of fast approaching morn. She stirred or moved not, save when the hoarse croak of some northern-bound fowl or Nell Gwynne's bark startled her.

Her soul was at war within her. She was thinking intensely. "Was it but a few short years since she was twenty?" she asked herself, unable to believe it. She was young yet, but she told herself wearily that she was forever old, that her youth was gone, and now she was a woman who had learnt some of the bitter lessons of life.

She gave vent to no emotion; her eyes were neither dim nor dewy, but burning with a dearth of tears.

> "Oh, that word Regret!
> There have been nights and morns when I have sighed,
> Let me alone, Regret; we are content
> To throw thee all our past, so thou wilt sleep
> For aye. But it is patient, and it wakes,
> It hath not learnt to cry itself to sleep,
> But plaineth on the bed that it is hard."

"What have I to regret? What has been my sin? What is life?" she asked herself at last, without either bitterness or rebellion, as all those who ever achieve the greatness of humility must ask themselves sometime.

Her whole life and theories seemed to rise and pass before her mental vision. She had defined life for them at the Court of Inquiry. It had been love and joy and peace and light and hope. She had sat unsullied and untried on a great white throne behind Virgil's gate of ivory and jasper, with a nature as warm and permeating as the summer sunshine and as high, calm, pure and lofty as the virgin snows on the high hills of her country home, whilst outside and far down below, the bitter tide, the mud and dross and miry labyrinth of the world had surged and swelled and passed on without either touching or soiling her. She had seen it and been with it, but she had walked distinct from it. She had never been harsh to it, but ever had looked upon it with comprehension and pity. She had said to Lord Averton at her country home, "We rise to higher things on the grave-stones of our dead selves," but this had come from her mind, not from her nature.

Her faith had been that of a Goethe's, a matter between **man** and his own heart. His conception of immortality had been hers also. She had felt that immortality was not an inheritance but a greatness achieved by purity of purpose and courage. She was intensely humanitarian, and her immortality must come through the world. She had felt that it must come through doing something which would bind her to humanity, which would make her live in the hearts of people when she was gone. She was too practical to become poetical, and so could not associate herself with mankind by the fine threads of thought which bind such great souls as Hypatia, Ovid and Dante to the world of to-day. But there was in her what has been in all great women of the world, the immense consciousness that she was born for a nobler work and higher standards of action than those which exist in everyday life, and with this conception born within her she had centred her life in the world. It had seemed so natural for her to concentrate her life thus. It was to her the only great life.

She had had her ideals, and her ideals had been high. Patriotism to her country and loyalty, in the true sense of the word, to her principles had been her profession. To see her country and its people prosper and progress, materially, intellectually and morally, had been her constant prayer, and that this could best be accomplished by the party who upheld the prerogative of ruling had been her persuasion. To see justice, truth and peace prevail among their people had been her life's politics.

These had been her ideals. And it had always seemed to her she could have no others. But there had come a change. To a certain extent she had become disillusioned. She had dwelt in the holy of holies and had seen it as it was, and the knowledge had saddened her. Things were not as she had believed them to be. They had been stripped of their rosy veils of youth and the alchemy of love, and appeared in their nudity. The reality had shown her that man, left to his own free will, was as noble, as unselfish, as patriotic as of old, but that there existed at the present time so many hydra-headed forces against which he had to contend that they rendered him almost powerless to act in accordance with his sense of honor and justice.

Education had been the only alternative, but in individuality she had learned that many of the forces against which they had to contend were ideas based on prejudices, ignorance and superstition, and which are infinitely more tenacious and harder to uproot than the strongest opinions founded on reason; and to a person who takes life seriously and sincerely, and who has born within him the conception that immortality is gained by leaving the world infinitely better than when he came, no doubt to such a one the sorrow of all sorrows consists in the existing disproportion between his ideas of greatness and goodness and the realities of the world.

The disproportion in Modena's case was immense, and the knowledge of this had saddened her to dejection. During the last year she had seen it, but she had not ceased to try. Like Sibyl, she had felt, " I have been a dreamer of dreams. I have awakened from my hallucinations as others before me have done, and, like them, I feel that the glory of life has gone." But she had not admitted it. To have done so would have been cowardly, and she was no coward.

Old eagles, when they no longer have feathers to warm their nests, seek shelter in tottering towers, often the home of the lizard and the sport of the winds of winter. There, though in misery and solitude, they are as proud as in their strength and glory. She had had within her the spirit and pride of the eagle. But to-night she felt that she was undone. Her strength and pride had failed her. Her personal feelings were embittering her against the life which had been her all, while now she knew that her desire was to go away with him to Italy, to Africa, to the ends of the earth, and she scorned herself for the desire. She hated herself for allowing it to be there. " She! She! Modena Wellington, thinking of and desiring the husband of another woman! It couldn't be possible! It was some hideous dream!" and she shuddered at the vision. In her abandonment of grief she felt she was powerless to act. Like the knights in their search for the Light, " if God would send the vision, well; if not, the Quest and she were in the hands of Heaven."

" Know thyself," said the sage of old. To-night Modena's introspection and reflection brought her to a bitter realization of herself. The workings of the Divine Will are mysterious; the prouder the person, the more desperate the struggle; the stronger-willed, the bitterer the battle. Her battle was a bitter one.

The friends who serve us best in time of trouble are the immortals with whom we have conversed. In her need of light and guidance her thoughts naturally turned to what great men had said. What had been the cry of Solomon, Homer, Virgil, Euripides, St. Paul?

" Zeus tames excessive lifting up of heart." Had she been proud? She had been proud to arrogance in many matters, but she had always looked upon her pride as courage and humility. Where had there been vanity in her pride? She valued, and had been extremely thankful for their great wealth, for their position, for the attributes and qualities within herself and her home, which are the best heirlooms of a long line of courage, courtesy and culture. She had accepted these in trust, conscious of their obligations and responsibilities, and had faithfully striven to fulfil them. It could not have been these of which she had been vainly proud. They were yet intact. It must have been of herself, of her will power, of her strength. Had she been stubborn and headstrong? Had God spoken in her heart, as her cousin Jack had said, and she had not listened? Should she have followed the dictates of her heart? She did not know.

She paused, her mind a blank. Then many, many things which she had been taught in childhood came to her. Was she not free to act as she willed? Did she move herself, or was she moved by some Unseen Power? Was her will and her strength not her own? She wondered if it were her duty to say it was not, and to submit to Fate. She had always thought a submission to Fate another form of cowardice, that Fate was only the shadow of one's own weakness standing up before one in battle-array. Zeno-like, she had thought man's noblest work in life was to do his duty. But now the thought sprang unbidden to her mind, was life what the cynical stoic of old found it to be and taught it to be?—" Life leads man to indifferentism and teaches him to go from moment to moment with his eyes on his navel." But she could not yet view life as Zeno had viewed it. Some power within her prevented her from doing so.

What had her friends done in time of trouble and temptation? She thought of the intense warfare which waged between Dante's Satanic pride and his sensitiveness, and of the internal misery it had caused ; she thought of how Michael Angelo had secluded himself for years in a soul's agony, of Byron's soul cynicism and moral abandonment, of Goethe's misery even to suicide, of Shelley's heart cries, and of De Stael's melancholy. But Dante's warfare had become immortal in his " Inferno "; Angelo had peopled the vaulted roof of the Sistine Chapel with prophets, sibyls and sublime Titans in a soul's agony; Byron's abandonment had culminated in " Manfred," Goethe's suicide in immortal " Faust "; Shelley had given the world a Man, and De Stael had poured out her soul in " Corinne."

Castelar had said that immortality's crown of stars on the head must be accompanied by a crown of thorns round the heart, and its pages must be written by the ink of one's own blood. Her friends had persevered and won their crown of stars, but where was hers? She had her crown of thorns and her heart was bleeding. She knew that the night was writing pages of history on her face with her own blood, but what crown was before her? She had given her life wholly to the world, and the world had failed her. There was no crown before her.

Wearied and perplexed to exhaustion, she raised her eyes and looked out to where the first rays of the rising sun were lighting the world; but to her they brought no light, she saw only the darkness of an eternal loneliness and regret. Life wore its darkest robes.

At the break of day she rose from her chair, bathed herself, and, putting on a morning gown, threw open the window. Her head ached and throbbed from pain, but she could not close her eyes. The fresh morning air, wet with rain mists, blew in and cooled her burning brow. She looked out over the valley to where the rain mists, before the approach of the morning sun, were sweeping like spectral armies to the hills beyond, and the sun's rays were slanting heavenward from the surface of the Idlewylde to a bow in the sky, like the spears of an advancing host saluting the colors of their king.

At her country home she had invariably said, "Nature teaches resignation, hope, willingness to labor and to love, and submission to the inevitable, and in sight of its beauties and uses the heart of its own accord goes up in peace and praise to its Creator." God had come nearer to her through nature than through all systems of teaching or doctrine. She was sensitive to any display of emotion, but she worshipped before nature.

Nature did not fail to move her now. It had helped to mould her character. It now soothed and calmed her. She looked out to where the rain mists seemed to float to Fernwylde and the bow to pour its golden coin into its lap. The passive consciousness that Fernwylde in all its beauty and peace lay over there seemed to renew some of her old strength and hope. If only she had something for which to live she might perhaps pick up the threads of life and go on. She was a woman who could not live without definite plans, definite work, definite objects in view. All her life her activity had been her religion. Now it seemed to her that her religion was taken from her, leaving her without pilot or rudder.

From the Catholic cloisters close by the bells chimed out on the bright morning air, summoning the faithful to early morning matins. She sat at the window and watched the sisters with their crossed prayer-books as they went to worship, and from her window she could see the white-robed chorister boys, and hear their young voices as they passed from the vestry to the chancel. Very soon myriads of other chimes rang out over the city. It was the week of prayer. She heard their own cathedral bells calling, and, as she had done for years, she arose, and, ringing for her maid, ordered her to dress her in a street costume, and then went to early service. She knelt in her own pew and bowed her head, but her lips moved not, neither did she pray.

She returned home for breakfast, and after she had driven her father to the House, she spent an hour with Helen Lester and the remainder of the forenoon with Grace Vivien. But what she did she did mechanically, from the force of habit, without warmth or feeling; her heart was not in it, for it seemed to her that her heart was dead.

She drove by the House on her return and brought her father home to lunch. She was awakened from her apathy when she saw him.

"Are you ill?" she asked, anxiously.

"My head aches," he replied, wearily, "but I am more worried over Keith."

His daughter's heart seemed to stop beating. Her intense pride and sensitiveness had exaggerated her own feelings and intensified her misery, and, like all proud people, she did not wish her misery to be known. "What had he said or done?" An uneasy, vague feeling of what he might do had haunted her since his departure. Since her own weakness had come home to her so forcibly, she had feared his power of resistance, and she now felt herself in the presence of a power which she was unable to hold in check.

Mr. Wellington remained silent, buried in deep thought, while the horses sped up Wellington Street. His daughter's suspense became unbearable. When she could compose herself she asked, "What is the matter with him?"

Mr. Wellington, turning to look at his daughter, seemed to realize for the first time that she, too, was looking far from well. A deep sigh, almost a moan, broke from his lips as he answered her, "He is ill. I am afraid, very ill. He came up to my office at the House this morning. We made a sad mistake, my child. I never knew it until this morning. He has not been well for some time. One feels public life more and more wearying and worrying every day. God forgive me for my part in it. It almost makes one feel that power is a misfortune. Have you spoken to him lately?" he asked her, as they reached Dufferin Bridge, but before she had time to reply he leaned forward to speak to Jackson. "Drive to Kenyon Court before we go home," he said; then remarked to his daughter, "I must see if he is any better. They took him home."

Neither spoke until the carriage drew up at the side entrance.

Mr. Wellington stepped out and entered the side door, where he learned that Sir Keith was in his own room, seeing no one, and was very ill indeed.

CHAPTER XLV.

Sir Keith was indeed very ill. When he turned from the woman he loved and went out from the conservatory into the stillness and serenity of the night, his blood was on fire, his brain reeled almost to delirium, his lips were grey, and his frame trembled with the exhaustion of emotion. He had emerged from a battle which had torn his life to shreds. He had conquered, but a great weakness was upon him.

He knew he would have given years of his life to have lawfully tasted of her lips once more, but he had left while there was yet time; he had not even allowed the desire to express itself. His instincts, his honor, his reason, all told him he had done well in remembering his marriage vows, but his love had so wrought through his life into the flesh that he feared his powers of resistance.

Lifting the hat from his head to cool the fever which burned on his brow, and looking up into the stars of night, " Oh, Modena! Modena! It must not be. It shall never be!" he cried to the night and silence, as some men in their extremity call upon their God.

He replaced his hat and descended the steps. The darkness of a great weakness was upon him. Mechanically he turned towards Kenyon Court and made his way wearily and abstractedly to his own apartments.

But wearied and exhausted as he was, the force of habit was strong within him. He looked up some records to compile facts for the next day's debate, but his mind refused to carry the data, so he laid them aside and, after resting for some time, retired.

He awoke at the break of day and tried to rise; there was much to be done; but his head ached and his brain reeled. Ringing for his manservant, he ordered, for the first time in his life, a powerful stimulant. Temporarily strengthened by this, he arose, breakfasted, and went to the House. But when he arrived at the House a great weakness again overcame him. Soon he recovered somewhat and made his way to Mr. Wellington's rooms, but he had said little when his memory forsook him and they took him home. For many weeks he had felt far from well. His social duties had been exacting, his work at the House had doubled itself. Calls for assistance had come to him from all parts of the Provinces, and he had invariably responded. A cold, contracted a few weeks previous to this from a night ride in a draughty car to a distant county, followed by a long country drive in a drizzling rain, had settled into a low, malarial fever, from which he had found it impossible to free himself. The strain under which he had been laboring had served to increase the fever, and at last nature had collapsed.

When he arrived at Kenyon Court he sent his man Walters to his mother's apartments for her, and when she saw him she sent at once for their family physician. He sat down by his desk and took a pen in hand to write, but his hand shook, his head reeled and his mind wandered. "Mother," he said, "I am very ill. I am afraid I am going to die. Will you write a letter for me?"

"My son, do not write it now," she pleaded. "You must have complete rest. I have warned you, I have pleaded with you, but you heeded not. You must now submit. You must rest at once."

But he replied, "I cannot rest until I write," and to humor him until the physician's arrival she sat down and wrote to his dictation. But as she wrote she saw that his mind was clear and his desires rational, and that he did in truth fear death.

"My dear," the letter began, "I am ill—going to die—and you will have to live alone. I am to be envied—you pitied—for death is but a freedom from the mortal weaknesses of the flesh and an entrance into a life of the soul. It is hard to live, but easy to die. We have so often said that the soul unblinded can see Truth. I know now that this is true. There are no words forcible enough to tell you what I see, what I hear; but one message, a hope, a consolation, a sustenance, I leave to you—I shall be ever with you to the end, and then I see, I feel that all will be well. Do not come to bid me a last farewell, for she knows all and will harm you. I tell you this to shield you. We have been strong—"

"Mother, emphasize that word, write it in letters of blood!" and his voice grew stern and strong and deep as the fever burned in his veins, while his mother rose and implored of him to go to bed.

"There is but one thought more," he said, as he bowed his head within his hands; "tell her I have loved her always. I have loved her in life, I love her in death, and I shall love her in eternity."

His head dropped back as he finished. The physicians came immediately afterwards, and they removed him to his chamber, where for long weeks the strong man battled with death.

CHAPTER XLVI.

WHEN Mr. Wellington arrived at Apsley House the same day, he went direct to his own room, and a few minutes afterwards sent for his daughter. "Modena," he said, wearily, "I, too, have been overworking myself of late. I must have rest, but one cannot rest within sight and sound of work. Will you come with me to Fernwylde for the week?"

When Modena had entered the house with her father she had gone direct to her own apartments, locked the door behind her, and paced the floor in deep agitation. Ungoverned natures would have wept or cried aloud in their distress, and would to a certain extent have found relief, but she remained silent, although her heart swelled and beat with an unspeakable emotion.

When she obeyed her father's summons, she was drawn out of her own great sorrow by the haggard appearance and look of suffering on his face, and saw that his words were only too true.

Going away from the city while Keith lay dying was like going away from all there was in life. She felt as Persephone might have felt when she was forced to return into the bowels of the earth. She felt that in leaving the city she was relinquishing the one last forlorn hope, but on reflection she decided that if she could not go to him, could not be with him to bathe his burning brow, kiss his fevered lips, and give her life for his, she would rather go away where no one would see her. A wistful desire sprang up within her, to go to him and give her life for his, nurse him back to life, and then and there to die. But she could not do this, and there was nothing for her but to take up the routine of life and do what its duties called upon her to do. "Yes, father, we shall take the afternoon train," she said, and the afternoon found them at Fernwylde.

On arriving at their country home Mr. Wellington brought out a low, padded, lounging chair to the shaded terrace, and, reclining upon it, soon fell fast asleep, with the early autumn sun quickening and warming his sluggish pulse and slowly beating heart.

When his daughter saw that he slept, she left him in charge of his manservant and went out over the lands for a long walk. Returning by the Fernery, she paused by the stile and sat down on a sheltered seat. She saw Father Jacques come from the shadows of the cloisters to his boat by the lake shore and pass over to the chapel on the Idlewylde shore. Did he know of Sir Keith's

32

illness? Was he thinking of him? Was he sorrowing for him?
Was he praying for him? She wished that she could cry, or feel,
or suffer, but she felt that her eyes were strained and sightless;
and she could not pray, for she felt that her heart was hard and
cold as lead within her breast. She felt as though she could
never rouse herself again. She knew that now, in his illness, the
whole city would connect their names and would pity her. But
she was indifferent to its comment or its pity. Nothing was
very clear to her, but that her life seemed blighted. Should he
die, what was there left to live for? and should he live, she must
never see him again! She could never again take up the threads
of life and go on. So sick at heart was she that she doubted her
own individuality.

She remained seated, silent and still. The monks' voices murmuring as one man's, their Latin words of prayer came up to her
like the sound of a great sea rolling slowly on a lonely shore,
having in it the echo of some *Miserere Domine.* It pierced her
to the heart and brought with it a sense of the loneliness and hopelessness of the long years before her, and at the sense of this
unending weariness came a revulsion of feeling. "If he were
only spared!" and on the impulse of her misery she threw herself
down on her knees to implore that he might be spared.

But when she knelt she could utter no words. Her heart
refused to speak, and she remained mute and motionless in a soul's
agony. For the first time in her life she seemed to realize that
there was a mighty Unseen Power who knew her as she was, and
in whose presence she was powerless to speak.

Silently and with rending of soul came the consciousness of
her own infinitesimal nothingness and helplessness, and as this
came home to her, as silently did there appear before her mental
vision, as the Holy Grail had appeared to the sister of Percival,
a blinding radiance which seemed to be a vision without a visible
form, and from out the vision came the words, "My will be
thine." Silently her lips responded, "Thy will be mine," and
at these words the blinding radiance seemed to recede, growing
in brilliance and intensity as it receded, until when it had left
the darkness of the world far behind, its brilliance and its
intensity centred in itself and it vanished in the form of some
glorified being.

Modena arose from her knees. She had asked nothing. She
had given all. The sound of the chanting voices of the monks
in the vesper, "In Domino Confido," came up over the still
water to her ear. "Is life trust?" was all she said.

CHAPTER XLVII.

WHEN Sir Keith went to his bedroom after dictating his letter, so great was the disorder of his mental faculties that he felt the prayer of the unhappy Œnone rise to his lips, "O death, pass by the happy souls who wish to live, and let me die," but before many days had come and gone, so fiercely did the fever burn within his blood and brain that he became unconscious of all things round.

His mother, fearing that in his delirium he might say something of the trouble that was on his mind, had taken the precaution to exclude from the room all but his own confidential manservant and the old family nurse, while she herself never left his bedside.

But he said little. The great reserve which was so instinct within him, and which had been increased by the habits of his life, was yet stronger than the fever which burned within him. Through all the long weeks he lay, sometimes in a stupor, sometimes flushed and restless, and oftentimes with a sudden gesture or an impatient shake or turn of the head, as a thoroughbred shakes his stately head to escape the persistent sting of a poisonous fly. His fever was great, and his mother's heart ached as she stood by him and saw what he was silently suffering.

On learning of his illness, his wife had gone to his room, but by his own implied desire the physician had allowed no one to enter. She turned away in ill-concealed mortification, and during his illness was moved more by her feelings of embittered anger at this request than she was by any thought of his danger. Now and again, when the nurse or manservant went in or came out, she saw through the open door the bed on which he lay, and heard the murmuring of his fevered wanderings, or saw the outline of his form as he lay in deep exhaustion, but the sight moved her to little pity and no remorse. The hushed and darkened chamber near by failed to awe her hatred into silence.

Many days and nights passed by. They were to Lady Kenyon one long, hideous nightmare. She could not go without. She could but restlessly pace her room or the corridors of the house, which were hushed as the grave. A pall hung over all. The servants were filled with grief at the danger of their master, while his mother's face was pitiful to see.

It seemed as if the pall had overspread the city. Groups gathered in the corridors of the House and spoke in hushed whispers. Two of their members, the two whom they most loved, were near the borderland. It seemed to them as if the House had grown suddenly silent, the central figures missing.

At last they learned that one was gone. There were times when they thought the other, too, had passed away, but his magnificent strength and unabused manhood, rallying to his aid, conquered the onslaught of the disease, and the physicians at last said that he would live.

When the delirium had passed away and consciousness returned, and he gazed out for the first time across the lawns of Apsley House (which could be seen from his chamber windows) to the wind-blown, cloudy sky, Orpheus-like, he felt he had been dwelling in the land of death and shadows and had once more come back to life and reality, and, Orpheus-like, one thought did he bring back with him, his memory of a woman. He had gone to sleep thinking of her, and now he awoke thinking of her.

In the after-days of exhaustion and convalescence, in which they believed he was without consciousness, the memory of all that had happened was ever with him. He said little, only to ask his mother had he spoken in his fever. When reassured he seemed relieved; but he suffered much—much more than when in strength, for he had not the power to put his trouble from him. It lay there turning itself over and over again in many shapes in his weakened brain. " If I were only free!" was his constant cry.

It was the thought of his unhappy union which irritated, troubled, depressed, pursued him now, more than his desire for another. His desire for Modena was a temptation of the past. His illness had been its reliquary. But how was he to live his life out beside her who was his wife? At the thought he almost wished he had passed away. But his union with her was irrevocable. He turned from the light as if to hide the thought from view, but it remained there eating into his little remaining strength, sapping it away like a rusted nail eats into, corrodes, and in time kills a stately oak tree.

His exhaustion magnified his dislike. His wife was ever as a spectre before him. He was haunted by her invectives, her presence, and her threats, as Orestes had been haunted by the Furies. He had no desire to leave his bed or to resume his duties in life.

At length the men of science told Sir Keith that he must rouse himself and go away; the cold which he had contracted had left his system sadly impaired. He must have complete change and rest. Nothing but renewed vitality could counteract the germs of disease which yet lingered and which threatened to become permanent. At the end of the fifth week he was so far recovered as to leave his room, and as his physical strength renewed itself he was enabled to meet his wife with a passive equanimity. At the end of the following week he went to her apartments, bade her a kind good-bye, and left for a year's sojourn on the Continent.

CHAPTER XLVIII.

"Why did you come to Fernwylde? I thought you were too busy to leave the city at the present time?" asked Helen Lester of Jack Mainton, one afternoon, as they stood together near the Fernery.

"I came down on purpose to see you."

"What do you want to see me for?"

"When are you going to marry Linden?"

She looked at him in great surprise. "How do you know he has asked me to marry him? Has he ever given anyone reason to think so? And even if he has, what right have you to ask that question? I am responsible to no one but Lester."

"I have no right. I am not claiming any right. He has asked you. I know it. Are you going to marry him?"

She was very pale and agitated, though she remained outwardly calm. She moved from him and sat down in a seat in the Fernery. He followed her and sat down beside her, his arm resting on the back of the seat.

"You had better marry him," he said at length.

She did not speak for some moments, and then her face grew proud and cold, and she looked away from him. He had hurt her again.

He knew what was passing through her mind. The Colonel, it was reported, was in a very bad way, and *she* would then be free. Her name had never passed between them. He could not speak of her in Helen Lester's presence.

"A woman, you know—" he continued, brokenly, not quite knowing how to express himself. "Every woman dreams of a home and —and children. It is their only heaven. Linden loves you; he would make you happy."

Helen did not speak. She could not. She was trying hard to keep back the indignant tears which were forcing themselves to her eyes.

She turned her head away to hide her emotion. He saw by the

heaving of her bosom and the quick throbbing of the pulses of her temple that she was much moved.

"She will soon be free, and he wants to marry her. I have never made any claims upon him. He might have spared me this insult," were the thoughts which sprang unbidden to her mind. But she did not harbor them. Self-respect and pride came to her aid, and when she had recovered herself she said very coldly, "Perhaps you are right. I shall seriously look at it in that light. He has gone away for several months, but he will return in the spring. No doubt it will be for the best."

Jack bent his head and, without knowing it, sighed very wearily.

She turned and looked at him, and in the fading light noticed how tired and worn he looked. She expected that her reply would bring him great relief, but it had not.

His mien touched her. "And you?" unconsciously she asked.

"I shall never marry," he replied, but as he spoke he raised his arm from the back of the seat, and drew her to him for the first time in many long years. "A man has the same instincts—as a woman—regarding home and children. After—after what has passed I could not ask anyone. I shall live it out as it is," he said, and he drew her closer as he said it, and something very sweet entered his soul as he felt her form relax, while she tenderly pushed back from his temples the locks of hair which were now fast becoming very grey.

CHAPTER XLIX.

Grace Austin sat alone in the Seaton library. Lord and Lady Seaton were attending a Drawing Room at the Senate Chambers, but she had preferred remaining at home. She had completed her latest book and was in no mood to meet the world. This was now her second great work. On her first she had labored long and earnestly to make it a work of art. But this one had been the outpouring of her best thoughts and feelings in their mellowness and maturity. She had loved her work; the best of her life was in it; and when she took it up to-night and gazed upon it in its entirety, and realized that it was now going from her, beyond recall, as the child of one's heart goes to the heart and home of a stranger, and that it needed her no more and belonged to her no more, a great void seemed to enter her life.

It seemed to her as though she were sending herself out into the world to be buffeted by the rude blasts and cold rains of an ever-changeable climate. " Will it be read by eyes which see and ears which hear?" she vaguely wondered. But its reception by the world was of little moment to her. Once she would have cared, once she would have craved and prayed for the world's applause, but not now. To the world's praise or censure she was alike indifferent. The wise sage of old has said, " A wise man's kingdom is in his own heart, and the opinion of a select few." Her heart was at rest, for she had poured the deepest desires of her life into it, and she knew that, even if rudely expressed, they were good, and the few for whom she cared loved her and would see it as she saw it and would understand. It was only a little thing, one of the little things of life, but the little things of life had become to her the big things; for many months she had filled her life with this little thing, and it had sustained her, but soon it would be hers no more.

The table at which she had written it, the pen she had used, stood by her side. She looked at them as a mother looks at the empty cradle of a lost babe. But the babe was gone and her breast was cold.

Mechanically she stretched out her hand and touched a blank piece of paper, as a woman might stretch out her hand in the dead of night only to learn that her loved one has gone.

Then she arose, locked the manuscript in a cabinet, turned still lower the already subdued lights, drew a chair before the grate and seated herself in it. " He loves her," she thought, sadly. " One cannot wonder at it, though, for she has won all hearts to her, and he has been much to her. She does not love Sir Colin. Her heart belongs to another, but in her loneliness she may turn to Mr. Lester, for she holds him to her and is jealous of his intimacy with another; and where no love exists there is no jealousy. He will win her yet, and then—" and she paused for some moments, " and then I shall return home."

" Dear Southern home," she thought, as she sat in the warm library, with the fitful glare of the hearth casting mellow shadows over her face, while the autumn winds moaned dismally without. " Dear old South," she repeated, as she thought of her far-away home, with its magnolia-covered hills, its sluggish rivers, with the chimes of the cities floating melodiously out over the water, the echo of their notes reaching her country home; its cotton-barges on the water with their singing rowers, its happy negro children amid the gorgeous flowers, its cotton fields, its laughing lights, its sunny skies and linden-laden air. " Dear old home! Oh, happy days!" she cried to herself, as memory recalled the climes and the times, oh, so long ago, when in her native South the sun had smiled on her days and the moon had illumined her nights. " I shall go back and end my days there. There one is as happy as the song-birds in the trees, happy in the mere sense of living, but here one's heart is as cold as the winds without. I—"

Her thoughts were interrupted by a servant, who opened the door behind her and approached with a card pencilled with a few words.

The atmosphere had changed. The winds without were soft, southern sea-breezes, their moans music; the thoughts lying locked away securely in the cabinet filled the room with living flesh; visions rose from the table beside her; her pen spoke, her heart beat as of old, her mind was in sweet confusion.

The servant was waiting.

" Turn the lights a little and show him up here," she said to the servant.

It was Mr. Lester, who had gone to the Drawing Room to see her, but not seeing her there, had returned to Seaton House. When he entered the library he noticed the warmth on her face, and stood for a few moments looking at her in softened, saddened tenderness.

" I thought you were at the Drawing Room," she said, in order to break the silence.

" I was there, but came away. Why did you not go?" he asked her.

" I did not care to go; such things weary one at times."

" They should not weary you. You are young. It is only when age has laid its hands on one, as it has on me, that one loses desire for such things," he continued, rather regretfully.

" You are not old," she said, coloring slightly as she felt his eyes dwelling upon her.

" Not so very old in years, but continual defeat and disappointment discourages one. One accomplishes so little in life," he replied, rather wearily.

" You should not be discouraged, Mr. Lester. You know there is always a season of stagnation before any reform, and no doubt this is the season. They have had great successes; they always bring their avengers like Job and his afflictions. Haven't you always said, ' Reaction is the law of life'? The public is impulsive and often not just, but when it reflects it will do justice. As Carlyle says, ' It is always revising its opinions.' You have been patient, persevering, patriotic, and are sure of success in time; and even if it does not come, you have the honor of a noble, unsullied name," she replied, with an unconscious tenderness and sympathy in her voice.

"Will you have that name, Grace?" he asked her, abruptly and without any prelude.

She was so startled and surprised that she dropped the book which she held in her hand. Surprise and confusion of feeling kept her silent, and he repeated his question.

"Will you have that name, Grace? Will you marry me?"

In a moment's time she raised her eyes slowly and looked at him as he stood before her. His persevering, chivalrous life passed in panorama before her vision. Here was a man loved and revered by all, a man of noble family and great wealth, the man she loved, asking her to be his wife. What more could any woman wish? And yet—and yet she could only say, "But you do not love me, Mr. Lester."

"What makes you say so? Why do you doubt me?" he asked, quickly.

"Because I know there is only one woman you do love, and that is Modena Wellington," she replied, without any bitterness, but with poignant regret.

He paled visibly, and laid his hand on the high back of a carved oak chair to steady himself. "Who told you so? I thought no one knew that," he said in a low voice, with a touch of sternness in it.

"I saw it in your eyes the first time I ever saw you," she replied.

He was silent many moments, his eyes dwelling on her but his mind absent. It had gone back to the past. "What should he do? Tell her all? Would she understand? Candor is the virtue for which we pay most dear," he thought. "Should he ignore it and press his suit? No, he could not do so. Deception was foreign to his nature. He could not ignore that which was obvious. He must be honest with her."

He drew nearer and took her hands in his. He was a man of few words. "I shall lay my heart bare before you," he said. "When I was a young man, quite young, I loved Modena's mother, but she married Mr. Wellington. That was in youth, and I recovered quickly, but it left a tinge of regret for something I had loved and lost. I think it was that feeling which prevented me from ever caring for anyone else until Modena grew up; then seeing her continually, I learned to love her with a strong man's love. You know, Grace, at my age a man is not fickle or feverish.

I have loved her for years, but it is useless. I saw it and sought consolation from you."

"Then, loving another, you would come to me, Mr. Lester, and ask me to marry you?" she replied, without either anger or resentment in her words, for she knew he was sincere.

He dropped her hand. His brow clouded and his face grew grave and sad.

She pitied him, and her eyes filled with a mist of tears. He looked at her and his tone softened as he continued, "My love for Modena is not now as it was. It is not dead, but it is buried for aye. You should not hold that against me; I cannot help my past feelings; I have buried them, and out of their ashes is growing a great longing for you. I think in time it would grow into a love which would satisfy you."

He leaned his arm on the mantelpiece and looked down upon her. He saw she was much moved. He knew that she loved him.

"Grace, trust me," he said, very earnestly. "If you do, I promise you that you will never repent it. I shall make you happy."

"Have you ever told your love to Miss Wellington?" she asked him, without looking up at him.

"No, it would be useless," and despite himself his countenance grew harsh and his voice stern, while he looked past her into the stars of the night, as if unconsciously asking why it was so.

The woman before him looked up, and sighed as she looked.

"Why useless?"

"Because she loves another."

"But that other is not for her. She has always sought consolation from you. If you now ask her she would turn to you for solace, shelter and safety. In time she would turn to you for love. Keep yourself free and go to her, dear. She will make you happy. I cannot," she said, her face intensely pale.

"You do not love me?" he replied, quickly.

She was silent, while her face still remained very pale.

"Do you love me, Grace?"

A warm flush passed over her face. "Did she love him! Could he open the drawer of her cabinet and read the lines written there, would he need to ask the question?" But the cabinet could not keep the secret; the very atmosphere of the room was charged with it.

"You are too proud to admit it. You do love me," he said again, as he took her hands, and a new light came into his eyes. "You love me, and yet you would send me to another woman!"

"I cannot admit anything," she said. "I will only leave you

free while there is hope. Go to her and try. If she refuse you and her decision is final, then come to me."

"I cannot, I shall not. She would refuse me. It would hurt her to do so, and even if she should accept I would not marry her. I would not marry a woman whose soul belongs to another."

The woman before him drew her hands away quickly, and the first cold look he had ever seen came into her face.

He had hurt her. He was offering her what he would refuse to accept. She had loved him so well that she had sent him to another, and he had repaid her greatness with an insult.

He had not meant it that way. It was not because the other woman belonged to another that he could not go to her, but it was because he realized that there was something which was lofty and lonely in that other's nature which his nature could not reach or satisfy. He was not a mate for her. He could make this one woman happy, but not the other. The one lived in the heavens and was beyond his reach. He wanted a warm, human heart to beat by his own and warm his. But how was he to tell her this? A great wave of tenderness and longing overcame him as he realized her love, her magnanimity and her self-effacement. Her beauty moved him, almost to desire. In affairs of the heart he was a poor philosopher, and was moved chiefly by events, instincts and natural desires.

His desire now overcame him, and he moved towards her. "It is not what you think, Grace, dear. I cannot explain it, but trust me; no one ever repents who trusts me. I want you and you only. Will you marry me now, to-morrow, any time, soon?"

CHAPTER L.

THE mistress of Fernwylde remained at her country home for some time after her father's death. The management of his estates demanded her presence at Apsley House, but she had purposely refrained from returning there until after Sir Keith Kenyon's departure for the Continent. On learning of his departure she immediately repaired to the city to meet and confer with her lawyers. His affairs had ever been kept in the strictest order, yet there was much to be done, and it was some weeks before she again felt herself free to seek the solitude of her country home.

She had always loved Fernwylde, but never before had she been so glad of it as at the present time. Her trials and temptations, her father's death, the subsequent passing away of the chief, their loss of prestige and power, had all told upon her naturally fine constitution, while Sir Keith's suffering and the letter which he had written had again touched her life to a great unrest akin to a remorse. With nature and the air of Fernwylde she hoped her physical health would soon return.

Sir Keith's letter had touched her so profoundly that she felt she must have time to regulate her life before she could again meet him; and within the amphitheatre of her country home, behind its screen of mantling woods and waters, she would be free from the gaze of the world, free from the presence of his wife, and from the baser leaven of human nature, which were so apt to bias and influence her in her course of conduct in life. She accordingly passed the following year in retirement and quietness, she herself having grown much quieter and graver, giving those around her the impression of being far away in spirit though present in person. But although outwardly calm and self-possessed, inwardly her life knew little peace or rest.

She had come to Fernwylde to regulate her life. She was one of those women to whom a consciousness of their own consistency is absolutely necessary as an attribute and essential of self-respect. There are natures that are as unstable as water, as capricious as the winds, as changeable as the weather. Hers was not one of these. If she had once forsaken her intuitive and philosophic line of conduct in the least thing she would have become contemptible to herself. She would scarcely have known herself any longer. She was a woman who could not live without a creed. Dogma was a necessity to her life. She could no more live without a positive creed upon which to feed her soul than she could live without bread to feed her body.

During the last few years she had learnt many of the deeper meanings of life. Formulæ, phrases and creeds, some of which had been hers from childhood, others the fruit of her study, had now through suffering become knowledge. Life, she had learned, was doing the work of an Unseen Will, and that freedom of the human will must be merged into and made subservient to a Will that knows everything and is working for the eternal good of everyone.

She had learnt that His ways are mysterious and incomprehensible, an " Isis hid by a veil." When she had thought that Sir Keith would die she had said, " Thy will be mine." He had written her that he would be ever with her to the end. Had he died she could have lived happy all her life on this assurance, but he had lived, and, although her spirit was willing to say otherwise, yet this very assurance at times made her flesh so weak that life became a very agony.

She knew that she must put this love from her once and for all. But how was she to do so? She could not banish it from her life, for it was her very self, but she might so fill her life that her days would have no time for remembrance of it. She had Fernwylde and her city homes, and her interests and her social and charitable work. She had read much and deeply, had thought over what she had read, and possessed theories which were very dear to her. Great wealth was hers, and she could enjoy that happy power of realizing and embodying her own theories in these places and interests and pursuits. Duty was generally conceded to be dull, but with wealth and imagination she could make it interesting. She could give her heart and her mind wholly to these. All was well when she thought him dying; all would be well did she fill her life thus.

And she tried to do so. There were times when she succeeded, but there were times also when she failed. There were times when in the very midst of her work she seemed, as it were, to be listening to her life, finding a great silence in it. He was wandering in a foreign land, and there was no echo in her life of the voice she loved. Then her heart would swoon within her. Nor did time assuage this feeling.

There were rumors of his home-coming. The summer was passing, and with the advent of the winter season she knew she would once more have to resume her place in the world and meet him, and this she was yet unable to do.

Sir Colin Campbell was acting with great delicacy and with great patience. She had filled her time with her duties at Fernwylde, but her heart and her mind she had failed to fill. Could she fill them with Sir Colin? For several months after the play she had filled her time with him, and he had thought that she would accept him. She knew that it was not well for a woman to live and die without a man's heart to beat by her own. If she allowed his to beat by hers, perhaps in time she would forget. Her reason now told her that it would be better for her to do so.

But there are natures to whom the thought of physical surrender of self is almost an impossibility; natures in which the mind predominates and over which only a great love can prevail. Hers was one of these. Her reserve had been overcome by one man, and she knew that her love for him was stronger than ever. This very love made her strive against herself with the self-punishment of an ascetic. Had passion not yet reigned supreme in her heart, her acceptance of Sir Colin Campbell would not have seemed so sovereign a duty. She knew that he was but waiting until she would again return to the world. Her year of retirement was nearing an end, and she did not know what she should say. All her life her ready judgments had come quickly to her aid, and she had ever been resolute and serene in action, but now in this crisis of her life she was irresolute and harassed continually by doubt.

At times she wondered if she had been wrong in her reading of obligation and duty. For several years after his marriage she had gone her way strong in the sense of pride and duty, never once doubting the wisdom of her actions. It had seemed to her there was no other way possible. "One's honor, one's pride and one's duty are the essentials of life," she had said. And so it had always seemed to her. But of late misgivings had arisen within her. There were now times when she thought that her pride was humility, and there were times when she thought it was only a species of self-love, and that her humility had been the self-arrogance of purity, rather than the triumph over sin and self.

Had she done wrong in being guided by her reason, honor and traditions, and not listening to the promptings and impulses of her heart? Had God spoken in her heart and had she in her arrogance turned Him aside? It was something which she could never tell, and for this very reason she hesitated long before deciding what she should now do. Although her sufferings had taught her humility, yet she knew that her pride and her self-will were there as they had ever been before. They may have been chastened, but yet they were there, lying away in the background of her life, as the burnt umber and siennese lie behind a Madonna's head, giving to it the strength, the beauty and the power which is never seen save in the face of some angel in exile. If she had done wrong she was surely doing penance. Her life had become one of chastened, saddened regret, a life of long, lonely expiation.

Or had she done right? Almost she thought that she had, but even yet, sometimes it seemed to her, were that time of temptation and decision to be lived over again she would not send him from her. She would say to him, " Our loves and our lives are one. We will live it out together." Sometimes it seemed to her that she must yet stretch her hand out over the gulf which separated their souls as the ocean separated their bodies and bring him to her. Sometimes when she would go to sleep at night his presence would be so near that she would start up thinking she heard the echo of his voice, and then would the days be long and lonely.

There were times when she wandered over the moonlit gardens of Apsley House, or the slopes and meadow-lands of Fernwylde, where he so often had lingered with her, when memories of past joys came so vividly to her that her heart seemed to die within her and she felt she could bear to look upon those scenes no more. There were times when the storm of passion returned in such force that she felt she would have given the rest of her life to feel his lips upon hers once more.

Again and again, unbidden, all the early hours of their love came to her with aching remembrance which was sweet in its very pain. Again and again her whole soul yearned for him with an intense longing. Again and again would her eyes, tired of their long denial to look upon what they loved, seek the East, where he had gone, as if to meet him there.

Sir Colin had written, and she took her pen in hand to reply. She wondered if she could banish her love from her life. She wondered, were she to marry Sir Colin, would her heart in time turn to him. She wondered if she should accept him, but time passed on, and passed away, summer faded into autumn and the words were left unsaid.

The first flush of autumn came upon the woods. One day she wandered out into the embrowning woods. Already the dead leaves were being heaped in the hollows of the groves; the uplands were brown and sere, the vines were being dismantled by the touch of early frost; the late summer flowers were drooping and dying, and the chill air moaned dismally through the trees. The woods weighed wearily upon her, and she turned her steps towards the village rectory. She knew that Mrs. Kenyon was spending the day there. She spent the afternoon with her. His mother said nothing of him, but she overheard the rector express his pleasure at Sir Keith's restored health and his intended return in a few weeks' time.

As she walked home through the same woods her heart sank at the feelings which stirred within her. She knew that the words to Sir Colin must now be said, and she was ill fit to say them. The sound of Sir Keith's name but now had awakened within her all the echoes of past passions and past joys. She tried to put these memories and desires from her, but she could not; they remained to torture her as the visions which had assailed the saints of Thebiad had tortured and tempted them. She knew that her whole soul was yearning for him, longing for him, hungering for him, and this very weakness and craving made her acceptance of Sir Colin seem so imperative a duty.

When she reached her room she bowed her head. She had not forgotten the strength which had come to her when she thought him dying. Prayer to her had ever been one continual and continuous state of heart to herself, to her world, and to her Maker. Her prayer now became a silent contrition, a humility, a submission, an admission of a great uncertainty and perplexity, and a desire for guidance.

When she raised her head she knew what she should do. "Love is eternal. She belonged to him, but for some reason unknown it had been decreed otherwise for a while. Hadn't he written her that the union of two souls on earth was sacred, being a passage and preparation for their union in eternity? Her body was the receptacle of her soul. She would not dishonor it by giving it to another. Wasn't it true that a great love must be as exhaustless as the ocean and as profound in its comprehension? What was love if not one long endurance, one infinite patience? What was human love if it had not gathered within it through all these years enough of the divine to keep it from sin? What were its merits to eternal life, if it had not gathered within it enough to sustain and console for a few short days of pilgrimage here? His love was as a halo about her life. It would keep her to the end."

"Oh, my love! My love!" she said. "Though our bodies are separated by a barrier strong as death, yet our souls are one. We will live it out as it is, and then—" His soul, unblinded, had seen how it would be. Life at its longest was very short. This Hope, which he had seen, would be her sustenance.

CHAPTER LI.

Sir Colin Campbell had been called to England in haste. He was impatient of the delay, and had written from London urging his suit. He had said he would not wait a reply, but would return in the next steamer and plead his cause at Fernwylde.

She could not meet him at Fernwylde and say to him what she had said she would say. She would go up to Apsley House and tell it to him there. She would tell Sir Colin all, and he would understand. What was love but one infinite patience and comprehension? She was sure he would be her friend for life.

33

The steamer was due that morning. She ordered the carriage and with Mrs. Gwen drove to the village station late in the afternoon. A few minutes after their arrival at the station the train came in from the east. It slackened its pace, and when it paused she approached to enter it, when Sir Keith Kenyon stepped out from the one first-class coach attached to the express, his wife having telegraphed him she would meet him at Idlewylde on his return.

He had been absent now for a year. He had travelled from one country to another, almost with an aimless purpose. Time and weakness hung heavily upon him, like a load of lead. He knew not whither to turn either for solace or occupation. His life seemed to be at a pause, and he had not the courage or the strength to pick up the threads and go on.

Rumors of Sir Colin Campbell had reached him. His mother had written him almost every day, and his hand had invariably trembled when he opened the letters for fear of learning of any change in the life of the mistress of Apsley House. But his mother had refrained from mentioning her name, or if she had done so, it had only been with a casual reference.

There were times when his weakness was so great upon him that he almost wished she would marry Sir Colin, that it might aid him in putting her from him. There were times that his longing to see her was so great that he feared to return. There were times, before he fully recovered his strength, when he thought of how it all was, that he looked into the deep black waters of the Seine, or at the rugged cliffs which broke the angry waves of some yawning lake. But as time passed, the rest, the invigorating air of the mountains, the warm breezes of the sunny, southern seas, soon began to tell on his naturally fine constitution, and as strength revived his manhood returned and the desire to live renewed itself within him. As the summer drew to a close he began to realize that he must necessarily once more face the complexities of life.

He was young; the shadows of life had not yet begun to lengthen into afternoon. She had been proud of him in the past. He would live that she would be proud of him to the end. Glory and honor had been his in the past. He knew that in the years to come greater glory and greater good awaited the men who were now guiding the ship of state.

His star had only begun to rise. One generation was rapidly passing from the ranks. In him was centred the rising hopes of a younger generation. His country was in its infancy, holding in its lap the greatest of all possibilities. A great future lay before him. The desire for fame had passed from him; his one desire now was to live well. He would go home and take up life anew. He cabled his mother that he would return, and soon afterwards left the Continent for home.

As he neared the home station, and as every sight and sound became familiar to him he felt a new life spring up within him. "Life is very sweet, after all," he thought, and then he remembered that in reply to the cable to his mother his wife had replied, stating she would meet him at Idlewylde. At the thought a revulsion of feeling overcame him.

When absent he had put all memories of her from him, as he would put away something which was very loathsome. In so far as she touched his life, nothing but her actual presence ever disturbed his peace of mind. The message informing him of her presence now brought him to a knowledge of the one cancerous spot in his new life. His marriage vows entailed upon him duties and obligations he had never fulfilled. If he were to live in peace, he must now accept her into his life. Could he do so?

He had not allowed himself to dwell upon the thought. He was not a man who was given to worrying over things. He had been blessed at birth with a happy disposition and the happy faculty of meeting the crises and complexities of life as they came. He had lived his own life and gone his own way. A good genius had attended him and brought him safely through—until he had met her.

But there always comes a time in one's life when one is forced to take sides with the good genius or be overcome by its shadows. As the train slackened its pace the knowledge came home to him that he was now face to face with one of the decisive issues of life, and one for which he was ill prepared. With her expected presence, visions of the old life came up before him, and his brows drew together in deep lines.

And the day served to increase his depression. The weather was dull, grey and depressing, but rainless. The first frost had touched the trees and vines. Dead leaves rustled to and fro in the arms of a bleak, north wind, which swept across the platform of the station with premonitions of the long, cold winter in its blasts.

When Sir Keith stepped from the train at the little wayside station he was looking well. His illness had not impaired his great personal beauty. To the blending of strength, decision, geniality and reserve, the little arrogance and the little insouciance, which had ever been seen in his countenance, were now added a tinge of melancholy, suggestions of some shadows and some storms in the

past, and the tenderness of an awakened sympathy, all which only
served to add to the power of an already attractive personality.

He had grown much older; threads of grey now shone on his
temples, and his cheeks were bronzed with tropical suns. As he
stepped from the train he saw Modena, and at the same instant
she saw him. He paused and bowed very low, but did not
approach her.

It was the first time Modena had seen him since their parting
in the conservatory, now some eighteen months previous, and his
unexpected appearance in the chill autumn twilight at the little
wayside station, as she was about to leave to meet another man,
startled and for a moment unnerved her. She had thought of how
she would meet him, and of how she would treat him, but she had
overrated her own powers and underrated the powers of the past.
A great faintness, mingled with a sweet confusion, passed through
her. She did not approach to welcome him home. She was not
very sure that she returned his bow. She heard the train's warning signal of departure and she passed into the waiting coach,
while Sir Keith remained standing in the chill shadows of the
little station, now made dark by the lowering clouds of early snow
and by the passing away of day.

His eyes had grown luminous with a great light, and they now
wistfully followed her as she passed in. He had forgotten that
his wife was to meet him here, until the station-master informed
him that the express from the city was late, and orders had been
given for the train to proceed and pass the other at the next station,
some seven miles distant.

He re-entered the now departing train—why, he did not know—
and seated himself in a corner of the coach farthest from them,
his thoughts and feelings much more disturbed than he had thought
they would be at meeting her. He did not go to her, but remained
where he was, seated in shadow, while the express flew with lightning rapidity, past boulders and cataracts, over bridges and through
gulleys, so as not to keep the other train waiting. The shades
of night had come down; the lights in the farm-houses began to
appear, now here and then gone in the gloom. The high hills and
rushing waters flew past; the train swayed and oscillated in its
mad rush to cheat silent time.

But there had been a fatal mistake somewhere. "Crash! Crash!
Crash!" shrieked the engines, and the air was one appalling chaos
of hissing steam, flying fragments, torn girders and human cries.
And it had happened, without any word or note of warning, at
the turn in the ravine where the waters leaped in torrents close to

the track. The train from the city was thrown from the track to the foot of the rocks, while the other was so precipitated that at any moment it might reel into the foaming waters on the other side.

Sir Keith was uninjured and free. He sprang to his feet and, utterly forgetful that his wife was on the other train, searched in frantic haste for his late companions in the coach. It seemed an age before he found Modena. She was standing, uninjured, but unable to free herself, a heavy beam barring her exit. She looked very pale in the fitful light, and was evidently unnerved. Her dress was stained with blood from a wound received by Mrs. Gwen, who had been stricken senseless by her side.

"I have found you at last! Are you hurt?" cried Sir Keith, as he bent over her.

"No, but I feel faint. Where is Mrs. Gwen? This beam is holding us in."

Sir Keith had but recently passed through a heavy illness, and the herculean strength of his manhood had not yet returned, but with all the power within him he set himself to the task of removing the weight. But this he found it impossible to do, and turned to seek help.

At that moment Sir Colin Campbell came hurriedly upon the scene. "Oh, Modena, my darling! Are you hurt?" he cried. Then he saw Sir Keith Kenyon. "Kenyon, did you know your wife was on the other train?" he said, in a tense voice. "She is in a worse state than this—near that boulder—there by those flames."

Then came the crucial test of Sir Keith's life. He seemed to live a life-time in the next few seconds. He saw the fire creeping towards where his wife lay, and he knew that the coach where he now stood might at any moment be precipitated into the black, seething waters below. A thousand thoughts flashed to one pulse-beat. "What can I do? I cannot risk her life, and she will despise me if I prove a coward." He looked at Modena. She said, and smiled as she said it, "Go, Keith," and at that moment kind train-hands came to her rescue, and he turned and left her in Sir Colin Campbell's care.

Hastily improvised litters were made, and the best care possible under the circumstances was given the suffering until a train was telegraphed for to the city, and arrived for the wounded and dead. Sir Colin did not leave the woman he loved until she was in her own room under the care of her old family physician and nurse.

That same night Sir Keith Kenyon sat alone by the bedside of his dying wife. "Raise me, Keith. I cannot breathe," she said.

"I have done wrong, but I loved you so. Tell me you forgive me before I die."

He raised her up and for the first time pressed his lips to those of his wife. "Do not speak of it now, Verona. Keep quiet and there is still hope."

But there was no hope, and in less than an hour he laid her lifeless form back on the bed.

CHAPTER LII.

THE mistress of Apsley House did not improve as the physicians wished to see her improve, so they ordered her abroad to escape the severity of the northern winter. She went to Rome, and from there to the South of France, and some time later on sailed for the East, where she soon regained her old health and strength.

On her return the following spring she had gone to Fernwylde. She had gone there because she couldn't remain away. She was glad to be home again. The place seemed dearer to her than it ever had been before. She had always loved it, but she had loved it with the pride of birth and possession; now she loved it with the humility born of sorrow. She had been glad of it for its security and serenity. It had been her refuge in time of trouble. It was now her home in time of—. She did not stop to analyze her feelings. A sweet confusion was ever with her. She expected something, but yet she never admitted to herself what she did expect. A hope and a joy were lying back, not dormant, but unasserted, but she was conscious that they were there; and this consciousness made her want Fernwylde, where the lights and shadows now ever seemed like soft sunlight and clear moonlight.

She now stood, late one afternoon, leaning over the balustrade of the terrace, watching the afternoon shadows creep up the side of the high hills surrounding her country home. "Why do we ever wander?" she asked herself, as her eyes turned and dwelt on the scenes which had been familiar to her from childhood, and of which she never wearied. "Exile is a mortal malady of the heart," she said again as she had once said before. When absent her heart had yearned for her home. She had wanted to return and take up the threads of life where they had been so rudely rent asunder. Her life for so long had been so broken that it seemed to her that too many of her noondays were passing away with their work undone.

She ever recognized the possibilities which lay before her. She was ever conscious of her ability, and she was ever conscious of her responsibility. Her trials and sufferings had brought home to her many of the deeper meanings of life. She had learned much, and her suffering had taught her in a measure the lesson of submission. But there were many things which she could not yet understand, and the one to her most patent, most powerful, most appalling, was that the world was full of endless suffering, rank injustices, cruel contrasts, and mental and moral inherited maladies, which were out of proportion to the joys and the brevity of human life. This knowledge had come home to her so vividly that individual life seemed now to be but one great sympathy, solace, and sustenance. " Only in so far as one has suffered and sorrowed can one truly sympathize with the sufferings and sorrows of those who are sorrowing," she said, with all the honesty of conviction, as she stood on the terrace steps.

Eighteen months previous to this she had said to herself that she would give her life wholly to such work, but now—now—she told herself that half her life must belong to the—the—State. Pericles had realized the brotherhood of man and the patriciate of accomplishment. He had created and established the Golden Age, and had placed his country as the cynosure of all the eyes of the civilized world. What had been done could be done. She felt that it lay within her power to do great good. It might only be a woman's fancy, but she was honest and sincere. She felt that a woman had a finer instinct, a subtler sense, a greater tact, a comprehension for and with the smaller things of life. She was competent for the details, while the generalizations, the broader questions, might be left to the male representatives of her race, or to her—her husband. And although she was all alone, as these thoughts passed through her mind, a warm color suffused her cheek, a color almost equal to the roseate hues of passing day.

A servant came noiselessly through the open door behind her. In his hand he carried a silver tray. On it lay a letter, sealed with armorial bearings, which she had once known well. They were those of Sir Colin Campbell—a shield with a thistle, a sheaf of grain, and an open book supported by a sword, with the motto, " *Fidelis ad finem.*"

Her heart contracted as with a sudden chill, and a look of pain passed over her face as she reached out and took the missive from the tray. For once in her life she had forgotten.

The servant withdrew, and without waiting to open the letter she passed down the stone steps of the rotunda with Nell Gwynne, who had now grown very old, by her side. The little lake lay at the foot of the hill, emerald and sparkling as the many jewels on her hands. Father Jacques and the monks were coming from the village to prepare for vespers. He smiled and spoke deferentially as he passed along the narrow path leading to the lake shore monastery. She crossed the terrace as they disappeared within, and seated herself under the shade of a spreading maple on the brow of the hill overlooking the waters.

Then she opened the letter. Her eyes followed the lines, but she knew not what she read. For some minutes she could not comprehend. The letter fell into her lap and her eyes dwelt absently and dully on the waters below.

Slowly other scenes rose before her vision. "Was it all some hideous nightmare, those scenes of long, long ago?" Ah, no, they were not dreams! They had been real, but she had put them behind her, or rather something so sweet had come into her life that its sweetness had banished the other to the background of her life. But now they once more stood before her like ghosts coming from the graves of one's dead self.

Nell Gwynne was lying by her side, and she laid her hand on the dog's shaggy head. The dog raised its head slowly, and her great brown eyes looked towards the village.

The afternoon train from the east had come thundering and oscillating into the little wayside station. From where she sat she could see, in the distance, a few passengers descend and wend their different ways. With some hissing and spluttering of steam and a warning signal the train started up again and was gone. Eighteen months ago he had come out of the same coach. She had gone to the city, and then she shuddered at the recollection.

But she had forgotten. Sir Colin had saved her life, and had waited with great patience. He had not approached or addressed her, and she had thought that he had understood. But his letter told her he had only been waiting. She had given him reason to believe that his presence was desirable. She had given him encouragement. He had come to meet her with great hopes and great desires. It had been her intention to tell him her life's story, and then trust to his magnanimity and comprehension to retain his friendship for life.

But Fate had intervened, and Verona Kenyon had died. Slowly all that had passed rose up before her mental vision. How could she tell him now? Did not Verona Kenyon's death bind her in honor to Sir Colin? Sir Keith Kenyon had dallied with another woman. By her silence and her pride, she, Modena Wellington, had forced him to marry that woman. She could not yet see how she could have acted otherwise.

She had meted out judgment to another, and now she was afraid to meet this same judgment herself. What had come over her? Always she had been stern to herself, but indulgent to others.

"If only she had told him before this had happened he would have understood," she thought, with a great regret. "But how could she tell him now? He had been so kind."

"*Fidelis ad finem*," said the motto on the shield which looked up at her from the ground where it had fallen. She picked up the square of paper. "Faithful to the end," she exclaimed, "and how am I about to repay him? Is Fate forever to be unkind to me?" unconsciously came the thought, and she turned her eyes from the water to the path which led to Idlewylde. As she did so she noticed her cousin approaching from the house. He had returned from the city. In a few moments he was by her side.

"Do you know what brought Sir Colin Campbell back?" asked he, abruptly and without any prelude, as he seated himself by her side on a low seat under the spreading maple.

She handed him the open letter.

He took it, and, without reading it, folded it and replaced it in the covering. "He came to see me yesterday," he said, "to learn if you were perfectly well and felt strong enough to have an interview with him; and then he told me all."

"Well?"

"Well, I told him, not all, but a few things."

"What?"

"Need you ask me?"

She was silent for a few moments, too moved to speak.

"Don't you think I am in honor bound to him?" she said, when she had recovered her self-command.

"He does not consider that you are."

"What do you mean?" she asked, not being able to grasp what he implied.

"When he came to me yesterday I told him part of your life's story, enough to send him back on the last steamer to England," replied Jack, and he smiled as he saw the intense relief and radiant

warmth of color which came slowly to his cousin's face as she began
to realize what his words meant. But his smile saddened as he
thought of the noble man who had loved her better than himself,
and who had only written a tender letter of farewell to the woman
he had loved so long and so well, and then returned home without
her.

She remained silent. Nell Gwynne rose and laid her great brown
shaggy head on her mistress's knee, and looked peacefully up into
her face. She laid her hand fondly and caressingly on the dog's
head, while her cousin remained silent by her side, his eyes on the
armorial bearings of the letter.

"*Fidelis ad finem,*" he said, as he returned it to her. Then he
took from his inside pocket the other and handed it to her, and
then rose and went to meet the nurse, who was coming from the
house with his little daughter in her arms.

She did not open the other. She could not. For the first time
in her life she was afraid. She knew what was in it. There would
be no reproach within; only what she herself would put there,
but there would be pain. It was the first pain she had willingly
or knowingly inflicted upon anyone. "Would she have borne the
pain instead of Sir Colin if Jack hadn't spoken?" And then she
paused and repeated to herself, "If Jack hadn't loved her?"

"They—these men are all wrong," she said, thinking of the
scientists and cynics whom she had studied. "They do not know.
They do not comprehend. Self-love is not the basis or motive of
a good man's action. Is it, Nell Gwynne?" she asked, as she
reverently touched the letters on her knee.

"What should she do with these letters?" What did it matter
what she did with them?

Hers was a nature upon which the very smallest things of life
left an indelible impression. She might bury or burn the shadow,
but the substance would be with her for evermore.

"*Fidelis ad finem!*" She would never forget!

"Will you take Pet down to the Fernery for a little while?"
said her cousin to her presently. "She seems fretful for her
mother's return. I have something which must be attended to,
and then I shall return for her."

"Certainly," replied Modena, as she rose from her seat.

They went together down to the Fernery, Nell Gwynne and
Cavall lazily following, and there she let them play until the
little one grew sleepy. Modena then took her up, wrapped a
warm covering about her, and, seating herself in a low, easy chair,

sang a lullaby until the little eyes dropped in infant slumber like the star of Bethlehem shutting up its little leaves at sunset.

"I shall take her now," said Jack, who had returned. He bent over her and, taking his daughter tenderly in his arms, turned with her to the house, while his cousin lingered listening to the music from some stringed instruments in a boat out on the limpid waters of the little lake.

She stood by the sun-dial at the Fernery watching the sun go down. The evening air was redolent with the perfume of lilacs and lilies-of-the-valley. Nature was smiling and happy. The sheep bells tinkled with gentle rhythm in the valley below. A little boy and girl had driven their cows to the brook to drink, and were wading knee-deep in the running waters, laughing merrily as the little fish passed over their bare feet.

A whip-poor-will was calling from Maple Grove, while the bats and owls were coming out from the eaves and shrubberies round the Ursuline cloisters. Upon her ear fell the faint murmuring of many far-away waters rumbling and tumbling down the mountain side, while the voices of the monks murmuring their evening words of prayer and praise came up on the still air from the monastery, which nestled in the arms of the great oaks bordering the lake, whose waters flowed away green and emerald into the long deep shadows of its pine-clothed shores.

Behind her rose the great pile of Fernwylde, with its turrets and keep towering into the low-lying clouds. The evening sun, now hanging on the tops of the distant mountains as if loth to leave so fair a scene, shone ruddily on its many metalled roofs and emblazoned windows, lighting up the great pile until it looked like the citadel of the Sleeping Beauty waiting for the knight with his hounds and horns to come and waken and claim his own. The western sky, where her eyes dwelt, was all aglow with the dying light of passing day. Its roseate hues fell upon and softened and brightened that look of proud humility which had become so habitual to her face.

She had always been a beautiful woman. Added to her great physical beauty had been that intangible and indefinable charm, grace and dignity which are never seen apart from a long line of tradition, culture, courage and cult. Instinct within her had been the spirit of the *noblesse oblige;* and she had been a proud woman. But her beauty and pride were now softened and chastened. As one gazed upon her one could easily imagine that a "perfect woman nobly planned" had stepped down from the canvas of the hand that played in Leda's hair.

As she stood on the terrace overlooking the waters, her form clad in the soft, clinging folds of some white oriental cloth, with no ornament save the many gems on her fingers, and a massive string of pearls which clasped her throat, her hand resting on the old sun-dial which had recorded the passing away of four generations of Wellingtons, her favorite dogs at her feet and the green boughs of the Fernery as a background, almost it seemed as though many centuries might have passed away, and in the evolution of time and of things Hypatia had come back from the tomb, or the lovely Queen of Camelot had come again to the woods of Cameliard. Almost it seemed that the green boughs behind her might part and admit to her presence Sir Knight as King, with her glove against the plume of his hat, and the tenth diamond, made pure in the waters of Lethe, set in his sword-hilt. Almost she felt so herself.

In the twilight she looked across the ravine towards Idlewylde, and as she looked a form came from out the gloom. She knew that sometime he would come, and she was waiting.

In a few minutes Keith Kenyon stood by her side. His eyes sought hers, and soul spoke to soul. Then he stooped over and with one great passionate gesture drew her within his arms. As they stood thus the monks' words of prayer and praise came to them from below. Almost it seemed to him that they, too, so greatly were they blessed, must kneel in the hush and holiness of the hour, and also praise God.

He drew her within to a seat in the Fernery, while the monks' murmur of prayer swelled into the sound of chanting voices, and the deep, slow melodies of the organ grew in volume until the hills and woods echoed back in one grand Magnificat.

As the last notes died away on the darkening day she raised her eyes to his face, where the illumination had chased away the recent shadows of sombre pain and remorse, and as his eyes met hers and she felt the throbbing of his heart warm against her own, she knew then the greatest joy of earth, and her life was at peace.

When their engagement was announced to the world, the world, having surmised the story of their lives, said little. Silence is so often more expressive than words. But men approached her with a respect almost amounting to reverence, while women deemed it a privilege to be numbered as one with her, and children loved her as they did the sweet sisters and saints of mercy of long ago.

She entered the old life once more, with sweet sympathy and solace for the sorrowing and suffering, and, even in her joy and gladness, ever afterwards was there about her that tinge of sadness which is the inevitable reliquary of sanctification through suffering.

Her old beliefs still remained with her; the prerogative of the best to rule and the spirit of the *noblesse oblige* were too instinct within her to become eradicated even if she wished to rid herself of them. She did not wish to rid herself of them; without them she would not have known herself; but she saw that in this age they were impracticable and impossible, and as her father and her husband had buried them, so too did she bury them, and lent herself to the spirit of the present age.

She had come to realize that, theoretically, responsible government is an excellent institution and a necessity, but that corruption is as inherent within it as it is within human nature, and its tendency is to degenerate to manipulation, place-seeking, tyranny of trusts, and tyranny of mobs. She believed that to a certain extent it had degenerated to this, but she saw that the time had come when men were beginning to think, and reason, and demand better things. Man as an individual was becoming more intelligent and enlightened, and was becoming conscious of the possibilities before him and the possibilities within him. His rights and his duties were becoming to him living realities. The country was awakening to a knowledge that it was on the threshold of a new era, an era pregnant with unlimited politic possibilities, aggrandisement, prosperity, progress, and the spirit of the Amor Patriæ.

Her husband, she knew, had been thinking. She knew he was now thinking. She learned now that such had been his knowledge and his creeds for many years. She should have known it before, but her sentiments and prejudices had blinded her to facts. Her husband, however, was clearsighted and far-seeing, and knew that a change could not be wrought in a few years. However faulty, frail, frothy it may be, nature will not relinquish in a moment cults and creeds of its cradle, which it has been taught to look upon as an element and essence of life itself.

Sir Keith was a man of great knowledge and high ideals. The motherland had been his model. He had mastered the secret of her great success and great endurance. Her foundation and her strength had been built upon her love and fear of God, her code of honor and her sense of duty. The foundations of her greatness had been laid when the Church was militant, her fathers had been true sons of the Church, yet had they ever been more ready to take their swords in the sunlight and go where duty and honor bade them go.

She had for her basis a knowledge of things. Her conscience was her king, and her king her conscience, and upon these principles had she given to the world a nation which, since the time of

Pericles, has never been excelled. Her works shall praise her in her gates. Her children shall rise up and call her blessed.   The bonds of birth are strong. Its instincts, its traditions, its inheritances, are heirlooms which ever serve as a basis for a sound national life.

Sir Keith was aware that his country was doubly blessed—blessed with the inheritance of these heirlooms and blessed with unlimited resources and possibilities—and he saw what his country now most needed was men of great knowledge, strong character, and keen common sense, to mould and develop these into shape and form. He never ceased placing before his contemporaries and his compatriots the necessity of high ideals in statesmanship and citizenship, and of consistency and veracity in public life as well as in private life.

His work lay like a bright morning star before him. He gave of his time and his energies freely and fully to it, while his wife, who had ever within her the ready resources necessary for progression, became in a measure his inspiration and his sustenance in making this star what it has been born to be—A Child of Destiny.

A year afterwards, when the last drop was added to their cup of happiness, she called the little one Margaret Lester, in memory of her mother and her dear friend Lester.

And here we will leave her now, the beloved and the helpmate of a noble husband, whose devotion is divided between his country and his home, that country of which the statesman has so truly said, " Never has any people been endowed with a nobler birthright or blessed with prospects of a fairer future. She is the star towards which all men who love progress and freedom shall go," and that home, the country's progenitor, in which she reigns as " the centre of all things, the balm of distress, the mirror of beauty, the motherhood of a perfect blending of the human and the divine." And with our soul's sincere desire for the spiritual, material and political elevation, progress and purity of My Lord and My Lady and all their national children, we will bid a kind farewell to " My Lady of the Snows."

9 781442 651531